Destiny's Crucible

Book 3

Heavier Than a Mountain

by

Olan Thorensen

copyright © 2016 Olan Thorensen

The is an original work of fiction. Any resemblance to people and places is coincidental.

All rights reserved.

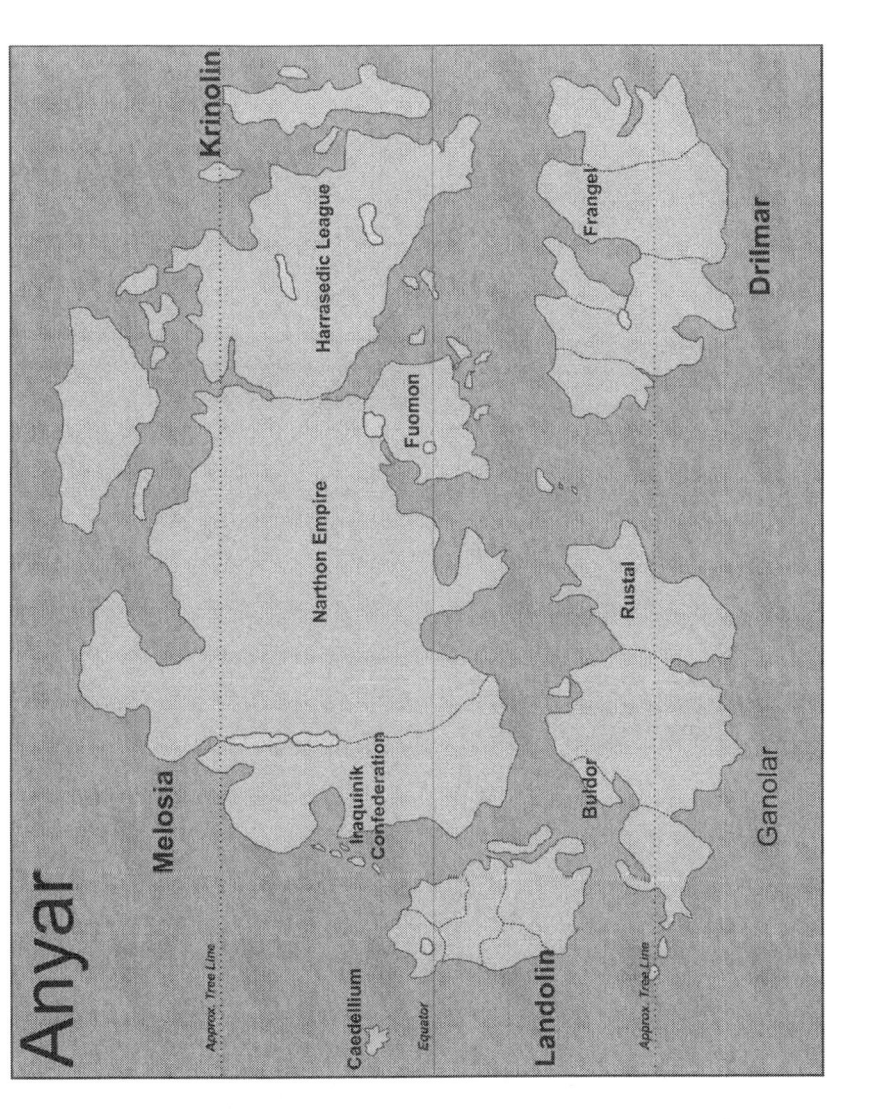

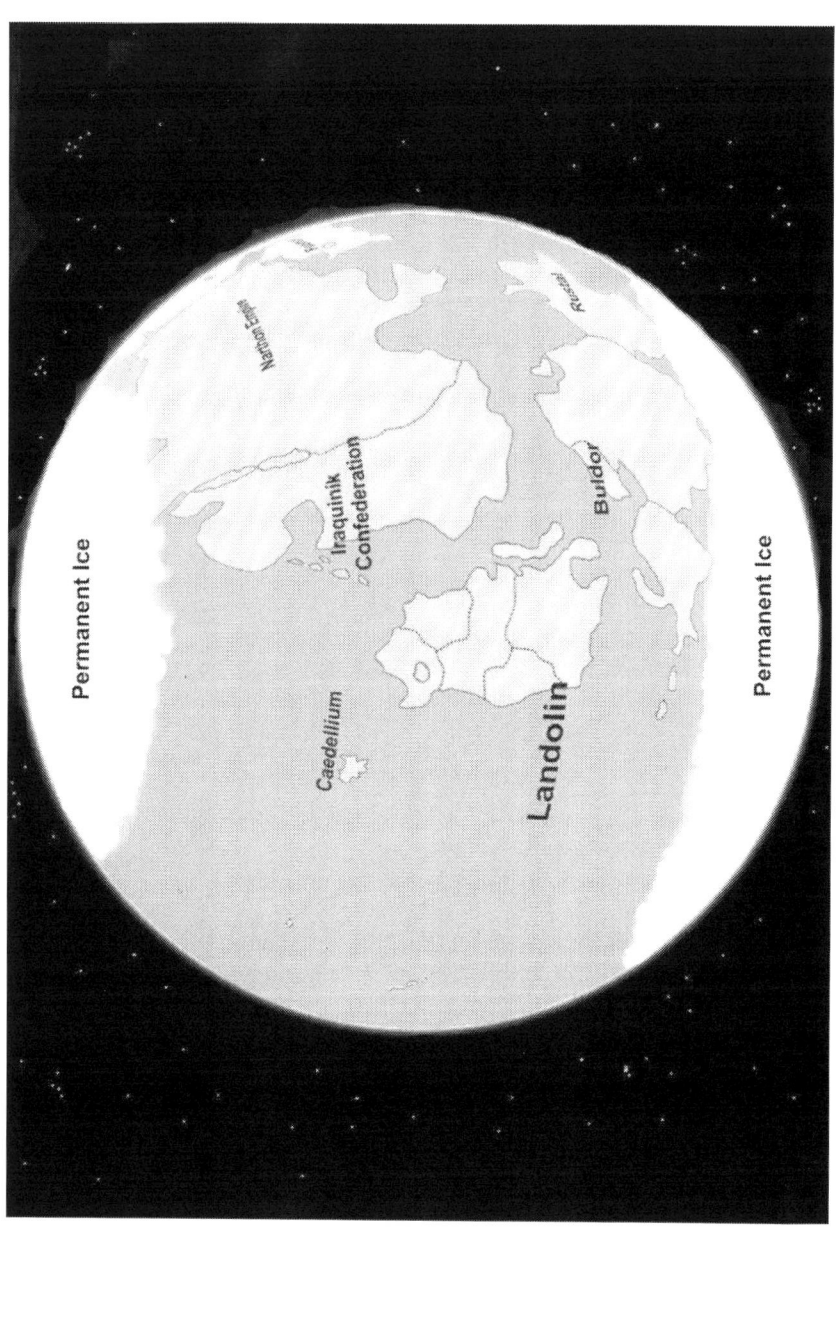

Caedellium

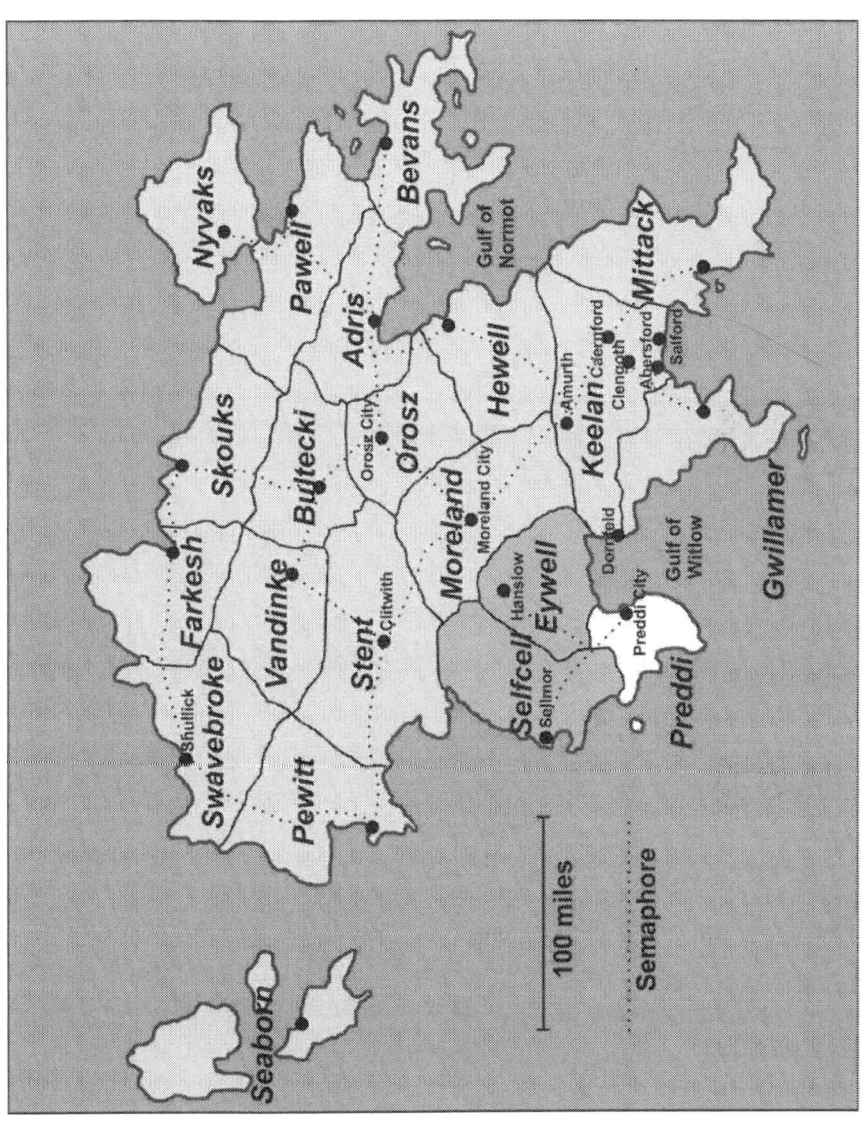

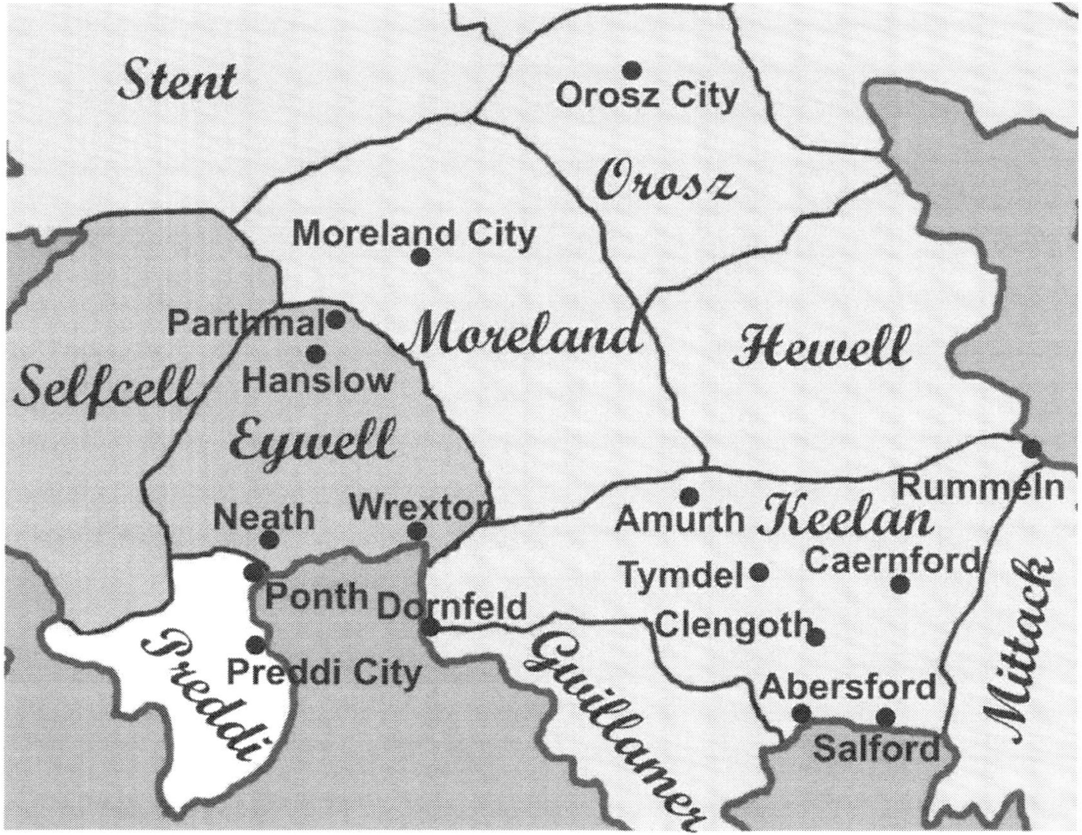
Stent
Orosz City
Orosz
Moreland City
Moreland
Hewell
Selfcell
Parthmal
Hanslow
Eywell
Neath
Wrexton
Rummeln
Amurth
Keelan
Caernford
Tymdel
Ponth
Dornfeld
Clengoth
Preddi City
Preddi
Guillamer
Abersford
Salford
Mittack

Acknowledgments

Thanks to my wife, Kathleen, for encouragement, tolerating my sequestering away for endless hours writing and revising, and for reading drafts. Thanks to editors Felicia Sullivan and Patricia Waldygo for contributions and teaching me those things about writing and grammar that I didn't learn in school. Cover by Damonza.com.

A list of major characters is given in the back of the book.

Color maps of planet Anyar are available at olanthorensen.com.

CONTENTS

PROLOGUE		
1	WOMEN WHO WAIT	1
2	TARGET, PARTHMAL	11
3	ESCAPE	19
4	LOSS OR DRAW?	29
5	LEARNING	36
6	PRISONERS	50
7	DIGGING IN	61
8	THUNDERSTRUCK	72
9	OBLIGATIONS	85
10	DECISION	101
11	CATALYST	106
12	MOVE	117
13	"YOU POOR BASTARDS"	123
14	STRIKE AT THE HEART	135
15	OFF TO OROSZ CITY	140
16	ALL-CLAN CONCLAVE	151
17	RETURNING TO CAERNFORD	179
18	WEAPONS REDUX	186
19	READINESS	196
20	AGENTS	215
21	ANARYND	219
22	HAIL TO THE HEIR	235
23	DISRUPTION	242
24	HOME LIFE	251
25	DANGERS IN HEALING	259
26	PLANNING	278
27	IF THEY DO THAT, WE DO THIS	286
28	BEWARE THE SERPENT	295
29	A DAY IN THE LIFE OF YOZEF KOLSKO	308
30	WHAT LURKS IN THE NIGHT	326
31	FINAL PREPARATIONS	333
32	OUT OF THE DARK	341
33	SWAVEBROKE	366
34	RETALIATION	374
35	THREE DAYS LATER	387
36	FOUR DAYS LATER	395
37	FIVE DAYS LATER	411
38	SKIN OF THEIR TEETH	421
39	NO TRUCE	435
40	THE CLANS UNITE	443
41	THE BEST-LAID PLANS	450
MAJOR CHARACTERS		453

"Not for ourselves alone are we born."
— Marcus Tullius Cicero

"Duty is what we expect of others, only to find out the other is yourself."
— Culich Keelan, Caedellium, Planet Anyar

"Duty doesn't melt away, no matter how much we might wish it to."
— Claudia J. Edwards, Taming the Forest King

"Duty is a debt you owe to yourself to fulfill obligations you have assumed voluntarily."
— Robert A. Heinlein

"Our duty is to be useful, not according to our desires but according to our powers."
— Henri-Frédéric Amiel

"Not once or twice in our fair island-story,
The path of duty was the way to glory."
— Alfred Tennyson

"Duty is heavier than a mountain, death lighter than a feather."
— Japanese Proverb

PROLOGUE

The planet was ordinary. The planet was extraordinary. Its orbit lay within the zone that allowed liquid water, but most such planets remained airless or barren or under gasses, such as carbon dioxide blankets, all conditions inimical to life. This planet rated among the exceptional by five criteria. First, it contained water; an ocean covered 80 percent of the surface, with major landmasses concentrated on one hemisphere. Second, single-cell life had emerged from those waters. Third, life had, in its earliest stages, generated organisms whose metabolism gave off oxygen as a by-product. This step opened the door to an explosion of evolution in multi-cellular organisms, a leap not every biosphere achieved, which constituted the fourth criterion and which placed this planet among the rarest of its siblings.

Yet with a hundred billion stars in its galaxy alone, the planet rested as only one of a myriad with complex ecosystems, not unique enough to entice those who watched the planet so closely. The lure was humans, a self-named sentient species. Again, that alone, while interesting and worthy of attention, paled beside the fact that humans did not originate on this planet. Nor did humans have the technology to transplant themselves, along with a selection of animals and plants, to this planet.

The AI and its creators did not know how the transplantation had been done, how long ago, or by whom. Thus, they watched and waited, unobserved by the humans below, in case those who had carried out the transplantation returned.

As with other planets harboring life, the planet glowed like a jewel in the darkness: the blue of the ocean on one hemisphere, blues supplemented with brown and greens of continents on the other half of the planet. Its position relative to its yellow-orange sun kept most of the planet ice-free. Despite two permanent ice caps, the small axial tilt resulted in moderate seasonal changes. The Watchers had observed this planet for two thousand revolutions around its sun. They saw cities grow and sometimes burn, ships sail the waters, and armies fight battles.

The Watchers were not always present, but an artificial intelligence (AI) kept constant surveillance: receiving, collating, and cataloging data coming to it as a constant stream. Rarely did new data require action, such as whether to alert its creators. But rarely was not never. Now, the AI had to decide.

On a large island, west of the major landmasses, the AI observed a battle. The AI didn't know the combatants' identities and their reason for fighting; its programming did not account for such details. However, the AI had never observed a battle of this magnitude on the island. Normally, the AI would simply have cataloged the observation, except that it paired with another datum specific to the island. The coincidence of two pieces of data relating to the same island raised an internal flag within the AI's programming.

Two years earlier, the AI's creators had cast away a single human on this island. A creator vessel had accidentally destroyed a human aircraft while observing humans on their planet of origin. The creators felt obliged, by their mode of reasoning, to ameliorate the accident. They saved and treated a human who survived the collision. Unable to return the man to his normal life—because he now knew of alien observers—and unable to either keep him aboard their vessel or take him to their own worlds, they gave the human, once recovered, a choice: either be painlessly terminated or be placed on one of the other worlds populated with humans. The man chose exile, the selected destination the same small island where the battle had come to the AI's attention.

For a long time—at least, several microseconds—the AI considered the probability of a connection between the two events. It deduced no likely scenario where the introduction of the single human could affect a battle involving tens of thousands, but, unable to conclude a negative, it passed the observations on to its creators.

The message sent, the AI allocated a tiny fraction of its attention to watch for other anomalous data points originating from the island, and waited.

The parameters of the AI's programming did not include interest in what happened to the humans who participated in the battle or the humans who waited for news of the outcome.

If he had known of the AI's assumption that no one human caused the battle, Yozef Kolsko (aka Joseph Colsco in an earlier life on Earth) would not have argued, though he would have admitted he influenced the outcome. However, the orbiting AI's conclusion matched what Harlie (the separate AI that Yozef interacted with after the destruction of his airliner) had told Yozef: that his impact on the planet would be "like a drop of water in an ocean."

Although angry at his fate and at Harlie's indifference, Yozef had determined he would transfer as much twenty-first-century Earth knowledge as he could to Anyar, his destination planet, whose technology level approximated Earth, circa 1700 CE. However, Yozef limited his goal to introducing knowledge, not embroiling himself in political and military affairs. His contributions to all three areas were unexpected by both himself and the AI's creators.

Unknown to the AI, the battle it observed contributed to an ongoing transformation of Yozef Kolsko, from the man he had been to the one he would become.

CHAPTER 1

WOMEN WHO WAIT

The battle of Moreland City took fewer than three hours. The clansmen who participated knew the outcome immediately. The dead were dead and cared no more. The seriously wounded were fortunate if in the care of medicants and mercifully unconscious. Others experienced the agony of waiting for either help or death. Those unharmed or the walking wounded felt the elation of victory or numbness from what they had witnessed or endured.

Beneath the orbiting AI, other humans waited. While the logical, disinterested sentience observed the battle from space, tens of thousands of other beings, emotionally invested, waited for news. For some, word came within hours. For others, days. For some, months—if ever.

Urlwina Moreland

Even from the highest building in Moreland City, the wife of Hetman Gynfor Moreland couldn't see the battlefield, but she heard the thunder of hooves, the cannon and musket fire, a pause, more firing, then nothing for two hours. Finally, a long trail of horsemen and wagons moved over hillocks and to the city. Her eyes were still good enough to see that the wagons held wounded and dead. She didn't see the banners of the Moreland leadership.

Maybe they're still at the battlefield, she told herself. *Particularly, the hetman and his sons.*

Not that she worried for the safety of her husband or even for her oldest son, Owain. Gynfor had not been the husband of her dreams, with his harshness, overweening self-importance, and stubborn refusal to face his own stupidity, and she had hated every day of her marriage and life in Clan Moreland. Unfortunately, as a daughter of Hetman Pewitt, she'd had no choice in the political marriage. The only lights in her life had been three babies: two sons, Owain and Caedem, and a daughter, Nissa.

Owain she'd loved until, by age seven, he began changing into a copy of his father. Now, only a dim memory reminded her of when she had loved her eldest son. Caedem, the younger son, demonstrated everything his older brother lacked: kindness, inquisitiveness, and strength. He was strong enough to avoid emulating his father and brother. She knew that other clans, particularly Keelan, chose the next hetman among all of the sons and not by primogeniture—and even then, only with the approval of the boyermen. She had never suggested to Gynfor that he choose Caedem as heir, knowing her husband would dismiss copying Keelan.

So far, Owain had three daughters but no sons. Despite her efforts to suppress the thought, which caused her intermittent guilt, Urlwina admitted to herself that if Gynfor died, she wouldn't mourn if Owain followed suit and Caedem became hetman.

Footsteps on stone announced someone behind her. Slow footsteps, as if made by an old or feeble person or someone hesitant to approach. She turned to see Abbot Kelvan of St. Worlan's abbey. He was young for an abbot and not feeble, but his pale, grim expression foretold distress.

"Urlwina," he said softly, confirming bad news by the use of her first name. "News came. The Narthani are withdrawing back to their territories, but Moreland suffered grievous losses, far worse than we first feared."

"Who is dead?" she asked, her voice emotionless. The abbot needed no further words to know she asked about her husband and two sons.

"God knows, I'm sorry to tell you, Urlwina, but it's confirmed that the hetman and both of your sons fell in a charge on the Narthani."

She didn't speak for a long moment. "And there's no doubt?"

"None, I'm afraid."

"Thank you, Abbot. I'd like to be alone now."

"Of course, but I'll be in the main hall, if you want to talk or need me for any reason."

She turned back, looking out to the west, as the abbot's footsteps receded. She would mourn Caedem later. For now, nothing held her in Moreland. She would take Nissa and within two hours be on her way back home to Pewitt. She could do nothing for Caedem, but Nissa needed to be out of the reach of Moreland factions. Her daughter was a simpleton—a good-natured girl of fifteen with the mind of a five-year-old. If Nissa stayed in Moreland, she would become a pawn in the struggle to define the new clan leadership. With the hetman and both of his sons dead and with no grandsons, Nissa might be forced into a marriage to secure a hetman claim. When Nissa was safe, *then* Urlwina would mourn her youngest son.

Breda Keelan

Another hetman's wife also waited, but the news took longer to reach her at Caernford, capital of Keelan Province, 130 miles south southeast of Moreland City. In Breda Keelan's twenty-seven-year marriage to Culich Keelan, she had seen him off into danger many times, mainly in the early years before his father died and Culich became hetman. But those times were nothing like now. When Culich had left this time, she watched him lead five hundred armed Keelan men on the way to joining hundreds more Keelanders and men from the Gwillamer and Mittack clans—2,200 men going to the aid of the Moreland Clan, invaded by a Narthani army and the allied Eywell and Selfcell clans.

The last report, now two days old, said that men of ten clans faced a Narthani army on the plain west of Moreland City. Since then, no updates had arrived. Whether her husband survived was surely already determined, and so she waited.

After the men headed north to whatever fate lay ahead, Breda insisted that she and her three daughters eat every meal together. She needed her children around her and intuited that they needed to stay near her and not retreat into solitary fears.

The four of them ostensibly went about their daily lives, which fooled no one. Their meals were quiet affairs. Strained conversations interleaved with draining silences, as each groped for words without voicing what consumed everyone's thoughts. Despite doing their best to maintain the strength expected of the hetman's family, they had limits. One night Breda woke to find her youngest daughter, twelve-year-old Mared, huddled next to her in bed. The child had part of her nightshirt stuffed in her mouth, stifling sobs so as not to wake her mother.

When Breda enveloped Mared in an embrace, the child spit out the cloth.

"Oh, Mother! I'm so scared! What's happened to Father?" she sobbed in a strangled voice.

"I know, child, I know. I'm afraid, too. But all we can do is pray and wait for news."

Breda had no sooner spoken than her two other daughters, Anid and Ceinwyn, stood in the bedroom door, holding onto each other, listening to their mother's words.

"And Yozef," said a sobbing Anid, the second youngest daughter.

"And Yozef," agreed their mother.

Anid and Ceinwyn rushed to their mother and sister, and the four held tight to one another.

After several minutes, Breda cleared her throat. "We all will keep praying for good news soon, but your father would want us to keep faith that everything will be all right." She comforted the others as best she could and fought not to show the depth of her own fear. An hour passed before mother and daughters, huddled together, fell asleep.

The stars had begun to fade with the approaching daylight when Norlin, the teenage boy who worked at the manor, pounded on the bedroom door. Breda jerked upright, followed by her daughters.

"Sen Breda, there's a rider with a message from the hetman!"

Breda untangled herself from her daughters and ran to the bedroom door, not thinking to put a robe over her nightdress.

Norlin appeared anxious and held out a sealed envelope. "The rider said he changed horses four times and rode all night. He looks it."

She tore open the envelope to reveal a single folded sheet.

Dearest,

I am scratching out this short message and sending it by rider instead of semaphore before dark, since the station manager said clouds and rain were stopping transmission between here and Keelan. More news will come later, but I wanted to assure you I'm safe. As are Yozef and Vortig. We are calling it a victory, since the Narthani are withdrawing back to Eywell Province. You will hear more later, but all I'll say now is that it was terrible. We fought a battle, and although the Narthani turned back, we estimate about 100 Keelan dead and many wounded. I believe I will be here in Moreland City for another day before we start home, so I should see you in 3 to 4 days. With all my love, Culich

She read the words again and started a third time when Anid called out, "Mother! What is it? Is it about father?"

Breda looked up to see three fearful faces circling her. "Oh, sorry, children. Yes, it's from your father, and he says he's all right."

Shouts and tears ensued, then Mared spoke. "And Yozef? What about Yozef?"

"Your father says Yozef is also safe. They should be back here in three to four days."

"We have to send word to Maera!" said Mared.

"It'll be light in another two hours," said Breda. "The sky is clear here, so a semaphore message can go out as soon as the stations can pass signals. Ceinwyn, run get me quill, ink, and paper so I can write a message to Maera. We'll have Norlin take it to the semaphore station in Caernford, to go out as soon as possible."

Two hours later, Breda sat on the manor's front veranda and gazed at clear skies dotted with scattered clouds. She assumed her semaphore message to Maera had been sent on its way through the intervening stations between Caernford and Abersford.

Her emotions were conflicted: exhilaration that her husband was safe and guilt at her contentment, when so many other Keelan families would soon hear the news she had avoided—of a loved one dead or seriously wounded.

She stood to go inside. She had things to do. Halfway to the manor front door, she caught movement from a corner of her eye, and she turned her head. A rider approached on the tree-lined drive leading a hundred yards to the manor. It was Esyl Havant, one of the workers at the Caernford semaphore station. Delivering messages from the station to Keelan Manor occurred so often, Culich had joked they should have built the station next to the manor to save on horses and the station workers' time. Havant frequently made several trips a day to the manor, so often that Maera once said they should count him as part of the manor's staff. A friendly, though nondescript man, with thinning hair, he always had a good word for everyone.

Normally, Breda passed a few pleasant words with Esyl, but this seemed like the wrong time to receive new messages. She stopped, her hand touching her throat. What if the first message that morning was in error or something had changed? Her husband hadn't come home yet—anything was possible.

Havant pulled up by the front steps and called out from his horse. "Sen

Keelan! Wonderful news came in on the semaphore. The clans defeated the Narthani!"

He pulled out a sheet of paper from a saddlebag and waved it in the air. "This message is to all Caedelli on the island. The stationmaster is having copies printed in Caernford as fast as possible and distributing them. I'm delivering copies, and, of course, one is for you and your family."

By now, Breda had descended the steps and rushed to the horse. Havant reached down and handed the sheet to her, and then he turned his horse and rode off.

She read the paper immediately.

```
From: Hetman Orosz
To: All clanspeople of Caedellium
On the fourthday, third sixday, month of
Mefilton, year 414 of the settlement of
Caedellium, on the plain west of Moreland City,
the free clans of Caedellium met a Narthani army
supported by Eywell and Selfcellese clans. After
desperate fighting, the Eywell clan was crushed
and the Narthani suffered severe losses and are
withdrawing. Praise God.
```

She went inside and called her daughters to come read it. Then she had them gather all workers at the manor that day, so that they, too, could read a semaphore message that would live in Caedellium history.

Breda proposed a celebratory libation. They read the message aloud, over and over, and after the final reading, Breda went to Culich's study, put the sheet on his desk, and smoothed out a few wrinkles created after numerous hand-to-hand passages. Her husband would want to keep this paper, perhaps even frame it.

Maera Kolsko-Keelan

Maera determined that today she would work on being nice to everyone she interacted with—in penitence for her behavior the last several days. The previous evening, she had cursed at Elian for dropping a dish, as the elderly woman cleaned up after evening meal. Elian's intimidated look and glistening eyes jolted Maera.

"Oh, Elian, I'm sorry I said that to you. Please excuse me. There's just so much going on."

"That's all right, Sen Maera. What with the baby coming and Ser Yozef away to Merciful God knows what, it's no wonder you're . . . you know . . . excitable."

An apology given and accepted, Maera still noticed Elian keeping a cautious eye and excusing herself for the evening with more eagerness than usual.

Only when preparing for bed did Maera reflect on her behavior the last few days. It hadn't been the first time she'd snapped at Elian and Brak; plus, she'd brusquely declined an invitation for a mid-day gathering in Abersford with several women she knew. She also recalled sniping at Sen Myrfild, Yozef's partner in papermaking.

She even stewed over delays in developing the University of Abersford. Her husband, Yozef, had asked her to take on the responsibility of serving as chancellor of the university—a scholasticum, as Caedelli termed formal collections of scholastics—but with expanded numbers and a dedicated building complex. Inherently interested in the concept, she had eagerly taken on the task. She also recognized it as a venue to establish an identity based on her ability and not just on being someone's daughter or wife.

Dealing with the myriad details of planning infrastructure and recruiting scholastics, her worry about Yozef and her father, and the need for naps and relieving her bladder all made for a cranky pregnant woman.

Thus, she decided—for the next day and for as long as she could—to remain civil, no matter what preoccupied her mind.

She apologized again to Elian the next morning and went to the barn to find Brak, who responded to her apology with a grunt and returned to cleaning stalls. Maera then walked in to Abersford, slowly, given her condition, and found Myrfild in the paper factory. She didn't outright apologize, but she did her best to sound pleasant and tried to seem spontaneous when mentioning how much Yozef respected him. She then sat on a bench in the town square for an hour, practicing smiling at passersby and chitchatting with those she knew. She didn't return home until near mid-day, to find a nervous Elian pacing on the porch.

"Sen Maera, where have you been!? A semaphore message came for you, and the Abersford station operator has looked for you the last several hours. He's been by the house twice."

Maera's throat constricted, and her eyes widened. "A message? From who?"

"I don't know," said Elian, "but he left it the last time he came by. It's on the dining room table."

Maera rushed into the adjoining room. There, on the table, lay a single sheet of paper, folded, not sealed, and wrinkled as if it had been carried around for several hours—which it had been. She snatched it off the table, unfolded and read it, then sank onto a wooden chair by the table and wept.

Elian rushed to her, knelt, and put one hand on her knee and the other on a shoulder. "Sen Maera, I pray it isn't bad news about Yozef."

Maera choked back tears enough to say, "He's safe. Father, too. That's all it says. Yozef will be home in a few days."

Maera wiped her face, as she hiccupped in her attempt to stifle sobs. "I'll be all right. Thank you, Elian. Don't be concerned."

An hour later, Maera sat on the front veranda, looking out at the ocean. She couldn't remember the last time she had cried so hard, even though it had lasted only a minute. She ruminated on the cause, which led to a conclusion both surprising and soothing.

I knew the marriage to Yozef was a logical decision for both of us. We never expressed words of affection. I felt comfortable with him, as he did with me, and obviously, he found me attractive, or at least enough to enjoy sharing a bed. I told myself we had a good marriage, but it's obviously more than just acceptable. When he left with Father to go to Moreland and face the Narthani, I hardly spoke to him. Then, the thought of him dead . . . I can't bear even the thought. A life without him seems desolate. I'm overjoyed that Father is safe, but I don't think I would have cried like that only for Father's safety. It was Yozef. I love him the way I know Mother loves Father.

Even so, part of her shied away from saying the words. After all, he hadn't said them either. But why should that hold her back, except for a fear he didn't feel the same? She knew what the *Word* would say or her mother; her love of him shouldn't be conditional on his love for her.

Serlip Dogen

Far from Moreland City, 7,258 miles, a Narthani woman washed the clothes of her husband, two daughters, and three of her five sons. Hands rough and red from decades of that task, she kneaded the clothes in a tub of water, brushed aside hair streaked with gray, and stretched joints stiffened from a lifetime of work. The Dogen family labored on farmland belonging to Nuthrat Metin, a colonel in the Narthani army. Her husband worked as the property's blacksmith, with two sons apprenticed to their father and a third son who oversaw teams of slaves working the crop fields. The latter work made the Dogen family constantly aware that even with their hard life, many others suffered in worse conditions. The Dogen family derived from a people conquered by the Narthani seventy years earlier, a people now recognized as Narthani, even if from among the lower levels of that society, whereas the Metin slaves had descended from peoples conquered within the last two generations.

Her grandparents were their family's first generation released from slavery. Narthani custom required their release, because the family had served faithfully and without rebelling when in slave status. Serlip remembered stories told to her by grandmother, Sirona—the only knowledge passed on of the family's origin.

Serlip comforted herself that three of her sons had solid positions in service on the Metin estate and that her daughters would likely marry men also in Metin service or men from neighboring estates. She would have those five children near her. Four years previously, the Narthani had ordered her eldest two sons, Ergin and Yazar, to report for induction. Serlip and her husband had known the call would inevitably come. Yet they felt consoled when the estate's master, Metin, was pleased enough with the family's service to promise to keep the two sons within the units he commanded. He assured the parents that no further call would come to claim their other three sons.

Serving under Metin also meant the sons could communicate with their family more often than most men in the Narthani army—where service might be thousands of miles and months of travel away. There had even been two visits home when the two sons accompanied Metin, who, while in distant posts most of the time, made rare inspection visits to the property. Once, the entire family reunited again for two months, when Metin brought his family to stay at the estate after his long tour at an Iraquinik front.

The precious reunion turned bitter when the two sons left again, this time for an extended duty serving under Metin in a distant land Serlip had never heard of. In the following four years, the family received three short letters, both written by Yazar, because Ergin had never taken to the limited schooling workers' children could attend.

Metin granted troops originating from his estate the privilege of sending their letters with his in a mail packet. When a year passed since Serlip had received the last letter, she told herself it was due to the distance, the mail having to come by ship and then overland, and the burdens of her sons' duties. Still, yesterday she felt disappointed yet again when a mail packet from Metin to the estate overseer arrived with no letters from her sons.

Two years passed before Serlip learned that Ergin had fallen in a battle on an island named Caedellium. The fate of Yazar remained forever unknown.

CHAPTER 2

TARGET PARTHMAL

Moreland City

The hetmen meeting that followed the Battle of Moreland City ended with the sun just touching the western mountains. Welman Stent, the hetman of Clan Stent, stood outside the stone meeting building alongside Hetmen Adris and Hewell, while the Stent and Hewell clansmen prepared to ride hard for the Narthani supply base at Parthmal, just inside Eywell Province. They would attack the encampment only if they surprised the garrison before it received word of the battle. An hour of light remained, and they planned on covering as many miles as possible before darkness. Since the Stent clan contributed more men to the raid than Hewell did, by agreement, Hetman Stent would lead the raid.

Four other clans, Adris, Bultecki, Orosz, and Pewitt, would harass the withdrawing Narthani army, picking off individuals and patrols and setting traps and ambushes until the Narthani crossed into more secure Eywell territory. None of the six clans was to engage the Narthani in battle. Although the clansmen were mounted and thus more mobile than the Narthani, the clans would be no match for the formidable Narthani infantry and artillery in a direct confrontation.

"The three of us saw firsthand what the Narthani are capable of," said Klyngo Adris, shaking his head. "It will take the Moreland Clan a generation or more to recover from the number of their men killed in only a few minutes."

"Aye," agreed Lordum Hewell, "which is why all of us need to be cautious and audacious at the same time. Especially you, Stent, as we ride for Parthmal. I've agreed to let you lead this raid, because someone has to and more of your clansmen will go than mine, but only as long as I don't see Hewell men wasted to no purpose."

Hewell's statement didn't offend Stent. He would have said the same in the Hewell hetman's position. Coordination among clans was critical to resist the Narthani, but his own clanspeople came first.

"We'll push to get ahead of the Narthani, while the other clans harass and slow them," said Stent, "then look to take Parthmal only if we catch them unawares. If not, we'll circle back and help snipe at the Narthani army. I might also send scouts on toward Hanslow, depending on what happens at Parthmal."

Lowering his voice and stepping closer to the others, Stent switched to first names. "Lordum, Klyngo . . . what do you think of this Yozef Kolsko from Keelan? I've heard reports and know of some of the innovations he's brought to Caedellium, but your two clans are joining the Tri-Clan Alliance. Do you know more about him?"

Lordum Hewell shook his head. "Probably most of what you've already heard, except that Culich Keelan thinks highly of him . . . enough so he's let Kolsko marry his eldest daughter."

"Maera," said Stent. "I've only seen her a couple of times, but I hear the stories."

"Whatever you heard is probably true," said Adris, laughing. "She'd be a handful for any man. Smart as can be, with a tongue that can flay at a hundred feet. I know that suitors have come and gone for several years, either not wanting her for a wife, no matter the advantages of a marriage link to Keelan, or her running them off at the first meeting."

"I think she's pictured unfairly," said Hewell. "I've met her a few more times than Klyngo and found her extremely honest, possibly to a fault. She's certainly got a mind of her own, and I've heard that scholastics within Keelan think she could have been a scholastic of the highest order if she hadn't been a Keelan hetman's daughter."

"So, I wonder even more about her marrying this Kolsko," said Stent. "Culich Keelan is as canny as they come, so he must see a major advantage to the clan to approve the wedding."

"Pardon," said Cadoc Gwillamer, as he walked up to the threesome. "I couldn't help overhearing. You're wondering about Yozef Kolsko."

"Yes, Cadoc," said Hewell. "You're part of the Tri-Clan Alliance. What do you know about Kolsko?"

"I've met him once, and I've talked with and exchanged letters with Culich. He's mentioned Kolsko many times. At first, it was just casual comments, but then, during the last months, it's been obvious Kolsko is important in Culich's thinking and planning."

"What of these rumors he washed up on Caedellium a few years ago?" asked Adris. "That's what Culich told me, but I wasn't sure what to believe."

"That seems to be true," said Gwillamer. "Culich told me the same story, plus, in Gwillamer we've heard the tale from other sources, including some who live in the Abersford area. They found Kolsko on a beach, naked and not speaking Caedelli. I've also heard some people believe he didn't wash in from the sea, and that somehow he was 'placed' on the beach."

"Placed?" queried Stent. "What does that mean?"

"My God . . . ," mumbled Hewell, in a tone that got the other men looking at him. "That would go with another rumor I've heard, and one I'd discounted as fanciful."

Hewell looked around as if to check whether anyone outside their foursome stood within hearing distance. "Septarsh," he whispered.

"What!" exclaimed Stent, who also looked around and lowered his voice. "Are you serious? Some people consider this Kolsko to be a Septarsh, an agent of God?"

"I know," said Gwillamer. "I've heard the same rumor, though I'm not subscribing to it myself, but you have to wonder. Kolsko arrived in Keelan only a few years ago and now has introduced new products that are making him exceedingly wealthy, has married the Keelan hetman's oldest daughter, and is obviously important in our struggle against the Narthani.

"I don't know if you've all heard the stories about the Buldorian raid on St. Sidryn's Abbey on Keelan's southern coast?"

Adris and Stent shook their heads, while Hewell nodded and spoke. "Culich told me a little of it one evening over ales, but no details."

"I know more," said Gwillamer. "St. Sidryn's isn't too far from my clan's border with Keelan, and there's regular travel and trade. Plus, Culich came to their western town of Dornfeld some months back. Dornfeld sits on the Gwillamer/Keelan border. The Narthani and the Eywellese seemed to threaten an attack on that part of Keelan province and might push on into Gwillamer. Culich came with advisors to Dornfeld, and I met them there. We discussed what response to make. The evening before all of us met, Culich and I talked, and he mentioned bringing Kolsko along to see if the man might have any useful suggestions. That's when he told me details of the Buldorian attack on St. Sidryn's Abbey. Evidently, the Keelanders saw no way to stop the Buldorians until Kolsko suggested a tactic, one that was successful in repelling the raiders with major losses, compared to relatively few casualties for the Keelanders."

"And now this Kolsko was instrumental in our victory over the Narthani," said Stent, running a hand over his shaven head. "I don't think there's any doubt things might have turned out much worse today if it wasn't for Kolsko's analysis of the situation and suggestions for attacking the Narthani flank."

"And none of you have seen for yourselves up close the effect of artillery," said Gwillamer. "I know you saw what happened to the Morelanders slaughtered by the Narthani muskets and cannon, but my clansmen and I were nearby when those odd artillery pieces of Kolsko's first fired at the end block of Narthani infantry. When that block was destroyed, Keelan and Gwillamer horsemen overran the nearby Narthani cannon, and I saw Kolsko turning the Narthani's own cannon on the next infantry blocks.

"No," asserted Gwillamer, "there's no doubt that whoever this Kolsko is, and wherever he came from, he's been a God-send to us all and I believe we need to pay close attention to anything he says."

"I'll have to meet him myself," said Stent. "I'm sure there'll be an All-Clan Conclave as soon as the Narthani have returned to Eywell Province and don't appear to be contemplating another invasion too soon. We need to be sure Culich brings this Kolsko to the conclave."

"I agree," said Hewell, "but for now, three of us need to get back to our men. They should be ready to ride by now. Stent and I need to reach Parthmal before the garrison gets word of what happened here today."

"And you, Cadoc. You get back to your province," said Stent. "The Tri-Clan Alliance has done the most to turn back the Narthani and has taken the most casualties, except for the Morelanders. Get your men home and back to their families. I only hope the rest of us can do the same soon."

The four men took turns clasping forearms or hands—the customs varied among clans—and rode off in two directions: Cadoc Gwillamer to rejoin his men and head south toward home, and the other three hetmen to gather their men in an attempt to strike more blows against the Narthani.

Parthmal, Eywell Province

One day later, in the middle of the night, Welman Stent, Lordum Hewell, and a dozen of their senior men crowded into a makeshift shelter of blankets and hides held up by clansmen—the men pressed together around a small fire that reflected off their faces. They had pushed their horses as hard as they dared. Plus, Stent had sent a hundred men with extra horses riding even harder to maneuver themselves in advance of the Narthani force's line of march—with the purpose of preventing messengers from reaching Parthmal. The main Stent and Hewell force had passed south of the Narthani army the previous afternoon, but they didn't know whether word had reached Parthmal about Moreland City.

"Men sent ahead confirm earlier reports about the Narthani encampment," said Stent, his face grim but determined, his shaved head hidden by a leather helm with inlaid iron strips that reflected the firelight. "It's just east of the village of Parthmal. The village has no obvious defenses, but the encampment has a six-foot-high earthen berm three hundred yards on a side, with twenty-foot towers on the corners and midway between the corners. Under each tower is a cannon, though our men couldn't see if these were manned.

"At least two of the tower platforms must have fires within them, since our men could see light and the outlines of men. Maybe four or more men in each tower. There also must be firing positions on the inside of the berm, since they saw a few men's heads and shoulders outlined against lights within the encampment. However, they're likely just individuals standing in position, instead of a continuous rampart, since those men never moved from the few places where they were seen.

"There's a single opening in the berm—on the western side, with a wooden gate attached to tree trunks sunk into the ground. We assume the gate will be closed and barred."

"And no sign of any watchmen outside of the encampment or moving patrols?" asked a grizzled clansman.

"None they saw. But we need to be aware that our men could have missed them. That's why we'll start the attack only when we're all in position and there's no sign the Narthani are on alert. We know what can happen to men attacking a Narthani position that's ready for it, so if there's any sign they're expecting us, we'll abort the attack."

Stent turned to face a lanky, black-bearded clansman. "Wym, you have a critical task and the most dangerous. I don't want to commit everyone to the attack unless we think we've surprised them and can breach the berm. Once you commit, your hundred men will ride for the part of the berm between the southeast corner and the adjacent tower in the middle of the south berm. You have ten men carrying shielded lanterns. Once they reach the top of the berm and see that they can ride down the other side, they're to uncover the lanterns and drop them on top of the berm. We'll assume that if they survive to reach the top, then they've surprised the Narthani. Another seven hundred men will wait until they see the signal and then follow. Eight hundred of our men inside the encampment are about all the area will hold, and the rest of the men will stay outside in case they're needed."

Wym Terrell's solemn expression conveyed he knew his and his men's fate if the Narthani were waiting, but he nodded. "We'll do our best to open the way. We're only lucky the Narthani evidently didn't want to dig too deep. If there was a ditch in front of the berm, we'd never be able to try this."

The soil for the berm had been dug from the adjacent ground. But instead of digging a three- to four-foot-deep ditch, the builders had taken the easier route and kept to looser soil on the surface. The Stent and Hewell riders would face only a half to one-foot drop about thirty-feet wide before reaching the berm and urging their mounts up the berm's slope—hoping their momentum would be sufficient to reach the top.

Three hours later, Wym Terrell peered through a thin screen of trees at the Parthmal encampment. Light provided by the stars and by Haedan, the smaller moon, at half phase gave enough light for his acclimated eyes to examine the berm two hundred yards away. He estimated it would take them half a minute to reach the berm, starting from a standstill and pushing their horses to a full gallop. Half a minute. He wondered, if he were a Narthani at watch, how long it would take to hear the hoofbeats, see the clansmen coming, register what he saw or heard, give the alarm, and fire whatever weapons were at the ready. Half a minute.

He looked behind him. Twenty yards to either side and stretching back into the brush sat his hundred mounted men. They had walked their horses the final mile, each man with a hand at his mount's muzzle to suppress neighs, all metal tied down or wrapped to minimize sound. No one had spoken a word, not even to whisper.

It was time. Terrell climbed onto his horse and signaled to those near him to do the same. Men mounted in a wave stretching to the end of the column. Terrell drew his sword. Another wave passed to the rear as men drew blades. No one carried a musket or a lance, both being too cumbersome to wield in the dark and with horses packed so tight. It would be sword and pistol.

Looking back, Terrell saw stars and moonlight reflecting off steel. There could be no hesitation. Any Narthani on watch, if they looked in the right direction, might see a multitude of faint flashes, as if fireflies infested the sparse woods.

Terrell turned to look ahead and urged his horse forward. After fifty yards, he assumed all of the horses behind him were in motion, and he spurred his mount into a full gallop by one hundred yards. No Caedelli spoke, but the sound of four hundred hooves rose from a faint rumble to a thunderous roar.

Munjak Salamun hated the last watch tour. Since regular duty followed immediately, it made the day seem endless before he could sleep again. Also, he hated his unit's current duty posting—sitting in a forward encampment with few amenities and having to play nice with the Eywellese contingent sharing the post. He hated the Eywellese. Not that he knew many of them, but he was more comfortable with his Narthani compatriots—at least, those he came with in the final infantry levy from Narthon.

In contrast to his opinion of the islanders, Salamun appreciated the island's weather. Narthon was bone dry with winds and dust, except twice a year when wind shifts brought drenching rains and suffocating humidity. In contrast, the weather on Caedellium was closer to perfect than a Narthani at home could imagine: moderate humidity; rain, when it came, relatively short-lived compared to week-long seasonal spells at home; constant gentle winds; and daytime temperatures usually varying from a little chill to not quite hot. One of the other men had heard the climate was due to the island's location in global wind patterns and the moderating effect of the surrounding ocean.

Salamun glanced up at the eastern horizon, the sky turning a light blue, with pink and yellow tinges on clouds announcing the coming arrival of the sun. Another hour until the night watch would be relieved and he and the other men could line up for morning meal.

Then, as he faced south, something caught his eye. A glint of light off... what? There, another one, then more. He squinted and raised a hand to shield his eyes from the lightening sky. There was movement—a waving or rippling of shapes and shadows at the forest edge. He noticed a sound like distant thunder getting closer but too quickly for a weather system. Suddenly, his eyes made out horses. Horses with riders. Riders holding swords. Ten seconds passed from his first notice until he shouted out an alert and fired his musket at whatever was coming his way.

Wym Terrell was one of the ten men carrying shielded lanterns. Nine of them made it to the top of the berm. A musket round struck one lantern carrier. *Probably from the first guard to see us*, Terrell thought. There had been a flurry of other musket shots, though no cannon and nothing else to stop their charge across the shallow depression formed when the Narthani had dug the berm. The clansmen spurred their mounts up the berm's outer slope and poured over the top. A few horses fell or struggled, but most managed the slope with little problem. At the top, Terrell and the other eight men uncovered their lanterns and dropped them.

The few men on watch were swept away by the tide of horsemen. Of the hundred clansmen in the first group, eighty-eight rode down the inner slope and into the encampment that had just begun to stir. Close behind came seven hundred riders who had waited for the signal. The attack caught the Narthani and the Eywellese by surprise.

In the dark, the clansmen roared through lines of tents and small buildings. They assumed anyone on foot was Narthani or Eywellese—to be cut down with sword or pistol. In the confusion and darkness, no organized resistance was possible, as a seemingly endless stream of horsemen surged through the encampment.

The clansmen gave no quarter.

Twenty minutes later, Welman Stent and Lordum Hewell watched the last of the encampment and the adjacent village of Parthmal's buildings added to the conflagration. The light from fires was bright enough to read small print or identify the hair color and the beard length on scattered bodies.

"I think we've done all the damage we can do here," said Hewell.

"Right," said Stent. "I'm tempted to go farther, but prudence says we take this victory and get back to safer territory. However, I think I'll send few dozen men to scout toward Hanslow. As for the rest of us, let's gather up whatever firearms we find and see if we can hitch up the Narthani cannon to those small wagons we've seen them use. Then we'll go directly east, sending scouts well ahead to find the Narthani army and the clans harassing them. Once we find the other clans, we'll assess whether we're needed or can head back to Moreland City."

CHAPTER 3

ESCAPE

Hanslow, Eywell Province Capital

Anarynd Moreland watched with conflicted feelings as the Narthani army left Hanslow and moved east toward Moreland. After two and a half months of Narthani language immersion since her capture, she understood enough of Erdelin's conversations with subordinates to gather that the Narthani had prepared a major move into Moreland.

She worried because her clan and family lay in the Narthani's path. However, she felt thankful when she heard Erdelin would be away for several sixdays or more, a time she wouldn't share his bed.

She refused to accept that she might never escape—a capitulation made by many other captive women such as Gwyned Walstyn, the Preddi slave who had advised Anarynd on that first night to do whatever necessary to survive. The two women had become friends in the manner that happened when sharing what they couldn't share with others.

Gwyned's master was a Narthani supply officer—one of the breed that armies depended on to keep functioning but who was not part of a fighting unit. He had deigned to give Gwyned a name after she bore a child, a name Gwyned never told Anarynd.

After being a Narthani slave for two years and with a half-Narthani child, Gwyned didn't foresee a better future. Her family was dead or scattered, but she had assumed that whatever her future held would be on Caedellium—she hadn't considered that her master might take her away from the island forever. That assumption proved false, when, two months ago, her master informed her that when he returned to Narthon, he intended to take her and the child with him—a promise given as a reward but received as a sentence.

Anarynd had risked speaking to Gwyned about her thoughts of escape—

something Gwyned discouraged because of the unlikely success and the consequences. In the last two months, Anarynd had met a score of other Caedelli women slaves and a few from lands beyond Caedellium and brought to the island with their masters—both military and tradesmen. A quiet network had formed among the women, spreading news and providing a semblance of emotional and physical support.

One secret shared among a few women, and only among those most trusted, was a brew made from the bark of a native Caedellium root, which reduced the chances of pregnancy. It was a dangerous game. If a master decided a woman was barren, he might discard her to the brothels. Gwyned began taking the herb after the birth of her child—hoping the one child would convince her master of her fertility and allow her to delay more children as long as possible. Anarynd had initially been so despondent that Gwyned feared she would attempt suicide, but sharing the herb's secret had assuaged Anarynd's dread of becoming pregnant.

On the occasions when their masters were away, Anarynd, Gwyned, and other women spent a few quiet hours together, either in silence or talking of inconsequential matters—as if to pretend they were back at their original homes.

On one of those days, just past sundown, six women sat under trees adjacent to Erdelin's villa. A sixday after the army had left, rumors spread that the army was moving slowly through Moreland, burning towns—but with no major fighting yet.

A ratcheting up of the city's background noise interrupted the women's recollections of home. They heard shouts of many voices raised in emotion but didn't know the cause. One of the women served an officer of the town defenses, and she left to find out more news. She returned walking fast and breathing hard.

"Word is spreading that there was a battle at Moreland City, and the Narthani may have lost!"

Anarynd's heart jumped into her throat. *Moreland defeated the host that left here? That's not possible, even if other clans came to Moreland's aid! Or is it possible?*

"Are you sure that's what you heard?" pressed Gwyned.

"Yes, yes, and more. Word just came that the clans overran a Narthani and Eywellese supply base in Parthmal, and clan riders were seen only a few miles from here. The entire remaining garrison—Narthani and Eywellese—are called to the defenses. I heard them say the clans might attack this city."

"But the clans couldn't possibly take Hanslow," argued Gwyned. "Not with the defenses, the cannon, and so many Narthani and Eywellese fighting men."

Suddenly, they could hear Narthani horns and drums beating rhythms.

"Calling to stations—that's what it means," said another woman. "Maybe the clans can't take the city, but that's the signal to man all defenses."

Suddenly, Anarynd knew this might be her only good chance to escape.

"Will all the men be at the defenses?" she asked.

"At first. If they decide an attack isn't imminent, then they'll reduce those standing to."

"The defenses of Hanslow are mainly on the three sides of the town away from the river, aren't they?" asked Anarynd.

"Yes," answered a puzzled Gwyned. "Why? The bluff on the river bank is too steep for a major attack, so they only keep a few men on the walls."

"Does anyone know of a way through the defenses from inside without being seen?"

"Anarynd! I hope you aren't thinking of trying to escape!" warned Gwyned. "You would never make it out, and if you did . . . then what?"

The woman who had gone for news spoke up. "I know a way. Several times I've accompanied my master as he inspected the fortifications. I think he liked to show me off to the common soldiers," she added bitterly. "There's a partially collapsed section of wall that can be squeezed through. From there, it's a steep climb down to the river."

"Would they have men at the opening?" questioned Anarynd.

"How would I know?" asked the woman. "I only saw it twice and only in daylight, with no alert ongoing. What they're doing now, I can't say."

Anarynd could hardly believe what she contemplated. "Can you tell me exactly how to find it?"

"No. But I can *show* you. I think you're right. This may be the best chance to escape."

"You're both crazy!" snapped Gwyned. "You know what will happen when you're caught!"

"*If* we're caught," countered Anarynd. "If we get there and can't find the opening and we're asked, we'll just say we were frightened and looking for a place to hide from the murderous clansmen we heard were coming to rape us." She spit out the last words with venom.

Breathing hard, Gwyned wrung her hands. "I still say you're both crazy . . . but . . . I'm going, too. Let me get Morwena."

Two of the other woman voiced they would also come, while the sixth thought them all insane, but she would go back to her quarters and wish them God's protection. The remaining five huddled together.

"Take nothing but the clothing anyone would normally wear around the city," said Anarynd. She waved a hand over the florid and expensive robe Erdelin had insisted she wear. "The clothing we're wearing now would identify us as officers' slaves. Change into less conspicuous clothing. Nothing else—otherwise, it will raise suspicion if we're stopped."

"When should we try it?" asked a woman.

"Now," said Anarynd. The five women scattered and reassembled again thirty minutes later, but now there were seven of them—three with small children.

"They were there when I went to get Morwena," said Gwyned desperately, clutching her asleep two-year-old daughter. "I couldn't leave them if there was any chance."

"You idiot," hissed one of the original five. "You'll give us away!"

"I didn't see a single Narthani or Eywellese soldier *anywhere*," said Gwyned. "There's no one to *see* us."

Another woman agreed—all the men were on the walls and the fortifications. They started off. By the halfway point to the river side of town, they had seen only women, children, and a few of the oldest men, until they came near a walled compound with a single guard at the door. They were about to detour around the street when Anarynd stopped and stared at the compound.

"That's a troop brothel, isn't it?" she asked, emotionless.

"Yes," whispered Gwyned.

"How many women do they keep in there?"

"I think around thirty to fifty," said Gwyned, "depending on how many are still alive and when they brought in new ones."

Anarynd peeked around the corner at the guard. "So far, we haven't been stopped. I think we'll make it to the opening. I'm thinking that if we get away, will I spend the rest of my life remembering the women left behind those walls?"

"Oh, merciful God, Anarynd! Don't tell me you want to try to bring them along, too!" blurted Gwyned. "There's a guard at the gate and who knows how many more inside! Why don't we just run through the streets screaming 'We're trying to escape!'"

"I have to try. Will you help or not?"

"Of course, I will, you stupid bitch, but what about the guard?"

"There's only one at the gate. Surely, four or five women who happen to walk up to him, asking for information about what's happening, can take care of him."

"Like how?" asked a short, black-haired woman holding a two-year-old boy.

"Like this," said Anarynd, pulling out an eight-inch bone-handled knife of Erdelin's.

"Or this," said Gwyned, holding a kitchen butcher knife.

The seven women produced five knives of different shape and length.

So much for not bringing anything except innocuous clothing, thought Anarynd.

While they watched, two Eywellese women scurried down the street and past the guard, who gave them a cursory glance and leaned back against the wall by the door. A scruffy dog ran up to the guard and then off again, dodging a boot.

"What if there are more guards inside?" asked one woman.

"Look at the key ring he's carrying," said Gwyned. "Why would he have so many keys and be outside the building if there were more men inside?"

"Too many of us and he'll be suspicious," said Anarynd. "I think three of us can surprise him if we walk up and pretend to ask him something."

"Which three?" asked a trembling woman Anarynd didn't know.

"I'll be one. I can get him to look at me," Anarynd said and clenched her jaw. She lowered her hood and shook out her long blonde hair.

"I still think you're insane, but then so am I," offered Gwyned. She volunteered a third woman, who nodded assent and flashed a wicked-looking, curved, bladed weapon.

Anarynd put a hand on each of the other two women. "When we get to him, I'll try to get him to turn to face me, and the two of you move behind him. Then we'll do what we have to."

The three of them walked out from around the corner and toward the guard. He noticed them at thirty feet away. His eyes scanned all three, then settled on Anarynd, who tried to transform herself back to the young girl and woman who used to tease boys and men with the way she walked and tossed her hair. He licked his lips, and his eyes reflected his thoughts as they roamed over her body and face.

"Pardon me," she said in her broken Narthani, putting her right hand on the wall a foot from the guard, "we hear all the horns and drums but don't know what's happening." She flicked her hair away from her eyes back to her shoulders. He turned to face her.

The other two women didn't exist at that moment but reappeared as Gwyned drove a knife into his back under the ribs.

He gasped and rose on his toes from the shock, but before he could move anymore, the other woman hacked at the side of his throat, and Anarynd jabbed her knife into his stomach.

All three women jumped back, as the man flayed his arms around—dying as he stood but still, by reflex, reaching for his sword. Anarynd leaped forward again and thrust her knife into his throat so hard, she lost her grip, and the hilt end of the blade ripped a gash in her palm. His eyes wide in shock and disbelief, the guard sank to his knees, Anarynd's knife in his neck, blood flowing down his neck. His hands grasped at his wounds and his legs kicked out several times. He never made a sound.

"My God, my God, my God," Gwyned chanted over and over.

"Quick, get him inside," ordered Anarynd.

"And pray to Merciful God there are no more guards on the other side of the door," moaned Gwyned.

Anarynd tested the door. It was locked. She pulled the key ring off the guard's belt. There were ten keys. The fifth one turned the lock, and she opened the door slowly and looked inside at a small, spare room with two desks and two hallways, one to each side. No one was in the room. She pushed the door open wider, and they dragged the motionless body of the guard into the room and to one side.

Suddenly, a woman's voice rang out from the left hall.

"Is the warning over?" called a woman.

"Well?" asked the voice again, and then a middle-aged woman in an expensive red robe and sandals appeared. She stopped when she saw the three women.

"Who . . . ?" she started to say and then noticed the guard's body and a blood trail. The woman turned to run, but Gwyned slammed her against the wall, threw her to the ground, and held her knife at the woman's throat.

"Shout and I'll cut your throat," hissed Gwyned. The blood-covered knife and the expression of the wielder made no other convincing necessary.

"Are there other guards in the building?"

The woman shook her head, her eyes wide and frightened.

"Where are the women?"

"They're locked in the commons rooms at the end of the hall," the woman gasped, with an arm toward the rightward hall.

Anarynd raced down the right hall. It was sixty to seventy feet long with open doors every eight feet. As she ran, she glanced into the open doors and got quick glimpses of narrow rooms with no windows and in each room, a low, wood-frame bed with a bare mattress—nothing else. Unbidden, her mind flashed that here was where the women "worked" to an endless line of Narthani soldiers. She shut the images out, as she reached the door at the end of the hall and fumbled with the keys.

This time, the eighth key turned the lock. She shoved open the door. Light from candles reflected off a sea of faces with blank or frightened expressions—all looking at her. None of the women uttered a word.

"There is no time for anything," barked Anarynd. "All the Narthani soldiers are at the city's walls. There are supposed to be clansmen about to attack. I and some others are trying to escape out of the city before the soldiers come back. Anyone who wants to come with us has to come RIGHT NOW."

Dozens of women talking at once broke the silence. "Escape?" "It's not possible!" "Who are you?" "It's a trick!" "Escape to what or where?"

The din rose and rose until Anarynd screamed, "SHUT UP or guards will come back!"

The tumult quieted.

"Is there *really* a chance to escape," asked a slender, brown-haired girl of perhaps seventeen years, tears running down her cheeks.

"It's a chance," said Anarynd. "We don't know if we can make it, but it's all we have."

"They'll kill us if we leave the building," stated a woman in the back of the room.

"Would you rather be killed trying to escape or stay here to service Narthani until you die?" grated the young woman.

"There's no time for talking," reiterated Anarynd. "Those who want to come with us follow me right this moment. We're leaving NOW. Any others just stay in this room and wait for the Narthani to come back."

Anarynd turned and started back down the hall. She heard the drum of many footsteps behind her. By now, the other four of their original seven women had gathered with the children in the anteroom.

"Oh, God," said Gwyned. "They're going to hear us just from the dust we raise and the drum of footfalls."

Anarynd turned to the women who had crowded into the room. "Pass the word on down to follow us and keep quiet!"

"What do we do about the woman?" asked Gwyned, referring to the richly dressed woman cowering in a corner.

The young woman, plus several other women, glanced to the corner. A feral look came over her. "She won't be a problem," she said, as the woman in the corner disappeared under a mass of brothel women. Choking sounds followed an aborted scream . . . and then nothing.

The woman nearest the outer door would guide them to the supposed opening in the defense wall. She peered into the street, then turned her head back. "No one in sight. Let's go."

Had there been Narthani or Eywellese men in the streets, the sight of a mob of women hustling along might have raised alarms. The few people they passed were women and children. Then they turned a corner, and in front of them walked a single armed Eywellese man. They froze. He looked them over, jerked his head to indicate move on, and strode away. All the women breathed again.

The cluster of women wound along streets and alleys for four hundred yards until they reached a tumble of stone blocks against the inner side of the city's outer riverside wall. Their guide walked up to the pile, then picked her way around and over blocks, Anarynd following. And there it was—a slit in the bottom of the wall. The two women could feel air coming through. They squeezed through a four-foot passage to stand on the other side of the main wall. A moon rose just over the horizon and cast a faint yellowish glow in the night. Before them lay a steep slope down to the river. The press of women squeezing through the gap forced them to move along the base of the wall. Soon, all were standing outside, and Anarynd got her first estimate of how many women there were. At least thirty!

Some started talking—to be hushed by others. Word got to Anarynd and Gwyned that some women said they couldn't go down that slope and others said they couldn't swim. Several turned and walked back into town. Anarynd had no time for them. It was their decision. But they *might*, deliberately or inadvertently, raise an alarm.

"We go NOW," said Anarynd, and she stepped onto the slope. The lucky, or most agile, women stayed on their feet part of the way down. Several tumbled the entire distance to the river. Two went directly into the river and disappeared. Two women lay dead at the bottom, and six had injuries severe enough to be helped or carried by the others. Anarynd felt bruises on every part of her body, and she had blood coming from a dozen superficial cuts. She didn't notice.

Crossing the river, they lost several more women. They never knew how many, since there had been no exact count at the beginning. Once across, exhausted, wet, bruised, if not worse, and with no idea where they were going, they headed for a line of trees a mile away.

Spurred on by adrenaline flowing through their veins, the exhausted women hurried as fast as their bodies would allow, while looking back every few feet, fearful of pursuers.

"We're almost to the trees," said Anarynd, gasping for air. "We can rest there."

They ran and stumbled the last few yards. Anarynd's legs trembled from exertion, but before collapsing onto the ground she turned to ensure the last of the women had reached the trees.

Suddenly, a man's voice called out. "And who in God's creation are you women?"

Anarynd spun and her throat constricted in fear before she recognized that the man spoke Caedelli and not with the Eywellese accent. She pulled her knife from her belt and held it against her side, so he wouldn't see it. Gwyned and the brown-haired girl did the same.

"Who are YOU?" asked Anarynd.

"I'm Stentese, and we've been out killing Narthani and Eywellese. However, Hanslow is more than we can chew off, and we're about to head back. There. I've told who I am; now *you* do the same."

"Oh, my God," blurted a woman. "Is it true, then, the clans have beaten the Narthani in a battle?"

"Well, I suppose it depends on what you say is a victory, but at least we drove them out of Moreland Province."

"Please," begged Anarynd, "we're all slaves captured by the Narthani and the Eywellese. We escaped when they sent all men to the defenses, but they'll be coming after us once they realize so many of us are missing. Many of us are Morelanders, plus Preddi and a few from elsewhere on Anyar."

The man cursed, then spit to one side. "Well, *that's* not part of our plan. We need to get out of here fast. Once the Narthani realize there aren't that many of us and we aren't attacking, they'll send men out to look for us."

Anarynd feared he meant he wouldn't help them.

"Please," she implored, "at least take the women with babies. You have to do *something*!"

He grunted. "Oh, we'll take you all. It's just got to be quick."

With that, he turned and whistled. Another whistle answered, followed by sounds of horses—many horses. In the darkness, Anarynd couldn't tell the number of men, but with a lot of shouting and shoving, all of the woman and children doubled up with riders, and they headed east at a trot.

CHAPTER 4

LOSS OR DRAW?

Preddi City

Despite Akuyun's determination to keep focused on the endless paperwork, his mind roamed to the east, and he imagined events playing out in Moreland Province. He had seen Brigadier Zulfa and 6,500 Narthani troops and 2,500 Caedelli allies start for the Moreland border. Part of him had wanted to lead the invasion, but his responsibility was to all the Narthani military forces, army and navy, and the 100,000 Narthani non-military colonists on the island.

He sighed. The waiting stack never seemed to grow smaller, no matter how many hours he spent attacking it. The current papers spread before him included cargo manifests of the latest supply ship from Narthon: uniforms, Narthani civilian clothing, replacement muskets for those becoming unserviceable, six fortification cannons of the thirty he had requested, bags of correspondence for the troops and civilians, twenty more priests of Narth who had usurped berths of new junior officers, on and on—plus ten vats of Narthani ale. The latter unrequisitioned and all spoiled; he suspected graft through someone in their quartermaster corps. He acknowledged the receipt of all the cargo—those of use and those not. As soon as he finished with the incoming cargo, he moved on to the items for the return trip to Narthon, including a few well-connected traders, five Narthani broken from their rank and from families too important for Akuyun to consider executing, and hulls filled with grains and cured meats.

He also suspected the paper stack contained the yearly performance reviews of all officers under his command. Although he made only the primary evaluations of those immediately under him, he routinely reviewed all the evaluations and concurred with or put aside any evaluations where he needed to talk with the evaluator. Beyond that, he didn't care to speculate on the rest of the pile, as he doggedly continued. As usual, he made it a routine to quit by sundown to be home for evening meal with his wife, Rabia, and children.

As much as he disliked such paperwork, he normally disciplined himself to work efficiently. But not on days like today. The latest news from Zulfa outside Moreland City reported that the first day of direct contact with the Caedelli army—if clansmen mobs could be called an army—proved inconclusive. The islanders had massed in front of the Narthani positions, milled around for hours and feinted attacks twice, but never came within firing range. Zulfa reported he would give them the next day to attack, and if they didn't, he would continue to advance on the city to force a battle.

If a general engagement has happened, it might have been days ago, thought Akuyun, *so Zulfa would have sent notice back to the closest Eywell semaphore station. In which case, I should get news any time now.*

He had barely finished the thought when a knock on his office door preceded an aide, unbidden, rushing in with a piece of paper. Akuyun's intended reprimand of the young officer for his decorum faded, as he saw the shocked look on the aide's face.

"A semaphore message from Brigadier Zulfa, sir," choked out the young officer.

Akuyun's displeasure vanished, to be replaced by a knot in his stomach. "What . . . ?"

He took the paper and read the few lines.

```
From: Brigadier Zulfa
To: General Akuyun
Engaged Caedelli large force.
Right wing collapsed.
Lost half cannon.
3 squares destroyed.
Withdrawing to Eywell.
More later.
```

"Great Narth?" he exclaimed, shaken. *Forced to withdraw? What could have happened?*

Remembering the young officer standing in front of his desk, Akuyun composed himself. "Thank you. I take it you read the message?"

"Yes, sir. Standing orders from Major Saljurk are to read all incoming messages and prioritize getting them to you. I know anything from Brigadier

Zulfa would be considered high priority . . . Should I not have read it, sir?"

"No, no. Nothing to worry about on that account. Of course, the news is not what we expected, is it?" Akuyun managed a tone he hoped conveyed his reception of disappointing news but not disaster.

"No, sir. Not expected at all. Pardon me if I'm out of line, but what does this mean for our mission?"

"Mean? It only means things didn't go as well as we hoped, and we'll just have to work harder, doesn't it?"

"Yes, sir," said the relieved young officer. "Only a minor setback, I'm sure, sir."

Only after the door closed and Akuyun sat alone again did he let his calm façade fade.

Beaten by the islanders? How can this be? Well . . . not beaten, I suppose. Zulfa says they are withdrawing. Aivacs is not one to play with words, so if they were beaten badly, he would have said they were retreating. It must mean the battle was indecisive, but the army is still intact and Zulfa has decided to break off contact.

Another message, delivered that evening to his villa, and further messages the following several days bore out Akuyun's prediction. By then, Akuyun knew the basic elements of events. The Eywellese had abandoned their position protecting the right flank and had fallen into an islander trap, resulting in over a thousand Eywellese dead, including the Eywell Hetman and his two sons. Before the Narthani commanders on the scene realized the right wing's exposure, the islanders attacked by enfilade and rolled over the first infantry block and the right artillery position and mauled two or three more infantry blocks, before other units could reposition. The islanders didn't pursue further attacks, except for harassing the army as it withdrew into Eywell. There, Zulfa found the Parthmal base destroyed, and he ordered the army to continue to Hanslow, the Eywell capital.

Zulfa waited until the army reached Hanslow and for confirmation that no major islander forces had crossed the border before he rode hard back to report in person to Akuyun in Preddi City. He came straight to Akuyun's office without changing clothes or doing more than shake off the worst of the dust. Four men stood hunched over a diagram of the Narthani deployment in front of Moreland City: Zulfa, Akuyun, Accessor Hizer, and Admiral Kalcan.

"And Hetman Eywell gave no indication of what he was doing or any other warning?" asked Akuyun angrily.

"Nothing," answered Zulfa bitterly. "The combination of lingering morning mist, gun powder smoke, and grass fires set by the Caedelli made it difficult to see the entire field. Somehow, the Caedelli enticed Hetman Eywell to chase after several hundred clansmen who seemed to be fleeing to the south. Unconfirmed reports say the clansmen might have included the Keelan hetman—which would fit, since the two hetmen were long-time enemies. Whatever precipitated his leaving his position, Hetman Eywell took two-thirds of his riders with him and ran straight into an ambush, where the clans decimated them. The Caedelli then attacked the flank of our right-most block and rolled right over them and into the artillery position. Neither the block nor the artillery batteries realized their danger in time to react. The islanders then pushed farther and savaged two more infantry blocks before other blocks wheeled in formation to face the flank. Plus, I had much of my own cavalry moved to back up the infantry. At that point, the Caedelli pulled back. Faced with losing half the artillery and with three of the infantry blocks destroyed or badly mauled—and, of course, most of the Eywellese—I decided it best to withdraw to reassess."

"And your reasoning for not counterattacking at that point or at least trying to retake the artillery?" asked Akuyun.

"Colonel Erdelin reported that his men saw the Caedelli hauling our cannon away. In the confusion and limited visibility, it was impossible to be sure where the cannon were. If they had left them in place and tried to use them against us, I would have considered such a counterattack.

"However, under the circumstances, I didn't think a counterattack advisable. The Caedelli were on two sides with large mobile forces. We didn't have enough cavalry, and the infantry was unlikely to force them to stand."

Zulfa wiped sweat and dirt from his face with a cloth.

"In addition, what we faced was completely different from the intelligence we used in planning. We expected a mass of uncoordinated light cavalry, and we based our plans on trying to force them into attacking under conditions where we could crush them. While we inflicted significant losses on a cavalry charge into our prepared fire zone, we didn't catch as many of their riders as we had hoped, and the attack on our right flank was far more coordinated and well carried out than we had any reason to suspect them capable of. Yes, enticing the Eywellese to break position was the key, but reports are that both at the ambush of the Eywellese and the flank attack, the Caedelli had light cannon."

"Cannon?" said a startled Hizer. "We had no reports of any field cannon among the clans."

"Well, reports or not, they had them. Not many, and witnesses say they were odd pieces with three barrels about the size of swivel guns. It's doubtful they had much range, but at close quarters they delivered canister effectively. Once the islanders got through the Eywellese screen, they got their artillery within a hundred yards of the rightmost infantry block and began firing before they were seen. In the confusion and limited visibility, I suspect the leaders of that block had no idea what was happening.

"The final factor in my decision to withdraw was that they didn't act like an enemy inexperienced in modern warfare. Fixing our attention to the front by sacrificing as many as a thousand men, then attacking an exposed flank and pressing hard until they came against more prepared positions, upon which time they withdrew, all speaks to me of significant military experience and planning."

"But we found no indication of any such capability with the Caedelli," said Akuyun, who turned to Hizer. "Did I miss anything in reports?"

"No," said the Assessor. "Everything we learned says the islanders have never fought engagements of this size, never with cannon, and they certainly have never faced a modern mixed army of infantry, artillery, and cavalry. All of which leads to an obvious conclusion."

"They had help from outside of Caedellium," stated a grim Zulfa.

Hizer nodded, as did Kalcan, who added, "That occurs to me as well. But who?"

"It could be any one of our enemies," said Akuyun. "The Iraquiniks and the Fuomi are the obvious possibilities, since they're the ones we're currently in direct conflict with, but any of the other realms could be worried about the expansion of the Empire and our one day turning attention to them—certainly, any of the nations on Landolin are possibilities."

Zulfa wiped his face again and took a long draught of water. He appeared drained.

Akuyun looked grimly at his subordinate.

"Aivacs . . . I expect a full written report tomorrow. But for now, go and clean up, and get some food and sleep. I doubt you've had much of either the last few days. We'll meet again after I read your detailed report."

After Zulfa had left the room, Hizer turned to Akuyun. "What do you think? Did he do the right thing by withdrawing, instead of counterattacking?"

"It's impossible to be sure. My own inclination would have been to counterattack and still try to accomplish the mission, but Zulfa was the commander on the scene. He's the only one who saw everything in real time and had to make the judgment. Without other indications, I'm inclined to support his decision. In addition, I've had high confidence in his abilities for several years, and that experience weighs in his favor."

"I've also known Aivacs for several years and have always thought him one of the better troop commanders I've worked with," said Kalcan, who then added, "But again, what does this do to the mission objectives and timetables?"

"Obviously, the best-case outcome isn't going to happen. We're not going to take all of Caedellium easily—certainly not with what we have here now," Akuyun said with a scowl.

Hizer frowned. "So, you don't think you could mount a more deliberate campaign, such as the circum-island strategy—moving on the coastal clans using the navy for support and mobility?"

Akuyun looked at the Caedellium map on the wall and waved toward the western coast. "For example, if we moved against Stent Province, they could withdraw inland while the clans gathered forces. If they refused to give battle, we don't have enough men to hold the province and move on to the next one, such as Pewitt. The Stentese would just move back in and they would be in our rear, and so on around the island. Yes, we can take any one clan's province, but we can't hold it and take more. We've just not got enough men. Plus, the more we stretch out our men, the easier it would be for the islanders to whittle us away a little at a time."

Akuyun kept facing the wall map as he ruminated.

"Also, remember that they put upward of twelve thousand men against us this time. Now that they've pushed us back, I'd be surprised if the clans that didn't oppose us this time won't be emboldened, and we could face twenty to thirty thousand the next time. When you add their greater mobility and cannon they already have and those they captured, I think the best we can do is hold what we have."

"You haven't mentioned it, General," said Hizer, "but I know what else is on your mind. You have to protect the Narthani noncombatants on the island. There are sixty thousand Narthani, plus another forty thousand servants and slaves in Preddi Province. For all practical purposes, they are part of the Narthon Empire. If you used enough forces to try a further campaign against the islanders, wouldn't this put Preddi in danger?"

"You're correct, Sadek, it's on my mind. If we send troops, with navel support, to attack other clans, it would weaken our ability to defend Preddi Province. We would be forced to pull all nonmilitary personnel back into cities and towns, which would prevent growing the food and mining the ore that make this expansion possible. Given all these considerations, I'm suspending the status of this mission and restricting it to holding the existing three provinces and continuing whatever non-direct military activity is still possible. Full reports will be sent to Narthon immediately. Unless I hear compelling arguments against, I will recommend that a substantially larger force is needed to subdue the island."

Akuyun paused and looked for comments. "Assessor Hizer?"

"I'm inclined to agree, but I would like to read the reports in more detail before I write my observations to the High Command."

"Will one day be sufficient?"

"I think I can finish tomorrow, if I get Zulfa's written reports early enough."

"Good. Admiral Kalcan, prepare your fastest sloop for return to Narthon with dispatches. Take no cargo or passengers. Instruct the captain on the urgency to make the fastest time possible."

"There will be complaints about no cargo or passengers from at least the trading houses and Prelate Balcan," cautioned Kalcan.

"That's why there are to be no exceptions. A blanket prohibition is easier to enforce than a leaky one."

The next day involved a flurry of report writing, including Assessor Hizer's concurrence with Akuyun's recommendation. On the second morning tide, a Narthani sloop left the harbor and hoisted full sails within three hundred yards of shore. Catching the winds northeast around the northern tip of the Landolin continent to Ezarkin, the closest Narthani port, would take the sloop a month and a half. From there, the reports would travel 3 to 4 sixdays by riders and semaphore to reach the High Command at Umasya, the Empire's capital.

Five months, thought Akuyun. *It will be a minimum of five months to hear any response to our reports. And given how slowly the decision wheels turn at such high levels, and then factoring in time to gather reinforcements, I expect it will be six months or more. I'm afraid we have some tense months ahead.*

CHAPTER 5

LEARNING

Three Things

Yozef Kolsko acknowledged three things in the month since the battle of Moreland City. First, he realized he couldn't decide whether his actions during the fighting at Moreland City meant he was braver than he'd thought or stupider. Despite gut-wrenching fear and his intent to stay as far from bullets, blades, and cannon as he could, somehow, in the heat of the battle, while the Keelanders tried to use their own small artillery pieces and the larger captured cannon against the Narthani infantry formations, he'd forgotten his fear and rushed to help organize the Keelan gunners. When he looked back at those minutes, how he'd acted didn't fit his own self-image. Episodes of cognitive dissonance recurred, as his mind tried to reconcile that he had done something he couldn't imagine himself doing. If he'd witnessed anyone else behaving that way, he would have viewed the person as *heroic*, a word he would never have associated with "Joe Colsco." Perhaps "Yozef Kolsko" was a different person?

Brave or stupid? He found it hard to use the latter label, because what he did had been necessary. The Narthani infantry blocks had repositioned to face the clansmen. Both sides had begun serious musket fire exchanges, which would have only one outcome; the islanders weren't disciplined enough to stand against professional soldiers. The only hope, and one Yozef had recognized, was to get the artillery pieces into action. Keelan gunners had tried to bring their three-barrel swivel light artillery into position, but one of the three carriages had overturned, its crew disorganized, and Yozef felt sure they intended to abandon the carriage.

He could only remember thinking that they needed every piece in action as soon as possible to suppress the Narthani muskets. He had no recollection of making a decision but found himself organizing the overturned carriage crew and helping other Keelanders get the captured Narthani 12-pounder cannon into action. Now, it was all a blur. He had no doubt that if they hadn't gotten the artillery into action, the Narthani would have crushed the Keelan attack and killed most of the men, including Yozef—though he arrived at this judgment in hindsight. It had come down to his doing what was necessary, without considering the potential cost to himself.

As a result, whenever someone raised the topic of what he had done during the battle, he diverted the conversation, claimed he couldn't remember details, or he found a reason to be somewhere else.

The second realization Yozef came to happened gradually, but he only fully acknowledged it when he woke one morning, rolled over, and looked at Maera still sleeping. The previous evening had been one of the best he could remember. They had lingered over evening meal, her talking about plans to organize the university, him describing ideas for new projects, both of them listening intently to what the other had in mind and offering comments and suggestions at the right moments, both of them knowing the other had truly *listened*.

Later, they played the Anyar version of the game GO. Maera, a master at the game, had played at the Snarling Graeko pub with the best local players until her pregnancy progressed to where she wanted to spend evenings at home. Still, she missed playing and coerced Yozef to play whenever she could. He usually obliged, though he hadn't yet won a game from her. At the pub, he felt proud of her skill and pleased to watch her intent focus when she played. Although he didn't mind her being so much better than him, it irked him that he didn't win *occasionally*.

"You must not concentrate enough," said his wife after his third loss.

"Somehow, I don't believe that's the problem," he said. "I'm concentrating as hard as I can—just to see if *once* I can win a game against you."

"And you would want me to lose a game now and then?" Maera asked, the smile at the corners of her mouth indicating she already knew her husband's answer.

"It would have to be a real win." Yozef paused. "I don't mind losing as much as wondering how you do it. Let's play a game, and you tell me why you made each move. Maybe I can pick up some pointers and at least make our games more interesting for you."

They played again, and Maera explained her reasoning when she could. By the twentieth move, it became apparent he couldn't learn how to play better.

"I'm sorry, Yozef. The best moves simply seem obvious to me."

"No need to be sorry. It's what I suspected. You have some of the characteristics of a savant."

"A what?"

"*Savant.* A word my people use for someone with an extraordinary intellectual talent that can't be explained." Yozef didn't tell her that another definition of *savant* pertained to someone with an extraordinary talent who also had a significant impairment, such as autism. *Savant* was the only word he could think of at the moment, and the Caedelli wouldn't know the difference.

"Then you must be one, too," said Maera, "with all the knowledge you have."

"No. I'm smart enough, but more the normal level. Having knowledge doesn't necessarily have a direct correlation with intelligence, though obviously it helps, especially in *using* the knowledge. If anything, I might be called a *polymath,* someone with broad knowledge in many areas."

"So many new words, Yozef. I wonder if you'll ever run out of them. I hope you realize every time there's a new one, it makes me all the more curious about exactly where you came from."

Yozef frowned. "Now, Maera, we agreed—"

"No, no," said Maera, laughing. "I'm not going back on our agreement. I won't press you for details of your mysterious origin. You said you'd tell me someday, if you could, and that the secrecy has nothing to do with Caedellium and its people."

"As for new words," said Yozef, looking to divert the conversation from the sensitive subject, "that's part of expanding knowledge. The more you know, the more you need words that weren't necessary before."

"As you say," replied Maera. "So, if I'm a savant and you're a polymath, our child will be what?"

"A treasure. A miracle."

The rest of the evening, they talked of the child, of their house, of inconsequential things, all the while communicating about being together, even if they never spoke the words.

As he lay in bed, looking at Maera and remembering the evening, his throat tightened, his gaze softened, and he resisted the urge to reach out to embrace her. He told himself he didn't want to wake her, but he knew it wasn't the only reason.

I love her. Yes, I liked and respected her, and the marriage was the logical thing to do.

But now there's more to it. I don't know when it happened, or whether it was a single event or a gradual development, but I have to admit it to myself. Yet neither of us has said the words to the other. Why don't I say them? As if I didn't know. Maybe she doesn't feel the same way. I'm sure she cares for me, but that's not the same as love. If I say them first, I'm afraid of what she'll say back. Maybe what I feel for her is only one way. It would put her on the spot: either she'd have to admit she doesn't love me that way, or she would be obliged to pretend.

What a dork I am, and I feel like a coward, but maybe it's best not to have the answer for certain, rather than risk hearing what I don't want to hear.

The third thing Yozef realized during his first month back from Moreland City was that his status in Keelan society had changed yet again. As he introduced products and knowledge, became wealthy by Caedellium standards, and was acknowledged for his role in the defense of St. Sidryn's Abbey, he became aware of his increased stature: from destitute, strange man to major figure in Abersford. He was recognized by everyone, respected by most, and accepted as somewhat odd. His marriage to Maera, the eldest daughter of the Clan Keelan's hetman, had bumped up his status several steps, with people paying him more deference than in the past, although those with whom he had the most contact had come back to considering him the same, or nearly so, as before the marriage.

Yet he occasionally sensed that even those closest acquaintances acted differently around him, although sometimes the difference was subtle—if he wasn't imaging things, as he often reminded himself. Carnigan remained the one exception. Yozef wondered whether the big man didn't perceive a change in Yozef's position or if he didn't care.

Yozef didn't delude himself that he didn't like being seriously listened to, but it got exasperating when people listened because of *who* he was, instead of *what* he said. The consequences hit home when, while walking through Abersford two sixdays after returning from Moreland City, he passed a man and a woman, presumably married from their tone of voice, arguing over whether to repaint their house white or brown. Yozef jokingly suggested blue as he passed, never looking back. Three days later he passed by the same house, now painted an awful blue. The same man walked out the door as Yozef approached.

Although Yozef almost felt afraid to ask, he did. "Ser, I see you painted your house blue. Why?"

The man looked startled. "Why, Ser Kolsko, you said to paint it blue, so we did."

"Because I suggested it?"

"Well . . . you're Yozef Kolsko. We figured it *must* look better if *you* thought so."

Yozef groaned. *Christ!* "It was only a suggestion. Would you have painted it this color if I hadn't said anything?"

The man didn't respond—only stared in confusion at Yozef, who prompted the homeowner again. "I heard you and your wife discussing either white or brown. I assume you preferred those colors."

"Yes, I wanted brown, but Willa wanted white. I had almost agreed to the white when you told us blue would be better."

"I only offered an opinion of another color, in case you couldn't decide," said Yozef, which was only half true, because he'd given his passing remark in a flippant manner, not meant to be taken seriously. "In fact, now that I see the blue, you and your wife had the correct idea. The white would look best."

The man smiled with obvious relief. "I'm glad you think so, Ser Kolsko," he said, lowering his voice to just above a whisper. "To be truthful, this color is awful. Our neighbors have already complained about it, and I hate seeing it. We'll go right ahead and repaint the house white as soon as possible."

"Good idea," said Yozef, who wished the man enjoyment of the color change and left before he made another offhand comment that might be taken too seriously.

I've got to be careful what I say, thought Yozef, chagrined. *Hell, can't a man relax into a good mood without worrying about everything coming out of his mouth?*

It was several sixdays before the answer became apparent. No.

Icon?

Yozef listened with one ear to Abbot Sistian's Godsday service message. The topic was God's commandment that a person should expect to be treated only as well as he or she treats others. He thought it another statement of the Golden Rule. Something similar to "Do unto others as you would have them do unto you." Sistian varied this common theme frequently. Usually, Yozef found the variation in approaches to the topic interesting, but the abbot must have been pushed for time, because today Yozef began mouthing the sermon almost word for word. Although what the Watchers had done to him gave him an enhanced memory, whether they'd intended the effect or not, it was a sporadic gift. He could recall whole pages, even chapters, of science texts he'd used in college, although he ran into annoying gaps. But memories of other topics, such as a political science course, were not as forthcoming. Even if he'd taken the course and read the text, his focus must have been below a minimum threshold, because he could recall only scattered bits, if that.

Yet he must have paid special attention when the abbot gave almost exactly the same sermon two years previously. Yozef wondered whether anyone else had noticed the similarity. He caught himself mouthing a phrase and Maera watching him, an odd look on her face.

Shit! Next thing, she'll think I'm reading Sistian's mind.

He leaned and whispered in her ear. "The abbot's given this same sermon before."

She nodded, but he wasn't sure she bought the truth.

The service ended with a prayer and a charge to "Go out and do good" or something close. Yozef was already mentally running through poems and wondering, as long as his memory insisted on bringing up non-science memories, whether he should write snippets of literature as part of his secret journal on the history of Earth. In his mind, he was just finishing *The Destruction of Sennacherib* by Lord Byron when a woman carrying a baby blocked his way down the aisle.

"Ser Kolsko, would you bless little Sulyn here? It'd mean so much to me, you having saved us."

He stared at her. She stood only a few inches shorter than he, stout figure, a plain, pleading face, brown hair gathered into a bun, clean but rough clothing, and holding a sleeping baby perhaps six months old. Other attendees flowed around them, as Yozef continued staring. Maera nudged him with an elbow.

"What . . . ?" he uttered.

"A blessing, Ser Kolsko. I know it's probably too much to ask a Septarsh, after all you've done for us, with the ether helping Sulyn be born and the wonderful employment for my husband at the lantern shop . . ." She broke off, as if hoping for an affirmative answer from Yozef.

Maera came to his rescue. "The baby had to be cut from her. It was in breach position, and they couldn't turn it. Your ether has made this operation far safer and, needless to say, infinitely less painful."

Yozef didn't ask Maera how she knew details about a woman he didn't recognize. More and more often, he simply took for granted that his wife just *knew* things.

"I'm sorry," Yozef addressed the woman, "I'm not a theophist, so I don't . . . urk!"

Another elbow from Maera, this one sharper than the last.

"Oh, for God's sake, put a hand on the baby's head," Maera hissed in his ear.

He did as directed, and the woman beamed back at him, curtsied, and melded into the flow exiting the cathedral.

"What was that all about?" Yozef whispered to Maera.

"I'll tell you later."

The next hour they occupied themselves with exchanging greetings and polite conversation with more people than Yozef recognized, though evidently Maera knew them all. Then there was an after-service potluck he hadn't known about. A hundred or more people spread out blankets on the grass among trees near the abbey complex. Maera had given Yozef a basket to take with them to the service. He hadn't bothered asking about the contents.

They met with Filtin Fuller's family, and Carnigan appeared with a wooden block for Maera to sit on, her pregnancy making it difficult to sit upright on a flat surface for more than a few minutes at a time.

"Why thank you, Carnigan, that's very kind of you. Otherwise, I'd have been lying on the ground before long."

"Your lout of your husband should have thought of it," said Carnigan.

"Well, he has other qualities, though thinking of the small things isn't necessarily a strong point."

"For that snide comment, I've half a mind not to invite you to join us," said Yozef, laughing.

"Join you? Well . . . I didn't bring anything to share," said Carnigan, shifting his feet and looking embarrassed.

"Nonsense," said Yozef. "If I know Nerlin, she brought enough for three times as many people. Meaning that by adding you, there's still enough for twice as many."

"Certainly, Carnigan," said Filtin's wife. "Sit down, and Maera and I will spread out the food."

The group of friends ate, commented on the service, exchanged words with other clusters of people, and then sat on the grass for another hour, while the Fuller children joined the mobs of other children doing what children do. When they departed in various directions, Yozef felt relaxed and almost forgot about the woman asking for a blessing—until they came within sight of their house and the memory surfaced.

"Maera, you were going to tell me what the woman in the cathedral was all about. And what's this 'Septarsh'? I've heard the word before a few times but haven't had it explained to me."

She glanced up at her husband. "It's an ancient word believed to originate somewhere on Melosia. It refers to a person who has a special relationship with God. Exactly what that relationship is seems to vary with how different peoples view a Septarsh. Here on Caedellium and other realms on Anyar, it refers to someone to whom God speaks."

"Speaks?" Yozef frowned. "Like . . . in a burning bush?"

"A what?" asked Maera, wrinkling her eyebrows. "Why would God speak from a bush on fire?"

"Never mind," said Yozef.

Couldn't resist, he thought. *Though I need to watch getting* cute *with too many of these snippets.*

"So, God speaks to a Septarsh," said Yozef, changing the topic, as he usually did when he dropped an out-of-context phrase from English into the conversation. "But why did the woman call me one?"

"I wondered whether you'd noticed the word before, but you never asked me about it or said anything, so I assumed you knew some people have started to associate you with being a Septarsh yourself."

Yozef stumbled in a rut in the road.

"Me!? Why would anyone think I'm on speaking terms with God?"

"Yozef!" said Maera, with a roll of eyes and an exasperated tone. "Think about it! A strange man appears naked on a beach. He can't speak Caedelli, and yet within a few years he's introduced products no one has ever heard of and is becoming wealthy. He introduces knowledge unknown on Caedellium and then saves everyone from the Buldorian raiders—at least, that's what most people believe. Not long after, he marries the hetman's daughter and has a major role in turning back the Narthani when they invade Moreland Province. Why would you think it strange that at least some people *would* wonder you're somehow inspired by God?"

"Well, shit. I can't have people thinking I'm some kind of saint!"

"Trust me, Yozef," Maera said dryly, "those who know you don't think you're a saint."

He didn't know whether to be relieved or curious enough to ask why not.

"Maera, I've tried endlessly to be sure people here know I'm just passing on knowledge from my homeland. It doesn't originate from me, and God certainly isn't telling it to me. Trust me, I'd recognize him if he were."

"How exactly would you know it was God?"

"Uh . . . well . . . I don't know. I just would."

Her sneer didn't require a verbal explanation of her opinion of his incisive logic.

"Okay," he conceded, "maybe I don't know how I'd recognize the old guy, but I'm not a Septarsh. I'm just like any other person but with more knowledge than most people."

"Yozef, we haven't been married that long, and I admit I felt uncertain about many aspects of you and your mysterious history, but one thing I do know is you're not just 'any other person.'"

He remained silent for almost a hundred yards, until they were within the bounds of their property, when he asked seriously, "Then what do *you* think I am?"

"I'm not sure what you are, with the exception that you're my husband and the father of my child, and I thank God every Godsday to have met you."

He pulled her to him with a firm hug, kissing her gently, not saying anything, his throat suddenly tight. Elian appeared on the veranda, and they broke apart.

The elderly woman smiled at them. "Still behaving like you just wed? Keep the feeling as long as you can. Brak and I still have it, thank Merciful God."

Maera's claim that people thought of him as a Septarsh, whatever exactly that was, disturbed Yozef enough that he resolved to confirm what she had said with others. The first one was Carnigan.

"Yeah, I hear it occasionally. I don't know exactly what a Septarsh is supposed to be. I don't pay much attention. Ask Filtin."

Yozef cornered his friend and worker at the distillation shop after midday meal.

"Sure, everybody knows about the rumors of you maybe being a Septarsh."

What the hell! Everybody but me!

"I try not to get into discussions or arguments about it," said Filtin. "What do I know about such things? Anyway, who ever heard of a Septarsh telling stories at pubs? But that's just me. I know more than a few people who do believe it or at least consider it possible."

Filtin looked straight at Yozef. "What do *you* believe?"

"I believe I'm a Septarsh about as much as I believe I can pick up Carnigan with one hand."

The same day, after gathering his thoughts about what to ask the abbot, Yozef approached Sistian Beynom's office door. He wanted to assure the chief theophist at St. Sidryn's that he made no pretense of being any fashion of holy man, messenger from God, or whatever attribute people might want to foist on him.

The abbot motioned for Yozef to take the chair across from his desk, and after they exchanged pleasantries, Sistian said, "We've had enough conversations in here for me to sense the tenor of what brings you here. From what I see, it's something you're *concerned* about, not excited."

"It's this nonsense about people thinking I'm something I'm not."

"And that is . . .?" asked Sistian.

Yozef shifted in his seat, uncomfortable with even saying the word. "A Septarsh."

The abbot leaned forward in his chair, folding his hands on the desktop. "Diera and I have wondered when you would come to me with this. I will say that I'm a little surprised it took you this long."

Yozef groaned. "This long? I was hoping it was something new."

"No," said Sistian. "There were murmurs after the Buldorian raid. I suspected it would happen. Then, after the Battle of Moreland City, the rumors have only increased. The impact you've had on Caedellium, with all your innovations and roles you've played in defending us against our enemies, made it inevitable.

"There are always people eager to believe a Septarsh is among us. Usually, a furor over an individual candidate dies down after some precipitating event fades with time and nothing else happens that's taken as a sign of God's favor."

"I want to assure you, Abbot, I've done nothing to encourage this. I would never pretend to be a religious figure. If I'd realized what was happening, I'd have done something about it."

"It's one of your idiosyncrasies, Yozef, that one moment you present a novel idea or insight and in the next moment are oblivious to what others see as obvious. Don't tell Maera I told you this, but she once told me you were the most interesting and exasperating person she'd ever met.

"As for your thinking I might believe that you encourage the Septarsh rumors, don't worry. I never thought that. I've always assumed you were unaware and would come to me when you found out. A person who's declared a Septarsh is not equated with being a theophist, a saint, or another role involved in direct worship of, and service to, God. Also, be aware that no formal mechanism exists to determine the authenticity of a Septarsh, but it's more like a consensus develops among all the people, not only the few who want to believe so hard they grasp at any hint.

"There have been writings about this, a few that have made their way into the *Commentaries* on the *Word*. It's when those who were skeptical or even opposed to the belief come to firmly accept a person as a Septarsh that a consensus develops. At least, that's how it happens on Caedellium. I know it's different in other parts of Anyar, and, of course, even the title might be different. In Landolin, such a person would be called a *Vajarjunatra*.

"Our word, *Septarsh*, comes from an ancient language and people who no longer exist. The Humari people lived in the south-central part of the Melosia continent. When the Narthani came out of the northern part of the continent after consolidating other tribes, the Humari were the first of the major *civilized*, as we would call them in comparison, peoples to fall under the invaders. The Narthani ruthlessly suppressed the Humari. They enslaved those they didn't kill and forbade the Humari to speak their own language. My understanding is that no speaker of Humari has lived for more than two hundred years, and their written language exists only in copies outside of Narthon.

"Caedelli has a few Humari words—*Septarsh* being one of those."

Yozef started to ask a question, but Sistian anticipated him and held up a hand. "And why do we use the Humari word, *Septarsh*, on Caedellium? No one knows. Although I suspect the origin is an interesting story, it's lost somewhere in the past."

Yozef remained quiet as he listened, but he spoke up as soon as the abbot paused.

"Abbot, how do I stop this?"

The abbot shook his head. "You can't. In fact, if you made too much of an open effort to discourage such a belief, it would only fuel the rumors. According to our lore, one of the characteristics of the true Septarsh is a vigorous insistence he or she isn't one."

"Well, shit," said Yozef, in English.

The abbot laughed. "Somehow I don't need to understand your language to suspect the meaning of those words."

"So, what do I do?" asked Yozef, discouraged.

"There's nothing you *can* do," said Sistian. "Just do your best to live your life as if none of this existed or mattered. After all, that's essentially how the *Word* tells us to live—to the best of our ability and without pretense. However, I'd caution you to choose your words carefully, especially around common people. What you say can be taken more seriously than intended."

Orosz City

By coincidence, the same day and two hundred miles north, another conversation occurred about the Septarsh question. The Bultecki were one of the smallest clans in population, and their landlocked mountainous province bordered seven other clans, more than any other clan. This proximity, their position next to Orosz and the Conclave site, and the marriage of the Bultecki hetman's eldest son to a daughter of the Orosz hetman all contributed to the Bultecki hetman being one of the more astute students of inter-clan relations and political currents.

On this particular day, Teresz Bultecki and Tomis Orosz had excused themselves from their respective spouses and other family members to retire to the Orosz Manor balcony outside the main room. The intermarried families lived fifty miles apart and managed reciprocal visits several times a year. The evening meal finished, the women had shooed the children out to play for an hour before dark, to allow the two hetmen to discuss clan affairs.

"I needed this visit, Tomis," said Teresz Bultecki. "Seeing the families together and all the children always lightens my mood, although it seems to get harder every month."

"The Narthani," stated Orosz, sharing his friend and fellow hetman's thoughts. "I also have trouble getting them out of my mind. What Yozef Kolsko told us when we met after the battle is right. The Narthani aren't going away. We only drove them back, but what about next time?

"Yes, we won at Moreland City," said Orosz, "at a terrible price for the Moreland Clan, and, let's be honest, we had more a share of luck than we had any reason to expect or are likely to get again.

"Culich Keelan said the same to me before returning to Keelan after the battle. The plan suggested by this Kolsko worked out, and the Tri-Alliance clansmen made heroic efforts, but it still took two incredibly stupid mistakes to gain the victory. If either the Morelanders hadn't held the Narthani's attention or the Eywellese hadn't left their position, we might be having a very different conversation."

Bultecki grunted agreement. "Where does it leave us? We cooperated at Moreland City and afterward until the Narthani were back deep in Eywell territory, then we all returned home and are doing what?"

"Waiting for the next Narthani move," answered Orosz.

"And then what? Who knows if all the same clans will respond to the next call, much less the clans that didn't this time? And then hours of argument about what to do."

Orosz glanced at the closed balcony door to be sure no one overhead what he was about to say. He leaned closer to Bultecki.

"I spoke of this briefly with Culich Keelan before he left Moreland City. Since then, we've exchanged several letters, ones I've burned after reading. I'll share the salient points with you. This needs to be kept between us, for the time being. Keelan has some radical ideas. At this point, it's just talk, but with all we face with the Narthani, the more I think about it, the more I believe it's something to keep under consideration.

"Keelan believes the only way we can drive the Narthani off Caedellium is to unify all the clans under some form of central control. He doesn't see how that can easily happen, though one thought he's had is that if the clans could rally around a central authority, they might be willing to cede control temporarily to drive the Narthani off the island."

"A central authority? Like who or what? It couldn't be a hetman. Too many of the clansmen would never take orders from another clan's hetman. Even getting them to *listen* to advice from another can be discouraging. It would have to be someone else. The only figure so widely respected is Rhaedri Brison, but he's not someone to lead the fight against the Narthani."

The theophist was highly regarded and revered throughout Caedellium and assumed to be a candidate to be named a Septarsh for his additions to the *Commentaries* that accompanied the *Word*.

"I agree," said Orosz. "However, Keelan and I think it might be possible for Brison to act as a spiritual leader supporting a temporary central leadership, perhaps a group of three or four hetmen who would plan whatever we do against the Narthani. Then, the other clans would be obliged to follow the plan."

Bultecki stroked his beard, while one eyebrow raised. "I can see that working in theory, but in practice? I don't know. Would Brison agree?"

"He might, if it was presented to him as the best hope to save our peoples."

Orosz looked around again. Still no one else in hearing range. "Keelan has another thought, this one more speculative. You've heard the stories of this Yozef Kolsko, how he came to Caedellium, all the changes he's influenced, and his role at Moreland City?"

"Moreland City, of course," replied Bultecki, "and the kerosene lanterns and other things he's brought to Caedellium, but only partial reports about the raid on St. Sidryn's Abbey. I assume you've heard the rumors about Kolsko being a Septarsh? My own cousin is convinced Kolsko is an agent of God sent to deliver us from the Narthani. Then again, my cousin is not the brightest member of our family and is constantly dreaming up fantastical plots and mysteries. Yet he's not the only clan member wondering if it might not be true. It does seem unlikely that a strange man shows up on Caedellium with innovations and advice on defeating the Narthani just when we're under such a dire threat."

Orosz shrugged. "A skeptic would say it's a coincidence, while someone grasping for hoped-for help from God could easily assign the role to this Kolsko fellow. Whatever the truth, Keelan wonders if Kolsko might also serve as a unifying figure, maybe not leading, but giving advice. His warnings about not attacking the Narthani line directly at Moreland City and his plan for the flank attack give him a reputation as someone to listen to."

"I don't know," said Bultecki. "He's not from Caedellium, and he's married into Hetman Keelan's family, so it's difficult to be sure how these factors will affect whether hetmen would follow such advice, although I agree he has considerable influence at the moment."

"Yes, it's hard to predict," said Orosz, "although there's certain to be an All-Clan Conclave coming soon. That's where such issues will be raised."

"And argued and argued," said Bultecki.

Orosz laughed. "At a meeting with all the hetmen, what else would you expect?"

CHAPTER 6

PRISONERS

Following the raid on St. Sidryn's, the citizens of Abersford wished that everyday life could be as before. After Moreland City, no such dream was possible, not after eyewitness accounts circulated. Everyone knew nothing would ever be the same, though they didn't know what the future *would* be.

For Yozef, his work focused on a stronger commitment to finding ways to defend against the Narthani. The swivel carriages had played a critical role in the clans' success at Moreland City but could not provide a long-term solution to the islanders' lack of artillery. Neither could the captured Narthani 12-pounders. Although those were useful, the clans needed ten times as many or more. The solution to the problem with casting larger cannon barrels came from an unexpected source, and the solution itself was simple, to Yozef's considerable consternation. A month after the battle, two wagons with guards arrived in Abersford. Their cargo? Narthani and Eywellese prisoners captured at Moreland City and kept alive for questioning, as ordered by Denes Vegga at Yozef's urging. The prisoners were questioned at Moreland City and then transferred to Caernford, because keeping them alive had been Keelan's idea.

No one in Caernford knew what to do with Narthani and Eywellese prisoners. After cursory questioning, Vortig Luwis, one of Hetman Keelan's chief advisors and in charge of the prisoners, decided they needed to be disposed of and sent them on to Abersford for Denes and Yozef to determine whether more questioning might prove worthwhile.

Yozef was in the foundry when a disgruntled Denes found him.

"They've sent us two wagons of Narthani and Eywellese prisoners, either to question or get rid of. Why couldn't Luwis handle this in Caernford?"

"Prisoners?" said Yozef, surprised. "I'd heard we had a few at Moreland City, but I'd assumed they'd been dealt with by now."

Denes slapped his riding gloves against his pant leg in frustration. "The guards who brought them want to head back to Caernford right away, but I told them they'd have to keep guarding the prisoners until you and I decide what to do with them. However, it'll have to be tomorrow, since the rest of today I'm taking one of our Thirds north of Abersford to practice riding to a battle site and deploying. We've expanded the numbers again, and there are twenty men who've either no experience in being part of a battle or practice in being a dragoon."

"All right," Yozef said, "we can look at them tomorrow morning."

Denes nodded. "I've already appropriated the cellar of the empty warehouse Filtin Fuller says you're planning to convert to a workshop. We'll keep them chained there overnight. The guards will complain it's not their responsibility, but the hell with them."

Yozef met Denes the next morning outside the warehouse. A sour-looking, rangy-built man stood next to the entrance, his arms folded tightly on his chest, glaring at the cause of his delay in leaving.

"All right, you're here, and we guarded the prisoners last night. *Now* can we formally turn them over to you and be out of here?"

"*I'm* the magistrate in this area, and you'll be released when I say," snarled Denes.

The guard spat to one side, said nothing, and followed them inside and down a rickety wooden stairway to a dank basement. Denes lit a lantern, casting a yellowish glow over the scene. Men lying chained together covered the floor. The few clothes they wore didn't hide bruises, with some fresh enough to have occurred the previous day. All appeared borderline emaciated, as if they had been fed barely enough to keep them alive. A few turned heads to look listlessly at their visitors. Most didn't move at all.

From their condition, Yozef assumed they had been beaten regularly, perhaps every day. If no new information had been produced for sixdays, then the beatings served only to appease the urge for vengeance. The casualties at St. Sidryn's and the carnage at Moreland City had scrubbed out more of the delicate sensitivities Yozef had brought to Anyar, but he wanted results. His only remaining qualms were against gratuitous violence. He would have been less concerned if the Caedelli had taken no prisoners or had executed them after a useful interrogation.

Yozef wanted to race back up the stairs and clear his head from the stench. Instead, he breathed as shallowly as he could and fought to keep his stomach from retching.

"Denes, I don't think questioning them while they're in this condition will get us anything. Let's clean them up, feed them, and try again tomorrow. Also, move them out of this place and up into the warehouse and take the chains off. They look like they can hardly walk, so I think armed guards aren't going to have trouble with them."

Denes appeared dubious, but the guard was outraged.

"You're going to *what*! They're all ignorant scum of Narthani, and we're wasting time. We should have killed them on the way here and been done with it."

"Are you sure about this, Yozef?" said Denes. "The man has a point. Shouldn't we just cut their throats and be done with them?"

Yozef counted Denes as a friend or close to it, but he didn't have any illusions about Denes's ruthlessness, brought to the surface by a perceived threat to the island, his clan, his family, or anyone under his responsibility.

"It may be that they have no information of use to us," he replied, "but I could try some of the techniques my people have found effective . . . if you would allow me to take over the questioning?"

No point in telling Caedelli their interrogation manner leaves something to be desired. Nor is it likely to produce the best results. Hmmm . . . I wonder if whoever questioned them even did it systematically or went straight to beatings?

"I think you'll waste your time, but go ahead. I have more urgent matters to attend to. Let me know when you give up, and I'll have them buried," said a skeptical Denes, leaving Yozef wondering whether Denes would have them killed prior to their internment.

Before leaving, Denes gave firm instructions to the guard leader to follow Yozef's orders, no matter how much he disagreed, with the promise that the guards would be released to leave in two more days.

Thus, Denes left Yozef in charge of seventeen Narthani and eight Eywellese, all well-tenderized.

Well . . . they've certainly had the "Bad Cop" treatment, so I might as well take advantage by becoming the "Good Cop."

"Wait here," Yozef told the guard leader. "I'll be back in a few minutes."

He escaped back up the stairs and out of the warehouse into the open air. Several lungfuls of air settled his stomach, and he hustled next door to the distillation facility.

"Filtin," he called out over the talking workers and the clang of metal and glass, "I need help. Can you and the other men stop what you're doing and come with me?"

The five men gathered around him.

"They've sent Narthani and Eywellese prisoners here for us to question. Now, I know what all your views are, as to what should be done with such men, but I believe we might get useful information from them that might help against the Narthani."

The men murmured uneasily, and one turned red-faced and opened his mouth to speak before Filtin cut him off. "Don't say it, Biwan. If Yozef says this may be important, then we all should know by now to listen to him." Filtin turned back to Yozef. "I suppose you called us together because you want us to do something about these prisoners?"

"Yes. The men are in too bad a condition to question them right away. I need you to help get them ready to question. Filtin, I'll leave the details to you, but I want medicants here as soon as possible to treat them. Also, get them some clean clothes, water, and hot food.

"While you're getting that organized, I'll go over to the foundry and fetch Yawnfol to translate into Narthani."

"He's not going to be happy," said Filtin. "He's a Preddi, and he witnessed what happened to his clan and most of his family. Plus, although I believe he knows some Narthani, I don't know if it's enough to trust him as a translator."

"I know," said Yozef, "but he'll have to do for the moment. I'll impress on him I'm trying to get information from the prisoners. We can never be sure when even the smallest piece of information could be important."

"What!" screamed the guard, when Filtin showed up at the warehouse with several women carrying baskets of food and buckets of water. "For these animals!? They're not getting any treatment except for the knife, and I'm certainly not feeding them!" The other guards growled in agreement.

Yozef knew his stock had risen since the battle. It was time to see whether it meant something in situations like this. He stepped to within inches of the guard's face. He kept his voice as deadpan as he could, trying not to reveal he was primed to run for it, if necessary. From the guard's build and scars, Yozef knew the man could turn him into mincemeat in short order. "You . . . will . . . do . . . as . . . I . . . say."

At first, the man just stared, as he processed Yozef's words. Then, when he started to turn red and prepared to do God knows what to Yozef, two other guards pulled him aside. One merely looked nervous, while the other was pale. They whispered together for almost a minute. By the time the lead guard turned back to Yozef, his visible ire had vanished, replaced by a wary look.

"As you wish, Ser Kolsko," he ground out. "We'll guard them, but you'll have to find others to tend to the scum." With a slight but definite and insolent bow, he and the others hustled out.

Yozef exhaled. *Whew.*

A fourth guard had observed all that transpired and remained with an amused look.

"Who are you?" asked Yozef in a cold voice.

"My name is Balwis Preddi."

"Preddi? As in clan Preddi?"

"As in the Preddi."

"So, are you from the hetman's family?"

"Not hardly," said the man. "But it's the name I choose to go by."

Whatever, thought Yozef, who learned in the next few minutes that Balwis was an escaped Preddi who had fled to Moreland and had been working on a ranch for the last year. He numbered among the survivors of the Moreland hetman's disastrous attack on the Narthani center. Being fluent in Narthani, which he'd learned during the two years before his escape, he had been called on as an interpreter for prisoner questioning. From the condition of the man's knuckles, Yozef suspected he had been among the men administering beatings to the prisoners.

Balwis looked calmly at Yozef, who got annoyed.

"No comments?" Yozef asked.

"No," said Balwis, with an expression that had elements of humor. "I'm just curious how you expect to get more information out of the Narthani."

Yozef laughed. "Wondering if I'm crazy or something for wanting to feed the prisoners and treat their injuries?"

"From what I hear, one would be wise to listen carefully to any ideas coming from Yozef Kolsko, even if they *seem* crazy."

Yozef laughed again, relaxing. *I think I might like this guy.*

"Our goal is to get information, however possible," Yozef explained. "Trying it your way sometimes works if time is short, but the experience of my people is that if time is not a factor, there are other ways. Based on their previous treatment, I think the prisoners expect only the worst, so why should they cooperate? What I intend doing is to convince them that I mean them no harm and will protect them from people like you and the guards, though only if they cooperate with me."

"And this works?" asked Balwis skeptically.

"Sometimes yes and sometimes no. At this point, with these prisoners, it's a matter of what's to lose?"

Balwis nodded in understanding, if not belief.

"I'm going to need your help," said Yozef. "Since I don't speak Narthani, you'll have to continue interpreting. I'll send back the worker who I sent for to translate and let you do it. It's important that you understand what we'll be trying to do and get the meanings accurately across to the Narthani. Since they already have experience with you, you'll be the 'Bad Man' who disapproves of my new methods but has to obey and do translating at my order. Call it the 'Good Man, Bad Man' method of questioning."

Balwis nodded understanding with a bemused expression. "What if they don't cooperate?"

"Then we're no worse off, but I think at least some of them will. Of course, we can also mix up the method. Since you're the 'Bad Man,' we can always include some of the previous methods, but only if I order it. We want them to think I'm sympathetic to them and the only positive part of their existence."

"This should be interesting," said a now fully amused Balwis. "Either I will learn some of the tricks of the great Yozef Kolsko or I'll have incredible stories to tell at pubs for the rest of my life."

Yozef smiled. "It's a winning situation for you, no matter what happens. I have other matters I need to attend to, so I'll leave you in charge here to see that the Narthani are treated, fed, and given some blankets to keep warm tonight. One of my workers will return with medicants. See that he gets whatever assistance he needs. We'll start questioning tomorrow."

Yozef arrived at the warehouse at mid-morning the next day. Balwis Preddi sat against the outside wall and rose when he saw Yozef.

"As you ordered, our Narthani friends are waiting for you," Balwis said sardonically.

"Let's see them," replied Yozef, entering the building and expecting to see the prisoners lying on the floor. Instead, to his surprise, men in plain but clean clothes sat or slept on rows of cots.

"What the—?"

"Since we're being nice to them now, didn't seem right to leave them on the floor, so your man, Fuller, found enough cots."

The guard leader was huddled with the other guards and strode quickly to the entrance when he saw Yozef.

"I hope everything is to your satisfaction, Ser Kolsko," gushed the almost obsequious man. "All the prisoners were given clothes, soap and water to wash, and fed as much as they could eat last night and this morning."

Yozef eyed the man and wondered about the change in demeanor.

"Yes, everything seems in good shape. Thank you for your effort."

With that, the guard half-bowed and hurried back to his companions.

"What's gotten into him?" Yozef mumbled into the air.

"We've gotten an earful from several of the locals on exactly who Yozef Kolsko is. My companions got somewhat vocal last night at a pub, and one particular fellow took exception to some of the comments about your parentage."

"The pub wouldn't happen to be the Snarling Graeko, would it? And the 'particular fellow' large and red-haired?"

"Right both times," said Balwis. "You can sure grow them big around here. I thought Grawan was going to shit his pants when he got picked up by the front of his shirt."

"Grawan?"

"Our brave guard leader."

Yozef envisioned the scene and felt grateful Carnigan had only warned the idiot.

It was time to begin with the prisoners. He addressed the guards. "We'll use one of the warehouse's front rooms. You'll see some odd pieces of furniture scattered around the warehouse. Set up a table with two chairs. We'll work with the prisoners one at a time and see which ones are willing to talk and if they have anything to say of interest.

"Balwis, you'll stand behind me and a step back. The reason you'll stand is not because I don't want you to sit down, but so we make the prisoners see me as more of an authority figure they might want to please and you as the subordinate. Some of them might be more likely to talk with the threat of you visible if I'm not pleased. Translate everything as accurately as you can."

"Oh, I'll translate for you. I just don't see this working."

"Maybe not."

One by one, the guards brought in the prisoners. Still bruised, wary, and fearful, they looked better than the previous day. Yozef had writing materials and started off with name, rank, age, origin, and a few other items of information.

More than half of the men were too incoherent, too defiant, too frightened, or too ill-informed to give much in the way of answers. Yet he could mine the rest of them. Those men were open books, either eager to curry better treatment and protection from Yozef or relieved to no longer be under Narthani authority. After midday meal, Yozef and Balwis, this time both sitting, brought back the men individually and started in-depth questioning. Although much of the information was redundant, by that evening they had the names and ranks of the Narthani command structure down to at least some of the lower command levels, depending on the experience of the prisoner; consistent estimates of the numbers of Narthani troops of each type; numbers of cannon; a rough outline of the conditions in Preddi Province; and knowledge of the almost complete supplanting of the original islanders in Preddi Province.

Most immediately interesting, Yozef got an estimate of how many Narthani military and civilians resided on Caedellium: 10,000 to 12,000 of the former and 70,000 to 110,000 of the latter. That evening, he summarized the first interrogations and sent a copy to Culich Keelan in Caernford.

The Eywell prisoners provided details that complemented those from previous prisoners' interrogations: they had knowledge of conditions within Eywell Province, but little, if any, information about the Narthani or Preddi Province. Unfortunately, even their familiarity with their own province was scanty, because they originated from a sparsely populated part of Eywell. One of the men felt so relieved when Yozef said they wouldn't be killed if they cooperated that he broke down crying. When he recovered, he relayed to Yozef that most Eywell captives had been killed outright even more eagerly than were the Narthani.

Yozef decided that *had* to change. He needed information on conditions within Eywell and Selfcell.

By the time they quit for the evening, Balwis was a convert.

"I admit I thought you were pretty stupid to think playing your 'Good Man' to the Narthani would get us anything. I was wrong. We can always kill them later. Now I see how cleverly you got them to give us information, even if I'm not sure how much of it will be useful."

"Do we have to kill them in the end?" asked Yozef.

"What else would we do with them?" questioned Balwis, confused.

"They're Narthani." He uttered the last words with deep bitterness and ignored the Eywellese.

"What about the last Narthani we questioned today?" asked Yozef. "He can't be more than seventeen years old. From what he tells us, he lived with his family working at the estate of a Narthani lord of some kind back in Narthon. Almost slaves themselves. At age fifteen, he was sent to a troop training camp, where for the next six months senior troops brutalized him into becoming a disciplined soldier who would obey any orders given. What choice did he have? If he had refused, he thinks he would have been executed and his family punished for not raising him to be a *proper* Narthani."

Balwis remained quiet, conflicting thoughts vying in his mind. "I don't know," he said finally, remembering how the youth had cried when Yozef suggested he might be allowed not only to live, but not to be sent back to the Narthani.

"Everything they say about you is true," said Balwis thoughtfully.

"Everything they say? Like what?"

"That you do things and know things like no one else has ever seen, and that everywhere you go, things change. Most think for the better, even if many are uneasy at the speed of change. Something tells me we have only seen the beginning and that you're probably important for us against the Narthani."

Balwis stomped back and forth in the room, mumbling to himself, as if arguing or trying to make a decision. Yozef waited.

Finally, he said, "Yes. I want to kill every living Narthani. Yet as much as I want that, I know driving them off Caedellium is more important. You will need more interpreting, not just with these prisoners, but more times in the future. You'll need someone you can trust to translate. *I'll* be your regular interpreter. I can also do whatever more unpleasant tasks are needed that you cannot or will not do. There. That decides it. I'm now in your service."

"Do I have any say in this decision?" countered an amused Yozef.

"No."

Thus, did Balwis Preddi become an aide to Yozef.

As useful as the background information was on the first day of conducting in-depth interrogations, on the second day they hit paydirt. The next to last of the Narthani prisoners was a scruffy older man with weathered skin and graying hair. He had been the crew leader of one of the 12-pounder cannon captured during the battle and was a twenty-year veteran in the

Narthani army. Despite those years of service, the older man felt no loyalty to the Narthon Empire. It simply *existed*, and he could do nothing about it, so he did what was necessary to survive. While he never clarified exactly where he came from, he transferred whatever loyalty he had to Yozef, as the most expedient action at the moment. Yozef had no illusions that his allegiance wouldn't transfer back to Narthon with changing circumstances, yet that was irrelevant.

What *was* relevant was that the man had served the last twelve years as an artilleryman and had collected tidbits of knowledge along the way, such as how to cast cannon whose barrels didn't inconveniently tend to burst when fired. Bingo!

Yozef's elation at possibly solving the cannon foundry problem was quickly replaced by embarrassed chagrin after hearing the old Narthani's advice translated by Balwis.

"I'm surprised all the barrels didn't burst with no reinforcing bands," was all he had to say for Yozef to recognize one obvious and trivial solution. Not only the thickness of the breaches presented a problem, but Yozef could improve the general strength along the tubes' length by adding reinforcing metal bands at several sites along the barrel. The Narthani didn't need to use such bands, because they had cast the original barrels with even cooling of the metal after pouring. Yozef's foundry workers had poured the barrels as a solid cast, with a clay mold holding the position of the bore. After cooling, they had bored out the clay and smoothed the inside of the barrel. As the metal cooled from the outside inward, the solid outer layers pulled away from the still molten interior, creating small cavities. These created weak spots in the finished barrels. With the smaller swivel guns, the cooling proceeded fast enough to minimize imperfections, but not so with the larger bores. The solution was to use a hollow casting core in the center of the mold. They would pump water in and out of the core, while keeping the exterior hot, thus cooling from the inside out and pulling molten metal *toward* the interior, instead of the reverse.

After hearing the old man, Yozef sat quietly, as his memory dredged up references to these exact suggestions. It wasn't that his memory didn't have the information; he simply hadn't asked himself the right questions to bring it forward. It was a chastising lesson for him. Even with enhanced memory, he had to conduct proper searches, as with the Internet back on Earth. Everything was there, but he just had to implement a specific search to find specific answers. Even so, he didn't understand how he had missed the information.

I know I can excuse myself by saying I simply have too much to do, but I just can't *make these kinds of mistakes* too *often.*

They finished with the last prisoner on the evening of the second day. Yozef was surprised that Balwis or the guards didn't object when he ordered the prisoners who had cooperated to be transferred to another building with actual beds, bedding, and better food. The old Narthani artilleryman, Razil Gurbuz, would work at the foundry, where Yawnfol would translate and Balwis would check regularly. With the ideas about reinforcing bands and the different method of cooling the cast barrels, Yozef felt certain they could successfully cast larger cannon.

Cooperative Narthani prisoners found jobs in trades or shops, also under close observation. The young Narthani whom Yozef had used to ask Balwis what *he* would have done in the boy's situation was sent to work on a ranch in eastern Keelan, along with the Eywellese prisoners.

He tried to think of a future for the other Narthani prisoners. When he failed, they disappeared the morning after he informed Denes.

CHAPTER 7

DIGGING IN

Narthani Headquarters, Preddi City

General Okan Akuyun held a cup, as he stared at the map on the wall, the bitter taste of kava matching his mood. Instead of the Caedellium map showing Narthani expansion from Preddi, the province they controlled, and the two neighboring and allied provinces, Eywell and Selfcell, a line meandered parallel to the eastern border of Eywell and separated almost a fifth of the province no longer inhabited by the Eywell Clan. Incursions and raids by the other clans had been frequent and severe enough for the Eywellese to abandon farms, ranches, and villages, even to within ten miles of the clan capital at Hanslow.

He could hear the rustling of papers, the shifting of chairs, and low murmurs of men behind him, waiting for him to start the meeting. His mind went back to another map, one that had hung on this wall before being taken down and stored: a map with arrows indicating their invasion route into Moreland Province, then on to Orosz Province, and eventually to the sea, splitting the island in half. They had been confident that most of the other clans would capitulate to Narthani control, to avoid the fate of the Preddi Clan during the early phases of the Narthani mission to subjugate Caedellium and bring it into the Narthon Empire.

For the month since Moreland City and more times than he had counted, Akuyun had gone over written plans, meeting summaries, and reports, trying to find where he had erred. He was in command. Therefore, the failure of the Moreland invasion fell to him. Yet no matter how hard he tried, he couldn't find fault with himself or any of his subordinates. He was honest enough with himself to recognize that not finding fault didn't mean fault was lacking, only that he couldn't see it. In the end, he came down to two possibilities. One was that, indeed, his shortcomings were at the root of their problem. The alternative was that they had done everything possible, given what they knew, but some unknown new element had come into play. In the latter case, they had no way to factor an unknown into their plans, and thus they were caught unawares. Either way, they had to accept their situation, and he had a duty to deal with what lay before them.

He took a deep breath and turned to face the room full of men. A senior staff meeting usually involved Akuyun, his three most senior subordinates, and the assessor. Those four men sat at the table before him: Brigadier Aivacs Zulfa, commander of all Narthani ground forces; Admiral Morfred Kalcan, naval commander; Nizam Tuzere, civilian population administrator; and Sadek Hizer, the mission assessor assigned to give the High Command independent evaluations of mission progress and evaluations of senior leaders.

An infrequent participant in staff meetings was Mamduk Balcan, the senior prelate with the role of overseeing conversion of the island's people to worship the only true God, Narth. While Akuyun preferred not to have the man in meetings, today was different. The focus of the mission would formally change as of today and would remain changed until new instructions came from Narthon. Akuyun had already briefed Balcan, and the prelate had reacted irrationally, just as predicted. The fact that the military situation made it temporarily impossible to expand conversion efforts made no impression on him. It had taken Akuyun over an hour to placate the prelate enough so that he would keep silent in today's meeting. Fortunately, Balcan had changed his tone, because Akuyun had come close to deciding an unfortunate accident needed to befall the prelate.

Those five faces were turned to him, as were thirty others, of men sitting in chairs to the back and sides of the table: colonels, senior majors, commodores, a dozen select civilian administrators, and two of Hizer's assistants. The expanded staff meeting signaled to all attendees that the mission was about to undergo a major reorientation.

Akuyun didn't take his seat. He would stand for the meeting, as was appropriate for what he had to say.

"Gentlemen, let us begin."

Those heads not already turned to Akuyun did so, backs straightened in chairs, pupils dilated in their focus to the head of the room, and for a moment, the only sound was breathing.

"I need not explain that Phase Four of the subjugation of the Island of Caedellium did not go as planned."

It was an understatement; no one laughed.

"We predicated our move on Moreland Province based on the assumption the clans would not unite in numbers enough to be a threat and on their inexperience in field tactics. We expected to inflict one or more decisive defeats on the battlefield, followed by individual clans accepting Narthani suzerainty. However, the enemy our men fought outside of Moreland City was not the foe we anticipated. Although we faced ten clans, more than expected, it should not have affected the outcome. The critical factor was that the clans showed a tactical sense far beyond what we believed they had any right to have, and they possessed light artillery, something else unexpected.

"Granted, the Eywell desertion of their flank screening position precipitated what followed. What we didn't expect from the Caedelli was their willingness to sacrifice so many men to focus our attention on a charge straight into our guns, luring away and destroying the Eywellese contingent, and the rapid follow-up of the opening provided by our exposed flank.

"Our men were not defeated, though were badly hurt. Brigadier Zulfa withdrew in good order back to our base territory. The clans also suffered significant casualties, and no further major engagements occurred, although our force was harassed on their way back. At the same time, the clans overran the launch base at Parthmal. After that, the clans made no further major moves against us. However, while Moreland City was a tactical draw, there is no purpose in pretending it was anything other than a strategic defeat."

A subtle shift in bodies, subvocal vibrations, and a sense of gloom pervaded the room. Knowing about the battle was not the same as hearing the respected mission commander's blunt assessment.

"Naturally, we will continue to analyze what happened, but our main concern is what next. Not all of you are aware, but the High Command knew from the beginning that the resources committed to this mission were not sufficient to ensure success. I will tell you now that when I was assigned as commander, the High Command confided that the odds of complete success were no better than fifty/fifty. Privately, I had indications the likelihood was even lower. The High Command assessed that the relatively minimal resources committed were a reasonable gamble.

"None of that changes the fact that we've failed in our primary mission. After lengthy discussions with all senior commanders, and after careful consideration of possible future courses of action, I have decided that for the time being, our focus will no longer be on efforts to subdue the other clans.

We will secure and maintain our current positions, while we await directions from Narthon. In plain language, we are shifting from an offensive posture to a defensive one.

"Before we continue, are there questions or relevant comments?"

One of the civil administrators rose from his seat. "General Akuyun, I think we all suspected this was coming. I know you have considered all options, though it's still a shock to hear. So, is there *really* no way to continue as originally planned, even with this one setback?"

"No," said Akuyun firmly. "We lost eight percent of our men at Moreland City, with another two hundred wounded seriously enough to be unfit for duty for months, some permanently. In addition, we lost twenty artillery pieces, captured by the Caedelli. We can cast more here in Preddi City, but now the islanders have field pieces and can use our own guns against us.

"Although the ten clans we faced in the battle equaled our numbers, they didn't commit all their men. Now that those clans that didn't come to Moreland's aid have seen the results, it would be foolish to ignore the fact that additional clans will likely join future resistance. In another field engagement, we could see ourselves outnumbered two or three to one by a more mobile adversary who knows the terrain better than we do and who now has artillery."

Administrator Tuzere raised a hand to get Akuyun's attention. The general nodded, and Tuzere rose.

"The other factor that complicates General Akuyun's planning is the hundred thousand non-military persons we have in Preddi Province. His duty is also to protect all of those from any threats."

"Good Narth!" exclaimed the shocked administrator. "You don't think the Caedelli could actually attack us here!"

"It's a possibility I'm obliged to consider," interjected Akuyun. "I hope you understand our position. It's apparent we can't risk field engagements with the Caedelli, nor can we expose the Narthani settlers to raids. The only option I see is to maintain a defensive stance until word comes from Narthon."

"When and what is that likely to be?" asked another administrator.

"I sent an unloaded sloop to our closest port, at Ezarkin on the northern border with the Iraquinik Confederation. Assuming good winds, the sloop should reach port in another two to four sixdays. Then the reports go overland a thousand miles to the end of the semaphore line being built to Ezarkin and on to Umasya, the capital. The High Command will take whatever time they deem necessary to consider options and then send the answer back to us. At the soonest, I'll be surprised if we get the response in less than five months from now."

"What is your assessment of what that response will be?" asked Colonel Nuthrat Metin.

Akuyun's face showed no emotion, though most of the men knew one possible response would be his removal from command. Arrest after defeat was not unknown in Narthani history.

"I and Assessor Hizer agree the High Command can decide one of three possible future courses of action. One is to abandon the mission to conquer Caedellium and withdraw all personnel back to Narthon.

"The obvious complication is that we have been bringing people to Caedellium for five years. Even by using every available ship, it would take a year to do the evacuation, and during the later phases we could come under Caedelli attack as our numbers diminished. It would also require abandoning the original reason for the mission.

"The second possible decision would be to tell us to hold our position as part of the effort to establish a supply and launching base for moves on the Landolin and the Iraquinik Confederation. In that case, there would likely be an increase in forces, but we would no longer have the objective of taking the entire island.

"And finally, the decision could be that taking the entire island remains the objective, and reinforcements will be sent, probably a force many times larger than we have here now."

Several arms raised for attention, and Akuyun anticipated the next question.

"I'm afraid there's no one clear most likely possibility. Each has factors in favor and against. If I were forced to predict, I would choose the third, only because of my perception of the High Command's level of interest, not because I have any specific information."

When several more hands waved for recognition, Akuyun shook his head. "Any more questions about what has happened or might come from Narthon should wait until later. Right now, we need to move on to what is most important. What we are to do until we hear from Narthon.

"Moving to a defensive stance will require significant changes for all parts of our enterprise here on Caedellium, both military and non-military. The actions that I've determined are necessary fall into three categories: actions within Preddi Province, those concerning the Selfcell and Eywell clans, and actions against the other clans. We'll go over them individually."

Akuyun motioned to Administrator Tuzere, who stood as Akuyun then took his seat.

Tuzere's visage appeared grim. "For the non-military Narthani living in Preddi Province, this necessitates effectively putting all of them under the demands of the military. That is, what is needed for the defense of Preddi Province is the top priority. The following steps are necessary.

"From this point on, expansion into new farm and ranch land will cease. Any such ongoing activities will also stop, and people involved will pull back to work on existing fully functioning properties.

"Export of foods, mainly grains and cured meats, back to Narthon will stop. All food production will go to provide for our people, the two allied clans, as necessary, and to build up stockpiles."

"Stockpiles!" blurted the administrator for the southern portion of Preddi, a region of cattle raising. "That implies you fear food production might be cut off! The only way that could happen is if the Caedelli attack right into Preddi and we can't depend on producing more food."

Akuyun answered before Tuzere could. "Under current circumstances, we must account for all possibilities. Before, we didn't believe the islanders were a direct threat to our settlements. Now, we have to recognize that's possible, though we can't judge how likely as yet."

The shaken questioner fell silent, and Tuzere continued.

"We must also prepare our non-military Narthani to contribute to direct defense. It is as General Akuyun has said, duty requires us to account for all possibilities, one of which is direct threats against our population. This will involve preparing local defensive positions where the populace of the surrounding area can go to wait for army relief. It will require forming militias of able-bodied men. I will coordinate with Colonel Ketin on the defensive positions and Brigadier Zulfa on the militia.

"We, and by this I mean mainly the local civilian administrators in this room and your staffs, will need to evaluate the numbers and distribution of slaves and servants from client peoples, including the remaining original Preddi, for potential sabotage. Any troubling individuals will need to be moved farther from the borders and into situations where they can be observed more closely.

"And finally, we know we have to maintain a functioning level of the economy, but consistent with that, men, slaves or not, can be called on for whatever labor or duty is necessary.

"I hardly need say that as soon as word of these changes spreads, there will be turmoil among our civilians. Most of them never imagined this situation, any more than we in this room did. At least, we've had time to anticipate most of what is necessary, whereas the civilians will be hit with it all at once. I'm afraid there's no way around this. My administrators and I will work to make ourselves available down to the smallest local level to reassure people and also to confirm the necessity of these actions and tamp down complaints.

"The first sixday will be the worst. After that, people will adjust to the new conditions. If necessary, stern measures will be taken against agitators, whether they deliberately resist what is ordered or are incapable of adjusting because of individual issues."

Colonel Erdelin stood. "Administrator, or General Akuyun, has it been decided how internal authority will be applied? By the existing internal security offices or the military?"

"It will depend on the location and circumstances, all to be worked out," Tuzere answered. "Where necessary, existing security personnel will be supplemented with troops. For example, to the usual two-man foot patrol within Preddi City we might add two troopers. Similar with mounted patrols, except toward the borders where the army may take over control. For now, local authority and judicial channels will remain the same, subject to conditions requiring full military control."

Tuzere nodded to Akuyun and sat down. At a motion from Akuyun, Colonel Ketin stood. "I've been tasked by General Akuyun to oversee preparing Preddi City to withstand a concerted attack. We don't think it likely, given the islanders' lack of experience in such matters and that they would have to fight their way here, but, as the general says, it is our responsibility to plan for any eventuality. We won't attempt to build complete fortifications but will lay out basic positions and do the most time-consuming work. Then, if necessary, the remainder of the positions can be completed in a reasonably short time by a concerted effort of all available workers. For example, should the worst happen, and we have to defend Preddi City, the navy will only be able to provide support near shore. However, naval 30-pounders can be moved to prepared positions onshore.

"Lesser defensive positions will be prepared in other selected locations, though those will be intended only as holding actions should we need all the people to consolidate at Preddi City."

Ketin sat, and Akuyun rose again. "Colonel Ketin served for many years with distinction as an engineering officer before transferring to combat units, and I have absolute faith in the fortifications he is designing."

Or, at least, that's what I have to say to instill as much confidence as I can, thought Akuyun. *As we will keep saying, we don't believe such measures are likely to be needed, but I've got a bad feeling we're playing in a game where we suddenly don't know all the rules.*

"We will also need to make changes to our military capabilities, as Brigadier Zulfa will outline."

Zulfa rose. "The main changes are that we need more cavalry and to retrain pike men with muskets. We didn't anticipate that we'd have to ward off large-scale raids or even attacks by the islanders inside the territory we control. However, we have to be able to respond faster and with more men. Since we're not going to receive any more cavalry from Narthon for at least five months, we have to create them here, and we'll do it in two ways. We'll convert some of our existing infantry units into mounted cavalry. Some of the men already have experience riding, so we'll pull those men out of their units and add more men who'll have to be trained in horsemanship, at least enough to ride to a fight. We don't expect them to be as good as the existing cavalry, so their mission will be to support the current units.

"Second, it was unfortunate the High Command decided not to bother sending any of the newer formations, where all pikes were changed to muskets. Mixed pike and musket formations were obsolete back home, but it was thought the islanders were so unorganized that no upgraded units were needed. Pikes are the traditional defense against cavalry charges, which we assumed would be the most likely offensive action we would face.

"Unfortunately, our expectation was wrong, and the islanders threw infantry at us after luring the Eywellese from their screening position. One problem is a shortage of muskets to rearm the pike men and still have a supply of replacement muskets. Preddi Province didn't have sufficient steel-making capability originally, but we had already expanded what existed, and the first blast furnace has been operating for three months, smelting iron ore into pig iron. The first finery forge and trip hammers are now operating, and we're beginning to turn out steel for making muskets.

"The startup process is slow. We estimate three to four months to turn out enough new muskets to replace those lost at Moreland City and be well on the way to rearming the pike men. We've already started the retraining, using wooden mockups and a limited number of muskets. As the pike men are rearmed, the training will intensify. We haven't made a final decision whether the new musket men will be incorporated into existing units with experienced men or formed into entirely new units. Exigencies will be the determining factor.

"Administrator Tuzere mentioned forming militia from the civilian population. Some of these people already ride as well as our cavalrymen, particularly workers on the cattle and horse ranches. Others who have any experience with horses will be formed into local mounted units. None of these will be expected to fight battles alone but will serve to patrol and support the cavalry units.

"As for other militia formations, we will work out the training with Administrator Tuzere and his staff. These units will be intended to defend against any raid until the army can arrive. They would also serve in fortifications, should the need arise."

"What about the Eywellese and Selfcellese?" asked a grizzled commodore. "What happens to them?"

"They are one reason we doubt the islanders will form a direct threat to our people in Preddi Province. Admiral Kalcan and his ships control the waters around Caedellium, so any threat to Preddi would have to come through either Selfcell or Eywell.

"We'll maintain our garrisons within those two provinces and will replace the pure infantry with mounted infantry as soon as possible. Both of those clans will mount vigorous patrols along their borders, although I will confirm that the effective border of Eywell is well within the original border. They lost so many men when they broke position, they've been forced to pull back farther into their province. There's a twenty-mile zone that's not controlled by Eywell or the other clans. Both sides run patrols, and there are occasional skirmishes, though nothing major.

"We are holding to the policy not to allow an influx of Eywellese into Preddi Province. We don't want to give the impression that Eywell is in imminent danger, nor do we want the Eywellese spreading too many details about what happened at Moreland City to incite unnecessary panic among our own people.

"We are also considering operations to discourage islander moves toward our three provinces. General Akuyun will summarize those."

"Thank you, Brigadier," said Akuyun. "Yes, we need to prevent the islanders from massing enough forces to threaten our positions. Plans are still being formulated, but the basic concept is to present a significant enough threat to the coastal clans that they are unable to send too many fighting men out of their provinces."

"Excuse the interruption," said another of the civilian administrators, "and no disrespect intended, but isn't that the strategy that failed to discourage the clans from uniting? I believe it was expected that only five or six clans would come to Moreland's aid. However, *nine* came. What's the reason to believe it will work this time?"

Akuyun could see several officers redden and clench their teeth. He wasn't offended. It was a reasonable question, and the purpose of the meeting was for the leadership to listen, ask questions, and, hopefully, leave understanding the situation and committed to filling their new roles.

"There is no such assurance," admitted Akuyun. "It's been argued that those earlier raids were not extensive enough to tie down the clans, and that larger raids or even overt attempts to take over a province by direct assault from sea with a major force might be necessary. The argument against that approach is that it might encourage the other clans to finish uniting and try to attack us here with all their forces. It may be a delicate balance my staff and I have not yet come to understand satisfactorily. At the moment, it's merely an option to be considered."

Akuyun Villa, Preddi City

After evening meal, Rabia sent the two children, son Ozem and daughter Lufta, to their rooms to finish their studies before an hour of family time. Rabia also dismissed their serving girl, so she could speak openly with her husband.

"How did the civilian administrators receive the change in focus, Okan? I assume they must have known some of this was coming and Tuzere had prepared them," said Rabia.

"Well enough," he replied. "While you're right that they must have suspected some of it, the scope shocked a few of them. I tried to reassure them that many of the measures were only to provide for unlikely eventualities. I think most of them believed me."

"Do *you* believe you?" probed Rabia. She knew her husband.

"I want to. By Great Narth, I want to. Still . . . some instinct is jabbing me in the spine that we've accidently stirred a greater morthan's nest." The Narthani admired the beautiful Anyarian insect-like flying creature for its iridescent mating swarms and feared its mass stingings whenever anyone disturbed a normally docile nest.

"Do you *really* think the clans would unite enough to attack us here? It seems so impossible, given everything I've heard you say since we came to Caedellium."

"Logically, the answer is no. However, logically, they should not have turned Zulfa back at Moreland City. That result can only have emboldened them. Enough to unite and come after us directly? I doubt it, unless another factor comes into play."

"Like what?"

"I suspect many of the clans are content to think we're confined to these three provinces, and as long as we stay here, they'll be willing to let us be, especially the clans farthest away. But what if the High Command sends twenty or thirty thousand reinforcements? Any delusion the islanders had about our intentions would disappear, and they might feel they had no choice but to launch an all-out attack. In that case, we would see thirty to forty thousand of our troops engaged against fifty thousand islanders fighting to the death. What might happen? We would likely prevail, but who knows?"

Rabia reached across the table and laid a hand over her husband's, neither of them saying anything for several minutes before she spoke again.

"I met with several officers' wives today. We had mid-day meal and several bottles of wine. They probed whether I had any insight into what was happening and if they should be worried. I tried to be encouraging, but was I right? Could we be in serious danger?"

"My professional side says no. Another part of me is not so sure. I've been thinking of something I'd like you to take on for me. It needs to be only between the two of us for now, since I hesitate to bring it up with Tuzere and Hizer. There are questions I'd like you to think about. What if we had to get as many children off Caedellium as fast as possible? If not in an emergency, what about gradually moving families back to Narthon? What would such moves do to military and civilian morale? There's no timetable for this. Just consider it, and we can talk when you want."

For the first time, Rabia fully understood how serious her husband considered the recent events.

CHAPTER 8

THUNDERSTRUCK

Abersford

Yozef had doled out to Diera the medical knowledge he thought the culture could handle, although he constantly agonized over what he *had* transferred and what he *could* already have given the Caedelli and all of the peoples of Anyar. Unfortunately, if he pushed too hard, he had no way to predict the consequences. Even after he'd established his current position and reputation, he still feared pushing too hard could lead to total rejection or his demonization.

There was also practicality. He had no reason to attempt to introduce knowledge that people couldn't utilize. That didn't mean he ignored new possibilities, such as one triggered by a comment of Hulyun Linwyr, the Gwillamese trader who had helped Yozef start kerosene production and had taken over operations as a partner, becoming wealthy in his own right.

Yozef had only casually listened until Linwyr said, "Too bad Watmer lost his arm at Moreland City. I hate losing one of my better drivers."

It took several moments for the comment to edge into Yozef's consciousness. Vynin Watmer, an Abersford man, drove tanker wagons filled with crude oil from the seeps in the Gwillamer Province border to the kerosene distillation facility growing ever larger near Abersford. Watmer was also one of the swivel gun crewmen who had suffered a wound at the battle.

Linwyr had continued talking, though about what, Yozef had no idea.

"Watmer," said Yozef, interrupting Linwyr. "He lost his arm? I saw him at Moreland City and then when we arrived back in Abersford. His arm was bandaged, but he acted like it wasn't that serious."

"It didn't seem to be, but it festered, and the medicants couldn't save the arm. Now, he can't drive a wagon anymore. The Keelan Clan is providing some coin to the men whose injuries stop them from their previous trade, but he makes less coin than when he worked for me. I'm trying to find him some other task he can do, so if you have any ideas, let me know."

"Yes, yes, we'll have to take care of him. I'll think about all my other shops. Maybe we can find something more for him."

Though Yozef was sincere, his mind had moved on. *Christ! At least, we have the ether now!* He remembered the elderly man with the badly shattered leg from an accident at the Snarling Graeko. Yozef and Carnigan had helped transport the man to the abbey hospital. There, Yozef learned no painkillers were available, and the man later died during the amputation.

The event had triggered Yozef into realizing he could produce ether. Success, with monetary help and the prestige of Abbot Sistian, had laid the foundation for all of his other enterprises.

Now, a similar stimulus compelled him to seek out Diera, the abbey's chief medicant, who had overseen his care when he was cast by the Watchers onto a Keelan beach. She had developed into a friend.

St. Sidryn's Abbey

Diera Beynom looked up from the piles of papers scattered in front of her and around the edges of her desk. In the month since she'd returned from helping attend to the wounded at the Battle of Moreland City, she only seemed to get further behind with paperwork: issues delayed for the two sixdays she was absent from the abbey; updates on the wounded; reports to Hetman Keelan and other medicants throughout Caedellium on her observations during and after the battle and recommendations for future action; correspondence with influential medicants, once again throughout the island, on changes in medicant knowledge and treatments resulting from interactions with Yozef Kolsko; and the never-ending flow of ongoing issues involving the operation of St. Sidryn's abbey's hospital, overseeing the medicants, and acting as the district training center for new medicants.

Thus, she felt both a sense of anticipation and a sinking feeling when a knock on her door presented her with the same Yozef Kolsko. He entered her office with an expression she recognized as accompanying some new idea he was about to share with her.

"Hello, Yozef. Please come in."

"Thank you, Diera. Sorry to bother you, but I've had this new idea."

She laid down her quill and sat back, sighing at the realization of her hopes and fears.

"Excuse me, Yozef, but I wonder if you'll ever run out of new ideas."

Not if I can stay alive, thought Yozef.

"And so soon after you were wounded."

"Takes a lickin' and keeps on tickin'," he mumbled before he could stop the words from spilling out of his mouth.

Diera's puzzled look brought him back to alertness. "Sorry, Yozef, what did you say?"

"Oh, nothing, just some children's rhyme. I can't remember how it all goes." *Well, hell, the Timex watch commercial is* sort *of like a nursery rhyme*.

"Anyway," he hurried on, before she could ask for more explanation, "I talked with Hulyun Linwyr, the Gwillamese who runs the kerosene production. He mentioned that one of his drivers, Vynin Watmer, had his arm amputated when the wound he got at Moreland City festered."

"Yes, too bad," said Diera. "We thought it was healing, but a sixday after he returned, he came to the hospital complaining about increased pain and fever. When Brother Bolwyn examined the wound, he could see festering had set in. We tried all the treatments we knew of, but it spread, and we were forced to remove the arm. Thank Merciful God once again for the ether you've given us, so at least Watmer remained unconscious during the operation.

"Festering doesn't always happen with open wounds, but this one was deep. Your comments about microorganisms have helped explain how the festering occurs, and we're taking more precautions, as you've suggested. Unfortunately, it didn't help Watmer."

"That's what I wanted to talk to you about, festering. My people know of treatments that can provide additional prevention and can help once an infection has started. It involves using substances called *antibiotics*."

Diera sighed again. Another new word. Another treatment she'd never heard of. Another case where she wanted to ask, scream at times, why Yozef hadn't mentioned this one earlier. Usually, he said it just occurred to him, which fed into the rumors that this stranger who had appeared on the nearby shore might be a Septarsh, one to whom God spoke. Lore had it that often the person was not even aware of the source of inspiration, but simply that God "whispered" into his or her ear.

At moments like this, Diera was tempted to ask Yozef whether he heard voices. Instead, she merely asked her usual question. "What is this *antibiotics* and how does it work?"

Yozef launched into a description of how some microorganisms excrete antibiotics to suppress competing organisms. He didn't go into injections yet, since he had no idea how long it would take to work out a method of purification sufficient to risk introducing crude extracts into the body. However, he remembered that the filtrate of antibiotic-producing fungi and bacteria had been successfully used to saturate cloth applied to open wounds.

It took only a minute for Diera to decide she had heard more details than she had time or understanding to appreciate.

"Let's go talk to Brother Willwin about this," said Diera, and they walked to one of the abbey complex's workshops used by the resident biologist. They found Willwin Wallington in his work area, today worrying over another flat of pea seedlings, the same type of peas Yozef had used to demonstrate genetic inheritance to the naturalist scholastic.

"Willwin," said Diera, "Yozef has another of his ideas he'd like to explain. Do you have time to listen?"

"For Yozef? Always," said Wallington, smiling and setting aside the plants. "What is it this time?"

"He says his people have a treatment to prevent or help with wound festering. He started explaining to me, but I thought we'd let you listen, since it involves the microorganisms you're studying."

"Well, right now my main focus is the peas," said Wallington. "I have too much to do with the 'genetics' Yozef explained. However, one of the new scholastic trainees is concentrating on the microorganisms, although I work with him whenever I can."

"Best fetch him over, then," said Diera. Wallington walked toward the far side of the room where two young men and a woman huddled over something.

"Trainees?" queried Yozef.

"That's right. I don't think you've visited Brother Willwin since you returned. His communications with other scholastics around Keelan and other provinces created quite a stir, as seems to be usual when you're around. Three abbeys have sent students interested in becoming scholastics here to St. Sidryn's to work and study with Willwin."

Diera shook her head. "This seems to be only the beginning. Willwin tells me that six scholastic brothers and sisters around Caedellium have asked to join the university you and Maera are planning. What with others voicing interest in doing the same, Willwin says he needs to discuss with Maera whether they should limit the number in the beginning."

"But we hardly have any of the new buildings started yet," Yozef protested.

"That's what I advised Willwin," said Diera. "His work area here is already overflowing, and now with the three students, the clutter is even worse, which I was surprised could happen. It's the same problem in the hospital. We have requests for more student medicants to come here than we can either house or train. Plus, there's all the knowledge that relates to treating patients. We also have eight visiting medicants from other abbeys in Keelan and have had to postpone visits from abbeys in other provinces—which doesn't make St. Sidryn's very popular."

At least, it shows the ideas in medicine and biology I've introduced are spreading, mused Yozef.

Willwin returned with one of the students, the other two trailing behind.

Without preamble, Yozef addressed Wallington. "As I told Sister Diera, there are microorganisms that naturally produce substances poisonous to other microorganisms. Think of it as similar to herd animals with horns for defense or predator animals with fangs, a characteristic that aids in the organism's survival. In the example I'm speaking of, a microorganism secretes a substance to prevent itself from being attacked or having to compete for space with other microorganisms."

"So, these ones that produce the poison—do you know which ones?" asked Wallington.

Yozef spent the next half hour answering questions, mainly from the scholastic, but an increasing number from the students and Diera. It was a discouraged Wallington who summarized.

"Please correct me if I've misheard, Yozef, but this sounds like an enormous task with uncertain chances of success. This antibiotic you speak of, you call it penicillin, comes from only a specific mold—a fungus. You can't identify which one, only that you think the fungus is green when growing on food. From what I've learned and from your information, there are thousands of different molds, many of them green. We would have to try each one to hope to find at least one producing this penicillin.

"Then, to test each one, we'd have to grow it in a plate containing a growth medium. We've been experimenting with this 'agar' you told us comes from seaweed. We had seaweed shipped to us from the port of Salford, east along the coast. It took time for a man we paid to collect different types of seaweed and ship it to us quickly enough before it rotted. We've only recently had some promising results, but I think it will be many months before we're ready to try growing microorganisms on top of a solidified bed of agar.

"We've also been experimenting with liquids containing nutrients that allow the creatures to grow, but the only liquids that show promise are acid-treated cattle blood and milk with the fat removed. You weren't able to tell us why the acid treatment was necessary, but so far all we get is incredibly foul-smelling slop, although I'll admit microorganisms grow readily on it. Too readily, in fact."

Yozef stared, mentally stepping back and assessing the scope of what he'd proposed. He swallowed. It was too much. He had carefully avoided suggesting projects that involved too many steps, especially those requiring materials that needed to be made, each of which required other materials, and on and on. In his enthusiasm for antibiotics, he'd broken his own rule. It would be years before anything useful resulted, if at all.

Based on the little he knew of how to recognize specific strains, because his enhanced memory didn't work for subjects he hadn't studied, they would have to test thousands of samples, and *only* after working out growth and maintenance conditions. The latter facet hadn't occurred to him until now—how to keep cultures alive without refrigeration. He knew that deep cellars kept food and drinks cold, but were the conditions constant enough to store long-term cultures? As for the common practice on Earth of freezing such cultures, he could forget it until reliable sub-zero refrigeration became practical.

Wallington had continued pointing out problems, while Yozef went through his own list. He felt discouraged and chagrined.

What was I thinking of? I know I need to consider the probability of success, yet here I go blabbing this all out to Diera and Willwin with hardly a thought to practicality. Shit.

"Sorry, Yozef," said Diera, "It doesn't sound as if this is one of your better ideas, not until much more work has been done in preparation. However, I'll ask Brother Willwin to write up the idea and let him circulate it to other scholastics. Who knows? Maybe some of them will have ideas that might help."

"I don't know what I was thinking of," admitted Yozef, dejected. "Everything Willwin says is true, and I'm embarrassed I missed the obvious problems."

"Nothing to be embarrassed about," said Diera, laying a hand on Yozef's shoulder. "With all your other positive ideas, when you have an occasional bad one, it's somehow reassuring to me."

Diera gasped and jerked her hand way. Yozef looked at her, surprised to see that her face was red.

Is Diera embarrassed about something?

"I . . . uh . . . what I meant to say was that no one has good ideas *every* time."

"True," said Wallington. "I often have wonderful thoughts when I wake in the morning, only to realize the absurdity later in the day."

Wallington and the three students laughed, but Diera occupied herself with looking at her hands as she rubbed them together.

"Well, this was all interesting," she said, "even if not immediately useful. However, I need to get back to a desk covered in paperwork. Willwin, as long as Yozef is here, maybe he'd like to see how your work is progressing and what the students are doing, since he hasn't even met them yet."

"Of course," Wallington said enthusiastically. "The latest genetics results with the peas are fascinating, then the categorization of protozoans, along with lovely pictures Erwilina here is making . . . oh, and just so much else."

"In that case, I'll leave you all alone." With those words, Diera spun and left.

She's flustered. Yozef realized. *Maybe it pleased her to know I could make mistakes and it embarrassed her.*

Yozef felt more than ready to retreat to his workshops and to more concrete successes. But when he looked at Wallington's eager face, he figured he needed to let one of his most enthusiastic converts to new knowledge show off his work—for a few minutes, anyway.

"Of course, Willwin, I'm eager to see the latest," Yozef said, the lie evident only in his stiff smile.

The next two endless hours tested Yozef's patience. As much as he respected Wallington's commitment to delve into new and unexpected realms of biology, the man demonstrated nothing Yozef didn't already know and no items to interest him.

Yozef perceived that the tour was winding down, when Wallington said he meant to ask Yozef about something. He led Yozef into a side storeroom piled to the ceiling with wooden boxes, crates, and loose objects of all shapes and sizes.

"A herder brought me something several years ago that he found half buried in one of his pastures. It looks like intricate artwork, but neither I nor anyone else has any idea what it is. I've wondered if you might recognize it."

Wallington rummaged through boxes, mumbling to himself. "Now where did it go? I haven't seen it for about a year, but I know I put it somewhere in this area.

"Ah! Here it is." He pulled out a flattish object about eight inches across. "Let's go back in the workroom where we have more light, over next to the window."

Yozef followed Wallington, who blew dust off the object, gave it a quick swipe with a cloth, and then held it out.

Yozef reached for it, then his whole body froze, as he stared thunderstruck at the object. Seconds passed. Almost a minute.

"Yozef? Yozef? YOZEF! Are you all right?" said Wallington, as his prompting morphed into concern.

Yozef's shaking hand moved closer to the object, barely touching it with a forefinger. He jerked his finger back, then forward again, and this time his hand gently folded around the cool surface. Suddenly, he grasped the object and snatched it from Wallington's hand, eliciting a yelp, as a sharp edge cut a shallow furrow in the startled brother's palm.

Still speechless, Yozef pulled the object closer to his face. His pupils dilated, as his eyes bored into every detail. For moments, his mind searched for an explanation for what he held. He groped for and discarded the even remotely plausible and moved on to the fantastical before coming back to the first jolting impression.

There was no doubt in his mind. Though he had never seen the exact form and design, there was no question he held a fragment of a printed circuit board—a piece of technology three or four centuries ahead of anything that should exist on Anyar.

He turned it over. Minute metallic-looking lines snaked over the surface, intersecting small areas of different shapes, shapes he assumed were components whose purpose he had no clue. The circuits and the components were finer than anything he had seen on Earth. Though he reminded himself he wasn't familiar with the most advanced technologies, it had the *look* and conveyed an innate sense of technology well advanced beyond Earth's.

Wallington gripped his left forearm and shook him. "Yozef! What's wrong?"

Momentarily shaken from his stupor, Yozef looked up from the board. An anxious Brother Wallington stared wide-eyed, the students flanking him with faces concerned or puzzled.

Yozef felt the need to say something, but what clamored to exit his mouth couldn't be said . . . not aloud and not to these witnesses.

He cleared his throat, started to say *something*, then stopped. More moments passed. Wallington had quit shaking him but still gripped his arm.

Yozef cleared his throat again.

"Ah, sorry, Willwin. I think you're right that this is a piece, or more likely a fragment, of an artwork. For a moment, it reminded me of a decoration my parents had in their house. Naturally, that reminded me of home and that I likely won't ever see any of them again."

It was lame, yet all he could think of. He felt desperate to be alone so he could process what he held.

Wallington's face relaxed. "Oh, sorry it brought back sad thoughts."

He didn't know whether Wallington believed his explanation, but Yozef thought that for once, his reputation of being a bit odd had come to his aid.

"Maybe this will give a clue to where your homeland is, Yozef," said Wallington. "If it's a style of art characteristic of where you originated, then there must have been other contacts between there and Caedellium besides yourself."

Yozef needed to deflect the scholastic's thinking and get himself somewhere alone and in possession of the board.

"No," he said. "Now that I look closer, it's not as similar as I first thought. It just reminds me of things I don't want to forget. Would it be all right if I borrow this for a few months?"

Wallington hesitated. "Well, it's unique, so I don't want to lose it."

"I won't lose it," said Yozef, "and will return it any time you want to study it. I'll probably only want it to remind me of home for a little longer."

Yozef didn't say he thought the absent-minded scholastic might forget it existed, as months passed and he remained engrossed in the new realms of study revealed by Yozef.

"Yes, please, take it. Just bring it back if you ever think you don't need it anymore," said Wallington with an almost apologetic tone, as if thinking he shouldn't have hesitated to grant Yozef's wish.

With a stuttered thanks and a perfunctory nod to the three students, Yozef hurried off the abbey grounds. Instead of taking the common road toward his house, he cut through a grove of trees, the same grove where he had temporarily fled to gather himself after the Buldorian raid. There, in a small clearing, a decaying log provided a seat, or a prone platform, depending on

Yozef's mood. Today, he sat on the log and held the board in both hands on his lap.

"A circuit board," he said to the trees. "Good God Almighty, a circuit board—or something that serves the same purpose. Harlie told me the Watchers kept hands off the people on planets they observed. Had he lied? I have no way to judge the truth of anything he told me. I've just assumed things I had no reason to trust. For Christ's sake, they're *aliens*! Beings from a culture that has to be so different from ours that it was stupid of me not to think harder that they might not tell me all of the truth. Or maybe their version of the truth and mine aren't the same."

He stopped talking aloud and brought the board closer to his eyes.

"Wait a minute," he uttered, using a fingernail to pry at a broken edge. What he'd first taken to be a single layer he could tease apart into multiple layers, like thin paper stuck together. He worried at the edge for several minutes before he gave up trying to determine the exact number of layers.

"Must be fifty or more," he mumbled. "Might even be hundreds, and I just can't separate them."

He set the board back on his lap and looked up, not concentrating on anything specific, his eyes unfocused as he ruminated on the shocking revelation.

"So, there is evidence of beings besides humans on this planet—if not now, then in the past. The board's dirty. When I rub and scratch at it, the underlying surfaces are unmarked, so I can't estimate how long it lay in the ground.

"And it's a broken piece. What broke it? An accident like the one that led me here? A battle between . . . who? Or should I say, what?

"The technology is way ahead of anything on Earth. Although I shouldn't try to second-guess how fast things developed there. Still, it's well ahead of Earth, but is it enough ahead to be the Watchers? Maybe. Then again, maybe it's not the Watchers, but whoever they said transplanted humans—some other alien race, ones the Watchers haven't identified."

He shook his head. Once again, too many questions arose, to which he'd likely never have satisfactory answers.

"I suppose all I can say for sure is that probably either the Watchers or the . . . what the hell should I call them? The *Others*? One of them visited the surface of Anyar and left a fragment of a computer or something using advanced printed circuits? The original got damaged by accident or conflict and then discarded or lost when they left?"

Yozef stopped speaking aloud, as another thought hit him. "Hell, why assume they've *left?* Harlie said they were observing, and I assumed from orbit, but why not from the surface or *invisible* drones? Whatever cloaking technology failed in the vessel that collided with my flight might also be used for occupied or robotic surveillance in the atmosphere. Shit. One could be hovering right over my head, for all I know!"

This disconcerting thought made him reflexively scan the sky and the air space within the grove of trees. Nothing was visible.

Of course, it wouldn't be visible, you dimwit, he told himself, unconsciously switching to internal monologue, instead of speaking aloud where *something* might overhear. Then, realizing what he had done, he flushed with anger and yelled skyward.

"Okay, so it's stupid to think you're monitoring me, but if you are, fuck you and whatever horse, jabberwocky, slimeball, robot, or whatever you rode in on! Thanks for nothing! Yeah, you 'repaired' me, but it was *your* fucking mistake that caused all this!"

A two-handed, middle-fingered salute to the sky completed his statement, followed by his breaking into laughter so hard, it took several minutes to subside, as he held onto his stomach with both arms.

When his semi-hysterical outburst was over, Yozef sat back on the log. "Okay. Get yourself back in control. Nothing has changed. I'm here. Even if I'm being observed, I'll never know it, and I still have to live my life and deal with all that involves. The Narthani, my projects, Maera, the coming child, and the one already here."

He looked again at the sky, knowing once more that nothing would be the same. He would never again look up without lingering wonder, even if deep in a corner of his mind, whether someone or something watched him.

It was time to go home. He stood and walked to the edge of the grove, then stopped short. He hadn't asked Wallington whether he had any other objects like this.

Yozef retraced his steps back to Wallington's workroom. The three students had left. Wallington was bent over a flat of pea seedlings, examining some feature and making notes in a ledger.

"Excuse me, Willwin, I forgot to ask you something."

The surprised scholastic jumped at the unexpected voice. "Yozef, back again? Did you forget something? Oh, you said you had a question."

Yozef held up the circuit board fragment. "Is this the only piece like this you have?"

"Yes," said Wallington. "I've never heard of any such object before. I asked the herder who brought this one in if there were any more like this. He said he had only seen it because he'd dismounted to check his horse's hoof. Only a portion of it was sticking out of the ground. A month later, he was in Abersford and we ran into each other. He told me he'd gone back to the same spot and dug quite a bit, but he didn't find anything else."

"Too bad," said Yozef. "Next time you see him, would you ask him to come see me? I might be interested in going to the same spot and looking around myself."

"Of course, Yozef, I'll let him know. I only see him every month or more, so I don't know when I can give him your request. Unfortunately, I also didn't get his name or where exactly he lives."

"No problem," said Yozef, "and no hurry. Thanks. I'll let you get back to your peas."

Yozef turned to leave, walked three steps, then stopped when yet another thought occurred to him. He turned again. "Besides this object, is there anything you or anyone else has ever come across that is odd?"

"Odd," Wallington repeated. "In what way?"

"Just different from anything else people are used to seeing or something that is unexplainable and a bit mysterious."

"Well . . . Nothing I can think of . . . except for possibly Flagorn Eggs."

"Flagorn eggs?" repeated Yozef, suppressing an insane urge to giggle. *Are they like dragon eggs or maybe the ones of Fabergé? Best to keep the former out of the fire and the other ones locked up safe.*

Wallington's face appeared blank with incomprehension.

Then Yozef *did* giggle briefly, before choking it back down. "Never mind, just some random thought of mine."

Like I'm going to explain the dragon eggs from Game of Thrones or the jeweled Russian Easter eggs of the Tsars.

"Flagorn eggs?" repeated Yozef. "What in the world are Flagorn eggs?"

"They're supposed to come from a mythological creature that doesn't exist on Anyar anymore. I only know they're referenced in a few of the oldest known writings. It's just legend, of course, but there are these odd-shaped rock formations that people have named Flagorn eggs. None around here, and I've only seen one myself, in Hewell Province. I know people who have seen the ones in Vandinke and Pawell Provinces, and I understand they're found elsewhere on Caedellium. They look like two-thirds of a big egg sticking out of the ground, with the small egg end up. Now that I think about it, I wonder if anyone's ever dug down to see if the buried part is the other egg end. Anyway, they're about three feet high, completely smooth, smoother than polished marble, a dark blue color, and—I have my doubts about this part—some say they occasionally feel warm, even in the coldest weather.

"Again, as you can imagine, there are rumors of strange happenings associated with the eggs, as happens with all phenomena that superstitious people can't explain. I'm sure they're just an unusual type of rock with a rational explanation for whatever they are."

Half an hour earlier, Yozef would have blown off Flagorn eggs. After seeing the circuit board fragment, however, and his thinking session on his log, he was of a mind to allow that anything could be possible.

I'll give it two options: either, as Willwin says, it's probably some weird rock, or it's a device of one of the alien races. If the latter, pick your favorite BEM—although I guess they could be slime blobs, instead of Bug-Eyed-Monsters.

"That's all I know about them," said Wallington, "At the moment, I can't think of any other strange objects like you asked about."

"Okay, thanks, Willwin. I'll take my leave again and quit bothering you."

"No, no, Yozef," said Wallington. "Any visit from you is always interesting, even in cases where I don't understand what you're saying."

Yozef grunted and left. He took the common road home this time, and it gave him enough moments to decide that if the opportunity arose, he'd try to get a look at Flagorn eggs.

CHAPTER 9

OBLIGATIONS

Yozef questioned the ten surviving Narthani prisoners several more times while they settled into living around Abersford, and he added to his interrogation notes. Maera volunteered to organize his notes into a coherent report when they ran to fifty pages of his scribblings.

"Father, Vortig, and Pedr need to read this," she told him, after reviewing the final pages. "But not in this form. Pedr could make sense of it, but Vortig wouldn't have the patience, and I wouldn't want Father to miss any of the points."

During the next three days, Maera pestered Yozef to explain his atrocious penmanship and clarify written comments that had seemed clear to him when he wrote them but that needed translation for Maera. Not for the first time, he appreciated the clarity of his wife's thinking, as she produced a readable report that included salient points Yozef had missed.

Maera sent the report to Caernford in the regular mail packet, and a sixday later a response came in an unexpected format.

The Kolsko house hosted a pleasant social evening with the Beynom family: Diera, Sistian, Cadwulf, and Selmar. Elian and Serys Clithrow prepared and served the evening meal. Serys was a new widow from the Moreland City battle and worked at the Kolsko house as part of Maera's efforts to provide for families of the dead or incapacitated. Elian Faughn, the wife in the elderly couple employed by Yozef when he moved out of the abbey guest quarters to a home of his own, was still spry for her age but had noticeably slowed down, especially by evening.

During the meal, they deliberately kept the conversation away from weighty matters, though without overt intention. Sistian recalled stories of his youth in Caernford and mischief he and his best friend, Culich Keelan, had gotten into. Maera laughed so hard at previously unheard antics of her father's past that tears covered her face and she got the hiccups.

Diera, Maera, and Yozef all recalled their own family tales, and the two Beynom sons elicited stories of everyone's days as students and the common experiences with good and bad teachers, tests, homework, and wondering what all of them would do with their lives and where their studies would lead them.

When the evening wound to a close, the Beynoms bade Maera and Yozef thanks, collected a promise of a reciprocal evening at the Beynom house, and left walking toward the abbey. The two moons of Anyar and a sky full of stars provided more than enough light.

"Thank you, Yozef," said Maera, sliding her arm through his.

"Thank you? What for?"

"For being you. For agreeing to marry me after my pathetic proposal of marriage. For our life together. For seeing me for who I am and not trying to fit me into a fixed role. Oh . . . I don't know . . . just because. Thank you."

Her words touched him, but he was unsure what he had done to elicit them. Not certain what to say in return, he fell back to his stock reaction to awkward moments and said nothing.

When the Beynoms faded into the darkness, Maera gave his arm a squeeze. "I didn't have time to tell you between when you got home and the Beynoms arrived, but Father is coming to Abersford next sixday."

Yozef looked down at his wife's face, lit by lantern light from the windows of the house. "Culich? Coming here? Why?"

"Ostensibly, it's part of his yearly tour of the province. He's always tried to make a circuit to visit each district, meet with leaders and others, and get the pulse of the clan and let the people see him. With everything that's happened the last year, the tour has been delayed again and again, and now he's doing it."

"Do I detect a 'but' in that explanation and did it start with the word *ostensibly*?"

"Oh," said Maera. "I don't doubt he regrets delays of his yearly tour, but I suspect a major contributing factor is to meet with you."

She could feel the muscles in his arm tighten.

"Any idea why he wants to meet?"

"Not specifically," she replied. "I got news of the visit in a letter from him today, and he only mentioned seeing you in passing. Most of the letter consisted of updates on the family and questions about the baby. However, with what's been happening, I know Father well enough to suspect two topics he wants to talk with you about."

"Let me guess one of them—our moving to Caernford."

"When we married, you *did* tell him you'd think about it," Maera said.

"I did, and I have, and I'm still happy living here. Here's where I've lived since coming to Any . . . Caedellium. All my projects are here, my friends, the university . . ."

Oh, Christ, Yozef thought, *am I whining? I hate whining, and here I am doing it. Is it because I think the move to Caernford is inevitable? The move is logical, but it would put me more into the middle of clan and island affairs. Haven't I done enough for them?*

And I need to watch what comes out of my mouth! I started to say "coming to Anyar," instead of "coming to Caedellium." Some people might pass it off as a slip of the tongue, but Maera's liable to remember and eventually begin to suspect the truth.

"All right," he said, sighing in resignation. "I promise I'll give it more thought. What's the other thing you think your father wants to see me about?"

"I'm afraid it's just as difficult for you as the first one. He'll want you to become more involved in planning what to do about the Narthani."

Yozef didn't react this time. Although he'd asked the question, he was already sure he knew the answer. He also didn't fool himself about one reason for his reticence to move to Caernford: it would put him in the middle of planning and people looking to him for answers.

* * *

Culich Keelan and Vortig Luwis arrived five days later in a carriage accompanied by twenty escorts. Maera told Yozef her father had given up trying to travel with fewer guards. With her mother, his daughters, Luwis and Kennrick, and others—more than he cared to count—nagging about his safety, he accepted the inevitable.

Yozef was in the cannon foundry when Carnigan walked in. The clue to his presence was when he filled the open doorway and cut off outside light.

"Yozef, Abbot Beynom asked me to let you know the hetman arrived. Maera's already headed there to see her father, and you're to come for evening meal at the Beynoms' house."

Yozef opened his mouth to say something, he wasn't sure what, but he looked at an empty door. Carnigan, his task complete and evidently having nothing else to say at the moment, had departed. Yozef went to the door in time to see Carnigan heading for Abersford, instead of back to the abbey.

I'll bet he's bee-lining for the Snarling Graeko to sneak in an ale before returning to work.

* * *

Evening meal was a pleasant occasion, to Yozef's relief. Culich was staying with the Beynoms, and neither Culich nor Vortig Luwis broached any subject related to Yozef's moving to Caernford or taking on an expanded role. Yozef found it so enjoyable that the return to reality felt all the more jarring when, as he and Maera departed for home, Culich, the friendly father-in-law, turned back into Hetman Keelan.

"Yozef, Vortig and I will meet with you tomorrow after morning meal, as soon as you can get to the abbey."

There being no evident acknowledgment expected or any objection anticipated, Culich turned to continue a conversation with Diera. Maera tugged on her husband's arm to lead him away before he thought of something to say.

"Just accept it, Yozef," she said, when they were out of hearing. "You're going to have to meet with him, so you might as well get it over with. At least, you can confirm for him that we'll be in Caernford for the baby's birth, which means I'll need to go to wait for it."

They spoke little until halfway home, when Yozef said, "What do *you* think I should tell him when he brings up the two topics you predicted?"

"I only know what I would do. I'm sure you are even better aware than the rest of us of the advantages for your projects to be in Caernford, instead of Abersford. As for the other topic, that's something you have to decide for yourself. I've come to terms with knowing you're different from other men. What seems best to others might not be to you, and I trust your judgment."

He reached over and laid his hand on hers. "Thank you, Maera. It means a lot to me to have your support when I make decisions I know you don't agree with. I may not always say it, but I appreciate how exasperating I can be."

"That's putting it mildly," she said, laughing. "But that's part of what makes being married to you such an adventure."

The sun had risen well into the mid-morning sky when Yozef and Maera reached the abbey the next day. Yozef had found reasons to delay, a bit of deliberate passive resistance against the hetman's preemptory directive to meet immediately after morning meal. His pleasure at his self-acknowledged petty gesture was spoiled when Culich took no apparent notice. Compensating for his disappointment was Culich's surprise that Maera accompanied Yozef, with the obvious intent to sit in on the meeting. Not that Culich minded his daughter's presence. She had attended boyermen meetings for years as his scribe, and Culich assumed she would be his ally in the discussion to come. He was to be disappointed.

"Let's get started," said Culich, sitting in one of three straight-backed, armed wooden chairs arranged facing one another in a small meeting room. Vortig Luwis followed suit, as did Yozef and Maera, after he pulled a fourth chair from against a wall for her.

"Yozef, I'm not one for meaningless preambles when everyone knows the real purposes of a meeting," said Culich, in a tone attuned to reasonable people having a reasonable discussion. "It's time for you to move to Caernford. Your work here has outgrown Abersford, and we need you closer to the clan center."

"I'm aware of the arguments, Hetman, but I am still considering the possibility and will be the final judge of whether such a move is in mine and my wife's best interests." Yozef didn't know for certain what his decision would be, but he wanted to lay out that it would be *his* decision, although Maera's input and desires would be part of the process. His use of "Hetman," instead of "Culich," was a flag signaling his intent.

Culich's eyes flickered imperceptibly, and Luwis stiffened.

"I realize this, Yozef. However, I would ask you to tell me the advantages of staying in Abersford for expanding your current projects, developing new ones, starting up this university of yours, and contributing to the defense of your family, the Keelan Clan, and all of Caedellium against the Narthani. Can you do that? If you can and are convincing, I won't bother you again on the topic."

My God, he's ruthless, thought Yozef, both amused and resentful, *resorting to logic and reason. He knows as well as I that there are no such arguments, and that I don't want the move simply because I don't want to leave my relatively sheltered life in Abersford.*

"First, let me say that Maera and I have talked, and we're agreed that soon she will go to Caernford," Yozef replied, delaying an answer. "The baby's still a few months away, but we think she shouldn't delay the travel. We agreed the child would be born in the clan capital, and we will abide by that commitment."

He paused to let the prospective grandfather express pleasure at the news and make a comment to Luwis about preparing an announcement. Maera, bless her heart, managed several minutes of chitchat to give Yozef more time. When the delay timed out and heads turned back to Yozef, what had solidified in his mind was to be honest.

"Culich," he said, starting off with the familiar address, "everything you say is rational. My problem is that I simply don't want to make the move, not permanently. Much of the reason is that I view the Abersford area as my home. I was already taken from one home and cast here on Caedellium. It took two years before I could accept Abersford as my new home.

"Now, you, and yes, logic, want me to uproot from *this* home and start again somewhere else. While I know it sounds childish, part of me wants to rail against the sense of unfairness. Haven't I had enough change for one lifetime? Is it too much to ask to live quietly where I choose?"

Luwis stirred in his chair, his jaw clenched, and Yozef felt certain he was about to storm at Yozef's attitude. By comparison, Culich sat calmly, a sympathetic expression softening his face.

"Alas, Yozef, would that the world let us live the lives we want. In my youth, I wanted to be a horse breeder and trainer, which was impossible once my father chose me to be the next hetman. Then, and to this day, what I would like to do is work to provide for a life of security and peace for all my clanspeople. Yet I've always known there was more to it than my personal desires. Even before the Narthani threat, I spent most of my time dealing with other hetmen and clans, petty conflicts within Keelan, boyermen focused on their own districts and not always on the good of the entire clan, and on and on. Then there's the Narthani. Never in my worst imaginings of what it would be like to be hetman did I conceive of fighting battles such as at Moreland City or the level of threat presented by the Narthani. What you call an *existential* threat.

"In life, we often must do what is necessary, irrespective of our own wishes. I have done what I perceived to be necessary, and this is a reconciliation you'll have to come to for yourself."

Yozef felt afraid. Not like during the fight in the courtyard at St. Sidryn's or waiting to ambush the Eywellese at Moreland City, but more of being forced to take a step in life that he dreaded.

"It's not just my moving to Caernford that you want, Culich, is it?"

"No, Yozef, it's not. You *know* things. Things we don't know here in Caedellium or ways of thinking we're not familiar with. You've proved that over and over. Not just the ether, the kerosene, and all the other innovations. The advice you gave at St. Sidryn's and Moreland City and the insights you've shared with Abbot Sistian and me on likely actions of the Narthani. We need these from you."

"Culich, I'm not the source of all knowledge. I could tell you things, give opinions and advice that might be wrong, and people would die because of my errors."

"How is that different from what many do?" rejoined Culich. "Life is *acting*. That our actions sometimes have tragic consequences is simply the way life is. To not act, to not give advice, is to act by inaction. You don't think of yourself as a leader, but what is a leader?"

"I see a leader as someone at the front of whatever is happening. Someone others want to follow."

"Those are reasonable descriptions of some leaders, though not all. Rhaedri Brison can be called a leader of theophists, yet he holds no position of authority over anyone. Diera Beynom is a leader of medicants, because of reputation and the fact that other medicants place great emphasis on her opinions. Gynfor Moreland was not a great leader, though he was hetman of his clan. His people followed him because of his position, not because of their regard. You are a leader whether you want to be or not, because your past actions have proved to be worth following or considering. Whether you call yourself a leader or not is irrelevant."

"What if some advice I give leads to disaster?"

"It could happen. Still, others are required to evaluate what they hear and make their own decisions. After all, advice is just that, not commandments. You also have to ask yourself the cost of not giving advice. Answer me this honestly, Yozef. What would have happened at St. Sidryn's if you hadn't suggested letting the Buldorians into the courtyard?"

Yozef hesitated to say what he knew would support Culich's arguments. Silence dragged on, as the other three waited and watched. Finally and reluctantly, Yozef replied, "Denes believed there was no way to defend the abbey with the number of men they had. The Buldorians would have come over the walls, killed most of the people, enslaved the rest, and burned the abbey."

"But they didn't," said Culich, "because you took the risk of giving an opinion."

"It could have been the wrong thing to advise," complained Yozef.

"Yes, it could, but it wasn't. In the same manner, what would have happened if you'd been silent at Moreland City?"

Yozef didn't say anything. The answer was obvious. He felt depressed that he couldn't think of a single argument that wasn't selfish and felt angry that he couldn't *be* selfish.

"What do you expect of me?" asked Yozef, his manner and tone suggesting defeat.

Culich did his best not to smile. He sensed he was going to get his way and Yozef would concede in doing what Culich thought he should be willing to do without convincing.

"Besides moving to Caernford," said Culich, "we need every bit of advice you can muster up on options in dealing with the Narthani. You've already shown you have priceless advice, with what you did at St. Sidryn's and Moreland City. What more can you do?"

"Culich, I'm not a military genius of any kind. I don't know why I advised what I did those times. My only experience has been reading books on military history and playing some games of my people that involve tactics and strategy."

Luwis grunted, and Culich smiled. "There you go, Yozef. Just when you try to tell us what you don't know, you pull new words out of the air. Tactics. Strategy. I sense these are important, but what do they *mean*?"

"Sorry, Culich," said Yozef. "Once again, whenever I can't find a Caedelli word, I automatically fall back on my own language, English, without thinking.

"In a conflict, like we experienced when the Narthani invaded Moreland, strategy is the overall goal, while tactics are the details of how we achieve the goal. We wanted to drive the Narthani back: that was the strategy. How we did it was the tactics—pretending a general assault on the center of their line, ambushing the Eywellese, and attacking the Narthani flank.

"By another definition, strategy is concerned with the future, what you want to happen, and tactics involve the present, what you do at the moment to achieve the strategy."

"Then," said Luwis thoughtfully, "by those definitions, when the Buldorians attacked St. Sidryn's, letting them inside the abbey walls was the tactic to accomplish the objective of defending the abbey? And what you did in both instances was advise on tactics, since the strategies were obvious. Is that how you see it, Yozef?"

"Well, yes, I suppose that's how it seems," Yozef said hesitantly.

"Then that's what we need from you," said Culich. "Let us assume that the strategy is to stop the Narthani from absorbing any more clans. How do we do that? Vigorous defense of the existing border between the Narthani and the free clans? Attack the Narthani, even if they don't move first? What would be the best ways to stop the Narthani?"

Luwis shook his head. "The words and definitions seem obvious, Culich, but it doesn't help us understand how Yozef comes up with the specific ideas, or tactics, as he calls them. I agree that we need his advice, but he can't be everywhere, and I have been around him enough to sense he doesn't believe himself infallible. We need others, including you and me, to better evaluate his ideas and come up with those of our own."

"Yes, Vortig, though I wonder if what he describes as 'tactics' is something that our people would learn from experience. Consider Moreland City. If we had attacked the Narthani line directly, without forewarning of the consequences, we would have learned not to do it again. We would have learned a tactic: don't attack the Narthani strength. The problem is, the learning experience would have been exceedingly painful. What Yozef did was state a principle: don't attack a strong point."

"Or the complementary statement," said Vortig. "If you must attack, do it at a weak point. Yet these seem obvious things to do or avoid."

"True," said Culich, "in hindsight. We will, unfortunately, gain experience in this magnitude of fighting. Yet experience can be a hard taskmaster.

"Yozef, you told me before that you had read about the history of military conflicts and that was where you might have gained insights that helped you give advice. Are there general principles of tactics you can teach?"

Yozef pondered the question. As a teenager and into undergraduate college, he had been part of gamester groups. They would argue for hours over details of tactics, in their naiveté pretending to be experts. He felt embarrassed to remember self-important arguments over which of three famous military treatises was the most influential: Jomini's *The Art of War*, Clausewitz's *On War*, or Sun Tzu's *The Art of War*.

An idea rose to Yozef's consciousness. The way Culich explained it, maybe there *was* a way he could help.

"You mean help those commanding in the field to flatten their learning curve?"

Culich grimaced, and Luwis clucked disgustedly.

"Yozef . . . ," said Culich, with feigned patience.

"Oh, sorry," said Yozef. "Ah . . . what I meant to say is that you're asking if I can remember basic principles of battles, then maybe the clansmen can avoid some of the worst errors?"

"Yes," said Luwis. "What you advised us at Moreland City now seems to me mostly obvious, though I wouldn't have thought of it at the time. We need to get our minds thinking differently."

"To get you . . . ," Yozef stopped himself before he said *kick-started*. ". . . ah, pointed in the right direction?"

"That's a way to put it, Yozef. Can you help? Can you *point us in the right direction?*"

"I'll try to remember what I can and write it down," said Yozef. "I can't guarantee how complete it will be, and for God's sake, don't assume it's authoritative. At best, it will be general principles." At the same time, he wondered exactly how much he would remember. It would be the first time he'd tried to use his enhanced recall for extensive non-science writings. Even if he could image entire works in his mind, he hadn't yet dared attempt complete books or even chapters. After all, a normal person couldn't do such things. Besides, how would the Caedelli understand whole texts on subjects that had no foundation in this world? Even with military theory, too much that didn't fit this world would seep through. He would have to give it careful thought and summarize parts that would be understandable and acceptable on Anyar.

"All right, Culich, I'll do the best I can."

"Good, Yozef. If possible, have something done in another month. Hetman Orosz has sent notice to all clans for an All-Clan Conclave in Orosz City. The only topic will be the Narthani and what we plan to do about them. I'm hoping all the clans finally realize the danger and we can come to an agreement on our actions. Naturally, you will need to come with me."

Oh, hell.

"Now, I think Vortig wants to look at progress in the cannon foundry. We'll set up another foundry in Caernford, as soon as you succeed in casting a larger barrel than the swivels you've done so far. You two go ahead, and I'll visit with Maera."

Yozef guided Luwis to the foundry, leaving Culich and Maera sitting in the meeting room.

"I must say, Maera, I'm a little surprised and, yes, disappointed that you didn't speak up to help me with your husband. I know how much you want to move back to Caernford, and you also know how duty to the clan comes before personal desires. Yozef may not originally be a Keelander, but he's a member of both the clan and our family now, so he should better recognize what he's obligated to do."

"First, Father, he *is* my husband, and if there's a loyalty conflict between him and you, he will always come first. And no, I don't see a conflict between duty to the clan and husband. As you say, Yozef is not from Caedellium, and how he reacts will never be the same as someone raised his whole life in Keelan Province. That doesn't mean he won't support the clan; it just might not be with the timing and level of enthusiasm you want. I believe you'll find him important in ways probably neither of us can predict or even possibly appreciate.

"Yes, he can be frustrating, including times when he dithers about doing something we believe is obvious and necessary. He once told me a quote that had been used to describe his people. An allied realm leader had said that 'They will always end up doing the right thing, after trying everything else.' I believe all of us just have to be patient and trust that he will always, or at least most of the time, come around to doing what's necessary."

"I understand, Maera, and I didn't mean to sound critical. It was just my own expectation obscuring that you might see things differently than me, and I have to trust your instinct about Yozef. So, do I perceive correctly that your moving to Caernford is certain?"

"Yes, Father, I think you can. As Yozef and I have talked the last months, I've seen him slowly accept what's necessary. What you saw today is simply some residual resistance. Don't worry. I'll work on him, gently, and I've several ideas and arguments to ease the transition for him."

Maera's Machinations

Yozef fought a persistent and futile rearguard action. "One negative about moving is I won't have Wyfor Kales to give me my monthly sparring lesson. I suppose I could find someone in Caernford, though no one else is likely to be as good as Kales."

"Didn't Kales tell you? He's moving to Caernford. His wife is originally from Salford on the coast, and she has many relatives there and around Caernford."

Maera saw no reason to bother Yozef with details, such as how she had talked to Kales after having to ask half of the town where he lived. She learned that he and his wife had a cozy, well-maintained and furnished house on the western edge of Abersford.

Teena Kales was a plain-looking woman until she smiled, and her friendly, down-to-Anyar personality shined. She was suitably impressed when the hetman's daughter and the wife of Yozef Kolsko came calling, more so than her husband. He received a stern look and a preemptive order to show proper respect and fetch their pregnant visitor a chair to their porch. There, the three of them sat facing a lovely view of hills to the west.

"Don't mind Wyfor, Sen Kolsko-Keelan, he never did learn proper respect for visitors, and ignore the scowl. His look is far worse than his bite."

Maera wasn't so sure. Her few exchanges with Kales had fit Yozef's description of a dangerous man with a murky off-island history, but his gaze of open affection and tolerance for his wife seemed real.

In the next quarter hour, Maera learned from the vociferous woman that she had been made a widow during the raid on St. Sidryn's. Her husband was one of the few to die defending the courtyard. He had been one of Kales's cousins. She and Kales had known each other as children, before he sailed off Caedellium and returned twenty-three years later. Her three children were on their own, and she and Kales had married only two months ago.

Maera, in return, recounted a few items of her own history, though she downplayed being the hetman's daughter. As soon as she could slip it into the conversation, she mentioned that she and Yozef would be moving to Caernford.

"Which is why I wanted to talk to you, Ser Kales. Yozef values the training you've given him and how you looked after him during the Moreland City battle."

"I suppose I did at times," said Kales. "Other times I was keeping up with him, especially once he decided to operate half the Narthani cannon by himself."

Maera was sure she detected approval in the normally blasé man.

"We both appreciate how you kept an occasional eye on him since he came back. You know, with worries about possible Narthani agents and how valuable Yozef has been. I've been talking with the hetman. My father would value your moving to Caernford to help keep a safe eye on Yozef and train Keelan men in the things Yozef says you're so good at."

Another detail Maera omitted was that neither Yozef nor her father had thought about Kales moving.

Kales tugged at his pointed beard. "Caernford? Well, it's a real city, not that I have anything against Abersford, but I wouldn't mind it." He turned to his wife. "What about you, Teena? You've lived here a long time. Would you consider moving to Caernford?"

"Why, Wyfor, I'd have to think about it. I have friends here, but not much family. Two of my children are in Caernford or nearby, and you know I have a sister and a brother there. The rest of my family is in Salford, and Caernford's a little farther away than Abersford, but I don't visit Salford that often."

"It's probably easier to visit Salford from Caernford than Abersford, since there are regular carriages and wagons to and from Salford," suggested Kales, who sat farther back in his chair and spoke more to himself than to Maera or his wife. "You know, it's certainly a lot more interesting with Kolsko around, and Carnigan's right that the man needs someone looking after him. If Kolsko moves, then I assume Carnigan and Balwis will go, too. I'd miss the three of them. Then there's nothing here for me to do during the day. We don't need coin, but I wouldn't mind helping to get other Keelanders ready for whatever comes against the Narthani."

Kales refocused on the two women. "Sen Kolsko-Keelan, Teena and I will talk this over and let you know what we decide."

Maera bid her goodbyes and walked home humming to herself. Now she'd have to tell her father that she knew of an expert hand-to-hand combat man who could be persuaded to move to Caernford and become involved in training Keelan men. She'd also let Yozef know that Kales intended to move to Caernford.

"Hello, Carnigan," Maera said, when she found the big man weeding flowers behind the cathedral.

"Maera. How are you this day?"

It had taken Maera several months to convince Carnigan to address her by her first name, and once he acquiesced, it was as if he switched to a different personality. Now he seemed comfortable treating her as a true friend.

"I'm fine, and the baby has started to make itself known, kicking and squirming," she said, stroking her abdomen. "But there's something else I wanted to talk to you about. You may have heard that Yozef and I are moving to Caernford?"

Carnigan's usually impassive face fell. "No, I hadn't heard. I suppose that makes sense, what with Yozef's projects expanding so much and his becoming more important to the clan."

"Yes," said Maera, "though I'm worried about him. As you know, he sometimes doesn't take enough care of himself, and I'd be so relieved if you were still around. You know he thinks of you as his best friend. Is there any way you could also move to Caernford?"

Carnigan's face lit up for a moment, then settled back into passivity. "I'm not sure. I would have to talk to Abbot Sistian about that. I don't know if it's possible."

"Why don't you see him as soon as you can and talk about it with him? I'm sure something could be worked out."

"Okay, Maera, I will," he said doubtfully.

"Thanks, Carnigan. I'll let you get back to work."

Maera walked off, thinking, *Now I need to talk with Sistian about how good it would be for both Yozef and Carnigan if his friend could move to Caernford the same time we do.*

***

"Hello, Filtin, I see you're busy as always," Maera said, interrupting Filtin Fuller and three other workers. "Is that the new kerosene distillation column you're working on?"

"Yes, isn't it a beauty! Almost thirty feet tall and able to produce three hundred lanterns-worth of kerosene in a single run. There's still more residue than we'd like, but . . . " Filtin rambled on into technical details that didn't interest Maera.

She let him run down his enthusiasm and waited for an opening. "So, Filtin, have you heard that Yozef and I are moving to Caernford?"

"Wonderful, Maera! My family and I will also be moving there. We just decided. I'll set up a new distillation *factory*, as Yozef calls them. Nerlin was unsure of the idea, but the increased pay was too good an opportunity to miss. I'm excited about building the factory brand new, instead of constantly modifying the original here in Abersford. I've discussed it with Yozef, and the plan is to produce daily three times as much as here. The distance to transport the crude oil is farther, but we will build much larger wagons and have people looking at oil seeps in northern Keelan. And, of course, anywhere Yozef is has to be more interesting than where he's not. We're already packing our possessions, and I'm planning to be in Caernford in two sixdays."

Maera congratulated him on his new position and made her exit. *Well, that was easy*, she thought. Yozef had said he wanted Filtin to move, but she hadn't realized it would be so soon and so definite. One more person Yozef felt comfortable with accounted for.

She visited Cadwulf Beynom but had doubts he could be enticed. Only a few moments of discussion confirmed it was not practical for Cadwulf to move to Caernford. The plan for the University of Abersford called for four initial departments, one of which was Applied Mathematics. The Beynoms' son had taken all of the mathematics Yozef had to teach and had gone beyond. Even before the university formally functioned, a small cadre of mathematics scholastics and aspiring students had gathered in Abersford. When Maera mentioned the possibility of moving to Caernford, Cadwulf declared he had no intention of moving, for unspecified personal reasons, no matter what happened to the university plan. She would have to talk with Yozef about what to do with the university.

Maera also considered whether it was practical to convince Bronwyn Merton-Linton to relocate, but she immediately dismissed the possibility. Yozef had had an affair with Bronwyn before he and Maera met, and a child resulted. At Yozef's suggestion, Bronwyn had joined the marriage of her sister and her husband, and they had merged the two farms inherited from the sisters' parents. The child, Aragorn, was developing well in a healthy family and felt secure in that environment.

Her final stop was at the Snarling Graeko inn and pub, whose lower floor had been the main social stop for Yozef since he'd arrived in Caedellium. He spent at least one night a sixday there, usually with Carnigan, regularly with Filtin, and occasionally with Cadwulf and Kales, drinking ale and telling stories that no one had ever heard. At the pub, he'd had the initial inspiration to produce ether, and there Maera suspected he first felt part of the community.

It was mid-afternoon when she walked into the pub. Only four patrons occupied tables, though she knew the number would steadily increase as people ended their workday, to peak well after most people's evening meal. No one noticed her, neither the few patrons nor the single barmaid snoozing at a table. She was about to wake the barmaid when the innkeeper walked in from a back room carrying a tray of steins. He set the tray down on a table and hurried over to her. She occasionally visited the pub with Yozef, either sitting with an ale, until she became with child, or participating in a corner of the pub dedicated to Go players, the game Yozef said was nearly identical to one played in his homeland.

Yet she had never come to the Snarling Graeko alone or at this time of day.

"Sen Kolsko-Keelan," said the innkeeper, "can I help you?"

"Hello, Ser Kuwaith, could we sit and talk for a moment?"

"Certainly, certainly," said the surprised man, conveying his puzzlement at what Yozef's wife and the hetman's daughter had to say to *him*. He pulled out a chair for her from the nearest table and sat across from her.

"Ser Kuwaith, my husband, Yozef, has enjoyed his evenings here at the Snarling Graeko, and he has told me that your beer is considered the best in Abersford. Unfortunately, we are moving to Caernford in a few sixdays, and Yozef will miss being your regular customer. I was wondering if you might consider establishing another inn and pub in Caernford?"

"Why . . . no . . . I can't say I have," said the obviously surprised Kuwaith. "Why would I? Abersford is my wife's and my home. We were both born here."

"I didn't necessarily mean to ask if you yourself might move to Caernford, only that you open another establishment there. You might be the owner or part owner to ensure that the business was properly set up and the beer equaled the quality you have here. Another person could be the proprietor, either working for you or a partner."

Kuwaith listened with a puzzled expression, resting his chin on his palm.

"I realize there are already many pubs in Caernford," Maera continued, "but I'm certain that when we move, Yozef and some of the other people who move at the same time would become customers. Naturally, I would accompany Yozef occasionally, and it's possible patrons of the other pubs would come to a new pub known to be the favorite of Yozef Kolsko and members of the hetman's family. You might even give it the same name, the Snarling Graeko. You know, if it was successful, you might even open other pubs in other cities and provinces."

Kuwaith licked his lips, his eyes taking on a distant focus, as if making a mental calculation. "Yes . . . such a pub might do quite well. I could spend a few days each month there. My cousin Aberlol brews for the Happy Stallion, and I know he's wanted to operate his own pub. I wonder . . ."

Maera allowed a smile to play at the corners of her mouth. She had been prepared to offer coin incentives to get Kuwaith interested. There was no need. Once he was committed, she would persuade him and his cousin, if that's who ended up operating the Caernford franchise, as Yozef called such arrangements, to make the Caernford Snarling Graeko structure and ambiance look as much like the one in Abersford as possible.

CHAPTER 10

DECISION

Kolsko Home, Abersford

After meeting with her father, Maera didn't press Yozef about moving to Caernford. She knew he took time to mull over decisions and would reinitiate the discussion on his own. She felt satisfied that she had facilitated his thinking without appearing *too* manipulative. She was learning patience, a trait she recognized that she'd often lacked before marrying Yozef. He *listened* to her like no one else ever had. Yet even more important, he could almost always be convinced by her or she by him. The sole exception concerned her desire to learn more details of how he came to Caedellium. She had acquiesced to his refusal to tell her more, after he had admitted he felt he couldn't share certain facts with anyone. She took comfort in his statement that she was the one he wanted to tell the most and would do so, if he ever found it possible.

While she waited to continue the discussion about moving, she had more than enough to keep her busy.

During the next two sixdays, Maera noticed Yozef's changing mood. After meeting with her father, Yozef acted quieter than usual, an indication he was chewing over something. He bordered on terse with her and the Faughns several times, a trait unlike his normal behavior. Within ten days, he seemed more relaxed and commented several times about Filtin moving to Caernford to set up the new distillation facility and Wyfor hinting he and his wife were considering the same move.

The morning after a storm had moved through Abersford, they finished a meal of kava, fruit, and French toast. Yozef had introduced the toast two years previously, and it had spread over Caedellium, even into Narthani-controlled territory by an unknown route. Maera had been a fervent convert the first time she tried it, but Yozef still wasn't satisfied with the taste, because duck eggs didn't taste the same as those from chickens. And chickens hadn't been included among the assorted terrestrial animal species, along with humans, transplanted to Anyar by an alien race.

Elian Faughn had eaten with them that morning, an occasional routine left over from before Yozef had married Maera. When Yozef had lived alone, the gentle elderly woman often delayed her eating until she'd prepared the meal for him, rather than having breakfast with her husband, Brak, who always started work well before dawn. Yozef had long ago given up trying to tell the man he didn't need to work so hard. Brak was prickly about not taking charity.

After a morning meal of French toast, Elian cleared the table and went to the kitchen to wash up, leaving Yozef and Maera alone. Yozef sat back in his chair, a calm expression on his face.

He's decided, Maera thought. *And he doesn't seem nervous, so he probably isn't worried about my reaction.*

"Thanks for being patient, Maera. I know I'm withdrawn at times. As you well know, I'm badly conflicted about moving to Caernford. I'm happy here in Abersford. More so than ever in my life, more so than I've only recently realized. I think I'm afraid that if we move, I'll lose that feeling and never get it back. I can't say that I've assuaged the fear, but I believe I'm coming to terms with it."

Maera watched him with a hopeful expression but not commenting.

"All the arguments are solid, and the fact is that everything we're doing here in Abersford has outgrown the location. Oh, it could continue the way it has, but to expand, it needs a larger base of population and skills, things readily available in Caernford. That area is also a more central location for transportation and politics. I can't avoid the latter factor, with the constant threat of the Narthani hanging over the island. As much as I want to sit here and enjoy our life, it's childish of me. The reality is, we have to face the Narthani, and the *we* includes me. I've worked hard to devise weapons to improve our chances, but I have to work even harder, though it eats into time I'd prefer spending on our university idea, conferring with Wallington and Diera on science, and writing in my journals."

"What *about* the university?" asked Maera. "The workers broke ground last sixday for the first building, and Cadwulf is already assembling the mathematics staff. How would it work with you and me in Caernford, since we're supposed to lead the Chemistry and Nations departments until we identify permanent leaders? Don't some of the same arguments for us moving also apply to the university?"

Yozef gave a rueful shake of his head. "The building will start over again in Caernford. At least, they haven't gotten too far, and we can use the same building plans. Fortunately, only a few of the identified scholastics who've agreed to join have made the move, so that's not a serious problem. As for the mathematics scholastics, if they're like those in my homeland, I doubt they'll care, except possibly for Cadwulf, since this is his home, and I think he has a young woman in Abersford."

"Don't forget about Willwin," said Maera.

"Oh, shit. I forgot. He's got several students." Yozef paused. "No. I don't see a problem. The students aren't from Abersford, so I doubt they'll mind. Willwin is something else. I'd prefer him to come with us, but I expect we could find a replacement."

"I doubt that'll be an issue," said Maera, laughing. "All we need is a good workroom for Willwin, and he'll be happy looking through his microscopes and experimenting with the peas."

"Diera is more the problem," said Yozef. "We'd planned for her to head the Department of Biology and Medicine, but not only is her family here, she's the abbess and the head medicant at St. Sidryn's."

"That may solve itself long enough to get the department established," said Maera. "Diera confided in me that she expects to spend extended time in Caernford for the next several months, possibly stretching into next year. Father asked her to help organize and train more medicants in those . . . what did you call them? . . . MASH teams, in case of future fighting against the Narthani."

Yozef ran a hand under his beard, pursing his lips and shaking his head. "Just too many things to do, Maera. Sometimes I feel like I do nothing but run from one thing to another and never get anything finished."

"We do what we can," said Maera. "The *Word* says God only expects us to do our best."

"Yes," said Yozef, "but it doesn't say how to stop worrying about the things we can't get done even *with* our best."

"God leaves that part to us and to understand that to do the best we can, we can't dwell on negatives."

"Easier said than done. Now, if I could just clone myself . . ."

Maera grunted and frowned. "Another new word, Yozef? Were you planning to tell me what this one means? Clone?"

"Ah . . . it means wishing there were two of yourself for when there's too much to do. A wishful fantasy."

"Well, wish about this," said Maera, "and getting back to the university, will we keep the same name? The University of Abersford was appropriate, if built here, but I think we will need to change it to the University of Caernford or possibly the University of Keelan. Those names would be better to gather support from throughout the province."

Yozef thought for a moment. "That would be the obvious decision, but I have another idea. Using your arguments, what if we call it the University of Caedellium?"

"But the university will be in Keelan and is being supported by Keelan and not the other clans," said Maera.

"The university will help everyone on Caedellium. Naming it after the island and not a single clan will help gain the support of more clans, which would then be more likely to help support the university. There could also eventually be other departments or campuses, as they're called, in different provinces.

"Maera, the clans must stop thinking of themselves as independent of one another. A major strength of the Narthani and a weakness of the Caedelli is unity. Even though the name we choose for the university is a minor factor, naming it after Keelan reinforces our clan's independence, while naming it after the entire island encourages people to consider everyone on Caedellium one people."

"I'm sorry, Yozef, but I'm skeptical. I know you think Caedellium must eventually have a single ruler, but from all I know of the history of the clans, I have difficulty seeing how it would happen. Few people think of themselves as citizens of Caedellium. If you ask what they are, they will say a Keelander or Stentese or Swavebroker. No one will say 'Caedelli.'"

"I never said I thought it would be easy, only that it would be inevitable. Without the Narthani, it might have taken much longer. Now . . . well . . . there's a saying from a time when my people were divided like the Caedelli and faced with an outside threat. A famous man said, 'We shall either hang together or hang separately.'"

Thank you, Ben Franklin, for the quote. It's one of those sayings that translates, since execution by hanging is known here.

"I know most of the mainland peoples are part of large realms," said Maera, "but the clans are all we've known here on Caedellium. Does that make us backward?"

Yozef shook his head. "No, only you haven't faced situations where survival required larger numbers of people. It's an unavoidable progression. Larger groups tend to absorb smaller ones, so that over time, the groupings get larger and larger."

"Well," said Maera, "I suspect we'll have this discussion over and over. However, I feel a need to visit our voiding house. It's one part of childbearing I didn't fully appreciate until now, because I seem to have to empty every hour. But I'm glad we've settled on the move to Caernford. That was the hard part—deciding. Everything else will take time and effort but will flow logically from the decision."

Yozef held back laughter, as Maera made her way to the voiding house. He didn't want to delay her, given her urgency. However, her words reminded him of something he'd recently remembered from the military writings of Clausewitz: "Everything in war is simple, but everything simple is difficult."

He waited on the front veranda for Maera to return. He had a clear view to the ocean this morning, with the usual haze having burned off early. Gulls and murvors cruised up and down the beach, their calls and whistles combining almost as if scripted. Now, they didn't sound as strange to him as when he'd first heard their blending.

He felt relief in having decided to move, and he noticed his lack of anxiety at the idea. Very different from the Joe Colsco of Earth, who would endlessly agonize after a decision such as this one and its uncertain consequences. In contrast, he felt calm, having put the negatives behind him. Now his mind worked in the details to carry through on the decision. He was almost proud of himself.

CHAPTER 11

CATALYST

Sistian was surprised when an aide came to his office with Carnigan's request for a meeting. Although he met with Carnigan at least once a month to offer the big man an opportunity to unburden himself or ask advice, it had always been a one-way meeting, with the abbot asking and Carnigan taciturn. He had never sought a meeting. Until today.

The firmness of the knock on the abbot's door announced a large fist.

"Come on in, Carnigan," said Sistian.

The abbot moved a pile of papers from one chair to the other, of the two facing his desk. The now empty chair was the sturdiest and less likely to collapse under the weight of Carnigan Puvey.

To the abbot's surprise, Carnigan said, "Thank you for seeing me so soon, Abbot." Carnigan seldom initiated any conversation.

"Of course, Carnigan. I always have time for you. What's on your mind?"

"I would like your permission to move to St. Tomo's Abbey in Caernford."

Maera had primed Sistian for the possibility, and he was prepared for the proposal.

"Is it because Yozef is moving there?"

Carnigan kept eye contact with the abbot and spoke slowly, carefully choosing his words, not as if to weigh the words for the listener's reaction, but to convey the meaning accurately.

"Yes, I suppose so. I feel I'd be more useful being near him than staying here. At St. Sidryn's I serve a purpose, but let's be honest, Abbot, it's a role almost anyone could fill. Not that I think I'm above cleaning voiding vats or weeding gardens, but is that how I can best serve, being who I am?"

Sistian could not have been more surprised if Carnigan had declared he proposed to fly to Landolin. Surprised not by the proposal, but by the depth of thought behind it.

"And who do *you* think you are, Carnigan?" asked the abbot.

Carnigan remained silent. Sistian sensed he was gathering thoughts, not avoiding an answer. Normally patient, the abbot was doubly so with the man sitting in his office, a man who had opened up as never before. The gathering of thoughts going on in the red head facing him deserved whatever time was needed.

A minute passed. Two. Four. Then . . .

"When I came to St. Sidryn's, I felt I didn't deserve to be among other people. That if people knew the things I'd done, they would shun me. To be . . . *safe*, I guess is the right word, I assumed they didn't want to interact with me, so I acted to keep them away. It became a habit. The more I pushed people away, the more they stayed away, and the more I grew convinced they wanted to stay away."

Carnigan stopped speaking, as if not quite knowing what to say next.

Sistian prompted him this time.

"And now?"

"While I don't want to push people away, I'm afraid it's become a hard habit to break."

"And you worry you can't change if you stay at St. Sidryn's?"

"No, only that it will be harder," Carnigan said. "There's more, Abbot. I'm *useful* around Yozef. Whether it's true or not, I don't know, but I believe he's most relaxed when he's around me, even with Maera, though don't tell her I said so. Obviously, they're husband and wife, though I think he's very cautious about what he says around her."

Surprised by Carnigan's statement, Sistian asked, "Why would you think that, Carnigan?"

Puvey shrugged. "How would I know? Perhaps it just is. Maybe I don't ask him too many questions. He needs others looking after him. Yes, he's taken fighting lessons from Wyfor Kales, and Kales says he would be quite a dangerous person, except for lack of experience, though he still needs . . . maybe not looking after, but *protection* is the better word. He's important to all of us. I'm already around often when he might need protection, as are Kales and Balwis more and more, but when he moves, he'll still need me. It's a gut feeling I can't shake."

Carnigan stared at the abbot, as if the door to his vocalizations had shut. He had stated his position and now awaited an answer.

Sistian considered the man's words for less than a minute, long enough to confirm the conclusion he'd come to in the last few months.

"Carnigan, I see no problem with agreeing to the move. Your period of probation ends in six months, and I had already decided I would see no reason to extend it. I will write to Abbot Walkot at St. Tomo's. I'm sure he'll have no objection, especially after I explain the situation. He'll have to approve transferring the probation oversight to St. Tomo's. Although it will then ultimately be Abbot Walkot's decision to end probation, he'll have my strongest recommendation."

Diera walked into the abbot's office when she saw Carnigan leaving. "Sistian, why was Carnigan here? Unless I lost track, he wasn't due for his monthly counseling session for another sixday."

Sistian set down the quill he'd just picked up to write to Abbot Walkot. "He wanted to talk."

"Carnigan? *He* wanted to talk?"

"Surprised me, too," said Sistian. "Not only that he wanted to talk but *how* he talked. He wants to move to Caernford when Yozef and Maera do. He thinks he will be useful there as both a guard and a friend to Yozef. Although he didn't quite frame it this way, I think he also believes it's better for him. He sees himself opening up more to people and badly wants it to continue. He senses it's easier when he's around those he knows best."

"And that's Yozef," stated Diera.

"Beyond a doubt. I remember when Yozef first came, and you saw him and Carnigan drinking beer together, talking and laughing like old friends, even though they couldn't understand a word the other was saying. You speculated they might be good for each other, and you were right. Two lost souls somehow finding in each other a kindred spirit.

"I told Carnigan I would write Abbot Walkot to ask to transfer the probation to St. Tomo's, and I will give my recommendation that the probation be ended in the minimum time in six months. I've sensed the changes in Carnigan, and my meeting with him confirmed it. He's a different person, and I believe he'll have a contented future. Whether it's a happy one, only God can know, but at least there's a chance."

"Yozef is a factor, though I'm sure he didn't know what he was doing," said Diera.

The abbot rose and walked to the gardens window. "It's hard to ignore that Yozef has that effect on many people. Though, as with Carnigan, I doubt any of it is intentional."

"Like a catalyst," said Diera.

Sistian turned to question the strange word.

Diera shrugged. "Yes, another of Yozef's words from his homeland. As he often does, it came out spontaneously when he spoke out loud. He explained it to me as a substance that facilitates other substances to change without changing itself. I know, I didn't understand it either. There were more words related to his 'chemistry,' but he lost me quickly. Once I got him back from wherever he goes when his mind's wandering, we settled on an example, such as a person who affects others just by being present. For example, Brother Petros. Often, it seems like people are more pleasant to one another whenever Petros is around. Same with Rhaedri Brison. Although I've only met Brother Rhaedri once, from my impression and stories from others, it's evident his mere presence encourages calm and rational thought. Yozef wasn't completely happy with the example but agreed that Petros and Rhaedri might be considered catalysts."

The abbot returned to his desk chair, placing his hands on the desktop edge, his arms straight. "So, you say we could call Yozef himself a catalyst?"

Diera sat in one of the chairs facing the desk, folding her hands in her lap, smiling at her husband. "I think it's a reasonable analogy. Look at what's happened with people he's been in contact with."

"Carnigan's a good example," said Sistian. "He's become more outgoing. Several brothers and sisters have commented over the last months. He greets them, asks how they're doing, offers help, and has even been seen playing with children several times. Plus, there's his protective attitude toward Yozef and, unless I misread, also toward Maera. More change is evident from his coming to see me today. Not just that alone, but the reason is based on him looking to the future. I'll even say looking *forward* to the future."

"Speaking of Maera," said Diera, "she's always been a dear child, yet she was so serious. Now, she seems more relaxed and, yes, even more cheerful. Some of that is likely because of the coming child and filling roles she takes seriously. However, much has to be due to Yozef and how he treats her as an equal. And there are others. Denes is becoming more important to the clan, as he adopts suggestions from Yozef. There's Willwin and microorganisms. Medicant treatments. I confess a modicum of pride, but St. Sidryn's has become arguably the most important center of medicant treatment and training in Caedellium, all due to Yozef."

Sistian stroked his beard and sat back in his chair. "We don't have to look further than our own family. Consider Cadwulf. I admit I didn't know what to make of his fascination with numbers and mathematics, I suppose because I didn't see them as a calling in life. Now look at him! In charge of this bank Yozef established and earning good coin at it. And if that isn't enough, he's become well known throughout Caedellium for the mathematics he's learned from Yozef and has expanded on. Either of those professions would be enough for any one person, and he's succeeding at both."

"And Selmar," said Diera affectionately, thinking of their youngest child.

"Yes, Selmar," said Sistian. "He was always an indifferent student, never showing interest in his studies more than was necessary to keep his teachers and us reasonably satisfied. I tried not to reveal too much frustration, but I felt he was wasting his abilities. That's one reason I chose him as Yozef's language tutor. I don't know whether I had an intuition it might interest Selmar or if it was just good luck, but he became fascinated with teaching Yozef to communicate."

Diera smiled. "When Yozef introduced the microscope, we could hardly get Selmar out of Willwin's workroom to eat and sleep," she said. "I finally had to order him to limit the number of hours a day he spent finding new creatures everywhere he looked, and the order had to come from me as his mother, since he ignored my warnings as a medicant. Now, he's expanded his interest in other parts of Willwin's work, and unless I'm missing the signs, he's getting interested in how bodies work, ours and animals'. I'm fairly certain he will end up as a scholastic in biology or even become a medicant, something I would have not thought possible two years ago."

"Imagine it, Diera," said Sistian. "We worried what our two sons would do when they were mature, and now both will be scholastics and one even a medicant. Who knows the ways of God? I almost wonder if the rumors about Yozef are right and he's somehow an agent of God, if not actually a Septarsh."

Both Beynoms remained within their own thoughts. After a long moment, Diera asked, "Sistian, do you regret that none of our children are destined to be theophists?"

He sighed. "While I'll admit I hoped at least one would, I think I'm honest enough to know each of us makes his or her own future. I always knew Orla would be happy as a wife and a mother, but I once thought Pyrma would make a theophist. She disillusioned me of this notion by the time she was fifteen, and then she married a theophist brother in Clengoth and seemed happy. I can truly say I'm pleased that all four of our children seem to have found their places or, in Selmar's case, are on that road."

"And there we are, back to Yozef," said Diera. "We have to credit him with how our sons are developing."

"If Yozef is a *catalyst*," said Sistian, "then has he stayed unchanged by his interactions with others?"

"Neither Yozef nor I were happy that it was the best analogy, only the closest I could come to understand. As for whether he's changed, I don't know, although he's certainly adjusted to Keelan, but has his *core* changed? Since we didn't know him before his arrival, how can we be sure? Still . . . for myself, anyway, I'm comfortable thinking of him as a catalyst and then wondering what further changes he'll bring and to whom?"

Diera took on a serious demeanor. "Another way to look at him is to think of people 'orbiting' around him, like our moons circle Anyar. Wherever we look, more and more things relate to Yozef, directly or indirectly, if we look closely enough."

"So, we're all moons orbiting Yozef?" said Sistian, laughing.

"Well, some are big moons, some are small ones, and others are just little rocks, but yes, in a way we are all orbiting around him."

"That includes you, dear," said Sistian. "Not only the new treatments you're spreading but also Yozef's idea for these MASHs, as he calls them. You're deeply involved in these mobile medicant teams that can accompany men to a fight and treat wounds as soon as possible."

"I wish we didn't need the MASHs, though they're necessary. We saved lives and helped in the recovery of men wounded at Moreland City—many of whom would have otherwise died," insisted Diera.

Sistian touched the amulet to God he always wore. "And I've thanked God for Yozef bringing the idea, but it still comes from Yozef. Also, as much as I acknowledge the importance of the MASHs, I confess to a shade of resentment that it will take you away from St. Sidryn's more than I like."

"I feel the same," said Diera. "I never dreamed we'd be away from each other as much as we might have to be in the next year. Besides the MASHs, there's the university. Changing the location to Caernford is logical. Abersford is just too small, and with Yozef moving much of his current and all his future enterprises to Caernford, having the university nearby is necessary. Although I hadn't mentioned it before, I've always wondered about the rationale for so much development in Abersford. Well, besides Yozef being here."

"The same thoughts occurred to me," said Sistian. "However, it was speculation then, instead of reality now."

"I'm sure Saoul Dyllis can be head medicant at St. Sidryn's while I'm away," said Diera, "It's my role in the university that worries me more. Within the year, I'll be spending half of my time in Caernford, before Yozef and I identify a replacement head for the Biology and Medicine Department."

Sistian smiled in a way Diera knew from experience indicated he had a surprise, but the accompanying forehead frown lines meant that whatever it was didn't completely sit easily on her husband's mind.

"Ahem . . . I supposed that's my opening to mention something I've thought hard about. A request . . . no, that's not quite right . . . a *proposal* from Culich. And, of course, it's something related to Yozef, as seems usual these days. Yozef has talked to Culich about the need for what he calls a 'general staff,' an established group of people that a leader depends on for advice and that takes over responsibility for specific duties. Yozef says it's important when too many duties are put on a single leader and when the duties require experience in different areas than is reasonable to expect a leader to have."

"I assume Culich is considering establishing such a *general staff*?" asked Diera.

"Correct."

"But Culich already has Luwis and Kennrick, plus all the boyerman," said Diera.

"True, although the boyerman are committed to duties within their districts. Luwis and Kennrick would naturally be included, but Culich believes the circumstances now and in the future will require more than those two."

Diera divined where her husband was going. "He's asked you to be part of the general staff."

Sistian nodded, tugging his beard as he did when conflicted or irritated. "Yes. He originally broached the idea when I was last in Caernford, and I listed all the reasons why I couldn't be away from St. Sidryn's for that much time. In his last letter in today's mail packet, Culich expounded in great detail how, while he appreciated the importance of my duties at St. Sidryn's and the Abersford area, there were counterargument considerations relevant to the Keelan Clan and all of Caedellium."

"Again, the Narthani," said Diera. "Two names we can't escape from—Yozef and Narthani. What does Culich see you doing?"

"Culich intends to embark on a more concerted effort to bring all the clans into a united alliance against the Narthani. He says the results from the Moreland City battle make this the time to do so. He believes it's critical to keep such an alliance functioning, despite inter-clan differences, so he wants to recruit theophist assistance. I'm afraid he'd thought of making this a battle against the Evil One, with the Narthani and their God, Narth, in that role. I told him I felt uneasy about trying to use God in such a manner, and I believe we've agreed not to be so explicit."

"Some see it that way, anyhow," said Diera.

"True," said Sistian, "but we've both read enough accounts of mainland conflicts based on differences in worship, even different Gods, to know the viciousness such fighting can devolve into. I would hope we could avoid the worst of that here on Caedellium. However, as much as I hate to admit it, he has arguments on his side. What if the Narthani *do* take over the entire island? Is there any doubt the worship of God, as we believe is correct, would be lost and replaced with Narth? I am more comfortable in framing it as a desperate defense of our worship beliefs, and to do this we need the active support of theophists throughout the island."

"I assume getting Rhaedri Brison's support is prominent in Culich's mind?" Diera asked.

"Naturally," grunted Sistian, "and it hardly passed my notice that Culich is aware I studied with Rhaedri and we've remained friends. The Theophist Order on Caedellium has no formal structure or leadership, but Rhaedri's reputation and the regard all hold for him make him as close to a theophist leader as we have."

"All very rational of Culich and very sneaky," said Diera, grinning. "Which brings us back to the problem of my spending so much time in Caernford. I'll admit I'd love to have you there, too, but what about here? You're the abbot."

"As with your belief Saoul can substitute for you while you're away, I believe Brother Villner can do the same for me."

"Villner?" said Diera, surprised. "Isn't he young for that responsibility? Would the senior theophists agree?"

"Yes, he's only twenty-nine, though it's no secret I've envisaged him as my successor when the time comes for God to call me home. Most of the other theophists in St. Sidryn's agree he'll make an abbot someday, somewhere else if not St. Sidryn's. The others will see this as a reasonable way for him to get experience in a temporary role, especially if I intend to return as soon as the

Narthani threat is over."

"So," said Diera, "are we talking around the fact that both of us will spend much of the next year in Caernford?"

"It does appear that way. I want to get back here as often as possible to assure myself the abbey is functioning and serving the people, and I assume you'll feel the same about the hospital. It won't be a permanent move, and we'll have to arrange a temporary home in Caernford. Cadwulf will stay here in the house, but we'll have to decide about Selmar. Just remember, we'll be back to St. Sidryn's as much as possible."

"If the worst happens, there would be no St. Sidryn's to come back to," said Diera, the words forced out of her mouth.

They both fell silent again, each deep into dark thoughts that neither wanted to express more openly. Finally, Diera made an effort to steer the conversation to more everyday matters. "Let's talk about something more removed from the Narthani. We had four births today, more than any one day in over a year. Two were in the hospital and two at the family homes. Brothers Alber and Bolwyn attended the home ones. All mothers and babies are doing fine, though one was in breech position, and Brother Alber was afraid they would have to bring the mother to the hospital for the surgery Yozef calls . . . oh, my. There it is again. I can't help Yozef from coming up.

"With the ether, cutting babies out from breech position is safer. He calls the procedure a 'caesarian' and explains that is named after a famous person named Caesar, who was born that way. Of course, neither I nor anyone else has ever heard of this 'famous' person, but I suppose we should be used to this happening with Yozef."

Sistian laughed. "Oh, Diera, it's even worse. In searching for something else to talk about, the first thing on my mind was a counseling session I had with Elwela Noswyn. Do you remember her?"

"Noswyn?" questioned Diera. "Wasn't Bellton Nolswyn one of the Abersford men killed at Moreland City? He had a smithy shop at the edge of Abersford and was part of Yozef's artillery crews. Yes, I remember his wife, Elwela. They had two children. Maera arranged a position for Elwela working in Buna Keller's clothing shop and made certain the pension coming from the clan, added with what she earned sewing, would support Elwela and the children."

"That *seemed* to be the plan," said Sistian. "Elwela came to me today for advice and approval. She proposes to marry the smithy worker who will take over her deceased husband's shop, a man already married. He had worked for Bellton many years, and the two families were friends. Elwela wanted to be sure the *Word* allowed two wives. I told her the *Word* did not disallow it, but the *Commentaries* emphasized care for children, and an original wife had to be honestly agreeable. Elwela assured me this was the case, something I advised her I needed to confirm with separate meetings with all three of them."

Sistian shook his head. "And here we go again, with Yozef's name appearing. Elwela argued it must be allowed, since everyone knows Yozef had an affair with Bronwyn Linton, and a child resulted. Bronwyn married into her sister's family and made it clear the idea came from Yozef. Furthermore, Ewela implied that if *Yozef Kolsko* thought it was appropriate, then it *must* be."

From Sistian's expression, Diera could see he wasn't pleased with Elwela's assumption.

"What did you say?" asked Diera.

"What could I say? Oh, I repeated something about responsibilities and approvals, but my mind was elsewhere. While it's true the *Word* doesn't disapprove of multiple wives, it's not a common custom. Certainly not in Keelan or most other clans, except for some of the northern ones. However, this may be changing, and if fighting the Narthani continues, it might be more common in the future."

"Widows," said Diera. "So many widows from husbands killed in the fighting."

"Especially in Moreland," said Sistian. "A thousand men died in Gynfor Moreland's insane decision to charge straight into the Narthani line. That's close to a thousand widows, since most were married men, and several thousand fatherless children. The theophists throughout Moreland had many meetings trying to come to an agreement and have just issued a proclamation throughout Moreland Province approving multiple wives. Other clans are considering the same, and Culich has asked that one of the first things I work on, if I come to Caernford, is to see if there is a consensus within Keelan on the same issue. I'll study the question, of course, but I don't foresee forbidding the practice. In fact, at least for the current generation it might be the best way to ensure strong families and sufficient support for the children and widows. I'm afraid there will be many more widows in times to come."

"Yozef and the Narthani," said Diera. "So intertwined."

"Diera, I remember when Yozef first arrived, the day they found him naked on the beach. I wondered then how he would affect our community. Never did I imagine the eventual reality."

CHAPTER 12

MOVE

Abersford to Caernford

Once Yozef acquiesced to the inevitable, he figuratively stepped aside to avoid the juggernaut named Maera Kolsko-Keelan and her sidekick for this purpose, Pedr Kennrick. Although the rotund, red-headed hetman's advisor might not have looked like a man of action, he was a whirlwind organizer. When paired with Maera, even in her increasingly gravid condition, the two of them swept aside all obstacles they encountered. Yozef had imagined himself involved in an orderly progression of their household and prioritized projects moving to Caernford over time, but progress went so smoothly that he left details of moving their household and relocating workers to Maera. Kennrick assured them via semaphore that he would handle securing property for a new industrial park in Caernford, and the groundbreaking for a new house was underway.

Yozef occupied himself by focusing on his shops and projects. All existing production factories would remain in Abersford: ether, alcohol, paper, soap, kerosene, gunpowder, and musket cartridges. New factories would be established in Caernford, if not already operating via previous production expansion, such as those for paper, soap, and cartridges. All development projects would move to Caernford as soon as expedient, except where key workers wouldn't or couldn't make the move.

Yozef broke the news of the move to Elian and Brak Faughn when he called them together one afternoon.

"Brak and Elian, I want to let you know Maera and I will be moving to Caernford in the next few sixdays."

Brak took the news impassively. Elian put a hand to her throat, and her eyes widened.

"Maera and I would like you to come with us and continue working for the Kolsko household in Caernford."

Elian looked sideways at Brak. Her husband didn't hesitate to reply. "I'm not moving. Abersford is my home. When will you want us to move out?"

Yozef wanted to ask what kind of home they would move into, because when he first hired the couple, they lived in a lean-to behind the candle works—having lost their small farm, due to low prices for farm products since the Narthani blocked off-island trade. However, he didn't ask, knowing Brak was prickly about being independent and not receiving charity.

Hell, where are they going to go, back to another shack they put together? Yozef thought.

"That won't be necessary. The move might not be permanent, and even if it is, we need a place to stay for times we return to Abersford for visits. Therefore, the two of you can stay here, maintaining the grounds and the structures." Yozef detailed projects he expected to be completed, most of which he hadn't thought of earlier, but he intuited that there needed to be enough work to keep Brak active.

The elderly man appeared satisfied and went back to whatever work he'd been doing when called in.

"Thank you, Yozef," gushed Elian, once Brak was out of hearing. "I would come with you, but Brak has lived his whole life within ten miles of Abersford and is set in his ways. He is not in the best of health either, so it's best if we stay here. Thank you for letting us remain in the cottage."

Yozef waved off the thanks, already thinking about who would maintain the getaway cottage on the coast west of Abersford, where he and Maera had spent their honeymoon. Providing for the Faughns also allowed him to procrastinate indefinitely about whether to sell the house and the cottage.

The last sixday in Abersford blurred with activity. Saying goodbye to everyone took a major portion of their time. The Beynoms hosted an evening at the abbey, where testimonials choked Yozef more than once. What was said varied with the speaker: Sistian, on Yozef's arrival and impact; Diera, on his initial condition and adjustment; Brother Fitham, with kindly words; Medicant Bolwyn, on the first use of ether and other medical innovations; partners in trade; workers; and recipients of new medical treatments.

Although most of the guests were abbey staff, a notable exception was the Merton family, which included Bronwyn Linton, now Merton-Linton, and five-month-old Aragorn. Yozef and Bronwyn's affair had lasted two months and ended amicably. Subsequently, Bronwyn had given birth to their son, Aragorn, and she married into her sister's family nearby, after Yozef mentioned the possibility—multiple wives being unusual but not prohibited by custom or the *Word*. Yozef had planned to take most of a day to visit the Merton farm, despite the crush of time before leaving, so the Linton family's presence at the abbey affair let him hold and play with Aragorn for almost an hour. He deflected a query on the origin of "Aragorn," recalling the "naming day" when he was called on unexpectedly to name the new baby, and the first name out of his mouth was from *Lord of the Rings*. He also remembered and relived the wonderment of publicly acknowledging his paternity of a child in the cathedral with the mother now married to her sister and her husband. And he did this with his currently pregnant wife at his side, and no one, including Abbot Sistian, thought anything unusual.

The evening at the abbey ended with laughter and tears, some of both from Maera and Yozef. After leave-taking, they walked home, slowly for Maera's sake.

"Are you sad to be leaving Abersford, Yozef?" asked Maera.

"I confess, more than I expected, and you know how reluctant I was at the idea. This is where I first adjusted to being cast on Caedellium. The Abersford area is 'home' more than any place I've ever lived, even more so than the three houses my family lived in where I grew up. By the end of the evening at the abbey, I already felt homesick and now am a little melancholy. While I know the feeling will pass, yes, it's hard for me."

"It's hard for me also," said Maera. "More than I expected, even though, in a sense, I'm moving back 'home,' but it's the home of my childhood, not of our time together. Abersford was where we began our marriage, where we conceived our child, and where I felt I was involved in the daily lives of people, more than in Caernford, where I was the 'hetman's daughter.' But I won't lie, Yozef. As much as I'll miss Abersford, our first home, and the people, part of me is drawn to Caernford. I'll see my family again regularly, and I confess I miss being around the center of clan activities, where I attended boyermen meetings as father's scribe, edited and made suggestions on his correspondence, and felt in the middle of where decisions were made. Not that I haven't been more than busy here, what with involvement in Abersford affairs and helping you."

They walked the rest of the way in silence, holding hands, and both in their own ways and minds coming to terms with their lives' new paths.

They had politely declined invitations for social occasions in Abersford, including a proposal by the town's mayor to hold a major farewell event—their excuse being the press of time and preparations. However, most of the same guests of the mayor's planned affair attended a night at the Snarling Graeko.

Carnigan laid down the law. "Forget it, Yozef. Kuwaith and I have already arranged the evening. The pub is reserved for that night, and everyone likely to want to be there has been invited."

Yozef and Maera gave in, not wanting to dash the only social event Carnigan had ever been known to plan. They arrived, by carriage this time—Maera wouldn't be drinking, but she wasn't sure what Yozef's condition would be later. Kuwaith, the Snarling Graeko owner, had outdone himself with the abundance of food and beer. Yozef never inquired who paid for the largesse.

Although the intent was to hold the event inside the pub, word spread widely. Most of the populace of Abersford showed up, and a spontaneous fair spilled into the streets, with the other pubs moving their night's business to support the Snarling Graeko. It was a night to remember.

Two sixdays after their decision to move, a wagon convoy left Abersford, composed of a carriage for Maera and Yozef and two wagons of possessions. They took only what they couldn't readily replace in Caernford, such as pieces of furniture made by Dyfeld Fuller, Filtin's father and an excellent furniture maker, and their growing collection of books, mementos, and clothing. A fourth wagon contained gifts from individuals and families throughout the Abersford area, along with the few possessions of Balwis and Carnigan, who came with them and rode their own horses. Seabiscuit walked along, tied to a wagon, along with a carriage horse given by the Mertons.

They would live with Maera's parents until workers finished a house of their own. Yozef groaned when informed of the initial arrangement, and it took time for him to explain the jokes among his people about married children returning to live with parents.

"Okay, Maera, it's logical we live at the Keelan Manor until our new house is ready, but why don't we use one of the guest cottages? That way we'd have more privacy."

He hadn't expected his question to gain much traction, and his prediction was correct.

"No," said Maera in a tone implying that further discourse was useless.

"My old quarters in the manor are more spacious than a cottage and more convenient to the rest of the manor and my family. I'm also sure we can arrange a workroom for you, where you can continue your writings and other planning."

Yozef swallowed a feeble protest, recognizing the futility of mounting any counterattack.

After a long day's journey, they reached Keelan Manor outside Caernford, as the last of the sun's light faded behind the eastern mountains. Mared, Maera's youngest sister, served as the lookout at the entrance to the manor's drive and ran back to the manor to announce their impending arrival.

The Keelan family waited on the veranda, and the women engaged in an orgy of hugs and tears at Maera's return and ooh'ed over her swelling. Maera proudly allowed strokes and pats. Even Culich beamed at his eldest daughter and enveloped her in his arms as soon as an opening appeared, although he ignored Maera's offer to feel the location of his first grandchild.

Yozef, initially forgotten, was eventually recognized, first by Culich and then by the females of the Keelan family. The affection showered on him made him glow inside, even as he felt uncomfortable at more effusive demonstrations than he'd experienced in his own family.

They settled into Maera's old rooms. Their clothing and a few belongings found places on shelves and in closets and chests, while staff unloaded the rest of their possessions into an older, seldom-used barn. By the third day, Yozef had appraised the progress in establishing new workshops and factories in Caernford. His concern that his workers' families get proper accommodations and aid in finding permanent homes was assuaged, as Maera handled everything. She recruited the St. Tomo's abbot to encourage the citizens of Caernford to make the newcomers feel welcome and do everything they could to help find housing, be it temporary or permanent.

Progress on the house impressed Yozef and didn't need his attention. The day after they arrived in Caernford, he and Maera visited the construction site, only a half-mile from Keelan Manor. They met the lead builder, went over the plans for the house, and made adjustments for their specific needs and wants. Culich had picked out the location before the wedding, and basic preparatory work had begun before the Kolskos made the decision to move. The builder said the hetman had placed the house as a priority, and the builder had pulled in workers from other projects. He estimated completion in one month. They gave him the go-ahead, and in another sixday the site went from staking out the house's position to progress on the roof trusses.

Three small cottages were included in the construction plans, one to be used by Carnigan and Balwis. Carnigan also had accommodations at St. Tomo's, and Balwis, somewhere in Caernford. The two shared duties with Wyfor Kales, so that one or more of them remained near Yozef and Maera at all times, along with their other duties, such as helping train Keelan men.

With all of the activity, Yozef shunted aside thoughts of Abersford, except for feeling occasional regret in his few idle moments. Yozef and Maera ate meals with her family in the manor, and the warm familial setting was welcomed by her and appreciated by him.

With the house plan out of mind, Yozef returned his focus to various projects, especially those on weapons. He had to return to Abersford to check on progress, oversee packing, and, in some cases, alleviate his worry about workers burning or blowing up buildings, themselves, or others. However, before he could leave to return to Abersford, Hetman Keelan once again changed Yozef's plans.

He and Maera had just arrived back at the manor after visiting the site of their new home. Yozef felt so encouraged by the progress, he reflected with satisfaction that they wouldn't have to live with the in-laws any longer than the six sixdays of an Anyar month. His mood changed when Culich called him into a private meeting.

CHAPTER 13

"YOU POOR BASTARDS"

Being asked to come to Culich's office was not one of Yozef's favorite experiences. This day was no exception.

"Yozef, while you were looking at the house site, I received confirmation an All-Clan Conclave is called for two sixdays from today in Orosz City. All the clans coming to aid Moreland voted for the conclave call, as did enough other clans to require mandatory attendance by all hetmen. This conclave is crucial for what we do next against the Narthani. Every hetman will bring his main advisors. Naturally, Vortig Luwis and Pedr Kennrick will come with me. I also want you there for advice and Denes Vegga, because he has been at the front of fights against the Narthani. In addition, Denes has adopted suggestions from you, perhaps faster than others might have."

Yozef wanted to object that he was in the middle of the move to Caernford and needed to get back to Abersford, but he felt stuck. Whether or not he knew what he was doing or had any business giving military or political advice, Culich, Maera, and the others expected it of him.

He stood looking at his father-in-law for several moments, silent while he considered and discarded arguments against going as immaterial or fruitless. His most cogent reservations related to *who* he really was and *where* he came from, neither of which he could voice.

Do I have any business giving advice? No, but so what? I've done it before, at St. Sidryn's and Moreland City, and it worked out, which I strongly believe was due to luck. On the other hand, might I actually have useful things to contribute? What if even with my abysmal lack of qualifications, I'm still the best the Caedelli have?

Through his mind flashed an old movie, a bad one he'd seen on TV. Richard Burton played the jaded owner of a small hotel in Haiti when the people are terrorized by Papa Doc Duvalier's secret police, the Tonton Macoute. Alec Guinness played a British army ex-major in Haiti on business.

Both characters fall afoul of the secret police, with Guinness being killed and Burton taking refuge with a small band of freedom fighters who mistake him for the major. The movie ends with Burton standing in front of eight bedraggled French-speaking Haitian men, who expect expert military advice from a British officer. In English, Burton starts his first address to his "troops" with "You . . . poor . . . bastards." That was what Yozef felt tempted to say.

Oh, these people are *poor bastards, if defeating the Narthani depends on me!*

They were by no means a stupid people. Well, not all of them anyway. The Moreland and Eywell hetmen surely would have fallen into that category. Certainly not Culich, Maera, Denes, Cadwulf, and many others. And they didn't lack for bravery. Even the stupid Morelanders showed that by their willingness to charge the Narthani, an incredibly dumb tactic.

Culich waited patiently for Yozef's response. The hetman had learned from Maera and his own observations that rushing Yozef while he remained in deep thought was futile. A part of Culich's mind wondered whether the rumors were true. Did God whisper in the man's ear? And in case God did, why interrupt?

"Sorry, Culich, could you give me a moment?"

Yozef didn't wait for an answer. He turned his back on the hetman and walked to a garden window. Culich sat and waited.

As always seemed to be the case on Caedellium, flowers bloomed outside the window. Yozef noticed the coralin vine blossoms just opening. In another sixday, their aroma would reach for hundreds of yards. Below the vines, in partial shade, Yozef saw what looked like pansies with black faces against yellow, blue, and maroon petals. He experienced a brief memory of Earth until a flock of small green and purple murvors landed on and around a birdbath. The distraction gone, his mind came back to the moment.

The Conclave. I have to go. And who's to say what I should or shouldn't say to the clans? Despite myself, I have to be there to argue against ill-advised actions that even I *can see. I have to do it for myself and Maera and all the others. Those I know and all the other Caedelli.*

Yozef turned back to Culich. "Of course, Hetman, I'll come and offer whatever I can."

"Bring what you wrote about—what you remember of military operations," said Culich.

Oh, shit! I haven't finished it, Yozef moaned to himself.

When the hetman had pressed him to recognize and accept his

responsibility to give advice, if he had it, Yozef had said he would write up sayings of famous theorists of military campaigns. In fact, on Earth, he had read only the single most well-known writings of Jomini, Clausewitz, and Sun Tzu. He hadn't studied any of them as well as he did texts for his classes but only perused them more casually, so he could pretend to be knowledgeable with other video gamesters. As a consequence of his less-intense study, his enhanced memory could dredge up only fragments, instead of whole pages and chapters, the way he could with chemistry and other science texts. Of the three writers' works, he liked Clausewitz's the most, though Jomini's offered more practical, detailed advice. Sun Tzu's was duplicative, as might be expected, because common principles would naturally occur to different writers, even if they'd lived millennia and thousands of miles apart. However, Sun Tzu's work required the most summarizing, because Yozef thought the Chinese writer sounded too much like Yoda, the Jedi Master.

Although Yozef couldn't remember whole pages from the three writers, he *could* recall versions of "bullet points," pithy summaries of major principles. If nothing else, this might help the Caedelli leaders avoid the most egregious errors and get them to *think*, instead of emotionally reacting. After witnessing the Moreland and Eywell behavior at Moreland City, Yozef feared that too many of the clan leaders didn't appreciate that cold logic during battle surpassed emotions or delusions of honor and glory.

"Of course, you'll go with Father to the All-Clan Conclave," Maera said to Yozef that evening, when Culich announced the upcoming trip at the Keelan family evening meal.

"Naturally," replied Yozef, when what he wanted to say was, "As if I have any choice."

Yozef excused himself as early as he could after the meal and retired to Maera's old quarters, where he had set up a temporary work area comprising a small desk, two six-foot bookcases that partly walled off the area from the rest of the sitting room, and lamps and writing materials. As he concentrated, oblivious, Maera's hand on his shoulder startled him, and he jumped.

"Sorry, Yozef, I thought you heard me come in. What are you working on?"

"The summary of what I remember about tactics and strategy, as I mentioned that your father asked me to write. I've worked on it off and on, but now he's asked me to have something ready when we leave for the conclave in eight days. I have forty or fifty pages of notes, but it's all disjointed, so I'm trying to boil it down to major points. I hope I don't mislead anyone who reads it into thinking they know anything about military theory."

"I'm sure you'll do fine, and it'll be helpful."

Yozef grunted, conveying his lack of conviction at her reassurance. "What I'm trying to do is summarize everything I remember in a list of short statements. I'm afraid it's disorganized, duplicative, and contradictory in places, since I'm pulling pieces from different sources I can remember. I'm not sure if the clan leaders reading this will be helped or confused. However, I'm about finished doing the best I can."

"Can I read what you have?" asked Maera.

Yozef sighed, sat back in his chair, and handed three sheets of paper to Maera. She settled into a cushioned armchair next to a kerosene lamp and turned up the flame.

Looking at the title, she asked, "*On War*? That's the title? What's this word *war*?"

"Remember the last sixday when I asked you about Caedelli words for fighting and conflicts?" said Yozef.

"Yes, and you said there was a word missing from Caedelli, although certain words in other languages matched the word you were looking for."

That day, Yozef couldn't recall an appropriate word from his knowledge of Caedelli. Maera confirmed words that connoted fights, feuds, vendettas, battles, skirmishes, conflict, and more, though none that he believed were appropriate for fighting on a scale that might soon happen on Caedellium. Only when Maera described words from Narthani, Fuomi, and Landolin that seemed appropriate for "war" did Yozef realize Caedelli lacked an exact word.

"We need a word to describe what the clans face," said Yozef, "and I doubt the people here would want to use a Narthani word or even one from another realm. I've chosen to use the word from my language, English. The word is *war*, a prolonged military conflict between peoples or realms, where the outcome is total victory or defeat."

While Yozef's definition wasn't strictly accurate, he decided the clans needed to come to a frame of mind consistent with the level of threat they faced. He couldn't judge the Narthani depth of commitment toward the subjugation of Caedellium, but the clans needed to prepare for the worst.

Maera set down the sheets. "Explain it to me clearly, Yozef. What *is* war?"

"I'll define the word with the example of the Narthani against all the peoples of Caedellium. The Narthani intend to turn Caedellium into part of their empire and convert the people into Narthani, whether they want to be or not. Those who resist will be killed or enslaved. Every surviving Caedelli will live and serve at the will of the Narthani. Within a few generations, all memory of the history and language of the island will disappear. If the clans and the people of Caedellium want to prevent this, they must commit themselves to use every possible means and make every conceivable sacrifice to fight the Narthani. The Narthani are waging *war* on Caedellium, and the clans and people must wage *war* on the Narthani, at least those here on the island."

"Using 'all means' I understand," said Maera "What do you mean by 'every conceivable sacrifice'?"

"What if the only way to stop the Narthani resulted in one-fifth of the island's people dying?"

Maera paled and put a hand to her face. "One-fif . . . that would be . . . good God, over a hundred thousand people!"

"Would the clans be willing to pay that price?" asked Yozef.

Maera shook her head. "I don't know. I've never considered something that horrific. Give me a moment."

She sat quietly for several minutes, her arms hugged to her body, as she chewed on her lower lip. Then she put her hands on her lap and with a firm jaw looked at Yozef. "If the alternative was for the Narthani to win, then I think we would be willing to make that ultimate sacrifice."

"Why do you think that would be the *ultimate* sacrifice?" Yozef asked quietly, with a sad expression.

Maera stared for several seconds, her eyes narrowing as she took in her husband's face. "I see where you're going. You'll keep increasing the sacrifice until you find where I say to stop, the level of sacrifice I don't believe my people are willing to pay."

Yozef only nodded.

"Then I think it would depend on the individual, which is the same for any level of sacrifice. There are those who would capitulate to the Narthani under threat to even one member of their family. Others would resist even if everyone were to be killed."

"But the whole of the Caedelli?" Yozef asked "What would most do and what would be the combined will of the people?"

"I think . . . " Maera paused. "It would depend on whether there was hope. If we had a chance of victory, then the whole of the people would fight on. As long as there was hope. Is this what you foresee? That sacrifices beyond what most have imagined might be required?"

"It's possible. I just wonder if the hetmen coming to the conclave have any concept of what may come, and if they do, what will their reactions be? Should I say things like I just said to you or not?"

"I'm not wise enough to answer, Yozef. I don't know if anyone is. However, maybe this isn't the time to say these things. The situation isn't dire enough to make such decisions or judgments. For now, I would advise waiting. Maybe the Narthani will leave on their own. Maybe the clans can come up with a plan to drive them off the island. Maybe God will intervene. I don't know, just wait."

"That's what I was thinking," said Yozef. "I just wanted to hear someone else say it."

"Remember, Yozef, everything that might go wrong doesn't rest on you. And don't assume some of the hetmen don't already foresee what you think only you can foresee. Maybe they don't speak of it aloud, but similar thoughts have surely gone through the minds of the better hetmen, including my father."

Yozef grunted. "In other words, quit agonizing and just do what you can."

"*Your* words," said Maera with a definite sniff, "but good advice. Now let me read again what you've gotten so far for Father."

Maera picked up the sheets once more, leaned back and toward the lantern to get full light, and began reading.

* * *

On War

War is the total commitment to defeat an enemy using whatever means and making whatever sacrifices are deemed necessary. War is compelling an enemy to do your will. Blood is the price of victory. Nothing is accomplished without risk. War is a trinity of violence, chance, and reason. War is totality. Anything else is fantasy, if victory is the goal.

The ultimate goal must be clearly defined. Once that is done, then the necessary steps can be identified.

The three parts to fighting a war are: strategy, tactics, and logistics.

Strategy: Strategy is defined by the goal and involves planning before battles.

Tactics: The actions used to implement a strategy, especially how men are used in battles.

Logistics: Providing men with food, ammunition, medical care, transportation, and anything else required to fight battles.

Strategy is future oriented, tactics deal with the here and now. Strategy is the art of using battles to win a war. Tactics are the art of using men in battle.

For example, the defeat of an enemy is a strategy that may take many battles, while the details of using men in battle are tactics. Supplying everything that's needed is logistics.

A war may involve many battles, but remember that only the last battle is decisive.

Planning:

Careful planning of strategy and tactics is essential, but the perfect plan is a fantasy. No plan survives first contact. You must be ready to abandon a plan if necessary, and any plan must take into account the enemy's ability to frustrate it. None of these principles are to be followed without reasoning whether or not they are appropriate for each individual situation. Rigid adherence can be as bad as ignoring a principle. Principles are more what to avoid than what to do. Theory must never be used in place of judgment but used as an aid.

General Principles:

1. When absolute superiority is not attainable, you must produce a relative one at individual points by making use of what you have and defeat the enemy in detail. However, be aware that this weakens other positions and puts the rest of your force at risk.

2. Do not divide your force in the face of an equal or superior enemy (do not risk defeat in detail).

3. Keep the initiative. It is better to be the ones deciding on battle conditions than to let the enemy do it.

4. In the face of the same information, audacity is better than timidity.

5. Surprise the enemy at every opportunity. The essence of surprise is the security of your position and intentions and the speed at which you act. Security and reconnaissance are opposite sides of the same coin. All warfare is based on deception.

6. The harder the training, the easier the fighting.

7. Do not run out of options. Never place yourself where there is only one course of action.

8. Impede the enemy's lines of communications and supplies without endangering your own.

9. Concentrate at decisive points.

10. Mobility of forces and rapid movement expand options and limit the enemy's.

11. Be first to the battlefield.

12. Always factor in the enemy's strength.

13. Maintaining the discipline to follow the leaders' orders is essential.

14. A central authority is critical to carry out both strategy and tactics.

15. It is more important to outthink than to outfight.

Faults of a Leader:

1. Recklessly committing to fight without weighing balances and consequences.
2. Being afraid for his own safety.
3. Letting emotions make decisions, instead of reason.
4. Worrying about honor. There is no honor in war, only victory or defeat. To worry excessively about honor is to foster defeat.
5. Too much solicitude toward his men. Decisions must be made that will lead to men's deaths. Attempting to prevent any deaths will only lead to more.

In addition, leaders must be men of ability and not only because of birth or influence. Even a hetman should not lead men into battle if there are other men of more ability.

The balance of forces:

1. If you have ten times the enemy's strength or more, surround them and they will probably surrender.
2. If you have three to five times the enemy's strength, attack if it will achieve a goal worth any losses.
3. If your strength and your enemy's are equal, engage to hold in place but not to defeat, unless the enemy makes a mistake.
4. If your strength is less than the enemy's, evade and look for opportunities where the balance is more in your favor.
5. If your strength is much weaker than the enemy's, retreat and live to fight another day.

Defense versus offense:

1. You can prevent defeat by defense, but victory usually requires you to attack.
2. Defense is inherently the strongest, but to win, you must force the enemy to attack where you have the advantage.

3. If you entrench behind strong fortifications, you compel the enemy to seek a solution elsewhere.

Do not force an enemy into a corner. Leave your enemy a retreat avenue. To get an enemy to do what you want, you must put him in a situation even more unpleasant than what you want him to do; otherwise, he will wait for things to improve. If you determine to leave no retreat for the enemy, you must have an unassailable position and be willing to take losses inflicted by a desperate opponent.

* * *

Maera read the pages once again quickly, and then, without looking up, read them the second and third times slowly, the last time making notes in the margins. After the last read, she sighed and looked at Yozef.

"Part of me now wishes I hadn't read this."

"What do you mean?" Yozef asked in surprise.

"I haven't experienced any of the fighting itself, though God knows I'm aware of the consequences and I've talked with eyewitnesses and read reports, but what you wrote . . . somehow it makes it more real. The cold rationality of what you lay out as principles. Although I've no doubt they're all logical and needed, now I envision men doing these exact things. I also imagine you doing them, or worse, having them done to you by the Narthani.

"Enough of my reaction, though. Father was right. The other hetmen need to read this. And not just hetmen, but any Caedelli in a leadership position. However, therein lie problems. You say that even a hetman should not lead in battle if there are more skilled men. I don't know how many hetmen will agree or follow your words. You'll risk some hetmen ignoring the rest by telling them they shouldn't lead. I worry about the same effect where you warn about leaders who might fear for themselves. To even mention the possibility that a hetman might be afraid will antagonize some of them. As for honor, I know of a couple of hetmen for whom honor is like life. Most of the rest of what you wrote either seems logical to me, or I can't judge. You might consider removing the most contentious parts."

"No," said Yozef. "If I start taking out parts, there's no stopping it. Culich wanted what I could remember, and this is it. Plus, those parts are real concerns. The clans will have to learn them as soon as possible, so they might as well start now. We can only hope the parts they ignore will not be too damaging before they learn or accept them."

"All right then, I'll smooth out some of the language for you. Your Caedelli is quite good, but there are a few grammar details I'll correct, and I'll suggest different wording in a few places."

Two days later, Yozef sat with Culich, Vortig Luwis, Pedr Kennrick, and Denes Vegga. The four men had read *On War* and were full of questions.

"Yozef," said Denes, "there seem to be contradictions. You write that planning is essential but should be abandoned without hesitation if necessary. In another place, it says to concentrate your force to have numerical superiority, then warns of the danger of doing so."

"And how do you decide what is a 'decisive point' to concentrate your men?" complained Luwis. "How can a leader know for certain how strong an enemy is until a battle is joined?"

Yozef sighed, fully aware of contradictions. "The hetman asked me to write what I remembered about military theory, and that's what you have. I've always said that I wasn't trained to be a military leader, and I only know what I've read. I'm sure there is more I didn't recall, and these principles are from different writers. It's more important to realize that nothing can substitute for the judgment of the leader who has to make decisions quickly. These are only guides. The good leader has to evaluate each situation individually. Unfortunately, the best teacher is experience in taking actions that involve life-and-death decisions."

"I'm sorry, Hetman," said Luwis, addressing Culich, "but while some of this is only common sense, I don't see how useful other parts are."

Denes disagreed. "I understand Ser Luwis's questions, and I share some of the concerns. I'll need to study this more and let each part be compared to what I've experienced or situations I've imagined I might find myself in."

"I'll agree with Denes on the point that we need to think more about this," said Culich. "All three of you give this more thought and share what Yozef has written with a few other men in leadership positions. We'll talk more before the conclave."

"How did they receive what you wrote?" asked Maera, when Yozef returned to their quarters.

"No surprises. Some doubts about the usefulness, especially from Luwis. Denes wasn't enthused by any of it, although he's taking it seriously. He'll absorb much of it. As for your father and Kennrick, I don't know. Neither gave much of any opinion, though my sense is they'll consider it. In all, it's about the best I could expect. I just hope it's useful and helps prevent the worst mistakes without causing any."

"Well, you did what Father asked, so I assume you'll be off to Abersford?"

"Yes," said Yozef, "I wanted to leave today, but I'm tired. I've told Carnigan and Balwis we'll leave tomorrow morning after eating. A day to get there, three days working with the shops and projects, then back here. I should be back in five days, six at the most. I hope it's the last trip to Abersford to complete the move."

CHAPTER 14

STRIKE AT THE HEART

Akuyun Villa, Preddi City

General Okan Akuyun's meeting with subordinates in his family's villa was unusual, but so was the situation. One of his teeth had become too decayed to save and had to be extracted. Because the Preddi medicant, a fervent convert to the Narthani God, Narth, would perform the procedure, he recommended repairing two other teeth with minor cavities. The medicant had also suggested using some of the limited supply of the new substance ether, captured in a raid on a Mittack coastal abbey, along with a Caedelli medicant who explained its use.

The surviving Preddi medicants and the Narthani medical staff were excited about the potential of ether, though none knew where it came from or how to make it. They put finding out on a priority list, once the island was firmly under Narthani control. In return, the knowledge of drilling and filling tooth cavities with mercury alloys had already transferred in the other direction and spread across the island.

While Akuyun felt tempted to use ether for the unpleasant session in store, Rabia discouraged the ether being tested on the mission commander, her husband, because the medical staff didn't have enough experience to know about any side effects.

The medicant had carried out the procedure the previous day, and Akuyun was still unsteady on his feet. Rabia failed to convince him to take two days' rest at home. He compromised by agreeing to limited meetings if the other men came to the villa, instead of his going to the headquarters building in Preddi City.

The meeting this day was small. Only Aivacs Zulfa and Sadek Hizer joined Akuyun in the courtyard so he could enjoy the sun. All staff members and family had been warned to stay well out of hearing of the three men sitting at a garden table.

"You've had time to discuss options," asserted Akuyun carefully, his jaw visibly swollen. "Let's hear the plan the two of you have agreed on for eliminating some of the Caedelli hetmen."

"I'll let Aivacs summarize," said Hizer. "His men will carry out the operations, with the help of my agents in place."

"The plan depends on Sadek's agents," said Zulfa, "both for information and in several cases to guide my men through the countryside, for which we have little, if any, details. Our previous attempts on the Stent and Hewell hetmen failed, so we both agree that for this to be a serious attempt, we need more planning and to use more than one or two agents-in-place. I was in favor of six- to eight-man teams, then Sadek gave good arguments for more, and we settled on twenty men. Enough to account for injuries and handle the number of guards likely to be present, but not so many men as to be too noticeable."

Zulfa pulled a single-sheet map of Caedellium out of a pouch, turned it around to General Akuyun's view, and pushed it toward him.

"The main factors in selecting targets are our perception of the importance of any individual hetman and his clan and the hetman's location. Since the teams can't be running around trying to find the hetmen, we have to rely on hitting them at their residences in the capitals. Clans with inland capitals are different propositions than those on the coast. The latter allow the most straightforward operational plans. The strike team will land at a remote location not too far from the city. Our agents will meet them, provide detailed maps and information on what to expect as far as security, and guide the team to the target. The agents won't take part in the strike and will blend back into the population.

"The lack of up-to-date information will mean that a strike may be aborted at any point, if the agents or strike leaders determine it's not feasible. We don't see these as suicide missions; our men will have reasonable chances of getting out in the end.

"The teams will also not come ashore without the proper go-ahead from the agent. For example, every targeted hetman might not oblige by being in the expected place in the capital on the day of the attacks. We need to carry out all attacks on the same night, so there will be no warnings by semaphore to the other hetmen until the next morning. If a hetman is absent or surrounded by unexpected levels of security or for any other reason the details change about the target's availability, then the agent will signal the ship that the strike is scratched.

"The target at an inland capital presents a more difficult challenge. The distance from landing to the capital is too far for the team to attempt the strike the same night they land. They'll have to come ashore several nights earlier.

"Returning to the coast will likewise be more difficult than for coastal targets. Stealth will no longer be a concern, so they will travel as fast as possible, using the same wagons or available wagons and horses. To slow alarms going out by semaphore, once the strike is made, the team or agents will destroy one or more semaphore stations heading in the direction of withdrawal. An obvious problem is that it will take the agents most of a day to reach the extraction point, although once there, they can be taken back aboard ships even in daylight, since the navy can support any landing. The same restrictions on whether to continue will apply for the inland strike. The agents and team leaders can call off the attack if conditions make success impossible."

"The men, especially those carrying out the inland attacks, are fully aware of the danger?" asked Akuyun. "If things go badly, it will be best if they aren't taken alive, even if the Caedelli are inclined to take prisoners."

"They know, Okan. I've talked with every team leader individually, to be as satisfied as I can be. They, in turn, have screened the volunteers for the most loyal and those of the strongest mettle. Realistically, it might be too much to think none will be captured, but if they are, it will be beyond their control."

Akuyun nodded, then looked down again at the map. "And the targets? Are they still those we've discussed?"

"Yes," said Hizer. "We've selected two of the eleven clans with coast capitals: Skouks and Bevans. We picked Skouks because our agent reported discord among their boyermen about going to Moreland's aid, so there's a chance we can sow more confusion. Also, they may be one of the more unsuspecting, since they are so far from Preddi. We would have preferred Farkesh, because our agent reports the Farkesh hetman is moving to support a united front against us, and he's influential with the other northern clans. However, we haven't been able to pin down his movements. Bevans was chosen because we wanted one more coastal target, and it's located on a section of the coast we haven't raided yet, so they shouldn't be too alert."

Akuyun drummed the fingers of his left hand on the tabletop. "What about the inland target, Keelan?"

Hizer gestured to the Caedellium map. "Arguably the most important, but also the most difficult. Of the seven inland capitals, only three are priority targets: Keelan, Orosz, and Stent. Keelan and Stent because they are two of the strongest clans, best led, and most committed to opposing us. Orosz would be another logical target, since their hetman chairs their clan hetmen meetings and tries to promote clan amity. However, our agent reported that the Orosz hetman's residence is in the middle of Orosz City, which has formidable walls, a leftover from a distant hetman who loved building fortifications.

"Of all the hetmen, Keelan is the most important. Both Eywell and Narthani witnesses from Moreland City confirm it was Keelan banners and presumably the hetman himself who lured Eywell into abandoning their flank screening position and trapped the Eywellese in a brilliantly performed ambush. Then it was the three allied clans, Keelan, Mittack, and Gwillamer, that carried out the attack that collapsed our right flank.

"We still don't have evidence to support our initial suspicion of outside advice providing the tactical sense the Caedelli shouldn't have. Despite what seems a likely explanation, there is one argument against it—the Moreland clan sacrificed themselves as decoys to divert our attention. Given the independent nature of the clans and the reported antipathy of other clans toward Moreland, particularly the hetman, I find it difficult to believe Moreland acted deliberately."

"In that case, we would attribute the outcome to what?" asked Akuyun. "A confluence of errors? Chance?"

Hizer shrugged. "I'm just stating a reservation to the outside influence theory. However, if my suspicion is correct, then it points an arrow even more so at Keelan. It was the failed Buldorian raid on a Keelan abbey that preceded the Buldorians leaving for home. We never found out why that raid ended so badly, only the short report by our local agent that it had been a disaster for the attackers."

"If the Keelan hetman is that important, should we consider increasing the size of the strike team for Keelan?" Akuyun inquired.

"I'd like to," said Zulfa. "Even doubling or tripling it, though the arguments for keeping the number at twenty still holds. More men equals more risk of detection."

"Stent is also important and was originally on our target list," Hizer continued. "They're the strongest clan in western Caedellium and influential with Pewitt and Swavebroke. Both of those clans surprised us by coming to Moreland's aid—we think probably because of Stent. Stent also led the attack on our base camp at Parthmal. The clans got there before word arrived of our withdrawal and the warning to be alert. We were surprised that they attacked a position in Eywell territory."

"I believe I'm getting weary of hearing the word *surprise* when we reflect on our previous assumptions about the Caedelli and the outcomes of our efforts," said Akuyun, his irritation real, stoked by his aching jaw.

"No more than Aivacs and I," said Hizer.

"Unfortunately, we had to scrap plans for a strike at Stent," said Zulfa. "He spends too much time away from his residence and is almost always surrounded by too many men."

Hizer sat back. "That's the summary, Okan. Three teams to attempt to kill three hetmen. If only the Keelan team is successful, I would call it a success, though I'll be pleased if any of the three strikes succeeds. However, even if none of the three succeeds, it will force the clans to tighten internal security and will sow confusion, giving them a sense of not knowing when and where we might strike next."

"Perhaps," said Akuyun, "though our experience at Moreland City makes me cautious about predicting the clans' responses. Still, I can't think of a good rationale not to proceed."

Akuyun looked at the map once more, then pushed it back across the table to Zulfa. "All right. Go ahead with alerting the agents and training the teams. They may all be good men, but they haven't worked together before, since they were picked from different units. We have time before we commit to this, so they'll have some months to train together. That might seem like an excessive focus on training, but this will be a one-time operation. After the first failed attempts and now these more serious assassination tries, the islanders are bound to increase hetmen security enough to preclude more attempts."

Zulfa and Hizer detected the undertone of distaste from Akuyun. Their commander preferred direct combat, rather than tactics such as assassination, but both also knew he wouldn't hesitate if it was effective in completing their mission and conserving the lives of their men.

CHAPTER 15

OFF TO OROSZ CITY

Yozef had been back in Caernford three days, long enough for Maera to drag him to inspect progress on the construction of their new house, spend an entire day with Filtin Fuller and other workers who had moved from Abersford to oversee projects and factories, and barely let his rear recover since he had ridden Seabiscuit on the Abersford round trip. The gentle gray gelding was still the only horse he trusted for any distance. Thankfully, the trip to Orosz City would be by two carriages, accompanied by a fifty-rider escort.

Two carriages were necessary because Abbot Sistian Beynom had arrived from St. Sidryn's the day before they planned to leave, which, with Culich, Luwis, Kennrick, and Yozef, would have meant five men for a carriage that normally accommodated four. Luwis could have ridden, but he would be part of a mobile Keelan clan advisory meeting during the two-and-a-half-day trip. Maera also saw that Yozef was accompanied by those he called his "three amigos" but what others called his "three shadows": Carnigan, Wyfor Kales, and Balwis Preddi. Not that all three could be called friends of one another, though they maintained an air of respect, and they each had personal reasons for staying close to Yozef when he traveled. Carnigan, because Yozef was a friend; Balwis, because he didn't want to miss anything Yozef came up with; and Wyfor . . . well, no one quite knew his reasons, except both Maera and Culich had asked him to come on the trip. He'd acquiesced, to everyone's surprise, because the wiry, sardonic man was seldom impressed by station. Carnigan thought Kales had become fond of Yozef; Yozef didn't see it.

On the morning when they left for Orosz City, all of the Keelan family women saw Yozef and Culich off from the manor veranda. Yozef hugged Maera tight, his hand resting softly on her bulge.

"I'll miss you and whoever's in there," he said.

"*He* will be fine," Maera stated.

"You still insist it's a he? Even though more daughters are born than sons?"

Yozef still considered it a mystery why the male-to-female ratio of new births was the reverse of that on Earth, where 105 male babies were born to every 100 female.

Maera's laugh brought smiles from her parents saying their own goodbyes. "Of course, I am. I *am* Maera Kolsko-Keelan. Who is there to argue with me?"

"Not I, assuredly. Besides missing *you*, I wish you were coming to the conclave, so you could educate me more on the different clans and their histories with one another."

"Not in this lifetime, Yozef. Women do not attend conclaves. Father pushed custom hard enough to have me at his boyermen meetings."

"I know, and I try not to judge, but it's a custom that has no logical rationale. From what I hear, you'd make more of a contribution than some of the hetmen."

Maera planted another kiss on Yozef's mouth, then laughed. "Thank you for that, but custom is what it is. Maybe when you rule the island, you can change the custom."

"It's a promise, although I'd advise you not to plan for it."

"All right, you two," called out Culich, laughing and untangling himself from his other three daughters. "The men in the family need be on their way."

"We'll look for you sometime at the end of the next sixday," said Breda. "Hopefully, the two of you will stay put for a while after that."

"Please, God," prayed Yozef aloud. "Horse or carriage, I'd rather walk or stay in one place."

"You're not *that* bad a rider," quipped Mared, Maera's youngest sister and an avowed defender of Yozef from any hint of criticism.

"I'll point out you didn't say I'm a *good* rider," said Yozef.

"Well . . . ," said Mared.

"Hush, Yozef," shushed Maera. "You'll put Mared in an awkward position between telling the truth and worrying she'll offend you."

Yozef gave the twelve-year-old a hug, then a firmer one and a kiss to Maera, and climbed in the second wagon with two of his three amigos. Carnigan would drive, and Kales would ride shotgun, a term he took to with barely hidden pleasure when Yozef explained the reference. Balwis would go on horseback, having said many times he saw no reason to ride in or on a wagon of any kind if he had a horse available. The first carriage would start with Culich and the three advisors accompanying him. The hetman stated that the arrangement of passengers would vary during the trip; one carriage could only hold four passengers inside.

The route to Orosz City followed the same roads that Yozef had already traveled when Keelan answered Clan Moreland's call for help against the Narthani invasion only a few short months ago, although that time 2,200 armed clansmen traveled from the three Tri-Alliance clans, along with extra mounts and scores of wagons. This time they could have moved faster, getting to Orosz City with two hard days' push, but instead, they went at a more leisurely pace to fill most of three days and planned on arriving at dusk after spending two nights at inns.

The second day, Yozef started riding with Culich and Sistian, the latter not having previously seen Yozef's summary of what he could remember of military theory. Culich had given the abbot a copy the night before, and the abbot had read the three pages several times. Sistian echoed Maera's reservations about how the other clans would receive some of the "principles." Culich kept his opinions to himself.

Yozef had received extensive descriptions from Maera about the history of the All-Conclaves, but he hadn't heard firsthand experiences.

"Culich, I know something of how these conclaves work, but could you summarize what will happen? I'd like to be aware of what's going on."

"There are two different kinds of conclaves," said Culich. "A 'conclave' and an 'All-Clan Conclave.' Each year there is an All-Clan Conclave. Every hetman is obliged to attend or to have a legitimate excuse and send a son or another highly regarded clan member in his place. No formal penalty falls on a hetman who misses too many of this type of conclave, but if decisions are made, meaning the hetmen vote, no substitute can cast a ballot."

"Smart," said Yozef. Not attending means no vote or input in any discussions. No chance to convince other hetmen of your position.

"Are votes a regular thing? And what are they usually about?"

Culich shook his head, as he gripped the inside locked door handle when the carriage hit a bigger than average rut.

"Sorry 'bout that," called the driver.

"Voting is rare," Culich continued. "Perhaps once every five years. All the hetmen try to avoid voting, preferring to settle issues one on one or in smaller groups—sometimes with Hetman Orosz moderating, if opinions are too hot and diverse. The reason for avoiding votes is that the outcome is binding.

Before the Narthani came, any issue that got 18 votes from the 21 clans required mandatory compliance. Naturally, no clan wants to be forced to do anything it disagrees with, so all try to avoid votes, in case the next vote goes against them. And, of course, being on the losing side of the vote can inflame tensions."

"Can a clan refuse to follow the decision?" queried Yozef.

"Yes, though it hasn't happened in over two hundred years. Then, there was a major border dispute between Stent and the Raslyn Clan."

Raslyn Clan, thought Yozef. *Who's the Raslyn Clan? There's no such clan I've heard of.*

Sistian saw the puzzlement on Yozef's face. "The Raslyn Clan doesn't exist anymore. When the Raslyn hetmen, presumably with the support of most boyermen, refused the results of the vote, the clan was expelled, meaning they were no longer considered part of the conclave. The other clans joined and occupied the province. The Raslyners didn't resist, except for a few who didn't face reality. The hetman, his family out to second cousins, and the immediate families of all the boyermen were banished from Caedellium. They were given enough silver to establish themselves comfortably somewhere else on Anyar and forcibly put on a ship. The history is that the captain of the ship was told to drop them someplace where they might be able to safely live the rest of their lives but not to reveal to anyone on Caedellium where they went."

"Wow," said Yozef, "that seems harsh. Couldn't the clans have simply forced compliance?"

Sistian shook his head. "Understand, Yozef, the conclave was only ten years old. Most of the hetmen remembered what it was like before then—constant feuding, border skirmishes, raids, and even battles with hundreds to a thousand men. Those ten years had been the most peaceful times of any of the hetmen's lives, and they were afraid that if they let one clan ignore a conclave vote, then the entire structure would collapse. Banishing a few hundred people was an easy decision to avoid reversion to the past."

"I would have agreed with the decision had I been Hetman Keelan at the time," said Culich. "The correctness of the action is attested to by the fact that no All-Clan Conclave decision has been openly challenged in the last two hundred years.

"What we will attend for the next several days is also an All-Clan Conclave, with the same requirements, except that these can be held at any time, if half of the clans call for it. One clan makes the proposal, and the others say whether they agree. This time, Orosz made the call, and twelve other clans supported him. This is also rare, but not so much as expelling, and it's only the fourth time in my life that it's happened. Usually, it's to deal with a single issue."

Yozef nodded thoughtfully, trying to imagine himself living here in those times.

"The last call occurred when the Narthani took over Preddi," Culich said, "and compelled the Eywell and Selfcell clans to ally themselves with Narthon. The Eywell hetman seemed eager to collaborate with the Narthani; then the Selfcell hetman, Roblyn Langor, called for a conclave. Only eight of the twenty-one clans approved. Since it wasn't the required number, they still held a conclave but with no requirement for any clan to attend, and only fifteen sent a representative. When Langor appealed for help to resist the Narthani, no clan came to their aid, including Keelan, to my everlasting regret. I still hadn't woken up to the threat, although by the time Selfcell was forced to ally with the Narthani I realized my mistake. Yet it was too late and Keelan too far away."

For the next hour, Yozef asked more questions about the conclave structure, and Sistian asked questions about *On War*. When questions flagged, Yozef watched the countryside.

Twenty miles from Moreland City, they turned northeast and missed seeing the site of the battle where Yozef had picked up his second and, he hoped, last scar. When they turned right at a fork, instead of left, he felt a sense of relief at not having the opportunity to re-imagine what had happened that day.

They climbed through a range of hills and then onto a plain higher than the river valley that ran through central Keelan Province. The plain's soil was lighter colored and the grass sparser at the higher altitude, which Yozef estimated to be around three thousand feet. Farms appeared farther apart, with more barley than in Keelan.

"Good beer in Orosz," asserted Carnigan, when they stopped for the night at an inn just across the Orosz border. "A little too strong for some people, but I prefer it. Reminds me of the beer at the Snarling Graeko in Abersford. The new one in Caernford is not bad, but I keep telling them it still isn't quite the same."

On the third day, they passed through several miles of scrub brush, the soil rocky with shale. While Yozef rode on top of the carriage, Kales pointed out a small herd of animals moving up and over a hill a half-mile away.

"Gwindles," said Kales. "Not many in Keelan anymore. Used to be lots of them in western Keelan when I was a boy. Now you hardly ever hear of anyone seeing them."

"Tastes terrible," added Carnigan.

"Yeah," Kales agreed. "My father used to bag one occasionally, and Mother would try different ways to cook them. Nothing helped. Tough, and reminds you of rotting leather."

Yozef decided this was one Anyar experience he could forego. He did wish he had a telescope. From a distance, he could only make out that gwindles appeared brown with a greenish belly and had a head that looked vaguely like a gnu with a short proboscis.

They continued north on the same plain. A mountain range appeared, first just a hint of purplish haze on the horizon, then growing larger and turning green and cream as they got closer. Orosz City sat abutting mountains that rose sharply from the plain and formed a formidable barrier on two sides of the city, part of which bulged into the plain, with more buildings filling a cleft in the mountains, though how far in, Yozef couldn't see. The plain itself narrowed to no more than three or four miles across, with a river running along the steep slopes of hills on the opposite side from the city.

The Keelan party stopped outside the city walls, a twelve-foot-high masonry construction separating small houses and shops outside from taller, more substantial structures inside.

Yozef again rode in the carriage with Sistian, this time also with Kales.

"How big is the population?" Yozef asked the other two.

The abbot answered, "About the same size as Caernford. Maybe twenty-five thousand. It's large for the population of the province, and it's the only city of substantial size. I understand the population has increased in the last year, mainly due to you, Yozef."

"Me?"

"Yes. Hetman Orosz has paid considerable attention to any reports about or from you. The largest musket cartridge factory is here, except for the ones in Abersford and Caernford. There are also some of your 'franchises' here for soap, paper, and there's talk of a kerosene production facility. I'm surprised you don't know all this."

"Uh . . . well . . . I confess I don't pay much attention to projects operating on their own without my attention. Cadwulf, partners, and factors take care of those details."

"How do you keep them all honest and giving you the proper shares of profits?" asked Kales.

Sistian chuckled. "Obviously, you haven't heard the story of a man named Pollar Penwick. He had a soap-making shop in Abersford. Yozef showed him how to make new kinds of soap, and they were supposed to share the new profits. However, Penwick hid profits from Yozef and said that since they didn't have a written contract, he was under no obligation to share anything."

"Damn shithead," said Kales. "I'd have threatened to cut out his tongue for starters."

"Oh, Yozef is not that vindictive. All he did was start another soap-making shop and sold at prices less than it cost to make the soap. Penwick naturally lost all of his customers and left Abersford to start soap-making in Adris Province, with the understanding that Yozef still receives his share of the Adris profits, or Penwick will risk being run out of his business again."

Kales looked at Yozef with unmistakable approval. "Hmmm . . . effective. Though I'd prefer my way, I can see that method could work, too."

The anecdote about the perils of stiffing Yozef Kolsko ended with a rap on the carriage door.

"Culich will meet with Hetman Orosz," Vortig Luwis told them, "then we'll have dinner together. In the meantime, we'll go to the inn reserved for us."

Yozef noticed that Luwis didn't address Kales. The two men had a testy relationship. Luwis felt ill at ease with a man he considered disreputable, someone who should not be so close to the clan hetman. Kales tolerated Luwis's view, Yozef presumed because Kales didn't give a shit what Luwis thought.

* * *

The first morning after arriving in Orosz City, they had no formal commitments for Yozef and most of the Keelanders. Denes Vegga asked Yozef to go over *On War* once more. For two hours, in a small meeting room on the second floor of the inn, Denes asked questions and Yozef answered, often with hypothetical scenarios to illustrate a principle. Balwis Preddi and Wyfor Kales listened, but only Balwis commented and only during the last hour. Carnigan remained in the same room, dozing across three chairs in a corner. His snores finally chased the other three men to a balcony.

When Denes exhausted his questions, he wore a discouraged expression.

"Yozef, all the principles seem reasonable. Well, most of them, but how do they all interrelate? Some even seem contradictory. How am I, or anyone else, to make quick decisions in the heat of battle by trying to remember and apply all these?"

"Believe me, Denes, I sympathize. I'm afraid only experience will help, and even then, not everyone can lead men in battle. That's one problem with the clans—there's not enough selection of leaders based on ability. Keelan was fortunate to have you at St. Sidryn's and Moreland City. Things might have turned out much worse if someone else had led those days."

Denes waved off Yozef's compliment with his hand. "I only followed your advice, so the credit goes to you."

"I'll accept some of that, though it took someone with flexible thinking when faced with new ideas and perilous situations to accomplish what we did. That's what I hope *On War* will do: present leaders with principles to keep in mind when faced with critical military situations. They still must make the real decisions, but they'll have tools to help their reasoning."

"I'm afraid Yozef is right, Denes," said Balwis. "Until a person has to make such decisions, it's hard to imagine doing it. Hopefully, it becomes easier."

"The problem is getting that experience, and how many men will die from making bad decisions?" asked Denes.

"Too many," answered Yozef, "but that's the price to be paid."

A quarter-mile away, in another small room, this one in the Orosz Clan headquarters building, seven hetmen sat around a rectangular table. Five of the hetmen were leaders of the now official Five-Clan Alliance. Hewell and Adris had formally applied for, and been accepted into, the previous Tri-Clan Alliance of Keelan, Gwillamer, and Mittack.

"What do you think the chances are that we can get all the clans to unite against the Narthani, Culich?" asked Lordum Hewell.

"To hetmen outside this room, excellent," said Hewell. "To everyone here, I'm afraid the answer is uncertain."

"We never had reason to think all would agree," said Orosz. "The task is to convince enough men to force a vote. Then, even those most against a united front will be forced by conclave law to cooperate."

"By Merciful God, if Moreland City wasn't enough to convince them, what will?" Klyngo Adris said bitterly.

"A Narthani knife at their throat is about all that will work with a few hetmen," said Stent. "However, and God forgive me, at least we don't have Gynfor Moreland around anymore."

"I think God will cut you some slack on that one, Welman," said Tomis Orosz. "If only he hadn't taken so many of his clansmen with him."

The late Gynfor Moreland's name brought forth a question from Adris. "Speaking of Moreland, who will represent them?"

"Virmir Orlan," answered Orosz. "A Moreland boyerman from one of the southern districts. They hadn't been able to agree on anyone to represent Moreland, since several factions are arguing over the next hetman, and none wanted to give the others an argument for their own candidate. I had to remind them that if Moreland doesn't have a vote on any decision, they will still be bound. They finally chose Orlan, because he's old, from a poor district, and isn't part of the factions vying for power."

"It hardly needs stating that Moreland will be in favor of anything that helps protect them from the Narthani. What can we do to bring in the others?" asked Stent.

Orosz cleared his throat. "Culich and I have been talking, and we have an idea. It's also why I'm glad no theophist is here listening to us. It involves Yozef Kolsko."

"I might have guessed," said Cadoc Gwillamer, with an acknowledging grunt. "I've wondered when he might come up. The man's everywhere, it seems. Innovations, advice against the Narthani, and my men witnessed him at the forefront using cannon at Moreland City. Now let me guess for real. It's about the rumors of him being a Septarsh?"

"A Septarsh!" Stent exclaimed.

Culich raised a hand to stifle further comments. "Let me be clear, I'm taking no position on whether the man is a Septarsh or not, only on how the rumors might help us convince hesitant clans to join an alliance against the Narthani."

"And not just those clans," said Orosz. "Even a couple of clans that came to Moreland's aid might still not be willing to go further. We need to hold on to such waverers."

Stent frowned and was about to speak when Hulwyn Mittack preempted him. "I think perhaps the rumors have not spread yet to Stent. Am I right, Welman?"

Stent nodded.

"With everything that this Kolsko fellow has introduced and then his roles in defending St. Sidryn's abbey and at Moreland City," Orosz said, "it's hardly surprising that many attribute his mysterious arrival on Caedellium to God answering our prayers for deliverance from the Narthani."

"Yes, but—"

"What has also been slowly spreading," Culich interrupted Stent, "is the rumor that Yozef's ideas and advice to us have been whispered in his ear. He often acts as if that's happening. And often, when he's asked how an idea comes to him, he says something like, 'Oh, it just occurs to me.' It wasn't much of a leap for people to wonder if the whisperer was God. Then, with everything else, the rumor took root and spread fast."

"Last night I had Feren Bakalacs ask me about Kolsko and the Septarsh rumors," said Orosz. The Farkesh hetman, known for his piety, was a close friend of Rhaedri Brison, the island's most respected theophist.

"We've heard the rumors in Adris for almost a year," said Klyngo Adris. "Just two sixdays ago, before I left for the conclave, I met with Zitwyn Bevans to encourage the Bevans Clan to join an alliance against the Narthani. One of Zitwyn's daughters is married to my eldest son, and our families have had a long and friendly relationship. I'm afraid I wasn't able to get a firm commitment from Zitwyn, though he was quite curious about the Septarsh rumors. While I didn't say I believed them, neither did I rule it out. Don't be surprised, Culich, if Zitwyn corners you while you're here and pesters you about Kolsko."

"All right, so there are rumors. How will they help us *now*?" insisted Stent.

Culich was about to speak, until Orosz motioned that he would answer. "All the clans at Moreland City know Kolsko's role there and his innovations before that. He'll be listened to by those clans and some of the others. If the opportunity arises, we can ask Kolsko to advise on our next actions. I already know the things he will say. Not all of it will be well-received, but I doubt anything he says will discourage clans from joining an alliance, and there's the chance a few might be influenced by Kolsko's words."

Stent's expression conveyed he wasn't convinced. "Maybe, but it wouldn't be a good idea for Kolsko himself to make such a claim."

Culich laughed. "No worry there. Yozef hates the rumors and at every opportunity has denied he has any direct communication to God. Unfortunately for him, he still hasn't realized that the more he denies it, the stronger the rumors."

"Because *everybody* knows a Septarsh will deny he is one," finished Stent.

"Precisely," said Orosz. "We'll hold onto this possible argument to judge whether it's needed."

An Oroszian man opened the room's door and poked his head in. "Pardon, Hetman. There's a problem I'm afraid you'll need to resolve. We didn't plan well and put the Nyvaks and Pawell representatives in the same inn. There have already been a couple of fistfights, and neither hetman is willing to be the one to change inns."

Tomis Orosz displayed a mastery of invectives, to the appreciation of the other hetmen, who joined in his frustration with the two neighboring clans. Their members never seemed able to pass a tranquil moment when in the other's vicinity.

"All right," said Orosz, when he wound down. "I think we've finished most of what we wanted to talk about. I'll have to go see about our two brother hetmen. Please continue without me."

Stent and Culich looked at each other, then both shook their heads.

"No," said Culich, "I think we're finished for now. We can all think about what we've discussed and try to convince some of the other hetmen. For myself, I need a good night's sleep to gird me for tomorrow."

CHAPTER 16

ALL-CLAN CONCLAVE

The Conclave Begins

The Seaborn delegation was the last to arrive. Word of the conclave reached the clan's islands off the northwest coast of Caedellium via a four-man sailboat. They crossed the separating strait under cover of darkness to avoid Narthani sloops and the cutters built in Preddi after the Narthani took control. Even the cutters, with their six 12-pounders, were a danger to any clan boat, none of which had ever been armed.

Once the Seaborn hetman received the conclave summons, he and those he brought with him had to cross back to Caedellium on the same craft that brought the news, again avoiding Narthani vessels. Once ashore, they had a three-day ride to Orosz City.

Some clan parties had waited three days for the last delegation, so when Seaborn arrived two hours after sunrise, all the delegations were summoned to begin. Seaborn would rest that night.

It took an hour to gather all the delegations, and as soon as the last one, Nyvaks, arrived at the conclave hall, Hetman Orosz stood at a low dais and struck the two-foot ceremonial gong that called all attendees to attention. Eighteen hetmen and seventy-three accompanying advisors slowly ended their side conversations and turned their attention to Orosz.

"Hetmen and Sers, this All-Clan Conclave of Caedellium is called to order. All eighteen free clans are present. The only topic for this conclave is the Narthani threat to Caedellium and what the clans intend in response."

Before Orosz could continue, Hetman Nyvaks rose and called out, "A point to discuss before we continue, Hetman Orosz. When all twenty-one clans were in attendance, and a vote was taken on any issue, it took eighteen supporting votes before a decision was mandatory on all clans. Since eighteen clans are here today, then all eighteen must support a mandatory decision."

Groans, sighs, and calls filled the room.

"For God's sake, Nyvaks, sit down!"

"Nonsense! When would any vote ever be unanimous?"

"No, no, it must be fifteen out of eighteen. We can't include the three Narthani provinces."

Nyvaks wouldn't be shouted down. "If the vote is not for all eighteen, then that violates the written rules of the conclave, and Nyvaks will not follow any decision made with fewer votes!"

"Nyvaks will comply with the will of the conclave or be subject to expulsion," said Orosz, his voice icy, the ultimate threat laid bare.

Nyvaks started to say something, but a gray-haired advisor sitting behind him grabbed him by his sleeve and whispered in his ear. Nyvaks sat down, glaring at Orosz, who let the responses continue for almost a minute, then struck the gong again. It took an additional blow to quiet the room.

"Hetman Nyvaks has a point," Orosz said. "The written rules of the conclave are clear. It mentions twenty-one clans and makes no provision for fewer. However, rationality demands we adjust to the current conditions and reduce the needed number. Are there proposals for how this might be done?"

Almost thirty minutes passed to settle that it would take sixteen votes out of eighteen clans for a binding decision on all clans. Culich had hoped for fifteen, but Nyvaks persisted in sixteen, and enough other clans felt leery of being forced to abide by decisions that the more difficult number prevailed. It would take only three votes to block action.

The vote number determined, Orosz moved for the second time to formally open the conclave.

"All eighteen free clans are present, and with the agreement that a binding decision requires sixteen supporting clans, this All-Clan Conclave is open. There is only one topic, and that is the Narthani threat. Hetman Keelan will summarize where we stand at this moment. Questions will wait until he is finished."

Culich took the next hour to overview the history of the Narthani presence on Caedellium, starting with their first trading station on Preddi, through crushing Preddi, co-opting the Eywell and Selfcell clans, carrying raids either through Buldorian mercenaries or their own forces, and ending with the invasion of Moreland. He made particular note of Selfcell's rejected appeal for help at a previous conclave.

"Thank you, Hetman Keelan. Are there questions?"

Although everything Culich said was known to everyone in the room, it took another hour to finish with questions and clans such as Nyvaks and Skouks trying to interject opinions—efforts quashed by Orosz as premature. On too rare instances, certain hetmen asked reasonable questions to clarify history where ambiguity existed. When Orosz ruled that questions had been sufficiently answered, and with no objections, he adjourned the conclave for a mid-day meal, which waited on tables outside under tents.

An hour later they began again. Orosz struck the gong.

"The question we have before us is, what action should the clans take to deal with the Narthani?"

Seven hetmen rose to be recognized. Orosz had arranged with Stent that he would be recognized first. Orosz wanted to keep the session focused on the main issue and not let clans such as Nyvaks cause diversions.

"Hetman Stent," Orosz intoned, "what say you?"

Welman Stent waited for the other six hetmen to reseat.

"Fellow hetmen, I see three possibilities. One is to accept that the Narthani are a permanent presence on Caedellium and to do everything possible to restrict them to the three provinces they now control. The second possibility is to drive them off Caedellium by force. The third is to do nothing and pray to God they take no further action against other clans."

Orosz had to ring the gong a dozen times before the tumult died. Stent's third option was quickly dismissed, when Hetman Farkesh reminded two hetmen who seemed inclined to favor that option that men may pray to God, but God expected men to act. "And not be like a stupid Neslender murvor and close your eyes, hoping danger thinks you're not worth its time."

The large flightless bird was originally found in western Caedellium thickets and was renowned for freezing and relying on camouflaged plumage to escape predators' notice.

The first possible action proposed by Stent could not be easily rejected.

Hetman Pawell was recognized. "Who is to say that if we leave the Narthani alone, now that they lost at Moreland City, they won't realize taking over the rest of Caedellium will be too difficult? They're like the hornet's nest. Best left alone."

"Hetman Pawell," said Culich, "what do you do if the hornets move and try to establish a new nest in your house? Is that not what the Narthani have already done? First with Preddi, then Eywell and Selfcell, and most recently their invasion of Moreland? What do you do if you wake up one morning and find a new nest already in your house? Do you live with them and hope the nest doesn't proliferate, or do you take whatever action is needed to remove the first nest? No. All of us here would take action."

Hetman Pewitt rose. "I appreciate your analogies, Hetman Keelan, but we have to balance the perceived threat and the costs of any action we take. What if we simply wait and see what the Narthani do next?"

"What if their next action is to attack a clan from the sea?" asked Stent. "We stopped them when they came inland, but they also gave us time to gather the clans. Remember how they moved slowly and then waited in place for several days when they neared Moreland City? They obviously wanted us to gather so their army could defeat us in a battle. They won't make that mistake again. They could directly invade Gwillamer or Stent, moving fast and with the support of their navy. Before other clans could come to those clans' aid in enough numbers to stop them, the Narthani could have burned every structure in the province to ashes, killed or run off all animals, and killed or captured who knows how many of the provinces' people."

"I agree with Stent. They don't have to do it by land," interjected Adris. "With their complete control of the sea, they could land thousands of men, cannon, and horses on the shores of any clan on a coast. No one clan could stop thousands of Narthani from destroying the province before more clans came to help. Even if clans did come, as soon as the Narthani felt their men threatened, they could just re-board their ships and go elsewhere to attack a clan on the other side of Caedellium. Maybe a clan whose men were sent to help the first clan."

Stent rose again. "Each hetman needs to ask himself what he and his clan would do if the Narthani invaded, either by land or by sea, and moved quickly. Hetman Skouks, what would *you* do?"

The rough-looking, scarred hetman with long gray hair appeared grim. "I pray to God I would act wisely and not waste the lives of my clanspeople in a futile fight. If necessary, we would flee inland to the mountains, where we would fight until the other clans came to our aid."

"A wise decision, Hetman," said Stent. "However, what happens to Skouvona? I've been to your capital. It has some of the oldest buildings on Caedellium and is unique. The Narthani would burn it to the ground. What of the other towns and villages? How many of them would suffer the same fate? And your animals. Would you have time to drive all of them to safety, or would you have to focus on saving the people and leaving the herds to the Narthani?"

The Skouks hetman's face became even craggier, as his jaw clenched and unclenched. "Then we would rebuild Skouvona better than before, and animals can be replaced."

"Yes, and I'm sure your people would try to endure the consequences, but then what if you rebuild and the Narthani come again and repeat the destruction? How many times could your people endure such a cycle?"

Skouks didn't respond.

"And you, Hetman Swavebroke, what would your people do in such a situation? Would you abandon Shullick, your capital and one of the largest cities on Caedellium?"

"We would defend Shullick until help could arrive from the other clans. Although their army might be too much for us in the open, it would be different among city streets, where we know every corner and turn."

Two of the six men sitting behind the Swavebroke hetman shook their heads, and the six murmured among themselves.

Stent pressed harder. "What if you couldn't stop them before help arrived, *if* it arrived? What, then, for the people of Shullick? You would be gambling with their lives to think you could stop the Narthani."

Swavebroke's confident expression melted into desperation. "Then what are we to do? Neither Shullick nor any other town in our province has mountains to fall back to for protection. Thousands of my clanspeople might be captured or killed if the Narthani landed their soldiers and we tried to flee, no matter how bravely our men tried to slow them in the open country. Yet how could we abandon Shullick and move our people away from the coast?"

"You should stand and fight them to the death, that's what you should do," scolded Eldon Vandinke. "Better all should die than end up slaves of the Narthani."

"Easy for you to say, Vandinke," said Teresz Bultecki, the Bultecki hetman. "Your clan and mine have no coasts, so the Narthani can't get to us without first going through other clans. And we have plenty of mountains to hide in. If anything, we would be among the last clans overrun by the Narthani. But make no mistake, if the others fell, our turn would come. You talk bravely about dying. But what about the children? Do you decide their fate so easily?"

Orosz held up his arms. "I think we can get back to what we should do. No one doubts the threat the Narthani pose to all our clans. However, we have to do *something.*"

"Could we try to negotiate with them?" asked Milton Ernmor, the Pewitt Clan hetman. "I know it's something none of us want to do. Even if what we want is to have the Narthani gone from Caedellium forever, we have to face all options, one of which is the first possibility Hetman Stent listed. If we could come to an agreement with the Narthani that we cede control of those three provinces, would they be willing to leave the rest of Caedellium alone?"

Culich stood. "Milton, while I understand your desire to settle all this with as little additional bloodshed as possible and with the security of our clans assured, how could we ever trust the Narthani to keep such an agreement? They will do anything necessary to further their goals. Look at the two assassination attempts. Hetman Stent was fortunate to have enough armed men nearby to foil the attempt on him. Lordum Hewell also survived, but only because the assassins mistook his brother for him. Consider how they brought in the Buldorians to raid and kill and then continued with their own men. Look how they turned the Eywellese loose onto Moreland, burned two towns, and killed over six hundred Morelanders. Can you honestly say you would trust them?"

"No, Culich, there is no way I'd trust them, but what is the harm in at least trying to have representatives meet with them? The worst that would happen is they refuse to meet. Still, on the slim chance something positive may result, shouldn't we try? Maybe it would make them pause, if they are planning further attacks."

Culich didn't respond. He saw the conclave slipping away from united clan action. He believed the argument to try negotiating, while rational on the surface, had no chance to succeed and would only provide an excuse to do nothing, while waiting for the outcome. Months could slip by, months he intuited Caedellium didn't have.

Two hours passed with the hetmen arguing back and forth, stating and restating reasons to act or do nothing, and repeatedly returning to the negotiation proposal. Culich limited his participation and waited for the next break, which would come just before dusk. The men would eat, the clan delegations would talk among themselves and with other clans, and all clans would reconvene for an evening session. He needed to get ready for a last chance to influence the direction of the conclave.

When they reconvened, Orosz rang the gong to gather the men's attention.

"Hetman Keelan has asked to speak."

Culich rose, walked to the front of the room, and faced the room full of men. "I will yield to someone who has played an important role in fighting the Narthani. Some of you have met him, others have not, though you know of him. He has unique perspectives on what we face, and I have asked him to speak to the conclave."

Culich motioned to the Keelan delegation. "Yozef Kolsko."

Culich had told Yozef he might be called on, if necessary. They needed to bring the clans back to facing the imminent threat of the Narthani. Yozef had spoken to a group of hetmen and others previously, at the end of the Battle of Moreland City. However, at that time his head throbbed from the wound whose scar he carried and his body was coming down from the physical and emotional consequences of having survived the fight. Thus, he hardly remembered what he had said, though Denes told him he had warned that the Narthani had merely withdrawn, had not been defeated, and were still a threat.

Today was different. Both conscious of the setting and aware of the stakes, Yozef didn't feel optimistic. Everything he'd heard so far showed that too many clans still hoped to avoid becoming involved and still remained incognizant of the level of the Narthani threat, because it hadn't yet impacted their clans. Nevertheless, he had to try. If nothing else, perhaps something he said would influence them later when they remembered it.

At least, there had been good news. A semaphore message had arrived from Caernford the previous day. It took the station in Orosz City several hours to track him down, the station assistant explained, as he handed Yozef the folded, sealed sheet.

"Not sure what it means, Ser Kolsko," said the assistant. "Sounds like gibberish. Tell me if you want us to ask Caernford to resend the message tomorrow."

No secrets could be kept from the semaphore station staffs. Thus, Yozef had cautioned against sending information too sensitive, in case a Narthani agent had been placed at a station anywhere on the island. This also limited loose lips that couldn't resist spreading titillating news.

Yozef had broken the seal and read.

```
To: Yozef Kolsko
From: Maera Kolsko-Keelan
News from Yawnfol. Success 6.
```

```
10 test okay.
Triple burst.
Mounting and 5 more.
```

He was sure it meant that Yawnfol Nyfork, the foreman at the Abersford foundry, had reported the successful casting of a 6-pounder cannon barrel, based on ten successful test-firings without damage to the barrel, and it taking a triple charge to burst the barrel. They were proceeding to mount barrels on carriages and would cast five more barrels. He would tell Culich the news and let the hetman decide whether to tell the others. For now, he faced the room full of bearded faces.

Yozef remembered being nervous on boarding the flight from San Francisco to Chicago, but that was because of flying and not at the prospect of presenting his research results to a room full of hundreds of scientists and engineers. He knew he would speak about a topic he had supreme confidence in—his chemical research and its implications. He could remember giving talks in undergraduate and graduate seminar classes on topics new to him and how petrified he felt the first few times, although it gradually became easier the more he did it. For the Chicago meeting, it was a topic he considered himself an expert on. Now, he would be talking about subjects on which he remained a dilettante. He feared leading astray this room full of leaders.

Yet here he was, facing clan leaders, most of them older than he was, most having many years of responsibilities beyond his experience, and he faced them ready to launch into what he believed they needed to hear. He couldn't control whether or not they understood.

He cleared his throat and did his best to look calm, confident, and wise—a troika that seemed, respectively, true, false, and in the realm of "in your dreams."

"Hetmen and Sers, I stand before you as someone not originally from Caedellium. I came to your island unexpectedly three years ago and now consider myself a Caedelli, if only by adoption. Wherever my origin, now my life, my future, and my family are irrevocably tied to the same fortunes as your own. I believe I bring a different perspective than most of you. One built on the history of my own people and the histories I have read of other realms. Many of those histories are apparently not available here on Caedellium. Therefore, I consider the Narthani problem from that background.

"The first thing I would ask you to consider is simple. Why did the Narthani come to Caedellium? The island is not on trade routes, and while the island has admirable natural resources, they aren't enough for the Narthani to spend the effort so far from their closest port. Although I have no way to be positive, *it comes to me* that the Narthani plan to use Caedellium as a base to attack Landolin or the Iraquinik Confederation, perhaps both."

Yozef had deliberately chosen to use the phrase "it comes to me" to play into the Septarsh rumors. As much as he cringed, the stakes were high, and he had to discount his personal qualms. He had no way of knowing that the Keelan, Orosz, Stent, and Gwillamer hetmen had casually sprinkled their conversations with other hetmen and their advisors with references to the Septarsh rumors, never giving a firm affirmation, yet leaving the impression they were open to the possibility.

His choice hit a nerve, because he thought at least half of the hetmen and many of the advisors sat a little more upright or their eyes widened slightly at his words.

"Whether this is true or not, there is no reason to believe they have any intention other than to conquer all of Caedellium. If you see a storm coming in your direction, do you assume it will pass you by, even if your neighbors are hammered by rain and wind, or do you close your windows and bring your children inside?

"You've already heard Hetman Orosz refer to the Neslender murvor. It closes its eyes and hopes for the best. Same with the storm. Who among you would close your eyes as the wind and lightning got closer and not assume you'd come under the storm? The Narthani *are* coming. When, I can't say, but as sure as the sun rises each morning, the day will come when a Narthani army comes for each of you. Together, you can resist them, but do any of you now think your clan can turn them back by yourselves? It may require working together in ways alien to you, even suborning the immediate interests of your own clan in favor of the many. Likewise, the time will come when the other clans will do the same for you.

"Imagine a single thin two-foot-long piece of a tree branch. You can easily break it. Yet bundle eighteen of these together, and none of you could break the bundle. United, you can stand tall; divided, you fall. You will either hang together or hang separately."

Yozef paused to let the last lines sink in. It wasn't the greatest oratory, but thanks to Ben Franklin again for the hanging quote and the fact that hanging for the most egregious crimes was known on Caedellium.

He remembered the bundling reference from once looking up the origin of the fasces—the symbol made of sticks or rods tied into a bundle, sometimes with an ax head protruding from the top side. The example came from an Aesop fable, and Romans adopted it as a symbol of strength through unity. Yozef's curiosity in the symbol's origin stemmed from seeing it on dimes in a coin collection given him by an uncle when he was nine years old. The Mercury dimes had the head of the Roman god Mercury on one side and a bundle of rods on the other side. No one he knew could tell him what the bundle represented, so he asked the librarian at school. She told him the bundle was a *fasces* and explained the symbolism. It was more than appropriate for what Yozef saw the clans facing. He saw no reason to soil the image by providing further information that Italy's Mussolini had used the fasces as the symbol for his political party, thus giving rise to the word *fascism*.

When the men in the room started to mumble among themselves, Yozef spoke again.

"Neither I nor the people I come from have personal experience with the Narthani, and I have asked four persons who *have* such experience to come today to tell you what it's like to fall under the control of the Narthon Empire."

Yozef had thanked Maera for suggesting that he bring in witnesses, because she believed personal stories would have more impact than general warnings.

"These four persons," Yozef said, "escaped from the Narthani and fled into Moreland, Gwillamer, or Stent Provinces." He gestured to Denes, who had moved to stand by the main door in the back of the room. Denes now opened the door and motioned to someone outside.

"The first person is Ubeladuhbando Badaleesha, as close as I can come to properly pronouncing his given name," said Yozef. "That name had not been used for twenty-eight years before he escaped. The Narthani simply called him 'Slave' for most of those years. He is thirty-six years old."

Through the door walked a man appearing closer to fifty-six years than thirty-six. He was short, his face bearing several scars, and he walked with a pronounced limp, yet he walked tall, as if proud of the scars and the limp. At the front of the room, he turned to face the clan leaders. He spoke passable Caedelli, though with a harsher tone than Caedelli's softer vowels.

"My name is Ubeladuhbando Badaleesha. Ser Kolsko has done well to come that close to saying it right. I took several days of trying before I remembered the correct way myself. It had been so long since I spoke my own language, because it's forbidden by the Narthani. Punishment is severe and swift, as it is for any transgression by a Narthani slave."

Badaleesha untied his shirt and pulled it over his head. Men throughout the room sucked in their breath at the sight of the scars: long raised welts, probably from whips; thin scars, as if from narrow blades; puckered skin, as if from burns; and others whose origin could not be guessed. Hardly a square inch of skin remained unmarred. The action of removing the shirt had also revealed Ubeladuhbando missing one ear entirely and half of the other, and one hand had only a thumb and two fingers.

"I was seven years old when my people fought the Narthani. I remember how frightened everyone was when my father and one older brother left our farm. I remember all the weapons they carried with them. We never saw them again. We heard a great battle had been fought and our men died, to a man. I remember Narthani soldiers sweeping into our village, forcing everyone to gather in the central square. It was women, children, and old men. They screamed at us in their own language, which none of us could understand. Then they divided us into two groups. The children and some of the younger women were put into wagons, our feet tied to iron rings. The youngest children, those not walking yet, were tossed into the arms of the women and children like me. I held a girl of about eighteen months old.

"From where I sat, I faced the square that held the rest of the people. A Narthani officer yelled something, I didn't know what, and the other Narthani drew swords and cut down everyone left in the square. Sometimes at night I can still hear the screams fading as the wagons pulled away. My last sight of the scene as my wagon turned a corner was a woman wearing a red and yellow dress and holding a baby being cut down. I couldn't see her face, but my mother wore such a dress that day when she was dragged from our home carrying my two-month-old sister.

"We joined wagons from other villages, dozens, then hundreds in a line of wagons that stretched as far as I could see. For two sixdays, we were kept in wagons, barely enough food and water given to keep most of us alive, our excrement coating the wagon floor and eventually shoved out the end of the wagon by our feet. Many died and were dumped alongside the roads.

"They took us to Narthani slave markets and sold us into whatever our next fate was to be. In the next years, I worked dawn to dusk in a large cloth-weaving shop, untangling threads within huge looms. Many other boys like me were maimed or killed by being caught in a loom that suddenly released from whatever had bound its action. When I grew too much to slip within the loom parts, I was sold to a farmer who was harsh, though when I think back, those were my best years as a slave. We had plenty to eat, were not beaten for no reason, and when I was twenty, I was given a woman as a mate. She was ten years older and had had seven children already by three different slave men, two of whom had died and one sold for a reason no one knew. We were mated for four years, and she had two more children. When the old farm owner died, the son who inherited the farm didn't want to be a farmer and sold it, along with all the slaves.

"The last time I saw my mate and children was when I returned from a field and saw them pulling away in the back of a wagon. When I ran after them, I was run down by the new master on his horse. My leg was broken, but they dragged me to a tree, tied me to it, and whipped me. The leg never healed properly, and I was sold for almost nothing to a horse breeder, who needed slaves to muck out stables and groom horses. You didn't need to move fast for those tasks. When this master came to Caedellium, he brought me and many of his slaves with him. He took over a ranch in the eastern part of Preddi Province. We never learned what happened to the previous owner. Besides the slaves the master brought with him, there were several newly made Caedelli slaves. It was from them that I learned your language.

"The ranch was only a few miles from the sea, and another slave learned of a fishing village. One night during a storm, eight of us ran to the village. It was hard for me to keep up with the others, though it was a minor pain, compared to what I had already suffered over many years. At the village, we stole a small boat and rowed east. One Caedelli told us if we stayed directly east, we would reach Gwillamer. It took three days. Several times, Narthani sloops passed so close, we thought they would surely see us, but they passed on. One of us died, and we finally landed on a rocky shore. We were found by people from a Gwillamese village. I've been living and working in Gwillamer Province for two years." He stopped for a moment. "Free for two years."

The prematurely aged man looked to Yozef, who nodded his thanks. He picked up his shirt, pulled it back over his head, and limped down the aisle and out the door held open by Denes.

Yozef waited until Badaleesha was gone before addressing the clan leaders again. "The next person is Savronel Storlini. His experience with the Narthani is different than Badaleesha's."

Denes ushered in a tall man about thirty years old, with a sturdy form and a strong stride so different from Badaleesha's. Balwis translated, because the man spoke no Caedelli. Storlini launched straight into recounting how the Narthani had swept aside several nations previously, separating Storlini's people from the Narthani. The other nations had resisted and been crushed. When faced with an overwhelming Narthani army, Storlini's people had surrendered without a fight.

The capitulation had saved them from immediate annihilation but failed by other measures. Storlini recounted how his grandfather and father had whispered at night to him that during the course of seventy years, the Narthani had systematically eliminated any trace of their past culture and language. Storlini was a horse handler and trainer and was formally a Narthani citizen, but he would never rise to any position higher than he had. The workings of Narthon dictated that those peoples absorbed had opportunities to rise in relation to how long it had been since their absorption.

Storlini had felt like a foreigner his entire life. The stories about his family's original people conflicted with what he saw of the Narthon Empire. When an opportunity arose, he took a leap of faith that he might find a better life among the islanders than he foresaw remaining as a Narthani.

Storlini didn't speak his family's original language, it having been forbidden for the previous fifty years, nor did he know much about his family's original people, except for a few stories passed on to him at home. The Narthani forbade any written records to serve as memory or rallying points for resistance. In another generation or two, even such small bits would be lost, and it would be as if his original people had never existed.

The third speaker was Balwis Preddi, Yozef's retainer, translator, and bodyguard. He told them that he was eighteen when the Narthani crushed the belated Preddi resistance. Bitterness at the Preddi hetman dripped from his comments, as did anguish over the futility and cost of the rebellion. He described watching surviving men being shipped off as slaves, along with many of the women, including an older brother and sister and his cousins. His father and an older brother died in the fighting. He survived only because his father had ordered him to stay at home to watch over his mother and five younger siblings. When news of the disaster in Preddi City came, they feared for their lives and fled south with others in three wagons to a horse ranch owned by his mother's distant cousin with a different last name. During the flight, they were accosted by a Narthani cavalry patrol. In the ensuing fight, they lost the wagon carrying two of his sisters, five and eight years old, being cared for by another woman. Balwis, his mother, and the three remaining siblings escaped and assumed new identities as members of the cousin's family.

A year passed before they found out that the captured sisters had been converted to slaves and assigned to Narthani owners in northern Preddi Province. Another year passed while they hatched impractical retrieval plans, before the mother and Balwis gave up, and he declared that he was escaping to free clan territory. He told his mother the only way he saw to rescue his sisters was if the Narthani were brought down, and he would do everything he could to contribute to that goal.

The cousin's family had not participated in the distant fight against the Narthani, and the distance further shielded them from the worst of the reprisals and the later influx of Narthani settlers. By showing proper obeisance, they kept the ranch, although they had to breed the horses for Narthani cavalry and farms.

The large number of horses and the lack of Narthani records made it possible for four of the best horses to depart with Balwis on a 150-mile dash from southern Preddi up the length of the province, through the middle of Eywell Province, and across the border into Moreland. He left before dark and rode hard, stopping only during daylight. He made it across the border on the fourth horse, almost dead, with the other three having been exhausted and let loose along the route.

When he finished, unlike the two previous speakers, Balwis moved to a chair behind Culich, in case people had questions later. Yozef let Balwis sit before he continued.

"The final speaker has great courage to come before you and tell what happened to her. Her name is Una Gower, and she was from Preddi. I trust you will show her proper respect."

Yozef motioned again to Denes, who opened the door and again summoned someone outside. A woman of about twenty-two years entered, wearing a shawl over her head, which she let drop as she turned to face the room full of men. She was brown-haired, of average height, and slender, and she had ancient, tired eyes. Like Balwis and some members of his family, she and her husband had been among the few Preddi who survived the destruction of their clan, due to the happenstance that the husband was at sea from their fishing village on the west coast of Preddi Province. Her husband owned a fishing boat crewed by other related men. When the Narthani finally reached their village, they tried to accept what they could not change, until one too many events made them give up. Six months ago, a Narthani cutter caught twenty-one of them trying to sail to Stent Province. Una was one of three women not executed. They were sentenced to Narthani brothels for the rest of their lives. The other women had died, wasting away within months, while Una had survived. In an emotionless voice, she described her life after her capture. For three months, six days a week, she serviced whatever men the Narthani authorities deemed worthy: soldiers, administrative staff, and then a few Selfcellese collaborators when she was moved to Sellmor, the Selfcell capitol. With the help of sympathetic Selfcellese, she was smuggled across the border to Stent and then on the Orosz City, where she had lived the last three months. When Hetman Orosz heard from Culich that Yozef intended to bring in three people with personal experience of the Narthani, he suggested Una Gower.

When Una started her recitation, there had been murmurings from the male audience, which subsided into silence, then angry utterances. She finished by describing the escape from Selfcell, hiding by day and traveling at night to avoid Narthani patrols. Without another word, she raised her shawl again and walked down the aisle toward the back door. She had taken only three steps when Welman Stent rose in respect, followed immediately by his clansmen and several other hetmen and clan delegations. She stopped, startled, then continued. By the time she reached the door, every hetman in the entire room was standing. As the door closed, curses and oaths of death to Narthani rang throughout the room.

Hetman Orosz let the tumult continue for several minutes, then used the gong to bring back order, at which time Yozef resumed speaking.

"I hope you all understand the courage it took for Una Gower to stand before you. I also hope that after hearing just these four accounts of what the future holds for Caedellium should the Narthani prevail, you begin to understand the full nature of the cost of failure. I also hope you understand that nothing short of total commitment by every clan, every man, every woman, and, if necessary, every child will be required."

Yozef looked around the room. "The question you have to face is *what* price might need to be paid?" He turned to Feren Bakalacs, hetman of the Farkesh clan. "Hetman Farkesh, what price would you pay to stop your clan from ceasing to exist?"

"Anything and everything," the older man stated savagely.

"Hetman Stent, what price would your people be willing to pay to prevent from happening to Stent what happened to Preddi or what is going to happen to Eywell and Selfcell?"

"They will die to the last Stentese."

"Hetman Skouks? What would you do to prevent your five granddaughters from becoming Narthani slaves and some sent to Narthani brothels?"

The white-haired but still robust and multi-scarred hetman jumped to his feet. "I would do anything!" he roared. "All of them would die fighting the Narthani first!!"

The room exploded in anger and shouts of defiance.

When Tomis Orosz finally brought back order ten minutes later, Yozef spoke his last words.

"Although I was not originally from Caedellium, I now count myself as a Caedelli. Look around you at the other men in this room. Look, and look closely." He stopped and waited.

Slowly, the men looked at their own clan members, then to clans next to them, and then wider in the room.

"Until we defeat the Narthani, what you see are not 'other clans.' Disagreements, border disputes, raids, and old antagonisms have existed between many of you. Think hard, men of Caedellium. Pewitt versus Stent. Moreland versus Keelan. Pawell versus Nyvaks. On and on. I ask you to consider that whatever differences and conflicts have existed are nothing . . . *nothing*, compared to what stands between all the clans and the Narthani. Do not think of the other groups in this room as from other clans. Think of them as your brothers. Brothers in the mightiest effort ever undertaken on Caedellium. If we fail, there will be no history of Caedellium, no stories to pass on to future generations. It will be as if the people of Caedellium never existed.

"But . . . if we are victorious, legends, songs, and histories will be known for a thousand years."

The room exploded again. Hetmen and men whose names and clans Yozef had no idea of rushed to hug him, slap him on the back, and pledge death to all Narthani. For a moment, Yozef felt as if he had been in no more danger of injury at the defense of St. Sidryn's or the Battle of Moreland City. It took half an hour for Orosz to call an end to the meeting that evening and direct the men to return to continue the next day.

Yozef stood with the other Keelanders, as the room emptied. He felt almost euphoric. He had stood in front of the room full of Caedelli leaders and, along with help from four witnesses, led the men to an outpouring of defiance against the Narthani.

Who would have thought I could do something like this? My God. It was almost like something out of an epic novel or a scene from Game of Thrones.

He chuckled aloud, causing Balwis and Denes to look at him with raised eyebrows.

Yes, they're surprised, too, and wondering why I'm amused.

His thoughts turned from his own grand performance, as Culich left a cluster of hetmen and walked in their direction.

"What do you think, Culich?" asked Yozef, eager to hear confirmation that his speech had had an effect. "Do you, Stent, and Orosz think we can get the clans to unite against the Narthani?"

"Oh, no. Nothing that grandiose," said Culich.

Cold water dashed Yozef's elation. Then he noticed Culich's serene expression, with perhaps a hint of pleasure.

"We never thought we could get all the clans together," said Culich, "but several more are leaning our way. I even have hopes that the votes tomorrow will be enough to force the recalcitrant to join some form of action, whether they want to or not."

Culich noticed Yozef's downcast face. "No, no, Yozef, you did fine. Actually, better than I'd hoped. Asking questions to individual hetmen at the end about what they would do had an impact. Pewitt was wavering and now is firmly behind uniting. Similarly with Bevans, although I've always thought Bevans would be forced to join, if only because they would once Adris did. The two clans have close ties. More important is Farkesh. I was uncertain about him, and now I think there's a good chance he'll support us. If that happens, the two most resistant, Swavebroke and Skouks, will gradually come around. I never had any hopes for Nyvaks, and Seaborn wouldn't be much help, even if they joined, because they're physically separated by being on their islands."

Culich went on. "We have to be patient. The clans can't be rushed into anything."

"The voting tomorrow?" said Yozef. "What does this do for the chances of not just uniting against the Narthani, but forming a central authority to plan and carry out actions?"

Culich shook his head. "Let's not get ahead of ourselves. Agreeing to unite is the most we can look for at this conclave. Clans agreeing to submit themselves to a central authority is something entirely different."

Yozef started to protest, but Culich cut him off with a firm grip on his upper arm.

"I know you think a central authority is necessary, Yozef. I tend to agree with you, but even *I* shrink at the idea of someone not a Keelander giving orders to our men. Clan independence is too ingrained. If it does eventually happen, I think it will need one or more catastrophic events like what happened to the Preddi or Moreland to shock the hetmen."

Yozef made no effort to hide his dismay. "Giving the other clans time to get their heads out of their asses may mean we run out of time. What happens if by the time they wake up, there are fewer clans to unite? Remember, Caedellium started with twenty-one clans. Now there are only eighteen to fight the Narthani, and it's probably best to think it fewer. Nyvaks seems useless, Seaborn too isolated, and who knows what Moreland can still muster?"

"We can only do what we can do," Culich said, "and pray to God."

The room was nearly empty. Culich had kept his hand on Yozef's arm, and as they walked side by side with the Keelan delegation to the exit, he lowered his voice and leaned to Yozef's left ear.

"I haven't given your *On War* writing to all the hetmen, Yozef. We have enough trouble here without opening too many new ideas for some of these men. I *have* shared it with Stent and Orosz and, of course, the four other clans in our now Five-Clan Alliance. Let's see how tomorrow goes."

Yozef's anticipation of the next day's session was shaken, due to Carnigan. The big man had found a pub to his liking, presumably while Yozef and Balwis remained occupied with the conclave.

By the second stein of beer, Yozef had summarized his impressions. Balwis added his, then was reduced to a string of curses at the blindness of too many hetmen.

Carnigan had listened without interrupting.

"That's how it ended, Carnigan," Yozef finished. "We'll find out tomorrow whether the clans will vote on a mandatory united front against the Narthani."

"So, what if they do?" asked Carnigan blithely.

"Huh?"

"Let's say that, unexpectedly from what I hear you say, all the clans vote to unite against the Narthani. What does that mean? What *exactly* will they do?"

Yozef stared at his big friend. And stared. His mouth had opened partway to say something, but no words formed in his brain to be transmitted.

"I was going to ask the same thing," said Balwis. "I assume you or Hetman Keelan or Hetman Orosz have a plan? Would we gather and attack the Narthani, raid them to death, piss on them until they give up, or what?"

"Yozef," said Carnigan, after several more moments, "were you planning on doing something else with your mouth besides catching flies?"

Yozef's mouth snapped shut, his mind in full motion. What *were* they going to do if the clans united? He had been so caught up in everything else going on, moving to Caernford, Maera's pregnancy, his projects, the university, trying to maintain his writing and workout schedules, writing *On War*, and then coming to the conclave and preparing to speak, that he hadn't given thought to *exactly* what the clans could or should do about the Narthani.

Well, shit. What ARE we going to do? The topic came up this morning in the options proposed by Stent. The third option, do nothing, is so obviously ludicrous, the hetmen can't possibly go that route.

Attack the Narthani? How? I don't care how many clansmen can be mustered, I don't see how they could win an open field engagement, and if they somehow managed to, the losses of men would have to be as bad as what happened to the Morelanders.

Nibble them to death? The clansmen outnumber the Narthani, so hit-and-run raids could slowly whittle them away and with hopefully acceptable losses, if the clans only do it with greatly superior numbers in any action. That could take time. Many months, a year, who knows?

Directly invade Preddi Province and face the Narthani right in their stronghold at Preddi City? I don't see it. If necessary, they'd pull back into defensive positions. Digging them out by direct attack would cost as many men as a field battle, if not more, and who knows if it would work? What's left is a siege. That could take many months. I remember reading of sieges on old Earth that lasted years. The clans couldn't stay together and invest the Narthani positions that long.

I think there's only one real option for the near future.

Yozef's eyes focused again on his two companions. Carnigan was long since used to such introspective moments. Balwis hadn't accepted them yet and kept drumming the fingers of both hands on the tabletop.

"Well . . . are you back with us from wherever it is you go?" Balwis said in a grating voice.

"Just thinking," said Yozef.

"You're always *just* thinking," said Carnigan. "Are you about to share with us what you were thinking, or do we have to guess, as usual?"

"I think I'll let you guess," said Yozef, lifting his stein for a long draught. *I would share with you if I had a clear idea of what I think is our only option. I need to think it over to be sure I'm not missing something obvious, as I seem to do too often.*

Balwis gave a disgusted grunt. Carnigan just shrugged at Balwis. "Either it's a secret, or he doesn't have a plan yet. Be patient, Balwis. It usually comes out okay. Usually."

The next morning, the conclave room filled with the same men. Yozef hoped for better results than the previous day. Yesterday had been filled with uncertainty, whereas Yozef now hoped for a sense of purpose. Whether the purpose was real or a mirage, he would find out. Thus, as Orosz readied to call the conclave to order, Yozef sat behind Culich and hoped they wouldn't summon him again for a brilliant plan.

Orosz struck the gong three times. "Hetmen, Sers, we are ready to begin again. I will state what I believe is the summary of conclusions we came to yesterday. You all, of course, can correct me if I am in error. Of Hetman Stent's three options he proposed yesterday, I believe we can dispose of the third. That is to simply do nothing. That leaves two options. One is to contain the Narthani in their three provinces, by whatever means necessary. We can discuss later how we would do this. The second remaining option is to take the fight to the Narthani in their three provinces, with the objective of driving them off Caedellium. Once again, we can discuss how this might be done. I believe those are the only two realistic options we have, although there is another action that I believe several clans support: negotiations with the Narthani."

The hetmen argued for an hour, without the clan positions changing on the three actions. Finally, Yozef left his chair and knelt next to Culich.

"It doesn't have to be either/or, Culich," Yozef whispered. "The clans are in no position to attack the Narthani directly but might be with time, training, and planning. I forgot to tell you that Maera sent a message. The cannon foundry in Abersford claims to have successfully cast a 6-pounder barrel. Once mounted on carriages, 6-pounders can accompany horsemen and dragoons to battles, giving our mounted men more power. Also, if it's true the 6-pounder casting worked, then most likely we can move on to 12-pounders and possibly other cannon I have ideas about. All that will take time, though. Maybe in a year, with enough cannon produced and more training, perhaps the clans could consider an attack on Preddi. Until then, the borders with Narthani territory should be defended."

Culich had listened with his head canted to Yozef's mouth, his eyes taking in the focus of the other men in the room. When Yozef first knelt, all of the men were engaged in the general discussion. Within seconds, more and more heads and eyes left the ongoing session and shifted to watch Culich and Yozef. The noise level noticeably subsided, and Culich was about to cut Yozef short when his son-in-law finished what he wanted to say and returned to his chair.

Hetman Hewell had been the last speaker, stating why he thought a direct attack was the only final solution but worrying about cost. Having said his piece, Hewell then smoothly segued to Culich.

"It has been pointed out to me," said Culich, and many eyes briefly swiveled to Yozef, then back to the Keelan hetman, "that the action options are not incompatible. Yozef Kolsko warned us at Moreland City not to attack the Narthani line directly, because we were inexperienced in this type of battle and against this kind of professional army. This doesn't mean we might not be capable at some future time, but not right now.

"We also must agree that the Narthani not be allowed to expand from the territory they now control. The obvious solution is to affirm that we will resist with all our might any Narthani attempt to expand, such as they did at Moreland. How we do this would need to be worked out. It seems unlikely they will try the same type of invasion, although we can't be sure what else they might do. While we do this, we can strengthen our total fighting ability and prepare ourselves by training, planning, and gathering whatever supplies and weapons might be necessary, if and when we attempt to directly drive the Narthani off Caedellium, which would have to be decided by a future conclave."

Most clans immediately grasped the Keelan hetman's words as a way forward and one that didn't require a commitment to try to immediately retake the three lost provinces. After another hour, Orosz called for a vote. There were no objections. The formal proposal was for heavy patrolling of the borders of Narthani-controlled territory, with thousand man forces, contributed to by all clans, encamped near enough to the borders to delay any Narthani, Eywell, or Selfcell incursion until more help arrived.

Culich said the progress in cannon casting was promising. If it proved true, Keelan would share the technology with the other clans, and he hoped the other clans would follow the lead of the Five-Clan Alliance in developing significant numbers of cannon and trained artillerymen.

"Then," said Culich, "when the clans feel they are strong enough, the option to attack Preddi can be revisited."

Orosz forestalled further discussion by striking the gong and calling out, "All hetmen favoring Hetman Keelan's proposal signify by standing."

Sixteen hetmen stood. All but Nyvaks and Skouks.

"All those opposed, stand."

The sixteen standing hetmen took their seats; no one stood.

Orosz struck the gong once more. "The vote is sixteen in favor, none opposed, two not voting. The proposal is approved and is the formal decision of the All-Clan Conclave."

Conversations broke out throughout the room, and although several hetmen signaled to be recognized to speak, Orosz plowed on.

"There are several more proposals that need to be voted on. I see that some hetmen wish to speak, but I will invoke my position as conclave chairman to push on to other proposals. Otherwise, we'll sit here and talk until the mountains erode into the sea."

The hetmen who wanted to speak subsided and accepted Orosz's ruling.

"Another decision is whether to attempt to negotiate with the Narthani. This is not to be a binding vote, because such an attempt is not widely supported, though we have no reason to prevent the effort. As an indication of the interest in such an effort, we will now vote."

The result was eight in favor, five opposed, and five not voting, because the hetmen either had no opinion or saw no harm in trying.

"Since Hetman Pewitt and Hetman Bevans seem most interested," said Orosz, "I ask them to plan how the negotiating gesture will be made to the Narthani and suggest the composition of the clan negotiating team, should the Narthani agree.

"Hetman Stent pointed out to me that we can't have different individual clans trying to negotiate with the Narthani. All of you should have seen Hetman Keelan's report about the dangers of the Narthani dividing the clans by bribes and promises, trying to set clans against one another's interests. Therefore, I propose that no single clan be allowed to negotiate with the Narthani, and all such contact represent all the clans. Are there any objections to this proposal?"

Hetman Nyvaks looked grim but remained silent. The other hetmen suspected that Nyvaks had been in contact with the Narthani, in an attempt to gain favorable status if the Narthani took control of the entire island.

With no verbal objections to the vote, Orosz called it out. There were sixteen in favor and two opposed, Nyvaks and Skouks. No clan was to have private contact with the Narthani, with the consequence of expulsion from the conclave.

The next issue leading to a vote was Yozef's warning that they needed a command structure to properly coordinate all the clans. The sticking point was that it would require any clan to follow directions given by someone who, in some cases, did not belong to their clan.

After the first five minutes, Yozef had no doubt how the vote would go. The only question was the vote total.

It ended up with seven approving, five against, and six abstaining. Culich later assured him the vote wasn't that bad, considering what had been proposed and the clans' staunch focus on independence. The six abstentions meant those clans didn't rule it out and could be convinced, just not yet. The five no votes meant that only three had to be convinced, if time and circumstance provided the opportunity.

Culich had expected the rejection of a unified command, as pushed by Yozef, but there were two follow-up issues for which Culich had garnered support from Orosz, Stent, and the other four clans of the Five-Clan Alliance.

Hetman Orosz recognized Culich to speak.

"Fellow hetmen," said Culich, "while we have agreed to attempt negotiation with the Narthani and to aggressively patrol the borders of provinces they control, prudence requires that we prepare if these efforts fail and the Narthani launch more attacks. I can tell you what the five clans of the Five-Clan Alliance intend.

"Our preparations have several aspects. The first is producing more weapons. When we responded to Moreland's call for help, our men brought with them whatever personal weapons they owned. This is fine for blades, but not for firearms, if future battles against the Narthani happen. One problem is we don't have enough muskets. My own people saw this during the Buldorian raid on St. Sidryn's abbey. Many defenders used crossbows or only blades, whereas if all had had firearms, the outcome would have been more assured. We need enough muskets and pistols to arm every member of every clan, with extra firearms for replacements and for when a fighter needs more than one.

"At the moment, only Clan Mittack produces firearms in the Tri-Clan Alliance and only in limited quantities. Hetman Mittack plans to increase production as fast as workers can be trained and tools and buildings are available. Since the main iron deposits are in Mittack, the other four clans will send workers to Mittack to help the expansion and gain experience, should production begin in the other four clans.

"One issue that became apparent is the need to produce a single type of musket and pistol, so that the men and the clans can share ammunition and to expedite replacement parts for damaged or nonfunctional firearms. Keelan was fortunate that most of our men's muskets took the same-size ball. We refer to the ball size as the *caliber*. I've talked with other clans, however, and some of you will apparently field forces using three, four, even six different calibers. This means that not only will you have to produce different ammunition, but the right ammunition will have to be distributed to the right men at the right time in the midst of fighting. You can imagine the confusion and dangers.

"Then there is the problem of sharing on the battlefield. A man runs out of ammunition. Next to him is a dead or wounded fellow clansman. If they used the same ammunition, the first man could use that of the fallen one. If not, the only choice would be to abandon his own musket and used the fallen man's. We all know we are more accurate and can fire faster with firearms we're familiar with.

"We also plan to form firearm repair teams to accompany any large numbers of fighting men. Any damaged or malfunctioning firearm will be repaired on the spot, but this is possible only if the firearms are essentially identical, so that spare parts can quickly be substituted."

Culich could see that most of the hetmen paid close attention and several nodded at his points, motions he took to mean they understood and approved. Even more approval became evident on the faces of advisors sitting behind the hetmen. The notable exceptions were the disinterested look on the face of Hetman Swavebroke and disdain from Hetman Nyvaks.

"What about existing firearms in clans such as mine, where there are no standard calibers?" asked Hetman Bevans.

"In your case," said Culich, "I would advise to rearm as fast as possible and use the same calibers that we use. While it might be possible to replace only the barrels, even the existing firearms are still useful, if only for defense purposes and not in the field, where movement and speed are important."

"Should Keelan determine the type of firearms Skouks uses?" asked Skouks, his brow furrowed and his tone indicating irritation.

"It's not just Keelan," Stent answered. "You heard Keelan say their five clans have agreed to this, and I'll announce that Stent will do the same."

"As will Orosz and Bultecki," said Hetman Orosz, with Hetman Bultecki nodding agreement.

"I think Farkesh will also adopt the same ideas," announced Feren Bakalacs, Hetman Farkesh, to the surprise of all. Farkesh was the largest producer of firearms and traded them to the other clans. The province also had the most abundant iron deposits.

"I've exchanged letters with Hetman Keelan. We've discussed this idea of Yozef Kolsko's. Even before Moreland City, I could see the logic to it, and our firearm foundries have nearly completed switching to the same calibers as the Five Clans."

Skouks scowled at Farkesh, obviously angry that his neighboring northern clan hadn't informed him of the intention, then turned to Culich.

"What if a clan doesn't want to make the change?" he challenged.

Culich appeared unperturbed but resolute. "That is, of course, the decision any clan can make. However, if the time comes when the Five Clans are asked to come to another clan's aid, we'll have to consider the likelihood of the aid being decisive. Not being able to share ammunition would be one factor in deciding to commit our men.

"There is another consideration. You know of the 'swivel guns' we used at Moreland City. They were effective, though limited because of their size. We hadn't been able to cast larger barrels such as the Narthani use, the ones called 12-pounders. I have just learned that in Keelan, we have successfully cast the first real cannon barrel."

A quarter of the faces in the room rotated briefly in the direction of Yozef, as did another quarter of the pairs of eyes. Most knew where the swivels had originated, having read reports or heard accounts of the Battle of Moreland City.

"But that's exciting news, Keelan!" exclaimed Orosz.

Several other hetmen voiced similar approval, before Culich raised his hand.

"This was only the first success. We're calling it a 6-pounder barrel. It will be mounted on a carriage to accompany our horsemen, the heavier 12-pounders being more suited to accompany men fighting on foot or in defensive positions.

"We believe this means casting 12-pounder barrels will also succeed. All our barrel casting has, until now, been in a foundry in Abersford, a small town in southwestern Keelan. We are building a larger foundry in Caernford and are working with Mittack to build another big foundry there, because Mittack

Province has plentiful deposits of copper and tin necessary to produce the bronze for the barrels. We have also begun talking with Bultecki about the same, and, after hearing the news from Hetman Farkesh about adopting the same firearm standards as we are doing, I'm sure we could help Farkesh establish cannon foundries."

"What about Skouks?" asked Margol Skouks. "We also have copper and tin and need to make cannon."

"Naturally, we will want to help any clan," said Culich, his tone full of insouciance. "However, with so much to do, we have to first help the clans working closest with us in all facets of preparing for future Narthani attacks. We will share cannon with cooperating clans as soon as production allows."

Hetman Skouks's face remained expressionless, and he said nothing more. The inference was clear—whoever doesn't cooperate with issues such as standardizing firearm calibers can expect to be the lowest priority in receiving technological information on cannon casting.

By the other hetmen's expressions and side-conferring with aides, their responses varied. Some smirked at Skouks's put-down, while others felt mollified at the prospect of Keelan sharing.

"In addition to weapons production," said Culich, moving on, "we plan to escalate food storage, in case harvests are interrupted. We're doing this using deep, cold caves to store grain, cured meats, and hard cheeses. We're also enlarging the size of cattle and horse herds as fast as we can and making plans to pool the animals and drive them to inland sites, where we can better protect them. Increasing the number of mature animals takes time, but we're making a start on it. We're even working to expand the number and capabilities of the mobile hospitals, such as we used at Moreland City. They saved many lives and allowed faster recovery of many more wounded men than would have occurred had they not been near the battle. Every clan should do the same.

"Finally, we're trying to train all our fighting men to ride to a battle site and then, if the situation warrants, dismount and fight on foot, as some of our men did decisively at Moreland City. We call such men dragoons."

Eyes again flickered to Yozef, though fewer than before.

"The last thing I will mention is that in case the Narthani invade Keelan, we do not intend to defend Caernford but plan to have the people move to defendable areas, where mountains and rivers provide added protection. Caernford itself is too exposed, with no natural defenses. The city can be rebuilt, if necessary, but the people and their ability to resist are all that counts.

Other members of the Five Clans are considering similar plans.

"There you have it," asserted Culich. "You have already heard that the type of fighting that occurred at Moreland City was different from anything the clans experienced in the past—large numbers of men, combining horses, cannon, and men on foot. This type of fighting—*war*, as Yozef Kolsko defines it—is known on the mainland continents, and the nations there are experienced in ways we are not. Ser Kolsko has read many writings on such methods, and he has written a brief summary of some of the lessons learned by other realms. Copies of his summary are available to all interested clans, and Ser Kolsko cautions me that these general principles still require men of reason and controlled temperament to implement."

Culich had told Yozef the previous day that he didn't think it was time to share the summary with all of the clans. Obviously, he had changed his mind. Yozef hoped the clans would read the principles and think deeply about them, while he knew some hetmen would be oblivious to their meaning and application. Still, *some* understanding was better than complete naiveté.

"Hetman Orosz," said Culich, turning to the Orosz hetman and conclave moderator, "that's the summary of the plans of the Five Clans."

Orosz rose and faced the other hetmen. "Are there any questions for Hetman Keelan?"

There were, and the next hour and a half consisted of a rapid-fire interrogation of the details of Culich's summary. When the questions petered out, Orosz raised a final issue.

"Hetmen, we have agreed to heavy patrols of the Eywell and Selfcell borders. However, this is the decision of the entire conclave and not just the three clans with those borders, Stent, Moreland, and Keelan. It is only fair that the other clans provide men to participate in the patrols. I propose that we consider that each clan provides two hundred men on a constant basis for these patrols. I suggest that those two hundred be rotated by each clan, so that no man spends too much time away from his home and work, perhaps three weeks. Because of the travel problem, Seaborn could be excused, but we can discuss this with Hetman Seaborn."

Orosz neglected to mention that the idea had been plotted with Culich, Stent, and Yozef. Besides the true argument of fairness to the bordering clans, it kept the other clans actively involved in resisting the Narthani and provided opportunities for men from different clans to gain experience working together.

Another hour of discussion passed with a few heated moments; then Orosz called a vote, which was approved by sixteen to two. Each clan, including the two nay voting clans, Nyvaks and Skouks, was obliged to provide two hundred men for the patrols.

The sun had set and its last light still competed with the stars, when the conclave adjourned and all ensuing discussions between and among individuals and groups finally ended. Yozef had mainly listened, until the Keelan delegation remained alone, and Culich turned to him.

"What do you think, Yozef? This is your first experience with a conclave."

"I'm sorry, Culich, but even though I didn't know what to expect, I'm discouraged by the lack of progress with the clans agreeing to *really* unite, instead of this piecemeal approach."

Culich laughed, Luwis grunted, and Denes covered a grin.

"Yozef, this was the most productive conclave I have ever attended among the thirty or more I've gone to, either accompanying my father or as hetman myself."

Yozef looked at his father-in-law incredulously.

"My God! What must the others have been like?"

Culich slapped him on the back. "I'm afraid that sitting in conclaves and maintaining composure is a hetman duty that my father didn't fully explain to me, even though I saw him do it so many times."

"Will there be time to bring the others around?" Yozef asked, worried. "A famous general in the histories once said to a subordinate '*Ask me for anything but time.*' And another time, he said, '*Space can be recovered, but time is lost forever.*'"

"True," said Culich. "Being a leader also means knowing what is possible and doing the best you can with what you have, not thinking too much about what you don't have."

Yozef's respect for Culich's patience rose several notches, but his opinion of the conclave's outcome remained dubious, as they ate an evening meal and returned to their rooms. They would be up and on the road back to Caernford well before the first light.

CHAPTER 17

RETURNING TO CAERNFORD

They retraced their route to Orosz City, south through the high, dry plain of central Orosz Province, until they reached the spot where the road turned southwest through low hills to descend toward Moreland City. There, Yozef's carriage, along with Carnigan, Balwis, and ten outriders, split from the main party and headed into Hewell Province. The conclave's outcome or, to his persistent nagging thoughts, lack of outcomes remained ever present in Yozef's thoughts, but he had a purpose to the side excursion. Looking for Flagorn eggs. Willwin Wallington had told Yozef of a man-sized, egg-shaped object that protruded from solid rock on the western slope of Mt. Erbowyn, the highest peak in western Hewell.

Yozef had mulled over what Willwin said, then brought up the topic of the eggs on a subsequent visit to the abbey.

* * *

"I had heard about them since I was a child," said Willwin. "They're called Flagorn eggs after a child's tale from the northern clans. You know, those clans descended from the first people to come to Caedellium? Most of the rest of us are from a second immigration about a hundred years later. The legend deals with ancient gods that are no longer believed in, but it talks of strange and fearsome creatures that once lived on Caedellium and laid giant eggs."

Yep, dragons! Yozef wanted to blurt out but suppressed the impulse.

"Now, of course, we know such creatures are only legends, and the Flagorn eggs are simply a strange kind of rock or probably a crystal of some kind," Willwin continued. "All that's known about them is the surface is smooth and doesn't allow dust to settle on it. Someone once told me that efforts to cut them or hack them into smaller pieces always fail, so they're tremendously hard."

Further questions to Willwin provided no additional information. When Yozef said he planned to see the egg for himself, he got a fair description of the egg's location from Willwin, and the scholastic suggested asking locals to guide him on the final part of the journey. Yozef's casual queries about other locations turned up supposed eggs in Mittack, Vandinke, and Nyvaks provinces, though not exact locations.

* * *

Thus, when the trip to Orosz City for the conclave arose, Yozef decided to see one of the Flagorn eggs for himself. He would normally have considered this a waste of time, following up on a silly myth, if it hadn't been for the presumed circuit board Willwin had shown him. After that, Yozef was loath to discount any unusual report.

When he informed Culich that he would take a side trip on their return, the hetman had a quizzical expression but didn't argue. Yozef figured the hetman subscribed to the view of so many others that if Yozef thought something worth doing, you might as well concede the importance or score it as another of his idiosyncrasies.

The small Keelan caravan became two smaller parties, with Yozef's entourage turning onto a smaller road heading south-southeast into Hewell.

The plain gave way to dry, bare hills, which gradually changed to those forested by Anyar trees with no sign of terrestrial species. Hills became steeper and approached what Yozef considered mountains, through which the road wound within valleys and passes. It took a day and a half to reach the village described by Willwin. The villagers, though surprised to see a Keelan party, acted friendly, if bemused, to learn of the purpose of the Keelanders' arrival.

"You want to see what!?" exclaimed one elderly Hewell man, in a tone Yozef could imagine him using on a child. "That's a good day's hike up into the mountain from here. There's nothing there but that odd rock. I can just describe it to you and save you the trip."

Yozef could see Balwis, standing behind the man, roll his eyes, whether at the man's remark or in embarrassment at being part of Yozef's fool's errand.

"Thank you, Ser, for the offer, but since we've come all this way, I want to see for myself."

"Up to you," said the man. "I'm not the one to show you the way, though.

I'll admit I went there once when I was younger, but nothing up there was worth the trip, and I never went again." The man looked around. "See the older boy over there by the water trough? I think he's been up there recently and can guide you. You'll need to pay him some coin for the lost time working on his family's farm."

Yozef thanked the man, who walked away, shaking his head. Yozef found the youth of about fifteen more than willing to show strangers the way to the province's one and only, as far as anyone knew, Flagorn egg. Whether his eagerness was due to associating with the foreign party, being paid, or escaping a day or two of farm work, Yozef couldn't tell.

The next morning, the Keelanders, minus five escorts who were left to watch the carriage and horses, followed the youth east up the western slopes of Mt. Erbowyn, a craggy, imposing peak Yozef estimated at 8,000 feet. Fortunately, the egg's resting place was only at about the 6,500-foot level, 4,000 feet above the village. Still, they endured a strenuous seven-hour walk up a tenuous trail that crossed scree slopes and boulder fields.

The sun had risen past midday when it disappeared, as they moved into a cloud hovering around the mountain's higher elevations. Another half hour and the guide stopped at a bare rock face on a twenty-degree incline and pointed.

"There. You can see it from here."

Fifty yards away, a bluish-gray ovoid stuck up from an otherwise smooth surface. Carnigan insisted on tying a rope to a boulder off the slope, with each man connected to the rope by a six-foot section of rope. Otherwise, one slip and he might not be able to recover before reaching the edge of the slope, where it dropped into an abyss. They walked up to the ovoid, careful of their footing and small pieces of rock that acted like ball-bearings.

Yozef's first glimpse from the side of the slope sent a shiver along his spine, and the hairs on his arms stood up. This was no natural rock formation. Any lingering doubt vanished before they reached the object. As Willwin said, it was egg-shaped, with the narrow end of the egg pointed up and the lower one-third either *inside* the rock or sitting *on* the rock.

Yozef chipped at the bottom edge with a hammer he'd asked the guide to bring, exposing another inch of the object below the rock surface. It extended into the rock, and Yozef had no doubt that if they excavated completely, they would find it encased by rock millions of years old.

This was set into the rock after drilling out a cavity, he thought. He ran his hand over a surface as smooth as if covered with oil. He reached into his pocket for dirt he'd picked up before leaving the village. He took out a small handful and let it fall onto the top of the object. It ran down the sides of the egg as if it were water, leaving no trace, no speck of dust. Just as he'd been told, nothing could rest on the object.

He tapped it with the hammer. There was no ring, clunk, or anything he'd expect from striking an object as solid as this one appeared, only a faint thud, and the hammer almost felt as if it had struck a hard rubber surface.

Yozef didn't doubt that this technological artifact was far more advanced than anything that could have originated on this planet. He guessed it was far more advanced than anything that relied on Earth's level of technology.

"Holy shit," he uttered in English. "The Watchers or whoever brought plants and animals here from Earth? And what is it? You don't just put something like this here for no reason. A communication relay? An observation device? Observing what? There's nothing special to see around here, except other mountains and clouds."

He looked up. "Maybe it's not looking down, but up. Watching for something in the sky or orbiting or a communication device aimed at who knows where?"

"What is it, Yozef?" said a voice. He looked away from the egg.

Balwis stared at him. "Do you know what this is? It's more than just a rock, isn't it?"

"Yes," he said, "more than a rock, though I can't tell exactly what it is." He wanted to sit and simply stare at the object, letting his mind sort through the jumble of thoughts that ran through it. But he couldn't sit. Not on this slope. Not with the other men watching him closely, probably wondering what Yozef Kolsko made of this strange rock, if it *was* a rock.

Christ, I wish I had a camera. Better yet, I wish I could take this back to Caernford and have time and tools to make a better examination, although, if I had to bet, I expect I'd learn nothing more than what I see right now.

He stood next to the egg for half an hour, his hands alternately running over the surface of the egg and down his pant legs, as he contemplated the object and its meaning.

Once again, a contradiction to Harlie's assertion that the Watchers had no direct contact, unless this and the circuit board are from different aliens. More is going on here than I can guess at, and I wonder if even the Watchers are befuddled, more than Harlie indicated, by Anyar and the other planets and the transplanted humans.

"Sers," said their guide. "The sun lowers. We can make it back down the mountain before dark, if we hurry. Otherwise, we'll have to stay on the middle slope for the night. It's too dangerous to try to get down at night."

Yozef looked around. The seven other men stood around him and the object, their expressions varied: confusion, probably at why he found the object so enthralling; unease at being near something so unearthly, or in this case, un-Anyarian; wonder at whether Yozef knew what the object was and how; or a touch of fear, though they couldn't have expressed why.

They'd have to go. Other eggs existed elsewhere on Caedellium. He would find one that wasn't located in such an inaccessible place, dig it out, and take it to his shops. He doubted that he'd learn anything, but he would do it, just in case. And who knew? Maybe the owners would show up. Of course, maybe that was not such a good idea.

He stepped back, looked around, and then up.

Was it an observation device and someone or something was looking and recording him right now? Was it a relic, like the circuit board? Something left from an unknown age?

Questions. I don't need questions, especially ones for which I'll never find the answers.

"All right," he said. "We've seen it, and it's certainly interesting, but we need to get down before dark. We'll spend the night in the village, then push on hard toward Caernford. There's a lot to be done, and we've diverted enough for this trip."

As they turned to re-cross the rock face, he caught the eyes of Carnigan and Balwis. He didn't doubt neither believed that he'd revealed all he knew of the egg. Carnigan's expression accepted his friend's mysterious way, but Balwis's appeared uncertain, as if he wondered whether he should be annoyed at Yozef for not telling all he knew or glad he didn't know more and have to deal with what he'd learned.

They slept that night in an abandoned house at the edge of the village. The villagers were polite enough, though unimpressed by the Keelan visitors and with no idea who Yozef Kolsko was. Balwis was about to make the connection for them between Yozef and kerosene, soap, and kotex. Yozef dissuaded him with a shake of the head and a whisper, "It's nice to be someplace where nobody knows my name."

The next morning, they headed south on the same road, then turned due west at midday on a track that hardly qualified as a road but provided the shortest distance and time to get back to Caernford. The carriage wasn't built for the depth of the ruts and the uneven surface, and by the second hour they walked, horsemen and carriage passengers alike, more than they rode.

When the landscape changed and the road improved, they once again rode in the carriage, with Carnigan driving and Yozef and Balwis on top. Balwis had tied his horse to the rear of the carriage, so he could converse more easily. As they exited a stand of trees, they came upon a small herd of balmoths browsing a hundred yards away on the edge of a clearing.

"Good lord!" said Yozef, still uttering his surprises in English, then switching to Caedelli. "Look at the size of those things!"

The largest balmoth would look down on a basketball hoop ten-feet off the ground and might even be able to defecate into the net. Yozef didn't try to estimate an exact weight, except to think in elephant equivalents, maybe three units' worth?

He had heard they were once more common but now were restricted to the foothills near the border of Keelan and Hewell provinces, probably because the area wasn't heavily populated or on a commonly traveled route.

Although he had seen drawings and paintings of the huge herbivores, observing them live provided one more disorienting experience since he'd come to Anyar.

Yozef had had the usual young boy's obsession with dinosaurs, but in his case, the interest extended to extinct mammals. The balmoth was either a direct descendent of the Paraceratheriums of Earth, extinct for 25 million years, or the product of amazing parallel evolution. To be the former would contradict his estimate that the animals, including the humans, and the plants had been transplanted to Anyar around five thousand years ago. Yet the similarity was so striking, he believed the balmoth's ancestors had come from Earth. Had there been multiple transplantations over millions of years? He needed to look closer at what he had assumed were Anyarian species, to see whether they might possibly be long-ago descendants from Earth or truly products of a different evolutionary history. He already knew the biochemistries of Earth and Anyar were similar, but had this happened because they had the same origin or because of inherent biochemical limitations required to evolve life? One more mystery, as if he didn't already have enough to solve.

They watched for twenty minutes until the animals slowly browsed into the forest. As the last one turned to look at the interlopers, Yozef faced the other men.

"Well, Carnigan, I think we've finally found a mount for you that wouldn't suffer back problems."

Balwis broke into a braying laugh, and the escorts who'd heard snickered until Carnigan scowled at them. He bestowed the same look on Yozef, who ignored it, confident that the big man's look was far worse than his bite.

After two days of slow travel, they left the mountains behind and reached the river valley that ran through the heart of Keelan. They spent a night in the town of Amurth in northern Keelan, reveling in hot baths, food and ale, and individual beds at an inn.

One more day to reach Caernford. Yozef spent the day inside the carriage, talking to the others only at stops. It was a day of reflection. Of the conclave, of Flagorn eggs, of Watchers, of the balmoths. Of who he was.

He had felt dispirited after the conclave and had found no solace in Culich's assertion that the meeting had gone well. Hours of reflection led him to wonder if part of his reaction had been ego. He had stood before the hetmen and the advisors, given what he believed was a speech that should have moved them more, and ended up wondering whether it had had any effect. What had he any reason to expect? Was he becoming too full of himself? The journey from naked stranger to wealthy entrepreneur, military advisor, and husband of a remarkable woman had been dizzying, no matter how he viewed it. The rumors of his being a Septarsh had at first annoyed, then dismayed him. But over time, had he begun to accept the adulation, even be pleased? If so, what was wrong with him? Part of him wanted to quash the rumors; another wondered whether he shouldn't take advantage. Maybe the hetmen would have listened more if he'd played up the Septarsh aspect. Or maybe they would have scoffed and dismissed his words. What if . . . ?

By the time the first buildings of Caernford came into view, he knew three things. One, he felt glad to be home and to see Maera again. Two, whatever he'd thought he would achieve at Orosz City, he had done his best. And three, no matter his disappointment at the conclave, he still had more to do than he could possibly accomplish, and he had to give it his strongest effort.

CHAPTER 18

WEAPONS REDUX

Deciding on the Caernford move, making the move, writing what he could remember about military principles, and attending the conclave were more than enough for Yozef. All of these activities had to compete for his time with prodding his shops and workers for ideas and products to help against the Narthani. He had started working on some of the newer ideas even before Moreland City, and now they'd been moved to Caernford. With Pedr Kennrick helping with organization and supplies, Yozef revived several projects, including earlier ideas he had shelved for lack of workers or space or technical issues he hadn't had time to address.

The next month consisted of a seemingly endless succession of meetings: preparations involving the entire clan, meetings with Yozef's workers moving to Caernford from Abersford, meetings to orient new workers, meetings to start new projects, meetings to revise dormant projects, and, to his disgust, meetings with Maera and Denes to schedule meetings.

To Yozef's thinking, too many meetings were of the "keeping in touch" variety: maintaining contact with individuals and groups. Those meetings he endured, chafing to move on to what he considered productive topics, particularly weapons development and logistical issues.

Napalm

Yozef gathered several workers from the Caernford petroleum distilling plant still under construction and the soap makers from the Caernford franchise already operating at the new industrial park. He stood beside a chalkboard covering the front wall of his temporary park office. Denes and Balwis hung out near the back wall, along with two men from the gunpowder plant.

"I have a new project that requires you to work together. While I will leave it up to the foremen to choose the team to carry out this project, let me emphasize that it is not a side project, but something that needs to be accomplished as quickly as possible. If more workers are needed or more resources, see me, and we'll discuss how to proceed.

"This is to make a weapon to use against the Narthani. It's called *napalm*, and you can think of it as a version of pouring burning oil on enemy troops. Most of you are familiar with stories of using hot oil to pour on an enemy trying to break into fortresses and, in some cases, setting the oil on fire."

Yozef paused and looked around at his audience. Several men nodded, others shook their heads.

"If you haven't heard of it, take my word it's an effective way to discourage attackers. Napalm is a version of that tactic. You'll get written notes about what I'll describe, and those of you who can write have quill and paper to take your own notes.

"Napalm is composed of different components such as oils, acids, and kerosene. You'll need to experiment with various ingredients. The objective is to produce a semi-solid, viscous material that can be ignited. In the simplest use, a container of napalm could rest on the ground or be thrown at the enemy by catapult. The container would also be designed with a small explosive device that will detonate at the right time. The detonation will ignite the napalm and spread it over a wide area. You can imagine the effect of such a container exploding in or over a Narthani infantry block. Another ingredient to research is something that can be added to the mixture to make it sticky, so that when it lands on clothing or skin, it is difficult or even impossible to brush off or remove."

Yozef paused for a moment. "Let's be clear. The objective is to burn the enemy so badly that they die or are incapacitated."

Several of the men looked disturbed. One man from the soap factory blurted, "This sounds like an abomination! Deliberately burning people! I don't believe the *Word* would approve of this."

"It *is* a terrible weapon," Yozef agreed. "You and all the people are fighting for more than just your lives. You are fighting for the very existence of the Caedellium people."

"I'm willing to fight and die if necessary to protect my family and clan," another man spoke up, "but this sounds like something the Evil One would think of. What do the theophists think?"

Yozef sighed. "I have discussed this with the Abbot Walkot of St. Tomo's and Abbot Beynom of St. Sidryn's. They hate the very idea, as do I. But they reluctantly recognize the necessity of using every weapon at our disposal against the Narthani."

Denes surprised Yozef when his voice rose over the general buzz. "Many of our men will see this as a dishonorable way to fight, even if it is against the Narthani."

"I can understand that feeling," said Yozef. "However, if we do not defeat the Narthani, you and any sons who fought them will likely be dead. Your other sons will be castrated and sent to Narthon as slaves and your women raped, killed, and many sent to Narthani brothels. What is the price of your honor? If you had to choose, which would it be . . . freedom from the Narthani or your feelings of honor?"

Several of the men who had previously seemed hesitant appeared to reluctantly see Yozef's points. The first man who had spoken simply stood and walked out.

"And you, Balwis, how do you feel about this weapon?" asked Yozef.

"Personally, I hope every Narthani burns in hell for eternity, and if I can help them on their way, then I have no problem."

Most of the other men vocally agreed. Thus ended the discussion on the ethics of burning the Narthani.

Denes, however, had another question. "Yozef, is this *really* more efficient than gunpowder? If the fuse system can be improved, we could throw containers of gunpowder to explode among the Narthani. We did something like this with the crossbow grenades at Moreland City. Why bother with this napalm?"

"Good question, Denes. I see four major advantages of the napalm. One is that the effect lasts longer than gunpowder, which explodes and is finished. Napalm burns for many seconds up to perhaps a minute, especially the larger glops. Second is that napalm can set other things on fire—grass, shrubs, and wagons, for example. We could also lay petrol or another oil on the battlefield and let the napalm ignite it. Third is that when napalm hits a man, he is at least initially still alive and will forget everything else in trying to put out the fire. Enemy formations will disintegrate with such men running or rolling around. Even the men not touched by the napalm will try to stay away from those hit or will try to help put out the fires, either way further breaking up the formation. And finally, the psychological effect of the napalm. Humans have an instinctive dread of burning, and the napalm will affect the morale of the enemy. Anything to increase the Narthani soldiers' fear and erode the certainty of their invincibility will help us."

Denes stroked his beard and nodded through Yozef's points.

Satisfied that he now had both their attention and their commitment, Yozef continued with what little he knew about napalm.

"One formula I remember used one or two parts each of plant oil, naphthenic acid, and oleic acid. Those of you working with petroleum distillation are familiar with naphthenic acid. Other possible substitutes are olive oil, any other oil, and palmitic acids. When they're mixed, you get a powder. This is then mixed with kerosene to form a slush."

Yozef went on to describe the components and where local sources might be found.

"Depending on the form of the weapon, the final napalm might need to be thicker. This is something you'll have to work out. Try to find something to make it thicker and stickier, while still allowing ignition, which you will also have to work out. For example, we might want to use napalm containers placed on the ground to be exploded and ignited on command as Narthani troops come near. We will also need an ignition system for when we catapult containers at the Narthani to either go off on contact or after a specified time. The last possibility might be the most difficult, but you can imagine the effect of a large container of napalm showering flames on a Narthani infantry or cavalry charge."

Yozef called to the front a portly middle-aged man who had been sitting on one side of the room.

"Raywin will be in charge of the project. He has shown an admirably devious mind in coming up with novel solutions to technical problems and has worked on improving our petrol distillation equipment and procedures. He will coordinate and, I'm sure, come up with some good ideas, but this will require a group effort with all your skills and experiences. To give you some added incentives to work hard, you should assume that if napalm is going to be useful against the Narthani, you need to have it ready in no more than three months."

Yozef ignored the groans, the objections, and the rolling of eyes. "You men were chosen both for your known abilities and your readiness to try new approaches. Where I came from, it was commonly said that men such as yourselves will always say the task assigned is impossible in the time allowed

. . . only to get it done in half the time."

This brought some grins and a few laughs.

"However, we'll be satisfied if you succeed within three months."

Foundry

The new foundry in Caernford was under construction before Yozef moved from Abersford. Progress accelerated with the decision to move and ratcheted up several more notches after the conclave.

Most encouraging was progress with casting cannon barrels. Razil Gurbuz, a Narthani artilleryman, had been taken prisoner at the Battle of Moreland City. Although a career soldier, he descended from a relatively recently conquered people, and he claimed no loyalty to the Narthon Empire. Whatever his allegiance, he freely shared his knowledge of cannon casting. While Yozef had attended the conclave in Orosz City, Maera sent the cryptic semaphore message that Yawnfol Nyfork, foreman of the Abersford foundry, had reported successful casting of a 6-pounder barrel.

Before the conclave, Yozef had hoped the latest trip to Abersford would be the last one for a while, but he needed to see the successful cannon for himself. To his consternation, two sixdays passed since the conclave before Yozef could free two days to get to Abersford to see the new cannon. When the time window finally appeared, Yozef, Balwis, Carnigan, and Denes were off to Abersford in a carriage. Even Balwis deigned to forego traveling by horse, though his reason was that his horse needed a rest, and he hadn't found a suitable second mount.

They arrived in Abersford an hour before sunset. Yawnfol had been alerted to their arrival and had arranged a demonstration a mile north of Abersford at an open field backed by a forty-foot rock outcropping—their test range for anything needing to be far enough from Abersford to avoid blowing up or immolating unsuspecting citizens and buildings—a precaution justified by more mishaps than Yozef was comfortable with.

"Yozef!" exclaimed Yawnfol, running up to the carriage. It stopped thirty yards behind two cannon carriages and a two-foot by two-foot block of wood six feet long. The cannons Yozef recognized as 6-pounders, but as gratified as he felt by their existence, it was the block that caught his attention. It sat on the ground, lengthwise downrange, and fastened by metal bands to the block was a larger-diameter cannon barrel.

Yawnfol saw where Yozef's attention landed. "Yes, yes! A 12-pounder, Yozef! It just finished cooling yesterday, and we rushed to get it on a test block. We wanted to surprise you."

"So you haven't test-fired yet?"

"No," said Yawnfol. "I thought you might want to see the first test-firings."

"Yeah," said Carnigan, "and be the first to get blown up, if the barrel splits like all the others we saw tested."

Yawnfol's offended expression was comical or would have been, if Carnigan's comment hadn't had a kernel of truth to it.

"I'm sure we'll be safe enough behind the barriers," said Yozef, placating the young foreman and indicating the six-foot earthen berm fifty yards from the cannon's positions. "Go ahead, Yawnfol, give us the show."

"I'll let Razil fire them off," said Yawnfol. "None of this would be possible without him."

"Works for me," muttered Balwis. "If anything goes wrong, it's one less Narthani."

Yozef shushed him. "Remember, he's *our* Narthani for now. Think of how many of them you might get a chance to kill if these cannon work."

Given a positive image to dwell on, Balwis appeared almost cheerful—for him.

Carnigan took the carriage another hundred yards away and tied the horses to a tree. The other three travelers, Yawnfol, and the rest of the foundry workers moved behind the berm, leaving the grizzled Narthani artilleryman to do the honors.

Whatever his ultimate loyalties, Yozef had to grant that Razil appeared confident. Or perhaps indifferent. He stood next to the rightmost 6-pounder, holding a two-foot-long, quarter-inch-thick rod of wood from an Anyar tree known for slow burning. Yozef could see the end glowing red and giving off tendrils of smoke. The "firing rod" was the device used to fire the swivel barrels. The rod, once an end was lit, would smolder for hours without extinguishing under any but the hardest rain.

Once the other men were safe, with only their heads from nose up peering over the berm, Razil touched the vent on the 6-pounders with the glowing end of the firing rod. With a roar, smoke gushed from the open end of the barrel and the carriage recoiled several inches, despite an anchoring spike through a hole in the carriage trail and driven into the ground.

From his position behind and to the left of the cannon, Yozef caught a glimpse of "something" flying downrange, then impacting the rock face, sending fragments exploding outward. He looked back at the 6-pounder. The barrel appeared unaffected.

Razil waited a few moments, then fired the second 6-pounder with the same result. With only a glance at the observers, he moved to the 12-pounder barrel fastened to the wooden block and touched the vent. The roar was louder, the cloud of smoke larger, and this time Yozef felt certain his eyes picked up the cannon ball before it struck the rock face.

The foundry workers cheered, rushed out to Razil, and mobbed him. Razil's grin was the first emotion Yozef had seen from the man.

"They seem to get along with the Narthani," said Denes. "If he's willing to help us make working cannon, then I doubt we have to worry about him as a potential spy or anything."

Yozef ignored Denes's comment, along with others offered by Balwis and Carnigan. His mind ran through implications, as he strode quickly to the knot of men.

"Yawnfol, you say you test-fired the first 6-pounder barrel ten times?"

"More. The first one Razil lit off has now been fired twenty-six times. This is only the fourth firing for the second 6-pounder."

Yozef rubbed his palms together. "Let's have the men fire the second 6-pounder six more times and the 12-pounder nine times. I want to see them all for myself before we make more plans."

The foundry workers dove into the request with a vengeance. Yozef had to stop them several times during the next firings to remind them to get back to the berm. By the fourth time, he gave up and let them stay with the cannon and reload as fast as they could. For the last two firings, Denes and Balwis joined in and took turns swabbing out barrels between shots and ramming home charges and shot.

On the last firing, Yozef looked at Carnigan. "You want to have a try?"

Rolling his eyes, Carnigan said, "Why the fuck would I want to do that?"

Fifteen minutes later, Yozef, Denes, and Yawnfol met back at the foundry.

"Very impressive, Yawnfol," said Yozef. "You and the men can be proud of what you've accomplished."

The foreman beamed.

"Now that means there's more work for you all. Your message said you were casting five more 6-pounder barrels. Is that right, and did you do more than that?"

Yawnfol shook his head. "Only those six so far, Yozef. We didn't want to do more without your approval."

"No problem, Yawnfol," said Yozef, not wanting the man to think he'd made a mistake. "Now we need to ramp up production. I definitely need you and Razil in Caernford as soon as possible. When's the fastest you can be ready to move?"

"Uh . . . fastest? It'll take a couple more days to finish packing what we're taking with us. I've been turning over operating the foundry to Gilkor the last sixday, and we've trained replacements for the three men coming with us. I think we can all be ready and wagons loaded, ready to leave three mornings from now."

"Good, good. I'll expect you in Caernford by the coming Godsday. I think the Caernford foundry can be up and operating in another sixday after that. I want it to be as fast as possible. How many of the 6-pounder barrels have been mated to carriages?"

"All six," said Yawnfol, "although we haven't test-fired four of them."

"Okay, get the men to do that testing. All 6-pounders that pass ten test-firings are to be sent to Caernford immediately. Same with the one 12-pounder. Get it on a carriage and send it with the 6-pounders, along with a supply of shot. We'll need to start training as soon as possible. We'll let the foundry here focus only on 6-pounders. The Caernford foundry will cast all future 12-pounders and more 6-pounders." Yozef turned to Denes and asked, "What do you think?"

"I think we're going to kill a lot of Narthani. I also think I'm going to prefer the 12-pounders, especially where we might have to fight dismounted, like we did at Moreland City."

"It's the 6-pounders for me," said Balwis. "They should be able to keep up with horsemen better than the heavier cannon. We need to see exactly how fast they can travel."

Denes nodded. "I agree, Balwis. When we get back to Caernford, I'll ask you to take a couple of the 6-pounders and a dragoon platoon and see how fast they can move together, set up the guns, then move out again. I'll take the other 6-pounders and the one 12-pounder and work on training more crews."

Yozef let the two men discuss the details, both obviously enthused by their new toys.

While they planned, he took Yawnfol aside. "I spoke with you before about mortars. Once we have the Caernford foundry working, I want to revisit casting a few mortars. I don't know yet how we'd use them, but I want to get started, as least with some experimenting."

He knew mortars had been used as early as the fifteenth century on Earth, almost entirely in siege situations. More mobile mortars hadn't been developed until the seventeenth and eighteenth centuries, and only in World War I did they have widespread use. It had been one of many instances where the knowledge of a weapon had to wait for technical developments to be practical for large-scale use. Mortars would be most useful only when they had contact fuses that worked with fired shells. Otherwise, the only use Yozef could see for mortars would be as siege weapons throwing either stone or iron balls, or charges lit by hand or by the gunpowder flash sweeping around the projectile to light a fuse. Such bulky mortars would be useless in open field battles and would be a bitch to move quickly.

When he finished with Yawnfol, Yozef stood among the 6-pounders. *I know I should be pleased,* he thought. *The men have done a great job, and we're on our way to fixing the cannon shortage problem. But, Christ! With one tank or even a real machine gun, I could end the Narthani threat!*

A moment's reflection dashed those wishes, because even if he had either weapon, the tank would need fuel, ammunition, and maintenance, and the machine gun would eat through ammunition that would have to be made by hand, shell by shell.

He also reviewed in his mind the latest weapons development. Although the cannon were critical for offensive operations, napalm would be restricted to defense, as would the mortars, once they figured out the fusing problem. Mobile mortars with exploding shells were likely a year or more away, assuming they had the time and the resources.

He constantly reminded himself not to get too ambitious and that it was better to have many inferior weapons than one not yet fully deployable. He wished they had time to develop rifled muskets, but the few that existed on the island were imported, and even the Narthani soldiers didn't have them. Smooth-bore muskets were just so much more efficient to produce, and the longer time it took to load a rifled musket argued further against them.

Minie balls were the answer to the latter issue, but they hadn't been developed for another hundred years or more on Earth from where Anyar existed at this moment. The Caedelli would have to develop the crafts to make them, even if rifled muskets were an option.

He remembered a famous short story by Arthur Clarke, one of the great science fiction writers. "Superiority" was set in the far future, when two divisions of humanity fight a war. One side has slightly superior weapons and more of them, but its leaders are constantly looking for better weapons, instead of using what they have on the way to an inevitable victory. The other side stays with the weapons it has and slowly turns the war in its favor. The story, not one of Clarke's better ones, had been required reading in one university engineering major, the lesson being to use the technology you had, if it was good enough to do the job *now*.

Then there were the United States' jets and tanks in World War II on Earth. America had developed jets and better tanks in time to produce them for the war but had eschewed their production in favor of existing inferior planes and tanks. The reasoning was to swamp the enemy with what they had, instead of diverting resources.

Yozef reminded himself of these lessons every time he felt tempted by ideas for new weapons.

CHAPTER 19

READINESS

Weapons weren't the only part of the Keelan clan's preparations for whatever came next with the Narthani. Weapons required trained men to use those weapons effectively. The men needed logistics to fight, as did the rest of the Keelan populace, if the Narthani interrupted food production and if the people fled to secure locations farther inland.

In addition, Yozef believed that for the clans to create the most effective fighting force, they needed to learn and accept fighting together with men of different clans, which included taking orders from someone not of their own clan.

Training as Dragoons

Even if Yozef's ideas seemed strange to Denes, once he understood, he quickly moved on to implementation. Yozef often wondered whether Denes was a natural military commander. After Moreland City, no one needed further convincing of the futility of pure cavalry against cannon and massed infantry. Though the Caedelli might ride to battle on horseback, all of them needed to learn to fight afoot, if necessary, once they found the enemy. On Earth, the early dragoons had been infantry trained well enough to stay on a horse and be able to ride to the battlefield before dismounting and fighting on foot. Over time, the definition and function had changed in Earth history, but the basic concept remained relevant for Caedellium. In the clans' case, however, it would be more a matter of experienced horsemen learning to fight as infantry, rather than the other way around, as on Earth.

Dragoons had two inherent disadvantages. Losses of horses needed to be kept to a minimum to maintain mobility, meaning the horses had to be kept well back from the fighting and guarded from any flanking attacks that might drive them off. Second, someone had to do the holding and the guarding. Typically, one man in four held the horses, while the other three men fought. Thus, a hundred-man company would have only seventy-five men to serve as infantry facing an enemy. Where rapid changes in positions were not anticipated, fewer men could hold the horses.

To counter the disadvantages, a Caedelli dragoon often equaled an enemy cavalryman and could outmaneuver any pure infantry. Consistent with the necessity to move quickly, Yozef pushed producing enough light artillery to accompany the dragoons.

Culich had ordered all Keelan fighting men trained to operate in dual roles: their traditional role as cavalry and as infantry that rode to the battle site. Denes had begun with men at Abersford, then more at Clengoth and Caernford. These men then served as cadre for training throughout Keelan Province. Eventually, all Keelan fighters would be so trained, and Denes found himself, to his consternation, spending more time in an administrative role overseeing training throughout Keelan and coordinating cadre training for other clans. Mittack, Gwillamer, Hewell, and Adris already had sent men, and now Stent and Orosz joined in, sending men for training as dragoons and using the new 6-pounders.

The training itself was not complex. Having no formal experience in infantry tactics and with only what Yozef could dredge out of his memory, Denes focused on simply teaching the men to go quickly from mounted to dismounted and back, coordinate with the 6-pounder artillery, and stay together as companies, platoons, and squads. As primitive as this infantry training was, it turned out to be a fortuitous foundation for unexpected opportunities that would occur.

You're Caedelli, Not a Clansman

As Culich had said to the other hetmen at the conclave, Keelan would intensify preparation for whatever came. Two actions consisted of increasing the training and making a massive effort to store food, in case war interrupted production for up to a year.

All three of Yozef's "shadows" contributed to the training. Balwis taught horsemanship, because his years of growing up on a horse ranch enabled him and a horse to seemingly blend into a single entity whenever he mounted, even with a horse he had never before touched. Most Caedelli men were already experienced riders, though not all, especially men raised and working within towns, and even the experienced riders had things to learn.

Wyfor Kales organized group lessons in blade fighting. Watching one session reminded Yozef of historical movies and the training sessions of gladiators or legionnaires. Wyfor perfectly filled the role of the experienced warrior screaming at novices.

Carnigan's role came into being one evening while he shared beers with Denes, Balwis, and Yozef at the Snarling Graeko 2 in Caernford. The second round of steins arrived at their table, when Yozef noticed that Denes appeared even more dour than usual. The man, loyal to the clan and personally fearless, though not reckless, had turned into an important leader. He only occasionally appeared at the pub and even on his good days did not make the cheeriest of drinking companions.

"What's up, Denes? You're not your usual ebullient self."

Denes cast a baleful eye at Yozef's quip, then sighed and slammed his stein on the table. "With so much to do, I'm spending far too much time with the mixed-clan men we're training."

Yozef proposed the idea that on some occasions, men from different clans would have to fight together and even serve under the orders of a leader not from their own clan. Culich endorsed the idea, and Luwis and Denes accepted the reasoning. The historical focus on clan independence and chauvinism toward clan membership would cause chaos during a battle. To counter these effects, a battalion-sized unit composed of men from all members of the Five-Clan Alliance had begun training outside Caernford. The hundred men from each clan made up platoon-sized units composed of all five clans. The intent was to create a cadre of leaders with experience in commanding mixed-clan fighters. These men would lead and train other such units.

"I take it things are not going well?" Yozef queried.

"They would be a disaster," said Denes between clenched teeth. "The men are supposed to take turns leading different-sized units. Instead, they spend most of the time arguing against orders, refusing orders, deliberately misinterpreting or delaying obeying orders, and fighting with different clans' members or sometimes with one of the men working that day as a unit leader. I and the others in charge of this fiasco scream at the men till we're hoarse. Sometimes they listen, sometimes they ignore us, and even if they seem to understand what we're doing, as soon as we turn our backs, it all starts again. I know the idea is sound, but I think we should give up the idea of mixed-clan units or operations."

Balwis sat smirking as he listened to Denes's complaint. "I watched a field exercise last sixday. If anything, Denes is too kind. I almost fell off my horse laughing."

Denes glowered. "It's not a laughing matter!"

"No, of course not," said Yozef, heading off more heated words between the two men. Then he looked up, his eyes unfocused as he thought. The other three men waited, accustomed to Yozef's momentary absences while he considered a problem or listened to whispers.

Three minutes passed, with the other three men sipping their beers and eyeing one another as they waited to see if Yozef had a pronouncement.

"Denes," said Yozef, when he became present again, "let's say a Mittack man is a platoon leader that day and a Hewell man doesn't follow orders. Is there any way to compel obedience?"

"Only if the Hewell leader of the hundred does something. Even if he is so inclined, which isn't that often, he might be elsewhere at the time and minutes or more can pass before the order is obeyed. Obviously, this doesn't work in a battle situation."

Yozef's lips parted, exposing a flickering tongue running over his teeth. "What you need is a 'drill sergeant.'"

The English word *sergeant* was one of the labels Yozef suggested to identify men at different levels of command, but what a "drill sergeant" was, they had no idea and waited for Yozef's explanation.

"In many nations and armies, a drill sergeant is a man with authority over men in training. He may not be in the chain-of-command, but it's his duty to see that the men follow orders during training."

Yozef's explanation wasn't strictly accurate but close enough for his purpose.

"How is that any different from now?" complained Denes. "There's still the problem of obeying orders all the time and not just when someone with authority is looking at them."

Maybe it was the beer, but Yozef eagerly anticipated watching the result of what he was about to suggest.

"The drill sergeant has authority to impose physical means, as well as yelling. The men need to worry more about displeasing the drill sergeant than they think about obeying orders from someone of a different clan. The idea is to get them used to obeying orders from whomever is in command."

Balwis snorted. "That's ridiculous! No clansman will stand for anyone pushing him around, much less striking him, if that's what you're implying. All it does is change the fight from men of two different clans to a clansman and this drill sergeant of yours."

"Of course," said Yozef casually, looking at Balwis, "the drill sergeant has to be someone so physically imposing and dangerous that the men will do what he says."

Balwis stared at Yozef, his face blank, then his eyes flickered briefly to one side. Yozef didn't change his position, but from the corner of his eye, he could see Denes's head turn toward Carnigan.

Sergeant Major

Carnigan stood to one side and behind Denes Vegga on a platform, facing a mob of five hundred men. Efforts to get the clansmen to form into ranks had proved fruitless and been abandoned.

Denes wasn't a small man, but Carnigan could easily see over Denes's head and view all five hundred men facing them. Most of the men waited for what Denes would say, although as many as a quarter of the men remained engaged in conversations, despite having been told to pay attention.

"What a bunch of shitheads," Carnigan groused to Denes.

Carnigan was from Swavebroke, a northern province and the only clan whose members came evenly from the two colonization waves to populate Caedellium. As such, he was familiar with tensions between groups identifying themselves as from different backgrounds, even though members of the same clan.

He listened to Denes and watched the men's faces for their reactions to Denes's words.

"Sers, today I am introducing you to Carnigan Puvey. Ser Puvey holds the rank of sergeant major. For your purposes, the responsibilities of this rank are to see that all men conduct themselves as expected, as members of a fighting unit from several different clans."

As Denes spoke, Carnigan left the platform and walked toward the men. He didn't move quickly, but he strode directly at the mob, not saying a word. The front rank must have expected him to stop, but he didn't, and the first two men were jolted aside when Carnigan's bulk contacted them. Other men saw what happened and hurriedly pushed other men out of the way. Carnigan had bulldozed ten yards into the mass before a man refused to give way—a big man, scarred and defiant looking. Carnigan never lost a step, as he backhanded the man, sending him and those he was flung against to the ground.

Watching Carnigan's progress, Denes continued his speech as if nothing had happened. "Sergeant Major Puvey is the bodyguard of Yozef Kolsko, and for those of you who don't know, he played a major role in the defense of St. Sidryn's Abbey from the Buldorians and the fight against the Narthani at Moreland City. I advise you to listen to what he says, and it would be unfortunate if he is *obliged* to . . . correct any of your actions or inactions."

Denes tried not to let his stern expression morph into a smile. "Your hetman, and I'm referring to all five hetmen of the Five-Clan Alliance, has approved Sergeant Major Puvey correcting any of you by any means necessary, if, in *his* opinion, you do not perform as you have been instructed. Sergeant Major Puvey will observe individual platoons and report to me on whether your training progresses in a satisfactory manner. Platoons not performing to Sergeant Major Puvey's approval or mine will find themselves with extra training and duties until performance improves. I should also tell you that all of your hetmen agreed that none of you will be allowed to return home until your performance is acceptable, no matter how long it takes."

Outcries at this news ranged from surprise to shock to anger. Denes didn't explain that not all hetmen were pleased with the request that came from Culich Keelan to transfer, temporarily, authority over the clansmen. Only the Keelan hetman's reputation and their respect for him earned their acquiescence.

Denes waited for the complaints to die down before continuing.

"There will also be two changes to the training routine. First is that a platoon of Keelan dragoons, experienced from the Battle of Moreland City, will join the training. They will do everything your training platoons do and will serve as examples for you to observe and a gauge of how you're progressing. Although we don't expect you to equal the dragoons, a performance that falls too far below theirs will trigger extra training and duties. The other change is that your platoons will engage in mock combat with the dragoon platoon, who will wear copies of Narthani uniforms to let you more closely imagine facing the real Narthani."

Denes also neglected to mention the Keelan men's protests at the prospect of wearing Narthani colors and carrying a Narthani flag. It had taken Denes an hour of patient explanation to convince the men it was for the good of the clan.

Yozef had assured Carnigan and Denes that the first platoon Carnigan worked with would be the most difficult, if Carnigan played his role well. The men carried unloaded weapons, there being no reason to chance one of the men losing control when subjected to the modified training regime.

Each platoon was divided into four squads, with a platoon leader (called, for the exercise, a lieutenant), four squad leaders (sergeants), and two fire teams per squad (each fire team led by a corporal). The leadership positions rotated among the other platoon members to allow each man to gain experience leading mixed units and, not incidentally, enable identification of men slated for future leadership positions.

The exercise this day consisted of squad tactics. Denes gave the lieutenant a scripted list of maneuvers and commands that the squad and the fire team leaders would follow. Carnigan's first intervention came before the exercise began.

The lieutenant stood in front of the five clusters of men, ten from each clan and not intermixed. He looked at the sheets he had just been given, having no prior knowledge of their written contents. He started reading and stopped within seconds. He looked up quizzically to Denes, who nodded to continue. The Adris lieutenant shrugged and read.

"From now on, to begin training, at the beginning of each new exercise or when the training staff wants to speak to us, we will form up in squad ranks we are assigned to. You all know your current assignments for today, since they were posted on the announcement board at camp, and you were told to read the notice before training."

The concept of "parade formations" had been new to the Caedelli when explained, and the execution of these formations would have put a Marine drill instructor into catatonia, were he to witness the Caedelli. The islanders' disdain for the idea and grudging acquiescence, when it occurred, didn't help matters.

The Adris lieutenant looked at the sheet again, glanced up at the fifty men, and, in a hesitant and less than commanding voice, continued reading from the sheet.

"Platoon . . . fall in?"

The men looked at one another.

"I think it means to form into ranks, like they showed us," said the lieutenant apologetically.

The men murmured among themselves, then about half of them moved to approximate positions, while the other half stayed where they originally stood.

Carnigan walked over to the platoon leader. "Lieutenant, if you would stand over here," Carnigan said politely in a low voice, although the tone and the vice-like grip on the Adris man's arm brooked no argument, as Carnigan pulled the man to a previously marked spot.

Carnigan's mild tone vanished when he turned to the other men with a voice to shatter rock and a glower to shrivel walls.

"NOW LISTEN, YOU SHITHEADS! YOU KNOW WHO ARE SUPPOSED TO BE SERGEANTS AND CORPORALS AND WHICH OF THE FOUR SQUADS YOU'RE IN, SO MOVE YOUR FUCKING ASSES BEFORE I HAVE TO HELP YOU!"

Some of the men immediately began moving, though where they moved was not evident in the chaos. Others stood as if shocked or uncertain what to do. One man sneered and said something to a companion. Faster than anyone would have thought possible for someone Carnigan's size, a massive fist impacted the man's chest and knocked him to the ground, gasping for breath.

"WHICH SQUAD DOES THIS PARTICULARLY SHITHEAD BELONG IN?"

When no one answered immediately, Carnigan grabbed the prone man's companion with a hand on top of the man's head, his fingers splayed down as if in position to squeeze like a vice.

"Maybe you didn't hear me. I said which squad does this shithead belong in?" Carnigan's mild tone contrasted with his previous shouts and was, in its own way, more terrifying.

"He . . . he's . . . in squad three," said the man, hardly more than a boy. "I'm in squad two and going to my position right away." He ran toward the lieutenant before Carnigan could provide further assistance.

Carnigan grabbed the now moaning man on the ground by an ankle and dragged him to an approximate position for squad three. On the way, he called out for squad three's sergeant. A Mittack man came up to Carnigan, though he stayed out of immediate arm's length.

"You're the squad leader, and this is your man. It's your job to see he gets into rank as ordered by the lieutenant. NOW DO YOUR FUCKING JOB!"

The man blanched and grabbed the other ankle, to help pull Carnigan's example into position. By the time the squad leader dropped him, most of the other men were in or on their way to *their* positions.

Although the formation remained a disgrace, in a minute the men had lined up—sort of. The appearance would still have given a drill sergeant angina, but Yozef had told Denes and Carnigan not to push the formation concept *too* far. The point was to get the men used to following orders.

Carnigan shadowed the platoon for the rest of the morning, directly intervening several times. The men's constant glances to be sure they knew where Carnigan was inevitably slowed their responses to orders. Whenever he did step in, it was for failure to follow orders immediately and no longer for any instances of disrespect or laziness.

At mid-morning, the leadership positions rotated to other men, and disorder reigned again, although not at the same level as the first set. Whether the improvement occurred because the new leaders were more focused or were worried about Carnigan, it wasn't clear.

Near the end of the morning session, a drill at repositioning skirmish lines in a perpendicular position garnered Denes's grudging admission that the performance wasn't *too* bad, even when a squad leader barely seventeen years old found that keeping track of his men, watching out for Carnigan, and listening for orders from the lieutenant left little room to watch his own feet. He stepped into a hole, not injuring anything severely but dropping his musket, as his face hit a mud puddle. When Carnigan reached the boy, the lieutenant was already helping the miscreant to his feet and, red-faced, was about to begin yelling. Carnigan laid a hand on each man's shoulder.

"No problem, Lieutenant," whispered Carnigan, which was an effort, given the big man's normal rough voice. "You're all doing much better, and everyone falls occasionally. The important point is to get back up and do your job. I'm sure the squad leader can do that, can't you?"

The boy nodded, choked back tears, cleared his throat, and exclaimed, "Yes, Sergeant Major!"

"Good," said Carnigan, "now back at it."

Carnigan walked over to Denes, as the platoon started the drill over again. "I think I've scared them enough for today. I'll be back tomorrow to frighten another platoon."

Denes choked back a laugh. "I think it won't take much tomorrow. This platoon will be telling tales of Carnigan the Ogre and how best to obey orders before he rips out your throat."

Carnigan looked reproachfully at Denes. "I'm acting this way because

Yozef says it's for the men's own good, and I see his point. In a battle, not following orders can get everyone killed, but I don't like deliberately acting horrible."

It was on the tip of Denes's tongue to say that Carnigan growled at people so easily, it seemed to come naturally to him, but he could see Carnigan's sincerity and kept the thought to himself.

The second day required fewer interventions by the new sergeant major, and direct competition with the dragoon platoon solved most of the problems from men of different clans working together. Two sixdays later, Carnigan informed Yozef that he would host two platoons to an evening at the Snarling Graeko 2, the reward Carnigan had promised the first two mixed platoons who beat the dragoons in simulated combat.

"All of this is your idea," deadpanned the sergeant major. "I figured it only reasonable you put up a reward. Call it my 'taking the initiative,' as you say."

Ammunition

An increase in the guano mining fed the heightened paper cartridge production, now ongoing in six Keelan cities and towns.

In addition, the success at finally casting larger cannon added the need for cannon ammunition, and Yozef set up a factory in Caernford to produce 6- and 12-pounder powder bags, along with tin cans holding canister and grapeshot for the two cannon calibers.

The need for more workers at new tasks seemed never-ending: wooden crates to hold musket and cannon ammunition for transport; limbers to hold ammunition; gun carriages; extra wheels; leather traces for wagons, cannon, and limbers; and on and on.

They drew workers from every trade not deemed essential and likewise restricted orders for new work. A smithy had no time for decorative grills when cannon carriage parts and wheels were needed; a seamstress switched to cartridge or powder bags; a lantern maker switched part of his production to smaller lanterns that dragoons could carry for night movements.

Stockpiling Food

Culich had already ordered that all possible farmland go into production until further notice, and murvor fertilizer production ramped up in concert with gunpowder. Another commitment Culich stated at the conclave was to stockpile food, in case the Narthani interrupted food production. Caernford sat in a river valley, but deep caves penetrated the hills to the west and even deeper ones east in the mountains, and limestone caves honeycombed the valley. Interspersed among the many small cavities were a number of impressive caverns.

While talking with Culich about how to store food, Yozef found out how the Keelanders kept their beer cold. He'd wondered about that many times but never pursued the answer. He didn't realize that part of the answer lay with the odd tower structures common in Caedelli towns, villages, abbeys, and individual dwellings of the more well-to-do.

He'd assumed the narrow, mainly two-story towers were decorative when he thought about them at all. Culich explained that most towers rested above a limestone cavity below ground. Such cavities naturally stayed cooler than the ground above them. Some of the cavities had springs or streams running through them. When combined with the towers, which Yozef realized were "windcatchers," the cavity environment could be kept cold and, in some cases, near freezing.

Once prompted, he remembered reading about windcatchers in the Middle East on Earth. The windcatcher tower had openings at the top, facing the prevailing winds, with only a single opening if winds mainly came from one direction. The opening "caught" the wind and brought it down the tower to spaces below, and it exited elsewhere. With aboveground structures, the downward flow pushed out warmer air inside the internal spaces, while additional cooling occurred due to airflow over surfaces. He recalled Persian towers that kept water reservoirs near freezing and desert windcatchers capable of keeping the interior of thick-sided houses in frigid conditions, while the outside temperature blazed.

Culich also pointed out that in locations without limestone cavities, windcatchers were still useful in cooling, but in some provinces, ice-houses had become common: double- and triple-walled and roofed structures with straw and sawdust insulation. Workers brought ice blocks down from the mountains during the cold season and stored them for months in the ice-houses.

However, in certain locations those options still proved insufficient to keep food from spoiling. Yozef's solution was carbon dioxide. A space filled with carbon dioxide reduced or eliminated threats from pests such as rats, which unfortunately had made the transplantation from Earth, along with some insects and molds. The gas also had the effect of retarding spoilage of fruits, vegetables, and grains.

As with many of his innovations for the islanders, Yozef knew parts of the process but not all of it. In this case, he knew carbon dioxide gas was heavier than air and would sink, and he knew how to generate the gas. He didn't know the details of how to combine this knowledge with the existing cooling techniques, which he hoped the local craftsmen could figure out.

After Yozef talked with Culich and convincing him that the carbon dioxide idea would work under some circumstances, Culich had Pedr Kennrick assemble a team of workers to figure out the details. Yozef explained that heated limestone gave off carbon dioxide gas. The island had a plentiful supply of limestone. The trick would be to modify cavities or caves so that they had sealed spaces to trap the sinking carbon dioxide. Above ground, the limestone was heated and the carbon dioxide funneled down to the cavity. Yozef repeated to all the workers, ad nauseam, that once they'd begun to fill a cavity with gas, no one could descend until they'd blown out the gas, using bellows and piping. This negative feature meant that once they'd stocked a cavity or a cavern with food stores and carbon dioxide, to tap the stores would require clearing the gas, then refilling the place with carbon dioxide once the people removing food had finished. The method would be practical only for large stores that people would infrequently access.

A second method of making carbon dioxide involved heating sodium bicarbonate that occurred naturally as the mineral nahcolite, a random tidbit of knowledge Yozef's enhanced memory pulled up. Among the numerous pieces of information, he didn't have a clue why those facts and not others existed in his memory.

Of the two sources, they could gather limestone most easily, and it had the advantage of producing calcium oxide, known as quicklime on Earth, as a by-product. Quicklime might not be immediately useful, but Yozef knew it as a component in steel making, people had used it in historical times as an early form of poison gas (as a dispersed, caustic powder), and it could be used to make high-intensity lights, which was the origin of the word *limelight*, the illumination used in theaters before electricity. He told the men working on the food storage project to save the calcium oxide, figuring they'd have time and a need for it later. He had visions of flares and searchlights.

* * *

Two sixdays later, Pedr Kennrick updated Yozef on the food storage plans. The men working on his idea of filling storage chambers with carbon dioxide had progressed, although they decided to limit the gas-flooded chambers to only certain sites and foods, particularly fruits and vegetables and their processed versions, and sites storing meats and cheeses, where they expected access to be limited.

Cured meats, dry sausage, and hard cheeses would make up much of the prepared foods. They would also store grains, but, as much as possible, would turn them into island versions of hardtack, flour mixed with minimal water and baked completely dry. By keeping the hardtack from moisture, they could make it last years, especially under carbon dioxide to keep out insects. Yozef remembered reading a memoir about the U.S. Civil War, where soldiers in both the North and the South lived largely on hardtack they would crush and mix with water or coffee, sometimes frying the mush, if oil or fat was available.

Yozef didn't appreciate the scale of food storage being planned by Clan Keelan until he sat in on a meeting of Culich with Vortig Luwis and Pedr Kennrick. Kennrick was in charge of organizing the food reserves, and he summarized a massive program. With Keelan being so well organized, the clan headquarters kept a running estimate of animals and large grain stores, as well as data on the population. According to Kennrick's numbers, Keelan Province had 190,000 cattle, 270,000 krykors (an Anyar species roughly filling the niches of sheep and goats and about the same size), and 80,000 horses. Also, families commonly kept combinations of ducks, geese, ruktors (Anyarian flightless bird analogs), and coneys (rabbit analogs).

Currently, people had more cattle and krykors than usual, because the farmers' inability to ship grain off the island had led many to use excess grain to increase herds, a strategy Bronwyn Merton-Linton had explained to Yozef before their affair. They hoped that if the Narthani ever lifted the embargo, the clans could turn the animals into cured meats for external trade. In other words, food could be stored easier on the hoof.

Keelan put plans into place for meat to be salted, smoked, or turned into dry sausage. The processing would start up incrementally, with facilities prepared to ramp up production, if the situation with the Narthani worsened.

Unfortunately, plant products required different strategies, which brought the existing methods and Yozef's carbon dioxide into play. They had already stored grain in silos, warehouses, and below ground. Although farmers had reduced acreage, the equivalent of two years' crops still sat idle, even counting spoilage and pests. Similarly, both farms and families widely grew root vegetables (turnips, beets, and several Anyarian species with a similar look and taste to potatoes) but didn't store them in large quantities. Much of the current practice would soon change.

Culich intuited, as did Yozef and Maera, that the next year would prove critical. As part of the expanded crop production, Yozef's fertilizer project went from stasis to full-scale production, using thirty men mining at Birdshit Bay, transporting guano to Abersford and crushing it there, and distributing the fertilizer throughout Keelan. The worst-case scenario with the expansion of crop production would be if they were wrong: then the farmers would have wasted their efforts. Yet if their premonitions about the Narthani came true, the clan would require every pound of food it could generate.

Ranchers couldn't increase meat production as fast as crops, but the hetmen asked clan members to reduce beef consumption to half of normal and to allow calves that they would have butchered for veal to mature further. Krykor herders received different orders. Krykors provided wool, and while people considered the meat inferior to beef, it was edible and made respectable sausage, if spiced enough. A krykor ewe could give birth twice a year, with two or three young each time. Herders normally exerted population control by limiting the number of male krykors. The clans now lifted that limitation, which meant the krykor herds could easily double in size within a year. If the need for stored foods didn't materialize, the clan could severely cull the herds in a year or two.

Other, less extensive plans included increasing bird flocks and smoking the meat, the clan's fishermen hauling in everything they could to be dried or smoked, and encouraging farms and families to plant large vegetable gardens and preserve the products and the fruit by drying them. Yozef explained the principles of canning, a method of food preparation that he remembered hadn't been developed on Earth until after the Napoleonic Wars (early to mid-1800s). However, the lack of infrastructure to produce enough sealable glass or metal containers appeared to make this option impractical for the time being. Nevertheless, in a few places people used multi-gallon glass jugs for canning.

They developed several bulk storage sites, with a main one in the Dillagon Mountains. Only a single pass crossed over the mountains to the Dornfeld

District, and no army could force the pass if the clans even moderately defended it. There, within a series of high valleys to be protected at each end of the pass by impregnable fortifications, the clan's ultimate redoubt would be built. Every clan member would try to reach this location, should the worst happen. They would turn deep caverns into storage sites, and hundreds of men already worked to make chambers sealable to use Yozef's idea for carbon dioxide–facilitated preservation and to build windcatchers to cool chambers. Given the altitude, they also planned to use existing deep ice caves and to bring block ice to shallower caves.

Although housing for potentially tens of thousands of clan members would be primitive when they arrived, the heavily forested mountains would provide shelter and heat. If necessary, they would fell the entire forest to create a safe haven. Forests would grow again; clan members lost would be lost forever.

The biblical scale of Clan Keelan's planning awed Yozef. Yet it also made Yozef's blood run cold, because the scope of the planning clearly revealed the worst fears of the clan leadership.

Still Time for Home

Finding time to write in his journals became harder and harder, as did Yozef's physical workouts. He maintained a once or twice a month session with Wyfor Kales on blade fighting, combining the session with half an hour of target practice.

No matter how many demands pressed on Yozef, he scrupulously reserved time to eat morning and evening meals with Maera. His other pleasant moments consisted of waking up or just before he fell asleep, with him and Maera in bed together, sometimes holding each other, sometimes not quite touching. Their coupling became less frequent as Maera's stomach grew, with Yozef expressing concern for her and the baby and Maera assuring her husband everything was fine and that she would tell him if the time came to stop. The time hadn't come one night, when afterward they lay naked, arms and legs intertwined. A sheen of sweat from both bodies mixed and added to their sense of bonding.

"Is it still kicking a lot?" He ran a hand over the mound, then exclaimed, "Oh! I guess there's the answer." Her abdomen rippled with internal activity.

"No question," she laughed. "He's an active one. I think we'll have our hands full once he learns to walk."

"Still think it's a boy?"

"Keelan needs an heir, so, yes, it's a boy," asserted Maera.

Yozef didn't argue that her assertion wouldn't likely carry weight with nature. Yet when Maera made up her mind this strongly, he found it best not to contradict her without a good reason.

He stroked her bulge. "How soon before it . . . he . . . comes?"

"Another month to a month-and-a-half."

Another . . . ? Wait a minute, Yozef thought. *That's not right! That would be eight and a half to nine Anyar months, each of which is thirty-six days!*

Yozef kept quiet while he did quick calculations. That would make the gestation between 310 and 324 days, compared to an average of 270 days on Earth. Then he remembered to factor in that the days here equaled twenty-three hours on Earth. Taking the day-length difference into account, he figured the gestation period on Anyar was equivalent to about a month longer than on Earth.

The moon cycles? he wondered. *I know women's menstrual cycles are longer here, matching their moons, just as on Earth. Why would that change gestation? Maybe it's the higher gravity, making the fetus develop slower? One more thing to remind me this isn't Earth.*

His hand wandered up to a breast, massaging it gently and rolling the nipple with his thumb.

Maera tensed, as her nipple stood erect. "Don't tell me you're ready again so soon."

"No," he said sedately, "it's just a nice thing to play with."

"Play with?" she said with mock indignation. "Is that what I am, a toy?"

"Do you object?"

She giggled. "Not really. Though I'll admit it took time getting used to . . . having a man touch me everywhere. And the other way, too." One of her hands moved down below his stomach and cupped his genitals. "Yes, I see you're not recovered yet."

"Give it time, although if you keep doing that, the time may be short."

"I wondered if you would still be interested in coupling when I got so big."

"I think the last half hour answered that question."

"I worried that after the baby comes, I wouldn't look appealing, because some women have stretch marks, and their bodies never look the same. I'm glad you told me how to avoid the marks."

* * *

Yozef knew the marks were due to connective tissue fibers breaking under the stress of rapid growth, leaving scars. Months earlier, after hearing Maera voice that worry, he mentioned that some women in his homeland did things to avoid the marks, such as applying oils or lotions to their bodies as they swelled, exercising regularly, and exfoliating their skin to encourage new skin cell production. He didn't think to mention that the methods probably didn't have any effect. At that particular moment, he had been remembering how Julie had read everything she could find on the Internet and planned to follow every suggestion. He had researched it himself and found no evidence that any of the approaches proved effective. Genetics remained the best predictor of stretch marks: if a woman's mother had gotten them, a new mother-to-be would likely get them, too.

However, his reservations about the methods such as using oils and lotions subsided into silence when Maera informed him she had spoken with a major Caernford soap maker, who had decided to market a lotion for prospective mothers to prevent stretch marks.

Well, he told himself, *it won't do any harm and probably feels good.*

* * *

Yozef and Maera held and stroked each other for several minutes, then Maera unwrapped herself and looked at Yozef's face, lit by candlelight.

"Yozef, you've been . . . different somehow since you came back from the conclave."

"Different? How?"

"I'm not sure," said Maera. "Maybe calmer, though that isn't quite what I sense. More assured? No, that's not exactly right either. You tell me. Did something happen at the conclave you haven't told me about?"

"I told you what happened. I don't know myself how it affected me. It can be confusing. There I was, standing in front of that room full of hetmen and advisors and thinking to myself how every one of them was more experienced in life and at leading men than I am. Yet there I was, giving advice as if I knew what I was talking about, and somehow seeming believing I did—

or acting like it, anyway. I've talked in front of rooms of people before, but then I spoke about topics I felt confident about. That experience didn't match the one with the conclave audience. Still, I spoke and afterward thought I had done well.

"Then, by the end of the conclave, I could see that I'd convinced very few people of some of the major points I'd tried to make. Your father assured me I was wrong, and it just took a while for many hetmen to mull over things before acting. Even if he's right, my instincts are that we don't have time to waste. The trip back gave me time to think, and I have come to understand his point. I just chafe at the slow progress.

"I also seem to be coming around to accepting that I can't hide as much as I'd like in my projects, my writings, you, and the baby, when it comes. Like it or not, I'm involved in advising. Although things have worked out so far, I'm still afraid I'll advise something that turns into a disaster, but I have to stop forgetting that other people are part of all this, and it's not totally on me, whether the outcome is bad or good."

He remained quiet a moment, and Maera could tell he was gathering a thought.

"It's just . . . just that I don't see myself as a leader like the other men at the conclave."

Maera took a minute to think about what he'd said. "Yozef, what is a 'leader'? Aren't there different kinds? Father is certainly one. He leads the clan. Denes is a leader. He's led men in battle. Abbot Sistian is a leader. People listen to him and respect him. Maybe you don't lead a clan or hundreds of men in battle, but aren't you somewhat like Sistian? People *listen* to you. People like father, Denes, Luwis, and Kennrick. They don't just listen, they respect you.

"Carnigan is your friend, so it may be hard to tell, but I'm sure he has respect for you. If nothing else, I remember him being impressed that you stood and fought at St. Sidryn's, even when you admitted you were afraid. He respected that. What about Kales and Balwis? Neither of them may be a friend, but I can't imagine either of them attaching themselves to you as they have unless there's a high level of respect. Hard men like that don't hang around other men who are weak or fools. You *are* a leader, Yozef, whether or not you believe it."

He sighed. "I understand what you're saying, Maera, and part of me knows it's true. Still, I'm unsure about trying to *be* a leader. What if I make mistakes?"

"Everyone makes mistakes, especially leaders. Father readily admits when he makes one, but he forges on, trying not to make the same mistake again. I think you do what is necessary, Yozef, even if sometimes I wish you'd act sooner. I know you are reticent to give advice on serious matters, though I admit I don't understand why. I tell myself to be patient and let you do what is needed in your own time, not mine."

CHAPTER 20

AGENTS

Esyl Havant rode his horse at a canter from the Caernford semaphore station toward Keelan Manor. He had made this trip hundreds of times in the last eight months. During the two days between the news arriving about the Narthani invasion of Moreland and the Keelan men departing for Moreland City to aid the invaded clan, he had made the eight-minute trip between the Caernford semaphore station and Keelan Manor fourteen times. The other two assistants at the station had carried another eleven messages to the manor.

Although he delivered messages throughout the Caernford area, he had volunteered so often to deliver the messages to the hetman's household that the station manager had usually come to send Havant by default. The hetman's family was friendly, the daughters charming, and the hetman and his wife treated him and all others with respect. He liked them, which was unfortunate and irrelevant.

Becoming an assistant to the station manager had been far easier than he had anticipated. When he'd arrived in Caernford two years previously, his demonstrated reading ability, facility with numbers, and earnest manner had secured him a position as an apprentice registrar in the Keelan central registrar office. However, he quickly realized the better position was working at the semaphore station. He identified the station manager and found that he was a regular patron of the Staggering Stallion Inn and Pub. It took a month of casual interchanges, then beers, to become friendly enough with the manager to "reveal" his longtime interest in the semaphore and boredom with the registrar office.

Havant volunteered that he would like to learn more about the semaphore, and the inebriated manager told him to stop by, and he'd be given a lesson. During the next month, Havant became a regular, hanging around the semaphore station whenever he didn't work at the registrar office. He ran errands for the station's staff and bought rounds at pubs. When a flurry of messages flew in and out, during and after the raid on St. Sidryn's, Havant volunteered to help deliver some of the messages. On one of these deliveries, he first visited Keelan Manor and met the hetman and his family.

From there, it was easy. An arranged fall from a horse and a resulting broken neck eliminated one of the semaphore assistants. The manager offered Havant the unfortunate vacancy. After due consideration, he accepted the position, and for the last eight months Havant had read more than half of the semaphore messages going to and from the Keelan hetman.

His Narthani name was Istem Sokulu, and he had worked for Sadek Hizer, the Narthani assessor, for ten years. A gifted linguist and a graduate of one of the more prestigious Narthani military schools, Havant had an inability to hide disdain for most superiors, which limited his career options. Hizer recruited him as a confidential agent and over the years had tasked him as both an internal and an external spy. Internally, he spied to assess Narthani command structures that Hizer evaluated, and externally he spied against enemies of the empire on the missions where Hizer was assigned intelligence duties. Caedellium fell into the latter category. The work involved spells of boredom, but the possibility of discovery was a heavy dose of spice. If he were found out, it could lead to a most unpleasant end to his life. Still, despite having trouble with authority, Havant remained a fervent Narthani patriot.

Although most assignments required only observation, on occasion more active roles came up. Once he had served as an infantry company commander in a campaign against the Fuomi. A regiment colonel, an officer with important connections, was siphoning funds meant for supplies. Although the military usually ignored a reasonable amount of graft, the officer's need to pay gambling debts had led to a dangerous decline in both regiment morale and operational readiness. It took Sokulu two months to gather conclusive evidence against the colonel, during which time Sokulu led his company in several battles, gaining impressive medals along the way—enough so that he was offered to switch to line duty, which he declined. The advantage of working for Hizer was being able to work alone. In the case of the miscreant colonel, Havant moved on to another assignment, after arranging for the colonel to fall by a stray musket ball during a supposed encounter with Fuomi irregulars.

Havant found the current assignment both exciting and boring: boring, due to playing the role of an innocuous Caedelli semaphore station assistant, and exciting, because of being totally on his own. He also found poking around for information challenging. As a downside, when he did find potentially important information, he had limited means to get the information back to Preddi.

Being in an interior location meant he didn't have direct access to patrolling sloops. Another agent was stationed in Salford, the only significant Keelan port. Eluk Sargol was a Caedelli, a Nyvaks clansman. His hetman had assigned him to work with the Narthani at the time Hetman Nyvaks had toyed with cooperating with the Narthani. The Nyvaks hetman's enthusiasm for a Narthani alliance had waned, particularly after Moreland City. Yet Sargol had already been in Salford for two years, so there was no way for Nyvaks to recall him, and the Narthani liked him right where he was.

Sargol, aka Drifwich, was obviously an islander, but his mother came from Pawell, the neighboring province and clan to Nyvaks. Drifwich could turn on a Pawellese accent, making it easy to pass for a Pawellese who had moved to Salford to work on the docks. Besides working as a stevedore, Drifwich drove wagons of cargo between Salford and Caernford, to also connect there with Havant. The problem was, most communications back to Hizer occurred through light signals at night to Narthani sloops lingering offshore. Sending complicated messages was impossible, and Hizer had instructed Havant to provide detailed reports only if he deemed the information absolutely essential. In that case, Drifwich would signal the sloop to make physical contact, and a small Narthani launch would row to a secluded cove ten miles east of Salford, where Drifwich would pass on written reports. So far, Havant had not been certain that any information he had was critical enough to risk direct contact between Drifwich and the Narthani navy.

Yet he had agonized over one topic: whether to risk physical contact to pass on what he had learned about Yozef Kolsko. He had first heard rumors of a strange man found naked on a Keelan beach, and who had subsequently introduced products no one had ever seen before. The ether, new alcoholic drinks, soaps, and the like had not seemed important to Havant. Even after hearing vague rumors of Kolsko having a role in the defense of St. Sidryn's, Havant didn't evaluate the Kolsko information as important enough to include in the condensed messages Drifwich relayed to the sloops.

Besides gathering information and passing it on to Drifwich, Havant's other task was keeping an eye on Hetman Keelan, learning his routine, and using message delivery to the manor as the cover to map out the manor and all signs of defenses. Hizer had told Havant that Keelan was a key clan and its hetman widely respected. The time might come when the Narthani would deem it necessary to remove Culich Keelan, and Havant would play a key role in whatever move they devised.

CHAPTER 21

ANARYND

Maera rose well before dawn or, as she recently thought of it, *"rolled out of bed,"* because she often felt like a ball when she moved. She slept only three to four hours at a time, before discomfort and the need to urinate precluded sleep. She tried not to wake Yozef unless she needed help. That day he woke about dawn, they ate together, and he scurried off to the shops to check on various projects. Previously, Maera had accompanied him on his tasks, until her mobility kept her nearer to the house and available beds, rockers, swings, cushions—anything to get off her feet before they swelled. Intellectually, she knew the side-effects of pregnancy: swollen feet, frequent urination, and choppy sleeping. However, knowing and experiencing weren't the same.

As one saving grace, she had suffered little of the expected morning sickness that women had warned her of. For her mother, it had lasted almost the entire length of her pregnancies and had run in her mother's family. Maera had assumed she would endure the same. Thankfully, it hadn't happened. Despite the aforementioned symptoms, she felt better than at any time in her life, a continuation of her good health since marrying. She had been a chronic sufferer of minor illnesses, what Yozef called "colds," as long as she could remember. For whatever reason, she had had none since their marriage. Her sister Ceinwyn, when not pouting about something or another, usually pestered Maera for whatever new medicine Maera took, because Ceinwyn suffered from the same predilection for colds. Maera insisted there was no new medicine to explain her good health. Her mother attributed it to her being happy. Whatever it was, Maera felt . . . *good.* The swollen feet, the frequent urination, and the spotty sleep were relegated to being mere irritants.

Maera got a cup of kava from the kitchen and had just ensconced herself on a cushioned swing Yozef had had built on the front porch of the house, when Esyl Havant from the Caernford semaphore station rode up to the house, jumped off the horse as only a younger man could, and hurried up to Maera.

"How are you, Esyl?" asked Maera of the man who usually delivered semaphore messages.

"I'm fine, Sen Keelan-Kolsko. A beautiful day, and you're looking radiant. Being with child obviously suits you. I have a message for you from the station at the Keelan/Moreland border."

He pulled the message sheet from his pouch and held it out to her.

She felt curious why in God's name she would get a message from there, and who could it be from?

"Thank you. Please wait in case I need to reply."

Esyl bowed slightly and went back to his horse. Maera unfolded the paper and read:

```
From: Semaphore station, Keelan/Moreland border post
To: Maera Kolsko-Keelan, Caernford
22 Moreland women walked to the border post.
Leader claims to know Maera Keelan and begs asylum.
Holding women waiting instructions.
Leader name Anarynd Moreland.
```

Anarynd!

Maera gasped in shock. Since Anarynd had disappeared during the raid into Moreland four months previously, there had been no word of her. Maera had felt conflicted. First, she hoped that Anarynd was simply unaccounted for and would reappear. Then, when hope faded, Maera wondered whether Ana was dead or a captive of the Narthani. Given Ana's striking looks and the Narthani history, Maera shuddered to think what her life would be like as a Narthani slave.

But Ana *walking* to Keelan? Why? Who were these other women? Where had she been? Why no word earlier? Questions, questions—too many questions. The answers lay with Ana herself. Ordinarily, Maera would have been tempted to jump on a horse or into a carriage and ride the seventy miles to the border, but not in her current condition.

"Esyl," she called out to the messenger, "I'll give you a message to send back to the border post. Wait here while I write it."

She went inside, sat at a table, and wrote:

To: Semaphore station, Keelan/Moreland post
From: Maera Keelan-Kolsko, Caernford
Urgent you provide transportation of women to Caernford.
Commandeer wagons and horses as necessary. Expect to
see them here within 2 days.

She gave her scrawled message to Havant, with stern instructions to get the message off immediately. She felt appeased that he nodded nervously—no one wanted to get on Maera Kolsko-Keelan's bad side. He could not have gotten on his horse any faster, and he disappeared in a cloud of dust down the road, back toward the semaphore station.

That was an advantage to being the hetman's daughter; people didn't want to irritate her.

Maera sat back on the porch swing.

Ana! Oh, Ana, what have you been through, and what's going on?

She sat there until Yozef came back for the mid-day meal. He could see she appeared pale, yet more excited than ill.

"Maera, are you all right?" he asked.

She nodded, and one corner of her mouth rose in, not quite a smile, but more in reassurance. "I'm fine, Yozef. It's just that a semaphore message to me arrived this morning. From Ana."

"Anarynd? Your friend? She's been found? I know how hard it was for you to hear of her disappearance during the Eywellese raid. Did the message have word about her?"

"Yes, but it's very strange. The Keelan/Moreland border post writes that Ana and some other women walked up to the post."

"Walked? Nothing else?"

"Nothing. Of course, semaphore messages are brief. Still . . . I thought about asking for more information but simply ordered the station people to provide transportation directly here as quickly as possible, and that I expected them to be here in two days."

Yozef smiled to himself. Maera had had no formal position, except that she was the daughter of Hetman Keelan. She rarely invoked that status, but when she did, she left little doubt she expected results.

"How many women?"

"The message said twenty-one, in addition to Anarynd."

"Twenty-one!"

Maera merely nodded.

"Walking? Not wagons, horses . . . walking?"

"Walking," confirmed Maera with a worried look.

"That doesn't sound good," said Yozef. "Why in the world would they be walking? Maybe their transportation left them near the station for some reason, instead of bringing them all the way into Keelan."

Maera considered for a moment, then replied slowly. as if it were possible but unlikely, "Yes . . . I suppose that would be an explanation. Of course, then the question is why leave them?"

"Well, we'll see when they get here." Yozef thought for a moment. "This doesn't sound right. You say they're supposed to be brought straight here?"

"Yes."

"That means they will come by the main road from Moreland. Do they have food? Will whoever is bringing them here stay at villages or what?"

Maera looked at him blankly for a few seconds, then flushed angrily and let out a stream of Caedelli invectives that would not have been out of place in any pub. Yozef gave her another minute or so, then said reassuringly, "I'll go to the semaphore station and direct that provisions be provided in route. I'll pay any costs. I also think someone should meet them, just in case."

"Just in case what?" Maera's eyes narrowed in a worried expression.

"Just in case someone needs to meet them," said Yozef. "I'll ask Carnigan to go with me."

"Not just Carnigan. Take Denes and a few more men."

"I don't think that's necessary. Especially Denes. He's so busy right now with other matters."

"I do. You're getting better on horseback, but humor me. I'll feel better."

Yozef shrugged. "Denes really *is* too busy for something like this. I'll be fine with Carnigan, and I'll take Balwis."

It took two hours to gather the party, and three hours before sunset they rode off by horse. Yozef was accompanied by Carnigan, a medicant in training from the abbey, a disgruntled Balwis, who had an assignation planned that evening with a widow in Caernford, and seven other men, all armed. Yozef thought it overkill, but Maera had given in on Denes and would not be thwarted for less than a seven-man escort. They covered thirty miles before total darkness descended and it became dangerous for them and their mounts to keep up that pace. They dry-camped near a stream and were on the road again by first light, enough to see the roadbed clearly. Their obvious haste encouraged other travelers on the road to move aside. Yozef had wished he would never again have to make a long ride, but he felt encouraged that either his memory of the last time was faulty or he had gotten better at this. It could also be the new horse Maera had given him. Yozef named him Mr. Ed, to everyone's bemusement. The horse was strong and fast but easy to control, with a naturally smooth gait greatly appreciated by Yozef's butt. Seabiscuit had shown signs of getting along in horse years, and Yozef didn't want to stress the gentle gelding.

They alternately trotted, walked the horses, and took only occasional breaks throughout the morning and into the afternoon. Yozef got his usual odd looks when he began singing the *Mister Ed* theme song.

It was a loony moment, and Yozef laughed so hard, he almost fell off Mr. Ed. A five-year-old Joseph Colsco had watched the old TV series until disillusioned by an older sister that horses didn't actually talk. He still remembered the theme song lyrics. He sang in English, so none of the Caedelli had clues to the words' meaning.

"Are you going to tell us what's so amusing or keep us wondering whether you've lost your mind?" Carnigan asked.

"How could you tell?" asked Balwis, to the tittering of several escorts.

"It's a song for when you feel happy," said Yozef, "like in a pub."

"What do the words mean?" Carnigan asked.

"They don't translate well, so if you want to sing along, just try to copy the sounds."

"And let everyone who hears us think there's more than one idiot in this group?" snorted Balwis. "Think again."

Yozef broke into song once more, this time with Carnigan attempting to follow along. By the tenth iteration, four of the seven escorts joined in.

Oh, God, Yozef thought to himself. *If I just had a camera and a microphone to record this for YouTube, it'd go viral within minutes.* Ten armed men on horseback, six of them singing the *Mister Ed* theme.

* * *

On the second day, an hour before sunset, they saw two wagons heading south toward them. Within a few hundred yards, Yozef recognized them as the travel party. Balwis rode ahead, then Yozef got a close look at the wagon's contents when the rest of the men caught up with Balwis.

"Well, Jesus H. Christ!" Yozef spoke angrily in English, so naturally no one understood.

Each small farm wagon held ten to twelve women huddled together on the wooden bed, some of them gripping the side of the bed for support on one wagon. The other wagon had a simple flat platform, and the women had to be constantly alert not to be thrown off. They were bedraggled—dirty, with ragged or torn clothing, some barefoot, and if Yozef's first glimpse of their feet was any indication, they must have walked much of the way from wherever they'd come from. Several showed bruises, fading, so however they'd acquired these, it had been at least some days ago. All had haunted eyes.

Balwis was talking to one of the women when Yozef and the others arrived. The woman, a blonde—at least, Yozef thought her hair blonde underneath the grime and dirt—seemed to speak for the group.

Is this Anarynd Moreland? Yozef wondered. He waited impatiently until Balwis finished speaking with her and came over to where Yozef stood holding his horse's bridle.

"She says her name is Anarynd Moreland, and she wants to see Maera."

"Did she say anything about why they arrived to Keelan like this or who the other women are?"

"She wouldn't say. Just kept asking for Maera. One of the others mumbled something about escaping from the Eywellese."

"They look half starved. Have they eaten today?"

Carnigan shook his head. "I doubt it. Maybe no water either."

"We'll go back to the village we just passed through," Yozef decided. "What was it called?"

"Dilstin," said Balwis.

Yozef thought he noticed something in Balwis's expression. "What is it, Balwis?"

The other man looked uncomfortable. "You know I lived and worked in Moreland after I escaped Preddi. It just occurs to me that these women look like they have been cast out by their families. This sometimes happens if a Moreland family feels the woman has shamed the family honor. I heard in a pub that Stent clansmen rescued some women after the Moreland City battle. I'm wondering if these are some of them."

"Why would they be cast out by their families after being rescued?"

"Yozef," Balwis said gruffly, "think about it. These are all young women. What do you think the Narthani and Eywellese were doing with young women captives?"

Yozef stared blankly for a few seconds at the women clutching one another, not looking at the Keelan men.

He flushed angrily. "God damn it!" No translation was necessary.

He looked again at the women, this time looking differently at them, his eyes narrowed and focused. Two of them looked as if they might be pregnant. Then a bundle that one woman held let out a weak cry, and he realized, shocked, that the bundle was a baby. At least one more woman held such a "bundle." He looked straight into Carnigan's face, and, with a cold voice they had not heard from Yozef before, asked, "They were thrown out by their families because they were raped against their will?"

Carnigan looked uncomfortable, "Some families will feel they are dishonored. Not in all clans, of course, but I am afraid it does happen. Clans are different, and the Morelanders are among the pricklier in issues of honor— at least, as they think of it."

"Assholes," Yozef muttered, this time in Caedelli.

"Try to understand, Yozef. For the Morelanders, after all they have been through, any association like this with the Narthani will be difficult for them to accept. I can see that some of these women have a child or are with child. If what we suspect is true, these are children of their Narthani or Eywellese captors. It would be hard enough to accept the women back, but also the children of the hated enemy? It's just too much to expect of some families."

Yozef's face appeared no longer flushed but instead was made of stone.

I keep forgetting, he thought to himself. *I have to remember where I am, and even so, there were plenty of instances of similar attitudes back on Earth.*

Recently, he had been thinking about the rumors that speculated about him being a Septarsh. Usually, he studiously avoided saying anything to feed the rumors. Not today.

If they insisted on assigning mythological status to him, he might as well use it.

He raised his voice so all could hear and did his best "prophet in the pulpit" imitation. "It is against the *Word* of God to punish those harmed against their will. He who cannot give understanding and mercy can expect none from God."

Carnigan looked taken aback by this sudden change in Yozef. Balwis, jaded though he was, nodded and touched the amulet to God the Militant he wore around his neck. The leader of the wagons looked uncertain but a little fearful at Yozef's tone. He obviously knew the rumors about this man.

Yozef figured he might as well play the Septarsh card for all it was worth. He tilted his head sideways and closed his eyes most of the way, as if listening to some faint voice. All the others remained quiet. Even the women close enough to hear the exchanges kept silent, although, in their case, due to confusion about what was happening.

After a minute, Yozef opened his eyes and proclaimed in a loud voice, "I do not believe God is pleased by how these women were treated either in their homeland or here in Keelan. I sense that he is close to being angry." Yozef then changed his voice, so that he sounded like himself and not a prophet of God. "I think we need to get these women food, shelter, and let them clean themselves."

By now, the wagon master was pale and eager to appease whatever aspect of God he might have offended. "Yes, yes," he said. "We need to get to the nearest village."

It took twenty minutes for them to arrive at the village of Dilstin. Yozef did his best Old Testament prophet imitation stance, while the initial discourse went on. The wagon master's explanation to the villagers occasioned surreptitious glances in Yozef's direction and a few clutches at amulets and hand motions to ward off any present evil spirits.

Whatever the wagon master said to the village chief elicited an enthusiastic response from the villagers. Faster than Yozef would have predicted, a building, possibly a school, was cleared and bedding for the women laid out on the floor, with cushioning under the bedding. The women of the village led groups of the women to different homes, to return later bathed and in some cases with new, if plain, clothing. Later, Yozef's party and the women were fed plentiful plain village food.

Yozef didn't rush leaving the next morning, letting the women get as much sleep as they needed. The sun was well up when all felt ready to depart. Yozef thanked the villagers and told them he had a dream that God was pleased with them. An audible sigh ran through the seventy to eighty villagers who witnessed their departure. Yozef thought he might as well reinforce the lesson and gave the village chief enough gold coins to more than pay for all they had provided, along with an admonition to remember to practice God's mercy. Several of the Moreland women cried, as the wagons moved out of the village. It had been the first time in however long that people had been kind to them.

As Yozef rode to the front of the party of wagons and his travel companions/guards, he got his first real look at the woman who had to be Anarynd. The dirty, bedraggled hair was now clearly the golden blonde Maera had described, tied in a ponytail. He briefly glimpsed blue eyes in a haggard face.

Because the road paralleled the semaphore line, Yozef sent Maera a message from the next station, saying they were on the way back with the women. He felt undecided about whether to go slow and stop again for two more nights or push on ahead harder. He finally thought it would be best to get the women to St. Tomo's Abbey in Caernford and the medicants as fast as possible. They stopped once more at another village and repeated the theatrics of the first night. The next day they rose at first light, pushed on to Caernford, and reached the abbey at mid-day. The medicants cared for the women and provided shelter. Anarynd allowed herself to be checked briefly by the medicants and then insisted on traveling on to Maera.

It was dark when Anarynd and Yozef arrived home in a Keelan carriage sent by Maera and driven by Carnigan. Kerosene lanterns lit the front veranda, where Maera waited. Not a sound came from either woman, as Maera rose from a rocker and Anarynd stood by the carriage after Yozef helped her down. Then, as if in slow motion, Maera came down the steps, as Anarynd walked forward. They met at the bottom of the steps, then slowly, as if afraid to dissipate a dream, their arms encircled each other, and both women broke into deep sobs.

Yozef thanked Carnigan, who handed the carriage off to a manor worker, and the big man walked back toward Caernford. Balwis watched for several minutes, then headed for the cottage he slept in when staying on the grounds.

A good ten minutes passed before the torrent of tears slowed, and Yozef guided the women into the house and the parlor, the two women clinging as if afraid of losing the other. Yozef went into the kitchen and brought back water, wine, and glasses. He set them on a table next to the women and retreated to his library and writing in his journals.

It was almost three hours later when Maera came into his workroom, tear-streaked, happy, and angry all at once.

"She's sleeping in the bedroom next to ours. I got several glasses of wine into her, and she finally relaxed enough to fall asleep. I expect she'll sleep until tomorrow, and then I'll see what I can do to care for her."

"How is she?" Yozef inquired softly.

"She was a slave of the Narthani for three months!" Maera snapped bitterly. "How do you *think* she is!"

He didn't know what else to say at that moment, so said nothing.

Maera slumped into a chair, closed her eyes, and laid her head on the chair back, silent for several minutes, then . . .

"I'm sorry, Yozef," she said. "There's no reason to yell at you. None of this is your fault, and Ana told me how you took care of all the women. Thank you for that. It's just that . . . I'm so overjoyed that Ana is safe here, but at the same time I want to scream to the heavens that this happened to her."

Yozef moved to Maera's chair, sat on the edge of the cushion, and pulled her to him. She didn't resist, letting her head rest on his chest, and clutched him. After another quarter hour, Maera turned businesslike once again and insisted they find something to eat in the kitchen before retiring.

The next morning, Yozef left to meet with Luwis and Kennrick, while Maera waited for Anarynd to waken. She waited until almost midday, checking several times an hour on Anarynd. As soon as her friend woke, a hot bath awaited, followed by a clean robe, and food and wine on a small table under a pergola behind the house. They spoke little until they finished eating. Finally, Anarynd looked into her friend's eyes, her right hand gripped Maera's left, and she recounted the previous months. Maera listened without comment, a flood of empathetic emotions coursing through her. She remained silent while Anarynd recounted her escape and return home.

* * *

For Ana, the decision to leave her family was easy and heartbreaking. The Stent clansmen had been observing the walls of Hanslow, the Eywellese capital. Twelve hundred Stent and Hewell men had ridden hard to get to Parthmal, the Narthani staging base for the Moreland invasion, before the withdrawing Narthani force arrived back across the Eywell-Moreland border. After surprising and annihilating the two-hundred-man supply base, a scouting party had pushed on to the outskirts of Hanslow. The Stent party of fifty men was about to the leave the forest edge a mile from Hanslow when the ragged, bruised, and terrified trail of women staggered out of the darkness. Half of the women were hysterical with relief when they realized the horsemen were not Eywellese; the other half were too exhausted to talk. It was Anarynd who identified them as slaves escaped from Hanslow. The fifty Stentese needed to return to the main force ten miles away, but there was no question that they would take the women, even if it slowed them and risked an encounter with Eywellese or Narthani mounted patrols.

Thirty-eight women and children rode double the seventy miles back to Moreland City, stopping only once to sleep on the ground after crossing the Moreland border. A few women were left at their home villages or farms on the way, but most rode all the way to Moreland City, where the Stentese turned them over to the Moreland authority to repatriate to their families, if the families existed. Some women returned to find their immediate families dead or still missing from Eywell raids. These women were sent to their nearest relatives. Other women were Preddi whose families were lost or dead, had disappeared, or had been shipped off Caedellium to Narthon. Families took in these women or abbeys cared for them, until permanent places could be found. All these women were, in a way, the fortunate ones, because they knew their status, no matter how bad.

Not so for many of the Moreland women with still-living families. There, the receptions varied. Ana witnessed one woman embraced by parents, husband, and children, all crying with joy. Her own reception differed dramatically. Word was sent to her family, forty miles from Moreland City, that they needed to come get her. A sixday had passed before her oldest brother, Heilrond, came to claim her. They had never been on the best of terms, and his obvious disgust at seeing her foretold her reception at home.

Her father never spoke to her, and she later learned he had ordered that she never be in his presence. Heilrond left her at a cottage on the edge of the family land and told her not to come to the house. The next day, her mother came to the cottage, and Anarynd described what had happened to her. How she and Aunt Tilda, her mother's sister, had been taken captive in Lanwith when they had gone the ten miles from the family estate to shop—her aunt's thoughtful, and fateful, attempt to get Anarynd away from her father's baleful presence for even a few hours.

The last Anarynd saw of her aunt was when they, along with all of the other captive Moreland women and children, were herded into a corral to be dispersed to masters, brothels, or slave markets. Anarynd had been pulled out by a Narthani officer—Colonel Erdelin, she later learned, the overseer of Eywell Province and one of the highest-ranking Narthani officers.

Her mother's eyes teared up at the news about her sister, but not when Anarynd recounted her own fate as the concubine of the Narthani officer.

Anarynd admitted she had done what she had to, in order to survive and not be sent to the brothels, but her mother slowly pulled away from her as more details came out. Anarynd had no thought to hide anything. This was her mother. Only when she finished describing how she had kept from becoming pregnant by taking the root extract given to her by another woman slave, Gwyned, and how they had escaped, did Anarynd notice her mother had moved away from her with a face cold, eyes dry, and arms crossed in front of her.

She heard no words of consolation or welcome home.

"You're our child, and we can't send you away, but we don't need to see you more than necessary, and you're not to come to the house where others might see you and the rest of the family be shamed."

Shamed! Anarynd wanted to scream. *For this happening to me beyond my control? Merciful God, you're my mother!*

Without another word, her mother spun and left the cottage. Anarynd didn't see her mother again until almost a month later. Despite the rejection, her urge to glimpse any family member became too strong, and Anarynd walked along a path that wound through a grove of trees a hundred yards from the family home. She watched the house too closely and didn't hear approaching laughter until her mother and two brothers rounded a bend. The four of them stood staring, shocked or surprised for several seconds. For a moment, Anarynd thought her mother would come to her, when an anguished expression washed over her mother's face, and Heilrond grabbed their mother's arm.

"You were told not to come near the house! Now get back to where you belong, before we forget our charity for letting you stay even there!"

It was the last time she saw any of them before deciding. This wasn't *home* anymore. Home was where you were wanted, where people cared for you and you them. She had no future here. Out of her distant relatives, none came to see her or intervened on her behalf with her parents.

She returned to the empty cottage and yelled, "The hell with you all!"

Where could she go? Only one possibility rose in her mind. Maera. She hadn't had writing materials to send a letter to Maera, and even if she had, no one would have taken it to the closest registrar office to get in a mail packet. Should she ask neighbors or anyone in the nearby village for ink and paper? She would have to walk to the registrar and had no coin to pay even the small fee.

Gwyned. Another escaped slave. A Preddi. The one who had sympathetically advised her on how to survive. Gwyned, who had become a friend, a sliver of consolation in her months in Hanslow. Anarynd had said goodbye to Gwyned in Moreland City when distant relatives of Gwyned's came for her. Anarynd remembered that she lived in a nearby village, only a fifteen-minute walk from the city's outer wall. A village named something like Halsworth or Halston or something close.

Anarynd would go to Maera, who certainly wouldn't turn her away. She hoped. Moreland City was on the way, and she would try to find Gwyned, see how her friend was doing, and say goodbye. Maybe in Moreland City she could send Maera a letter.

Anarynd packed enough food for three days, almost all she had in the cottage, a wineskin of water, and a change of clothes. She put on her only pair of shoes and started walking at dawn the next morning.

Two full days later, the tops of Moreland City's buildings came into view. It was too late to try to find Gwyned that day, so she slept once more on the ground, covered by a cloak. The next morning, she asked and found directions to the village of Halstorn, the closest-sounding village to what she could remember Gwyned telling her. After an hour's walk to the village of perhaps three hundred, she was told Gwyned lived somewhere in Moreland City. Her distant family in the village had refused to let her stay, unless she got rid of the half-Narthani child she'd borne during her years as a Narthani concubine. Gwyned had refused and left for Moreland City.

Anarynd retraced her route back into Moreland City. Even with more than twenty thousand people in the city, news of the escaped women was widely known, and Anarynd needed only an hour to find one of the other women. Not Gwyned, but she knew where Gwyned worked, at a seamstress shop.

Their reunion was tearful and bitter. Anarynd learned that her experience and Gwyned's were not unique. While many of the women had been accepted gladly by their families, others suffered rejection or had no families to come back to, because they were from Preddi or even from elsewhere on Anyar and had been brought to Caedellium by the Narthani.

Anarynd stayed with Gwyned in a corner of the seamstress shop, and in the next sixday, the two of them tracked down all the escapees living in or close to Moreland City. Anarynd had already asked Gwyned to come with her to Keelan, sure that Maera would help. When seven others eventually asked if they could come, too, and Anarynd told them she couldn't ensure their reception, most of them asserted that things couldn't be worse in Keelan Province. When it came time to leave, word had spread, and twenty-two women had showed up, with two toddlers and two babies still nursing.

The women didn't have enough coin among the group to pay for transportation, so they started walking. They used what coin they had to buy food on the way and asked for charity when the coin was exhausted.

A number of the women were weak from hunger or illness, and the children had to be carried. Some days they traveled only five miles. Three times farmers with empty wagons gave them lifts for a few miles, with all of them packed on top of one another and hanging off the wagon beds. On the eighth day, they reached the Keelan semaphore station just across the border. There, Anarynd asked, then begged, then threatened the station agent to send a message to Maera Kolsko-Keelan.

"It costs twenty-five krun to send a semaphore message. Do you have it?" asked the agent, a disdainful curl to his lips.

"No," said Anarynd, "but Maera Kolsko-Keelan will pay it and more. I'm a friend."

"You?" said the agent. "Why would the hetman's daughter and the wife of Yozef Kolsko be a friend of yours? And a Morelander, at that."

"Do you want to take that chance?" Anarynd retorted. "If I'm telling the truth and you don't send it, you'll risk the anger of both Hetman Keelan *and* Yozef Kolsko."

The threat made the agent pause to reconsider. He looked at the station counter, bare for the moment of messages to be relayed in either direction, so should he risk that this bedraggled woman had told the truth? He thought for several moments, then decided, *Why not?*

"All right," he said. "What's the message?"

Although Anarynd wanted to slump to the ground in relief, she held herself firm. "Just say that Anarynd Moreland is at the border and needs transportation for herself and twenty-one other women."

The agent shook his head. "I'll send it, but you should figure out what you're going to do if no return message comes, or it comes and Maera Kolsko-Keelan has never heard of you."

To the agent's shock—and relief that he'd wisely sent the message—an answer came to arrange transportation to Caernford. He provided water and enough food for a few bites for each woman and child, and two wagons from a nearby village left the station heading south. He didn't know what was going on and felt relieved to be rid of them.

They slept in a barn that night, while the two drivers slept under the wagons. The next midday, a group of riders pushing their horses hard met them. All the men were armed, and many of the women cowered in the wagon beds. One man rode ahead to the wagons; a hard-looking man with a facial scar. Of the other men, one was a huge, red-headed man with a ferocious countenance. All the men seemed to defer to a third man, of average height, sturdily built, with brown hair and lighter fine streaks. When he came near the wagons, Anarynd could see that he had unusually light blue eyes, almost gray.

* * *

It was well past mid-afternoon when Anarynd got around to talking about herself. "I thought of killing myself. Oh, God, you don't know how many times I thought about it. I didn't, because I hoped for rescue or escape. Then, when hope faded, I knew the *Word* forbids it. I wondered if I believed in God anymore, then another thing stopped me. After what they had done and were doing to my people . . . and after what Erdelin had done to me, if I killed myself, I would let them win. If I died, Erdelin would only take another woman. So, to spare myself, I would condemn another victim to the same treatment. In the end, I couldn't do it."

Maera had sat listening as Anarynd unburdened herself, her eyes vacillating between fury at what had been done to her friend, more than a sister, and pain at hearing what Anarynd had endured. Though her eyes burned, she determined not to shed tears and to give Anarynd the time and space to be supported.

Anarynd stopped talking and stared out the window—one of the "thousand-yard stares" Yozef had described to her, of men too long in battle.

"When I accepted I wouldn't kill myself, I thought hard about what I would do," Anarynd continued softly. "I knew I couldn't simply accept being a slave to the Narthani. Erdelin would either keep me or eventually pass me on to another Narthani or even to the brothels, if I displeased him. But while I was alive, there were always options. I might have a chance to escape. If I failed and was killed, it wouldn't be suicide. Also, I could one day kill Erdelin while he slept. Again, if they killed me for it, God would surely not see it as taking my own life."

Anarynd stopped talking and for the first time had a warm look in her eyes.

"The thing that helped the most was you, Maera. I told myself, 'What would Maera do? She would be *brave*.' Therefore, I had to be brave, no matter what happened. Brave like Maera. Many days . . . " Anarynd swallowed hard, ". . . and nights, I had to be brave, as I knew you would be."

Maera wanted nothing more than to tilt her head to the sky and scream. *Brave! Me! Oh Merciful God, Ana. I don't know how I could have been as brave as you!*

She didn't say those words. Now was not the time, if ever. For now, the only thing that mattered was Ana being alive and safe, and Maera would do whatever she could to help her.

CHAPTER 22

HAIL TO THE HEIR

Move Completed

The complete relocation of projects and shops from Abersford to Caernford took time, during which Yozef made the round trip twice more, to his frustration. He used it as an opportunity to improve his horsemanship. In Abersford, he walked the routes to and from their home, the town, his industrial park, and the abbey. In Caernford, that routine became impractical, due to the longer distances, and he rode one of the horses from his expanding personal stable. He rode Mr. Ed for the round trips to Abersford, particularly after the ride north to fetch Anarynd, and Seabiscuit more often for short, local trips.

On the last trip to Abersford, he found himself reminiscing. With the final details of the move settled, he took an extra day to see the beach where they'd found him, his retreat cottage, Birdshit Bay, and the small valley with the jacaranda trees where he'd first kissed Maera. He also visited the abbey, where'd he lived those first months and made his first real connection with someone, Carnigan. He mentally replayed the courtyard scene of the desperate fight against the Buldorian raiders. He had no logical need to see these spots, but they were so much a part of who he had been and who he now was that he felt drawn to experience them one more time before he and his life moved on.

When it came time to leave, there was no ceremony. He spent only a few minutes with Abbot Sistian Beynom, because Diera Beynom had gone to Caernford to help organize medical planning for future contingencies.

As Yozef rode away, he stopped at the final hill to look back at the buildings of Abersford and the abbey.

I wonder when I'll see this again, he thought. *So much happened here, where I was so desolate, then so happy.*

He sat for several minutes reviewing the previous years, then urged Mr. Ed on, and closed that door.

Almost a hundred other Abersford citizens preceded or followed him and Maera to Caernford: Carnigan, Cadwulf, Filtin, Kales, Denes, Balwis, workers, and families. Cadwulf initially said no to moving, then agreed, on the condition he would stay only until the Narthani threat ended. Then he would return to Abersford to head the Applied Mathematics Department for the University of Caedellium at the Abersford campus. The reality of the Narthani threat, the Kolskos' move to Caernford, and the unrelenting arguments that the main university needed to be in a more central location than a relatively remote town forced all parties to accept that the planned university would have to be a lower priority than anyone involved desired, especially Yozef. Not that they shelved the idea, only delayed it.

Until then, Cadwulf agreed to relocate to Caernford and continue oversight of Yozef's ever-expanding commercial enterprises and the Bank of Abersford, which had evolved into a major financial institution. Yozef had stubbornly refused to change its name to the Bank of either Keelan or Caedellium. No one understood his argument that "B of K" or "B of C" didn't sound as good as "B of A," and his decision brought forth the usual shrugs and "Well, you know, it's Yozef."

Filtin spoke of returning to Abersford one day to take over his father's work, but Yozef didn't reveal his conviction that his chief technical troubleshooter would find endless reasons and fascinations to delay the return for the rest of his life. Yozef intended to introduce as much new information as he could, as fast as the culture here could absorb it, and he would need as many Filtin Fullers as he could find to make it happen.

In Yozef's mind, the Kolsko household relocation officially ended when they moved from Keelan Manor into their new home a half-mile away. In contrast to Maera's last time leaving home, this one was a celebration, with relatives coming from Caernford and as far away as Clengoth to help move possessions and take part in a family housewarming that lasted well into the night.

Yozef felt amazed and gratified that the builders had constructed the new home so quickly. They still had details to finish, and the smell of wood and paint would persist for months, but the house was now ready to be lived in.

Anarynd and Maera

Anarynd recovered quickly, in a physical sense. Within two sixdays, she had once again become the striking young blonde woman who turned men's heads, until they looked into a face with lines too prominent for someone her age, a closed expression, and sad eyes. Maera attempted to act as if nothing had happened during the previous months and they were the same two young women, best friends who told each other things they could tell no one else. It was only a pretense. After Anarynd's experience with the raid on Landwin, her months of captivity and enslavement to a Narthani commander, the escape where she helped kill a guard, her return home and rejection by her family, she would never be the same.

Though neither was Maera the same. Her feelings of being "out of place" had receded, as her life filled with multiple roles. Wife and mother-to-be were roles she had always expected, although with some trepidation. Yet she found it unexpected and exciting that her role of advisor to both the hetman and Yozef Kolsko became more formal. Yozef had been the first to tell people how he depended on Maera's advice and help, and her father, after some hesitation and prodding by her mother, had followed suit. No matter their personal opinions, no Keelander wanted to argue with Hetman Keelan and Yozef Kolsko.

Yes, Maera had changed, but not how she felt about Ana. Maera made efforts to keep Anarynd active, so she wouldn't withdraw. As her first effort, she assigned some of the household "chores" to Anarynd. Maera could, with some rationale, claim she found these more difficult now that she was less mobile.

Anarynd acquiesced without comment. Her evolution to being more animated began when Maera volunteered her to keep tabs on the other escaped women, who were only slowly finding places in Keelan society. Twelve of the women were employed by Maera, by Breda Keelan, or within Yozef's enterprises. The rest stayed temporarily at St. Tomo's abbey or were taken in by kindly families. Maera also asked Anarynd to maintain a written record of the progress of the other escaped women and keep up a regular written correspondence with those not in the immediate neighborhood. This gave Anarynd a reason to practice and improve her reading and writing.

Gwyned Walstyn, Anarynd's friend and co-escapee from Hanslow, and her daughter, Morwena, joined the Kolsko household when Maera initially thought to keep Gwyned nearby to help Anarynd adjust. Maera quickly found she liked the gruff, practical-minded woman and added her to the Kolsko staff with general duties, including secondary cook. While the Kolskos' new house was being built, Gwyned lived in one of the visitor cottages on the Keelan Manor grounds, then moved to a cottage on the Kolsko estate. Maera sensed that Gwyned would find her own role in Keelan society, but keeping her close for the moment worked well for all parties. However, after everyone moved into the new house, Gwyned's hybrid roles as worker and friend created awkwardness, and Maera soon decreed that evening meals would include Gwyned. Yozef took it in stride, eating with three women, but remained firm that morning meal was reserved for him and Maera, along with an occasional evening meal.

Although Anarynd had acted withdrawn in Yozef's presence at the beginning, Gwyned added a dynamic at evening meals that prevented Anarynd from staying silent. Anarynd gradually became more animated, and within three sixdays Yozef saw the Anarynd of Maera's stories.

Arrival of the Heir

One month after Anarynd's arrival, on the evening of fifthday, the third sixday of the month of Brunelon, Yozef, Maera, Anarynd, and Gwyned sat for evening meal, as two-year-old Morwena slept on a cushion in the adjoining great room. Maera had grown so large, she found it difficult to safely go from standing to sitting, so Anarynd helped her sit down. The meal started with a vegetable soup that Yozef insisted on calling *minestrone*. As usual, Yozef and Maera talked about their day. Anarynd still seldom said anything in Yozef's presence, until prompted by Maera or Gwyned. He had tried to engage her, to no avail, and finally gave up. Maera told Yozef they had to be patient with Anarynd and that she would eventually open up to him and others.

Maera lifted a spoonful of soup toward her mouth, then jerked, spilling the spoon contents back into the bowl, onto the table, and on herself.

"Urgh!" she grunted. The other three people stopped and looked at her. "Ahh!"

"Maera?" said a concerned Yozef.

She looked at her husband. "Just a sudden . . . urg! Pain." She leaned back, one hand on her bulging belly, the other on one side. "I had a cramp or something."

Anarynd looked at Yozef. His first thought was that Anarynd had never before looked directly at him, during the entire time since he'd brought her and the other women to Caernford. The anticipatory look in Anarynd's face triggered his second thought. *The baby!*

Maera began to breathe deeper and faster, her face in a slight grimace.

"It keeps coming and going." Light dawned in Maera's face. "I . . . I think it might be *that* time."

Suddenly, Maera jerked and looked down. "Ahrg . . . what . . . oh. I think my water broke."

That time it was. While Anarynd and Gwyned helped Maera to the bedroom, Yozef ran the half mile to the Keelan Manor. Running was faster than saddling a horse, not that Yozef was in a frame of mind to make that deduction.

Once he'd alerted Breda Keelan, she took charge, sent for medicants, and had a carriage brought to the Kolsko house. Yozef had already run back home. They took Maera to Keelan Manor, where the first grandchild of the hetman would be born. Although this would be the second child he'd fathered on Anyar, this time Yozef was on site and knew it would really be his, one he would help raise.

Within two hours, a crowd had gathered at Keelan Manor, including hetman advisors, boyermen who happened to be in Caernford, Abbot Walkot, and scores of others. Yozef wouldn't have recognized most of them, even if he'd been aware of anything except worry about Maera, as he wandered around, thinking he *should* be doing something. The father being present at a birth was not a Caedellium custom, so Yozef paced outside the house, waiting with the other men. Several medicants attended Maera, and Anarynd stayed with her the entire time.

When the medicants first arrived, they reported that Maera was definitely in labor, everything was progressing normally, and people should relax, because it would be many hours before the baby arrived. That advice proved faulty when, only four hours later, a squalling eight-pound boy made his appearance. When Yozef was allowed in to see the mother and child, several people commented that Maera looked better than he did. She sat up in bed, in one arm holding a small bundle of reddish flesh with squeezed-shut eyes. With the other arm, she tried to eat a bowl of beef stew. Yozef relieved her of the bowl and spoon-fed her until she fell asleep.

Two Godsdays later, Yozef and Maera formally presented their newborn in St. Tomo's cathedral. Attendance overflowed. Culich formally acknowledged the boy as his grandson, and when the time came for Yozef to declare the boy's name, he had prepared this time and gotten Maera's approval for the name: Aeneas.

When Maera had asked him about the origin of the name, Yozef told her Aeneas was a legendary warrior who wandered, then founded a mighty empire called Rome, and whose descendants included famous rulers named Julius Caesar, Augustus, and King Arthur. Maera merely nodded with satisfaction at the appropriateness. Yozef left out certain details, such as Aeneas fleeing the fall of Troy and that the Roman Empire was not all that different than the Narthani.

He figured that although no one on Anyar or Earth knew of his fate, if in some distant future contact occurred between the planets, he would have left clues that this future contact was not the first. He also wondered how many more clues he would eventually leave.

Home Life with Aeneas

Aeneas Kolsko was a sleeping, eating, squalling, shitting lump, and in the coming sixdays Maera expressed bewilderment at how eagerly Yozef held the little bundle—at least, until he needed changing. The Caedelli considered tending infants solely a woman's task, and Maera could remember that many months had passed before her father first held each of her two youngest sisters, and then only briefly. But this was Yozef—so different in so many ways. Why not this one, too?

Although Yozef wondered how he would balance helping care for a baby with all his other obligations, he hadn't factored in his and Maera's status, Caedellium customs, or the available assistance. The expected midnight feedings and changings never materialized. Gwyned amicably shared her cottage with Mirramel Killin, a young widow and wet nurse with a baby daughter, Dwyna. With Anarynd, Gwyned, and Mirramel on hand, Yozef had no required time with Aeneas, only time he made for regular holding. Even Maera spent less time with Aeneas than she'd expected. She nursed the baby several times a day, but Mirramel was on hand for other feedings, and Maera only partly supplied the constant attention a new infant needed. Within two sixdays, she found herself once more immersed in her activities, albeit not full time.

The newborn's parents talked about their perceived lack of attention to Aeneas, but both settled on spending time each day with the baby, more Maera than Yozef. They told themselves and each other that the baby wouldn't know the difference at this age. Yozef believed it, and Maera *told* herself she did.

Thus, did life at the Kolsko household settle into a routine, modified from the past only in that the baby and the attendants added to the general bustle.

CHAPTER 23

DISRUPTION

Narthani Headquarters, Preddi City

Brigadier Aivacs Zulfa, commander of their ground forces, and Nizam Tuzere, civil administrator, had just finished reporting on the status of defenses. Admiral Kalcan, commander of all Narthani naval units in the area, had reported no change in the Narthani's total control of the waters around Caedellium.

"All right," said Akuyun, "I think we can agree the defense preparations are far enough along to consider what we might do outside of Preddi Province."

Akuyun felt satisfied. Now it was time to decide whether defense required offensive actions. He looked over his three direct subordinates: Zulfa, Tuzere, and Kalcan. Assessor Hizer, the fourth man at the table, did not formally function as Akuyun's subordinate. Akuyun already knew their individual views, each having given opinions privately.

"My inclination is to stay with a defensive posture," said Akuyun, "except for Assessor Hizer's agent's reports you've all seen. Although we don't have updated reports from all the clans, it's evident many of them are preparing for war. Weapons production is way up, they're producing cannon, although we don't have a clear picture of what calibers, and training has intensified. Some clans are more involved than others, but it's clear the southern clans and Stent are leading this effort, especially the Keelan Clan in south Caedellium.

"We can't rule out them preparing to start offensive actions against us. With what they must think after Moreland City, along with their weapons making and training, they might decide to attack us here. I don't believe there's a real danger of them winning, but it would be bloody if they chose to push it, and there'd be no way to prevent damage to our fighting ability, in addition to suffering major civilian disruption and casualties. We need to decide whether we stay hunkered down in our positions here, or do we take actions to prevent or slow them from attacking us in force?"

"Aivacs, you go first," said Akuyun, addressing his ground force commander.

Zulfa had never been demonstrative. His serious manner and handsome face hid whatever emotions might churn beneath the surface. However, since Moreland City, more lines had been carved into his face. Despite Akuyun's private assurances and public comments that he had faith in Zulfa, he took the results as a personal failure. He recognized that although Akuyun had approved the campaign plan, and Assessor Hizer had avowed he had no reason to object, *he, Zulfa*, had still been the leader on the plain in front of Moreland City. *He* had been the commander of the thousand men left dead on the battlefield.

Whatever his feelings, he didn't hesitate to give his assessment. Akuyun expected it, and Zulfa knew that anything less would put him in more danger of falling out of the general's favor than the Moreland results had.

"I agree that any opportunity to subjugate the entire island with our existing forces is gone," he said. "We've no choice but to wait on what the High Command decides. If I had to guess, I'd say they will send reinforcements, whether under General Akuyun or another commander is unknown, and the same for whether I remain ground force commander.

"In the meantime, the question is, how do we maintain the security of Preddi Province, our troops, and the civilians? There's no way we can be sure *what* is the best course. I can propose good reasons to stay here within our most defensible positions and just as many reasons to strike at the islanders. What it comes down to is assessing the possible negative consequences.

"If we sit, we face four risks. First, we give the Caedelli time and inclination to organize themselves to attack us. Second, this also lets them focus on producing weapons. If they're now producing cannon and there's no threat to their provinces, then the cannon will be used to attack, whereas if they feared us invading their province, it's more likely they would place the new cannon in defensive positions at their cities and harbors. Third, it would allow them to concentrate men forward to our borders, instead of protecting their coasts. We can ignore for the moment the land-locked provinces we have no direct access to. And fourth, by sitting here we send the message to our troops and the civilians that the clans have the initiative. While there's some truth to that, I believe it dangerous to leave all the initiative to an enemy, even in worse situations than we find ourselves. We all know the axiom taught in our military schools, 'Attack is often the best defense.' Whether that's true in this case brings up the negatives.

"We have to ask about the consequences if we *do* take actions against the clans that stir them up. However, I suggest they're probably as stirred up now as they're going to be. We risk another failure—at least, from our point of view and likely that of our men and the civilians. Such an outcome would cause more deterioration of morale, something that's already a problem.

"Another possible negative outcome is further reduction in our fighting force, although I tend to discount this possibility, because we would carefully choose the action we undertake, and if it involved ground forces, we would use our navy as transportation and support. Even under the worst imaginable happenstance and we landed men, say, in Gwillamer Province and found ourselves facing thirty thousand islanders with cannon, we would simply re-embark on ships. Even that would work to our advantage, because we could sail to the other side of the island and attack Pewitt. The islanders would take a sixday to move from Gwillamer, and we'd have achieved our objectives by then and either be too entrenched for them to expel us or have left again by ship.

"We could envision a strategy of razing the coastal capitals and towns and moving on before they concentrated against us. However, any such plan would leave us open to what I believe is the biggest danger. We're already stretched thin defending Preddi Province. If we send thousands of our men to attack elsewhere on Caedellium, the clans could launch attacks and raids where we've weakened our defenses."

Zulfa paused and looked around at the grim faces of the other men. "So there we are. No good choices. Yet we have to make them. After hard thinking, I believe we need to take action to try to tie the clans to their own provinces. I know Assessor Hizer has other options, but I've stayed focused on our army and navy, with assurances Admiral Kalcan has given that the navy will support us in every way it can."

Kalcan grunted and nodded his head, his normally cheerful expression absent.

"I propose we attack at least one of the coastal clans with a troop landing," said Zulfa, "with naval support and the objective not to hold the province, but to burn the capital and pillage as much of the surrounding countryside as possible, before the clans can gather against us. Since we don't intend to hold the ground, two to three thousand men would be sufficient. As soon as we feel threatened or there's nothing left to destroy, we'll re-embark. Depending on the results, we then either return directly to Preddi City or circle the island to attack another province, thereby keeping the clans unsure where we'll strike next."

Administrator Tuzere had listened with set lips and small but noticeable shakes of his head. "What if the clans do as you foresee and they attack here while you're off with a sizable fraction of our fighting men? What happens to the civilians I'm responsible for and all the farms, ranches, towns, shops, and factories we've built up?"

"It's a risk," Zulfa conceded. "One way or another, though, we'll be taking risks, whether we act or not. In this case, any expedition force will be in regular contact with headquarters here. If a sizable raid or attack on your people occurs, the remaining forces will have to defend you until the others return. It might actually work to our advantage if they send a sizable force near enough to a coast to allow us to land the expedition force in their rear and catch them between us."

Tuzere slapped a hand on the table. "That all sounds well and good, but it's moving pieces on a map. The real result would be people dead and property destroyed!"

"Everything we do involves risk," Akuyun said calmly.

Tuzere flushed. "Sorry. I'm just worried."

"As we all are," said Akuyun, "but Aivacs has laid out the unpalatable options. We're here to consider those options. We've heard the recommendation from the troop commander. Nizam, do you have another option to suggest?"

Tuzere drummed the fingers of both hands on the tabletop, then splayed his fingers and sighed. "No, not really. I have to cede to Aivacs his logic from a military side and hope it doesn't backfire on us."

"Morfred," said Akuyun, turning to the navy commander, "any thoughts?"

"As Nizam says, it's a troop commander's decision. Nothing has changed in our control of the waters around Caedellium. With no outside threats, my ships can support any operation, including an attack on one or more coastal clans. As for responding to a hypothetical clan attack, my ships are limited to what we can reach from near shore, besides providing transportation."

Akuyun turned to the last man at the table, Assessor Hizer. "Sadek, any thoughts or comments?"

"No. I appreciate Aivacs's summary that we have no good options. Neither do I think there is a logical way to determine the best course. It will be using our best judgment and planning contingencies if things go wrong."

"All right," said Akuyun, "you've all had your say. I'm afraid I agree with Aivacs and Sadek about the uncertainties, and I'll have to fall back on the axiom of not giving up all the initiative. Aivacs, go ahead and work with Morfred and Sadek in planning an attack on a coastal clan. Anyone have suggestions for which clan to start with?"

"Keelan might be an obvious choice," said Hizer, "but I'll propose something else for them. They've shown the most capabilities, so I'd be disinclined to risk attacking with what I assume would be no more than two or three thousand men. We don't want anything short of an outright victory, lest we embolden the clans even more. I'm thinking one of the northwestern clans, Pewitt or Swavebroke."

"You say you have something else to suggest for Keelan?" said Admiral Kalcan.

"Yes. General Akuyun asked me for an assessment of all the hetmen and each clan's influence and the consequences if either a clan or its hetman were no longer a factor."

"Assassinations," stated Zulfa, never one for circumlocutions.

"A time-honored tactic," affirmed Hizer. "While the occasion is rare that a single leader is that much of a critical factor, often removing leaders at least makes an enemy pause to anoint a new leader and for that person to take the reins. With the Keelan hetman, all indications are he's a major player in organizing resistance, very likely the main leader. At worst, we'll disrupt the Keelan Clan's thinking, and it might hamper whatever action the clans might be contemplating. I had toyed with the idea of also moving against the Gwillamer and Mittack hetmen, the closest clans allied with Keelan, but we don't have agents in place near enough to the Gwillamese hetman, and the Mittack hetman seems to merely follow Keelan's lead and is not a factor himself.

"After careful consideration, I'm recommending in addition to Keelan that we target Skouks and Bevan. We already tried Hewell when we learned their hetman was considering joining the formal alliance with Keelan. We failed, and our agents making the attempt had to flee. Stent would be a target because of their hetman's influence, but their capital is even farther inland than

Keelan's and, like Hewell, we lost our agents there after a failed attempt on Hetman Stent."

Kalcan shifted uneasily in his chair. "But as you mention, the Keelan capital is well inland. Doesn't that complicate how your agents figure on escaping? I know your men are good, but I don't imagine they are so fanatical as to be eager for suicide missions."

"Hardly," agreed Hizer. "That's why I propose we send in strike teams for all three targets. My agent in Caernford, the Keelan capital, is the most advantageously placed of any of my men. He's too valuable to risk in an assassination attempt, even if aimed at Hetman Keelan. However, he's so closely connected to the hetman that he can give more information and guidance than agents in other clans.

"Then there's the issue of the hetman's security. Keelan took seriously our previous attempts on the Stent and Hewell hetmen, and my man reports too many guards of too high a quality for one or two men to try an attack on the hetman. And before you ask further, Aivacs, no, I don't view this as a suicide mission if we use some of your best men. I have another agent in Salford, the Keelan main port. He routinely takes wagons between Salford and Caernford. I envision a strike team landing near Salford at night, then going hidden within a large freight wagon to a secluded location near Caernford. The actual attempt would be coordinated with my Caernford agent. Your men would escape back south by the same wagons or by horseback. The horses are to be arranged beforehand or taken from the hetman's property. I don't pretend it's not dangerous, but I believe it worth the attempt, and we would apprise the men of the risks. Obviously, there are many details to work out, details that Aivacs and Morfred are in better position to deal with."

"I'll have to get my staff to study this," said Zulfa, "but *if* we can come up with a plan I believe has a plausible chance of success, I'm sure we can find the men."

"And, as before, my ships are no problem," said Kalcan. "We can just use sloops. The islanders are so used to seeing them off their coast, I doubt they pay them much attention anymore."

"All right," said Akuyun. "Sadek, get together with Aivacs and Morfred and come up with plans by next sixday."

"Swavebroke," said Zulfa five days later, when he met with Akuyun and handed his commander several sheets summarizing proposals. "Hizer points out that Swavebroke and the three clans of the hetmen we'll try to assassinate are evenly spaced around the island, so if we coordinate the attack on Swavebroke simultaneously with the attempts on the Keelan, Bevans, and Skouks hetmen, it should create maximum confusion and lessen chances of aid coming to Swavebroke."

"And the force size you recommend for the Swavebroke assault?" asked Akuyun.

"Twenty-five hundred men, mainly infantry, and a few 12-pounders. The main objective will be Shullick, the Swavebroke capital. The population is about eighteen to twenty thousand, with another few thousand in farms, ranches, and villages within ten miles.

"For us, cavalry is a problem. Horses don't like to be at sea, but the distance is short enough that we think those we take will be in reasonable shape. The problem is how many we can transport by ship, given they take up room, and then getting them quickly ashore. Morfred, of all people, suggested a solution."

The admiral detested horses and was an abysmal rider.

"He had experience as a young ensign when they needed to get horses ashore quickly. The solution was to cut a door in a cargo ship just above the loaded water line. They packed almost a hundred horses into the cargo hold of one ship. It turned out that having them so packed worked better, because they couldn't move around. We'll do the same but also have ropes around their necks, pulled up to keep the horses' heads high and their attention on breathing, and we'll have them hooded so they can't see. If possible, we'll go straight to the docks. Otherwise, the ships will get as close to shore as possible. Then we'll open the new doors in the sides of the hulls, and the horses will be forced out into the water.

"Morfred assures me they can arrange it so the hoods come off as the horses exit the ships. Men will wait in longboats to grab the ropes of the first few horses, those picked for being the most docile, and they'll row for shore. Horses are reasonable swimmers, and we'll test that as we pick the horses we'll use. Most of the other horses should follow the leaders and the boats. We'll lose some, but enough will get to shore to give us a couple hundred cavalry. We hope to capture enough horses to add to those numbers."

Akuyun nodded. "There are no plans to bring the horses back?"

"No, not unless we have enough time to ferry them back to the ships. I assume they'll be left. We'll see what happens, but I consider them expendable.

Anyway, the infantry will do most of the work. The city doesn't have strong wall fortifications, so we should be able to sweep through before the Swavebrokers can organize serious resistance. The people themselves won't be the main goal, and many, possibly even most, will flee inland in front of us. The cavalry we have will encourage them to keep moving. The main purpose is to burn the city to the ground and kill as many clan fighting men as stand against us. Looting and captives will be determined by circumstances, and as long as it doesn't interfere with the main objective.

"Assuming we take the city quickly enough and have enough active cavalry, we'll move outside the city proper to continue destroying what we can, including villages, farms, bridges, and anything else. The cavalry will also put out patrols to warn of organized forces that might threaten us. All of this is contingent, of course, on how things progress. What we won't do under any circumstances is remain too long and allow other clans to send help. I'm making an estimate of three days on shore, and then we re-embark."

"I see you're taking twenty 12-pounders." Akuyun perused the summary sheets. "Should be more than enough, since we don't have reports of Swavebroke having cannon—not yet, anyway," he added as a caution.

"I assume the coast-mapping reports are accurate," said Zulfa, "and Morfred assures me that if necessary, he can bring one or more frigates close enough to shore to provide support from their 30-pounders. Only solid shot will be possible out to a thousand yards onshore and grapeshot to 600 yards, but no canister. Still, that should be enough to discourage any Swavebroke artillery, if they have it. If the ships and our 12-pounders are not enough support, we'll simply pull back, do what damage we can, and leave."

Akuyun scanned the sheets again, while Zulfa waited.

"I'm sure I'll have questions, but I need to read this over carefully and give it some thought," said Akuyun. "What about the attempts on the hetmen? I don't see anything here."

Zulfa frowned. "Hizer and I are still discussing the compositions of the strikes."

Akuyun interpreted the *discussion* to be *arguing*, but he didn't interrupt.

"Hizer originally wanted a thirty-man team to go after Hetman Keelan, while I thought ten was the most that we could expect to remain undetected long enough to get from Salford to Caernford and make the attempt. The problem is balancing getting to Caernford, having enough men to fight through the expected number of guards, killing the hetman, and then escaping. As with too much of what we're doing, we have no best options. I argued that thirty men were too many to avoid alerting the Keelanders, while Hizer counter-argued that ten men might not get through the security."

Zulfa's mouth formed a grin or a grimace. "I think we'll end up with a twenty-man strike team, and neither of us will be satisfied, but the way things are, that seems to be the norm."

"And the other two hetmen?"

"There, the two capitals are on the coast. After considering smaller teams for these two targets, we've agreed to go with the same twenty-man teams. Escape afterward is not as complex as with Keelan, and those teams would have support from ships. Hetman Bevans lives on an estate outside the city, and reports are that he keeps six guards on the property. However, they rotate being on duty, so at night there will probably be only two guards awake, if we take them by surprise.

"Skouks may be the easiest, as long as we launch all the attacks on a specific day. Hetman Skouks routinely goes to a daughter's house on the same day every month and spends two days. She has six children he dotes on, and he almost never misses a trip. Naturally, nothing is assured, but with no information to the contrary about the Keelan and Bevan hetmen's schedules, we'll plan based on Skouks's schedule and hope to catch the others the same day."

"I could argue that Keelan is more important than the others and to concentrate on him," said Akuyun.

"True, but whether the attempt on Keelan succeeds or fails, we won't get another chance at any of the hetmen, because all of them will certainly change their routines and increase their security to make any future attempt impractical."

"Do you have a timetable?"

"It won't be right away," said Zulfa. "We'll pick good men from different units, and they won't have fought together before. It's best to give them time to train and become comfortable with one another. The mission will be risky enough without having the men uncertain about other team members."

"I'd like to set a tentative window," ordered Akuyun. "It can always change, but let's narrow it down."

"I think we can set it a month and a half from today," Zulfa suggested. "That gives us enough time to select the teams and do the necessary training."

CHAPTER 24

HOME LIFE

Yozef and Maera

Sixdays passed. The Kolsko household settled into a routine. Yozef and Maera had moved into their new house before its final construction details and those of surrounding structures were finished, but Yozef wanted to be in their home. The Keelan Manor, although large, was crowded with the new additions to the entourage, and it wasn't *theirs*.

They increased the originally planned three workers' and guest cottages to four. Balwis and Carnigan shared one, for when one or both had duty as bodyguards. Gwyned Walstyn and Mirramel Killin and their two daughters, Morwena and Dwyna, shared a second cottage. Anarynd completed the Kolsko household with a bedroom in the main house. A cook, Serys Clithrow, a widow who had relatives in Caernford, rode her own horse back and forth.

Balwis and Carnigan made themselves useful but hovered around Yozef whenever someone they didn't know came to the house: both took their bodyguard duties seriously. At other times, Balwis trained city Keelanders to stay on horses, and Carnigan played the intimidating sergeant major.

Gwyned likewise helped with a variety of chores, which included caring for Aeneas, cooking when Serys needed help or wasn't working, and, the most important to Maera, keeping Anarynd company when Maera was away from the house or busy in her study.

All the women wondered at Maera's speedy recovery from childbirth. Most men didn't notice—yet Yozef wasn't most men. He noted how quickly she recuperated and filed it away for future thought, pleased when Maera resumed many of her previous activities. Maera again managed his schedules and continued planning for the university. She understood the necessity of giving the plans a lower priority, but there were still things to be done. She insisted that planning for the future symbolized faith that the Caedelli would *have* a future, in which a university would play a major role. She also began contributing to Pedr Kennrick's logistics planning.

The resumption of work led her to question herself and her roles, particularly that of a mother. Her model of motherhood came from her own family, where Breda ran Keelan Manor and had only informal roles outside the family. It was a rare day when Breda didn't spend most hours inside the manor or on the grounds. For Maera, life was different. Many days she spent half of the day or more at St. Tomo's Abbey or at the clan headquarters in Caernford. And even when home, she might be in her study reviewing communications to and from her father or Yozef, keeping up with her studies of off-island languages, or poring over writings about other nations and people of Anyar, scrounged from libraries all over Caedellium.

On top of all these tasks, she was a new mother. Maera worried that she wasn't taking proper care of Aeneas and chafed at the endless amount of attention he needed, which took away from everything she *wanted* to do and felt she *needed* to do. She found herself almost angry at Yozef when he offered to help with the baby. Changing, feeding, and washing Aeneas fascinated him, although his opportunities were limited because of endless demands on him from his shops and factories, her father and his advisors, and seemingly everyone else. She caught herself wondering whether he passively criticized her for neglecting Aeneas, even though she recognized it was probably her imagination. Her internal conflict grew until she took the baby and walked the half mile to see her mother.

"I'm a terrible mother!" Maera exclaimed, almost in tears.

Her mother got within ten feet of her and stopped, surprised at the outburst. Breda recovered quickly and moved to embrace her daughter and grandson. "I wondered if such thoughts would hit my precocious daughter, as they do all new mothers. I thought maybe you were above such self-doubts, and I'm both relieved and sorry you're not."

"You're glad!?" exclaimed Maera.

"No. *Glad* isn't the word, but you have always castigated yourself for being different from other young women. This just proves you're not that different. Questioning yourself is something all good mothers go through."

"But I don't spend enough time with Aeneas!" she wailed. "And when I do, I find myself wishing I were somewhere else!"

Breda sighed, took her daughter by the arm, and sat with her on a veranda swing. "Do you love Aeneas?"

"Oh, Merciful God, yes! I love holding him and breastfeeding him and, yes, even sometimes changing him. At times, it's like he's the only thing in the world. Then I remember some work I need to be doing, and it all changes. What's wrong with me?"

"Nothing is wrong, dear. You're going through what all new mothers do. In your case, it's worse because you have tasks outside the home that are not only important to you, but are important to Keelan and all of Caedellium. I only had our family, so I didn't have these added pressures to put on myself."

"What do I do, Mother?" pleaded Maera.

"You have plenty of help with the baby, don't you?"

"Lord, yes. Anarynd adores him, and Gwenyd's always ready to take care of him. When I'm not around for feedings, Mirramel is a great wet nurse. She's not the brightest person but totally good-hearted and has plenty of milk for both her own daughter and Aeneas."

Maera smiled. "Oh, Mother, you should have seen Yozef's face when we first met Mirramel. He thought I would be the only one to talk to her, but he went along when I said he should be there, too, since her husband died at Moreland City. I assumed he'd want to give her condolences. Mirramel had her daughter with her, and while we talked, she started breastfeeding. After Dwyna finished, Mirramel assured me she had plenty of milk and how she loved breastfeeding. She said she needed another baby to feed because her breasts ached with more milk than Dwyna wanted. When she fed Aeneas, the little beggar went right for the nipple, which is bigger than mine. I think Yozef felt embarrassed by it all. No, there's plenty of help with Aeneas. And then there's you and my sisters, always begging me to bring Aeneas here and you'll watch him."

"Have you talked to Yozef about this?"

"I know what he'll say!" Maera's tone showed her annoyance. "He'll look all confused at what I'm talking about and then start offering reasons why it's not true, and if it is, he'll propose solutions, such as him trying to help more."

Breda had to restrain her laughter, and Maera missed the twinkle in her mother's eye.

"So let me see if I understand. You love your baby and caring for him, except when you recall other duties you want to do. However, when you *are* engaged in those activities, you have three women around the house, along with me and your sisters, all more than willing to help. And then, oh, Merciful

God, you have a husband who obviously does not think you a bad mother and wants to help more. Surely, this is a nightmare!"

Maera looked angrily at her mother, then broke into raucous laughter. "I knew I could count on you for motherly advice!" Maera roared.

Breda joined in, and minutes passed before their laughter subsided.

"Yes, yes," Maera admitted. "You warned me, as did Diera, my cousins, Gwyned, and who knows how many other women, to expect doubts and depression. I guess I didn't take their words seriously. After all, *I am* Maera Kolsko-Keelan and am *above* such frailties. If nothing else, it's a lesson in humility. Not that I expect to be content. I expect I'll always worry that I'm not doing enough."

"Which will only prove the positive, not the negative. Keep that in mind," said Breda.

Kolsko Estate, Bedroom

The coupling was as gentle as Yozef could manage. It had been only four sixdays since the birth, and despite Maera's insistence she felt fine, she still experienced a bit of soreness, along with awkwardness in finding a position that felt comfortable. However, she didn't begrudge her husband's need, and she made the overture and deflected his concern. Later, they lay together side by side, the back of her head against his face, his arms wrapped around her.

His thoughts dwelled on her naked body against his. With one hand, he stroked her abdomen, which had shrunk back to near its original shape. He thought about its previous contents, idly wondering whether he'd bumped the baby while it was in there or if it had felt the rocking motion during the last months before they'd stopped, a few sixdays before the birth.

Maera turned to face him, her breasts and belly pressed to him, her face against his chest. "Yozef, what do you fear most?"

"Huh? Where did that come from?"

"Oh . . . I was talking with Mother today. It made me think about what I fear. Although it should be the Narthani and what may happen, I find the fear that's most on my mind is that I'll be a bad mother, and then I think how selfish that is, and, oh . . . you know."

He hugged her tighter. "All I can say is that *I* don't have any such concerns. You know you can ask me for any help you need, but only you can deal with what goes through your mind."

His words relieved Maera, though she suspected people might think they sounded cold. She didn't doubt him when he said he had no qualms about her ability to be a good mother or about her being able to talk to him about it. His sincerity just *was*. She also appreciated his not thinking he could make her thoughts different just by something he said or did. It was ultimately up to her.

They stayed molded together for several minutes in silence until Yozef spoke.

"Maera. Wife, lover, mother of my child. I've always respected you, right from the first time we met. Such a lovely young woman, even if you didn't realize it. So smart. So responsible, though at times too much so. When we got married, it was a rational thing to do. It solved problems for everyone—you, me, your family's responsibility to have heirs. I think it's been good for you, but there's no doubt it has been for me."

Maera didn't know where her husband's words were going. He seldom spoke of his deepest thoughts or emotions.

"Things changed," he said. "Even before the baby came, and even before we knew you were pregnant, I knew I loved you."

She burrowed her face tighter against his chest, her free arm clutching around his back, her heart pounding.

"I know I should have told you earlier. I guess I was afraid of what you'd say, since neither of us ever used the words. I just thought you should know how I felt, but you shouldn't feel you *have* to say the words back. I'm content just having you for a wife."

"Oh, Yozef," she said into his chest, then pulled her head back to speak clearly. "I knew after the first few months that I loved you. Like you, I didn't know how you felt, so I kept it to myself. Maybe I was afraid of losing the hope that you loved me, too, and that kept me silent."

"Well, aren't we a pair?" said Yozef, his voice choked, though also indicating amusement.

They lay together for another ten minutes, both relaxing after the spoken words.

"Yozef, you didn't answer. What's your greatest fear?"

It was a question he faced regularly. His answer wasn't that he feared being exposed as more than a stranger from another part of Anyar. He suspected that by this time, his reputation would let him lie or evade any revelation. As with Maera, his mind told him the Narthani threat should be paramount, but it wasn't.

"I'm like you, Maera. I worry about something focused on myself. Maybe it's just part of being human. I'm afraid I'll give advice that people will follow, and it will turn into a disaster, with deaths and other consequences the clans can't recover from."

Anarynd

The travel from Moreland City to the Keelan border had been hard but liberating. Despite stepping into the unknown, her going to find Gwyned and the other women and their trek to Keelan had been the freest she'd felt in years. Whatever the future held, she felt as if she'd left nothing behind.

She first saw the man she suspected was Maera's husband the second day on the wagons, when the group of armed men approached. She hadn't known what to expect when she met Yozef for the first time. All she had known about him came from Maera's letters, which described the mysterious, interesting man found naked on a Keelan beach. Then the letters changed, with more descriptions of time spent with Yozef, her confusion about what she felt, her taking the step to propose marriage, and finally, before the raid on Lanwith, Maera's growing satisfaction with the marriage.

Anarynd's first hint that there was something special about Maera's polite but otherwise undistinguished husband was the obvious deference given him by the other men in the mounted party. Anarynd had picked up nuances of men's interactions during her months in Hanslow and saw how the Narthani behaved around one another. Their ranks and social positions laid out rules and formalities, even when the men didn't realize it.

That experience told her Yozef was, in many ways, the equal of Memas Erdelin, the Narthani colonel who had been her master. The difference was that she sensed caution or fear in the behavior of men under Erdelin, whereas with Yozef the men showed respect tinged almost with affection.

The reunion with Maera was everything she'd dreamed of and had feared wouldn't match the dream. Maera and Yozef quashed her doubts about where she would go and how she would live; she would live with them as long as she wanted. As sixdays came and went, the previous months didn't go away, but she could feel a scar forming, a sign of healing and evidence of past wounds.

The birth of Aeneas was a time of joy and sadness: joy at witnessing a new soul appear in the world and sharing the experience with Maera, sadness because it might be a joy she would never experience.

Anarynd expected Maera to take many sixdays to recover from the birth, but to everyone's surprise, except Anarynd's, Maera was up and active within days. Anarynd could only shake her head. After all, wasn't this Maera Keelan, Kolsko-Keelan, who could do anything she set her mind to?

The warmth and casual acceptance of her by all members of the household elicited an occasional embarrassed flicker of envy within Anarynd. She remembered her own family and her lost dream of marrying the distant cousin and starting a family, one she had sworn would be different than her own.

She didn't understand how Maera seemed somehow different. It had nothing to do with how Maera treated her, though it took a few sixdays for them to slip back into knowing what the other was thinking, based on the merest change of expression or bodily twitch. Maera was more relaxed. As long as Anarynd had known her, Maera had seemed to exude an aura that combined defensiveness and assertiveness. Now she exhibited a calmness that was missing in the past. Maera seemed surprised when Anarynd mentioned this, then she wondered to her friend whether it was due to Yozef and how he seemed to accept everything about his wife.

"Is it Yozef, or is it you?" Anarynd asked.

Maera looked thoughtfully at her friend. "You mean, is it *really* Yozef who treats me differently than others do, or is it how *I* perceive it? I suppose I can't be sure. Maybe it's a bit of both. I have no doubt he treated me differently right from when I first met him. Partly, it's because he's not from Caedellium, but somehow there's more to it.

"Maybe it's because since I married Yozef, so many new things have happened in my life. Oh, getting married and all that entails, of course. And then there's Aeneas. Although I helped Father by being his scribe and assistant, it was informal, something we didn't admit to everyone. Since Yozef, that's different. I do as much or more to help him as I did for Father, but Yozef has always publicly acknowledged it with pride—not that by now, anyone would have problems with almost anything Yozef Kolsko does or approves of.

"And the university idea I told you about. Think of it! A large center of scholastics with me in charge! When Yozef first proposed it, I felt as if I could *fly*. After my emotions settled, I became more aware of how much work it would be and of the responsibility, but by then, it had coalesced into determination and a vision of a long-term calling that would truly be Maera Kolsko-Keelan's. Again, things have changed since then. Not just Aeneas, but the Narthani and how everything has to shift to them, as the only priority for the clans. But the idea of the university is still in my mind as something that's *mine*. Something to return to when the time is right."

After listening to Maera's theorizing about her changed outlook, Anarynd said, "No matter what the cause, you're still Maera, but it's like you're 'Maera, the woman,' instead of 'Maera, the girl.'"

CHAPTER 25

DANGERS IN HEALING

As his status rose, Yozef's trepidations faded about people's reactions to his innovations and the knowledge he purposefully or inadvertently introduced. Although he still tried to restrain what he said without thinking, accidental lapses happened occasionally, and those that did, he could either explain away or attribute to his idiosyncrasies.

However, he couldn't ignore one issue—the consequences of the elements the Watchers had injected into him to help his body recover from the plane collision. Harlie had explained that the elements—or nanoelements/nanomachines, as Yozef thought of them—also conferred immunity against infections and cancer. The elements somehow recognized any foreign organisms or abnormal cells and eliminated them. As much as he appreciated never again becoming sick or getting cancer, a third feature Harlie had not enumerated was that Yozef healed from physical injuries faster than normal.

Although all three effects of the nanoelements were positive, the first two would go unnoticed, but healing fast could attract unwanted attention. The benefits of fast healing were obvious, and so was the complication of explaining *why* he healed so fast—an explanation that dare not mention advanced technology, so that Yozef risked being labeled a demon and an agent of the Evil One, the Anyar version of Satan.

After his transportation to Caedellium, Yozef became suspicious of how quickly his minor cuts and bruises healed. His first serious injury occurred when a musket ball slashed a shinbone during the courtyard fight defending against Buldorian raiders. Carnigan saw the wound, as did the medicant who applied stitches, but neither of them nor anyone else again examined the wound hidden by his pant leg. During the following hours and days, Yozef swore he could almost see the wound heal, it progressed so quickly. He recognized the danger;

how could he explain or reveal injuries healing so fast that they inevitably invoked thoughts of divine or demonic intervention?

During the next months and years, it would take additional healings and a collation of evidence for Yozef to understand the full implications of the nanoelements, for himself and others.

Abersford, after the Battle of Moreland City

Further conclusive evidence of Yozef's fast healing came after the Battle of Moreland City. As the battle drew to a close, a Narthani cannon ball shattered the carriage of a captured 12-pounder only eight feet from him. A chunk of wood scored a glancing but solid blow to the side of his head, nicking the bone and leaving a serious gash. Carnigan wrapped Yozef's head with cloth to staunch most of the bleeding, and when they reached their original positions, a medicant closed the wound with eight painful stitches.

The throbbing pain and an intense headache slowly subsided during the two days it took them to return to Abersford. When Yozef got home and surreptitiously examined the wound site with mirrors, he would have estimated it was ten days old or more.

If he had lived alone or with a wife less perceptive or assertive, hiding the wound would have been manageable. Unfortunately, neither of the two conditions existed.

* * *

"Don't tell me it doesn't bother you," fumed Maera. "You winced when you turned your head fast and were unsteady on your feet yesterday when you returned. You'll let the medicants at St. Sidryn's examine your hard head."

"Maera, it's not that bad. I was just tired from the trip."

"Oh, sorry, Yozef. Did I give the impression we were having a discussion on whether you were going? If I have to, I'll go get Carnigan, and he'll carry you to the abbey."

Well, shit, Yozef cursed to himself. *The big oaf just might do it, if she starts in on him. I wouldn't blame either of them. Normally, you should keep an eye on any wound to the head. She didn't see it after it happened, and neither did the St. Sidryn's medicants, so I should be able to bluff my way through.*

The two of them stood staring at each other, Maera waiting for Yozef to give up and Yozef imagining the medicant examination and the resulting comments on the condition of the wound.

He focused back on Maera, standing arms folded, looking back at him with her "I'm Maera Kolsko-Keelan, and we'll do it my way" expression.

"You're right, Maera. We'll go to St. Sidryn's."

When defeat is inevitable, you might as well pretend it's a good idea.

Maera had been in mid-pregnancy, and they walked to St. Sidryn's. Scheduled appointments were not available. Patients arrived and waited their turn. Yozef still felt uneasy about how he was now treated differently than an average citizen, especially since marrying the hetman's daughter. He finally capitulated and admitted to himself that he appreciated it at times like this. As soon as they appeared in the hospital reception area, an aide rushed them to an examination room. Yozef tried not to look at the patients waiting their turn, but as he and Maera passed them, he couldn't help himself and checked out their expressions. All were neutral, respectful, or even seemed pleased to allow Yozef Kolsko and Maera Kolsko-Keelan to go first.

The medicant aide had no sooner left them in the examination room than Saoul Dyllis rushed in. The middle-aged medicant was the chief surgeon at St. Sidryn's and served temporarily as head medicant, because Abbess Diera Beynom hadn't returned from Moreland City. Diera had sent word that it would be several more days before she came with wagons carrying the non-walking wounded Keelanders from the battle site.

"Maera, Yozef," said Dyllis, as he rushed in, breathing heavily. "Nice to see you. Especially you, Yozef. I heard you returned last afternoon and with a bandage on your head. I assume that's what you're here about, though I've sent for Sister Norla to check Maera, as long as you're both here."

"Yozef first," said Maera. "I haven't seen his wound yet, but it needs to be checked. He acted like it bothered him, and now he's trying to insist it was fatigue from the travel."

"Very right to come in," Dyllis agreed. "At least, you'll need to learn how often to change the bandage. Sit over here, Yozef, next to the lanterns."

Yozef sat, and Dyllis used flint strikers on four of the kerosene lanterns Yozef had introduced during the previous year. The lanterns were arranged in a vertical square, where a patient's chair or cot could be moved to allow maximum light on whatever body part was under examination.

When Yozef started to unwind the bandage, Dyllis stopped him. "Here, let me do that. We don't want the cloth to pull away scabs or break stitches. You did have stitches, didn't you?"

"Yes, Saoul, eight in fact."

"Eight? It must be a significant wound for that many," Dyllis said, as he pulled the small pin holding the bandage end closed and slowly unwrapped the cloth. "Tell me if you feel any pulling."

Maera stood looking over Dyllis's shoulder, her frown and eye focus reminding Yozef of his mother, making sure he behaved for the doctor when they visited for whatever reason.

The medicant had nearly finished unwinding when Yozef felt a twinge. He had glimpsed the bandage reddened with dried blood. "Something there, Saoul. Not bad, but like a little pull of skin."

"Only a little left," said Dyllis. "Let me dampen the cloth to lessen the chances of opening the wound."

The medicant moistened the last of the bandage with a wet rag, then carefully exposed the side of Yozef's head . . . and frowned. "Well, that doesn't look so bad," he said with a puzzled tone, gently probing the area with his fingers. "It appears completely closed. In fact, from what I'm seeing, I question whether it needed the stitches at all. A simple compression bandage might have served or maybe two stitches at most, but eight?"

"So it wasn't that serious?" asked Maera.

"Not that I can see. Oh, there's redness around the cut and stitches, maybe more than I would expect. It'll leave a surprisingly big scar for such a minor wound, but everyone's body is different, so it's nothing that unusual."

Dyllis stopped examining the wound and picked up the old bandage. "This is also puzzling. From the amount of blood, I would have expected a more severe wound. Of course, head wounds bleed profusely. Even minor cuts can give an impression the injury is far more serious than it is."

The medicant dropped the bandage into a waste receptacle and turned to Yozef and Maera. "I could cover it again with a smaller bandage, but there's no sign of leakage, so I'd be inclined to leave it exposed to the air."

No way, Jose, Yozef thought. *People seeing for themselves how fast it heals will raise red flags from here to Caernford, and Carnigan and Wyfor saw the original wound!*

"I'll be working in several of my shops in the next sixday, so maybe it's better to keep it covered so nothing gets in it or hits it directly." Yozef tried his best to sound sincere and resisted the impulse to check how Maera reacted.

"As you wish," said Dyllis. "I'll cover it again and give you several similar bandages. Change them until you think the area is sufficiently healed not to need protecting while at your work. If it continues to bother you or anything changes, come back."

Yozef and Maera walked back home, holding hands. Past the abbey's tended fields, Maera put her other hand on top of their clasped ones. "Sorry if I sounded so 'pushy,' as you call it. It's just that I worry about you and wasn't sure if you'd take care of yourself. I know it's silly. You'd do what was necessary. Maybe I'm just overly worrying because of the baby."

"Nonsense," said Yozef, smiling and patting her hand. "It's our responsibility to worry about each other. It's part of being married."

"I warn you," said Maera, "I'll keep pestering you about how you feel, and I'll change the bandage for you."

"Thanks, Maera, I appreciate it."

In a pig's eye, he thought. *Now I have to find excuses to change it myself for the next several days. By then, I should be able to get away with claiming quick healing on a minor injury.*

By the next morning, his headache was gone. Yozef peeked under the bandage to see further signs of healing and confirmed the need to keep Maera from too close an examination. He rose before his wife and changed the bandage, later showing her the lack of blood on the old bandage, confirming the injury to be minor and healing well. The second and third days, he found other excuses she grumbled at but seemed to accept. Finally, he let her take off the bandage, only when they prepared for bed.

"Well," she groused, as she finished touching the wound area with her fingers. "The candlelight doesn't let me see that much, but it seems all right, and there's no warmth of the skin."

"I feel fine. No headache or tiredness. I think it's safe to say that's behind me."

"Just don't do too much yet, and another examination by Brother Dyllis is a good idea."

"Okay. Tomorrow is too busy, but let's figure on the day after."

Fat chance. A few delays, and it'll all fade away.

Which was what happened. Safe from Maera and Dyllis, Yozef had two more people to be wary of—Carnigan and Wyfor. Both men had been present at the time of the wound and saw the gash, the blood, and Yozef's unsteadiness. They were the most pertinent witnesses who could cause trouble.

Fortunately, avoiding them proved easier than with Maera. Yozef canceled a scheduled monthly sparring session with Wyfor. By the time the next month rolled around, Wyfor would accept normal healing. Carnigan was more difficult. Yozef wore the bandages the first few days, then a cap hiding the wound site. By the end of the second sixday, Yozef risked exposure with Carnigan, who evidenced no interest in the wound.

Bronwyn and Aragorn

One consequence of Yozef's effort to hide his fast healing from Maera brought back to mind a separate concern. The Watchers had altered his biochemistry and physiology by modifying the genes of his mitochondria, the sub-cellular organelles responsible for energy production, to compensate for Anyar's higher gravity: 1.18 times that of Earth. He had grudgingly admitted the Watchers were trying to help him, short of returning him to Earth. Although the vast bulk of human genetic material existed within the 30,000 genes in the cell nucleus, the mitochondria contained only 37 genes, remnants of the genome of an ancient symbiotic microorganism that evolved into the mitochondria.

A concern that occurred to Yozef the first time he'd held Aragorn, his and Bronwyn's child by their affair, was the effect of the higher gravity on a child with one parent from Earth. Yozef knew Aragorn would not inherit the enhanced energy production, because all the mitochondria in a baby's cells descended from the mother. A mother's ovum contained mitochondria, but the father's sperm did not. However long since humans had been transported to Anyar, he assumed that during the intervening thousands of years, there had been natural selection for genes favorable to the higher Anyar gravity. How would having only half of his genes Anyarian affect Aragorn?

Yozef already assumed Aragorn would be susceptible to diseases, because the child didn't possess the nanoelements. Residual antibodies transferred from the mother initially bolstered a baby's immune system, though that protection faded and the child became self-dependent within months. The same reasoning that caused Yozef to worry about gravity also applied to disease resistance. Because half of Aragorn's genes came from Yozef, those genes might not be adapted to Anyarian microorganisms, and the child would be more susceptible than other Anyarian children. It would be bitter if Aragorn was doubly stressed by both Anyar's gravity and diseases.

It had been three months since he'd last seen Aragorn. The child was now almost six months old (seven Earth months) and should be crawling. Signs of impairment should be apparent.

The questions had immediacy, because Maera would deliver a child in only a few months. He needed to visit the Merton farm to see for himself.

At morning meal, Yozef broached a visit with Maera.

"Maera, I haven't seen Aragorn for several months. I'm considering a quick trip north to the farm to see how he's doing."

Maera had been buttering a warm biscuit and continued with only a slight glance up to her husband. "That's a good idea, Yozef. I meant to suggest a visit to you, but with everything going on . . . "

Yozef relaxed. Even after three years, he hadn't fully adjusted to the Caedelli customs about such matters. Here, adults were adults, and no stigma attached to a child conceived outside marriage, as long as the child was cared for. In Aragorn's case, the father had acknowledged responsibility in providing for the child. Yozef still shook his head at the memory of a Godsday service attended by himself and his pregnant wife, along with Bronwyn holding Aragorn, her husband, her sister/co-wife, and the sister's three children. Everyone took all of it so matter-of-factly.

"Do you plan to spend the night?" asked Maera, taking a bite of biscuit.

"No, I thought of going right after we eat and being back this evening."

"I think I'll stay here this time. I'm not looking forward to the carriage ride in my condition," said Maera. "I'll walk with you to Abersford and buy gifts for Bronwyn and Aragorn, do some visiting, and come back home."

An hour and a half later, Yozef bid Maera good day and mounted Seabiscuit. He tied a package to the back of Seabiscuit's saddle that held a bolt of cloth for Bronwyn and several shirts he assumed were too large for Aragorn now, but into which the child would grow.

No word of his visit preceded him, so when he arrived at the farm, there was no welcome committee. From Seabiscuit's back, he could see Bronwyn and her husband, Cynwin, working in a field with two other men. As he rode up to the house, Bronwyn's sister Dellia came out of the house. A child of about two years of age hid behind her skirt, and she carried baby Aragorn. The two older children, five and seven, stopped playing with a dog and stood watching Yozef rein in and dismount.

"Greetings, Yozef," called out Dellia, shifting Aragorn to her other hip. "It's been months since we saw you last and were relieved to hear you returned from the terrible fighting in Moreland." Dellia said to the oldest child, "Ginwan, run tell Mother Bronwyn and your father that Yozef Kolsko is here."

The seven-year-old ran to the field, followed by his sister and the yapping dog.

Yozef walked up to Dellia. She held out Aragorn, who clung first to Dellia, then relented and held his arms open while Yozef picked him up. The child scrunched his eyes at his new conveyance, as if in doubt, then stuck a hand into Yozef's mouth and burbled.

"He's crawling since you last saw him," Dellia commented. "Set him down and watch. We have to keep an eye on him every second, or he's out a door."

Yozef squatted and put Aragorn on the ground. The child stared into Yozef's face, then twisted around and crawled back to Dellia.

Yozef's doubts about his child's health eased. *Well, he's certainly healthy-looking enough. Not that I've handled him or any other baby that much. I was afraid I'd see him as struggling. He might not have my modified mitochondrial genes, but those genes he has seem to be sufficient for Anyar's gravity, at least when raised on it from conception.*

"And he's strong and hasn't been sick?" asked Yozef.

"No!" said Dellia. "As healthy as any baby I've ever cared for. This whole last year has been a blessing. The other three children had minor ailments, but the rest of us have never felt better. Darling little Aragorn brought good fortune to us all."

Something nudged the edge of Yozef's consciousness, but before he could identify it, Bronwyn and the others hustled in from the field, and for the next two hours the four adults sat on the farmhouse porch, Aragorn alternating among four adult laps or playing, then being breastfed by Bronwyn and falling asleep. Yozef asked questions about Aragorn, inquired politely into the three parents and their other children, and was, in turn, queried about Moreland City and what it meant for the future of Caedellium.

Halfway through the visit, Dellia went inside and came back with plates of bread, cheese, hard sausage, and water. When Yozef left to return to Abersford, he held Aragorn one last time to reassure himself, then bid goodbye with an invitation for the Merton family to eat mid-day meal with him and Maera the next time the family attended a St. Sidryn's Godsday service. His last glance back received a wave from Dellia and another from Aragorn, his arm controlled by his second mother. The other children played again, and Bronwyn and Cynwin were absent, presumably back at work.

The ride back was different from the time he'd returned home after Bronwyn told him of her plans to marry Dellia and Cynwin and that she carried Yozef's child. Yozef had known the affair was slowly ending and felt ambivalent. Part of him was relieved at the ease at which he avoided any commitment to Bronwyn and pleased that Bronwyn and the child were secure, yet at the same time he suffered from an aching loneliness.

This time was different. He looked forward to going back to Maera and *their* child swelling within her. To their home.

Maera, Curiosity Unquenched

When Yozef finally allowed Maera to examine his wound in full light, he strived to be nonchalant, and he assumed the view satisfied her. He was wrong.

"See, I told you it wasn't that bad," said Yozef. "The same as Brother Dyllis noted."

Maera stroked the pinkish scar tissue, with hair growing back a lighter hue than before, not quite white. The original gash and eight stitches were barely discernible.

"The headaches are gone now?" asked Maera.

"Yes. No twinges anymore."

Maera stood on their veranda, watching him walk toward Abersford. Her eyes narrowed at his obviously jaunty gait.

He sounded a little too relieved. Almost like he was afraid she'd notice something. He was right. Saoul did seem to think it wasn't serious, but he was also perplexed at the amount of blood on the bandage with so minor a wound, even considering that head wounds bled more than others. And eight stitches?

Then why all the excuses so that she didn't get to change the bandages? Yozef always did it himself or didn't have time or something else.

Carnigan Puvey and Wyfor Kales had been at the scene of Yozef's injury when it happened and were the first to go to him, with Carnigan tying a cloth around Yozef's head until they could get to the medicants. Carnigan had also been there for the stitches and saw how Yozef reacted to it all. On the men's return to Abersford, Maera quizzed Carnigan and found out that Yozef had under-reported to his wife details of his role in the fighting.

Maera considered Carnigan a friend, although what he thought on any subject was seldom clear. Yet she did know that when Carnigan and Yozef returned from Moreland City, it took little effort for her to get Carnigan to blab about Yozef's role in the fighting, details Yozef had conveniently glossed over. She now chastised herself that she hadn't probed for more details about the wound. She intended to rectify that oversight.

When no opportunity occurred after three days, she insisted that Yozef needed a relaxing evening at a pub—with Carnigan, of course. She accompanied him, and although she ostensibly watched Go games, she kept a covert eye on Yozef's table. As soon as he left to relieve himself, she hustled over to Carnigan. She had only a few minutes.

"Having a good time, Carnigan?" she asked, though before he could answer, she rushed on. "Don't you think it's wonderful Yozef recovered so fast from his injury at Moreland City? I was worried, but it turned out to be a minor injury."

If there was more to the wound than Yozef led her or Medicant Dyllis to believe, she gave Carnigan the opportunity to contradict or confirm.

"Yeah," said Carnigan, taking another of his prodigious quaffs from a stein, "bled like a river, and I feared the worst. I slapped a cloth on to hold him together until we got to the medicants, and they sewed him up. Kales and I pretty much carried him off the battlefield, and he was barely sensible the rest of the day, then he seemed better by the next morning."

"Oh, I'm sure you've seen worse," Maera said, as innocently as she could manage.

"Well, unless you get to heads missing pieces, not really. Short of those cases, I thought he looked pretty bad, but what do I know?"

Maera spotted Yozef returning, and she patted Carnigan on the hand. "Have a good rest of the evening." She gave Yozef a peck as they passed, he back to his own stein and she to her second hoped-for informant, Wyfor Kales.

The wiry, scarred man sat with two other men as disreputable-looking as himself. Those two men excused themselves when the hetman's daughter and wife of Yozef Kolsko arrived, while Kales simply eyed her as he would any unimpressive phenomenon.

"Hello, Wyfor . . . actually, I don't think I ever asked if I could use your first name," Maera said as cheerily as she could, though she suspected he wasn't fooled.

"Why not, Maera?"

She stumbled for a moment, as accustomed as she had become to Yozef's lack of deference based on family or position and the degree to which his attitude rubbed off onto those interacting with him the most. Kales's tone bespoke indifference. There was no reason to dissemble. She decided Kales would appreciate bluntness.

"Wyfor, you were there with Yozef when he got hurt at Moreland City. Can you tell me how it happened?"

Kales didn't hesitate. "Happened as we withdrew. We'd done all the damage we could without trying to fight the Narthani face-to-face. Must have been one of the last cannonball shots. It hit a Narthani 12-pounder our men were pulling off. Yozef was only about eight feet away, still giving directions to the men, as if they didn't already know to hurry. Anyway, the cannon's carriage shattered, and a piece several feet long and with blade ends took him in the head. I thought he was done for, but it just glanced along his skull."

His skull! Maera's pulse shot up.

Kales continued. "Since he's here in the Snarling Graeko I assume he's recovered, although it wouldn't have surprised me if it had taken several months."

"Oh, he recovered quite quickly," Maera said distractedly, as she digested Kales's account. "Well, thank you, Wyfor. I won't bother you anymore, and I think my turn at Go is coming up."

Later that evening, Yozef went straight to bed with a beer-fuzzed brain. Maera sat on the veranda, thinking.

I know I promised him I wouldn't pry. He's already told me there are things he can't explain to me, and I believe him when he says if there's anyone he can someday tell, it will be me. Still . . . it's almost certain his wound healed so fast that he was afraid it would be noticed and raise suspicions about who, or what, he is.

Diera also warned me not to press too hard and have him shut down in other ways. None of that means I can't stay curious and try to figure it out on my own.

She decided she would write down everything out of place she'd noticed previously, even if at the time it didn't rise to her consciousness. She'd add everything Yozef had ever said about himself and his homeland. What he hadn't told her, she could glean from others, such as Diera and Sistian.

Then I'll be alert for anything else that happens. I wonder if someday I end up writing a book on The Life and Times of Yozef Kolsko.

With a chuckle, she rose and entered the house, nestled next to her husband, and soon fell asleep.

It was years before she remembered that foresight could come when least expected, even in the guise of humor.

* * *

Revelation to Maera

As time passed, Yozef's worry about people finding out that he healed too fast faded under the press of responsibilities, not the least of which was Aeneas's birth. One evening after work, months after the events following the battle of Moreland City, Yozef was rocking Aeneas when a cry came from the kitchen.

"Ahrg!!"

It was Maera's voice. He jumped to his feet, held the baby tight, and ran toward the kitchen. He heard women's voices: alarm from Anarynd, directions from Gwyned, and curses and cries of pain from Maera. He burst through the door from the hall to see Maera clamping a hand over her forearm, dripping blood on the floor.

"Let me see it!" demanded Gwyned, trying to pry Maera's hand away. Anarynd held towels, waiting for something to do with them.

"What happened?!" exclaimed Yozef.

All that came from Maera was, "Damn, damn, damn!"

"Knife slipped," Gwyned said, as calmly as if commenting on a casual observation.

"Knife?" was all Yozef got out.

"We were slicing the harlon gourds into halves."

For the first time, Yozef noticed several oval-shaped vegetables on the table, three cut lengthwise in half. Blood had smeared on the table near one of the three chairs.

"Here, Anarynd, hold Aeneas," said Yozef, handing her the baby, who by now had picked up the tenor of the adults and wailed, adding to the clamor.

Maera appeared pale, her mouth set and her eyes smoldering. He felt relieved. He was sure it hurt like hell, though he thought she was mainly angry at herself.

"Let me see," he said, gently guiding her to the kitchen washing basin and a waiting ewer of well water. He held her arm over the basin, and when she took away her hand holding the wound, blood oozed up, lots of blood. She winced and sucked in air, as Gwyned rinsed the forearm with water.

I need to get running water into the house, rose unbidden in Yozef's mind. He'd noticed such seemingly inappropriate thoughts coming to him in stressful moments.

The water washed away the blood on the forearm, as fresh blood continually welled out of a two-inch straight gash running midway between elbow and wrist.

"Good grief, Maera! How did you do this while cutting a gourd?"

It was the wrong thing to say.

"Obviously, it was the easiest way to cut myself, you idiot!" Maera shot back, then drew in a deep breath. "I'm sorry, it was just so *stupid*. I was having a hard time cutting through a tough section of skin, probably where the gourd wasn't quite ripe, and I held the damn thing in the crook of my arm. It slipped, and next thing I knew—"

"Gonna need stitches," said Gwyned in an unperturbed voice.

"Well, no shit, Tonto," Yozef said in English. No one noticed.

Yozef held the gash closed with his fingers. The blood flow slowed to a stop.

No pulsing, he observed, *so no arteries cut. I think it's into the muscle, but no tendons either. Should heal okay. Gwyned's right, it should probably get . . .* The line of thought trailed off, as another took its place.

Yozef had heard of flashes of insight in science, moments when a set of facts, observations, and questions came together.

He had a flash of insight.

His own fast healing; Aragorn having never been sick; Bronwyn, Dellia, and Cynwin not getting sick since Bronwyn joined the marriage, although Dellia's and Cynwin's three children had minor illnesses; Maera not having colds since their marriage; Maera suffering minimal morning sickness; Maera surprising other women by how fast she recovered from childbirth.

Holy crap! he thought. *I passed the nanoelements to her! Sex! That's the connection. There must be nanoelements in my semen, and I passed them to Maera!*

Had Harlie said the elements were meant only for Yozef's physiology, or did he just assume it? He couldn't remember. If he passed them on, and they functioned in another body, then somehow they adjusted to new bodies. How the hell did they do that? That shouldn't be possible.

He took several breaths and a few seconds to calm himself.

Think. Just because I don't know how it's done doesn't mean the Watchers can't do it. Hell, they can fly spaceships around and design the nanoelements in the first place, so who knows what they're capable of?

Mere seconds had passed since his insight. He still held Maera's arm, she still cursed, and the other women still stood anxiously.

If he took her to the medicants for stitches, they would check her arm to see how the healing was going. For that matter, after any bleeding stopped, the wound would be left open to the air. Everyone would see it.

"No," said Yozef," I don't think it needs stitches. We just need to wrap it closed, and it'll be fine."

"What?" exclaimed Gwyned, her usual equanimity shaken by Yozef's idiotic statement. "That needs stitches. I've seen cuts like this, and sewing it closed will be safer from corruption and let it heal faster."

Yozef wanted to blurt, "I don't think infection or slow healing is going to be a problem." Instead, he said, "Trust me, I'm sure it'll be okay. It's not as bad as it looks, and by tomorrow it'll be better. If not, we can always go to the medicants then."

"I don't care if you're Yozef Kolsko or not, this needs stitches," asserted Gwyned.

"I don't know, Yozef," Maera said, "it does look bad. Maybe Gwyned is right."

Yozef hesitated, then did what he hated to do.

"I *know* what I'm talking about, Maera. It *comes to me* that we should wrap it and wait until tomorrow."

The "it comes to me" phrase had become Yozef's "go to" words when he didn't want to explain something. The phrase also fed rumors that he was being told something by unseen powers. He had never used the stratagem with Maera or anyone close to him and regretted he couldn't think quickly enough of another ploy to hide Maera's wound and the anticipated quick healing.

Yozef squeezed the sides of the wound shut again. Gwyned kept pouring water on it, which still mixed with blood seeping from the cut.

Maera looked at the wound, at her husband, back at the wound, and was about say something when he narrowed his eyes, looked hard at her, and imperceptibly shook his head. She focused hard back.

"Okay," Maera said, her voice shaky, "go ahead and bind it up."

"Aw!" complained Gwyned. "You're both wrong. If it's not better in the morning, we're going to the medicants if I have to go get Breda Keelan. Let's see if you can ignore *her* like you do me."

"Are you sure, Maera?" asked Anarynd, rocking the now quiescent Aeneas. "It does look bad."

"Don't worry, Ana, Yozef knows what he's doing."

Although Yozef wasn't sure Maera's voice conveyed complete conviction, he tightly wrapped the forearm with clean cloth strips the outraged Gwyned had procured, tight enough that Maera complained.

"I know it's tight, dear, that's what's best."

Later, when Maera and Yozef retired to their room, she had questions, as he knew she would.

She sat on the bed, cradling her injured arm in her lap, not saying anything, looking at him.

"What is it, Yozef? Why didn't you want me to go to the medicants? And why tell Gwyned and Anarynd it wasn't serious? I've seen injuries like this."

For the last two hours, he had interacted with the others only outwardly. Within, his mind turned over what to say and how much to say. He knew it was a time he couldn't get away with saying nothing.

"You couldn't go to the medicants right away because they might see the wound again in a few days," he said softly, yet firmly. "Either of your parents, maybe both, would insist on it. If that happened, the medicants would not understand why the wound healed so fast."

Maera's response was also soft, almost reluctant, as if unsure she wanted the answer. "How do you *know* this, Yozef? And this is one time your claiming you 'just know' is not going to work."

"I'm afraid part of the answer is exactly that—that I *do* know what will happen, but I can't tell you exactly why."

"You can't tell me or won't?"

"I heal faster than most people. So fast that many might wonder things we don't want them to. I don't know exactly why I heal fast, I only know it's true."

He wasn't lying *too* much. He really *didn't* know exactly how the Watchers' elements worked.

"While I can't be sure," he said, "I believe the same will be true for you. If others notice this, there'll be questions we don't need people asking or thinking about."

"Yozef, if anyone but you told me this, I'd judge them delusional, insane, or lying for some unknown reason. What am I to think of this? If what you say is true, this is like God intervening in the world, something the *Word* tells us he doesn't do, except on rare occasions, leaving most of life to our free will. *Is* this an act of God? Are you really a Septarsh or something else?"

"I'm a man who has no knowledge of God, except what I wonder about or what others say and teach. I can't say if I even believe in God, though I believe in much of what the *Word* teaches. I suspect this healing is connected to my coming to Caedellium. A devout person might believe it's a gift from God. Maybe a kind of compensation for my being cast here, never to see my homeland and family again. I just don't know, Maera. What I now believe is that somehow I've passed this healing ability on to you, probably through our intimate contact. But however it happened, Maera, isn't it a gift? How can it be evil?"

Maera's face expressed troubling emotions. "Good or evil, understood or not, this is hard to take in." She rose and walked to a window, not seeing anything in the darkness but using the time and the act to gather her thoughts. She spun back, facing Yozef, concern on her face. "Aeneas! What does this mean for him?"

"I believe it will be the same with him. He's only a few months old, so it's too early to know. He still has immunities from you that haven't worn off yet."

"Damnation, Yozef, this is not the time I want to hear your riddles."

Oh, shit. Watch out for blabbering without thinking. "Immunities" *is a word they don't know, and I'm not about to go off explaining about immune reactions or how newborns are protected with antibodies from their mother's blood before their own immune systems are up and running.*

"Sorry, Maera. I only meant we won't be sure about Aeneas for perhaps years. Let's assume that what I passed to you, you in turn passed to him. Isn't that a good thing? Our son will heal from injuries faster than otherwise. Would you take it away from him if you could? From yourself?"

Maera sat on the edge of their bed and looked down at her wrapped arm, blood showing through the cloth. "If I took off this cloth, would the cut be gone?"

"No, I doubt it's had time to close. The bleeding might be much less. The healing will still happen, and you'll have a scar."

Yozef unconsciously touched his own head scar. Maera noticed.

"Your wound at Moreland City, it was far more serious than you let me believe, wasn't it?"

"I think so. Of course, I'm not a doct . . . a medicant."

"I felt worried and annoyed when I never saw the wound," said Maera, "except when we visited St. Sidryn's hospital and the medicant said it looked minor. You were worried, weren't you, that he would be suspicious? As *I* was, after Carnigan and Kales both told me what the wound looked like after it happened."

"Think of it, Maera. Both of us have so much to do. The Narthani, the innovations I still might introduce, the university. What would happen if people saw us as different? While some might think of us as protected by God, others might see us as demons or agents of the Evil One. It's a risk or at least a complication we don't need. Things might change in the future. Can we just accept it as a gift from God and move on with our lives?"

"I'd like to think of it that way," said Maera. "Part of me doesn't see how this can be anything but a blessing, but another part of me still needs to think about it."

Maera went back to the window. Yozef waited, sitting on the bed's edge. He saw her stiffen, and she faced him again. "Is it just healing, Yozef? I've told you how my headaches and fevers have gone away since we married. It wasn't just good fortune or changing my moods, was it? It's not just the healing that's changed."

He had wondered how long Maera would take to make the connection. Her being Maera, he wasn't surprised it had taken only minutes.

"Again, I can't be sure, but since I don't get sick and you haven't since we've been married, I think it's a possibility *you won't* get sick."

"Ever?"

"Never," said Yozef. "If that's true, then neither will you get the tumor sickness you said one of your aunts died of. My people call it 'cancer.'"

"Anything else you want to hit me with, Yozef?" Maera said with barely hidden sarcasm. "Will I be able to fly or live forever?"

"I wouldn't plan on getting rid of the carriages just yet," replied Yozef, then he waited for her to follow up on the second part of her question. She didn't, to his relief, because he didn't want to add the possibility of extended life spans, something that he couldn't predict and wouldn't have clues about for many years and that would present an even greater complication, if it happened.

Maera walked from the window to the bed and sat on Yozef's lap, putting one arm around his shoulders and looking him straight in the face. "It's going to take me time to absorb all this and understand what I'm feeling. At the moment, it's a combination of fear of what I don't understand, worry about how other people would respond if they learned of this, wondering whether somehow all this goes against God's will, a residue of wondering if you really are insane, and awe at what it all means."

The next morning, as soon as they both were awake, they went to a bedroom window. The sun peeked over the eastern hills, and its rays shone through the glass. Maera unwrapped the bandage. Blood had seeped through, though no more than had been there the previous night. When the last of the cloth lifted away, they could see the cut: a thin line already closed, no blood seeping out. Maera probed the surrounding reddish tissue gently with a finger.

"It's a little warm and only a little sensitive. Most of the pain is gone, with barely a mild ache to the arm." She looked at Yozef with a sense of wonder. "I'm beginning to believe everything you told me last night. It's like a tale with magic you tell children, except it's real. And you're right; we need to keep it between us, until a time comes when we can reveal it, if that ever happens."

Yozef sighed with relief. As rational and bright as he knew his wife to be, he'd had doubts how she would receive what he'd told her. However, there was still one problem.

"Within our household, it will be difficult, but I think we can manage it, although at some point it will likely become evident to those closest to us that there is something unusual about the Kolskos. There's another worry. If it's true that I passed on to you the ability to heal quickly when we coupled, then I—"

"Bronwyn!" blurted Maera.

Yozef nodded, his face grim. "And her sister, their husband, and—"

"Aragorn!" exclaimed Maera.

Yozef nodded. "At least, they're on a farm and don't interact daily with other people, but it *is* a farm, and accidents happen. Not getting ill should attract no attention, but it's only a matter of time before there's an injury requiring medicants."

"What about bringing them into our confidence? Alert them what to expect and to be circumspect?" Maera suggested.

"Tell them what?" asked Yozef. "I don't know them well enough to predict how they'd react. What if they go straight to the theophists or medicants?"

Maera shook her head. "We'll have to hope no attention comes to them about this. If it does, we'll handle it when it happens."

It wasn't a solution that satisfied either of them.

Yozef didn't mention Buna, the woman of his other brief affair and the owner of a seamstress shop. Buna was past childbearing age, and he hoped he remembered that women she employed did most of the work. It was a reasonable risk that Buna would not be injured severely enough for her fast healing to draw attention.

Yozef felt satisfied with Maera's reaction to the revelations, which temporarily relieved one concern and let him return all his attention to the Narthani and how the clans could prepare for whatever came next.

CHAPTER 26

PLANNING

Although many of the clans had taken steps to prepare for further Narthani actions, most steps targeted weapons and ammunition, food and medical supplies, and training. While Yozef didn't want to push too many things at once on the Caedelli, when the initially agreed-on actions were underway, he felt it was time to address several other important issues that the clans might not appreciate. He waited until there was a scheduled meeting with Culich, Pedr Kennrick, Vortig Luwis, and Denes, and until they finished the agenda items. Maera also attended, after Yozef suggested that there was no reason she couldn't resume her earlier duties as recorder for the meetings.

Contingencies

"That seems to be enough discussion on how we're doing with training," said Culich. "That was the last item on the list. Is there anything else?"

"Yes, Culich, I have two items I believe are important," said Yozef. "One is the need for better maps, and the other is what you would call 'possible plans.' There's no exact single word in Caedelli for what I'm referring to, so I'll use the word from my own language—*contingencies*."

Yozef wondered how the Keelan leaders would react to contingency planning. It sounded logical when most people thought about it, but depending on the depth of looking for possible events, it could sound pretty weird. He remembered articles cropping up in the United States every few years about Pentagon's contingency planning, everything from invading Albania to a zombie apocalypse. The media either sensationalized it or made fun of stupid things the military concerned itself with, never bothering to understand the purpose of such planning, which was not the stated objectives but to create skeletal plans that could be adapted to unpredicted real-world events. He remembered someone mentioning how the Pentagon used to have a department that did nothing but contingency planning, which started a shell game of renaming the office and moving it around the Pentagon to hide it from the media.

It was time to see how the Keelanders reacted.

"It refers to anticipating what future actions you might need to take and putting together plans for how to accomplish what you would need to do. Clan Keelan is already doing something like this with food storage and plans to move the people into more defensible sites, should it be necessary. However, what I'm referring to is looking at the different possible actions the Narthani will take and how we will respond."

"Aren't we already doing this?" Luwis complained.

"In general, yes. I'm talking about more specific possibilities and what we would need to do in each case. What if the Narthani land an army near Salford and move toward Caernford? Or, instead of Caernford, they move west toward Gwillamer or east toward Mittack. How would our responses differ to the three possibilities? What if they attack Stent by land or Pewitt by sea? Those provinces are on the other side of Caedellium, and it would take a sixday or more for the Alliance to get help there. If it did, how would that weaken the defenses back here?"

"That's absurd!" exclaimed Luwis. "There's an endless number of possibilities. We couldn't conceivably plan for them all."

"Maybe not in details, no," said Denes. "But many possibilities would lead us to take similar actions. In Yozef's first example, whichever of the clans farthest away was attacked, wouldn't our responses be the same or similar?"

"Right!" said Yozef, jumping on Denes's grasp of a key point. "If we make a plan for what we'd do if the Narthani attack Pewitt, then wouldn't our response be similar, even almost identical, if they attack Stent or Swavebroke? We don't need every little detail, just the major decisions and requirements."

Yozef hurried on before the others could interject.

"If we have enough such plans, let's call them contingency plans, then no matter what the Narthani do, we can go to a contingency plan that most closely matches. Although a plan would have to be adapted, we would have a scaffold to build on."

Culich had listened without comment until now. "I can see the use of such 'contingency plans,' but it sounds like a lot of work, and who would do it? None of us here has that kind of time."

"That's a problem," admitted Yozef. "I don't know how much of this we could do for it to be useful. Still, I think it's worth trying. I suggest each of us individually or in pairs look at a few different scenarios and see what we come up with. Then we could bring in other people to take what we've done and adapt those plans to other scenarios. Naturally, we'd have to review the first plans that the new people develop, but hopefully they could eventually continue with only occasional supervision."

"Who would these other men be?" asked Kennrick.

"That would be other men *and women*," said Yozef. "Most will be men, but we need to become accustomed to including capable women to do any work that helps the clan prepare. That's *any* work and *any* role, except the main fighting units. Does anyone doubt that Maera could do this work? I suspect she's not the only Keelan woman of sufficient ability."

Maera had listened to the men without making a comment about the discussion. She still wasn't used to being an active participant in men's meetings, no matter how much confidence Yozef expressed to her. Customs and habits died hard.

"I suppose," Luwis said, in a tone Yozef interpreted as dubious and not wanting to get into an argument with Maera, which itself supported Yozef's point.

"Anyway, we just need to leave that possibility open," said Yozef, satisfied that he'd gotten a foot in the door. Maera had already made a list of women she thought could contribute to such planning, including two sisters at St. Tomo's Abbey and a third cousin, Riona Klofyn, whom Maera couldn't stand personally but whom she said was sharp as a honed knife.

Yozef hadn't mentioned that he thought such contingency planning would help the mind-sets of men who were likely to be leaders in fights to come. Leading and decision-making required learning to consider many factors, including logistics, intelligence, and terrain.

"Pedr and Vortig," said Yozef, using their first names, a recent familiarity, "you must have assistants and people you know who could do this work. If we work on the example plans, they could be involved and learn enough to take a bigger role."

Kennrick nodded enthusiastically. "My middle son. He lost the lower part of a leg from a stupid wagon race two years ago. He does much of the family's accounts, but he chafes at not being able to fight. He's bright enough and certainly would be diligent in working on these contingency plans. Even if the plans don't prove advantageous, I'd be inclined to put him working on them, if only to give him a chance to feel useful."

"He sounds like a good candidate," said Yozef. "Although don't rule out that he might contribute to fighting, if it comes to that. Any clan members might find themselves fighting or leading from defensive positions, and firing behind walls or barricades doesn't require running."

"As we proved at St. Sidryn's," said Denes, a satisfied set to his face.

Luwis didn't look happy. His forehead wrinkled, and he chewed on the side of his tongue, as if coming to a decision he didn't like. "My daughter Isla," he said reluctantly. "I confess I haven't known what to do with her. Even with Maera as an example, customs are customs, and I'm not the most flexible of men."

Culich and Kennrick both laughed at his statement of the obvious.

"You've convinced me," said Culich, still smiling and with an arm over Luwis's shoulder. "It's your idea, Yozef, so I'll let you work out the example plan details with the others."

"Actually, I thought of letting Maera do the organizing."

Maera stiffened in her chair. Yozef had said nothing to her about such a role.

"Clever," said Culich. "You think women should be involved, and Maera will have a better chance at recruiting them than a man would. I still think most will be men." He looked at his daughter. "You understand that ability and hard work will be the most important factors in recruiting."

"Of course, Father."

"Talk with Pedr, Vortig, and Denes and get their candidates. I assume Yozef will propose a list of initial 'contingencies'?"

"I'll do that and give you a list to look at by tomorrow," Yozef confirmed.

Culich glanced at Maera, who furiously wrote notes, her quill racing over a sheet. He waited until she pulled the quill away.

The hetman looked again at Yozef. "You said you had another item?"

Maps

"We need far better maps. I know you have extensive maps for Keelan Province, but we need the most detailed maps possible for all the provinces. This is part of the contingency planning, to have detailed knowledge of every place we might have to go on the island. Ideally, this project would involve all the clans. And by detailed, I mean there is no such thing as too much detail: every hill; rivulet of water; pond; boggy area; every bridge and its condition, meaning what load can it carry and what's the fastest way to destroy it, if necessary; the vegetation, meaning the type and size of trees. If there's a creek that's seasonal, we need to know approximately when there will be water in it, where there are reliable fords, no matter the water level, and we must be sure it shows up on every map of the area. The thing is, we will never know what piece of information is critical until we need it. Therefore, no detail is too small in the information-gathering stage. Later, we can winnow out all but the most important facts.

"When we have maps we're reasonably satisfied with, they need to be distributed to relevant leaders, of both fighting men and noncombatants. There can't be different versions of maps. If an order comes to take some action, the order might include map information. The recipient of the order needs to look at a map and the coordinates and know he is looking at the same map as the person giving the order."

All four men nodded their understanding and agreement, almost from the first words out of Yozef's mouth.

Good, he thought, *no convincing needed for this one. No reason to get into details yet about relief maps, fake maps to let the Narthani "capture," or anything else I can think of.*

Yozef felt relieved when Kennrick took the lead.

"This is something I can look into, Culich. I already oversee the registrar offices and records, and most registrar agents have experience in surveying, so it should only be an extension of what they already do."

"One difference may be that the maps need to include altitude, how high a point of land is above sea level," said Yozef. "One type of map we'll make is called a topographic map, which has lines indicating altitudes."

Yozef laid on the table a hand-drawn example. "Here is a crude map of the Caernford area. Don't take it as accurate. I just drew it to demonstrate a topographic map. See these wavy dotted lines? They represent one-hundred-foot altitude differences between lines. If you look east of Caernford on the map, you see lines indicating where the land is one hundred feet higher than at the previous line. As you get into the hills, the lines get closer together."

"As the hills become steeper," said Denes.

"Right. Once you are used to looking at such maps, you can get a quick picture of the terrain."

"I can see the usefulness," said Kennrick, "though our registrars don't usually concern themselves with altitude, only straight distances."

"That's okay. I can show them methods of measuring height differences. One way is called triangulation, where points on the ground are at the vertices of a chain or network of triangles. By measuring angles, the sides of a triangle can be computed or measured directly. Those measurements are then used as sides of adjoining or related triangles. It's tedious work but can be very accurate, if care is taken.

"The second method involves levels like a carpenter uses. A bubble level is attached to a cross-haired eyepiece that can be magnifying or not. Once the eyepiece is on level, the surveyor looks at a calibrated pole placed some distance away. From where the eyepiece crosshairs lie on the pole, you know how much higher or lower a pole is, compared to the spot with the eyepiece. Again, this can be tedious, but with care, extremely accurate relative heights can be determined."

"I don't think the tedium will be a problem," said Kennrick, smiling. "One of the qualifications of a registrar is obsessive care in handling numbers, maps, and records. I expect many of them will take to this new task with enthusiasm."

Kennrick's smile faded. "However, I have to caution that getting maps for all of Caedellium will be a problem. Some clans are unlikely to either share mapping data or allow Keelan registrars into their provinces."

Luwis and Denes both cursed, but Culich seemed unperturbed.

I guess he expected this, thought Yozef. *He's more used to dealing directly with the other hetmen.*

"I'll communicate with the other hetmen about this," said Culich. "I think once ten or so of the clans agree, the others will be forced to cooperate. If necessary, some form of pressure can be applied, such as delays in sharing cannon or the resulting maps. Yozef, do you think it sufficient to have registrars carry out work on improving maps or do we need more men?"

"Culich, I suggest that we start with a few registrars and add some selected other people to learn the type of surveying I'm talking about. I'll work with them until they understand what I think we need."

Yozef made no more comments, and the meeting adjourned.

Battlefields

Yozef had one more item he'd planned to include at the meeting, ultimately deciding it wasn't the right moment.

No matter how much the Caedelli trained and produced more weapons, he didn't relish the thought of an open field battle against the Narthani army. The islanders would probably win, but the cost would be far higher than he thought any hetman understood, especially after their belief in a stirring victory at Moreland City. In contrast, Yozef believed they had been extraordinarily lucky. The terrain features the clans had taken advantage of, the two incredibly stupid errors by the Moreland and Eywell hetmen, and the Narthani being unprepared to expect a clan flank attack had combined to lead to a tactical draw, not an outright victory.

He didn't believe they could hope to be lucky again.

A major class of contingencies, perhaps the most important, involved a situation where the clans might have to face the Narthani again in a field battle, one where the clans couldn't rely on luck or Narthani mistakes to save them. Although Yozef recognized that he was no general, he knew that where a battle took place was often decisive, if one side had terrain features in its favor. He didn't doubt many clan leaders would intuitively use terrain wherever they could, but he feared they weren't ready to appreciate the importance of terrain being a decisive factor, if they had the opportunity to choose the battlefield.

Compounding the problem, Yozef had no doubt the Narthani leaders understood the use of terrain, and they would work on their side to pick sites favorable to them and unfavorable to the clans.

When he was a teenager, Yozef and fellow gamesters had endlessly argued and discussed the strategies used in famous battles, pretending they were qualified to critique military campaigns. He remembered multiple examples of famous battles where terrain was a major factor, although histories, novels, and movies tended to attribute victories to more glamorous factors, such as leaders, weapons, and noble causes.

At the Battle of Crecy, the English defeated a large French army, with the longbow given credit for changing the nature of warfare. But the English victory was also due to a judicious choice of the battlefield. The English chose the site and waited for the French. Towns and a river prevented flank attacks by the French cavalry, the heart of the French army. The English positioned themselves at the top of a slope, so the French cavalry had to ride upward to attack the English, only to find the archers protected by pits and obstacles. It was a shattering defeat for the French, and the English suffered few casualties.

Less than a century later, not having learned their lesson, the French suffered another disaster at the hands of the English at Agincourt, where a combination of weather and terrain gave the English longbowmen an overwhelming advantage. Their flanks protected by dense woods through which the French cavalry couldn't maneuver, the English positioned themselves at the end of a large field recently plowed, a field that had turned to mud from a recent rain. Armored French knights had to slog through deep mud to get at the English and were slaughtered by longbowmen.

He recalled other examples: terrain that restricted maneuvering at the Battle of Chickamauga in the U.S. Civil War, the Russian winter's effects on Napoleon's and Hitler's armies, and the French ceding of high ground to the Vietnamese communists at Dien Bien Phu.

Military theory writers often emphasized terrain. Sun Tzu's *The Art of War* had an entire chapter on army positioning. Terrain played an especially important role in "first-generation warfare," as defined by a Pentagon report referencing battles with massed men using column and line tactics, before such tactics were rendered obsolete by rifled muskets, breech-loading rifles, and cannon, not to mention the first machine guns and indirect artillery fire.

Yozef saw only two ways to get the Narthani to leave Caedellium: either defeat them in pitched battles outside of Preddi City or besiege Preddi City until they withdrew by ship or surrendered. If it became necessary to fight the Narthani in a field engagement, he wanted to scour the island for battlefield sites that might give the Caedelli the advantage. It was not an appealing option. Then again, neither was a siege.

CHAPTER 27

IF THEY DO THAT, WE DO THIS

Yozef and Maera worked the next two sixdays organizing the contingency-planning group. Yozef also took the opportunity to begin setting up formal intelligence gathering and analysis. Without checking with Culich, he named the group the Military Intelligence Unit, MIU, and set it up on the top floor of a two-story building in Caernford. A clothing shop occupied the bottom floor.

Yozef also saw the group as a chance to inch the clans into closer cooperation, so he asked Culich to contact other hetmen to recruit at least one member of their clans to come to Caernford and join the MIU. Six clans responded, and the group began operation. Maera and her third cousin, Riona Klofyn, represented Keelan. They were also the only women, which proved awkward at the first meeting of the entire group, until Yozef sent home one of the two Mittack men for snarky remarks about women and rational thinking.

It took only two days for Yozef to determine that six of the remaining nine members of MIU were keepers. Naturally, this included Maera and Riona. From Clan Adris came Owill Brell, a forty-one-year-old man, tall and wiry, with receding hair and a seemingly endless talent for devious thinking. He was matched by Halwon Ristwyn, a twenty-year-old Stentese, whom Yozef identified as a certifiable nerd and a correspondent with Cadwulf on mathematics. Yozef thought he'd recognized the name when Welman Stent appointed Halwon as Stent's member of MIU, but it was Maera who made the connection that Halwon was already a candidate for the University of Caedellium's Department of Applied Mathematics. Halwon's main fault was not keeping his attention on the task at hand but instead wandering off on something that caught his attention but had nothing to do with contingency planning.

Two less astute members were Isla Luwis, Vortig Luwis's daughter, and Gartherid Kennrick, Pedr Kennrick's son. However, both were dedicated and bright enough to be useful.

Owill Brell emerged quickly a leader of the group, along with Maera, who soon suggested Brell might be the best leader of a larger intelligence operation, leaving her to focus on analyzing Narthani culture and on projecting Narthani intentions. One of Brill's strengths was getting Riona to be productive without letting her irritate him. Maera's cousin was forty-one, a widow, and the mother of three teenage children. They apparently ran their household, because Riona felt they were old enough to take care of themselves.

"I've always felt sorry for her," Maera told Yozef. "I'm afraid her husband and immediate family had very traditional ideas about the role of women, more like the northern clans, instead of here in Keelan. Ever since I've been old enough, I've realized that Riona was unhappy. Whether due to the situation or her own inherent personality, she always seems to alienate people, often by things she says, without judging or caring about the consequences. I've tried to avoid her at family gatherings when her family participated, but she's one of the sharpest members of the Keelans. Yet she has had no outlet for it."

Yozef spent the first day of MIU operations meeting with the group, mainly giving examples of contingencies they should consider and how all clans, not just Keelan, could respond. He then left them to return to his other projects, only stopping in one morning a week to be briefed on their progress. For the third such summary session, Maera alerted him that the group had something he needed to hear. She declined to give him hints, saying it was best that the entire group told him, although Maera hinted that Owill and Riona were the prime movers.

Yozef delayed, due to making a stop at the cannon foundry, and arrived a few minutes late to the meeting. The others waited around a table.

"About time you got here, Yozef," snarked Riona. "We've got more to do than wait around for your convenience."

Maera rolled her eyes, and a corner of Owill's mouth hinted at a smile. The other members ignored their insolent colleague.

Yozef sat in the only empty chair, and Maera started them off.

"Owill will tell you what we've discussed the last sixday."

The Adris man rose and went to one of the many maps tacked to the room's walls. He stopped at a map of the entire island.

"One of the scenarios you gave us was if the Narthani attacked one of the northern or western provinces. For this example, let's assume the target is Pewitt, Swavebroke, or Farkesh. You mentioned that distance can limit our clans from helping. We'd like to redefine the problem from how to respond to such an attack, to how to promote Narthani withdrawal and make them hesitate before any future attempts.

"What would the Narthani response be if, instead of coming to Pewitt's aid, we attacked *their* provinces? They would have needed to use enough of their men for the Pewitt attack to be successful. Therefore, they must have also weakened their remaining forces in the three provinces they control."

Yozef had had a similar thought but hadn't carried it through, too many other things always demanding his time.

"Where do you see our attacks aimed?" Yozef asked.

Brell pointed to the map with a forefinger. "We suggest three possibilities. One is from the coast of Stent into Selfcell Province. Two is from the northwest border corner of Eywell and Moreland, and the third from Dornfeld in Keelan into the southern part of Eywell."

"And the size of the force we would use?" asked Yozef.

"Well, shit, Yozef, it'll obviously depends on how far we want our people to go and how much fighting they expect to run into," said Riona, a snarl of disdain curling her lips.

Yozef again tried to ignore her, but his patience wasn't endless. Maera saw the look on his face and jumped in.

"At least a thousand men, Yozef, and some of the 6-pounder horse artillery whose crews are trained well enough to commit to action."

Yozef went to the map and stared for a minute. He missed Maera giving Riona a frigid stare and a shake of the head and Riona about to say something back and then restrain herself.

Yozef let his left forefinger rest on the first option. "Let's eliminate this possibility. The Selfcellese might be allies of the Narthani, but so far, they haven't seemed very enthusiastic. There's always the chance we might peel them away from the Narthani, so we don't want to get into battles with them where losses of life or property make it harder for them to change sides."

"Change sides!? They should be crushed along with the Narthani," said a man whose name Yozef forgot. He did remember that the man wasn't one of the team's sterling members.

Yozef tried to keep his tone civil, but he knew a trace of irritation crept in.

"If the clans have to fight the Selfcellese, there will be casualties that could be avoided if we can get Selfcell to either be neutral or come over to us. I think it's best to remove option one. I like the other two options. Eywell is severely weakened from their losses at Moreland City. In this scenario, the Narthani garrisons we learned about by questioning prisoners have to be weakened or are less likely to be aggressive, with so many other Narthani troops gone on the northern clan attack. For option two, Stent or Orosz would have to lead it, since Moreland is still chaotic, trying to settle their leadership vacuum. For the southern option, Keelan would be the lead clan. Both raids would be *coups de main*."

Maera cleared her throat loud enough to alert Yozef that he'd done it again, except this time he'd used a French term.

"Oh, sorry. A *coup de main* is an attack that uses speed and surprise to reach its objective. In this case, the objective would not be holding territory or inflicting casualties, but to destroy and threaten. If we made the Narthani feel as if the Eywellese were threatened or even their own territory was, in the original Preddi Province, they'd be more likely to withdraw from their northern clan attack to bolster defenses at home."

They talked for another half hour before Yozef decided. "I'm satisfied that you've identified a course of action we can bring to Hetman Keelan's attention. I'll ask the hetman and a few others to join us here tomorrow morning."

That evening, Yozef watched Maera breastfeed Aeneas on their back porch. It was one of his favorite things to do. As she switched sides with the baby, Yozef asked a question about Maera's cousin.

"What's with Riona, Maera? Is she always like she was today?"

Maera sighed. "Unfortunately, yes. It's one reason I've never had much to do with her. I suggested adding her to MIU both because I thought she would be an asset and because I hoped that giving her something important to do might mellow her out."

"I can predict that she won't last long with that kind of behavior. No one wants to be around someone who spits acid every time she opens her mouth."

"I know. Yet it was an interaction between her and Owill that came up with the diverting attack idea. I don't know if the rest of us would have seen it without her."

"Then get her settled down. If you think it might work, I'll talk to her, although I don't know whether I should try patient counsel or scream and threaten to dump her from the MIU."

Yozef was on time the next morning and half expected another testy comment from Riona, maybe about being early this time, but she ignored him. Culich, Luwis, and Denes arrived shortly after that, and Brell gave an updated version of the briefing from the previous day.

Culich sat with a hand cupping his chin, while Brell spoke. Once he raised a hand to restrain a question from Luwis, his attention remaining on Brell and the map, and he only briefly glanced at Yozef.

"Thank you, Ser Brell," said Culich. "An interesting idea. I like how it both has the potential to restrain the Narthani from future attacks and keeps our men closer to Keelan. Luwis and Denes, what do you two say?"

"As you mentioned, Culich, I also like our men staying closer, instead of sending them off toward the north," Luwis answered, "not knowing what was happening to them or if they had any effect helping the invaded province. And I'd worry about them being so far away, in case the Narthani turned on us.

"However, for this to work, we would have to respond quickly after the first word of the Narthani attack. There wouldn't be time to spend sixdays gathering men and supplies, then get them to the Eywell border and across. By then, the Narthani might have destroyed the attacked clan and even returned to Preddi, where they'd be in a position to threaten our raiding force."

"I agree," said Yozef. "The southern option, attacking along the Eywell coast, would have to be Keelan and allies, and the men would have to be within days of the border, all supplies in place, and a maneuver plan ready."

Denes went to the map. "It's a hundred miles from Caernford to the Eywell border north of Dornfeld. Starting from Caernford, it would take three days to reach Dornfeld without breaking down the horses, unless we have multiple changes of horses."

"Pre-position," Yozef almost blurted, before catching the English words. "Uh . . . we could have horses and supplies already at Dornfeld or on this side of the Dillagon pass to Dornfeld. That way, we'd just have to get the men there the fastest way, connect with horses and supplies, and be off toward the Eywell border."

"Wagons," said Denes. "The men could get to Dornfeld by wagon, so they wouldn't have already ridden a hard hundred miles before even starting the attack. I suggest modifying existing wagons to handle a load of men or perhaps building wagons dedicated to this purpose. The more comfortable the men, the better shape they'd be in for the attack. If we have wagons to hold twenty-five men each, that's forty wagons for a thousand men, plus supply wagons. We could change horses several times and make the trip in one long day. Give a day to link up with horses and supplies, rest, and be ready to move on Eywell two days after getting word of a northern attack."

"Is a thousand men the right number?" asked Luwis.

"It needs to be enough to brush aside most opposition," said Yozef, "and enough to fight their way back to friendly territory, if they run into major Narthani and Eywell forces. In fact, to help tie down the Eywellese and some of the Narthani, it would be best if option two were also implemented."

"A raid staged from Moreland territory toward Hanslow?" said Culich.

"Yes," replied Yozef, "though a more cautious raid, since we know there are concentrations of Narthani troops and Eywellese fighters in and around the Eywell capital. The raid's main objective would be to fix those forces in place and secondarily do whatever damage they can to the province."

"I'll have to communicate with Stent and Orosz to see if they would agree," said Culich. "An attack on a northern clan is only one scenario. Yozef, if your MIU comes up with too many like this, we wouldn't be able to make plans and commitments for them all."

"Of course," said Yozef. "However, this one scenario would account for attacks on the coastal clans from Stent on western Caedellium to . . . " he went to the map, " . . . all the way to Bevans on the eastern tip. We would only have to adjust the details."

Culich nodded, looked across the map again, and then sat. "Back to the question of how many men. I agree with Yozef's advice that it needs to be enough of a threat to the Narthani, yet we have to balance that with how many men can be away from Keelan."

"Bring in other clans," Yozef suggested. "We already have men from six other provinces rotating through Denes's training site, where they're learning to fight as dragoons and using the new 6-pounders. Part of the purpose of this training is getting clansmen from different provinces to work together. Why not expand the role of these men into what we can call a 'ready reaction force,' in the event they're needed for the scenarios we've been discussing?"

"I like that idea," said Luwis, with more enthusiasm than for many of Yozef's ideas. "But one problem is, what if we need this reaction force right when a new rotation of men from other clans has just arrived? They wouldn't have had dragoon training, used the cannon, or trained together. It'd be asking for disaster should they run into major opposition."

Maera had been sitting quietly, scribbling notes. Yozef happened to glance her way. She bit her lip and shifted in her chair.

She's got something to say, Yozef recognized, *but still isn't confident how much she can participate.*

"Maera," he said, "you have a thought?"

She looked at him with gratitude and launched quickly into what she was holding in, as if she were about to burst. "Have the rotations overlap. The men are in Keelan for a month, six sixdays. Ask the other clans to have the next rotation come halfway through the previous rotation. That way, there would always be men who've had at least three sixdays of training."

Culich shook his head. "That would mean the clans would have more men committed to being away from their provinces at any one time. I'm not sure if they would agree."

"Perhaps," said Maera, "but there's no harm in asking."

"Even if they do say no," said Yozef, "go back to them and propose that the overlap will be just two sixdays. That way, their clans would have a hundred men away for four of the six sixdays of a month and two hundred for the other two sixdays. After refusing your first request, I'll bet they'll feel they have to agree to the second."

"That gives us between six hundred and twelve hundred men, depending on how the clans answer," said Denes. "The low number isn't enough men."

"We already have five hundred men either in Dornfeld or within range of the Dillagon Pass," said Culich. "Gwillamer has had three hundred men in the northern part of their province, in case the Eywellese or Narthani come at Dornfeld and on to Gwillamer. Those men would be available."

"How many of those have had the training as dragoons and using the 6-pounders?" asked Denes.

Culich looked at Luwis, who shrugged. "I'll have to check," said Luwis, "but at least some of our men. As for Gwillamer, I don't know."

"I see Denes's concern," said Culich. "It would be best if all the men going on a raid into Eywell have the training, but it may not be possible, if events happen too fast. I'll communicate with Cadoc Gwillamer and apprise him of what we've discussed. I'm sure he'll support the idea. I'll also ask that the men he stations near Dornfeld include as many as possible with the training. For now, we'll have to be satisfied that *most* men have had the training and the others will follow along."

"That worries me," said Yozef. "It's a recipe for confusion at the wrong times. Keelan is in better shape, because we started earlier and have more experience. By now, most Keelan fighting men have been trained enough to be considered dragoons. The other clans need to come along faster than just one or two hundred men at a time. They need to set up their own training programs, either using their own men who have been through the training here, or we could send experienced Keelanders to their provinces for a month to get them started."

Culich let the discussion go for another ten minutes, then ended the session.

"I'll contact the other hetmen with all these ideas and proposals. Something else occurs to me. We should run a semaphore spur line to Dornfeld. If it comes to carrying out this raid, we'll need faster communication than riders. We should probably also run a line to Rummeln, on our east coast. Luwis, check with Pedr on how long it will take to get new lines operating."

Damn, thought Yozef. *There's just too much to do! Here's another case where a functioning telegraph could be vital.*

The meeting broke up, with the MIU members going back to thinking up scenarios and contingencies, Yozef heading back to his shops, and Culich and Luwis walking the quarter mile to the clan headquarters building in Caernford. Culich acknowledged greetings of clan members the whole way, but his mind was elsewhere.

I wonder whether any Keelander would have dreamed up a plan like this a year ago, Culich thought. *Listening to Luwis and Denes talk about tactics, logistics, reserves, line-of-retreat, and other concepts new to them makes me wonder, once again, about Yozef's influence. Even if it's true that most of the ideas behind this plan came from others, it has Yozef's handprints all over it. Maybe it's simply that he's introduced new ways of thinking, but would these ideas have surfaced if he hadn't come to Caedellium? I doubt it. Thank you, God, once again.*

By the next sixday, Culich had answers from the other clans. Gwillamer, Mittack, and Hewell agreed to double the number of men sent for training, seeing it as getting more of their fighting men accustomed to new tactics faster and approving the rapid reaction concept.

Adris declined the increase, citing their distance from Keelan but asking for the loan of fifty experienced dragoons to assist in setting up a training site in Adris. Stent and Orosz were not asked to send more men. Stent would be fully occupied if a northern invasion occurred, and both Stent and Orosz approved the concept of the diversion raids and began organizing their own reaction force to carry out the feint into northern Eywell toward the capital, Hanslow, or other operations.

CHAPTER 28

BEWARE THE SERPENT

Narthani Headquarters, Preddi City

Okan Akuyun stood next to Admiral Morfred Kalcan and Assessor Sadek Hizer, watching the sloop clear the breakwater and catch the wind past the harbor.

"There we go, Sadek," said Akuyun, addressing Hizer. "Now if the messages to your agents just get there without detection, we should have all their acknowledgments in five or six days."

Akuyun had let his hair grow longer than usual, and it billowed from the wind gusts. "I think the orders will jolt your agents when they get them."

"Certainly, from the delivery method," said Hizer. "They're aware they might be called on for direct action, if necessary."

Hizer held his hat on with both hands to keep the wind from sending it flying. He appeared satisfied with seeing the sloop off. "After this, we'll have the three strike teams launched in two sixdays, once we have the dates set for all three provinces."

Kalcan clasped his hands behind his back, as he watched his sloop turn and head along the coast. "Sadek, will you still consider this a success if you kill only one of the three hetmen?"

Hizer shrugged, never losing his grip on his hat. "Strictly speaking, I could count a success if none of the teams are successful. The main point is to focus the clans' attention on protecting their own people and territory, so they don't get ambitious about what to do about us here in Preddi. The one exception is the Keelan hetman. He's proving too successful in rousing the other hetmen to action and cooperation. If we get only one of them, I hope it's him."

"Two sixdays until two of the strike teams land at dusk, then the assault force on Swavebroke hits shore at first light the next morning," recited Akuyun, more to himself than to the other two men. "Aivacs was right to suggest starting the Swavebroke attack at dawn. Word by semaphore of the hetmen strikes won't have come yet and alerted Swavebroke."

Brigadier Aivacs Zulfa, commander of Narthani ground forces on Caedellium, had pointed out the impracticality of landing twenty-five hundred men in the dark and expecting to coordinate it with the attack on Shullick, the Swavebroke capital. First light would be best, and by first light, Zulfa meant the lead units would be on the docks of Shullick before enough light existed to read large lettering. The local agent had reported that Swavebroke hadn't implemented regular patrols along the coast or lookouts at strategic points. The Shullick harbor piers were empty of ships, since the Narthani naval blockade kept trading ships away. The Narthani intended to sail straight into the harbor and use the Swavebrokers' own piers. They should be able to approach almost to the docks before being spotted, because the two Anyarian moons would have already set.

Since no semaphore message could go out until there was light enough to read flags from however many miles' distance lay to the next station, alerts from the hetman attacks would not reach Swavebroke until the twenty-five hundred men, two hundred horses, and twenty 12-pounder cannon were ashore.

The three men watched another five minutes, each with thoughts about the coming operation, their roles, and the consequences, if anything went wrong. When the sloop, now almost a mile offshore, disappeared behind a headland, Akuyun finally pushed hair out of his eyes. "Good. Now back indoors for me and the endless stack of papers."

"I'm afraid you're looking at the wrong man if you want sympathy, Okan," said Hizer. "I'll admit that while my stack might be more interesting than yours, it's still a stack that never gets smaller."

"That's the trouble with you ground-walker leaders," said Kalcan, laughing as the men turned toward the headquarters buildings. "You're too in love with pieces of paper."

"As if you don't have your own to do," said Akuyun, amused at the incorrigibly cheerful naval officer.

"Oh, I do, but that's what a flag lieutenant is for. The good ones anyway, and mine is *very* good. Especially once he understands what I really need to see and what he can do himself, with occasional perusals by me."

"I'm going to pretend I didn't hear that, Morfred. Otherwise, I'd be shocked to think any Narthani officer did not understand the importance of properly completed paperwork."

"Oh, but I *do* appreciate it, General, that's why my selection of flag lieutenants is so important."

"As long as everything is done to proper standards," cautioned Akuyun.

Amusement at the Narthani bureaucracy was one thing, but none of Akuyun's subordinates doubted that their commander expected the paperwork to pass any inspection.

Akuyun Villa, Preddi City

"Okan, how did you feel seeing the sloop off and the assassination plans going forward?"

Rabia Akuyun already knew what her husband thought. She'd waited until they finished evening meal and their two children with them on Caedellium, their son Ozem and his twin sister, Lufta, left them alone at the table.

"Knowing something is necessary to a mission is one thing, but liking it is different. No matter how many times I tell myself that killing one man by stealth is no different than ordering men to their deaths in a battle, it still makes me uneasy. Neither does the logical assessment of expected casualties seem to change things. The three hetmen attempts may result in fifty to a hundred deaths, Caedelli and our men. The attack on Swavebroke will certainly cost many times that number, but my mind lingers more on the assassinations than on the Swavebroke attack."

"You've said many times that a commander needs to balance the short and long term."

"Now, dear, it's not appropriate for you to use my own words against me."

They laughed, and Akuyun poured himself another glass of wine and a half glass for his wife. He knew without asking how much more she would drink at this point in the evening.

"But yes, you're right, and so am I. The island *will* come into the Empire. It was never explicitly told to me, but I can read the signs. The High Command is firmly committed. My task is to accomplish this, and I hope to do it with the least destruction of properties and lives as possible. But it will happen, and the longer it takes, the more lives and property will be lost.

"We may be in a holding position since the Moreland setback, but one way or another, the basic mission stays the same. I've determined we can't subjugate the island with the forces we have, so it's wait to hear from home. Until then, I need to keep the clans focused on their individual security and on keeping their men close at hand. If that takes the lives of several hundred or even thousands of people, then that has to happen.

"If the clans launched all-out attacks on us, the number of lives lost, theirs, our troops, and especially Narthani civilians, not all of whom could we keep safe, would be far higher than attacking Swavebroke and the strikes against three hetmen."

"You believe what you've planned is the best way forward?"

"That, dearest, is one of the dirtiest secrets never fully explained to young officers. You *never* know if any decision is the right one."

Port of Salford, Keelan Province

Gethin Drifwich was not a happy man. Spying for the Narthani, at the behest of his Nyvaks hetman, had been exciting, and the monthly pay amounted to more than he could earn in a year back at home—not that he saw the coin himself, because it went to his family in Nyvaks. Neither did he see himself in particular danger. After all, he only passed on simple messages once or twice a month to Narthani sloops on scheduled patrols along the Caedellium coast. No one noticed him in the secluded, hidden location he'd picked out to send lantern codes to the sloop. He would never know that after the Keelanders caught the Abersford agent, an alert went out to look for other spies sending encoded messages by lanterns to Narthani ships. He hadn't been caught solely because the spot he'd chosen recessed into a cliff enough that the small boats watching a few hundred yards offshore couldn't see his light.

Until now, sending the messages had been routine. Tonight, all of that changed. After arriving at his signaling location, he was halfway through the time it took him to send light codes, when he nearly had a heart attack. Three armed men appeared behind him and threw him to the ground, jamming cold steel against his throat. Under the light of both Anyarian moons and the stars, he glanced down and saw the blade of an impossibly large knife under his chin.

"Your name!" hissed a Preddi-accented voice.

His throat constricted, and he croaked a staccato of sounds, his knees lifeless, and his whole body trembling.

"Your name!" came the voice again, even harsher, and he felt the blade break the skin on his throat.

"D-Dr-Drif-wich. Drif-wich. Drifwich. Gethin Drifwich," he said.

The steel withdrew, and he sucked in the best breath he had ever taken. The man with the knife turned to the other two and said something that sounded like Narthani.

The man released him, and he fell to the ground, only to be picked back up by the same man. The man unsealed a watertight pouch and pulled out a package.

"We're here to deliver a message. This package goes to your contact in Caernford. You are not to open it. The contact will tell you anything you need to know. You will be back here in five days to signal whether the package was received and the message inside acknowledged. Are there any questions?"

Questions? Drifwich thought hysterically to himself. *Why would there be any questions? I'm risking being shot for spying for the Narthani when three men put a knife to my throat and then give me a package. Why would I have any questions?*

"I-I'm . . . to give this to my contact in Caernford?" he said, trembling.

"And?" prompted the voice.

"And . . . " *What was it?* "Oh . . . .I'm not to open the package. The agent will tell me anything I need to know."

"Where's the report you were sending?" the man said.

"It . . . it's here somewhere," said Drifwich, waving toward the ground. One of the men partly lifted the flap on the unblackened side of the lantern used to signal and swept the ground. He grunted and picked up three sheets of paper, now crumpled and smeared with footprints. The men exchanged more unintelligible words.

The Preddi officer put the sheets into the pouch from which he'd taken the package now held by Drifwich's death-grip. "Your report is complete. Leave and deliver the package as you're told."

The man said nothing more to Drifwich, uttered a short phrase in Narthani to the other men, and as quickly as they had appeared, the men vanished. Drifwich didn't see where they went, nor could he hear their movement. They were just . . . gone.

He collapsed to the ground, scraping his hand against the rough rock face that provided one side of his signaling spot. It took him fifteen minutes to gather himself enough to walk back to where he had tied his horse, borrowed from the stables of his employer.

The transport business had been almost nonexistent since the blockade, and the Salford port had been dying for several years, as workers and their families left searching for work elsewhere on Caedellium. The elderly owner left the near-defunct business's details to Drifwich, who remained the only full-time worker of the original eleven. Thus, he had access to wagons and the horses not yet sold. He made a point of driving a wagon to Caernford twice a month, every three sixdays, to maintain an observable routine, even when the wagon remained near empty of cargo. His real purpose was to meet the Caernford agent whose name he didn't know and didn't want to know.

He rode back to the stables outside Salford, restabled the horse, and collapsed on his cot in his quarters attached to a tack room. He lit a single candle and looked at the small package. Though he wondered what was so important that the Narthani risked making physical contact, it never occurred to him to open the package.

He had just returned from Caernford three days ago and was not scheduled to leave again for fourteen days. Nevertheless, his instructions were to be back in Salford in five days to signal a sloop the message had been received. He would have to leave first thing the next morning.

Keelan Manor, Caernford

Esyl Havant trotted his horse down the lane to Keelan Manor. He'd been here more times than he could count, but each time he scanned for details of any changes since his last visit, even if only the day before.

The grounds were well-maintained, the house impressive. He often imagined himself owning such an estate, though with a more modest-sized house. He'd had such imaginings during the many years he'd worked for Sadek Hizer. This wasn't the first time he'd served as a spy among enemies, but, to his surprise, he found that he felt comfortable among the Caedelli.

He hoped they didn't have to destroy too much of the island, because he'd begun to think it might be his ultimate destination when his days of working for Hizer ended. He had become used to the moderate temperatures and the air freshened by sea and vegetation, much different than the bone-dry air and alternating cold nights and scorching days of his native central Narthon. As he neared the manor, he pictured his house on these grounds. But no, he wanted to be nearer the sea. Maybe similar grounds near Salford, with the sea within sight of the house but not *too* close, so that he had to contend with salt spray. Yes, to always have the endless water within sight, so different from endless arid wastelands.

He reached the manor and tied his horse on a rail in front of the veranda. He'd hardly put a foot on the first step when the manor door opened and a girl came out. She wasn't quite a young woman yet, but showed the budding signs of it.

"A pleasant morning to you, Sem Mared," greeted the friendly semaphore messenger.

"Hello, Esyl, and yes, it's a fine morning. I saw you coming from my bedroom window. Father is just dressing. Is there an urgent message you need to get to him right away?"

"Now, Sem Mared, you *must* be aware the semaphore messages are confidential. We at the station know what's in them, since we receive and send, but besides us, only the recipient can know the contents."

Mared wasn't fooled. She and Esyl had had this exchange many times. They played this game regularly.

"But no," said Havant, "I can say that the message isn't urgent, so I can wait for the hetman."

"Oh, Ser Havant, who knows how long Father will take to dress? And I'm sure you haven't eaten yet this morning," said Mared, taking on the tone of the innocent fair maiden. "I would be happy to show you the kitchen, where we could find you some fine food. Of course, I'd have to hold the message for Father, so you can eat properly."

"Sem Mared! I'm shocked that you'd think to bribe me to hand over the message I'm bound to give it only to the hand of the hetman. Shocked!"

Mared giggled, and Havant's outrage morphed into avuncular fondness. "Now, I might overlook this attempt, if you were to lead me to this kitchen you mention."

Mared put a hand to her chest. "Now I'm the one shocked by your attempt at blackmail!"

The ritual satisfied, Mared grabbed Havant's hand and pulled him into the manor. "Father will be down in a few minutes, so let's get you a couple of the fresh biscuits. I smelled them when I ran to greet you. I want to hear about that young lady you mentioned meeting, the one with the Orosz accent."

"And you can update me on the new litter of puppies you were so eager to see born," said Havant.

Ten minutes and two biscuits later, Hetman Keelan entered the kitchen, greeted Havant familiarly, then took and read the message.

"Hmmm . . . if you don't have other urgent messages to deliver, Esyl, could you wait while I compose a reply? I'll probably take twenty minutes or so."

"Of course, Hetman. I'll wait here with Sem Mared, with your permission. She advises me that it takes at least three biscuits to fully judge if they were made properly."

Culich smiled. "A wise plan. I'll also begin my own assessment." He picked two of the still hot biscuits off the oven top and left the room.

Before Mared launched into the puppy report or asked about Havant's supposed new acquaintance, he had other topics in mind.

"Sem Mared, I noticed last time I was here that Sen Maera is back living here, and I assume the baby is the hetman's new and first grandchild."

"Yes," said Mared. "She and Yozef stayed here while their new house was being built. It's only a half mile from here, and they just moved in."

"So they've moved from Abersford? I know Ser Kolsko has his shops in Abersford, so I'm surprised they would move here."

Mared grabbed a biscuit for herself and, with a mouth full, began a detailed explanation of why Yozef Kolsko moved to Caernford, so he could expand weapons production and become more involved in plans against the hated Narthani.

"They don't know what they're dealing with, those shit-eating Narthani," said Mared, then looked around to see if her mother was around to chastise her language choice. When she confirmed the coast was clear, she continued. "Yozef will try to tell you he wasn't a hero at St. Sidryn's Abbey when the Buldorians attacked it, but I know better. I've talked with men who were there, and they assure me it was Yozef who saved the abbey. And when the Narthani invaded Moreland, wasn't it Yozef's artillery and plans that won the day? I mean, really? If he's not a hero, then who is? That scar on his head and the one on his leg, you know, the one you see only if he's swimming or something, do people think he got those at the dinner table?"

Havant's casual interest in Yozef Kolsko changed to alarmed interest, as Mared recounted more details about her brother-in-law. His interest in the manor layout long forgotten, he led the youngest Keelan daughter on for more details before her father arrived, which he did just as Mared was about to recall overhearing Yozef tell Maera about something called a "balloon" and how, if he could get it to work, it would allow clan fighters to see Narthani troop formations while still miles away.

"Ah, Esyl, thanks for waiting. Here's the return message," said Culich, as he walked in the kitchen. "I'm sure you have other messages to deliver."

"No, he doesn't," Mared said.

"Actually," Havant said hurriedly, so as not to give the Keelan leader any reason to question his lingering, "I do need to get back to the station in Caernford. I'm sure other messages have come in, and I'm due for my time up on the scaffold changing panels at mid-morning."

"Mared will see you out then."

Havant let the girl see him to the front door of the manor and gave her a friendly, playful farewell. Well, he later hoped it had come across that way, because his mind kept racing in other directions.

By Great Narth, was everything the silly girl said true? If it was, how had he missed it? No, that wasn't fair. He'd read many of the semaphore messages to and from Hetman Keelan and other leaders, though not all. There had been little mention of this Kolsko. Who knew what could have been in other messages? And there'd been no reason for him to question people about Kolsko. Until now, anyway. That had just changed! He'd talked to many of the Keelan men at Moreland City, but from what he heard, most of them had not been involved with the artillery or the direct attack on the Narthani infantry. He had to immediately seek out anyone from Abersford. The Keelan girl said many workers and their families already had or would move from Abersford to Caernford. He had to find them and learn more about this Kolsko.

Havant waited until his horse had trotted out of sight of the Keelan manor before spurring it to a gallop. Not that he saved much time in getting back to Caernford, but the unconscious act matched his urgent need to get more information.

Caernford, Central Plaza

The morning prayer service at St. Tomo's Cathedral had ended a few minutes earlier, when Havant crossed the Caernford central plaza. The attendees usually numbered around two hundred, and now they mingled with the citizens of Caernford out to shop, workers going to and fro, and a group of men replacing broken paving bricks. His mind still obsessed over the visit to Keelan Manor and the alarming new information about Yozef Kolsko, when he passed the Great Hall of the Keelans and turned down a street, then left to a lane of shops. He took the same route any time he traveled in the vicinity of the plaza, even if in the opposite direction of his destination, which in this case was the semaphore station on the other side of the city.

His mind remained so unusually distracted that he almost missed the single two-inch-long chalk mark on one specific brick sitting among thousands that made up the outer wall of a two-story building. The mark, six feet off the ground, appeared there only when Gethin Drifwich was in the city and waiting for him at their prearranged rendezvous site. Havant had passed within two hundred yards of it on his way back from the manor.

Havant froze when he saw the mark, then recovered, looked around for anyone watching, and erased the mark. Drifwich was not due for his twice-monthly trips to Caernford for more than a sixday, so Havant had not expected the signal.

What's the miserable little Nyvaksian doing here now? Havant wondered. He detested Drifwich, though he tried to keep the opinion from being obvious whenever they met. It was unprofessional and stupid to do otherwise, because Havant's assignment depended on the other agent serving as a go-between to the sloops and Hizer back in Preddi City.

Havant circled a block, instead of turning around, to avoid anyone noticing his change of direction. It was a small thing, but accomplishing his assignment and even his very life depended on a myriad of small things to keep suspicion from falling on him.

It took him twenty minutes to retrace his path to the outskirts of Caernford and then take a smaller road that passed a patch of whoresthistle bushes. The plants dropped leaves that crackled when dead, even after a rain. It was impossible to move through such patches without announcing your movements to anyone within a hundred yards. Havant had picked this spot so that he and Drifwich could both check for anyone in a small clearing and hear another person approaching.

He passed a wagon with its two horses tied to a tree, their feet hobbled. Down a narrow path to the clearing he found the Nyvaksian pacing nervously back and forth. Havant put on an expression of camaraderie.

"Drifwich. You're not due. What's up?"

"I'll tell you *what's up*! I almost shit myself two nights ago when I was sending the latest report. Out of *nowhere*, there's three men dressed all in black and me with a knife big enough to gut a steer at my throat. They were from the sloop, I assume. I mean, where else would they be from? One of them spoke Caedelli with a Preddi accent, but he spoke Narthani to the other two. All they said was to see you get this." Drifwich held out a small square package, still tightly wrapped.

Havant snatched the package from Drifwich and used the three-inch-blade knife he kept in his boot to slit the wrapping. Inside was another layer of wrapping, the second layer made of resin-impregnated gingo cloth. When the stalks of the gingo plant were soaked in lye, the released fibers could be used to weave cloth with such a tight thread count as to be almost waterproof. Further treatment with a tree resin finished the waterproofing, and the resin made the cloth self-sticking to complete the sealing of the contents.

A third layer consisted of ordinary paper that stuck to the gingo cloth on one side, next to a message. Havant unfolded two sheets of paper and glanced over the contents. He read them again, slowly, as he decoded. He had the cipher memorized and could read the underlying message without resorting to quill and paper. Drifwich stood rocking on his feet, waiting to hear what was so important to break security protocol and bring Narthani onshore to deliver whatever had been written on the well-wrapped sheets.

During the third reading, Havant spoke aloud softly, more to himself than to Drifwich, "Well, well, well. Things are about to get interesting."

Drifwich didn't like the sound of that. Boring was more to his liking.

Finally, Havant looked up at his nervous colleague. Drifwich didn't need all the details. In fact, it was best if he knew as little as possible.

"Gethin, there are two things you need to do. First is to return to Salford and signal that I received the package as instructed. Do you have anything to write on? No? When we leave, we'll go first to your wagon, and I'll carve five numbers on the side of the wagon bed. When you send the message, include those five numbers at the beginning and end of the message. That will authenticate that I've received the package and understand the contents.

"The second thing you need to do is have two wagons ready exactly nine days from now. They have to be large enough to hide ten men each under some form of concealment. Perhaps straw would work, since air can get inside. I'll meet you at your employer's stable at sundown of that day. The two us will drive the wagons to Caernford, so you should arrange to be gone four to five days without arousing suspicions."

"Twenty men? What men and what will they be doing in Caernford?" asked Drifwich.

"You'll get more information when it's necessary. For now, focus on your two tasks, getting back to Salford to send the acknowledgement message and getting the wagons ready nine days from now, exactly."

"But . . . well . . . all right." The Nyvaksian wanted more information, but he didn't expect to get it from Havant. "Twenty men," stated Drifwich. "How quickly do we need to get to Caernford? Making the trip in one hard day would require changing horses at least once. I assume you want to remain as unobtrusive as possible."

"Two days," said Havant. "The first night we'll travel until near dawn, then move off the road to a secluded spot and camp for the day. We'll make it the rest of the way the next night. I'll find a place near Caernford for the men while they wait. You will stay at the inn you usually use.

"Put in the wagons enough food and water for the twenty-two of us for four days. Come to think of it, I'll come to Salford a day early to see that everything is ready with the wagons."

Drifwich licked his lips, and he felt the hairs on his arms stand up. Whatever the Narthani had planned, he knew he wouldn't like it. For the last six months, he'd had a set of gear packed and ready for a quick exit from Keelan. He didn't know if he could make the three-hundred-mile trip back to Nyvaks by sticking to mountainous terrain without being caught, but it was his emergency escape option should the worst happen. When he got back to Salford, he would check the gear and add saddlebags of food and water. He also decided to see about trading existing horses for two younger ones.

Havant watched his colleague disappear, heading south back to Salford. He knew the man wasn't reliable enough for this situation, but he was all Havant had to work with. He couldn't be away from Caernford too long himself, so he'd have to trust that Drifwich would do what he was told. Not that Havant thought the Nyvaksian would tell anyone. He was too cowardly for that. More likely, he'd try to get back to Nyvaks, maybe hiding in the mountains and slowly working his way back. Even if that happened, Havant would get the wagons ready himself. At least one of the twenty men would surely be able to drive the second wagon.

Havant would be in Salford a day early, and the stable owner hardly ever visited the property, what with trade almost nonexistent. As for the other few occasional workers, if Havant encountered them, he could either bluff his way through, or they would meet quick ends, not to be noticed until the operation was finished or underway.

Assassinating the Keelan hetman, Havant thought to himself. *Hizer is ratcheting up the stakes. I assume he knows what he's doing and that the chances of succeeding here can't be better than one in two. Is this the only such action? Is he after other hetmen, too? Not that I need to know, for my part.*

Havant understood the logic of targeting Culich Keelan. The clan was far too strong and organized. However, headquarters likely remained unaware of the significance of Yozef Kolsko. Hell, even he himself wasn't that aware until the Keelan girl clued him in. She said Kolsko and the oldest Keelan daughter lived only a half-mile away from the main manor. He wondered if they could hit them both the same night, thinking it definitely worth a try and that Hizer would approve, if he had the same information Havant now had. He'd talk with the strike team leader and see whether they could agree to add Kolsko as a target. This assumed that a reasonable opportunity would present itself.

And if they succeeded, what would that do to his position? Only Hizer and he knew that one of the code numbers at the end of the message was Hizer's signal to him that he could decide whether to stay in position or come out with the strike team. He'd have to think about that now, during, and after the assassination attempt.

CHAPTER 29

A DAY IN THE LIFE OF YOZEF KOLSKO

As sixdays passed, and Yozef's days blurred, with every hour filled by something important, something he *needed* to do.

6th Hour

Yozef woke at 6:00 am. His mind still translated Keelan hours into the timekeeping of his former life. He knew the time because outside a bedroom window it was lighter than inside the room, and he heard a single distant ring from a St. Tomo's Abbey bell. Clan Keelan recognized twenty-four hours in a day, and the Keelan abbeys, by custom, rang once every hour. Thus, the first sign of approaching daylight and the single ring meant the beginning of sixth hour—6:00 a.m., to Yozef's brain.

It had taken an Anyar year, about nine-tenths of an Earth year, for Yozef not to reflexively look for a digital clock as his first waking act. He still did it occasionally, though now as an act of remembering what he used to do, instead of unconsciously looking for the clock.

Maera's absence in the bed was a further sign of the time. She must have left recently, because when he reached to her side of the bed, the sheets still held a hint of warmth. Her rising might have triggered Yozef's arousal. He had semiconsciously noted her getting out of bed two other times during the night and coming back minutes later. Aeneas was a regular feeder, and Yozef felt both relieved and half-guilty that fathers were not involved in feeding infants. No bottle feeding or breast pumping existed on Anyar. Thus, he was assured of complete sleep most nights, while Maera would take a substantial nap during the day to make up for Aeneas's multiple feedings and changings during the night. Thankfully, although the little bugger was a healthy eater and squawker, he slept solidly through the night, except for the feedings.

Yozef let himself enjoy the lassitude of the bed for another few minutes before reluctantly throwing off the covers and coming to his feet. It would be a full day.

After pulling on pants and a shirt, he padded barefoot to the kitchen. He could smell what passed for bacon in Keelan, and when he came to the kitchen door, he heard peals of laughter. Maera, Anarynd, and Mirramel. Hearing Maera laugh always lit a small glow in his chest. She had been *so* serious when he first met her. Anarynd had gradually relaxed after coming to them, though Yozef still caught melancholy expressions on her face when she thought no one was looking.

He swung open the kitchen door, and the merriment subsided at his appearance, though, by the looks on the three women's faces, it was likely due to their not wanting to share the cause of the laughter with a mere male.

"Good morning, Yozef," said Maera, smiling. Anarynd only nodded, her face still lit from the laughter. Mirramel bobbed her head, the only version of a curtsey she could manage while breastfeeding both Aeneas and her own daughter at the same time. The idea of a woman bare from the waist up and feeding two babies didn't strike the islanders as peculiar.

"I won't ask what was so funny—you might tell me," said Yozef, bringing on a burst of giggling.

Only then did he notice Serys Clithrow, who, like Mirramel, had been widowed by the battle of Moreland City. Serys served as cook for the household and was busy frying salted coney meat (aka bacon) and pulling a pan of biscuits out of the wood-burning stove.

7th Hour

"All right, Yozef, it's time for your writing," announced Maera. "You have a full day planned. It's seventh hour now, and you may not get time later. Remember, you meet with the glassblowers at eighth hour."

New child or not, her own activities or not, Maera continued to keep a schedule for Yozef, something she'd started when they married and moved to Abersford. He found it both helpful and annoying.

She knew the precise time by the pendulum timepiece hanging on the kitchen wall. Her parents had given her this expensive present years ago, but it ticked too loudly for Yozef to want it in the bedroom. Made by skilled craftsmen on Landolin, the closest continent to Caedellium, the clock face showed the twenty-four hours of an Anyar day, though the symbols depicted one of the Landolin dialects and not Caedelli.

Maera's pendulum clock was indicative of the more sophisticated timepieces he'd seen, although these appeared mainly in abbeys, official sites such as registrar offices and the Keelan clan headquarters, some town and village clock towers, and homes of the more well-to-do Keelanders. The rest of the people kept time by listening to abbey bells, if the listener was close enough to hear, and by consulting various versions of water clocks, hourglasses, and even sundials for the daylight hours.

Anyar had an advantage, in that the axial tilt responsible for differences in seasons was much smaller for Anyar than on Earth, leading to less distinct seasons. This resulted in year-round cropping on the farms, though the selection of specific crops varied within the year, and less variation in the length of daylight. A BBC sword-and-sandals series Yozef had watched on TV had mentioned that the Romans used twelve hours each of daylight and night, no matter the season. That led to winter hours of 45 minutes and summer hours of 75 minutes—oddly inefficient for the supposedly practical Romans, Yozef had thought at the time. In contrast, Caedellium had the same relative latitude as Panama, and with the lesser axial tilt, the length of daylight and night hours varied by only a few minutes. The same relative consistency in the sun's position as it crossed the sky in daylight made sundials more reliable than on Earth.

As for the average Keelander, farmers and ranchers needed little precise timekeeping, because their lives revolved around sunrise to sunset, while people in towns and villages listened to local bells and used the sun's position in daylight to judge time.

Pocket watches were known but expensively imported from Landolin.

Despite different methods of keeping time in Keelan, variations occurred in a single system, with the abbeys maintaining consistency across the province. Yozef didn't realize that this was not the norm for other clans, until he began interacting more outside Keelan.

Not only did differences exist in when to start counting the twenty-four hours, there were also differences in the frequency of bell rings, whether hours remained constant or varied with the season, whether a standard applied for the entire province, and whether the clan kept a formal time.

All of which led to Yozef's insistence on island-wide standards and the topic of his first session outside the Kolsko property on this day.

Yozef's daily writing schedule had been reduced because of all his other commitments, but Maera scheduled it for an hour three times a sixday. Today, he picked up where he had left off two days previously, in the middle of a chapter titled "Carbene Complexes" from a textbook on organometallic chemistry, a subject he remembered thinking interesting at the time he took the course, though in writing down what his memory recalled, he couldn't account for his prior interest. He finished the chapter and had moved on to organometallic reaction mechanisms when Maera rescued him by reminding him he needed to leave for Caernford and a meeting with workers from a glassblowing shop.

8th Hour

Yozef left the house, mounted Seabiscuit, and neared his destination when he heard St. Tomo's bell ring once. It had taken him six minutes to reach the newly developing Caernford industrial park, a planned expanded version of his shops in Abersford. He couldn't have been more than four minutes past the bell when he walked into the glassblowing shop. There, he met the three workers scheduled to present their latest results in making standardized hourglasses.

The project resulted from one of a seemingly endless parade of ideas occurring to Yozef, most of which he now turned over to craftsmen and left it to them to figure out how to make the ideas happen. This especially applied in cases where he had a concept in mind, but his enhanced memory lacked details on that particular subject. In the case of hourglasses, the Caedelli needed mechanisms for fighting units to maintain matching times. There simply weren't enough pocket watches, even the clunkier ones most commonly owned on Caedellium, to outfit more than the leaders of a hundred men or more.

The only solution he could see was to produce small and accurate-enough hourglasses that could be carried by horseback or wagon. He initially worried that time kept by a stationary commander might differ from that of men ordered to ride hard to a destination. Empirical tests proved the differences in times between stationary and moving hourglasses were not significant enough to be a problem.

Yozef had turned over to the workmen the task of producing two types of hourglasses, one for one hour and one for ten minutes. Any need for coordination would have to rely on multiples of those two times. For example, if two units needed to attack at the same time in one hour and twenty minutes, but the units remained out of visual sight and lacked any other coordinating mechanisms, the timing would depend on one flow of a one-hour hourglass and two of a ten-minute hourglass. Until they had access to more mechanical and portable timepieces, the hourglasses would have to do as stopgaps for daylight hours. Today Yozef would witness the results.

"We quickly gave up trying to blow identical chambers," said the lead worker. "We had no way to control the variation so any two hourglasses would go through a single flow cycle in the same time. We know you said you wanted matching times, which wasn't possible, no matter what we tried. However, we think we came close enough for your purposes. The solution was obvious once it occurred to us. We wouldn't make the chambers identical, so we adjusted the amount of the flowing material for a specific chamber and the size of the channel connecting the upper and lower chambers.

"Once this occurred to us, it went quickly. We simply made hourglasses with one end open, adjusted the amount of flow material to match the time it took to empty the upper chamber, compared to a pendulum clock standard, then sealed the top reservoir. We found that among the different flow materials commonly used, ground marble filtered for size gave the best results."

The worker showed Yozef two sets of six hourglasses, each of the two types about three inches tall, with different diameters. The set of more slender hourglasses was fastened to a board, and the worker turned them all over at the same time, starting when the pendulum clock's hand moved to a new marking. They stood watching until all the ground marble had run out of the six upper chambers. The difference in emptying amounted to only a few grains, hardly more than a second, Yozef estimated. As the chambers emptied, he looked at the clock just as the hand moved to a marker ten-minutes from the starting point.

"As you can see, Ser Kolsko, the six function almost identically. We also compared them to one another when some are stationary and others move by wagon or horse. We do see a small difference, but only a matter of five or six marble grain differences between moving or being stationary."

Good enough, Yozef thought to himself.

"We've done the same testing with the one-hour hourglasses. It takes longer to get the exact amount of ground marble for each hourglass, but the result is the same. If you have time, we can demonstrate the longer-timed hourglasses."

"Not now," said Yozef. "Send these to Denes Vegga and tell him I suggested he have some men test them many times to be certain of the consistency. Assuming Ser Vegga is satisfied, continue production to a hundred each of the two sizes of hourglasses. I can't emphasize enough that the quality of all one hundred, and any more you make later, have to be the same as with these twelve. Men's lives may depend on this accuracy, possibly your own lives or your relatives', if we have to fight the Narthani again."

9th Hour

The 9th-hour bell rang while Yozef talked with the glassblowers. After finishing, he walked a hundred yards to the foundry. Although no meeting was scheduled, he always felt better seeing cannon barrel production. The Abersford foundry had concentrated on 6-pounders and left 12-pounders to the Caernford foundry, which also cast 6-pounders.

He had vacillated in producing heavier cannon, but now that they'd begun to set up new foundries in Farkesh and Bultecki, he had told the Caernford foundry staff to try the 25-pounder barrel again. They were scheduled for the first pour today, and he couldn't resist looking in. However, he was to be disappointed. The intended mold had a defect they'd only just discovered, and they'd put off the casting for at least three days. He and the foundry workers discussed the defect and how to avoid it. Then, for another hour, Yozef inspected barrels already cast and visited the carriage mounting shop next door. Four 12-pounders and limbers were lined up outside and covered with canvas to protect them from the weather. When the workers finished casting a fifth, the five cannon would form a battery and be taken to Orosz City and turned over to the Orosz clan for training men as artillerymen.

11th Hour

When the eleventh-hour bell rang, Yozef hesitated outside the large shop being set up to produce muskets, a new enterprise for Keelan Province. He had visited the shop the previous day and had gotten into an argument with the foreman, who had decided to make production more efficient and bypassed steps intended to ensure that Keelan muskets be compatible with those made elsewhere on Caedellium. When the foreman had refused to back down, Yozef asked him to step into the next room, where they could speak privately. There,

Yozef told him he would be fired from his position immediately, if he didn't swear to abide by directions from then on. Unsatisfied with the foreman's response, Yozef had fired him and promoted the next senior worker to foreman, with warnings that he could also be replaced.

Now, Yozef decided he'd better check on the new foreman. He went inside and found that the old foreman had been hired by his replacement.

"I know he's an irritating bastard," said the new foreman, "but he knows the work and has a family to support."

After a moment of thought, Yozef replied, "All right. But he's your responsibility. If he starts causing problems, I expect you to fire him again."

"Yes, Ser Kolsko, I understand. I don't think there *will* be a problem."

12th Hour

Yozef left the musket factory and glanced up at the sun. Almost noon. He grabbed a satchel tied to Seabiscuit's saddle. He sat under a tree on the edge of the industrial park, took quills, ink, and a sheaf of papers from the satchel, and outlined concrete production. In the afternoon, he would meet with a group of masons. Brickwork and small-scale masonry work with something like aggregate-poor concrete was known on Caedellium, though not for large-scale works.

Masonry fortifications wouldn't stop a determined Narthani assault. So far, they had seen only 12-pounder cannon with the Narthani army, but they had to be prepared for more powerful cannon and siege mortars.

They needed reinforced concrete. Although Yozef couldn't be sure, he estimated two feet of reinforced concrete could be breached by heavy cannon firing point-blank for several sixdays or longer, although three to four feet might be impregnable with current Anyar technology.

He sat on a bench next to a tree and wrote, thought, trawled his imperfect memory, and wrote some more. The sun filtered through the leaves, and he leaned against the trunk, his face tilted up to catch flickering light.

"Hey, Yozef, you asleep?" said a deep voice.

"Huh . . ." mumbled Yozef. " . . . what?"

"Asleep! You're supposed to be building cannon, doing your chemistry magic or whatever it is, to save us all from the Narthani. How can you do that by sleeping all day?"

Yozef sat upright on the bench, as his head cleared. He could only see a large shape next to the sun. He leaned to his right to hide the sun behind the shape that changed into a very large red-headed and bearded man with a scowling face and amused eyes.

"Carnigan," said Yozef, "I liked you better when you weren't talking so much and certainly when you didn't have a sense of humor. I'd tell you to go hide someplace, but there's no place that big."

The big man roared, reached down, and grabbed Yozef by his shirt, pulling him to his feet. "Have you eaten anything yet? And where's Shadow Two?"

Carnigan was referring to the triumvirate of himself, Balwis Preddi, and Wyfor Kales—Yozef's official bodyguards. One was always supposed to be with him. This morning, the duty had fallen to Balwis. The escaped Preddi shadowed Yozef all morning and had last been seen sitting on the ground, his back against a building where they'd tied the horses. Carnigan was due to replace Balwis for the afternoon shift.

A puffing Balwis rounded a corner and trotted up to his charge and Carnigan, who scowled for real.

"Where were you?" Carnigan growled.

"Relieving myself out of sight behind the trees. I was only gone a few minutes," said Balwis, his tone defensive and his face flushed.

"Well, piss in your pocket for all I care!" snarled Carnigan. "You're supposed to never leave Yozef or be out of sight!"

Balwis reddened further and looked at Yozef. "Sorry. It won't happen again. But now that Carnigan is here, I'll be going off." Without another word, Balwis turned to gather his horse.

"He said he was only gone for a moment," said Yozef.

"That's what he said," Carnigan grunted, "but there's a whorehouse two blocks away, and I've seen Balwis coming out a couple of times. I wouldn't be surprised if he thought he could slip away for a quick poke before you woke up and missed him."

"Well, shit," said Yozef. He didn't care whether Balwis availed himself of prostitutes or not. The Caedelli had a relatively blasé attitude about sex, as long as people observed reasonable discretion and took good care of any resulting children. That Balwis might not be trustworthy enough to carry out assignments is what bothered Yozef—in this case, to provide protection. He wondered whether he could trust Balwis to protect Maera, Aeneas, or other members of the Kolsko household.

"That's not good," agreed Yozef. "I'll have to keep a closer eye on him."

"I will, too," said Carnigan. "I can't say I've ever completely trusted him. Right now, it's time for food. The Snarling Graeko is only three blocks away."

"No beer for me this time of day," Yozef remarked. "I have too much to do this afternoon."

"That's the trouble with you little people, no capacity," said Carnigan. He laughed and headed off to the pub, expecting Yozef to catch up on Seabiscuit.

13th Hour

Full of barley and beef soup, heavy bread slathered with fresh butter, and a cup of kava, to Carnigan's disapproval, Yozef led Seabiscuit two hundred yards to the clan headquarters building on the edge of the central plaza. The largest structure on the western side of the plaza, it faced the Great Hall of the Keelans on the eastern side. St. Tomo's Abbey and associated buildings occupied the entire northern side and several blocks farther north, while tradesmen's shops filled in the southern side.

Denes Vegga and Vortig Luwis met him in a meeting room on the second floor. A middle-aged woman Yozef didn't know accompanied them.

"Yozef, this is Kullyn Lorna," said Denes. "She owns a seamstress shop here in Caernford, and Pedr Kennrick advised that we might ask her to think about designing the flags, badges, and medals you suggested."

Yozef remembered some common advice from the military writers he drew on, Clausewitz, Jomini, Sun Tzu, and Napoleon, all four emphasizing the importance of morale. What he knew from his reading and, to be honest, movies and TV, was that men fought harder if they felt they belonged to something bigger, if they felt recognized, and if they were emotionally attached to their units and fellows. When the men fought with their own clansmen, there was no problem, but Yozef pushed for the clans to learn to fight in mixed-clan units. Without clan identification, Yozef worried that they needed symbols, and he wanted flags for each larger unit, battle streamers to signify actions they had taken part in, and badges to sew on clothing or medals to pin on.

For the next hour and a half, Lorna showed them designs for medals, cloth badges for units and ranks, and flags, all based on Yozef's suggested models. He was especially pleased with the results of the idea he'd given Lorna for the Caedellium flag, something that had never before existed. Each clan had flags and banners but no single symbol for all the clans combined. Yozef's proposed flag drew on flags from U.S. history, with stars representing individual clans. Lorna rolled out a green flag with eighteen small stars encircling a larger star. The symbolism was for eighteen free clans making up Caedellium. He didn't push the concept of eighteen clans as part of a greater political union—that concept was too early for the clans to accept.

Luwis commented several times in the first few minutes that he thought the entire meeting and idea trivial and not worth their time. In contrast, Denes participated and joined Yozef in interacting with Lorna. They gave the seamstress enough feedback and suggestions to go back to her shop and come up with a second round of proposals. As a notable exception, Denes immediately adopted one of the flag examples and declared it the official flag of the 1st Keelan Dragoon Regiment, the largest formal military unit yet formed by the islanders. The twelve hundred men were divided into three dragoon battalions and an artillery company, with Colonel Denes Vegga the commander. However, organization was not the same as readiness. The battalions and the companies, spread over southern Keelan, had yet to come together for regimental maneuvers.

14th Hour

Yozef heard the ring for the 14th hour. Not that he could have missed it, with St. Tomo's bell tower only a few hundred yards away. Through their meeting room's open window, they could see the tower. The bell rang loudly enough that they stopped talking until the reverberations faded.

When Yozef left the headquarters, he collected Seabiscuit and Carnigan, and they rode to the new industrial park, where eight masons waited in a planning room with no furniture, save a dozen straight-backed wooden chairs.

"Please have a seat, Sers," said Yozef. He proceeded to describe how he wanted them to work on developing concrete, a material composed of crushed rock and mortar.

"We already do this for some projects, Ser Kolsko," said a graying but solid-looking man, "but it's known that this 'concrete,' as you call it, tends to crack unless allowed to dry just right and is not as strong as one might think."

"Have you tried different combinations of materials to look for stronger ones?" asked Yozef.

"Occasionally, but there's little demand for structures made of mortar and rock combinations," said the worker, his manner conveying "Why are you bothering us with this?"

Yozef sighed to himself. *It's not their fault they don't see this as worth pursuing, since there's been no market until now. I need to light a fire under them.*

"It comes to me," Yozef said, with a dreamy voice and a pause, as if hearing something, "that the time will come when the safety of Keelan families will depend on fortifications made from what I've described to you as concrete. Therefore, it will be your task to determine the strongest possible concrete. I don't believe it's necessary to ask Hetman Keelan to talk to you about how hard you need to work on this . . . is it?"

"No, no, not necessary, Ser Kolsko," the man said hastily. "I'm sure the masons of Caernford will be eager to help. Uh . . . when do you want this concrete?"

"I wouldn't want to rush you, but you should have the details worked out and be ready for the first structure in one month," said Yozef.

The youngest of the eight masons spoke up. "If you want it in a month, you're going to have to help us with some of that knowledge you seem to have."

The original man blanched and elbowed his young colleague. Yozef could hear him whisper, "Ser Kolsko, you idiot."

"Ser Kolsko," came a grudging addition.

"Knowledge?" murmured Yozef. "Yes, there should be something I can help you with . . . " He let his voice trail off, as if searching his memory or listening. "Concrete. A combination of crushed rock and a special mortar called 'cement.' You make the cement by heating limestone with either shale or clay to produce something we will call 'clinker,' which is then ground with gypsum. The heating step has to be quite hot, so you'll need to work on how to get it hot enough, maybe with a coal-fired furnace."

The idea for concrete had been percolating in his mind for several months, which gave Yozef time to confirm the availability of the ingredients, though not all could be found close to Caernford. Limestone was abundant throughout Caedellium, as was clay. However, the closest deposits of shale lay eighty miles away in northeast Keelan, and the closest gypsum deposits were in Hewell Province. He saw no reason to go into the chemical compositions of the ingredients.

"You will need to have shale and gypsum shipped to Caernford, and you can see Cadwulf Beynom at the Bank of Caedellium building for coin. I'll let him know you'll see him tomorrow. Once you have the cement, mix it with rock crushed to pieces the width of a thumbnail or smaller. Add water, and pour the slurry into a mold you'll make with wood. Don't worry about the mold immediately. When you think you have the ingredient amounts worked out, send me a message, and I'll come look at the progress. Any questions?" Yozef asked as guilelessly as he could manage.

The eight men looked at one another worriedly, the youngest just shrugging.

"Good, then I'll let you get to work."

The men filed out of the room, leaving Yozef with Carnigan.

"I think you enjoy pretending you're a Septarsh," admonished Carnigan.

Yozef winced. "I didn't think about what I was doing, but I guess you're right. I get frustrated sometimes and tired of trying to convince people to do something I want done. It's easiest if they think it's something they *have* to do, instead of something they need to be *convinced* to do."

"Oh, I don't blame you getting frustrated," said Carnigan in his gruff voice, "but maybe you should save the Septarsh bit for when it's really needed."

"What do *you* think of all the rumors?"

"I leave such thoughts to those with nothing better to do. It's not worth worrying about whether Yozef the Mysterious is from a land where things are different from here or if he's communicating with God. It all works out the same, doesn't it?

"Maybe, in a way, but it's different in how people think of me."

"True," admitted Carnigan. "Though also how you think of yourself. I wonder whether it would make a person forget he can make mistakes, if he acts like God talks to him."

"I don't have that problem. Not yet, anyway. I know I've hesitated to give advice on things I don't have knowledge of. I'm afraid of making mistakes or having people give too much credence to my opinions. But with the Narthani always on my mind, I find myself more anxious to get things done. I go back and forth between not wanting to have too much influence to feeling impatient when people don't agree with me. It's confusing."

While Carnigan didn't respond right away, Yozef could almost see the wheels turning in the red head. Then he smiled.

"I was trying to think of a way to help. Certainly, nothing about your ideas, but I can keep reminding you that you're Yozef Kolsko and not *Yozef Kolsko the Septarsh*, all-knowing, all-wise man familiar with God."

"Which would you be, the angel or the devil on my shoulders?"

Carnigan gave Yozef his standard "I don't know what you just said, so why don't you say what you mean?" look.

"Okay," said Yozef, "you're big enough to be both, but stay off my back. I don't want to be crushed. Let's agree you can always tell me if you think I'm starting to believe in my own infallibility."

"That I can do," grunted Carnigan.

15th Hour

After leaving the masons, Yozef and Carnigan rode to the napalm project shop, located well away from the other projects, just in case. He had set the project's men to developing napalm and to join forces with a second team that worked on mines. Yozef had gotten a message from Raywin, the napalm project foreman, that they were ready to give a demonstration. They met in a field near the building used by the napalm team. Several tables had been set up, with numerous objects of varying sizes and shapes.

Raywin led the demonstration. He obviously felt pleased with their results and all but puffed up with enthusiasm. On that partly cloudy day, 50-some men and a few women witnesses had assembled. The development team had set up a triple line of 100 straw men to simulate a Narthani infantry line. Each dummy had paper coverings to allow better scoring of hits. Another hundred yards behind the line stood a block of 225 dummies, 15 to a side.

Yozef addressed the witnesses. "One of our problems is how to counter the Narthani infantry tactics and discipline. We want to not only kill Narthani but break up their major formations and destroy their belief in their invincibility. A group of impressive craftsmen has been working as a team to develop weapons that contribute to those objectives. What you will see is a demonstration of these new weapons. We need to be aware that this is a planned demonstration, and nothing works as easy in real life. Still, it will give you a rough idea of the weapons' capabilities."

He pointed to the line of straw dummies. "You'll see different versions of what we call 'mines.' Two are placed on the ground in front of the straw infantry. On the right side are mines that will explode and throw pieces of lead and metal at the dummies. The mine is designed so that the pieces go only in the direction of the dummies and not in this direction. We call these *claymore mines*. On the left side are containers of a flammable substance called *napalm*. The containers are thrown up from the ground and spread burning napalm in all directions. We call these *bouncer mines*. A similar bouncer mine sends metal and lead in all directions, instead of directional like the claymore. We won't demonstrate this version of the bouncer today.

"The third weapon involves napalm containers that will be hurled at the straw infantry block farther to the rear. The straw dummies have been soaked with water to more simulate the consistency of human bodies."

Yozef nodded to Raywin. "At your direction, Development Leader."

Along the hundred yards facing the "infantry," ten men lay on the ground, each one holding a wooden handle with twine wrapped around it. The twine seemed short, ending a few feet in front of each man. Raywin blew into a whistle once. All ten men pulled hard on the twine. Instead of being short, each length of twine suddenly elongated, as the dirt-covered remainder of the twine popped up from the ground. Four of five napalm and three of five claymore mines fired on the first pull. The three not firing with the first pull were subjected to repeated pulls. Two more fired on the second pull, and one failed to work. On the right, explosions from claymore mines were followed by clouds of straw bursting from the dummies. On the left, fireballs covered almost all the 50 yards of dummies.

Raywin then blew the whistle twice in succession. From the side where the observers had gathered, six small catapults, each with an 8-foot throwing lever, fired round objects that trailed a thin line of smoke as they arced toward the more distant block of dummies. One of the objects ignited into a fireball not 20 yards from the catapult—fortunately, far enough away to avoid incinerating the catapult's crew. Three of the objects landed near the square. Two hit the square, ignited, and merged into a fireball covering most of the square, while a third projectile hit the square dead center, didn't ignite, and bounced away.

After shocked silence, the crowd erupted in exclamations and a couple of quick prayers. Everyone waited for the team members to check the unexploded mine and napalm projectile to avoid the danger of accidently eliminating a good part of the Keelan leadership, then people walked out to see the result. On the right, the infantry lines had been decimated. Of the fifty right-side dummies in the front line, every dummy had at least one hole in its paper covering. More than half of the dummies had simply disintegrated. The degree of damage lessened in the second and third rows, with perhaps two-thirds of the dummies hit in the second row and a third in the last. On the left, all fifty front-line dummies were scorched to some degree, with more than half burned substantially and still smoldering, despite being water soaked. In the second and third rows, a few dummies had escaped apparent damage, but almost half showed major scorching. In the middle of the line, where some of the fake infantry had suffered the effects of both the claymores and the napalm, the dummies were blackened piles of smoldering straw.

They walked farther to the block. Although only two of the thrown napalm containers had hit the square and worked, three-quarters of the dummies were significantly burned and most of the others scorched to some degree.

Yozef let observers talk among themselves for another fifteen to twenty minutes, then asked them all to retire to the site meeting room.

"Remember, this was merely a test where everything had been set up to work. You can imagine what would have happened if the dummies had been real Narthani infantry. The firing line was destroyed. All the front line would be put out of action and most of the second and third lines impaired. For the infantry block, visualize the effects on the block's fighting ability and the ability of a commander to respond to changing enemy actions. If we are given time to set up these weapons, and enough of them, any Narthani efforts to defeat our positions will be incredibly costly, if not impossible. However, there is one major problem with these weapons. Does anyone see it?"

Yozef looked around. It was Mulron Luwis, Vortig's son and commander of the Caernford garrison, who saw it first. "It's mainly defensive. The Narthani would have to attack a prearranged position. In addition, it would fix our people in place. If we had to retreat, we'd probably have to abandon the catapults."

"You see the problem then," agreed Yozef. "It's only useful in very specific conditions, not in general field maneuvering, where we couldn't predict either the Narthani positions or their intentions. And one more important consideration. Anyone?"

Culich spoke this time. "Once we use these, the Narthani will know about them and change their tactics. How long would it take before they started to use the same weapons against us?"

"Hetman Keelan is correct. The Narthani are professional soldiers and will adjust their actions. Therefore, the best chance we have to inflict the most casualties will be the first time we use these weapons. After that, it will become more difficult to be as effective. As for the hetman's second point, it's true that once they know about our mines and napalm, it will be only a matter of time before they duplicate them."

Yozef concluded his prepared comments with, "In open field battles, it will be difficult to deploy what you've seen today. However, there is one scenario where we might have advantages over the Narthani; where they attack our prepared defensive positions. The only other time we could probably use most of these weapons is if we put their positions under siege. We also need to carefully decide when to use these weapons so the Narthani don't have time and opportunity to use similar ones on us."

For the remainder of the day, they discussed and argued how to most effectively use these new weapons, asked and got answers to detailed explanations of the mechanisms involved, reviewed the logistics of their production, were cautioned in their deployment, and emphasized the need to train the men in their use.

18th Hour

Yozef felt ready to sit on their veranda, take a turn at holding Aeneas, and have a large glass of wine next to him. Unfortunately, Wyfor Kales was waiting outside with Carnigan when Yozef exited the clan headquarters building.

Shit, thought Yozef, when he saw two of his Shadows standing by Seabiscuit, Carnigan's Percheron-like horse, and a roan Yozef recognized as Kales's. *I forgot it's the day for sparring practice.*

After the Buldorian raid of St. Sidryn's and Abersford, Denes had recommended Wyfor Kales, the wiry and disreputable Keelan man, when Yozef asked for someone to help him learn to defend himself. He had come to the jarring realization that Anyar was a dangerous place and, like it or not, he needed to know *something* of fighting, because hoping to never again experience combat might be a fanciful wish.

No one seemed to know what Kales had done during the twenty-three years he'd lived away from Caedellium, but scars and familiarity with blades testified that it wasn't gardening. Over several months, Kales had twice a sixday inflicted bruises on his one and only student. It was only after Yozef managed to stay "alive" for more than ten minutes during one of their sparring sessions that Kales admitted Yozef *might* manage to stay alive until help arrived, should he be unable to avoid a real opponent intent on mayhem.

Accepting his fate on this day, Yozef left with Kales and headed back to the Kolsko estate. Carnigan accompanied them, even though he had passed off to Kales the task of evening bodyguard.

"It's always amusing to watch the great Yozef Kolsko be humiliated," said Carnigan, oblivious to Yozef's glares.

Back at the estate, the stable master took their horses to be unsaddled and groomed. Kales would spend the night in the cottage shared by Yozef's Shadows, while Carnigan headed back to Caernford.

Yozef quickly changed into thicker clothing, to better cushion his impact on the ground, and walked to the sparring area set up behind his workout room. Then his resignation about attending the session and his determination to give Kales a run for his money took a morale-inhibiting hit. Wooden chairs had been lined up into observing positions. It wasn't the chairs that bothered Yozef, it was the occupants: Maera holding Aeneas, Anarynd, Gwyned holding Morwena, Mirramel holding Dwyna, and Carnigan, aka "the Traitor," standing behind the women's chairs.

During the next thirty-five minutes, Yozef refreshed last month's bruises but consoled himself that he had inflicted a few on Kales. It took all his willpower to ignore the laughter and jibes from the hostile audience. Yozef was so intense, he missed the silence that followed when he flipped Kales onto his back and his mock knife made a gutting motion.

Kales laughed, jumped to his feet, and slapped Yozef on the arm. "Very nice, Yozef. I saw that coming, but you were too fast and too strong."

"Let's say we let that be the last fall of the day, Wyfor," said Yozef. "I'd like to end it with a win, even if it does only make it thirty times of me dying to your once."

The women walked to the house, followed by the men carrying the chairs back to the veranda. Yozef again missed odd glances thrown back by the women and their whispering, as he listened to Kales explain Yozef's mistakes and Carnigan admit that Yozef might be able to outfight a drunk at the Snarling Graeko II, assuming the man was elderly enough.

20th Hour

The 19th-hour bell had passed while Yozef and Kales sparred, and the rest of the hour slipped by while Yozef bathed, donned fresh clothes, and took half an hour to review the day's mail and messages coming to their home.

Precisely at the 20th bell, they sat for the evening meal. Yozef and Maera ate alone several nights a week, but not this evening. While Mirramel cared for the two babies, the diners included everyone who was a regular in the house and present that evening, be they family, friend, staff, or bodyguard: Yozef, Maera, Anarynd, Gwyned, Carnigan, Kales, and Serys. As Yozef looked around the table, he thought it an odd collection. The women and two of the most dangerous men on Caedellium. Yet somehow it didn't seem all that anomalous.

21st Hour

The meal finished, Yozef said goodnight and made his nightly visit to Aeneas's crib to kiss the child's soft forehead, then he walked to his study to deal with more paperwork: filing, writing responses to mail and messages, and making notes. The incoming had been light this day, so he spent a half hour staring at a wall-mounted map of the island. He had marked X's at St. Sidryn's and Moreland City and, as he had many times, wondered where more X's would eventually find themselves on the map.

22nd Hour

On the strike of the bell for the 22nd hour, Yozef put away the paper still sitting in front of him on the desk, took a last look at the map, turned off three kerosene lanterns illuminating the room, and walked through the quiet house to their bedroom.

Maera met him at the bedroom door. She had just finished bathing Aeneas and left him with Mirramel.

"I asked Mirramel to take care of the feeding tonight. I didn't get much sleep last night and need to get up early tomorrow."

Yozef felt disappointed but understood. He had thought about him and Maera delaying sleep while they engaged in other activities in bed, but there would always be tomorrow night.

23rd Hour

Yozef didn't hear the bell for the 23rd hour. He had already been asleep for forty minutes. His last thought was that he didn't know whether he'd achieved much that day. Thus did the days blend together, with more to do than he could possibly accomplish.

CHAPTER 30

WHAT LURKS IN THE NIGHT

Beach

Esyl Havant's every sense probed for warnings, and every muscle was poised to act. He felt more alive at such moments than at any other time, and he honestly knew that these moments made his chosen profession the only one he wanted. He felt alive in a sense that he knew Gethin Drifwich never experienced. The Nyvaks spy crouched next to the rock face, as if making himself small would provide safety.

Tonight was the appointed night communicated by the hand-delivered message to Drifwich from the Narthani sloop. Havant pulled out a pocket watch, the only one of its type he had seen during his time posing as a Keelan semaphore station assistant in Caernford. He had brought it with him when he inserted into Keelan, then buried it along with other items that he didn't want found in his possession. They hadn't envisioned a specific use for the watch, but he and Hizer had planned for contingencies, such as needing accurate time at some unknown future date, like tonight. By prior agreement, they had synchronized the watch to the 1st-hour bell of Keelan abbeys. The Keelanders remained unaware that the effort to keep their abbeys on the same time worked to the Narthani's advantage on nights like this. Havant and the sloop offshore could hear the Salford abbey bell and ensure synchronization.

Havant held the watch next to the lantern and partly lifted the flap that allowed signaling to this sloop, with the other three sides of the lantern painted black. It was time.

"All right, Drifwich, send it," Havant said. He could have sent the message himself, but he wanted his nervous colleague to be involved. Doing nothing but crouching would only increase the man's trepidations about what they were going to attempt.

Drifwich sent a single word, "*go*," followed by a string of numbers that Havant gave him. Only Havant and the sloop captain knew that the numbers confirmed it was Havant sending the message.

Three spaced flashes of a lantern came within a minute. They couldn't see the sloop in the darkness, but the flashes came from where the ship should be. The message sent, they left the hidden signaling position and followed a narrow game trail down to the beach.

Then they waited.

Havant didn't check the time again, but his innate sense of passing time could not have been more than two minutes off when a longboat appeared, riding in on white surf. They could barely make out movement, and then men dressed in black jumped into the water. Several raced to shore, bypassing Havant and Drifwich and setting up a perimeter. The rest of the men pulled the boat ashore.

A figure in black walked up to Havant, intuitively ignoring the Nyvaksian. "Havant?"

"Yes," Havant answered. "And you are?"

"Uzcil. Captain. Are we a go for the mission?"

"Everything is set, Captain Uzcil. Gather your men. We'll have to hike a mile to where we left two wagons that will take us all to Caernford, the Keelan capital. Travel will be only at night. It will take two days, and I've selected a site where I believe we can stay during daylight tomorrow, but we'll need to move quickly to make the overnight site before light."

Havant looked toward the longboat. He could see several men standing with the boat, none of them carrying weapons or packs.

"I assume the navy men will take the boat back to the ship?"

"Boats," corrected Uzcil, as a second boat beached. "The seas are high enough that the sloop captain didn't want to overload one boat, and he said they'd need six rowers."

"How many men do you have?" Havant inquired.

"Twenty, including myself. As planned. We'll be ready to move out shortly."

Seconds

Twinor Madof wasn't supposed to be roaming the woods this far from home, and his father would have been furious if he'd caught his son disobeying—but not being caught was what made it fun. Besides, only in the thickest forests with heavy undergrowth did the adult flat-footed murvor come out of its burrow and forage for insects. The Anyarian avian was a delicacy, once the feathers were removed and the flightless murvor roasted. The canvas sack over his back could hold up to four of the creatures, all Twinor's eight-year-old body could carry. If he could catch even one, his father might scold him but nothing worse, and should the hunt yield three or four, the family might sell one or two at the village market for a price equal to several days' wages for a skilled craftsman.

"Shh," cautioned the sentry, as Uzcil crept near. They had pushed the horses to exhaustion to reach the site Havant selected for them to wait out the daylight hours before continuing to Caernford. Most of the men slept in the dilapidated barn a mile off the Salford-Caernford road. One of the four sentries had roused Uzcil and led him a hundred yards into the woods.

"There's someone nearby. I know it's not an animal, since there was a clank of metal to metal. Whoever it is, they're moving carefully." Both men froze at the sound of a branch breaking.

* * *

Damnation! Twinor cursed to himself. *What an oaf. How do I expect to sneak up on one of them tasty murvors if I clop around?*

He listened, not moving, breathing slowly and carefully. Despite their name, the word *stealthy* could have been invented for the flat-footed murvor. Twinor had once seen one cross a glade covered in dry leaves and twigs without disturbing whatever it stepped on or eliciting a sound. When combined with feathers mottled in greens and browns, the murvor was almost invisible.

He listened for a minute. Two. The tasty creatures were stupid. If he waited quietly, any murvor within hearing would eventually forget it had heard something and would continue foraging. Five minutes of silence satisfied him that no murvor had heard his misstep, and he shifted the sack and slowly moved again.

Uzcil's hand on the sentry's shoulder tightened its grip. Both men heard rustles of cloth against foliage. Whoever it was had gotten closer. If the person kept the same direction, heading straight for the barn, they would see the wagons or hear the staked horses at any moment.

A bush branch moved aside thirty feet away, and a boy carrying a sack stepped around the bush and carefully set the branch back in its original position. The sentry slipped a knife out of its scabbard and looked questioningly at Uzcil. The strike leader's face appeared stern. With a resigned nod, he released the sentry to silence the boy. Unfortunately, he saw no option. If the boy saw them, and they lost him in the dense woods, an alarm could be raised and jeopardize the entire mission. However, it was only three hours before dusk, and the boy might not be missed until it was too late to search the woods. They wouldn't find his body until the next day at the earliest.

The boy had his back to them. Uzcil pulled his hand from the sentry's shoulder. The sentry shifted the knife in his hand, placed the other hand on the ground to help catapult him out from cover, when—

"Twinor Madof! You answer me! I know this is where you go to hunt flat-footed murvors. You get back to the farm before your father realizes where you've been."

"Oh, Mother," Twinor moaned. "Every murvor within a mile heard you and is already back in its burrow."

Dejected, Twinor turned and trotted toward his mother's voice.

Uzcil had grabbed the sentry at the woman's voice calling out. They heard the boy's disappointed utterance and saw him disappear back in the opposite direction from the barn. They listened as the boy met his mother, her chastising audible until it faded with distance.

"Well," said Uzcil, "that's one boy who's never going to fully appreciate the rest of his life."

Six Miles from Keelan Manor

The stars had faded with the lightening sky when the two wagons left the Salford-Caernford road ten miles south of Caernford. They followed an old track another four miles to where it brushed a cluster of rocky hillocks, within which lay a depression forty yards across, where they made camp. They quickly set up tents and lit fires to prepare their first hot meal in two days. They extinguished the fires and coals before any smoke became visible in full daylight.

Uzcil made sure the camp was secure and his men fed before seeking out Havant, who had sat to one side—dozing, Uzcil thought, until his eyes popped open when the captain came within ten yards.

"Captain," said Havant, acknowledging the strike leader's rank and approach. "We'll go over the mission now. We need to confirm that I'm in charge."

Uzcil knew he had to establish lines of authority right from the beginning. The mission was precarious enough without adding a layer of confused command.

"According to my instruction, you are in charge of the mission's timetable and of providing the information needed about the target. However, *I* will decide the details of how we make the strike, given the information you provide. *You* are *not* in tactical command."

"Understood, Captain," said Havant. "The men are yours, and even if I was so inclined and felt I had the authority, it would make no sense for a stranger to them to assume command. However, up to the point of the actual strike, it's my duty to select time and place."

Uzcil nodded. "Within limits," he said. "I trust that your information will give us a reasonable chance at the hetman and a plausible chance to get away. This is not a suicide mission."

Although Havant didn't care whether any of the strike team survived, as long as they killed Hetman Keelan, he understood that the likelihood of success depended on Uzcil's cooperation and his men's belief they could escape.

His own priorities were, in this order, ensuring his own survival, assassinating the Keelan hetman, making a strike at this Yozef Kolsko, if possible, and safeguarding the strike team members. Least important was the fate of Drifwich, as long as whatever happened to the Nyvaksian didn't impact Havant.

"I believe we can work out any issues, Captain," said Havant. "The one change in the mission that I want to mention right off is an addition to the strike. The original plan was against the Keelan hetman, obviously because he's considered a focus of resistance. A weakness to my assignment is that I couldn't get detailed updates back to Preddi City. It's only recently that I've uncovered another individual who seems at least as important as the Keelan hetman and possibly even more important. The individual is named Yozef Kolsko and apparently has been instrumental in several of our failures. I'm invoking my authority to add him to the mission."

"Now wait," said Uzcil, "it's dicey enough to be hitting a hetman in the middle of his clan. We won't have time to race around more sites, I don't care how important you think this Kolsko is."

"Fortunately, Kolsko lives only a half-mile from the hetman," Havant said. "It turns out he's married to the hetman's daughter. I'm intimately familiar with both residences, and we should be able to make a pass at Kolsko after finishing with the hetman, since the exit route I've planned goes near the Kolsko house. If we miss him, there'll be no time lost, we'll just keep going."

Uzcil's expression told Havant the strike leader was dubious, but he hadn't outright rejected the proposed addition to the mission.

"Let's go over the plan I've come up with, Captain. You can evaluate whether the addition promotes any unnecessary risk, but I think your genuine doubts can be assuaged."

Havant pulled out two sheets of paper, and the two men moved to a blanket spread out on the ground. He laid the sheets side by side. The first sheet was a diagram with squares, rectangles, lines, words, and symbols.

"Here's the layout of the hetman's house. They call it the manor. The drive runs about eighty yards from the road to the front of the manor, here." Havant continued with a description of everything marked on the diagram.

"There are four regular guards for the hetman. Two of them have fixed positions: one at the entrance to the drive and one on the front veranda."

"Only four guards?" interrupted Uzcil. "You're sure? I would have expected at least ten. I had figured that unknown number to be the biggest obstacle. My men are good, but for the attack to go forward, I was prepared to cancel if the opposition strength made it seem impossible. Only four guards? I may start to think this might actually work."

"Four," confirmed Havant. "I've been to the manor dozens of times. Even four is something new. Until a few months ago, there were no guards, only whatever working staff happened to be around."

"Stupid of them," said Uzcil, "but that's fine with me. You mentioned two of the guards are stationary. What of the other two?"

"The times I've been at the manor when the hetman was at home, I couldn't detect a pattern to the other two guards. Often, one is at the rear of the manor, and the other one walks the grounds, though it's not consistent."

"No matter," said Uzcil. "With only four guards, we should go through them without hardly slowing. I assume they were picked for fighting ability, but so were my men, and we'll outnumber them five to one."

Havant pointed again to the manor house. "The obvious problem is that we can only attack when we're confident the hetman is at home. Fortuitously, the hetman's family keeps a rigid evening meal schedule. Within ten minutes of the Caernford main abbey ringing for 20th bell, the family is in the dining room." Havant had pulled a diagram of the manor to the top of the sheets. "Here it is—to the left of the main entrance, down a hall. The only two exits from the dining room, besides windows, lead to the kitchen and the great room. You'll have to account for the windows. We wouldn't want to get this far and end up letting him slip away."

"Besides the four guards, who else can we expect to be there?" asked Uzcil.

"Just the immediate family servants. The hetman, his wife, three daughters, ages about twelve to twenty years, three servant women, and a teenage boy around fifteen years. It's not uncommon for the hetman to have guests, but we can't predict who else might be there the night we attack. If there *are* guests, the number should be small—usually couples or families—so they shouldn't present a threat to your men."

"I agree, to a point," said Uzcil. "The other factor is you can't be sure the hetman will even be at the manor when we're ready to strike. You'll have to confirm the hetman is on site before I'll commit my men. We're not here to kill indiscriminately."

Havant didn't argue. Not that he had qualms about noncombatant deaths, but if the hetman disappointed them by his absence, there was no need to risk exposing himself. He would then send the strike team and Drifwich back to Salford as fast as they could travel. One of Uzcil's men had already planned to drive the second wagon on the return trip.

Tomorrow night was the assigned date. Havant would make a final scout of Keelan Manor and attempt to confirm the hetman's plans for the evening. For now, he needed to get back to Caernford to sleep and make final plans. He would arrive at the semaphore at dawn the next morning. If it turned out to be an average day, several messages should come in for the hetman, and Havant would establish whether the hetman would be home that night.

CHAPTER 31

FINAL PREPARATIONS

The sound of wind woke Havant, who rose and opened his front door to check the sky. They didn't need a storm to move over Caernford and potentially cancel the dinner at the Kolsko estate or leave the roads south muddy enough to slow or even stop wagons, the strike teams' primary escape method. His initial dismay at the wind eased when he saw the clouds move on, with a clear sky coming his way.

Havant entered the semaphore station office as planned, with the sun just below the eastern hills. Overhead, he heard footsteps and dull thumps on the roof, as other assistants brought out panels in preparation for the day's first messages. The station sat on a hill southeast of Caernford, the city's towers and taller buildings' roofs visible over another hill. The station had clear views to flanking stations six miles northwest, five miles southwest, and seven miles southeast. The Caernford station was one of only seven stations in the entire network that handled three-way traffic, because it received messages from all stations north of Keelan Province and passed relevant messages on to Gwillamer Province to the southwest and Mittack Province to the southeast. It was not the busiest station, since two of the links only connected to single provinces. The stations at the capitals of Orosz, Stent, and Moreland provinces passed on so many messages that those three stations had separate panel arrays for each direction. In comparison, Caernford's single array had its orientation rotated to align with the direction of transmission.

"Esyl, you're in early," the station manager called out. "You weren't due back until midday."

"That's what I thought, too," Havant said in his *I'm the innocuous assistant* voice. "I got back early, so I came on in."

"I'm glad you did. We still have a pile of messages that came in late yesterday and we didn't get delivered. A number of them need distributing to Caernford shops and tradesmen."

"How about for the hetman?" Havant asked nonchalantly.

"Naturally. Almost half were to or from Hetman Keelan. None of the late ones yesterday were marked urgent, so I held on to them until we had someone to take them to the manor. They went out not ten minutes ago."

Narth damn to eternal fire! Havant cursed to himself. *If I'd woken a few minutes earlier, I'd be on the way to the hetman's manor right now!*

The manager rose from his desk and went to a bench with a row of twelve two-layered wicker baskets lined up. Each basket held messages for a specific part of Keelan Province, the Gwillamer and Mittack provinces, and three sections of Caernford. The upper layer held messages coming from, and the other layer contained messages going to. The hetman had a basket to himself, larger than any of the others.

"Here you go," said the manager. "These for northwest Caernford. Be on your way."

Havant must have revealed his disappointment at being ten minutes late.

"Don't worry, Esyl. The day's still young. There's bound to be another bundle or two for the hetman before we shut down for the night."

Havant forced a laugh. He'd let slip, even if only a hint, his special interest in delivering the hetman's messages on this day. Part of his plan was for the team to burn semaphore stations, as the strike team fled back to Salford. He now wondered whether they should include burning the Caernford station and if he should eliminate the manager to avoid any suspicion arising from his interest in Keelan Manor.

Havant took the set of messages from the manager and raced to deliver them and be back for the next messages to the hetman. At late morning, a message to the hetman came in from Hetman Skouks. Havant grabbed it and headed for Keelan Manor.

At the 12th bell, Havant pulled up at the rail in front of the manor. The front door slammed open, and Mared Keelan raced out.

"Hi, Esyl! I didn't see you deliver any of the messages yesterday or the first ones this morning."

"Couldn't yesterday," Havant said, "but today I finally couldn't wait any longer to get a glimpse of a certain charming young lady."

Mared giggled. "You shouldn't let Father hear you say such things."

"It's worth the risk!" exclaimed Havant, feigning a noble pose. "But, alas, yes, I *do* have messages for your father. Is he inside?"

"Yes, in his office. I imagine he's working on the last batch of messages, so he might not be happy to see more."

Havant followed Mared inside and down the hallway to Culich's office. She knocked. "Father, it's someone to see you."

"Come on in," Culich called out.

Havant entered the office, and Culich frowned to see the semaphore assistant. "Hello, Esyl. I hope you have good news."

"I don't think it's anything to worry about, Hetman." Havant lowered his voice to a conspiratorial level. "Hetman Skouks asks why he hasn't received any of the new 12-pounders yet."

The semaphore station staff obviously knew the contents of messages, because they received and sent all messages. Only a very few had been written in simple codes. Most were plain text.

"Crap," said Culich. "He sends me an 'urgent' message every couple of days. Let's do this, Esyl. Every time Hetman Skouks sends me something, no matter how *he* rates the urgency, if it isn't about something going on at the moment, something I *really* need to know about immediately, just put it in a not-urgent pile."

Havant managed a friendly smile. "Is there a return message?"

"Not to Skouks. Let's let him stew a couple of days. If I answer right away, he'll only send something else. This way, it'll be several days before I hear from him again. But I do have several messages I need to get out, so if you wait a while I'll give them to you."

"Of course, Hetman. I wonder if Sem Mared will manage to find me a fresh biscuit or two."

He needn't have wondered. Mared was pacing outside the study door.

"Are you staying a while? You promised to tell me more about the latest rumors in Caernford—the ones you can share that don't come from semaphore messages."

"I'm sure I can dredge up a few new rumors," said Havant. "Naturally, a biscuit would help considerably."

Mared let the way to the kitchen, and Havant proceeded to pass on a few tidbits of gossip before turning the exchange to Hetman Keelan's plans.

"I thought I'd heard the hetman might be traveling," said Havant.

"Oh, no," said Mared, "not for a few days. Father wouldn't travel today, since tonight is Maera's birthday dinner at her and Yozef's house. We're all going, and I'm excited about the shawl I found for her in a Caernford shop. I hope she likes it. It's got several shades of green she favors."

Havant almost dropped the hot buttered biscuit, after he'd just taken a large bite. He swallowed, cleared his throat, then asked, "So the hetman's whole family will be at Ser Kolsko's tonight? I assume the dinner will be about the same time you usually eat, at the twentieth bell?"

"Well," said Mared, "I don't think Yozef and Maera mind the time, but Father's habit is so strong, he gets grumpy if evening meal is even a few minutes later. I'm sure we'll be sitting down before the twentieth bell finishes reverberating."

"Sounds like an enjoyable evening and not too many people. I assume the hetman's guards will go with him? You can't be too careful."

"Oh, yes. There's usually four of them around, no matter where Father goes. One of them will stay here, though, to be sure no one gets in the manor while we're gone."

"And Ser Kolsko? He must have guards."

"Not as many as Father. His Three Shadows usually take turns, one at a time."

"Three shadows?"

"The three men who came with him from Abersford. Carnigan is big but fun. I like him. Wyfor is also fun at times, but Mother feels uneasy about him. Something about his history. Then there's Balwis. I'm not sure about him." Mared lowered her voice and leaned closer to Havant. "If I didn't know better, I'd wonder whether he has eyes on my sister Ceinwyn. I caught him looking at her with a strange expression the other day."

Havant couldn't care less about Mared's other sister, but there was a chance to catch the hetman and Kolsko together after dark! He continued chatting with the girl, his mind plotting how to get a change in plans past Uzcil without too much argument.

One less hetman guard and only one for Kolsko, so no difference. Uzcil can't bitch about that. I don't know the Kolsko property that well. I've only been inside their new house once, while they were building it. I can remember the general layout. That should be sufficient. It's too good a chance to pass up.

Fortune smiled on Esyl Havant, whose Narthani name was Istem Sokulu. During the 14th hour, a semaphore message came for Yozef Kolsko. It was from Abersford and merely alerted Kolsko that a movement of equipment would leave Abersford the next day, as previously planned. The station manager had briefly left the station, allowing Havant to claim he didn't know whether the message was urgent or not, so, to be sure, he had decided to deliver it immediately. Even more fortunate, when he arrived at the Kolsko house, Yozef and Maera Kolsko were absent. He turned on innocent charm to convince one of the women at the house to show him their beautiful new dwelling. She demurred at a complete tour, saying babies and another woman were asleep in the bedroom wing, but she showed him the portion containing the kitchen, dining room, and great room—where he expected all the evening's diners to concentrate.

When Havant had ridden out of sight of the house, he stopped and drew diagrams of the interior and the grounds. His memory was sharp, but he left out one feature of the main hall, an omission to later have consequences.

In late afternoon, Havant picked up a final four messages to deliver into Caernford. He rushed the deliveries, then returned to his house on the eastern outskirts of Caernford. He had maintained polite relationships with residents of the few houses within eyesight, but none so close as to encourage curiosity. The neighbors were accustomed to his irregular comings and goings, so none who saw him that day thought anything odd when he came home, then exited his small barn fifteen minutes later with full saddlebags tied to one horse and packs on a second saddled horse. He hefted a pack to his back, mounted the first horse, and headed south, leading the second horse. The few people who noticed him assumed he had gone off on some business related to the semaphore lines.

Three miles east of Keelan Manor and the Kolsko estate, Havant uncovered a cache he had hidden deep within a thicket. He'd tried to plan for any contingency, and if things went wrong, he would come here for a fresh horse, food for a sixday, water skins, weapons, and heavy clothes appropriate for the mountains that straddled the Keelan and Hewell border. There, he could hide until he figured out how to get back to Preddi.

After staking out the second horse so it could graze alongside a small rivulet, Havant rode cautiously to within three hundred yards of the Kolsko house. He watched for thirty minutes through a small telescope, carefully re-familiarizing himself with the grounds and the structures. The only people he saw were an older man working around the barn and two women, one of whom held a baby and sat on the veranda breastfeeding. Uzcil and his men waited only seven miles away. To get to the house, the men would come in the two wagons that had brought them from Salford. Little or no traffic occurred after sundown, and anyone whom they met would assume they were trying to reach Caernford. A half-mile from the target, they would leave the road, conceal the wagons, and hike the rest of the way. Afterward, they would return to the wagons and push hard to the south, destroying several stations of the semaphore line south toward Mittack Province.

Havant had also privately discussed with Uzcil the possibility of alternative transportation. Both of them assumed the attackers would not go unscathed. Depending on the number of members killed or wounded, they might take horses at the Kolskos', along with those of the Keelan family and their own wagon horses, and ride by horseback toward Salford. They wouldn't take any seriously wounded men with them to slow the pace. Such men would be sent on to Narth with a martyr's death.

Havant took a last look at the grounds, then hiked back to where he'd tied his horse and made his way along game trails and creek beds, a route he'd scouted out when the target location was the hetman's manor, but it would serve as well for Kolsko's house.

At dusk, he reached the strike team's location. Each man had his gear spread out on a raincover. Uzcil and an older man walked among the other men standing or sitting near their equipment. In front of each man, Uzcil and the man Havant assumed was a senior soldier would pick up something, inspect it closely, and then either place it back or point out something to the man. Havant couldn't tell what the men said, because everyone spoke softly to prevent sound from traveling outside their rocky enclosure.

Havant walked closer to one of the raincovers. On it lay a short-barreled musket. All the action would take place at close range, so they didn't need longer barrels, and they could maneuver the shorter barrels more easily inside buildings. Next to the musket lay three pistols. Uzcil had told Havant that they intended to drop each pistol after firing. As with the muskets, they assumed that they would have little time or need to reload. Everything after the firearms would be hand-to-hand combat, with the short sword, the knives, and the cleaver-like small hatchet Havant saw on several raincovers. Three men had inch-and-a-half-bore shotguns, instead of muskets, and three more men carried axes, along with muskets. They would use both shotguns and axes to deal with locked doors.

"I don't like it," snarled the strike leader that evening, as he and Havant sat apart from the other men huddled around several banked fires. He didn't trust the agent, no matter how much confidence Assessor Hizer and Brigadier Zulfa had expressed in the man. Havant might be an exceptional spy, but Uzcil suspected the man would sacrifice the entire strike team, if it meant succeeding in their mission. Not that Uzcil was uncommitted, but he believed the risks balanced the chances of success, whereas he worried that Havant would throw them into danger, even if the odds of completing the mission were miniscule.

"Neither do I, Captain, but the Great Narth provides us with the opportunity to hit both men at the same time. Who knows the ways of God?"

Havant's ingenuous piety stemmed from noticing the tattoo on Uzcil's right forearm, a symbol signifying that as a youth, the captain had attended a Narth school for prospective priests. Obviously, the man's life had taken a different path, though Havant's experience told him such early indoctrination usually lingered.

"The only thing that changes is the building. Kolsko's house is only a half-mile away and hardly a detour from the direction we'd be going anyway. I've been to the house many times and know it well."

Havant figured Uzcil would never know his fabrication. He had been in the house only twice, once while the frames were still visible and his visit earlier that day. Even if the scouting was not as detailed as he would have liked, the strike team would enter the house and so overwhelm resistance that the team would only risk more casualties among themselves, something of no consequence to Havant.

The strike leader went to check on his men, then came back to Havant. "Everything is as ready as it's going to be," said Uzcil.

Havant waited for the captain to say more. He sensed the man was unsettled. "Last-minute worries, Captain?"

"Not of the men doing their duty, just wondering how many will be alive by midnight."

"And you are conflicted because the chances of escape will be better if not all survive?" said Havant. He and the strike leader had discussed the escape plan, and returning to Salford by wagon was less than optimal. If they had fewer men, and all were mobile enough to stay on a horse, their chances of escape increased. They could leave the wagons and use the light saddles they'd brought with them, to ride the horses they had to near death and then steal others on the way. By moving fast, they would outrun any word of what happened in

Caernford or about a group of horse thieves.

Havant wanted to placate the officer and get him focused back on the mission. "Narth will guide us, Captain. No use worrying about choices yet, since we won't know the options until tonight."

Uzcil grunted and grimaced. "I know, it's just . . . well . . . " He thought better of what he planned to say and slapped his pant leg with the gloves he held. "Time to tell the men to get some sleep, even if only a couple of hours. They need to be as rested as possible, and those still alive won't be sleeping again for quite some time."

CHAPTER 32

OUT OF THE DARK

Kolsko House

The sight was incongruous, and one that few people could have imagined two years ago: two-year-old Morwena Walstyn, Gwyned's daughter, laughing as she pretended to ride a horse, was actually rocking up and down on one of Carnigan Puvey's large legs. The little girl's delight and her mount's doting visage made Yozef look in amusement to Wyfor Kales, sitting next to him. Even Kales's normally jaded nature softened at the sight, although Yozef wasn't sure whether it was the influence of Kales's wife, Teena, who sat next to Wyfor on the veranda and had a hand on her husband's shoulder.

Teena Kales is not tiny, was Yozef's thought when first meeting her. Slightly taller than her husband and forty pounds heavier, Teena was a match for the wiry and disreputable Wyfor. A widow who had owned and operated a bakery in Abersford before the couple moved to Caernford, she immediately opened another bakery and was by all accounts an immediate success. She brooked no nonsense and could sound gruff but was kind in a way that no one could pretend. Yozef wondered how they'd gotten together and what exactly their mutual attractions were, but as for their bond, there was no question.

A week earlier, Kales had been hesitant about the invitation to attend Maera's birthday dinner, initially trying to excuse himself as not being a family member. Yozef had launched into reasons why Kales should come, when Maera settled the issue by telling Kales he was coming and his wife was invited, too. Kales deferred his objections when Maera said she'd stop by Teena's bakery to be sure the couple attended.

Not that Maera felt enthused about Yozef inviting all three of his Shadows. Carnigan she liked, but Kales didn't fit into social situations, and Balwis made her uneasy. She was never sure exactly who he was and how he would react to anything. Yozef's insistence and his pointing out the advantages of making the men protecting him, her, and Aeneas feel welcome and appreciated needed no further exposition.

As for the largest babysitter on Caedellium, Carnigan revealed his tolerance when Gwyned's toddler first favored him as a climbing target. Everyone present felt nothing short of shock to realize that the big man wasn't just tolerant, but he enjoyed the little girl's attention, to the worry and then bemusement of her mother.

Yozef completed the adult foursome sitting on the veranda, as he rocked a sleeping Aeneas. Yozef and Carnigan had volunteered to free up space and mothers while they prepared the dinner. The only image that marred the scene was the armed guard standing thirty feet away, near the door to the enclosed porch. He held his musket by the barrel, the stock on the ground, and his attention alternated between the darkness around the house and the sight of Carnigan playing with Morwena.

The hetman's family had arrived half an hour ago and was being entertained in the great room. As Maera updated her parents on details about finishing their new home, such as curtains, to her mother's interest and her father's disinterest, Anid and Mared watched Mirramel breastfeed her seven-month-old daughter, Dwyna, and waited for a turn to hold the baby. Ceinwyn Keelan had just asked Balwis Preddi why his last name was Preddi, if he wasn't a member of the Preddi hetman's family. The latter concerned Maera, considering her view of Balwis. It puzzled her at the same time, because Balwis studiously refused to talk about his past, yet continued to sit and dodge Ceinwyn's probes, instead of stomping out of the room mumbling to himself, as she'd witnessed him do more than once.

Ceinwyn was twenty Anyar years old and had had several visits from potential suitors. Her perpetual spiteful and put-upon manner had mellowed since Maera's wedding, supporting her parents' belief she had resented the older sister's not yet being wed, believing it blocked her path. She had inherited more of her father's looks, to her chagrin, as opposed to her three sisters, who more resembled their mother. In her mind, she needed as much time as possible to find a husband. She couldn't be convinced that as a hetman's daughter, there would be no dearth of suitors.

In contrast, Anid Keelan was by any criteria a beautiful young woman, seventeen Anyar years old, of kindly and cheerful disposition, and until recently she had been the family member most able to stay close to Ceinwyn. Culich and Breda laughed between themselves that in another year or two, when Anid was of age for suitors, they would need to improve the roads to Keelan Manor to handle the traffic.

The Kolsko cook, Serys Clithrow, was a whirlwind in the kitchen, moving between the large stove and the island cutting table and shouting orders to the night's assistants—Gwyned, Anarynd, and Norlin Rumney, the fifteen-year-old servant at Keelan Manor. Norlin had been volunteered by Breda Keelan to help with the evening's chores. His father ran the Keelan stable, and his mother washed and cleaned the manor and the guest cottages.

Gwyned served as a second cook under Serys's direction, while Anarynd and Norlin chopped, stirred, set the dining table, and carried out tasks to get ready for the thirteen people to be fed at Maera's birthday dinner—not counting the three to be fed by their mothers, two at breasts and one with her own small plate, as she sat on Gwyned's lap.

The three guards who accompanied the Keelan family would not sit for dinner, but Serys had already taken sandwiches and water to them at their posts, with a promise of more once the formal dinner started. Serys herself wouldn't eat with the others, despite Maera's insistence, only to find out there was one person more stubborn than herself. Serys said she couldn't do her job properly if she sat at the table and constantly jumped up and ran back and forth to the kitchen. Maera settled for Serys agreeing to partake in the birthday cake, a custom that Yozef had discovered seemed to be universal, no matter where humans landed.

* * *

Uzcil cursed when Drifwich fell for the fourth time, as they moved single file along a game trail leading near the Kolsko estate.

"Did we really have to bring that clod along?" he hissed into Havant's ear.

"I wanted to be sure he didn't scurry off at the slightest noise he heard, like a skittish coney. He can help gather the horses and saddles once we're finished with the target. I saw no reason for him to have a firearm, so I assured him your men would take care of that part of the night."

"I guess I should be grateful he's unarmed," said Uzcil. "He'd be more danger to us than any man or woman he faced."

Havant only grunted, to which Uzcil responded in kind.

"How do you know he won't run as soon as we're out of his sight and the firing begins?"

"Do you really think he could find his way back to your camp and the wagons? He can't show up in Salford if he's missing two wagons, and I made sure he didn't bring the escape bags I know he's prepared. They're back in Salford. Don't worry, he'll stay hidden, pissing himself until it's over. Anyway, I'll keep an eye on him, since I won't be going to the house until you signal it's all clear."

Uzcil understood that the assault itself was not Havant's responsibility, though he suspected the agent could well take care of himself in a fight. Havant's duties were gathering information, helping to plan the attack, getting them to the target, and then identifying the hetman's body.

* * *

Maera opened the main door and leaned out. "Everything all right out here?"

"Fine," answered Yozef. "Aeneas is still sleeping, and I'm starting to wonder who will tire of horse riding first, Carnigan or Morwena."

Maera laughed, shaking her head. "Maybe we need to get the two of you to help with the babies more often."

"Providing riding instructions and serving as a climbing object are as far as I go," rumbled Carnigan. "More intimate tasks I leave to women. I'd rather be fighting the Buldorians."

Morwena was in the middle of toilet training, and everyone was astounded that Carnigan could become even redder than his normal ruddy complexion when, a sixday ago, Morwena had asked him to take her to the voiding room attached to the house. He had declined and hurriedly found Gwyned, who compounded his discomfiture by cackling, as she led Morwena away by the hand.

"How much longer until we eat?" asked Yozef.

"Until Serys says it's ready. I was already told this is the one day I can't give her instructions. Since you men have the babies under control, I'll leave and get back to my family. And no, Teena, we've got things organized inside. Relax. First-time guests shouldn't be put to work. Don't worry, next time you visit we'll make up for today."

Kales's wife had been about to offer, for the third time, whether she could do anything to help. She had brought an impressively large decorated birthday cake, prepared in her bakery at the suggestion of Serys, who had had no issue handing off the cake, so she could focus on the other courses.

* * *

Havant stopped and crouched when he caught the first glimpse of lantern light from a window. Like a caterpillar whose rear segments sequentially took fractions of seconds to react, the twenty-one men behind him halted and did likewise.

"That it?" whispered Uzcil.

"Yeah," said Havant in a voice lighter than Uzcil's whisper. "Three hundred yards away. The brush and trees will only provide cover for another two hundred yards, then it's more open, with a few scattered trees, fences, and some outbuildings. Too bad there's no cloud cover tonight, but Haedan will be completely set in about another ten minutes."

The larger of Anyar's two moons hung over the western hills, just touching the treetops.

Havant leaned closer to Uzcil. "Another hundred yards and I'll check the front of the house to see how many wagons and horses are out front and confirm how many people we can expect inside. I'll also spot the locations of guards with static positions. I won't account for any guards who roam, so be aware. If all seems in place, you can proceed."

* * *

Breda Keelan put a hand on Maera's arm. "Dear, the house is coming along beautifully. I can see for myself why you're thrilled with it." Breda gave the arm a squeeze. "And with your family and life. I'm so happy for you. You know how your father and I worried about you."

Maera patted her mother's hand. "No one's more surprised than me at how much I enjoy being domestic. Me! Maera Keelan! Picking colors of curtains, shopping for just the right ceramic flowerpots for the back patio, and proudly showing Aeneas off to anyone even slightly interested. Oh, it's not all giddy. Changing Aeneas and walking him when he cries are no more fun than when I saw you with Anid and Mared, though somehow that fades when I feed him, wash him, or when he just sleeps in my arms."

"Any lingering regrets at how all this ties you down?" asked Breda.

Maera nodded. "There's still some of that, and I assume there always will be. But I manage to spend half my time at work outside the home, even if it's with Aeneas attached to me. I know how fortunate I am to have so much reliable help. Anarynd is wonderful with Aeneas, and Gwyned is a devil for getting things done. Serys handles most of the kitchen, and Mirramel seems unable to sit and do nothing, if she's not feeding her daughter or Aeneas. I saw all the help you had, and I might have even more. I'm only just coming to appreciate mothers who have to do it all on their own."

"Another ten minutes," a voice called out from the kitchen.

"That's Serys," said Maera. "I'll give it five minutes and go retrieve Aeneas from Yozef and tell the others in back it's about time to eat."

* * *

A low-pitched whistle alerted Uzcil. He replied, and a moment later Havant appeared out of the darkness.

"They're all there, although there might be a couple more than we expected, judging by the horses in front."

"A couple?" said Uzcil. "What does that mean? Two for sure or more?"

"Probably two," asserted Havant. "Nothing this many men can't handle."

"I don't doubt we can handle that many, but I don't like surprises."

"I'd hardly call this a surprise," uttered Havant, not hiding his irritation. "We always know any plan is only that—a plan, not an edict direct from Narth."

Havant brought the conversation back to the mission before Uzcil could respond.

"I spotted three outside guards in fixed positions. One each at the front and back main doors. There's also a third out from the road at the entrance to the lane leading to the house. A fourth guard is walking the grounds. He seems to take the same route each round and takes about ten minutes to complete a circuit. You take care of those four first, and the rest will be easy."

"*Easy* is never a word I use on operations like this, until my men and I are back in our own territory," said Uzcil. The strike team leader turned to two senior men crouched behind him. "Nirrem, take six men and work around to the front of the house. Leave one at the west side of the house, so no one gets out a window. Leave another man waiting for the guard at the road to come running. After he eliminates the guard, he's to rejoin you. Wait until you hear the rest of us at the rear of the house, then go in the front door.

"Arkol, you'll have seven men. You'll take care of the walking guard. Wait until he's out of sight of the house and be quiet about it. Send one man to the east side of the house to stop anyone from getting out a window on that side. I'll leave it up to you when to start off the assault on the house. Get as close as you can, then kill those on the back veranda and rush inside. I'll follow with the other four men. If you have little or no resistance, we'll follow you. Otherwise, we'll go in the windows on the right side of the house. Havant's diagrams show a dining room and a large room where we might expect people to have congregated.

"We can't tell exactly where they'll be, since we can't approach close enough to see in windows without being detected, so we'll rely on speed and shock. We'll be at them from two or three sides, and there can be no hesitation. We have to be in and finish as quickly as possible. Kill everyone who can be a witness. That doesn't include babes too young to speak. We're not savages."

The missing details about how to know in split seconds whether a child was speaking or not amused Havant. He knew any baby would be fortunate to survive this night, especially since the team's final act would be to set the house ablaze. This was war, even if no armies of tens of thousands faced each other. Noncombatants died, whether intentionally or not, and he didn't feel squeamish about the reality.

* * *

"Should be about ready to eat," declared Yozef, "although someone I'm holding already ate and, unless I'm mistaken, he's shit, even if he's asleep. Time to give him back to his mother or one of the other women."

He wouldn't have dared make such a comment in his previous life, for fear of the PC police, but equal parenting details hadn't yet developed on Caedellium.

Yozef gently stroked the soft skin of Aeneas's leg. There was nothing quite like the feel of a newborn's skin. He listened to the baby's breathing and watched the little belly rise and fall in the natural abdominal breathing that most older children quit after adults mistakenly told them breathing should be out of the chest.

Aeneas's breathing was so quiet, Yozef lowered his ear nearer. Then . . . the effort to listen carefully made him realize *something* was missing.

"That's odd," he said to no one in particular. "I don't know if I've ever not heard the niklons after dark."

The cricket-sized and sounding Anyarian insect-analogs were ubiquitous on Caedellium, even at higher altitudes. Although several species had adapted to different environs, they all sounded the same to Yozef, and they were always present . . . until now.

"What—" said Kales, sitting up sharply in his chair, his wife's hand slipping off him by his sudden movement. "What did you say?"

Yozef shifted Aeneas in preparation for standing, still with an ear cocked at the night. "I was just thinking I don't remember ever not hearing niklons as soon as it gets this dark."

Carnigan's horse imitation instantly ceased, to Morwena's complaint. Yozef heard the big man's chair creak, as he shifted his weight.

"Nobody move quickly," said Kales, his voice low, tight, and urgent. "Act normal, but one by one get up and go in the house. Keep talking loud about anything, like we were doing."

"What—" started Teena, but Kales put a seemingly casual hand on her arm to stop her from speaking. Yozef could see her flesh turn white with the pressure.

"Niklons don't stop making noise unless there's something or someone they sense is danger. I don't hear anything in any direction. It may be nothing, or it might be something is out there or someone. You need to get into the house and caution the others. *Now!*" Though the last word was whispered, the urgency *shouted.*

Yozef's breath caught in his throat for a second, his heart rate shot up, and he clutched the baby against his chest.

"Easy, easy," soothed Kales in a whisper, as he rose, pulling his wife to her feet but keeping his grip on her arm. "I think it must be time to eat soon," he said aloud. "You all might as well go in. I'll be in in a minute." He walked his wife to the door into the enclosed porch. Kales opened the door and guided Teena through, and the others followed.

Yozef reached the door last. On the way, he heard Kales tell the guard they needed to check the grounds and for the guard to follow him thirty feet behind.

When Yozef got to the door, he hesitated and whispered, "Do you really think it's anything, Wyfor? What if it is? You're unarmed."

Kales grinned his "*Are you shitting me?*" look, which Yozef recognized.

Kales opened his coat a few inches with the hand not holding the door, and Yozef glimpsed a pistol stock in a holster fastened to the inside of the coat and two knife sheaths. Kales let the coat close and nodded Yozef inside.

Yozef held Aeneas tight, his throat muscles tight, his mind racing from an idyllic mood to incipient panic.

No, no, no, this can't be happening, desperately exploded in Yozef's head, as, unbidden, he remembered attempts earlier on the Stent and Hewell hetmen. *Kales must just be an alarmist! Please, God, let him just be imagining danger!*

* * *

Arkol quietly grunted. The people sitting outside were going in. Another minute and they'd have had them like practice targets. He glanced behind at Uzcil, whose shrug was visible by starlight.

No matter, Arkol thought. *Outside or inside won't make any difference in the end. Now they'll just be bunched together.*

At the front of the house, all Nirrem knew was that he and four men were almost in position to rush the main door. One man carried a shotgun and another an axe, both to ensure that any door they needed to go through wouldn't stop them. He had dropped one man at the side of the house to block that escape route for the hetman, and a final man had crept to within forty yards of the guard at the road. In another few minutes, Nirrem expected to hear the chaos start, as Arkol and Uzcil launched their assault on the rear of the house. That would be his signal.

* * *

Inside the foyer, Yozef crossed to the front door and opened it. The front guard turned at the sound. The man had a questioning look, caused by Yozef's expression and Carnigan pulling weapons harnesses off a high shelf.

"Ser, listen carefully'" said Yozef. "Count to ten, then come inside. Do you understand?"

"Why—"

"No questions! Just do as I say! Once you're inside, wait and listen for anything happening outside. I'll be right back."

Yozef turned and Carnigan tossed him Kales's harnesses. "Get armed."

Even without the weapons Kales had on him, the harness was so heavy

Yozef almost dropped it. It took him five seconds to set Aeneas on the floor, jam his arms through the harness straps, cinch the belt, and pick Aeneas back up before the baby responded to being dumped on the floor.

Carnigan had somehow donned his own harness without setting Morwena down. Although Carnigan's harness had fewer weapons than the others, the size of the pistols and the blades more than made up for the fewer number. Carnigan leaned Kales's musket against a wall, keeping his own and Balwis's under his arm.

Under other circumstances, the sight of the huge man decked out like a cartoon pirate, holding a two-year-old in the crook of the same arm that held Balwis's harness, the other arm holding two muskets, would have been amusing. In these circumstances, it was terrifying.

Yozef followed Carnigan thundering down the hall. Carnigan stopped at the door leading to the kitchen and tossed Balwis's harness at Yozef. "Get Balwis! I'm giving Morwena to Gwyned and getting the people in the kitchen, away from doors and windows, and killing the lights. Then you or Balwis get back to the front door."

As he caught the harness, Yozef caught a glimpse through the door into the kitchen, where Serys and Anarynd stared at Carnigan rushing into the room. Then Yozef reached the great room. Eight seated faces turned to him. They had heard commotion and were just responding. The questioning or surprised expressions immediately changed to other emotions.

"Everyone," Yozef enunciated carefully and loudly enough to get their attention without yelling. "Get up, put out the lanterns, and come toward the hall, away from the windows. It's probably nothing, we're only being cautious. Kales thinks someone might be out behind the house. He and the back guard have gone to check."

"How do you know someone's out there?" demanded Culich.

"Goddamn it, I don't know! Better to look foolish than take a chance. I noticed the niklons quit sounding off! You tell me. When do the noisy buggers ever shut up? Kales is concerned enough to check it out."

"The niklons are quiet only if they're startled or afraid," said Maera, running to Yozef and taking Aeneas.

Balwis had rushed to Yozef and grabbed his harness.

"I'll ask the front door guard to also check the grounds," said Culich, turning to head down the hall.

"Wait, Culich," said Yozef. "I've asked him to come inside and station in the foyer, just in case. It's less exposed than standing out front."

"Just in case of what?" exclaimed Breda. Anid and Mared, holding hands, stood behind their mother.

Before Yozef could give another reassurance that there was probably no problem, a series of shots sounded from behind the house, followed by cries.

In a moment of chaos, exclamations threatened to overcome the group, before Culich yelled, "QUIET! Put out the lanterns, then do as Yozef says and move away from the windows. Drag furniture over here." He pointed to the interior wall of the room.

Culich looked at Yozef. "We're unarmed!"

Yozef gave Culich one of Kales's pistols and a knife to a pale-faced Maera, who held Aeneas. Balwis gave one of his two knives to Ceinwyn, standing next to him.

They heard another musket shot and shouts from outside the front of the house.

"I'm going back to help the guard at the foyer." said Yozef, giving Maera and Aeneas a look.

He ran down the hall again. As he passed the kitchen door, he could see that Carnigan had upended a table that Gwyned now crouched behind, cradling Morwena. Serys held a meat cleaver, the teenage boy Norlin grasped one of Carnigan's pistols in both hands (he needed two to hold the small cannon and aim), and Anarynd brandished a carving knife.

At the end of the hall knelt the guard, watching the front door intently. They heard voices, then feet on the wooden veranda steps.

"Quick, to the other side!" Yozef told the guard, grabbing Kales's musket. He knelt where the guard had been. If anyone unfriendly came through either the front door or the door into the rear enclosed porch, the two of them wouldn't be concentrated in the same place, and the intruder would face fire from two directions.

* * *

Uzcil had watched the people sitting on the back veranda rise and start into the house. *Too bad,* he thought. *We could have eliminated them first.* With three of the men gone right away, the rest of the attack would have been almost anticlimactic.

He wasn't worried until one of the three men didn't go inside but spoke to the guard. Then the two of them walked down the stairs and toward the spot where Uzcil and the other eleven men waited.

"No problem," whispered the man next to him. "We'll take care of them." The man and three others slunk away, spreading out in the direction of the two approaching men.

Uzcil watched, not quite holding his breath, uneasy with the wrinkle in what had started as a stealthy approach to the house. He watched the two men get closer, then . . . what? Where was the first man, the one walking ahead of the other by twenty or thirty feet? The lights from the house helped backlight the two men. The rear man, the guard with a musket, was still visible, but the other, smaller man . . . where had he gone?

In an instant, all plans at stealth disintegrated.

* * *

Wyfor Kales trusted his instincts. Not to say they hadn't proved wrong a time or two, but listening never hurt. Better mistaken than dead. The silence of a throng of annoying pests was not as significant to him as an intuition he recognized—a summation of too many years in too many situations where the slightest signal was too important to miss.

From the veranda and before Yozef had said anything about the missing niklon chorus, had he seen a flicker of movement in the starlight? Had there been a faint clink of metal that could have been a window latch or an echo from the kitchen? He didn't know the answers, didn't think about knowing them, and didn't care. All he knew was that every nerve ending was reaching out into the night.

Kales was a hundred feet from the house when he morphed from a walking man to a wraith. He dropped to the ground as boneless and casually as oil slipping down a glass surface, then moved silently on fingertips and boot toes.

To the men watching, it was as if Kales had disappeared. One man was only twelve feet away when his target vanished. His surprise lasted only ten seconds before the corner of his eye caught an almost imperceptible movement, and a coldness stroked his throat. An urge to say something was stifled by the warm flush that bubbled from his lips and the hot flood running down his chest. He rose to his feet, only to fall face forward.

Eight feet away, another man was shocked to see his companion stand.

What!? flashed through his mind. The next moment a blade plunged upward, under his ribcage, through his diaphragm, and into his heart. The blow prevented his lungs from expelling air, so he couldn't shout. It killed him that instant, though it took another twenty seconds for the rest of his jerking body to capitulate.

A third man had turned from seeing the first man rise and fall, and he became the first to see Kales after his disappearance. He fired his shotgun at a blur moving toward him, gratified to see the blur being smashed to the ground. Yet he didn't live to identify what he had hit. The flash from a pistol was his last sight before the ball hit his left eye.

Kales felt a terrible blow to his left side. His arm didn't work, but blackness waited to overtake him just long enough for him to pull his single pistol at the man illuminated by his own shotgun flash.

The guard following Kales saw the two flashes, the larger of the shotgun and the smaller of the pistol. The first bright flash appeared too suddenly and not in the field of view he directly faced. The second flash came when he had focused his attention where the first flash originated. It revealed men, many men, two only thirty or forty feet away. He only needed to turn his leveled musket a few degrees to fire at the closest man. His ball struck the crouched man six inches below his right nipple, breaking a rib and coursing through his liver and intestines.

The guard didn't see anything else, after three of the four musket balls fired at him ended his life.

* * *

Uzcil might have cursed to himself at the loss of his team's surprise advantage or because Arkol, the man to lead the initial assault at the rear of the house, was down, dead or wounded, but he had no hesitation about the appropriate action.

"That's it!" he yelled to the seven men who still functioned. "We'll check our wounded on the way out, spread out, and hit the house at doors and windows."

He'd hoped that he and the eleven other men at the rear of the house could burst through the back doors and be inside before the people knew they were coming. That hope was gone. The only option left was to hit this house as fast as possible and at as many points as they could, to prevent a concentrated defense. What worried him more than the loss of surprise was that four of the men now racing toward the house had empty muskets. Among their eight, they now had only two loaded muskets and two shoguns. After that, they'd have to attack with pistols and steel.

* * *

The five men at the front heard the firing at the rear of the house and took it as the signal to go in. Nirrem, the leader, gave the order. "At the front door! Munkun, you're first. Try the door. If it's locked, use your shotgun. Tonkel, if the shotgun doesn't get the door open, use your axe and get us inside. Let's go!"

* * *

Yozef's heart pounded as if about to burst from his chest. He hyperventilated, his breath coming in gasps. He heard sounds . . . low voices, then louder, then feet on wooden steps and the floor of the front veranda. Light from the single lantern on the veranda and from a hall lantern still flickering after the attempt to turn it off gave enough light for him to see the door latch quiver, as if someone were checking the mechanism.

Despite Yozef focusing all of his senses on the door, the shotgun blast that took out the lock and left a six-inch hole left him frozen for several seconds. A fortuitous delay. The door kicked open, and a man with a short musket leaped through, only to be hit by a musket ball the guard fired from the opposite side of the foyer.

Two more flashes and cracks came from outside, the flames and smoke pouring through the door jamb. The guard was flung backward, as both balls hit him, one on a shoulder, the other on a hip. As he reached to pull his pistol from his belt, a third shot struck him in the chest.

A man stepped through the door, slipping sideways against the wall, watching the fallen guard. Dressed all in black, he wore a cloth over most of his head, leaving only eyes, nose, and mouth showing. The man didn't see Yozef crouched only seven feet away, so close that the flame from Yozef's musket hit the man's chest. Yozef didn't watch as the man briefly stood straight against the wall, then slid slowly down, leaving a trail of blood on the wall from the exit wound.

Yozef didn't notice because he was busy. As soon as he fired the musket, he dropped it and pulled out one of Kales's pistols, in time to shoot a third man who tried to enter the door. The man pitched back onto the veranda.

A fourth man fired into the foyer, missing Yozef but causing him to fire back with the last of Kales's pistols. He didn't see whether he'd hit anything and cursed at himself for firing without a clear target. He was now down to two knives on Kales's harness.

Yozef listened for more men. He thought he heard two voices, then steps running away, down the veranda toward the great room wing of the house. He was about to run after them, when an axe crashed through the lock on the enclosed porch's outer door. He had locked it on the way in but realized, with a jolt, that he hadn't locked the next door, from the porch to the foyer. He stood six feet away from the door.

His split-second of indecision ended, as sounds of many feet and much cursing came toward the unlocked door. Later, he had no clear explanation for his next act: he pulled pistols from the two fallen attackers and jumped into the hall that led to the bedroom wing of the house.

Once again he seemed to have inane thoughts at the most stressful times. The one that popped into his head now was vindication. Maera and everyone else had expressed puzzlement and doubt when he'd insisted that the two halls leading from the foyer to the two wings of the house should not be straight but angled differently in their first twelve feet. When the house had been under construction, he'd stood in the framework and felt uneasy that from one end of the main hall in the bedroom wing, he had a clear line of sight to the great room. Although he couldn't articulate why it bothered him, he'd insisted on the angle change. This made it impossible to see down the hall more than fifteen feet in either direction from the foyer.

He ducked around the angled corner, as he glimpsed men rush into the foyer.

* * *

Uzcil was the second man into the foyer. He didn't need to be first, in case someone was waiting. He'd served his time being first through doors or point on patrols.

The only thing waiting were three bodies. He cursed aloud, there being enough din elsewhere not to bother suppressing his disgust. In the dim light, he could see that two of the bodies were his men, the third was one of the guards. Another of his men lay sprawled motionless on the front veranda. He looked around.

Who the hell designed this house and these weird hallways? Havant didn't say anything about this.

Shouts, screams, and gunfire drew his attention in the direction of the great room, the kitchen, and the dining room, where they assumed most people would have gathered.

"This way," he pointed, and they moved.

* * *

Carnigan and Norlin had the only firearms in the kitchen. The three women crouched behind the heavy wooden table Carnigan had overturned. All three held knives or cleavers. Sounds came from all directions: down the hall, in the great room. Then the kitchen door to the outside crashed inward, as its lock gave way from a kick.

Carnigan had left one lantern on low enough to see someone coming in. A man dressed all in black dove into the room, hit the floor, and rolled behind a counter. Carnigan held his fire, but Norlin shot at the figure, missing by two feet and losing his grip on the huge pistol. Another man stepped in, exposed partway through the door, and fired a shotgun into the room, spraying both Carnigan and Norlin.

Carnigan was hit several times but hardly flinched, as a one-inch ball from his pistol took off the top half of the man's head. Carnigan glanced to the side. Norlin lay back on a countertop, blood seeping from three hits to his chest and one to his throat. Anarynd jumped up and pulled the boy down to the floor. He gasped, choking on his own blood, and a frothy red puddle pooled on his chest.

Anarynd held her hands paused above the boy, not knowing what to do first. She looked at Carnigan. He shook his head.

Carnigan heard windows breaking in the dining room next door and shouts and shots from the great room, but he couldn't move yet. The other black-clad man still lurked in the room. Carnigan couldn't leave the women and Morwena.

In desperate need to both protect those in the kitchen and go help the others, Carnigan ducked down to the women. "Throw every pot and pan you can get your hands on toward the other side of the room. *Now!*"

Gwyned set Morwena on the floor and joined Anarynd and Serys in grabbing anything metal and throwing it from behind the overturned table. When the first one hit, Carnigan ran out and dove over the counter that the other attacker had disappeared behind. As Carnigan cleared the countertop, the man spun from six feet away and fired his pistol. The ball hit Carnigan's upper left arm, momentarily shocking him. As the man threw away his pistol and drew a hatchet, Carnigan moved faster than a man his size should be able to. He grabbed the man's knife arm with the hand of his unwounded arm. With a wrench, he dislocated the man's elbow, then a big fist broke his jaw and drove a splinter of bone into the man's brain.

His arm was on fire, but he had no time to deal with it. He could hear firing and shouts in the hall and the great room. He pulled another knife and ran to the dining room, not noticing that Serys and Anarynd followed him.

* * *

The sounds coming from the east wing of the house panicked Yozef more than thoughts of his own safety. Maera and Aeneas hid in the great room where the group of black-clad men headed. Yozef peeked around an angled corner. He couldn't see the four men. He raced across the foyer and peered around the next corner.

The four men had their backs to him. They faced down the hall. One of them fired a pistol, then dropped it, and all four, with blades and hatchets in hand, rose to rush the great room. Yozef ran after them. From twenty feet away, he pulled the trigger on one pistol. There was only a spark. A misfire. Without pausing, he dropped the pistol and grabbed a knife with the same hand. He pulled the trigger on the second pistol. It fired, and one of the attackers went down. He dropped the second pistol and drew another knife, as he reached the three men.

He felt more scared than he had during the raid on St. Sidryn's. There, he had taken cover behind a barricade alongside other defenders, including Carnigan and Denes. Here, it was only him. In the second before he reached the men, it flashed through his mind not to *think*, but let to his reactions take over, as Kales had drilled into him during those bruising sparring sessions.

As the three men turned, he stabbed one in the side and pushed the man into the others. For endless minutes or, in reality, a few seconds, it was a deadly dance of slashing steel, dodging, and ducking.

He later couldn't remember exactly what happened, but suddenly he stood alone, three of the men on the ground, one groaning, the other two silent, the fourth man running through a door to a side room. Yozef followed, only to see the man push another man back who was about to climb through a broken window. The man Yozef chased leaped out the window and vanished.

* * *

As abruptly as it had begun, the firing ceased, but not the shouting and crying. Yozef ran down the hall, glancing into the kitchen and seeing only Gwyned holding Morwena, the same knife still in her hand. Both looked okay.

At the hall doorway to the great room lay a sideboard that had been shoved across the opening. Yozef slid over it and into the room. The only light came from a single lantern turned low. Carnigan was stamping out a small fire from a lantern hit by a firearm. People lay or knelt everywhere. Balwis held his hand to Ceinwyn's face. Maera held Aeneas and Dwyna, Mirramel's daughter. Maera's face was streaked with tears. Breda Keelan sat holding her daughter Anid, with Culich's arms around them both, one of his legs a bloody mess below the knee. To his left, a woman lay face-down, not moving. Yozef couldn't see the face, but by her shape and clothing he recognized Mirramel. Next to her knelt Teena, holding one of Mirramel's hands.

"Is it over?" Balwis called out.

"I don't know," answered Yozef, with the first words he'd spoken since directing the front guard to move to the other side of the foyer. In the intervening time, no more than two minutes, he'd killed five men. He realized he didn't feel sick at the thought. Instead, he felt as if his blood were on fire, as he looked around for someone else to kill. Three black-clad bodies lay in the room. One had his head turned almost backward, Yozef assumed from an encounter with Carnigan. Another had a kitchen cleaver in the back of his head, the same or similar cleaver as Yozef had seen Serys carrying. The third was near a window, still moving, but with his chest soaked in blood.

Seeing no one who needed eminent death, Yozef let his blood slowly cool, until reason resurfaced—and fear. He raced to Maera.

"Are you all right?"

She nodded but didn't speak, her tears turning into a steady stream.

"Aeneas?"

She nodded again and pulled Aeneas slightly higher in her arm, so Yozef could see the bottom of his nightshirt and the round hole through several folds of cloth. A ball must have missed Aeneas by the tiniest of margins. Now, Yozef *did* feel sick and had to suppress vomiting at the image of a musket or pistol ball hitting the baby's soft skin.

Maera nodded a third time, toward her parents. Yozef looked over. Breda held Anid. Beautiful, cheerful Anid, with so much to look forward to, had a hole in her forehead. From the size, Yozef's shocked brain attributed the wound to one of the pellets from an attacker's shotgun.

Yozef rose, and for a moment, he and Carnigan just stood looking at each other. Yozef wanted to rage and cry at the same time. Carnigan appeared almost gray, the lines in his already lined face now more like chasms. Yozef glanced at Balwis and only then realized the man was holding closed a serious wound to Ceinwyn's face. Balwis noticed Yozef's look.

"She saved me," said Balwis. "I'd just shot one coming through a window, when another one came up behind me. Ceinwyn hit him with a small chair, and he turned and slashed her with a short sword."

Yozef didn't need to ask the fate of the attacker who'd hacked at Ceinwyn. He recognized the knife handle of Balwis's blade, completely buried in a man's chest.

Yozef forced himself to take three deep breaths, then spoke aloud to everyone in the room.

"We have to get help, in case they haven't all gone. And medicants for the wounded."

He hated to lean on Maera, still shocked by the attack and her sister's death, but they had no time.

"Maera, give Aeneas and Dwyna to Anarynd. The men need to stay here. We need you to get to Caernford for help. *Can* you do it?"

She didn't answer, just swallowed, as if ingesting an impossibly big pill.

"Carnigan, you stay here. Balwis, to me. We'll see if it's clear out front and we can get a horse for Maera. Teena, can you take Balwis's place with Ceinwyn?"

"What about Wyfor? Where is he?" asked Teena.

"I don't know," said Yozef. "I'm sorry, but we have to send for help before looking for him."

Kales's wife blinked back tears but nodded.

Balwis turned Ceinwyn over to Teena, and Maera handed the babies to Anarynd. They couldn't trust any firearm to be loaded, so they took a minute to reload two muskets and four pistols, giving two of the pistols to Maera.

"If your family's carriage and horses are all right, you'll use that. If not, we'll see if we can find a horse still tied up out front. We'll lead you to the road, in case any attackers haven't left. We'll also check on the road guard, though I doubt he survived, since he hasn't shown up. If it's okay that far, go to Caernford for men and medicants."

Yozef grabbed Maera in a fierce hug, then he and Balwis crept down the hall single file against a wall, Maera following. She spit on the first black-clad body they found. Balwis checked out the front door, then went to the rail. Two of the horses still remained tied, and the carriage and its two horses were under a spreading tree. All of the horses appeared skittish from the gunfire.

"I hate sending you alone, Maera," Yozef said, as he gave her a hand up onto the carriage.

"Oh, Yozef! Anid! Oh, God!"

"I know, but right now we have to think of those who need help."

They led the horses toward the road, passing two bodies on the way. "We'll check them on the way back," said Yozef. "They must be the guard and one of the attackers."

The bodies were the last sign that anything unusual had happened. When they reached the end of the drive, Yozef yelled, "Go!" and Maera used a buggy whip to speed the horses toward Caernford.

He wasn't religious, but in such moments, it never hurt to be sure. *Please let her be safe from whoever did this and from driving the carriage so hard.*

She was experienced with horse and carriage, but not at this speed and with the urge to be as fast as possible.

"Back to the house," ordered Yozef. He and Balwis started running, then stopped at the two bodies.

"This one's dead," said Yozef, as he checked the body dressed all in black.

"The guard is still alive!" exclaimed Balwis. "I can't see clearly in the dark, but his breath seems strong. Should we take him to the house or leave him here until help comes?"

Yozef thought for a moment. "It could be dangerous to move him, but he could also be bleeding to death. I think we have to risk carrying him inside, where we can see how bad he is."

They picked him up, each of them with an arm under the man's back and another arm under a knee. Their adrenaline still flowed, and they hardly felt the weight the fifty yards back to the house. Once inside, they laid him in the hall and began turning up or relighting lanterns.

Teena Kales appeared. "Serys is helping Ceinwyn. What about Wyfor?" she pleaded.

Shit! Yozef thought. *I forgot about him!*

"What about the injured in the great room?" Yozef asked. "How serious are they?"

"None are in danger of dying right now, and the dead don't care. *What about my husband?*" Teena begged.

"Balwis and I will find him, Teena. Please check the guard and see if you can help him."

More light came from the great room, as lanterns were lit or turned up, illuminating inside the house. Light spilled out the windows, those intact and those broken, onto the grounds. Yozef and Balwis cautiously exited through the enclosed back porch and onto the veranda. Balwis had grabbed a lit lantern and thrown a cloak around it. He set it on the veranda, and once they descended the steps onto the ground, he pulled off the cloak as they knelt. There was no movement as far as the lantern light could cast. And no gunfire.

"There," said Balwis, pointing to their left. Thirty yards away lay the rear guard and thirty yards farther was a cluster of bodies. They rose and trotted, backs bent as they scanned while moving. They found Wyfor and three attackers, one of whom was still alive, as was Kales. His left hand was mangled and his chest and head covered in blood, though whether his or the attackers', they didn't know.

"Let's get him to the house," said Yozef, and they picked up Kales as they had the front guard. He weighed considerably less than the guard, and they ran to the veranda and through the two doors to the foyer. Teena saw them, gave a cry, and left the wounded guard, who now lay moaning.

The lanterns cast enough light for them to see Kales's wounds. He had half a dozen shotgun pellet holes in his left arm and the left side of his chest. Yet from habit, he'd worn a heavy leather coat that had blunted the pellets, which had barely pierced his skin. However, his hand had taken most of blast, and he was missing two fingers. Although none of the wounds were life-threatening, he was unconscious. One of the pellets had struck his forehead with a glancing hit, enough to knock him out, but thankfully hadn't penetrated his skull. Teena cried, as she worked on putting a tourniquet on the hand, and

Yozef and Balwis left Kales to her and hurried down the hall to the great room.

* * *

Captain Bekir Uzcil had no desire to be a martyr. He accepted risks as part of being in the Narthani army and serving on such missions as this one, assigned by Brigadier Zulfa. When the possibility of success in a mission was lost, he saw his duty as surviving to serve and fight again on a later day. The strike's chances of success had always been problematic. Everything had gone well up to the point when a guard and a second man had left the house and walked straight into Uzcil's men. The attempt to quietly eliminate the two men failed and unexpectedly cost four of his men. By then, they'd lost the element of surprise, and their only option had been an immediate assault on the house from all sides.

Their only chance of killing the hetman, and possibly this Kolsko man Havant wanted to include, was to overwhelm the people inside before they could react. The unexpectedly stiff defense and his men's disadvantage at having to force the attack had led to short, vicious hand-to-hand fighting, each step of which whittled away at his men's numbers. Uzcil had led three men down the hall toward where they believed most of the defenders had gathered, when an attack from behind surprised them. The single attacker had shot and killed one of his men before they knew he was there, then stabbed another before they could respond. In the semi-darkness and chaos, the ensuing seconds were a blur, but Uzcil saw his third man fall and fought his own frantic defense against the man who had attacked. Then part of his brain noticed the fighting slacken off in the large room at the end of the hall, all of which convinced him it was time to save what he could, including himself.

He disengaged from the islander and fled through a window in a room off the hall. Outside, he called to two of his men, one standing next to the window and reloading his musket, the other running from the western side of the house, where he had been stationed to prevent anyone escaping out a window.

"It's over," Uzcil said, panting. "We're leaving."

"The others?" a shocked man cried out.

"Gone. Dead or wounded. There's nothing we can do for them. We did our best, and it went to shit. Time to get out."

Uzcil ran around the bedroom wing of the house to retrace back to where

Havant and Drifwich waited. A fourth man joined them, having withdrawn from the eastern side of the house when the fighting died and it became evident the attempt had failed.

* * *

Havant knew things hadn't gone well. Instead of hearing twenty attackers simultaneously firing, several sporadic shots could only mean they had been detected early. The following lull and then sounds of fighting that lasted five minutes before dying off momentarily gave him optimism. This was quickly dashed when he heard voices from the front of the house, then sounds of a carriage racing toward Caernford—obviously going for help.

He wasn't surprised when Uzcil appeared out of the darkness with only three of his nineteen men. "I take it the strike didn't go well?" Havant said, his voice conveying only information, no emotion or judgment.

"It went to shit," Uzcil spat. "You said the hetman would have only three guards and Kolsko one guard. We must have faced more than that, and some were trained and dangerous. One of them killed three of my men and alerted the others. I know of another man who killed at least three more by himself and almost gutted me before I got out." Uzcil's tone just short of accused Havant of incompetence in providing information and planning for the attack.

Not that Havant cared. He only dealt with what *was*, not what he *wished*. He had already gone over his own options, while waiting to see if any of the strike team returned. They had, so the number of options settled to three. He could return to Caernford to continue his role and hope Drifwich and the remaining men reached Salford and escaped without being captured. Their being killed while fleeing was also acceptable, as long as Havant wasn't compromised. He didn't like that option, because it depended on people and events over which he had no control.

The second option that allowed him to continue in Caernford was to eliminate all connections to himself, meaning to kill Drifwich and the four surviving team members. The killing didn't bother him, but with one against five, the odds were too great. Havant had a brief moment of regret that all of the men hadn't died in the attempt. He eliminated that option.

That left only one choice. He would flee with the five back to Salford and the waiting sloop.

"I'll be going with you," Havant told Drifwich and Uzcil. "With this few of us, we have plenty of horses. We'll run back to where they're waiting and take two each. As planned, we'll burn the first two semaphore stations along the road before the line turns away from the Salford road. If we push it, we should reach the signal point before dawn. If it's still dark, I can send a signal to override the captain's reluctance to send a boat ashore, even if the extraction is in daylight."

* * *

Eighteen minutes after Maera had left, whipping the carriage horses, a dozen mounted men galloped down the drive toward the Kolsko house. Half rode bareback, not taking the time to saddle up after Maera had stopped at a pub on the outskirts of Caernford. She'd raced inside, screaming that the hetman had been attacked and needed help at the Kolsko house.

During the next thirty minutes, more armed men arrived, some riding and some running, including a steady stream of medicants, more armed men, Luwis and Kennrick, and a hundred other Keelanders wanting to help in any way they could. It was Kennrick who finally ordered anyone else turned back. The grounds around the Kolsko house had filled with so many people and horses, it became too chaotic.

Following the first medicants was a fully equipped and staffed MASH unit that had prepared to accompany a training maneuver the next day. The medicants quickly decided to treat all the wounded in place, instead of first transporting them to the main hospital at St. Tomo's.

Yozef found that he had no duties, except to stay with Maera. Anarynd and Gwyned took Aeneas, Morwena, and Dwyna, Mirramel's daughter, to the bedroom wing of the house and away from the turmoil and carnage.

Culich's lower leg was hopeless, having taken most of a shotgun charge. The medicants amputated two inches below the knee.

Ceinwyn had received a slash that almost sliced a cheek off her face. Balwis had held the flap of flesh in place until relieved by Teena Balwis. He cursed, as he recounted to Yozef how he'd had to pull out a tooth hanging sideways from Ceinwyn's wound, so it wouldn't interfere with his holding the wound closed. In other circumstances, Yozef would have been impressed with Balwis's command of cursing, if he hadn't been involved in his own demonstration in both Caedelli and English.

Kales regained consciousness before the medicants arrived. Though in great pain, he worried first about his wife, then about what had happened. Balwis gave him a summary.

Carnigan refused to lie down for the medicants, until ordered to do so by Gwyned before she left with Anarynd and the youngest children. The pistol ball wound wasn't serious. His harness was more of a thick leather vest than simply straps. It had absorbed most of the force of seven shotgun pellets that penetrated Carnigan by no more than an inch.

Gwyned and Anarynd suffered minor injuries—bruises and a single shotgun pellet to a forearm for Anarynd, bruises and a cut on her shoulder from an unknown source for Gwyned.

Unscathed were Yozef, Maera, Balwis, Serys, Breda, and Mared.

The final death toll was six: three of the guards, Norlin, Mirramel, and Anid.

CHAPTER 33

SWAVEBROKE

Shullick, Capital Swavebroke Province

Margol Swavebroke was the fourth of his family to be Hetman Swavebroke. His great-grandfather had taken on the Swavebroke last name after the existing hetman died with no designated heir and no relative closer than third cousin. The struggle, and almost civil war, as to which family would fill the hetman role resulted in Margol's ancestor winning. However, the contentiousness of the succession still tainted elements within the Swavebroke clan, and Margol's grip on the leadership depended on a core of five boyermen. The most important of these was Boyerman Hargo, whose district comprised the capital, Shullick, and the immediately surrounding area.

The Swavebroke clan had suffered a single coastal raid by the Buldorians but none yet from the Narthani. When reports came of raids and attacks on other clans, Hargo and two other boyermen with coastal districts had resisted Margol's proposal to increase defenses and plan for evacuation, in case of raids or invasions from the sea. As their overt position, they stated that the economic cost would be too great for events that might never occur. Margol Swavebroke knew they also had not agreed with his decision to come to Moreland's aid, being among the islanders who thought the Narthani threat too distant and that it involved other clans, not Swavebroke. The perceived victory at Moreland City had blunted the boyermen's criticism of going to Moreland's aid, but Margol didn't feel his position was strong enough to fight the boyermen's resistance to spending coin on improved defenses and evacuation planning, in case of further Narthani attacks.

Margol's eldest son, Harmon, openly expressed disdain for his father's lack of will in facing down the boyermen. Margol passed off the clash to his son's youth and lack of experience about ruling the clan. His wife had arranged a family breakfast, in hopes of preventing a further breach between father and son. She had counseled the latter to understand the demands of being the hetman.

"Thank you for coming, Harmon, and I'm happy to see you, Marlina." Harmon's wife was in the mid-term of her third pregnancy. Both women wanted to prevent any larger rift and had worked on their husbands.

"It's been too long, what with our hardheads arguing constantly," said Marlina. "I have Harmon's promise to be good for this morning."

"The same with his father."

Both men merely grunted, eyeing each other cautiously. The foursome sat, and servants brought in the morning meal. Hetman Swavebroke had just buttered a roll, when his second son burst through the dining room door. Margol's wife frowned. She had left firm instructions the meal should be uninterrupted. Oblivious to her disfavor, her younger son addressed his father.

"A rider from the harbor, Father! He says the sea is full of Narthani ships, and they're headed directly at Shullick!"

Margol blanched. Harmon reddened, glared at his father, and was about to say something, when his wife put a hand on his arm. "Not now, Harmon. It's not the time."

Harmon took a deep breath and rose from his seat. "Father, we need to get to the harbor immediately to see what's happening."

"Yes . . . yes . . . maybe the sighting is wrong, or the Narthani are just passing."

Harmon didn't counter. His expression conveyed his opinion.

Fifteen minutes later, the hetman and his son stood on a promontory overlooking the Shullick harbor. At sea, within two miles of the city, what appeared to the Swavebroke hetman to be an endless number of Narthani ships under half sail pointed directly at the clan capital. Boyerman Hargo and boyermen of the neighboring districts stood flanking them. The three boyermen had arrived shortly before Margol—Hargo from his residence and the other two boyermen from where they stayed while visiting the city. The latter boyermen had supported their hetman's preparation proposals, and both had expressed dissatisfaction with their hetman's unwillingness to confront Hargo, who now shifted uneasily on his feet, as if about to run.

Margol remained calm. He had never been a decisive hetman like his father and grandfather. When necessary, he made decisions, even if not timely ones or as firmly as he wished. He had told himself that times had been different when he became hetman, while within himself the truth always lurked below the surface. His uncertainties and feelings of inadequacy had caused his vacillations in the face of decisions. Until now. He saw only one path forward.

"Hetman," said one of the other boyerman, "alerts have gone out. Fighting men from all of Swavebroke will head this way, as soon as they get the word and can get here. We'll do what we can to stop the Narthani at the shore, but you need to call on the other clans for help."

"No, Sers," replied Margol. "Look at the number of ships. The ocean floor is deep on this part of the coast. Their ships will come within a hundred yards of the shore or even right to the piers, and their cannon will control everything within range. They'll land men, probably cannon, and even horses under the protection of the ships. We can't possibly gather enough men to stop them before they land. Any defense has to be out of ship cannon range. The most important thing is to save the people. Send word out immediately for everyone to head inland. Without a plan for how to get people out of the city, we'll have to do the best we can."

Margol accompanied his last words with a deadeye look at Boyerman Hargo, who stood stone-faced under the implied reprimand.

"Ring all abbey bells continuously," the hetman said to all the men. "Spread word for people to gather only what they can carry. All other districts that can get men here should gather at St. Wilf's and help move the people and provide protection, if the Narthani try to pursue us inland. I doubt that they brought enough horses to stop the evacuation, but they might harass and try to slow movement enough for their men on foot to catch up. Your men's task is to keep that from happening."

"But Shullick, Father," said Harmon. "Where will we stand to defend the city and with what men?"

Margol's calmness surprised him more than anyone else. "If they land the numbers of men and cannon I suspect they will, there's nothing we can do to stop them from taking the city. Remember Moreland City and what they did to the charge at their line."

"But we defeated them," argued Hargo.

"Yozef Kolsko stated to us that the Narthani weren't defeated, they simply turned back. And although he didn't say it outright, I believe he wanted to caution us that only mistakes by Moreland and Eywell, and the Narthani being too confident, saved us. As chaotic as our defense is bound to be, do you *really* think we can stop thousands of Narthani?"

"But the city," blurted a desperate Hargo. "We can't let them take the city! They could destroy it!"

"You should have thought of that before opposing plans for its defense," Margol hissed, all forbearance and deference to the city's boyerman gone.

"Time is wasting," said Margol. "Pass the word quickly to leave the city. If they're coming ashore, we don't have more than an hour before the first Narthani are on Swavebroke land."

He turned to face Boyerman Hargo. "Boyerman, gather all your district's fighting men in the city central square. By the time they gather, we'll know more of the Narthani's exact intentions and then can plan to delay them long enough for most of the people to escape."

Hargo paled but didn't give a rejoinder, only nodded and issued orders to his aides. The other two boyermen left to help spread the evacuation order and send word to their own districts.

Standing alone on the promontory, Margol put an arm on his son's shoulders. "Harmon, ride back to the house and tell your brother to get the family inland. He's to stay with them and see your mother and sisters to safety. After you give him that word, you go to St. Wilf's Abbey east of the city, to the gathering place for fighting men from outlying villages and the other districts. You'll need to be in charge, but listen to the senior men and any boyermen who get there. All of you are to help move people inland and protect them as best you can, if the Narthani come after them."

"But, Father," said Harmon, his faced showing distress, "where will you be?" The son feared the answer.

"I'll be with Boyerman Hargo, helping to slow the Narthani. I can't trust him to do what will be necessary, and there's no time to replace him without creating more chaos."

Margol placed his hands on his heir's shoulders. "It's also my penitence for not being a better hetman and having the strength to do what I believed needed doing. If the worst happens, and I'm either dead or captured, you will be the hetman. If I'm dead, it will be clear, but if I'm their captive, we can't let them use me as a hostage. You are to consider me dead. In my office at home, in the lower desk drawer of my study, there's a sealed envelope. Inside is my declaration that in the eventuality of my incapacitation, you are to be considered the hetman. Use that as justification for assuming the hetman position. Enough of the boyermen will support you to carry the argument. I've already discussed this with several of them, and with Hargo likely out of the picture, there shouldn't be serious protest."

Harmon didn't need elaboration to understand that Boyerman Hargo's absence meant his father would be dead or captured.

"Harmon," Margol choked out, pulling his son into a tight embrace, "we've had our disputes, but I want you to know I've never been disappointed in you, and anything that's separated us has been more my fault than yours. You'll make a better hetman than me."

The hetman released his son and turned his back to face the harbor and the Narthani, as the closest ships started to furl sails. "Go now and save our clan."

Tears streaking Harmon's face, he mounted his horse and spurred toward the family home.

Aboard Admiral Kalcan's Flagship

"Your first men should be ashore in a few minutes, Zulfa," said Morfred Kalcan.

Both men stood on the admiral's flagship's forecastle, viewing the action. Four frigates had anchored just offshore and poured rounds and grapeshot into the neighborhoods bordering the harbor. Behind the frigates, troop carriers were a beehive of activity. The first longboats had neared the piers, and more were being unloaded, with men climbing down the sides of ships via rope netting. When the first men ashore secured the docks, more troop ships would tie directly to piers to unload.

"So far, no sign of organized resistance," said Brigadier Aivacs Zulfa. "It's one of those things you don't know whether it's good or bad. Did we surprise them so much they haven't gotten themselves organized, or do they have unpleasant surprises we haven't yet encountered?"

Kalcan didn't answer for a moment, occupied with a word from his flag lieutenant, then turned back to Zulfa. "I don't envy your men ashore. At least at sea, you see the enemy clearly and see what's coming. I'd rather be on ship."

Zulfa allowed himself a smile. "But then the ground doesn't open up and swallow you if things go badly."

Kalcan laughed. "There *is* that. To each his own. I'll still stick with my ships. I'm also sure my captains will be glad to get rid of the horses. The smelly, stupid things have no business at sea. We're lucky it was a short trip, not like the ones from home. Only half of the horses survived those voyages."

"Don't act too aggrieved for your sailors, and don't tell me they didn't enjoy the fresh meat." Zulfa couldn't resist a small tease. "I sometimes wonder whether some horses weren't helped along by sailors tired of salted meat and fish."

"I'm shocked to hear you say such a thing," said Kalcan, and both men laughed, a last moment of humor before Zulfa left to board a longboat. He would go ashore to direct the attack. He and General Akuyun had discussed, and argued about, who should command, Zulfa or one of the colonels, probably Ketin. Zulfa's point was that commanding the attack would take the three colonels away from their duties, while Zulfa had no direct day-to-day responsibilities once the attack force left aboard ship. Akuyun had reluctantly acceded to Zulfa's argument.

A whistle from mid-ship drew their attention. One of Zulfa's aides waved. It was time for the brigadier to head to shore.

Kalcan drew closer. "Don't get yourself killed, Aivacs. Okan might put that damn Erdelin in your place. I can't stand that ass."

"As a favor to you, Morfred," Zulfa whispered back, "I'll endeavor to stay alive, although with twenty-five-hundred of our men around me, I think I'll be safe enough."

"Nothing is safe when the action starts, whether on land or at sea, so just stay out of the forefront and let the junior officers take the risks."

Narthani Headquarters, Preddi City

Sadek Hizer walked up to Okan Akuyun, who stood on the roof of the headquarters building, looking over the now almost empty harbor. Most of the warships that had been anchored in the harbor or just offshore were now at Swavebroke.

"Can't get them off your mind, huh, Okan?"

"No, Sadek. I still have trouble seeing this many of my men off into action without me, and what happened last time doesn't help."

"I wouldn't foresee anything going wrong," said Hizer. "Well . . . at least not *too* wrong. The other clans won't have a chance to come to Swavebroke's aid before we reach our objectives. The men will burn Shullick to the ground and be gone within a couple of days, well before help arrives—if it does at all."

"Intellectually, I know that," said Akuyun. "Still, part of me can't help but wonder what can go wrong *this* time? And then there's the three strike teams.

Whatever happened is over. We won't know the results until the sloops return with the men we sent out. Realistically, we can only hope half of them come back."

Hizer understood Akuyun's feelings, having many of the same, in both this situation and many others he'd experienced.

"It's part of reality, Okan, as you well know. Men will be lost, if we are to advance the Empire. All men like you and me can do is be sure any sacrifice we ask or danger we send men into is justified. In this case, we judged the strikes on the hetmen and on Swavebroke to be worth the risks, in order to tie down the clans until we get word back from Narthon."

"Ordinarily, I'd agree with you, Sadek, but as you know, I've never been totally convinced that stirring up the clans like this is the best action. Oh, I understand the reasoning, and it all sounds fine, but it still depends on the clans doing what we expect them to do. That didn't work out so well for us at Moreland City. Part of me wondered whether we might be better off ignoring the clans and hoping they sit back and do nothing. However, the other part of me worried about giving them time to gather themselves to attack us directly here, and the opinions of the rest of you finally swayed me to approve the attacks. I just hope we . . . I suppose, I mean I . . . made the right decision."

Semaphore Station, Near Keelan/Moreland Border

Amyl Lewton had managed this semaphore station ever since its construction. He knew how lucky he was to hold the position. Besides paying well, the station lay only five miles from his home in Amurth, the most northern settlement of Keelan Province large enough to be called a town, and the horseback ride let him enjoy time alone, without being so long as to take too much time from work or family.

Normally, he enjoyed the work. He wouldn't admit, even to his wife, his voyeuristic attachment to reading other people's messages, and he made a great show of repeatedly reminding his three assistants to maintain the confidentiality of whatever information passed through their hands.

The messages usually tended to contain topics of consequence; otherwise, they wouldn't be sent over semaphore: announcements of meetings such as conclaves, relatives informing of the death of a family member, hetmen discussing issues from the mundane to the critical concerning Caedellium's future, and, only a few months ago, messages about the Narthani invasion of

Moreland Province.

However, the first message heading north from Caernford this morning had been a shock unlike any other he'd received. The Narthani had tried to assassinate Culich Keelan! The hetman had survived, but there had been deaths, though details weren't given in the alert sent out to all other clans. A message from Caernford had also alerted that a line south of the city was out of operation, and no messages could be passed on to Mittack Province until the line operated again. The message didn't mention the cause of the disruption, but Lewton assumed it was related to the attack on the hetman.

The station had just passed on the alert, along both lines heading northwest and northeast from Keelan. The northwest line went first to Moreland City, where it branched to Stent and Orosz, and from there to northern clans. The northeast line went to Hewell and from there toward the Adris, Pawell, Bevans, and Nyvaks clans.

Lewton's assistants manned the panels. As soon as the alert message went out, the assistants used mounted telescopes to scan the northern adjacent stations for inbound messages. Only seconds had passed since the panels had been turned black to signal no more outgoing messages, when the assistant watching northwest shouted, "Incoming message!"

Seconds later, the northeast assistant yelled, "One here, too! Just coming in."

It took time to read the panel settings via telescope on the adjacent stations' panels and then acknowledge reception in response. Lewton waited for the assistants to complete reception. Ten minutes passed.

"Holy shit!" came an exclamation.

Lewton jumped out of his chair in the office and raced to the stairwell leading to the array sets on the roof. He had reached halfway upstairs when he heard another assistant shout in confusion, "What the hell is happening?!"

CHAPTER 34

RETALIATION

Caernford

The only people in the Kolsko house who slept the night of the attack were two babies and a toddler. Aeneas and Morwena never left their mothers' arms, while Anarynd and Teena Kales alternately held Dwyna, who remained unaware her mother lay dead in one of the bedrooms, along with Norlin and the three guards. Anid's body lay in another bedroom, attended by Breda and Maera. None of the adults or Mared Keelan slept. A swarm of medicants treated the injured, the most serious of whom were Culich, Carnigan, and Ceinwyn. All would recover, though the hetman would live without his lower left leg, and Ceinwyn would carry a great scar on one side of her face from her chin up to just under her eye and back to her ear. Carnigan tried to insist a hole or two wasn't something to slow him down, but Gwyned and then Yozef ruled otherwise, and he allowed himself to be seated in a chair. He flatly refused to lie down, because he took that as a sign of a *serious* injury.

The sun was half an hour from appearing above the eastern hills before the Kolsko grounds began to clear. More than two hundred armed men had come to the house at various times during the night, in addition to medicants, Vortig Luwis and Pedr Kennrick, St. Tomo's abbot, Keelan relatives, and citizens living near the house or farther way. Two hours before dawn, Kennrick had taken charge of the chaos, thanked others for their concern, and, if they weren't essential, sent them home.

Mulron Luwis, Vortig's son and commander of the three hundred–man standing garrison in Caernford, had organized a sweep of the surrounding five miles and came up empty. There was no sign of the attackers or any encampment attributable to them. The search would continue at daylight. Yozef attested that at least some of the attackers still remained at large. He'd witnessed one of the four men he'd fought in the hall flee out a window, after stopping another man from climbing in. Yozef also thought he'd heard voices of more than one man outside the house, but he wasn't sure amid everything else going on.

Yozef couldn't have slept if his life depended on it. He would later wonder whether his adrenaline level had set any new records, but whatever the physiological basis, his agitation wouldn't brook any immobility. He listened in on Mulron and Denes making reports about no evidence of more attackers and Luwis and Kennrick saying something to someone, none of which registered in his brain. He went to the room with Anid's body and hugged Maera and Aeneas, then strode out to the grounds where fourteen black-clad bodies were lined up. He walked over to a tent where medicants treated two badly wounded attackers not expected to survive, and then he started the same cycle again.

He lost track of time. All he noticed was that the sun sat high in the sky, as he wandered among the remaining men and horses in front of the house.

"Are you okay, Yozef?" asked a familiar voice that cut through the fog in his brain.

He looked around, confused for a second about where he was, until he saw Balwis standing beside him, looking concerned.

"I killed five men," Yozef blurted without thinking.

Balwis didn't respond for several moments. His eyes narrowed, and he took in Yozef as if for the first time. "They got what they deserved," he finally said. "I killed two and only wish I'd had the chance to gut more of them."

"Have you . . . you know . . . killed before?" asked Yozef, his eyes haunted and burning at the same time.

"Yes," said Balwis. "When I escaped from Preddi, I killed a Narthani who caught me stashing food I was accumulating. I was stupid and didn't check carefully enough whether anyone was around when I went to my cache. He asked me what I was doing. I had no choice. I tossed him a sack of bread. He was startled and reacted to catch the sack, and while he was distracted, I pulled a knife and drove it into his stomach. He didn't utter a sound, just gave me a confused look, while I pulled the knife out and stabbed him in the throat. Blood gushed all over me, and I almost puked.

"The next time was easier. I had crossed into Eywell when four Eywellese men stopped me about thirty miles from the Moreland border. I was surprised I'd made it that far. I don't know if they recognized my gear wasn't Eywellese or what, but they demanded my identification and business.

"I'd taken two pistols from the first Narthani I killed, and I shot two of them before they reacted. One of the others fled, but one went for a pistol, and I drove my horse into his. Both of our horses went down, and he lay pinned under his. He was helpless and probably had a broken leg, so he wasn't going anywhere. Since the fourth had already fled, I had no real reason to kill him. But I didn't hesitate. I could only remember how Narthani had killed my father, and in my mind, at that moment, I was avenging my father's death. So, yes, I've killed, and I have no qualms. I only wish I could kill every last Narthani and Eywellese."

"This was the first time for me," said Yozef, his voice detached, as if noting a casual event. "At St. Sidyrn's, I wounded one Buldorian, more by luck than intent. At Moreland City I helped direct cannon, though I couldn't identify whether we hit anyone. I assume we did, but they weren't nearby. This time, I shot a man seven feet from me and saw him fall. I shot another one, and the light on the veranda let me see the impact on his chest. Another I shot in the back in the hall.

"Then I pulled a knife, and the rest is a blur. I do remember that one of the attackers was still alive. I stood over him, thinking we needed to keep him alive for questioning. I don't know what happened, but I stabbed him over and over. It was like I was a different person or insane, or . . . oh, I don't know . . . not myself? I should have kept him alive," Yozef said, looking at Balwis for an explanation or an exculpation. "All that seemed to matter was that he needed to be killed, and I almost felt disappointed when the fighting stopped and there were no more of them to kill."

"It's just the heat of battle," said Balwis, laying a hand on Yozef's shoulder. "We need that extra energy, or whatever you want to call it, to survive. Listen to yourself, Yozef. You say you killed five of them. How many lives did you save? What if those men had gotten to the great room? Who else might have died? Perhaps everyone. You and I are different, but if it was me, I would give thanks to God for giving me the strength to kill and save those who survived."

Yozef patted Balwis's arm. He didn't feel reassured about himself but appreciated the human contact. He opened his mouth to ask something—he later didn't remember what—when voices alerted them to get out of the way, as a rider tore down the drive toward the house.

Everyone's nerves were on edge. "Damnation, watch where you're going!" and "God's blood, who's this idiot?" were only a few of the imprecations hurled at the rider.

"Messages for the hetman!" shouted the rider, overriding all other noise. "It's the Narthani! They've invaded Swavebroke and attacked other hetmen!"

The previous level of shouts would have been lost amid what resulted. Only when Vortig Luwis burst from the house did the cacophony subside.

"SHUT UP! All OF YOU!"

The rider, whom Yozef identified as one of the Caernford semaphore station staff, ran to Luwis and handed him several sheets used for semaphore messages. Luwis read the first, clenched his teeth, and moved to the second sheet. If anything, his face turned redder than from reading the first message. By the time he finished the third message, the red had faded to pale, almost white. Not the white of fear, but the white of fury beyond mere blood. He read the messages several more times.

The forty or so men and a few women who'd crowded around Luwis murmured until Luwis gathered himself, his voice oddly emotionless, considering the expression on his face and the look in his eyes.

"The Narthani landed in force at Shullick, the Swavebroke capital. Their hetman has ordered the city evacuated inland, and they're fighting within the city to delay the Narthani from pursuing those who fled."

Questions and exclamations began, only to be silenced again by Luwis.

"The Farkesh, Vandinke, and Pewitt clans have started men moving toward Swavebroke, but it'll be several days before enough get there to stop the Narthani. The son of Hetman Swavebroke sent messages that they expect the city to fall completely before help can arrive."

Luwis held up both hands to quell a renewed chorus. This time a deafening quiet ensued, as if everyone dreaded what would come.

"There have also been assassination attacks on the Skouks and Bevans hetmen. Zitwyn Bevans is safe, and all of his attackers were killed. Elek Skouks is dead, along with his wife and the entire family of one of his daughters. If I remember, there were six children in that family." He spoke the last words softly, in wonder and anguish.

* * *

To find a quiet, unbloodied room, where they wouldn't bother the wounded and grieving, the Keelan leaders moved to the cottage used by Yozef's Shadows when they spent the night. No one sat, not that there were enough chairs. Vortig and Mulron Luwis, Pedr Kennrick, Denes Vegga, and Yozef stood in a circle, along with Abbot Walkot of St. Tomo's, who had returned as soon as he heard the news of the other attacks.

"The hetman is resting right now," said Luwis. "The medicants say he just got to sleep an hour ago, so I don't want to wake him yet."

"There are already plans in place for just this eventuality," said Yozef.

Denes nodded vigorously. "Yozef's right. The ready-reaction force must move to Dornfeld to re-equip with the pre-positioned horses and weapons. Then we move into Eywell and raid as far west as we can."

"That's a decision only Culich can make," asserted Kennrick.

"The decision was already made," Denes shot back.

"The *intent* was made, not the decision to do it," said Luwis.

"Father," said Mulron Luwis, "I agree with Yozef and Denes. "The hetman approved this action based on the same scenario that has happened—the Narthani attacking a clan on the other side of Caedellium. We couldn't send men to Swavebroke in time to help, and even if we could, I don't think we'd want too many of our men that far away. However, by raiding inside Eywell and threatening Preddi we might cause the Narthani to withdraw from Swavebroke before they do maximum damage. Even if that's too late, the idea is sound that it might prevent them from doing the same thing again."

Before a heated argument started, Yozef spoke up. "There's no conflict in both setting the reaction force in motion and getting Culich's approval. Given his condition, it could be hours, even a day or two, before he's fully aware enough to judge the situation. It will take that long or longer for the reaction force to get into position. I suggest they start off toward Dornfeld immediately. Time is a critical factor. If we wait, and it takes two or three days for Culich to give approval, it may be too late to act. If the force starts off and Culich does not give approval, the raid can always be canceled or even called back, if they have already crossed into Eywell."

Denes leaned forward, as if on a starting line. "I've already sent word to the RRF camp to prepare to move. We could be on the road in an hour."

Luwis still frowned but had a sense of hesitancy in his expression. "Well . . . I—"

"Vortig," Kennrick interjected, "I see no harm in letting Denes start. And let's be honest. Culich lost Anid. It's more likely you and I would have to counsel restraint, rather than him not agreeing to strike at the Narthani."

Luwis's face saddened at the mention of the dead Keelan daughter. "I hate making Culich deal with anything right now, except his family. God's mercy! I hope God doesn't think me blasphemous, but how can he allow something like this to happen?"

"God understands how you feel, Vortig," said Abbot Walkot. "Remember that he allows humans to make their own destinies. We can call on him for strength but cannot lay on him what is caused by ourselves."

"I know, Abbot, it's just . . . " Luwis shook himself and stood stiff from the dejected slump he'd briefly assumed. "All right. I agree there's no reason not to put the reaction force in motion." Luwis looked at Kennrick. "Pedr, do you agree?"

"Yes. Denes, get your men headed to Dornfeld."

Denes's mouth twisted into a snarl. "I'm sorry, Abbot, but may God curse every Narthani and give us strength to send them all to hell. I'll send word when we start off. As I said, it should be no more than an hour."

Denes walked to the door, and Yozef followed to stop him outside the cottage.

"Remember, Denes, we are not trying to achieve a victory in battle or even kill Narthani. Our objective is to cause damage and make the Narthani draw inward. Don't get carried away and put yourself and our men in a situation where you can be trapped. The Narthani should be surprised, but they still have thousands of men in Preddi, and they control the seas. Give them time and opportunity, and they could land troops behind you to cut off the direct way back to Keelan. Don't get carried away by a sense of either victory or vengeance."

Denes's face remained impassive. He wasn't offended by Yozef's reminder that at the Battle of Moreland City, he had almost continued the attack on the Narthani after they had repositioned from the clan's surprise attack. Only Yozef's grabbing his attention and yelling that it was time to withdraw had saved them from a potential disaster.

"I learned my lesson, Yozef. I'll bring the men back. We'll need every one. This second Narthani invasion won't be the last, but maybe we can buy time to get the clans better prepared when it happens again."

"Good man," said Yozef and let Denes hustle to his horse and several men waiting for him.

Yozef saw him say something to the men, who received his words with grim approval. The group mounted and galloped toward Caernford, and Yozef walked back into the cottage. The group there exchanged a few last words, before each man returned to what he saw as his immediate task.

Yozef stopped Balwis. "Wait a moment."

When they were alone, Yozef let self-control slip away, and Balwis saw an expression and a pair of eyes he had never seen before on Yozef. Balwis couldn't exactly define what he saw. *Cold fury*, *deadly intent*, and other phrases passed through his mind, without being an exact match.

"We hope the reaction force raid makes the Narthani rethink any future plans about attacks like the one on Swavebroke," Yozef said in a low voice. "The assassinations are something else. This is the second time they've tried multiple attempts at the same time. Just as the raid is meant to discourage them from not keeping all their forces at home, we need to send another message."

Yozef's eyes took on the distant look Balwis usually saw when Yozef considered ideas or heard a voice. Balwis waited. After almost a minute, Yozef's eyes refocused.

"Not now, Balwis," said Yozef. "I have to think more on this. We'll talk later."

Clitwyth, Stent Province

The Stent Clan capital lay eighty miles inland. The province's coast was so rocky and the waters so marked by reefs and shoals that the only settlements were two small fishing villages. Both of these had moved their families farther into Stent, and even the fishermen slept in tents three miles from the coast.

Although the news of the Swavebroke attack and the assassination attempts shocked the populace of Clitwyth, they didn't panic. The distance from potential seaborne attacks and the preparation plans Hetman Stent had put in motion gave the people a sense of focus absent in Swavebroke.

The planning had also accounted for their not being able to consult all of the clan's boyermen before major decisions needed implementing. Thus, within hours of news of the Narthani attacks, Stent's actions were in motion. The word went out, and fifteen hundred men from all over Stent moved to assemble near the location where the borders of the Stent, Swavebroke, Pewitt, and Vandinke provinces touched. Whether the men moved into Swavebroke and into action against the Narthani or assisted the Swavebrokers in some other manner would be left to later circumstances and decisions, but they were on the move.

The second action occurred in response to word from Caernford that the southern rapid-reaction force had deployed in preparation for a raid into Eywell and possibly as far as Preddi. Welman Stent had understood the reasoning behind that proposed raid and the one his own clan would participate in, but he felt uneasy, because their reaction force was not as well developed and trained as he would like.

He also felt disquieted because *he* would have to lead the foray into Eywell. He wasn't concerned about his own safety but because of the necessity that only a hetman had the stature to hold together a force composed of men from four clans. The 1,200 men included 500 of his own clansmen, 400 Morelanders, 200 Oroszians, and 100 Bulteckians. He would have preferred not involving the men from Moreland, but since the raid would launch from Moreland territory, it needed their titular approval. Welman had voiced his doubts in a meeting with Tomis Orosz. Although the Orosz hetman had sympathized, he had argued for the importance of not only integrating Moreland into any effort against the Narthani, but also that involvement in the reaction force might help divert the attention of various Moreland factions that kept jockeying for position, trying to replace the leadership ranks devastated by their deceased hetman's mistake at the Battle of Moreland City.

Welman briefly considered whether he could avoid using the reaction force and employ only his own clansmen. However, he had to quickly dismiss that option. It would take too long to gather enough men. The northern reaction force encamped only forty miles from the Eywell border, and he needed to ride hard to cover the seventy miles from Clitwyth. Before leaving, he would order four hundred Stent men to muster and head for the encampment. They would serve as a reserve, if the raid went poorly, and would be the only help available. At least, they would be his own clansmen.

Caernford

After leaving Balwis, Yozef had gone to Maera sitting in the room with her sleeping father. Breda sat in a chair with Mared asleep in her lap. Maera was breastfeeding Aeneas. The otherwise intimate scene was marred by darkness in her eyes and tracks of dried tears on her cheeks. He mouthed whether she needed anything, but she only shook her head.

He walked to the great room, still covered with evidence of the previous night. Furniture that had been pulled to form some protection was now pushed aside. Blood. So much blood, now dried into dark patches on the carpets and the wooden planks. Holes where shot balls had missed targets or passed through flesh. Discarded weapons.

Yozef picked up a heavy chair and hurled it across the room, overturning one of the few undamaged pieces of furniture. A man he didn't recognize rushed into the room in response to the noise, took one look at Yozef, and left.

Part of Yozef wanted to get away from the house, but the part that prevailed wanted to ingrain every image into his brain. The bloody room; Aeneas's nightshirt with the hole mere inches from his tiny body; Anid lying dead—the warm teenage girl would never grow into the beautiful woman who dreamed of her own family; Norlin, who would not finish his education or decide, as he'd confided to Yozef, whether he wanted to change the focus of his studies; Mirramel, Aeneas's wet nurse, relatively simple-minded but friendly and looked on fondly by all who met her; the three guards who had done their best to do their duty, who probably had families, and whose names Yozef didn't know; Culich, who would be fitted with a peg for his missing lower leg and, more important, who now had a dead daughter; the news about the slaughter of Hetman Skouks and many members of his family, including children; the attack on Swavebroke and the unknown number who would die fleeing or defending.

And himself. The five men he'd killed—four while fighting, the fifth only semiconscious and defenseless when Yozef had stabbed him enough times to kill him several times over. Part of him thought he should feel anguish or at least regrets over killing other humans, but he remembered how he'd been angry last night that there were no more Narthani to kill. He passed a mirror and deliberately avoided looking at his reflection, not sure what he would see.

Thud! He'd walked into a wall without realizing it was there. He'd been awake for thirty hours and needed to sleep before his mind shut down. He went back to the cottage where the six men had met and decided to send Denes and the reaction force to Dornfeld. He lay on one of the two beds, wondering whether he could fall asleep.

A hand shook him by the shoulder. "What—"

"Yozef," said a voice. "Wake up."

He looked up into Balwis's face.

"How long was I asleep?"

"I don't know," said Balwis. "Culich is awake, and the others are gathering to see if he's in shape to talk about Denes's raid."

Yozef hurriedly swung his legs off the bed and stood upright, staggering for a moment, then followed Balwis toward the house. He noticed the sun's shadows and estimated he must have slept at least three hours.

He and Balwis were the last to arrive. The others surrounded Culich's bed, where the hetman sat propped up against pillows, his face ashen with pain and grief but his eyes clear.

"They found some poppy extract on one of the attackers," whispered Balwis. "The medicants gave the hetman enough to dull the pain but leave him coherent."

"Yozef," said Culich, his voice ragged, "they've told me about sending Denes and the reaction force toward Dornfeld. I agree with the decision, yet I worry about them getting themselves trapped if the Narthani react faster than we expected when we dreamed up this plan."

"It's a danger," Yozef agreed. "Still, risks have to be taken. The Narthani have to learn they can't launch attacks without knowing we can respond toward their weakened home territory. However, I share your concern and think we need to move more forces to Dornfeld to provide support, if Denes runs into too much trouble. Keelan already has five hundred men at Dornfeld and the fort blocking the Dillagon pass. Not all those men are appropriate for offensive operations. Perhaps half are. With those and more we can muster quickly, we should put a thousand men and additional supplies across the Eywell border and set up a camp in a defensible position that Denes can fall back to. The reaction force has 6-pounders. This additional force can take more 6-pounders and several batteries of 12-pounders. If we pick the location properly, there should be nothing the Narthani can throw at the position before everyone can withdraw back to Keelan. I suggest Mulron Luwis be in command, and I'll organize the artillery and accompany this reserve force."

"That's putting another thousand Keelan men in danger," Kennrick protested.

"No, Yozef may be right," said Vortig Luwis. "It's been a few years, but before the Narthani came to Caedellium and the damn Eywellese went over to them, I spent a month in that part of Eywell. I remember the terrain. Although the hills aren't high, the sides are steep. There are any number of places where a thousand men and artillery could stop any Narthani force for several days. I'll feel better about this if Denes had a backup."

Luwis asked Culich, "What do you think, Hetman?"

Culich had closed his eyes while listening and opened them to answer. "I agree. Vortig, go ahead and muster the men. Mulron will command. Kennrick, work with Mulron and Vortig on the supplies and other needs. The reaction force will be well into Eywell before the support camp can start to be set up, so speed is essential.

"As for Yozef going along to help with the artillery, I approve, but Mulron, you are not to allow him to go farther than the camp. You have my permission to take whatever means necessary to keep him from doing anything heroic, like at Moreland City."

"Yes, Hetman," said Mulron, eyeing Yozef with a look conveying he wasn't sure which of the hetman's assignments would be the easiest.

Culich closed his eyes again. "I need to rest. I think you know what needs be done. Keep me informed of any news or problems."

Culich's eyes shot open again. "Before I drift off again, the news about other attacks? Are they confirmed?"

"Yes, Culich," said Luwis, his voice harsh with anger. "Hetman Skouks is dead. The attack on Hetman Bevans failed. The latest word from Swavebroke is that the people of Shullick are moving away from the city as fast as possible. Hetman Swavebroke and an unknown number of his men are fighting the Narthani within the city to slow them from pursuing the fleeing citizens. There's no further word on how the fighting is going."

Culich shook his head slowly and drifted off.

"He needs to rest," said Kennrick. "We can continue outside."

They went out to the front veranda. Reminders of the previous night were the hole in the front door where a shotgun had blasted away the lock, broken windows, and bloodstains where the second attacker Yozef had shot bled away his life.

"Mulron and I will organize the men to form the support force," said Vortig Luwis. "It would have been best to simply use men from the northwestern districts, but they haven't had enough time training as dragoons or using the new artillery, and our men in Dornfeld haven't had the training at all. That only leaves men closer to Caernford."

"We could compromise, Father," said Mulron Luwis. "I can put together six hundred men from the Caernford garrison and neighboring districts where the training has been ongoing. In a day, two at the most, we can be moving hard toward Dornfeld. We can add another six hundred men from the northwest districts and integrate them with the other men. It won't be optimal, but for this purpose it's not crucial that all the men know how to fight as dragoons. After all, we're talking about establishing a defensible position, not offensive operations like Denes is doing. Then there are the men already at Dornfeld. I could include perhaps two hundred of them to either go with us all the way or set up a second fallback position closer to Dornfeld."

Luwis looked at Kennrick for his opinion

"This is more your responsibility, Vortig," responded Kennrick. "Although, if we're sending Denes off, it isn't a bad idea to have support, in case it's needed."

"All right, Mulron," said Vortig, "set it all in motion. Let me know what instructions from the clan headquarters need to be sent out."

Luwis looked around. "Anything else?" No one responded. "Off we go then."

Yozef almost blurted out that he had another topic, but he caught himself just in time. It occurred to him that he didn't require input or permission for what he had in mind; he only needed to accept responsibility if things went wrong.

He wandered around, looking for his escaped Preddi Shadow, and found him standing outside the room where medicants attended Ceinwyn.

"Balwis, follow me."

They moved out of the house and stopped when fifty feet from the nearest person. Yozef didn't want anyone to listen in.

"You mentioned that you had been to Hanslow, right?"

"Yes, twice," Balwis responded. "When I was fourteen, I helped my father drive fifty horses from our ranch to Hanslow. It was unusual for Father to deliver horses so far away, but the price was too good to pass up. When we got there, the buyer was away, and we had to wait five days. I got to know the city fairly well, since there was nothing else to do. The second time was just before the Narthani took control of Preddi. This time I went alone to take possession of three mares my father had purchased from an Eywell horse ranch known for its breeding stock."

"So," said Yozef carefully, "do you consider yourself familiar enough with Hanslow that you could find your way around the city easily?"

"It's been a few years since I was there, but I don't imagine it has changed *that* much."

"Balwis . . . " Yozef paused, arguing with himself whether the potential reward would prove great enough for men to take the enormous risk he feared it would be. He tried to find reasons that the answer would be "no" and failed.

"Balwis, I have an idea. Something that would strike hard at the Narthani and, I hope, convince them to stop with these assassination attempts. However, it's *very* dangerous. How much so, I can't honestly estimate."

Balwis grinned. "I have the feeling you're working your way up to seeing if I would volunteer for this idea of yours."

"It *is* strictly volunteer. Let me tell you what it is, and you can tell me why I'm crazy to think you're insane enough to do it."

Half an hour later, Balwis had gone through a succession of opinions that ranged from curiosity about Yozef's latest idea to being incredulous that Yozef thought he would volunteer, to grudgingly admitting the idea might work but not with himself participating, and finally to wanting to know more details before he committed.

"For more details, we'll have to talk with Anarynd and Gwyned," said Yozef.

They found Anarynd holding Aeneas and sitting with Maera, who had finally fallen asleep in her chair next to her father's bed. Gwyned had been feeding porridge to Morwena in one of the guest cottages.

The four adults sat around a table in the cottage.

If this were going to be possible, they'd need Anarynd and Gwyned to remember all they could. As much as Yozef hated to press the two women, he only hoped they had the fortitude to help.

CHAPTER 35

THREE DAYS LATER

Shullick, Swavebroke Province

Brigadier Aivacs Zulfa panned his telescope across the vista from his vantage above the valley where the main road ran eastward from Shullick. Even from two miles away, he could see the jumble of belongings the citizens of the Swavebroke capital had tried to take with them, only to be discarded when word of a Narthani pursuit passed through the thousands of refugees. This part of the road was ten miles from Shullick, and the abandoned baggage had gradually lessened the farther from the city they went.

Resistance inside Shullick was quashed only the previous day. Although not that many of Swavebroke's fighting men had fought, they had been tenacious and had to be rooted out block by block. The delay had allowed most citizens to leave the city, though Zulfa wasn't discouraged, because taking captives was not an objective and would only slow down their main mission—property destruction. General Akuyun had warned against indiscriminate killing. They wanted to put fear back into the clans, not incite them.

Zulfa's ears picked up distant sounds of musket fire and the occasional 8-pounder. The smaller cannon were only recently cast and tested, ready for deployment. They hadn't brought horse artillery with them to Caedellium, because it hadn't been deemed necessary—just one of the surprises the island had presented to them, such as the clans being more capable than anticipated.

"Major," Zulfa said, not lowering the telescope, "I think it's time to pull back to Shullick. Resistance is increasing, and the latest reports say that Pewitt and Farkesh men have started showing up. We knew this would happen eventually, and we're not here to engage in fixed battles with an increasing number of clansmen."

"Yes, sir, I'll give the order. I'll admit I was about to suggest it myself.

This morning is the first time they've brought artillery out. We lost ten men to a grapeshot volley from three of their cannon when they ambushed a patrol scouting to the north. The officer in charge of the patrol estimated the cannon were somewhat lighter than our 8-pounders, maybe in the 6-pounder range."

Zulfa grunted. "General Akuyun will not be happy to get this news. It was annoying enough that they had those abortions of light artillery at Moreland City and then captured some of our 12-pounders, and now they're casting their own. If they have 6-pounders, I'd be surprised if 12-pounders aren't coming along."

"One positive about the new islander cannon showing up is that the men won't grouse as much when ordered to pull back," said the major. "As the people fled Shullick, they dumped more of what they were carrying, and the pickings over the discards got better. One platoon found a chest of silver coins and almost got into a fight among themselves about how to divvy it up."

Zulfa allowed himself a smile. Looting was acceptable, if it didn't impact achieving objectives, something that this mission had more than accomplished. Zulfa and the other officers could afford to look the other way about sporadic pillaging.

He put away the telescope and took his horse's reins from an aide. "Let's get them pulling back, Major. I want everyone within Shullick by nightfall. We'll finish razing the city tomorrow and be back aboard ship the day after that. I think we've timed it right and we'll have accomplished the maximum damage before the other clans can get here."

Town of Wrexton, Eywell Province

Denes Vegga watched the last of the eight hundred Eywellese citizens leave the town of Wrexton, ten miles inside Eywell Province from the Keelan border. They took with them only what they could grab, as Denes's men swept through the town at dawn and drove the populace to the north. What little armed resistance they offered was dealt with harshly and decisively. Otherwise, the Eywellese were unharmed physically. The emotional and economic consequences to the Eywellese people were not Denes's concern.

"Ser Vegga ... er ... Colonel Vegga, Major Sixwith says the town is clear," said a "captain." The use of ranks was still new enough to Denes and the men of the reaction force that all of them had to keep reminding themselves and one another to use the titles. Denes hadn't understood the need for such labels, though he accepted Yozef's arguments about delineating specific numbers of men into groupings, such as squad, platoon, company, battalion, and, as Yozef called the reaction force, a regiment requiring a "colonel" in charge. Thus, Denes was a colonel. Colonel Denes Vegga, commanding the 1st Regiment, composed of twelve hundred dragoons, twenty 6-pounders, and a hundred support personnel for supplies and medical treatment. The full name was the 1st Mixed Dragoon Regiment, to recognize that its members came from different clans, although the exact membership changed as men rotated through the training, with the exception of officers down to the captains. These were on semi-permanent loan from their clans, part of the effort to get clans accustomed to working together.

Denes didn't attempt to follow Yozef's reasoning on the naming system, except that Yozef said only that another regiment forming near Caernford and composed entirely of Keelanders would be called the 2nd Regiment or the 2nd Keelan Dragoon Regiment.

The captain, a Gwillamese, belonged to the battalion of Major Sixwith, a Keelander. The other battalion was commanded by Major Kildorn, an Oroszian, and the artillery by another Keelander. That second battalion and the artillery provided security west and north of Wrexton, while Major Sixwith's men cleared the town.

"Tell Major Sixwith he has thirty minutes to start the fires and have his men formed on the road west," said Denes. There would be no looting. Nothing to slow their passage, beyond the time needed to destroy what they could. When they left, the town of Wrexton would be burning, and the citizens literally left with only the clothes on their backs. As far as Denes was concerned, all Eywellese deserved whatever happened to them for betraying the other clans and allying with the Narthani, and they should thank God for the mercy being shown by the clans' not killing all the men.

Denes rode to Major Kildorn's position west of the town. He found Kildorn standing near a battery of five 6-pounders, talking to the battery commander, as smoke rose from Wrexton.

"Colonel, I take it the town is cleared, and you've given the order to burn it?" asked Kildorn. The major had taken to the rank structure and scrupulously used it.

"Yes. I gave Major Sixwith thirty minutes to finish and be here, ready to follow your battalion. Start forming up and signal to pull in the more distant pickets. Any interesting information from the Eywellese you questioned?"

A company of Kildorn's men had circled the town before daylight to block anyone escaping to the west with warnings. They didn't care about the north, because the nearest town that might have enough fighting men to be a threat lay fifty miles away. By the time word reached inland to the more populated parts of Eywell Province, the reaction force planned to have completed their mission and be back near or inside Keelan Province.

The blockage had worked. They stopped close to a hundred Eywellese heading west. Denes hoped that none got through to sound alarms.

Kildorn had instructions from Denes to interrogate as many of the Eywellese men as he could in the time available. "No information that might cause us to change the plan," said Kildorn. "The land is flat, as we see it, almost all the way to the Preddi border. There're five or six fishing villages, the men disagreed on the exact number, and no towns right on the water after this one. One of the men is from Neath, the Eywell town eighteen to twenty miles north of the coast. He confirms the population there is about three thousand. They have about two hundred fighting men, in addition to any others who are willing to pick up a musket or sword. No regular Narthani are stationed there, although fifty-man patrols pass through.

"If we stick to the coast, there's hardly anything to stop us until we reach Ponth, the town just over the border into Preddi. Another man claimed there were a hundred Narthani foot soldiers in Ponth. I would have expected their cavalry. However, Preddi City itself is only twenty miles farther, and he confirms there's a shitload of Narthani there. He volunteered that the Narthani have had a hair up their asses, building fortifications all around Preddi City, with what sounds like forts out as far as ten miles from the city."

An aide handed Denes a quill and ink, and he pulled a map out of his saddlebag and made notations. "We won't get close enough to Preddi City to stir up that nest. Ponth is our target. That's assuming we can move fast enough and surprise the Narthani. What about north of Ponth?"

"Three towns about the size of Wrexton to the north and northwest of Ponth," said Kildorn. "One is ten miles away and the other two a little farther."

"Well," said Denes, "the closer one might get our attention. It will depend on what we run into. Our scouts are only three miles out from Wrexton, which makes me uneasy, but we're assuming speed is better than being more cautious. Once we get to the Preddi border, we'll push the scouts out to ten miles and see what we shall see. At the first sign of serious opposition, we'll head back home."

"Both sound good," said the Oroszian major. "Destroying what we can and putting a scare into both the Eywellese and the Narthani and then getting out with our skins intact."

Moreland Province, Five Miles from the Eywell Border

Welman Stent read, for the third time, the written message from Yozef Kolsko. Between each reading, he looked again at the man who had given him the message and the four other men standing farther back, holding their horses' reins. The evident leader was of good height and a rangy build, but his distinguishing features were a facial scar and eyes that reminded Welman of a predator. The other four men all appeared just as rough-looking, especially a short, wiry man with one hand heavily bandaged.

Welman Stent held the sheet in one hand and slapped it with the other. "If this didn't come from Yozef Kolsko, I'd *know* whoever thought this up is insane. Since it is Kolsko, I'll reserve that I only *suspect* he's lost his mind. And you're the idiots he's convinced to try this?"

"That's us," answered Balwis, the description of himself and his four companions evidently having no effect.

Welman sighed and shook his head. "If you're set on committing suicide, who am I to naysay? I've enough to worry about, so you'll be on your own. I can't divert any attention or men. It will be hard enough controlling the mix of men I've got."

"I noticed your men are riding under clan banners, Hetman Stent," stated Balwis.

Welman grimaced. "I know the rapid-reaction force in Keelan has mixed up the men from different clans, but we started later and haven't yet had enough success in convincing the men to work together or take orders from someone of a different clan. I had no choice but to leave them in companies made up of just one clan."

"I'm not sure which of us has the harder task," said Balwis.

"It's going to take a lot more Narthani to give *us* trouble than it will for you," said Welman. "At first light tomorrow, we'll cross into Eywell territory and tear through several villages before getting to Hanslow. We know two thousand Narthani had amassed there at one time. The latest word is that only about twelve hundred remain. Of course, then there's the Eywellese and probably another thousand or so fighting men in the city or nearby. Although the Eywellese pulled their people back farther into the province, they still patrol heavily, mainly at the border and around Hanslow. If you can slip through the border patrols, you might get to within a few miles of the city, though it's far too risky, if you ask me."

"Not your concern, Hetman."

"The most I can do for you is let you talk to my man who has led a group watching the Eywellese patrol the border. We never see Narthani cavalry, except near Hanslow, and the Eywellese patrols cover only about a mile from the border. Farther into Eywell they don't patrol. He can tell you the best times to slip through. Once there, it's a clear path to Hanslow, if you travel at night and avoid main roads.

"The Narthani are mainly foot soldiers, though an escapee has reported they've been training more of their infantry to ride horses. The only cannon they have are their standard 12-pounders, like the ones we captured at Moreland City. Those are not suited to accompany their cavalry or our dragoons, so we should be able to fight off any Eywellese attack and outrun any Narthani we don't want to confront. My intention is to circle the city at about ten miles, razing villages, burning bridges and crops, and doing whatever damage we can. We'll feint at Hanslow, if the opportunity arises and we're not threatened, but our purpose is to arouse and threaten, not get into a serious battle."

"Thank you, Hetman, that's useful. However, I think we can also help *you*," asserted Balwis. "If we're successful, there should be chaos among the Narthani leadership, and they might hesitate to send men outside the city walls until the leadership is more organized."

"*If* you're successful, that may be true," said Welman, his manner making it clear he had slim expectations of Balwis and his men completing their mission. "Although you might be lucky. From the clouds we see coming from the south, there's a good chance of rain over the next couple of days. This time of year, the rain comes in waves in this part of Caedellium. Assuming you can get past the patrols and assuming no one sees you before you get to Hanslow and assuming the gap you say is in the city wall above the river is still there, then who knows? Maybe then your chances of coming out of this alive are somewhere above zero."

"Good luck to *you* also, Hetman," said Balwis, smiling. "We'll grab some sleep, and then, if your man can help us through the Eywellese patrols, we'll try to reach within a few miles of Hanslow before nightfall. Depending on weather and if we can find the way inside, we'll act and be out of the city before light. With your move into Eywell, we suspect they won't be as committed to searching for us as they otherwise would have been."

Welman shook his head once again. "God go with you. You're going to need all the help he can give."

Narthani Headquarters, Preddi City

Administrator Nizam Tuzere had dressed as impeccably as always, although Akuyun detected an unusual edge to the overseer of nonmilitary personnel on Caedellium.

"The civilians are nervous, General, as I've reported before. Not unexpected, what with Zulfa away with twenty-five hundred men, leaving fewer regular troops visible, plus the militia training and fortification construction contributing to the unease. No disturbances, but there's no question everyone knows things aren't the same as six months ago. One upside is that merchants and the more highly placed Narthani have made fewer petty complaints. I doubt they see their own problems as any less important, but at least they aren't as persistent as before."

Akuyun appeared attentive to Tuzere's report, though his mind was elsewhere, particularly three hundred miles north-northwest at the capital of Swavebroke Province. The regular command staff meeting would go on as always, minus two members: Brigadier Aivacs Zulfa, who commanded the attack on Swavebroke, and Admiral Morfred Kalcan, naval commander of the mission to Caedellium. Akuyun missed both Kalcan and Zulfa at staff meetings. Kalcan's perennial good humor and Zulfa's capability always reassured him. Not that the three other military men attending today were incompetent. None of them would have passed Akuyun's approval otherwise. Ketin and Metin were solid colonels. Ketin might rise higher, but Akuyun had identified him as an officer to take along to his next command and believed Ketin would make a superb engineering brigadier for a corps. In comparison, Metin also functioned as a respectable regiment commander, though Akuyun doubted he would rise further.

Erdelin, the outlier of the three colonels, was personally brave, just short of reckless. He had also shown more decisiveness at Moreland City than Akuyun would have expected. Despite it being his wing of the deployment that suffered the clan's flanking attack, Erdelin had responded quickly enough to save the day from being a complete disaster. However, Akuyun disliked the man personally and had to keep that opinion from slipping into his evaluations. Erdelin might rise higher and serve the Empire well, though not again under Akuyun.

Akuyun turned to Assessor Sadek Hizer. "Any more news about the strike teams, Sadek?"

"Still only the one for Skouks. The team got back to their sloop with only two losses and three wounded. The hetman was killed for certain, and they think possibly one of his sons. As for the other two teams, no word yet. The sloops will stay on station for another sixday. If they aren't contacted by the team, they'll return here."

Akuyun didn't bring up the part of the Skouks team leader's report that stated matter-of-factly that all persons at the site of the attack had been killed. Akuyun knew from pre-mission planning that the Skouks hetman had been at a daughter's home. If all died, that included the hetman's wife, his daughter and her husband, their six children, and whatever servants, guards, and other families were unfortunate enough to be present. He hadn't said anything, except to his wife, Rabia, to whom he wished the hetman's younger grandchildren had been spared.

Akuyun shifted in his chair and tried to put unpleasant images from his mind. "One out of three is still a success, Sadek. Along with the Swavebroke attack, these should cause the clans to pull inward to protect their own."

Akuyun saw no reason to express his concern that the exact opposite might result. Instead, he voiced optimism. "Last reports from Aivacs stated that all had gone well, and they would finish destroying everything within twenty miles of the Shullick harbor and be back aboard ship no later than tomorrow afternoon, then back here by the next morning.""

CHAPTER 36

FOUR DAYS LATER

Hanslow, Eywell Province

After leaving Hetman Stent, the guide led them past Eywellese patrols and left them a mile and a half inside Eywell.

"This is as far as I go. Even though the Eywellese don't run patrols any farther from the border, watch out for the Narthani. For the next twenty miles, there aren't many patrols until you get closer to Hanslow, and they don't keep to a schedule. Avoid villages and farms. My advice is keep to the forest patches, as much as possible. They curve southwest and back toward Hanslow. It'll take you some miles out of a direct line to the city but with less chance of being seen."

Following the guide's advice, after four hours of creep and hide, they had progressed only three miles closer to Hanslow.

"Fuck this," said Kales, after they hid from a farm wagon carrying hay. "There's only a couple of hours of light left. If we're not within sight of the city by midnight, there's no way we can get about doing this tonight. We'll have to chance it. Act like we have every reason to be on these roads."

The moon Aedan and the stars gave enough illumination to reveal the outline of Hanslow a mile from the forest where Balwis, Kales, and their three companions stood. From there, the trees and the brush gave way to grass across open terrain before reaching the river. Its far bank had a scree-covered slope a hundred and fifty yards up to Hanslow's main wall. Balwis had been here before. On his first trip to Hanslow, he and his father had camped not more than a half-mile away. They had let their horses graze in the grassy field before delivering them to their new owner in the city. Balwis remembered his fourteen-year-old-self swimming naked in the river, only to scurry for his clothes when women on the wall high above shamed him with their jeers. He smiled briefly at the memory and how his father had laughed at his red-faced son. The pleasant memory faded, as he returned to the task at hand.

Standing next to Kales as they perused the Hanslow walls, Balwis marveled at the man's toughness. He had survived the 180-mile ride in as good a shape as any of the others, even with the wound that must have pained him the whole way.

"Aw . . . I've ridden farther with worse," was all Kales would say when Balwis had checked on him fifty miles from Caernford.

* * *

Balwis had been dubious when Kales told him he would be coming along to Hanslow.

"Kales," Balwis said, "you lost two fingers not sixteen hours ago and got a shotgun pellet alongside your skull. Both have got to hurt like hell, and how are you going to ride a horse as hard as we'll have to ride? Then what? You're a one-handed man and would be a handicap."

Kales's curses would have melted bronze. After a minute and Balwis's admiration for the man's repertoire, Kales subsided enough to form complete sentences.

"I've been hurt worse than this. And I'm not one-handed, only missing part of one. Even one-handed, I'd be able to handle any Eywellese we're likely to run into. This won't be a battle, this will be skulking around and silencing any unlucky individuals who come across us."

Balwis didn't ask for further details of why Kales obviously considered himself expert in "silencing," though Balwis had his own suspicions about how Kales had spent the twenty-three years he'd lived off Caedellium.

"Yes, God curse it, the blasted hand hurts, but it's *hurt*, not missing. You get everything else ready, and I'll meet you in the Caernford central square in three hours, ready to go."

"I'm not convinced," said Balwis, "and we won't slow down for you. If you can keep up all the way to Hanslow, then we'll see."

Balwis hesitated, while he considered two thoughts. One was that he wouldn't bet against Kales being true to his boasts. He didn't have personal experience witnessing Kales in action, but the man had taken down three

Narthani in the dark before being struck unconscious. If he could make it to Hanslow in good condition, he might be an asset.

The second thought was that he saw no reason to bother Yozef about Kales's participation. Yozef would insist Kales couldn't go.

"All right," said Balwis. "See you there, but make it two hours. It won't take the rest of us any longer to get ready. We'll bring extra horses, including ones for you."

Two hours later, Kales waited next to a three-story building flanking the square. Balwis reined in and dismounted. The other three men he'd picked stayed on their horses. They had volunteered when told the target. All three were ex-Narthani slaves, one from Preddi and two from off-island, and all were members of the dragoon platoon of Narthani escapees.

Kales didn't say anything, just held up the arm with his injured hand. The bulky bandage had been replaced by a tight wrap covering the wound and fastened to the wrist. Around the forearm were several leather straps whose purpose puzzled Balwis.

Kales reached to his side and from a scabbard pulled out what appeared to be a spearhead. Most Caedellium spearheads had a hollow base that the shaft fit into, and rivets through the spearhead base and the shaft further held the two together. The spearhead Kales held out had a base of flat metal, an inch wide. Balwis had seen a few like this, where the base slid into a slotted shaft, and glue or twine held the two together.

Kales slid the base between straps on his forearm, pulled a loose strap end, and gripped the upper portion of the base with his thumb and two remaining figures. He waved it several times, then pantomimed stabbing and slashing motions. Balwis imagined the result. The blade was three inches wide and thick, with a rounded upper edge tapering to a point. Balwis could picture it serving as a short sword and didn't doubt the damage it could do.

"All right," said Balwis, "I can see you handling yourself in a blade fight, which is more what we're likely to face than firearms. What if there's climbing?"

Kales yanked on another strap end to pull the spearhead out and re-sheathed it. He reached into the pack at his feet for a metal hand-sized claw with a metal rod attached. He shoved the rod into the same position as the spearhead base, pulled a strap, and tugged on the claw to be sure it was firmly in place. Then Kales reached back into the sack for two larger claws he stepped into and fastened. Finally, a second smaller claw went on the free hand, the strap tightened by his teeth.

Kales turned to the stone building and started to climb, as if walking on all fours across a horizontal surface. At the top of the second story, he stopped and looked down.

"Satisfied, or should I go all the way up?"

"No, that's fine," said Balwis. "I knew there was a reason I wanted you along."

The four men laughed, and even Kales grinned.

***

They had watched the city for the last hour.

"What do you think?" Balwis asked Kales. "Wait another hour?"

"Too soon," answered Kales. "We'll wait till most lights are out. Otherwise, there'll be too many people on the streets."

"That'll only give us three or four hours to find the villa and get back out before the sun's up," said Balwis.

"Can't be helped," said Kales. "We'll have to be quick."

Balwis turned back to look at the city and the many lights still shining from tower windows. For a moment, he felt eyes looking straight at them, and the thought rose that they still had time to abort. He quickly quashed the thought, as he recalled the night of the attack. He remembered the man coming at him while he was occupied with another attacker, and Ceinwyn hitting the man with a small chair. The man had staggered, then slashed at Ceinwyn. Moments later, it seemed like many minutes, Balwis remembered going over to Ceinwyn, lying shocked on the floor. The flap of her cheek hung below her jaw, her teeth and tongue visible. He had held the flap back in place until someone came to relieve him, so he could go with Yozef to see Maera off to Caernford and then search the back property for Kales.

He also remembered Norlin and Anid, neither of whom he knew well, both young and full of life. Both now dead.

He remembered Yozef's icy demeanor, so different from how he usually behaved. For the first time, Balwis felt a personal kinship with Yozef. Although he had respected Yozef and knew he had been pivotal in how they'd resisted the Narthani, Balwis hadn't felt they shared emotions, until now.

Akuyun Villa, Preddi City

Okan Akuyun sat up in bed. Rabia stirred beside him, but she was harder to rouse. He crossed to the bedroom door and cracked it open. Lieutenant Nestor, one of his aides, stood rocking side to side, a tense expression on his twenty-one-year-old face.

"Sorry, General. Colonel Ketin sent a messenger. The colonel needs you at headquarters."

"Any word why?"

"No, General."

"Send the messenger back and tell Colonel Ketin I'll be there as soon as I can."

Akuyun closed the door. *Now what?* he wondered. *Some word from Zulfa? Has he gotten into some trouble? A ship from Narthon? No, not arriving in the middle of the night. It would be dawn before a ship could moor.*

"What is it?" Rabia called out drowsily from the bed.

"No idea," said Akuyun. "Ketin wants me at headquarters."

Rabia sat up in bed, the covers falling to her waist. She slept in sheer nightgowns, and, emergency or not, he took a moment to gaze on her form, which never ceased to please him.

"Should I get you something to eat or drink while you dress?"

"No, dear. Go back to sleep. If it's something I can handle, I'll try to come back to eat and get a little more sleep."

Nestor was a good aide. By the time Akuyun had splashed some water on his face, dressed, and rushed out the villa's front door, a saddled horse and four mounted guards waited for him. Another five minutes, and he arrived at headquarters and saluted the guards at the door as he rushed through. He took the stairs two at a time. The closer he'd gotten to headquarters, the more anxious he'd become. There had been too many surprises the last six months.

He found Ketin and several other officers in the planning room, where maps covered the walls, along with the desks and the tables that occupied most of the floor space. One man wore spurs, his uniform coated with dust. All of them stood around a map of Preddi Province and talked until Ketin spotted Akuyun.

"General, a messenger from Ponth. It's not confirmed yet, but several Eywellese rode into Ponth, claiming at least a hundred clan horsemen are headed that way. And they include cannon."

Akuyun remained calm. Although this was unexpected, he'd had enough experiences of being surprised that his instinctive reaction was to gather more information before making a decision.

"Not confirmed, you say? Has the commander at Ponth sent out patrols to try to find these clansmen?"

"Sir," spoke up the messenger, "four cavalry squads were sent out, fanning from the shore to twenty miles north and east of Ponth. They were leaving as I was, so there may be more information by now."

"Maybe," said Akuyun. "If there is, it's in Ponth or on the way here, but not here now." He turned to Ketin. "Colonel, let's not take any chances." He went to a wall map of an area showing twenty miles from Preddi City. "Let's push the ready infantry battalion out to the bridge and ford here." Akuyun pointed at the map. "They're supposed to be able to leave on thirty minutes' notice. Another hour and a half by wagon and they should be setting up defensive positions in two hours."

One of Akuyun's innovations, and one he hadn't yet convinced superiors of, before he'd left for Caedellium, was using wagons to transport infantry and the men fighting on foot only when at a battle site. More traditional officers had not seen a reason to use horses to move infantry, except in unusual circumstances.

"Get a semaphore message off to Erdelin in Hanslow at daybreak. Let's see if there's been any action he knows of. For here, let's make two plans. One, to send a cavalry battalion and 8-pounder batteries toward Ponth, and a second plan for two infantry regiments to begin moving after the cavalry. We won't move until we have more information."

Sadek Hizer had come into the room shortly after Akuyun. He stood looking hard at the wall maps.

"Assessor Hizer, what's your opinion of what we're hearing?" asked Akuyun.

"As you say, General, we need more information. However, I doubt this is a serious attack on us here in Preddi Province. Even though we have fewer agents than before, there's enough to have picked up on something as big as a serious attack. I suspect this is more a spoiling raid, a big-enough force to do damage. That's assuming this one report is accurate and not the imagination of some overexcited Eywellese."

Hanslow, Eywell Province

The five men stood at the base of the Hanslow main wall. Below them, down the steep, scree-covered slope, flowed the Falworth River, thankfully running relatively low, since no rain had fallen the last sixday. As they made their way from the thicket where they'd left the horses staked out, rain began to fall. Balwis gave a quick and uncharacteristic prayer that the drizzle would continue or intensify to help hide their escape, assuming any of them survived to flee.

"I wish that Moreland woman had noticed better where the gap in the wall was," whispered Kales.

"*That* Moreland woman is Anarynd," rejoined Balwis. He had not interacted much with Maera's friend, though he'd been impressed by her steely recounting of what had happened to her and her serious attempt to remember everything she could. She reported on the gap in Hanslow's riverside wall and the route to Erdelin's villa and went into great detail about the villa itself. Only with the latter did Anarynd's composure falter, especially when describing Erdelin's bedroom, including the location of the bed, when he usually went to sleep, whether he kept weapons within reach, and whether he kept a woman in the bed after he had finished with her or he sent her to sleep elsewhere.

"She and Gwyned did well to remember as much as they did," said Balwis, "considering what must have gone through their minds when they risked an escape attempt and shepherded a flock of women they hadn't planned on."

Kales grunted, which Balwis took as a grudging acknowledgment. "It still leaves us needing to find the fucking hole, if it still exists and the damn Eywellese didn't seal it."

"This section can't be more than four hundred yards long," said Balwis, recalling how the wall looked from the thicket. At the moment, they could only see thirty yards. A cloud cover and drizzle had moved in and blocked the light from the stars and Aedan. "I'll go to the right and you to the left," he told Kales. "Come back if you find the gap or reach the end of the bluff."

"You three stay here," Balwis ordered the other men.

Six minutes later, both Balwis and Kales returned.

"I didn't find it," said Kales.

"I did," said Balwis, in a tone Kales wondered whether showed pleasure or regret.

"It's about a hundred yards away. It's a tight fit with the packs, but I slipped all the way in, until I found the jumble of blocks on the other side, just as Anarynd and Gwyned described."

The drizzle had changed to a steady rain, and when they exited through the gap, they froze for a moment to hear voices thirty feet above them on the wall's rampart.

"Goddamn it, why do I always end up with night watch when it rains?" complained a Narthani voice, making no effort to maintain silence.

"I can only think of two reasons," came a loud reply from a second voice, "either you pissed off whoever makes up the watch list or the god Narth hates you."

Descriptions of what the second man could do with his private member were followed by raucous laughter, which faded as the men moved away along the wall's top.

Balwis translated, and Kales commented, "If God really *does* hate that idiot up there, maybe he loves *us*. I think the rain is getting heavier."

Kales had no sooner whispered the words than they could hear rain pounding on rooftops and getting closer by the second. They had crawled through the jumble of stone blocks facing the street that paralleled the wall when larger raindrops splattered on their faces. A torrential downpour shut out all other sounds and limited visibility to ten yards.

"Thank you, God, if you're real. I'll even go to cathedral and pray along, if you keep this rain going for another hour or so," tittered Kales, raising his voice to be heard over the drumming of the rain.

"For once, I agree with you," said Balwis. "No reason to try to act inconspicuous. Anyone not running in this rain will draw more attention than creeping around. Let's run."

And run they did. Up main streets, down alleys, and sometimes crossing streets they'd already traversed. Nothing looked consistent with Anarynd's and Gwyned's descriptions. Despite Balwis's memory of Hanslow and the information from Anarynd and Gwyned, an hour passed and their concern mounted that they might have to give up, because dawn was only a few hours away. They never considered leaving and reentering the city. The fortuitous rain and Welman Stent's force moving into Eywell Province in the morning would make getting back into Hanslow nearly impossible. Guards would increase, or Erdelin could be in the middle of Narthani forces, as they reacted to the incursion, if he were still in the city at all. It had to be tonight.

"I can see Aedan to the south," hissed Kales.

Balwis turned his head. There it was: the moon Aedan visible on the horizon as a hazy globe. That meant the weather front that brought the rain would soon pass. Though Balwis couldn't tell for sure, he thought the downpour had slackened.

"If we don't go soon, we ain't going anywhere, except into the ground," said Kales.

"Just to the end of this street," said Balwis. "This matches what Anarynd said about alternating two- and three-story structures. If it's right, there should be a plaza around the corner and Erdelin's villa on the other side. If it's not there, then we'll go. Shit!"

They continued trotting down the street, staying clumped together, as would any group of men in the rain—not single file, as assassins would act. They hoped. They turned the corner. There was enough light for them to tell that the side street opened to space. Thirty more yards and they stood at the edge of a plaza. They couldn't clearly see the other side.

"This has to be it. Anarynd just didn't remember the short street section between the plaza and the other street," said Balwis.

"We'll work our way around to the right," said Kales. "If this is it, there should be a cluster of trees along the side. We won't have time to study it, if we're going in. Time is too short."

Five minutes later, Balwis climbed down from one of a dozen trees clustered along the outside of the villa's outer wall.

"This is it. The front is exactly like Anarynd described, right down to the ironwork horse rail and two big urns flanking the front door. But there's a complication. There should only be one guard at the door. Instead, there are two. Both are right under a whale-oil lantern and are doing their best to stay out of the rain. I didn't see either of them look around or at each other even once in the couple of minutes I watched. I don't think we can count on knowing how many guards there are, anywhere."

"Erdelin's room should be the third to fifth windows on the second floor on this side," whispered Kales. "We don't want him moving around the house, so we'll have to get him in the bedroom. That means climbing and entering a window."

Balwis couldn't see Kales's face, but he'd have bet everything he owned that the wiry man was grinning.

"You can't go alone," said Balwis. "After getting this far, we have to be sure. What if Erdelin is awake or not in his room or you get injured or . . . hell, anything can go wrong. The villa is made from stone blocks, and it looks like the mortar is recessed enough for grips and toeholds, so neither of us should need your climbing claws, unless you need one for your hand?"

"I don't," whispered Kales. "The knife hilt can serve to jam into the crevices. I'll still be faster than you."

Balwis gathered the other three men. "Kales and I are going in after Erdelin. If we can do it quietly, we'll come back out the window and over the wall to here. If it's noisy, the guards will come running. We know there are three in front of the house, two by the door and one at the villa wall's main gate. There's supposed to be one at the back and one inside, but who knows? If the guards are alerted, we don't have any choice but to kill them all before we leave. Otherwise, word would get out too soon, and we'd never escape the city.

"We'll leave you our muskets and go in with only blades and pistols. Follow us over the wall. There's a bin ten-feet to the left. We can use it to get back over the wall. You'll have to judge whether the guards are alerted. In that case, don't worry about being quiet. Just kill them. Kales and I will come out the front door." In the faint light from a few lit windows, Balwis could just make out three nods of understanding.

"If any of you believe in God, this is a good time to call on him. Kales, I'm after you."

With those words, Kales dropped his pack containing the climbing claws and clambered up the same tree Balwis had used. Four men followed Kales. One by one, they jumped to the ground inside the villa grounds. Kales and Balwis handed off their muskets and, bending low, moved quickly to the villa wall. Kales ran his hand over the stone blocks and checked the gaps between blocks.

"Plenty of room," Kales whispered and started up the wall. Balwis followed. Kales swarmed up the wall as if it were horizontal, but Balwis had broader fingers than Kales, and he had to jam his fingertips between some blocks to secure a hold. When Balwis had scaled halfway up the wall, Kales already stood on the balcony, peering into one window and then the next.

"Can't see anyone inside," whispered Kales, when Balwis reached him. "There's a lantern burning low over by a desk at the right of the room. I think I could see a door in the middle of the far wall. We'll have to go in cold and hope to find Erdelin asleep somewhere in the room. None of the windows open, so we'll go in through the balcony door."

They crouched in front of the door, and Kales used his good hand to apply firm, slow pressure to the door's latch. There was a faint creak, and Kales froze, listened for almost a minute, then pressed a bit more. The latch rotated a fraction, then freely for a quarter of a circle before stopping. He pulled, and the door gradually moved outward. When it was ajar a foot, Kales stopped and waited again, then opened it further, pulled a second knife, and slipped inside. The opening wasn't wide enough for Balwis, and he pulled gently. The gap had just widened enough for him, when a hinge squeaked. There was a rustle inside the room. A flash illuminated enough for Balwis to see a tall man, naked and holding a pistol. Balwis ducked by reflex, but a zip and breaking glass before he'd reacted told Balwis the occupant had fired and missed.

A woman screamed. A man cursed. Balwis flung open the door and rushed in. The low lantern gave enough light to reveal two men grappling, then leaping apart. The lantern light reflected off metal, as blades seemed to fly around the two men. A woman started to scream, then choked it off. Balwis assumed Kales to be the shorter of the men, but he couldn't be positive enough to use a pistol, and he feared drawing his own knife and joining in. The men moved too fast in the dim light.

Balwis heard a musket fire outside. A second musket. Yelling. A third shot. More yelling. He thought he recognized one of his men's voices.

The shorter man never spoke a word, but the taller man cursed in Narthani. The tall man grunted and staggered back, catching his bare foot on the edge of a thick rug. Before he could recover, the other man was inside the Narthani's guard, his left arm jabbing outward. The tall man cried out in pain and shock, before the other man slashed across his throat with another blade. The Narthani fell to his knees.

"Here's for Anid, you fucker!" Kales yelled and stabbed Erdelin in the chest. "And Norlin and Mirramel and guards whose names I don't know."

Erdelin was dead before the second stab.

Footsteps pounded outside the bedroom door. Balwis stepped to the wall beside the door, as it burst open. A man in a Narthani uniform carrying a musket dashed into the room. Balwis shot him in the back, then looked into the hall. It was empty. More shots sounded, though from where he couldn't tell. He turned back into the room and went to the bedding in a corner of the room. A woman sat there, only a sheet covering her from the waist down. She wasn't screaming anymore, but her eyes flared wide as Balwis approached.

"Was that Erdelin?" he demanded. When she didn't answer immediately, he reached out, grabbed her by the hair, and turned her head toward the body. "Is that Erdelin?!"

She choked and nodded. "Yes. That's him, the bastard! May he rot in hell!"

"Who are you?" asked Balwis.

"His slave! Who the hell do you think I am?" she spit out, momentarily overcoming her fear.

Kales walked up. "We have to go, now! There's fighting outside, and we don't know who's winning." He looked at the woman. "She's a witness."

"So?" said Balwis. "She won't warn anyone faster than the firing has already done."

"Are you clansmen?" she asked, throwing aside the covers and rising to her feet. Adrenaline flowing or not and the need to move or not, Balwis couldn't help but admire her voluptuous, firm figure.

She didn't wait for an answer. "I'm from Pewitt. The Narthani took me in a raid on my village two months ago. That pig on the floor claimed me. You have to take me with you."

"You'd only slow us down," said Kales. "Just tell the Narthani it was clansmen, and we spared you only because you weren't Narthani."

"As if they'd give a shit. They'll probably torture me to see if I'm telling the truth, then either kill me or send me to the brothels."

"I could just slit her throat, and then all our problems would be solved," Kales offered. "She'll slow us too much."

The woman gasped and sat back on the bed.

Balwis asked, "And what would Teena think when she found out?"

Kales laughed. "I just wanted to see what you'd say. I might actually start to like you, even if you don't have much of a sense of humor."

"We won't have much of anything if we don't get moving." Balwis turned to the woman. "You've got seconds to get dressed and follow us. We won't wait for you. If you can't keep up, you're on your own."

Kales peered into the hallway, then hurried toward the stairs he saw at the far end. Balwis followed. There were no more firings or shouts. When they reached the stairs, Balwis glanced behind. The woman held clothing and dressed as she caught up with them. She had paused only to spit on Erdelin's body as she ran after them.

"Stay close," Kales told her, and they carefully started down the stairs.

"Keelan," said a voice in the dark.

"Caernford," Kales called back.

"That you, Fixton?" asked Balwis.

"Yeah. Everything finished upstairs? Did you get him?"

"Yes. Where are the others, and what about the other guards?"

"Synton went running after the last guard, the one from the back. He took off over a fence. We shot the guards in front, but one of them got Ulrith. He's gone. Right through the gut. He wouldn't have lasted long. He said a prayer and asked me to finish him."

A door slammed open, and they heard running footsteps. All three crouched with blades. None had loaded firearms.

"It's me," a form called out. "Couldn't catch the fucker." Synton walked into the lantern light and noticed the woman. "Who's this?"

"She's coming with us," said Balwis.

"We have an extra horse now with Ulrith gone," Kales stated, as if casually noting the weather. "So we invited her along."

"Whatever," said Fixton. "I think we need to get the hell out of here."

The woman had finished dressing, and the five of them ran out of the villa, past the bodies of three guards and Ulrith, and through the main gate and into the plaza. Several windows of buildings surrounding the plaza showed light, from people awakened by gunfire. A man leaned out of one window, saw five persons, four of them carrying muskets, and ducked back inside.

The rain had slackened back to a drizzle, and stars started to join Aedan, now fully shining. They ran across the plaza to the short piece of street and zigzagged through Hanslow streets toward the wall along the river. Three times they passed people without raising attention, until they were a few hundred yards from the wall. They turned a corner and almost ran into three Narthani soldiers carrying muskets over their shoulders. None of the three lived more than a few seconds, as Kales, Balwis, and Fixton each killed one before the Narthani could yell or brandish a weapon.

Another fifty yards and bells began ringing, not the deep-toned abbey bells.

"It's the Narthani ringing out an alert," said the woman. "The man who got away must have reached a watch station. There are several stations around the city, and each one has several gongs. They sound like bells. Three strikes like they're doing means a threat inside the city. Continuous is the city in danger of being attacked."

"Keep up or be left," Kales told her.

More lights came on, as the alarm roused people, and they knocked several people down as they ran. When they reached the wall, a guard on the rampart called out for them to identify themselves. Fixton shot at the man, who disappeared, whether hit or hiding they didn't know and had no further interest in finding out.

They raced around the stone blocks and through the gap in the wall and found themselves on the outside and leaping down the slope. They were almost all the way down when the woman fell and tumbled past the men the last fifty yards. When they got to her, she was moaning and holding her ankle.

"I think it's broken," she sobbed. "Please don't leave me."

Kales revisited his repertoire of curses, but Balwis didn't hesitate. He picked up the woman and headed into the river. Low flow or not, he almost lost his footing three times before reaching the other bank. They ran for the thicket, with first Fixton and then Synton taking turns carrying the woman.

They reached the thicket where they'd left the horses three hours earlier—a span of time that seemed much longer. The woman couldn't control a horse with her ankle broken, so they put her in front of Fixton and led the empty horse by its reins. They had barely an hour before daylight. They could still hear the alarms from Hanslow, and twenty or more riders thundered across the grassy flat between the thicket and the river.

"Eywellese," identified Kales. "Sweeping the perimeter of the city. There'll be more any time now. We need to *move*!"

First Light, Northern Rapid-Reaction Force

Welman Stent watched, as the first company started from its muster point a mile from the Eywell border. Its men were Stentese and would lead the force, as it punched across the border and into any enemy patrols. Once clear of the border, that first company would fan out to serve as advanced scouts to warn against more trouble than they could handle. The main order of advance in column consisted of three companies, the artillery unit with the ten 6-pounders delivered from Keelan—Stent's own foundry was not yet operational—and three more companies. Flanking the main column on both sides were two companies each. As they reached appropriate targets, companies would break off and rejoin the main column later.

Welman had commanded more men at Moreland City, but they had been his own clansmen, and their order had essentially been a single mass of riders, instead of the more complex organization of dragoon and artillery companies from different clans. Theory and training exercises would never prepare men for actual combat.

Not that their purpose was to fight fixed battles. They planned to raise as much confusion and consternation as possible and force the Eywellese and Narthani's attention toward northern Eywell Province and away from Denes's southern force, until it fulfilled *its* mission.

They advanced at a walk until they reached the border, then moved into a trot. Distance was not a factor, so they could save their horses for when and if they needed to gallop. The artillery remained one limiting factor, because the horse teams plus cannon and limbers moved slower than the dragoons.

It would take less than an hour to reach the ruins of the Eywell town of Parthmal. Welman Stent had led the attack on Parthmal after the Battle of Moreland City. They had surprised the Narthani camp, destroyed it, and gone on to burn the town. Stent didn't know how much of Parthmal's damage had been repaired, but now they would destroy whatever had been rebuilt.

Once past Parthmal, Stent would order the flanking companies to spread out and burn any farm, ranch, or small settlement they came upon. If possible, they would circle Hanslow. However, the entire force would rejoin at the first sign of a significant enemy force and withdraw back to Moreland territory.

Support Base, Eywell Province

Yozef followed Mulron Luwis, supposedly to give advice, but Vortig Luwis's son was a quick study and also possessed an inherent sense of how to use space, a talent his father lacked. Except for contributing to selecting the site for the support encampment, Yozef had felt more like a tag-along than an advisor. He had alternated between riding his horse or sitting in a supply wagon beside the driver, with Mr. Ed tied behind. Yozef's horsemanship had improved enough that by the time they arrived in Dornfeld, he wasn't sure whether a saddle or the wagon bench felt worse on his butt.

Mulron hadn't pushed the pace, to save the horses, because the men had ridden their own mounts all the way to Dornfeld. There hadn't been any pre-positioned horses for the rapid-reaction force. Once in Dornfeld, they spent the night, then pushed on across the Eywell border the next day. The one Eywell village they passed had been burned by Denes's men, and they didn't stop. The villagers who didn't hide at Denes's men's approach watched sullenly, while salvaging what they could.

Twenty miles past Dornfeld and six miles inside Eywell, they found what they were looking for. Just before the hills gave way to the coastal plain from Wrexton to Ponth, they came upon a jumble of small buttes left by millennia of erosion. The slopes rose no more than fifty feet high, but steepness and disposition provided multiple defensible positions. Yozef and Mulron agreed on a site where the road passed through a four-hundred-yard gap flanked by two buttes. Scouts confirmed that for at least five miles in all directions, the gap was the only place horses could move.

Mulron ordered six hundred men to dig positions for themselves and the cannon and sent two hundred men each to blocking positions north and south, should any Narthani or Eywellese force attempt to flank them. Mulron also sent a platoon as a picket forward to within sight of the still-burning Wrexton.

Then they waited.

CHAPTER 37

FIVE DAYS LATER

Keelan Manor, Caernford

Pain was Culich Keelan's constant companion. Alcohol was the only anesthetic the medicants prescribed for the stump of his leg. He ignored the medicants' advice. The pain from his leg helped dull the pain from Anid's death. The funeral ceremony had been held in St. Tomo's Cathedral in Caernford three days previously, with Abbot Walkot leading the congregation and giving one of several eulogies. Maera spoke for the family and broke down several times before gathering herself and continuing. No one paid attention to her tears, because many in the audience cried along with her. Of the four Keelan daughters, Anid had been most favored by the people who knew her. Maera garnered respect, Mared fondness, and Ceinwyn exasperation, but it was Anid who drew love to herself simply by her presence.

As sorrowful as the funeral was, it faded under the blazing anger of Keelanders from all corners of the province. It was bad enough that the Narthani had crippled their hetman, but to kill Anid and threaten Aeneas, the first grandchild, lit a fire within the people that would have shaken the Narthani, had they witnessed the consequences of the attack.

Nowhere did the fire rage more than within the Keelan family. Yet while Culich and Maera let their fury vent, Breda Keelan was the family rock. She tended both her husband and Ceinwyn, whose head was half-sheathed in a bandage covering her almost-severed cheek. The medicants said Balwis's quick action of holding the flap of flesh back in place had greatly increased the chances the tissue would live and heal. Yet they had no doubt Ceinwyn would bear a great scar, an expectation not yet apparent to Ceinwyn, as she dealt with the pains of her wound and the loss of her sister.

No one had seen Breda sleep since the attack, though she must have, because no one could stay awake for five days and still function. When Maera finally forced her mother to get some needed sleep, Maera sat with her father. By unspoken agreement, they didn't talk of Anid.

"Do you think we've done the right thing, Father, attacking Eywell and threatening the Narthani? All the action is so far from communication, we can only imagine what's happened."

"I hope we did, Maera. It seemed so simple a decision at the time. The last several days I keep asking myself whether I approved out of anger, rather than rational reasoning."

"The plan was already in place as one of the contingencies," Maera reminded him.

"Hypothetical situations on paper are not the same as sending men out to fight. Even if everything works as we planned, men will be killed. By God's grace, we pray it's not too many. Still, however many it is will weigh on me. Denes and our reaction force are the most vulnerable. They're going straight at the Narthani, whereas Hetman Stent is only feigning to keep the Eywellese's attention. Denes needs to remember their objective is not to fight battles, only to do enough damage that the Narthani and Eywellese are circumspect about future aggressions."

"Do we have any idea who the new Eywell hetman is or, should I say, who the Narthani installed?" asked Maera.

"No idea," Culich replied. "Almost certainly their dead from Moreland City included other members of the hetman's family, boyermen, and other leaders. It's not much different from the Moreland Clan. Who is now giving orders in Moreland seems to vary daily."

"Speaking of the Eywellese capital," said Maera, "I can't help but wonder if we'll ever see Balwis Preddi and Wyfor Kales again. I'm still surprised Yozef sent them to do something so dangerous. I'm afraid I can't see how they expect to succeed. I hope that at some point they realize how ludicrous the idea is and turn back before it's too late."

"I agree, Maera, I feel the same. If it weren't for everything else, I'd be mad at Yozef. On the other hand, he's had strange, even insane-sounding ideas before, and they worked out. Maybe this will be another of those times."

"Father, I also pray the support group isn't needed to help Denes's men, and if it is, that Yozef remembers he shouldn't be in the forefront of any fighting."

Culich didn't tell his daughter that he also worried about his son-in-law. None of the three men tasked with keeping Yozef safe were now with him. Balwis and Kales were somewhere north, hopefully safe and on the way back from their attempt on the Narthani colonel, and Carnigan was recovering from moderate wounds inflicted during the assassination attempt. Although Yozef avowed no interest in being directly involved in fighting, somehow the man managed to contradict that claim every time he was near a fight.

Unbeknownst to Culich, the same worry dogged Maera. She prayed that Yozef understood he was more valuable to the clan than anything he might do in a battle. To divert her thoughts, she changed the subject.

"No further word on the attackers, Father?"

"Not since searchers found the camp and wagons we believe they came in. Pedr traced the wagons to a stable in Salford. They found the only full-time worker in the stable dead beneath hay in one of the barns. A search of his home discovered enough to establish him as a Narthani agent, probably the one who passed messages to Narthani ships, as you found happening in Abersford.

"The problem is that it's difficult to see how he could have been the source of information about where I would be on that particular night. It's too much to assume coincidence, so I believe there had to be at least one more spy located in Caernford. I've just learned from Vortig that one of the Caernford semaphore station assistants is missing. The one named Esyl Havant. He's been to our home and, I assume, yours many times. It would have given him more than enough opportunity to keep track of all of us. I know the man and never noticed anything about him—"

"Great God!" said Maera. "Esyl? If he was a Narthani spy, not only did he pay regular visits to our homes, but he must have seen many of the semaphore messages! In fact, he was at our house the same day of the attack."

"As for Keelan Manor," said Culich. "I'm afraid I may know one source of his information. Mared was particularly friendly with him. She often fed him when he delivered messages. Just hours before the attack, he was in the kitchen with Mared. He always seemed too chummy and, I guess I'd say, innocuous. It might not have taken much for him to get information from Mared about our plans to eat at your house that night."

"Oh, Father! If that's true, you can't ever tell Mared. She'd never forgive herself for Anid."

The mention of Anid brought them both back to a topic they had attempted to avoid. The failure ended their discussion, and Maera sat silently until her father eventually dropped off to sleep.

Outside Ponth, Preddi Province

Denes Vegga worried, as he had done the last two days and for the same reason. The rapid-reaction force had moved across southern Eywell Province as fast as they could without exhausting the horses. Their pace was a compromise. If they moved too slowly, the Narthani and the Eywellese would learn of their presence and have time to gather forces. If they moved too fast, they risked their horses being unable to get them out of danger if they ran into trouble.

Three hours ago, they'd reached a crossroads six miles east of the Preddi border. The Preddi town of Ponth lay ten miles farther. The fork heading north led to the Eywell town of Neath, also ten miles away. Denes stood next to his two majors, their horses held by aides. He had to make a choice.

"Neath is an easier target," said Major Kildorn. The Oroszian had, like Denes and the other force's major, Sixwith, been at Moreland City. He'd lost a close cousin at the battle and had eagerly led the battalion that swept the right flank of the raiding force's path along the coast and, to Denes's thinking, took excessive pleasure in watching Eywell villages burn.

"True," said Sixwith, "but our main purpose is to threaten Narthani territory, not the Eywellese."

Denes thought the Keelan major more capable than Kildorn and had left written instructions with aides that if Denes were killed or incapacitated, Sixwith should assume command. While Yozef argued that such chain-of-command arrangements should be set in advance, Denes still struggled to integrate men from different clans and hadn't wanted it to appear that he favored a fellow clansman, a decision he regretted once the force committed to this raid.

"Both points are correct," said Denes. "I have sympathy for wanting to see an entire Eywell town the size of Neath burning, especially when we never thought we could do the same to Ponth, because we know the Narthani have men stationed there and those might have been reinforced. The Narthani *must* be aware of us by now and had to have reacted. Major Kildorn, I'm afraid you'll have to satisfy your urge to burn by destroying whatever villages and farms we find between here and Ponth."

Denes held up the map in his left hand. "From here on, we leave the poor soil along the Eywell coastal plain and get into good farmland. There will be more people and structures, so more opportunities to raise havoc. The road to Ponth moves farther from the coast, so we'll spread out a little more. Instead of moving in battalion column, we'll move the two battalions abreast, as the artillery stays with me and the support people between battalions. Major Kildorn, spread three of your companies in line, aimed at Ponth, and the fourth company screening our flank and a couple of miles to our rear. "Major Sixwith, you'll also put three companies in line, with the fourth aggressively scouting ahead. If we run into Narthani soldiers, I want to know as soon as possible. This is going to be a dangerous dance, Sers. Move and burn, while not getting burned ourselves. We have sixty miles to retrace back to Keelan territory, and we don't want to fight our way back."

Five hours later, Denes faced two more decisions. One was easy and expected, the second more difficult and unexpected. They reached Ponth only to find earthworks thrown up around the town of three thousand, with people still digging, as they watched just out of musket range.

"Like I told you, Colonel. A pisser," said Sixwith. "There's got to be a couple of hundred fighting men, in addition to what look like other citizens helping dig. If we attack, we could probably overrun them, but it's not certain and we'd take casualties. Getting the seriously wounded back to Keelan would slow us."

"We won't attack Ponth. And with what your forward scouts report, there's no time to waste here."

Sixwith's forward scouting company had circled Ponth and pushed a few miles farther into Preddi, until they skirmished with what appeared to be Narthani cavalry escorting wagons of infantry headed to Ponth. The company commander gathered his men and withdrew.

"Get your men turned around, Major. I think we've done all we can, and it's time to get our asses back to Keelan."

Denes looked to their right. Nearby was the leftmost company of Major Kildorn's battalion. Beyond, he made out the next company, though he hadn't seen Kildorn for more than an hour. He turned to an aide. "Ride and find Major Kildorn. He's to pull his men together and follow in column. We're moving fast back to Keelan."

Twenty minutes later, Denes wasn't sure *how* fast they'd be moving and cursed the Oroszian major. He waited for the last of Kildorn's companies to form up on the road back, when Kildorn arrived leading a dozen wagons loaded with people, thirty or more captured horses carrying double, and many of his men with people riding behind them in their saddles.

"What the fuck is this, Kildorn?!" Denes roared.

"The company came on a slave camp five-miles north of here. They were being kept in terrible conditions and were used to work all the farms in the area. The company was loading them on wagons when I got there."

Kildorn looked alternately defiant and desperate as he talked. "We didn't even take them all. Some were in such bad shape, they couldn't have traveled as fast as we need to. A few were too scared to come with us, especially Preddi who'd been slaves for years."

"God's curses, Kildorn," said Denes, sounding desperate himself. "Taking them will put all of us in danger."

"What the hell did you want me to do?! Leave them? Even if I wanted to, I doubt the men would have allowed it. These are mainly Caedelli, for God's sake."

Denes shook his head, sighed, and guided his horse along the line of wagons. Kildorn was right about the people's condition. All were lean, some nearly emaciated, and many bore scars and bruises. Ages ranged from children no more than eight years old to gray-haired men and women whose age could have been anywhere from forty to eighty, depending on how long they'd been enslaved and how severe the conditions.

"Damn, damn, damn," Denes muttered. He rode back to where Kildorn and other leaders waited.

"All right. We'll have to take them with us, but they'll have to keep up. I'll have no argument about this. If it comes to a point where we either leave them or risk getting all of us killed, we leave them." Denes's tone and harsh expression brooked no argument.

"Yes, Colonel," said Sixwith. "We understand and will see they don't slow us." Sixwith gave Kildorn a warning look. Kildorn nodded reluctantly.

"Sixwith," said Denes, "send a couple of riders hard toward the support camp. Tell them what's happening and that we're bringing . . . how many of these people are there?"

"About three hundred," answered Kildorn.

"Have the riders tell them we're bringing three hundred slaves we 'rescued' from the Narthani, and we'll make the best time we can."

Inside Ponth

An hour later, Colonel Erkan Ketin entered Ponth soon after his lead cavalry company ensured the town was secure. Akuyun had charged him with making contact with the islander raiders, assessing their numbers, and, if possible, pursuing.

"You don't think their scouts saw more than your company, Captain?" Ketin asked the company commander.

"I can't be positive, Colonel. My forward men say the islanders turned and galloped away, as soon as they saw those men. The next company was well out of sight, still not through the forest when the islanders came on us."

Ketin was pleased. "If that's the case, then they don't know exactly how many of us are after them. From what the officer in charge of the Ponth men says, they have something like a thousand men. They also saw a few cannon we can assume are cavalry versions, probably 6- to 8-pounders.

"We have enough men. I'd like to force them to stand and fight, although to do that we have to close with them. Also, General Akuyun plans to divert Brigadier Zulfa's force to land behind them, although the general doesn't know whether Zulfa will be back in time. We know he was supposed to sail from Swavebroke yesterday. We can assume the islanders came straight across the Eywell coastal plain and will head back the same route toward Keelan. If Zulfa does block their route, we might catch them between us.

"Major Torvik, I want you to take two companies and ride hard to Neath. The Eywellese are supposed to have a standing hundred-man force based there. Gather them up and fan out, paralleling the raiders' route, picking up as many more Eywellese as can ride and shoot. Your task is to be on their flank, in case they try to turn north or northeast. Also, if we can get them to stand to fight, you might have opportunities to come at them while they're busy with us or Zulfa."

"Major Seljunk, keep our militia cavalry organized as best you can. I realize some of them aren't the best horsemen, but don't let them lag."

Preddi City

"I'm afraid your instincts were right, Okan." Sadek Hizer's voice was full of regret, not congratulations. "I know you weren't convinced we should stir the clans up, when the rest of us weren't as worried."

"I had reservations," said Akuyun, "but it didn't take all of you too long to get me to agree, and it still was *my* decision, so the consequences rest on me."

Akuyun kicked a trash receptacle across the room. It hit a wall, and paper and various discards exploded in a fountain of debris. He paced to the window, hands clasped behind him, while he regained his composure. The empty harbor held his attention, as he went through a mental checklist taught to him many years ago by a captured Fuomi priest. By the eighteenth step, he felt calm enough to turn back to the assessor.

"The raids into Eywell and Preddi are obviously not intended to hold territory or win any battles. They just want to show us they can do it. As for Erdelin, that's either retaliation for striking at their hetmen or another warning or both."

The semaphore message of Erdelin's death had shocked Akuyun. He hadn't liked the man, but Erdelin was competent. Moreover, to strike right at the heart of the Narthani command structure showed daring and determination.

Akuyun couldn't help but imagine his family's house being attacked by assassins. His guard would now be doubled from eight to sixteen men, and two men would accompany Rabia and both of their children wherever they went. He also sent a semaphore message to Colonel Metin in Selfcell to be on the alert.

"So you think the raids and the strike on Erdelin were . . . what?" asked Hizer.

"While I'd prefer to think of them as pure retaliation, I'm afraid I see more behind it. The clans didn't simply retaliate after our attacks. They prepared all of this well ahead of time. Think about it. Two separate thousand-man raids and going after Erdelin, all within days of our attacks? No. It was all in place *before* we moved. If I speculated, I'd say they had already considered the possibilities and prepared their attacks in response. No matter what they did or didn't anticipate, the result is the same. Those are the last offensive actions we'll take against the clans until we get reinforcements from Narthon."

Hizer sat back in his chair. "I take it you now think it likely the High Command will send more resources?"

"I'm afraid the only other option I see is abandoning the entire Caedellium objective. If we give the clans too much more time, we might see them seriously coming after us here. Even though we control the seas around the island, they are going to eventually control the land. With their larger numbers and them now making cannon, it's only a matter of time before they judge their position strong enough to come after us.

"If I was them, I'd start by cutting out Eywell. The clan's already shaken by the losses at Moreland City, and with Erdelin's death and the damage done by these two raids, the clan isn't too far from collapse. Many of the Eywellese could pull back to Preddi Province, but we never fooled ourselves that every member of the clan was pleased by Brandor Eywell's alliance with us. It won't surprise me if we hear of Eywellese running to the other clans and asking to be taken in."

"Would other clans do that?" asked Hizer. "After what Eywell has done?"

"It would be the smart thing to do," Akuyun replied. "And the clans are making far too many smart moves for me. But this is all for the future. We need to deal with the *now*. In Hanslow, what's done is done. Erdelin is gone, and Major Jurna seems to have moved quickly. He reports the city calm, despite the clans' ability to evidently walk in and kill a Narthani commander. He's acting decisively against the raid. He didn't ask my permission to go after them, only informed me of his general intent. I've had my eye on him for some time, and this will tell me whether I promote him and leave him in charge or send in another officer."

"What if headquarters doesn't send reinforcements? What then?"

Akuyun had anticipated the assessor's question, and despite their good relations, he couldn't be sure of Hizer's response to what Akuyun saw as the only alternative.

"I believe the High Command is competent enough and my reports comprehensive enough that they will see the futility of continuing the mission with what we have. If I'm wrong, then there are hard decisions to make." Akuyun paused and looked Hizer in the eye. "Dangerous decisions. I'm not throwing away the lives of all my men, and Narth knows how many of the hundred thousand civilians we have on the island, to blindly follow orders I know to be suicidal. In that case, I would order Admiral Kalcan to start ferrying the civilians back to Narthon."

Hizer's expression didn't change, nor did his tone convey an opinion. "Even if contrary to direct orders?" he asked softly.

Akuyun stood on precarious ground. Although it happened rarely, a mission's assessor could, under what he deemed extraordinary circumstances, relieve a commander. Both men knew they danced around a fire pit. Akuyun knew Hizer could remove him from command, and Hizer knew how respected Akuyun was among all the men. Would Hizer act against Akuyun? Would Akuyun arrange a fatal accident before Hizer could publicly remove Akuyun? Hizer could, theoretically, rule that the High Command was not fully aware of the situation on Caedellium and could support Akuyun, though that itself would be a move with unpredictable consequences. So many unknowns.

CHAPTER 38

SKIN OF THEIR TEETH

Eywell Province, Thirty Miles from Keelan

Denes Vegga's serious worry began when Kildorn's rear scouts reported in.

"It's a large Narthani force," said Kildorn. "My men say they're five miles behind our last company. Before they were chased away, they confirmed at least a battalion of cavalry and cannon, and more dust rising behind the units they could see."

"I think we have to assume a Narthani force at least the size of our own," said Denes. "Our problem is, they aren't shepherding three hundred slaves.

"Major Sixwith, send two more riders to the support camp. Tell them to kill the horses, if they have to, but get to the camp fast as they can. Warn them we're being pursued by a significant Narthani force and will push our horses to the maximum."

"Do you expect them to send help out from the support camp position?" asked Major Kildorn.

"No," said Denes, who then turned back to Sixwith. "Your riders should say I'm not asking anyone from the support camp to move forward, only advising them of the situation. While I'm sure they're alert, we don't know that other Narthani or Eywellese aren't headed this way. The camp needs to be ready for whatever happens. Tell them that, at this pace, we'll be three or four hours behind the riders."

Gulf of Witlow

"That was an unpleasant surprise," Brigadier Zulfa remarked.

He stood beside Admiral Kalcan, who had returned to the aftcastle of

Kalcan's flagship. The two men had been hailed by one of the cutters picketed to intercept the squadron returning from Swavebroke.

"Yes," Kalcan said, "I'm afraid Okan's gut feeling about our actions may have been too prescient, and we might regret our arguments that convinced him. He must be right that the clans had plans in place to respond to our actions. This will almost certainly restrict us from any further land action against the clans. I can still harass them from the sea, but you won't be able to pull enough men away from defensive postures to carry out major actions, as we did at Swavebroke."

"We can still salvage all this," argued Zulfa, "if we can land behind the islanders who reached Ponth. We destroy this group, the clans might not try the same tactic again."

"I wouldn't be optimistic, Aivacs. We're two hours from where I'll anchor the ships. We'll still have to get the men and cannons ashore. You'll be completely on foot, since we didn't bring any horses back with us."

"All we have to do is set up a blocking position to delay them. Ketin is hot on the trail, and Akuyun wrote that a small Narthani and Eywellese force is racing to get into a flanking position. We can serve as an anvil, with the other two forces hammering the islanders."

Support Base, Eywell Province

"Well, fuck!" Yozef exclaimed in English, after hearing the rider's message from Denes. Mulron Luwis didn't need to have the words translated, because he was busy expressing similar sentiments in Caedelli.

"You said there were two riders sent," Luwis said, addressing the messenger. "Where's the other one?"

"When we were about halfway, we decided we risked both horses giving out, so we drew sticks and I won. I took both horses and, about ten miles back, turned loose the one I was riding and continued on with the second horse. The other rider is on the road, waiting to be picked up."

Luwis groaned. "Why the damnation did they take along three hundred slaves?"

Yozef put a hand on Luwis's shoulder. "We weren't there, Mulron. I assume the men found them and couldn't bring themselves to leave them as slaves, not when they had a chance to transport them back."

Understanding is not the same as approving, Yozef thought to himself. *Denes succumbed to a classic leader fault by letting emotions decide, instead of logic.*

Not that he blamed Denes. Yozef was honest enough to admit that in the same situation, he might have done the same. He couldn't bring himself to cast aspersions when he himself might have been guilty of an emotional decision. For two days, he'd castigated himself for sending Balwis off to kill the Narthani colonel in Hanslow. In retrospect, he couldn't be sure that pure anger and thirst for revenge at the attack on his home and family hadn't made him too eager to send Balwis and the others. He felt even worse when he learned that Wyfor had gone with Balwis, despite having just lost two fingers.

"The only relevant question now is not why Denes did what he did, but what should *we* do?" said Yozef. "How are they transporting the slaves?"

"Mainly in wagons from the slave camp or from farms," the messenger replied. "Most are overloaded for the number of horses pulling them, and I wouldn't be surprised if some haven't broken down. The rest are riding double with our men."

"We can't leave this position," said Mulron. "We're dug in here, and it's too good a defensive position."

"Maybe we can send wagons and horses forward to meet Denes," Yozef suggested. "We don't need the wagons we brought. We can dump everything out of them. If the rider is right, our wagons can hold more people, and we have full teams, so the weight of the load won't be a factor."

Mulron put his lower lip between his teeth, while he chewed over Yozef's proposal.

"What about men?" Yozef asked. "We can't just send wagons and drivers. They'll need enough escorts, in case they run into Eywellese."

Luwis scowled. "I hate reducing our strength here, but you're right. The wagons can't go naked. What do you think—one company?"

"I'd rather send two companies," Yozef said, "but I've got a bad feeling the Narthani coming after Denes aren't the only ones we have to worry about. I think we need to send pickets farther north and to our rear, just in case. Maybe a company's worth, to be sure nothing slips by them. That leaves us two companies short here, so I think one company is all we can risk sending with the wagons. We should also send a rider to Denes to alert him that the wagons are coming. It might change how hard he pushes the ones he's got."

Ketin

"Colonel," said a young lieutenant with the company leading the column, "a forward scout just reported. They've made contact with the islanders. They're only three miles ahead of us."

"They may be only three miles away, but they're also only fifteen miles from leaving this flat terrain and getting into broken hills, where we wouldn't be able to envelop them. Not only that, I remember some rock and boulder fields a few miles before that. That'll make it harder to get around them. At that point, to stop them from reaching Keelan, we'd have to go straight at them, and only a fraction of them could defend some position, while the rest escaped. Lieutenant, get back to your unit and tell the captain to push his horses and make contact with the islanders. Do whatever he can to force them to stop and fight. I'll bring up the rest of our men as fast as I can."

Ketin spun to his staff. "Now that we know exactly how far off they are, we need to pick up the pace. We still have two battalions of infantry too far back. Get the drivers to whip the horses continuously, if necessary. It's going to be tight. If Zulfa can block the road and force them to try to bypass him, we'll have them. Otherwise, we'll need to force them to stop and fight, before they get off this flat land."

"What about the Eywellese coming from the north?" asked a captain.

"Last word was they should reach the raiding party in the next hour," said Ketin's aide-de-camp.

Denes

"Get those people into the new wagons!" Denes shouted. "Don't ask them to move or offer to help, carry or throw them, if you have to! The damned Narthani are only two miles behind us!"

Denes's mind went over Yozef Kolsko's summary of tactical points and leadership issues. The one element he focused on was the necessity for a leader to think calmly and rationally. They were in trouble. Maybe they could make it to Mulron Luwis's position and the prepared defenses and maybe not.

He watched while the rest of the ex-slaves were moved to the larger wagons with bigger horse teams.

If I were Yozef, what would I be thinking? he wondered. *I need to think of how to stop the Narthani from attacking our rear without slowing us down. Think. Think! What are our advantages?*

A platoon of dragoons rode past where they stood.

Horses! We're all mounted. The Narthani don't have that many cavalry, so either we might outnumber them or they're bringing up infantry, maybe in wagons. They must have artillery, but with both artillery and infantry, it takes time to deploy. If we can force them to stop and bring up artillery and infantry, then they have to slow down.

"Kildorn, Sixwith, here's what we'll do. Kildorn, take ten of the 6-pounders and set them up about a mile farther from here. As soon as the Narthani get within range, start with solid shot and then switch to grapeshot as they get closer. Put two companies of dragoons to each flank to keep the Narthani from getting around you easily. To force your position, they'll have to deploy enough men and cannon to take you on. Before that happens, pull out. It'll take them time to reassemble and come on after us."

"That'll give them the chance to get cavalry around us," Sixwith warned.

Denes rubbed a hand over his shaven head. "So far, the scouts report cavalry, though not large formations. We'll have to risk that we have enough mounted men to keep any Narthani cavalry at bay, while our artillery forces them to deploy their own cannon and infantry. Sixwith, move your battalion another mile farther than Kildorn and set up the same as Kildorn does. The two of you will take turns setting up new blocking positions, while the other slows the Narthani. We only have to do it a few times to get the wagons to the camp."

Denes left the men to do their work and pulled Major Kildorn aside. "Kildorn, it's going to be a close call. We're still eight miles from the camp. If they catch us, at best it'll be a bloody fight to the camp. At worst, we'll have to leave the slaves and save as many of ourselves as possible."

Kildorn's face clouded over, his jaw clenched. "We can't just leave them. We don't know how many Narthani are following. If they catch us, we could still beat them off."

"That's not an option," Denes stated firmly. "We don't know exactly how many are chasing us. Neither do we know what other forces might try to cut us off, either from the north or landed from ships. We have specific orders not to engage in pitched battles. The purpose of the raid was to throw a scare into the Eywellese and Narthani. We've done that, but for everything to be successful, we have to get back relatively unscathed."

"You're right, I know," said Kildorn, his face taking on a desperate set.

Kildorn looked around to see if anyone was within hearing distance.

"Denes," he said, switching to first names, "if it comes to that, I'll take a company and delay the Narthani as long as possible. Hopefully, that will give you enough time to get the rest to safety."

Denes's throat clenched. He swallowed. "Raley, I hate to ask it, but I was going to, if you hadn't offered."

"That's okay, Denes. I remember Kolsko's summary, too. Better to save most than none. If it does come to that, I want you to know it's been an honor to be on this ride, and I hope I served you well."

"The honor is all mine, Raley. We may not get a chance to speak again, things may move so fast. I'll leave it up to you to do what you think is necessary."

Yozef

He stood on top of a higher butte, a hundred feet above the pass. He wore a pair of fox ears on his head. The leather, ear-shaped, foot-wide cups sat over his ears, connected by a strap that held the apparatus on his head. He'd had them made months ago and brought them along on a hunch. They were one of the sporadic ideas that had cropped into his head. He'd been inspired by the memory of seeing an enclosure of African fennec foxes at the San Diego zoo when he was nine years old. The little animal's enormous ears, for its size, made the creature look cartoonish, but visitors to the zoo could put their heads between a fennec ears mock-up and experience dramatically improved hearing, to the delight of his nine-year-old self. It was as if his own ears had connected to an amplifier. The sign next to the fennec enclosure said the little fox could hear prey moving underground.

The first time he'd tried the ears in Caernford, he had garnered odd looks, until witnesses recognized him. Almost anything he did was accepted by now as probably something important, even if it looked as bizarre as a grown man wearing a pair of giant ears.

Standing on the edge of the butte, he held on the fennec ears being assailed by the wind. He could just make out what had to be musket fire. Most of the sounds came from due west, but he also thought occasionally from the northwest.

He jerked the ears off his head and raced to a chute that led to the loose gravel of the butte's lower slope. There, he jumped out, landed on the loose rock, and let himself slide several yards before he slowed. Then he jumped again. It took nineteen seconds to descend the hundred feet, and he arrived, miraculously, in one piece with nothing broken.

"Mulron!" he yelled, running to the command tent. "I can hear them. Firing. Muskets. Can't be more than three miles away."

"That close?" questioned Luwis. "We should have heard it from here."

"It's these hills and broken terrain. The sound probably passes over."

Luwis looked west. He couldn't hear anything, but if Yozef were right . . .

"I can't risk taking too many men from this position, but the 12-pounders aren't best used here because the hills restrict the firing lanes. A mile, mile and a half west is a boulder field where the flat land begins. The 12-pounders would have clear firing lanes and might outgun anything the Narthani cavalry brought with them. I can take the 12-pounders and one company. If we hurry, I can set up in time to support Denes, if he gets that far. It's the best I can see to help."

Oh, shit, thought Yozef. *Why does this always seem to happen to me at these times?*

"*You* can't go, Mulron. You're in command here, and we can't afford any command confusion. It'll have to be me who takes the cannon forward. Anyway, I'm most familiar with them, so I'm the logical person."

Ketin

Musket fire came in clusters. A dozen, a score, a hundred shots were heard in rapid succession. They trailed off to nothing for minutes, before beginning again. Ketin couldn't see the action, but it wasn't more than a half a mile away.

A captain galloped from the direction of the firing and reined in his horse near Ketin's mount, which jumped aside.

"Major Torvik's compliments, Colonel. He says they haven't been able to close with the islanders. It's the same as they've been doing the past few hours. They deploy their 6-pounders if we get too close and pull them out before our own cannon can get forward. We tried again to send a cavalry company around them, but their horsemen outnumber us. We're out of the sand and clay terrain and into broken gravel and rocks. The horses have a harder time trying to flank the islanders before they pull out again. Major Torvik says unless the footing gets better or we can get our cannon deployed faster, the only way he sees overtaking them is a straight-out charge and absorbing the resulting casualties."

Ketin used the time to settle his horse to consider the captain's news. The prospects weren't good. "No, Captain, we can't go trading one-for-one with the islanders. They outnumber us, and we'd run out of men before they would.

Tell Major Torvik to do the best he can to break through their rear guard. Also, tell him that the Eywellese are supposed to have already hit the islanders' flank. If it's going to happen, it must be soon. That might provide enough of a distraction and diversion of their men that you can break through."

"Yes, Colonel. The major was wondering if we'd heard any news about Brigadier Zulfa?"

"Nothing yet. They should arrive any moment." Ketin didn't mention he'd been expecting Zulfa and his men to have blocked the islanders at "any moment" for the last two hours.

Zulfa

"I don't think you're going to make it, Aivacs," said Kalcan, watching the first two troop ships lowering longboats to row infantry ashore. The road lay only two miles from the beach. Pickets reported musket and cannon fire to the northwest.

"You're probably right, but we need to try. I wish we could also get the cannon to shore faster."

"The only way would be to beach the transport carrying the cannon, hack a hole in the side, and pull the cannon out onto the beach. We can patch the ship later and tow it off the beach. I'm willing to give the order, if you think you'd have a good chance to trap the islanders."

Zulfa's head swiveled to look at Kalcan. "Beach one of your ships? I thought all you naval types were in love with the things, even lumbering ones like troop ships?"

The admiral's eyes twinkled. "I didn't say I was giving one up, only temporarily stationing it on shore. I have enough carpenters on the other ships that we can get the hole plugged in hours. I checked our charts and tide records. The beaching would be before low tide, so when the hole is repaired enough, we'd pull her off at high tide."

Zulfa considered the idea for only a few seconds. "Let's do it, Morfred. There's no worry about getting the cannon back aboard. We'll let Ketin take them when he gets to us."

Denes

Sixwith reined in next to Denes and Kildorn. "My company to the north continues to skirmish with the riders coming south. Lots of them, hundreds. I'll send another company of dragoons to slow them more. They don't seem all that eager to attack, so I think we can hold them off long enough to get to the camp."

Denes cursed. "Must be Eywellese. As far as we know, there's no Narthani stationed this far south in Eywell, and I doubt they could have come from Preddi. How far off?"

"They're coming overland—no roads," said Sixwith. "There are enough gullies and rock fields that I think we can slow them down for thirty or forty minutes, no matter how many there are."

"How fortunate for us, then," said Denes. "We'll be at the support camp before they get here."

"How can you be sure about that?"

"Because we *have* to," replied Denes.

"So far, Kildorn and I have been able to slow them enough," said Sixwith, "but it's getting dicier. Either from practice or by changing procedures, they're getting their artillery into play faster each time."

"Maybe it's that time," said Kildorn, referring to his offer to take a company and delay the Narthani as long as possible.

"Thanks, Raley, but I think we're going to make it without going to that extreme."

Yozef

They set up the four 12-pounders thirty yards off the road, two cannon north and two south of the road. From their position, they had a small elevation advantage of the road west. Yozef dealt with the cannon, while the company commander deployed most of his men frantically digging and piling rocks, to provide minimal protection. They rolled some, because they were too heavy to lift. Ten men kept the horses in a draw out of shot exposure, and five men were sent as pickets north and south to warn of flanking attempts.

Sounds of sporadic musket and 6-pounder firings came closer by the minute. Eighty men were still digging when the first of Denes's dragoons—two companies, Yozef estimated—came racing down the road. They passed without slowing, waving in relief and greeted with cheers by the men Yozef had brought forward.

Following the last dragoons were wagons careening down the road, first visible five hundred yards away, each wagon filled with people hanging on. Harried drivers so intently urged their horses on that they didn't notice the makeshift entrenchments until almost on top of the cannon and the company.

The driver of the first wagon started to rein in, in panic, until he recognized clansmen, then he lashed the horses. The wagon's occupants only stared, as they flashed past Yozef, their fear palpable, though he didn't know whether it was from the Narthani or the wagon ride. Yozef shook his head. Denes was the man on the spot, and slowing down to rescue these people had been a risk. Yozef was glad he hadn't been the one making the decision.

The last two wagons carried wounded clansmen. Yozef estimated no more than twelve.

I hope that means not many dead. I don't believe Denes would have left wounded behind.

More mounted clansmen rode past—two companies, by Yozef's estimate. He stood on a mound and saw the first signs of fighting, smoke from muskets and 6-pounders. Then horses, he thought, and maybe men, but he couldn't make out what they were doing.

Damn, I left my telescope back at the support camp.

Finally, he saw a cluster of men galloping in his direction. One rider carried the green Caedellium flag he'd designed. Another carried a banner. Denes's command flag! Relief washed over Yozef. Denes was okay, and they would reach safety.

When Denes made it to their position, Yozef and the company commander stood off the road, waiting. Denes pulled up, took one look at Yozef, and started to say something, then closed his mouth and jumped off his horse.

I bet he was about to say, "What the fuck are you doing here!"

Denes didn't waste time. "I'll set up two companies and half of my 6-pounders on the next rise." He pointed to the small hill that the road disappeared over, about three hundred yards away. "They won't be able to see if we've got another position farther from here, until they get to the top after we withdraw. As soon as we're ready, you pull out and get back to the camp."

Yozef noted that Denes hadn't ordered him back to the support camp.

Orders about me staying out of action or not, Denes deals with the moment, and at this moment I'm manning the 12-pounders.

The company commander ran off, yelling orders to his men and sending runners to pull in the pickets and several men to those holding the horses.

"I see many of your men are riding double," said Yozef.

"We didn't have any standup fights, but it's been long-distance sniping and occasional probes by their lead units at our blocking positions. We lose a few horses every time we withdraw the blocking companies. Horses are too big of targets not to hit a few. Fortunately, not many men have been hit. The 6-pounders kept the Narthani cautious. Only once did they manage to bring up their cannon before we pulled back, which was fortunate, since their cannon seemed to outrange our 6-pounders. I couldn't see details, but by telescope I got the impression they were somewhere between our 6- and 12-pounders. That one time we lost a cannon, several limbers, and five dead before we got out of range."

Damn. The Narthani didn't have anything like that at Moreland City. We're casting our own, and certainly they know the craft better than we do, so it's hardly a surprise if they're putting out new cannon. We can't assume we'll always outgun them if they make something bigger, especially for fixed defenses. Damn.

"I'll finish seeing the next position set up," said Denes, "then I'll be back here to see this position withdraw, and *you* will get your ass back to the base camp."

I guess he didn't forget his orders after all.

Yozef didn't argue, being relieved and chagrined at the same time.

Forty minutes later, Denes joined the last men to withdraw into the support camp's position between buttes. Mulron Luwis had already sent the wagons with rescued slaves and the wounded on to Keelan, accompanied by four companies of worn-out dragoons.

"There's not enough room here for all the men to be useful," Luwis said to Denes. "I think we can start another three or four companies back, but I wanted to check with you first."

Denes perused the position. The 12-pounders Yozef had moved forward were being wheeled back into their original dug-in positions. Digging had gone on since the support force arrived, and by now an impressive layout of trenches would allow every musketman to stand upright to reload, then use a step in the trench to fire. They had positioned Denes's 6-pounders fifty yards to the rear and on higher ground.

Yozef noticed the object of Denes's gaze. "The 6-pounders are a backup, in the unlikely case the Narthani attack our position and break through. They can also be seen from where the Narthani would come at us, which should help discourage them."

"Here they come!" shouted a voice, and every man turned to look west. A triple line of infantry fanned out across the four hundred yards of the flat plain alongside the road. More men appeared on the smaller buttes on both sides. Yozef could see cannon being pulled forward and crews detaching them from limbers and wheeling them to face the islanders. The infantry line moved fifty yards, then stopped and knelt. Behind them came a score or more of cavalry and then a group of men, one of whom carried a large red flag and other men held banners.

Denes, Luwis, and Yozef all used telescopes to scrutinize the Narthani.

"They're not coming on," said Luwis. "Yet anyway."

"I recognize one of the banners," Denes said. "We saw it several times since sunrise. What's the other one? That's a new one."

Luwis turned and spoke to a man standing behind him. The man ran off.

"Denes, one of the slaves you brought back wouldn't leave. He seems to be something of a leader and insisted he stay, in case he could do anything to help kill Narthani. Half a dozen men joined him, and I have them carrying water to our people. I've sent for him. Maybe he recognizes the banners."

"What are they doing, just sitting there?" Denes said, more to himself than asking for answers, then his voice changed. "Are you *sure* there's no way to get around behind us?"

"Not quickly," said Luwis. "Their infantry could eventually work their way to our rear, but it would take a good part of a day. We don't plan to be here any longer than necessary. I think we're all secure now. Even if they follow us as we pull out, there's no way to get ahead of us."

"Here we go," said Luwis, as the man he'd sent off returned with a scrawny middle-aged man with fire in his eyes.

"Lonwyn, we're seeing Narthani banners. I think one is for whoever is leading the pursuit. A second one showed up that I haven't seen before. Would you recognize them?" Luwis handed over his telescope.

"I worked on the docks for a year, before they sent me outside Ponth to be a farm slave. I probably saw most of the banners of the top Narthani." Lonwyn put the eyepiece to his right eye and closed the left eye. "The big red flag tells you they're Narthani. Blood red with two crossed swords. One of them is supposed to be the traditional weapon where they came from, the other one what they currently use. Then there are personal banners for the most senior officers. Yeah. The one on the right is for Colonel Ketin. I think his first name is Erkin. He's the commander of the Narthani soldiers in Preddi Province and some kind of engineer. I've heard from slaves coming from Preddi City the last few months that there's been a frenzy of construction going on. Trenches and fortifications.

"Uh . . . I can't make out the other banner. The wind's got it coiled around the staff. Wait . . . the man holding it is untangling it. There. It's waving. I . . . well, what do you know? It's Zulfa's banner."

"Zulfa?" queried Denes.

"Brigadier Aivacs Zulfa. He's the top army commander. General Akuyun is also army, but he's in overall charge of all Narthani, military, and civilians. Zulfa is the officer who directly commands the army on Caedellium."

"That's odd," said Yozef. "I can see this Ketin being on the scene, if he were dispatched from Preddi to deal with us, but his commander showing up only later? Unless . . . oh, hell! I'll bet he showed up by ship and brought a shitload more soldiers with him."

"Could they have put that much together so fast?" asked Luwis. "They could only have gotten word of what we were doing a couple of days ago. In that time, they gathered men, got them on ships, and tried to block our way back?"

"Possibly," said Yozef. "Remember, this is a professional army. However, there's another possibility. If this Zulfa led the Swavebroke attack, it could be they were returning or had already returned to Preddi City and got diverted toward us."

Denes spat to one side. "That doesn't make me feel too good. That would mean we'd missed being trapped between two forces by maybe an hour. Perhaps minutes."

"Whatever happened, we're safe now from direct attacks. They can't get around us anymore before we reach Dornfeld," said Yozef. "It wouldn't surprise me if the general pursuit is over, and they just tail us to be sure we leave Eywell territory."

Ketin and Zulfa

"Look at the bastards, Erkan. That bunch under the green flag. Standing there looking at us through their telescopes."

"As you are doing to them, Aivacs," said the older man. "If I was them, I'd be taking a break after being pushed so hard these last fifty, sixty miles. And why not rest? They must know they've gotten away from us. There's no way we can force the position they're in, not with no room to maneuver and how it looks like they're dug in. We have to accept they're going to get away with the raid."

Zulfa glared at Ketin, who returned his look calmly.

"Oh, all right, Erkan. I know you're right. I'm just irked that we missed them. Kalcan's not going to be pleased either. He offered, and I accepted, that he beach the transport ship carrying our cannon. He had his men cut a hole in the side to get the cannon out. They should be halfway here, with men on foot pulling them with ropes and manually turning the spokes. First, it was through a couple hundred yards of sand, then over this damned rocky ground. Now I have to tell the men it was all for nothing."

"And tell them to turn around and take the cannon back to shore to . . . what? Put them on another ship?"

"No. Kalcan says they'll have the hole repaired and tow the transport off the beach at high tide. You'll take the cannon by road back to Preddi City."

"Which I suppose I should start my staff organizing. All right, we'll take your cannon. There's no rush now. I'll have two cavalry companies shadow the islanders and be sure they leave Eywell territory, unless you think there's still a chance to make them stand and fight where we can maneuver?"

"No. No chance that I see. Your two companies are more than enough to keep eyes on them. Let's head back to Preddi."

CHAPTER 39

NO TRUCE

Kolsko Estate, Caernford

After the last sixday, the trip back to Keelan seemed leisurely once the clansmen confirmed the Narthani had quit the pursuit. Scouts reported that the main Narthani force had headed back to Preddi, leaving a few cavalry to follow the islanders' withdrawal. The scouts also reported that five miles back west, a Narthani naval squadron reboarded a thousand or more troops amid a flurry of activity, as two frigates prepared to pull a beached transport back to sea.

Traveling the hundred miles back to Caernford took six days. Two days to reach Dornfeld on the Keelan/Gwillamer border, taking it easy on the horses and encamping in a defensible position just within Eywell territory, a day to rest at Dornfeld, then three days at a moderate pace back to Caernford.

Yozef rode most of the way on Mr. Ed. The moderate pace let him take his mind off events by concentrating in his horsemanship. Mr. Ed was younger than Seabiscuit but had a similar sedate manner. By the fourth day, Yozef forgot to concentrate on staying on his horse, as it became more natural.

He felt a strange unease develop, as he got nearer Caernford. By "home," he still thought of their house in Abersford. The new house in Caernford was now scarred by associations with the night of the attack. He thought of the hole in Aeneas's nightshirt, a few inches' difference and . . . he tried to shut out the memory. Anid was dead. Norlin and Mirramel, dead. Ceinwyn with the horrible wound to her face. Culich, losing the lower part of a leg. Yozef thought of the men he had killed, windows broken, doors smashed, holes in walls, attackers' bodies, blood everywhere. His own bloodlust. Could he ever get those images out of his mind?

And himself? For the first time, he had killed other humans. He knew he *should* agonize over what he had done, no matter whether the men deserved their deaths. He *should* hope he never had to kill again. He *should* feel guilt. He should . . .

Instead, he only wished he could kill them again.

They arrived in Caernford in late afternoon. A gray overcast sky and an intermittent drizzle too closely matched Yozef's mood. He only half paid attention, as words were spoken and men peeled off the column. He later remembered saying something to Denes about the next day, then rode alone the few miles to the house. Yozef hesitated as he passed Keelan Manor, seeing horses tied to the front rail and a one-horse carriage under a tree. He *should* see how Culich was doing. Were Maera and Aeneas staying with her family? Despite images he couldn't avoid, he needed to see their house.

He came to the turnoff to their drive, and his throat tightened. His heart seemed to beat faster and harder, and his hands felt cold.

The house stood empty, with no horses or carriages in front. No sounds came from within, as he climbed the stairs onto the veranda. A gap took the place of the front door, although someone had repaired the part of the jamb damaged when the shotgun blast took out the lock. He walked into the foyer. Bodies, splintered wood, and bloodstains were all gone. Sections of the flooring had been replaced.

Probably where bloodstains couldn't be completely removed.

He wandered through the rest of the house. It was the same everywhere—repairs in progress. He'd missed the workers, who had already left work for the day. *Despite what happened, Maera started cleaning up and getting repairs done almost immediately. I suppose it was a way to take her mind off what happened.*

The thought of Maera's sister brought regret that he hadn't been here for Maera. The regret mingled with sadness at Anid's death, renewed cold anger at the Narthani, an emerging sense of urgency to do something permanent to cleanse Caedellium of the invaders, and a sudden yearning to see and hold his wife.

He walked Mr. Ed back to Keelan Manor, conflicted by the need for Maera and reluctance to once again be "Yozef Kolsko." Someone must have seen him pass by the first time, for when he came to the manor drive, Maera was sitting on the veranda, holding Aeneas. His pace quickened enough for Mr. Ed to shy to one side, not knowing whether Yozef wanted him to move into a trot.

Maera descended the stairs. He dropped the reins, and they embraced, his arms around her, one of her arms around him, the other arm holding Aeneas between them.

They wandered away from the house and sat on a bench within a grove of trees. Maera told him about Anid's funeral, how hard it had been, how Culich broke down and wept from the bed he'd been carried on into St. Tomo's Cathedral for the service, how Ceinwyn cried, mewing through the bandage on her face, how the cathedral had been packed and overflowed outside, how no one had anticipated the way Anid had so much been another symbol of the Keelan family, and how the firestorm of anger against the Narthani burned fiercely throughout the clan.

When Yozef asked Maera how *she* was doing, she cried in his arms, sobbing so hard he wondered if this was the first time she had let herself go totally into her grief. She subsided when Aeneas made his desire to feed known by nuzzling a breast through her dress. She wiped her eyes with her sleeve, slid a shoulder free of the dress, and guided Aeneas to her nipple. He latched on quickly.

"Life goes on, Yozef. Anid is gone, yes. Aeneas is still here. I sometimes envy the little dear for not knowing what happens around him. Even during the attack, I can only remember him looking around as if wondering what all the commotion was about."

Maera glanced down at Aeneas, then back to her husband, her face sad more than grief-stricken. "Yozef, when we have a daughter, could we name her Anid?"

"Of course. It's a beautiful name, and I'm sure her namesake would have been pleased."

The first stars shone when they walked back to the manor. For the first time, Yozef noticed guards whom his distracted mind had ignored when he'd first passed. Two guards stood at the entrance to the drive and three at the front of the manor.

"There are four more in the back, and you'll notice weapons left more in the open within the manor than before. It's a different life now than we had before, and I know I'll come to hate it. For now, it's comforting, or as much as anything can bring comfort."

Mared met them at the door and jumped to hug Yozef in a fierce, quiet embrace.

"The meal is waiting," Mared said. "We didn't want to disturb you."

The manor dining room held a surprise. Instead of only the Keelan family, as Yozef had assumed it would be, with family members spread out at the large table, the table was crowded. The first person he noticed was Carnigan, naturally since he was the largest object at the table. Yozef quickly surveyed the others seated. Only Serys, their cook, was missing. Otherwise present was everyone who had been at their house the night of the attack. All of those still living. Culich and Breda, Mared and Ceinwyn, Balwis, Wyfor and Teena Kales, Anarynd holding Dwyna, dead Mirramel's daughter, Gwyned, holding Morwena.

Yozef felt relieved to see that Balwis and Wyfor had survived his rash idea to send them after Erdelin. Assuming they had turned back, he knew he would hear details later.

"Serys is visiting family," said Maera, as if reading his mind. "So many people wanted to hear what happened on the raid, we decided to have everyone from that night here for evening meal. Father and Balwis wanted to talk with you after we eat. It's also a little strange, but we all seem drawn to one another more than before. Maybe it was the shared experience . . . horror of that evening. I don't know."

Yozef sat with Maera on his right, Culich on his left. He glimpsed the hetman's bandaged stump. Culich appeared pale and winced every time he shifted his body.

The first question, from Carnigan, was about the raid, but Culich deferred such questions until they finished the main meal. While he ate, Yozef stole glances at the other diners: Wyfor, with his bandaged hand, Ceinwyn sipping broth with a crude straw, so she didn't have to work her jaw; the three babies; Breda with deeper lines and, Yozef could have sworn, a few more gray hairs; Carnigan, eyeing him back. For the next hour, their inconsequential conversation soothed, until it died out toward the end of the meal, there being only so many times the recent and future weather could divert their attention.

Finally, Culich said, "All right, Yozef. Give us all a summary of how the raid went."

And so Yozef did, eliciting grunts of satisfaction when he recounted how Denes's men had burned their way across southern Eywell Province and over the border around the Preddi city of Ponth. Then, concern followed by relief about news of the withdrawal and Denes's close call with the Narthani. A sharp look and a sigh of frustration came from Maera, as Yozef described the only part of the raid he had taken an active part in, moving a company and a battery of 12-pounders forward to provide Denes with a support position should the Narthani press him too hard. He assumed he'd hear more about this later from Maera and Culich.

People asked questions as he talked, and as he went over the return trip, Breda and Mared helped Ceinwyn return to her bedroom. Anarynd and Gwyned took the three children elsewhere in the manor.

Culich pulled Breda's chair closer and rested his three-quarter leg on a cushion that had lain by his chair. "Balwis, there's a bottle of Yozef's amaretto over there on the counter. Please bring it here, along with some glasses. I'm not normally for stronger alcohol, but somehow it seems appropriate."

Balwis complied, and when they all held small glasses filled with the amber liquid, Culich raised his glass. "To those missing."

They all drank.

"Death to the Narthani," Balwis said in a grating tone.

All glasses emptied, then were slammed to the tabletop. Maera rose and filled every glass again, then sat. She looked at Yozef, something in her eyes. A connection sparked between them.

Yozef raised his now refilled glass. "Despite all that's happened, we can't forget the good." He raised his glass even higher. "TO LIFE!" he pronounced.

After a second of silence, everyone present uttered the same pronouncement, and a subtle shift occurred in the mood of the table.

Yozef set his glass down. "I've told you about Denes's raid. What about the one in the north, and what about Erdelin?" As he said the last words, he glanced at Maera. He hadn't been here for her reaction when she learned he had roped Anarynd into recounting all she remembered of Hanslow and Erdelin's residence. Maera looked back serenely.

"The raid in the north didn't go as well," said Culich, "although I think it succeeded in the objectives. Certainly, the raids in both the north and the south make the Narthani know Eywell is vulnerable, and losing Erdelin has to have shaken their confidence."

Yozef jolted up and looked at Balwis. "You got him!?"

Balwis nodded. "I'd just as soon not try the same thing again, but yes, we got him. Me, Wyfor, and the other three men, only one of whom we lost. Wyfor had the honor, and I doubt we would have succeeded if he hadn't been along."

Kales waved off the compliment. "We might not have succeeded if *any* of us hadn't been there."

Carnigan snorted. "The two of them have been in a love-fest ever since they got back. If Wyfor wasn't already married and Balwis wasn't so disagreeable, I'd wonder when the wedding announcement would come."

The ensuing laughter washed over the table as a stream of water rinses away dust, perhaps not cleaning a surface, but at least revealing what had been hidden.

"The northern raid, Culich? You said it didn't go as well."

"We'll need more details from Hetman Stent, but on the second day, the Narthani sallied out from Hanslow. Stent had divided his force to cover more ground and raze more villages surrounding the city. The Narthani surprised three companies north of Hanslow. The companies weren't of mixed clansmen, as with Denes's regiment. These were Stent, Moreland, and Orosz companies. Welman reports they were working their way free of the Narthani when the Moreland company abandoned their position in the withdrawal. Both the Stent and Orosz companies found themselves isolated, and both lost half their men before escaping.

"Naturally, Welman was furious at the Moreland company commander, and we'll see that he is never again put in a command position. However, Welman also thinks they were surprised by how fast the officer taking Erdelin's place reacted. We thought the Narthani would be hesitant to act after the assassination, but whoever this new person is, he showed far too much initiative."

Well, shit, Yozef thought. *I hope in our . . . my . . . wish for revenge or teaching the Narthani a lesson, whichever it was, that we didn't end up with a more competent officer taking Erdelin's place. That would* really *be a pisser.*

Culich raised an eyebrow at Yozef. "Stent's angry at himself for violating several of the principles in your *On War*. He believes his emotional desire to cause as much damage as possible led him to let his companies get too far apart, so they couldn't all support one another. I think your stature with him has gone up quite a bit, now that he saw what could happen when he didn't follow your advice.

"I suspect the same can be said for Denes Vegga. He sent several long reports ahead by riders. He thinks he has you to thank for *On War* and his talks with you helping him get his mind around these complex ways of fighting. He told me it was almost like having you with him, giving advice. Even when he took the Preddi slaves, he says he knew it violated several principles about staying focused on the objectives, but he also remembered that a leader has to use *On War* only for general principles and that it was up to the leader to make decisions for any given circumstance."

The return trip to Caernford had given Yozef ample time to think about the Narthani and his own roles. He recognized that the attack on the birthday party had changed him in ways he didn't fully understand, yet he *was* changed. What he was about to say, and he hoped to set in motion, was proof of a Yozef Kolsko he would not have recognized three years earlier.

"I would thank Denes and Hetman Stent for their opinions, but we have something more important to consider. The Narthani attack on Swavebroke has been devastating for that clan. Although most of the people are still alive, they've lost their main city and all the history and cultural artifacts it contained.

"The Narthani killed two hetmen and almost a third hetman here in Keelan. They must want to hold the clans in place. I don't believe the Narthani are satisfied to simply maintain control of Preddi and the other two provinces. They must know the clans are getting stronger. Our counterattacks into Eywell and over the Preddi border, along with killing one of their top commanders, had to have convinced them that their time might be running out.

"I cannot imagine any scenario where the current situation, what my people would call the 'status quo,' can last. We have to do something permanent about the Narthani. It's untenable to leave the situation as it is. Even if our responses inhibit the Narthani from future attacks, the clans would be under potential threat as long as the Narthani are on Caedellium. I've also become more convinced the Narthani might want Caedellium so much, they'll send more troops. The fact that they've settled so many of their noncombatants on Caedellium indicates how serious they are.

"Right now, we estimate there are eight to ten thousand Narthani soldiers on the island. What would happen if they send another twenty thousand? Forty thousand? There's nothing we could do to stop them from landing while they have Preddi Province as a safe base. However, if they didn't have the Preddi infrastructure, the harbor, farms and ranches, and a supporting population, any more troops would have a much more difficult time. So much so, that the Narthani might be forced to reconsider, even abandon, attempts to incorporate Caedellium into their empire."

"That's what you're going to propose, isn't it, Yozef?" asked Maera. "That the clans *must* eject the Narthani from Caedellium, before they have a chance to land more troops."

Yozef hadn't told Maera of his thinking, but she'd known him long enough and was bright enough to fill in the blanks.

"He's right, Father," she told Culich. "We have to settle with the Narthani, once and for all. No more reacting to what *they* do."

Culich shifted his leg, wincing until he found a more comfortable spot on the cushion. He smiled the smile of a predator, an expression that seemed appropriate for the agony he felt.

"It will be painful for the clans," Culich said. "Pain in the losses of life that will ensue. But I believe, for the first time, that the clans will finally unite in a campaign against the Narthani."

He turned to Yozef. "You may not have heard, but besides Hetman Skouks being killed by assassins, Hetman Swavebroke died with four hundred of his men, as they slowed the Narthani enough to let the people of Shullick escape inland. His son is the new hetman, and, from semaphore messages, it sounds like he'll be a fervent supporter of any effort to eliminate the Narthani.

"I wonder if the Narthani will ever realize what a mistake these attacks were? Swavebroke and Skouks were two of the clans least interested in making coordinated efforts against the Narthani. Bevans is also now a believer. Although their hetman survived, he and his clan are furious. Pawell was shocked by the Skouks attack, and even Nyvaks, who we suspect of colluding with the Narthani, now seems less likely to resist any coordination.

"I've been communicating with other hetmen, especially Orosz, Stent, and Farkesh. We're calling a mandatory All-Clan Conclave for one month from now."

Yozef groaned. "Another—"

Culich cut him off. "I know, I know. Another conclave, but this time I think we'll get real results. The formal topic will be a united and coordinated effort against the Narthani. What you need to do, Yozef, is work with Denes and Vortig on exactly what action is feasible. This needs to be done quickly, so I can have input and then discuss it with key hetmen before the conclave."

"I've already been thinking, Culich," said Yozef. "I have to warn you that what I'll propose will be on a scale that dwarfs anything we've done, or considered doing, before."

CHAPTER 40

THE CLANS UNITE

The Plan

For the next month, Yozef made time each day for Aeneas and personal time for him and Maera, except for those minutes when he focused on preparing for the conclave. They continued living at Keelan Manor, with the others from their house staying in guest cottages. A room in Keelan Manor was designated for half- to full-day meetings planning an attack on Preddi, the manor site chosen to let Culich avoid moving more than necessary. They assumed the clans would finally agree to unite and the conclave would approve the plan. There were issues of command structure that Yozef didn't have answers for, but he figured he had no control over that aspect, leaving it to Culich.

The meetings' participants varied. Yozef, Denes, and Vortig Luwis almost always attended, with Culich, Pedr Kennrick, and Mulron Luwis taking part, depending on the topic and status of specific aspects of the plan. Maera attended most meetings, as both scribe and participant, and Owill Brell, the Adrisian in charge of the MIU, became a regular contributor.

As Yozef had predicted, the scope of his ideas initially startled the others. It took a full sixday and hours of convincing before everyone agreed this was no time for half measures. Yozef had to justify each part of what he formulated, and they modified many details. However, the three central parts remained, and Yozef summarized them at the end of the first sixday of meetings.

He stood next to a blackboard, another of his introductions, and pointed to three bullet points.

"First, we have to cut out the two allied clans, Selfcell and Eywell. This will result in the Narthani pulling all their fighting men back into Preddi Province. We also can't leave potentially hostile forces in our rear when we go after Preddi City.

"We would send large dragoon and artillery units south southwest from Moreland Province to cut off Sellmor, the Selfcell capital, from Preddi Province. We have reason to believe the Selfcellese are not enthusiastic allies of the Narthani, so there's a good chance they'll capitulate without serious resistance, if they find themselves greatly outnumbered. It's also likely the Narthani will pull their own men back into Preddi, rather than risk them against a large clan force. Such a withdrawal will give Selfcell more reason to surrender without fighting.

"Eywell is more difficult to predict, since they've appeared more eager to be Narthani allies. However, they've lost enough men already, at the Battle of Moreland City, and had so much of their province razed by our two raids that they might not resist. We've gotten reports of more and more Eywellese crossing borders into neighboring provinces and asking for asylum. But as I said, the level of Eywellese resistance is hard to predict.

"Assuming we isolate Preddi Province, we'll pursue the next two objectives at the same time. We will amass forty thousand dragoons, all the cannon we can muster, and extensive logistics support on the Preddi border. The Narthani will want to concentrate civilians in Preddi City and the larger towns. Our forces will cut behind Preddi City, moving south and isolating the city from the rest of the province. This objective serves two purposes. It prevents the province from providing materiel and manpower support to the Narthani military, and tens of thousands of prisoners could serve during any negotiations.

"The third objective is to invest Preddi City. This means surround the city and dig fortifications, so the Narthani can't leave. We must be prepared for a long siege, months, possibly longer. They won't be able to bring in more food, but we assume they've stockpiled enough to last quite a while. We will also divert three streams that flow through the city, although there are wells, and they can try to dig more.

"After the only major Narthani forces left are behind Preddi City fortifications, we'll start digging trenches deep enough to get closer to their defenses, while providing protection from musket and cannon fire. We'll try to avoid a direct assault, but the trenches will let us get close enough to use the siege mortars I've described. The first ones are being planned for casting as we speak and should be testing in two sixdays. We're also renewing our efforts to work out fuses for shells. I believe it will be some time before we have contact explosive shells for cannon, but the mortars have lower shot velocities, and their short barrels give the option of manually lighting the fuses before firing. We also hope to work out lighting the fuse when the flame sweeps around the projectile. I'm optimistic we can figure it all out.

"Once the mortars are close enough, we'll start a continuous bombardment of the city. Even if the fuses are unreliable, enough should work that we'll slowly destroy the city and fortifications. As this happens, we'll look for opportunities to dig our trenches closer and closer to theirs. At some point, they'll be forced to pull back in a shrinking defensive line.

"I hope that well before the city is totally leveled and everyone inside is killed, the Narthani recognize the inevitable, and we can negotiate their leaving the island. I also fervently hope it doesn't come down to us having to storm even weakened defenses. While I understand the wish to crush them completely, we have to remember that the goal is for them to leave. The sooner they do, the fewer clansmen will be killed.

"Hetman Keelan and Vortig Luwis voiced concern that the Narthani might not sit behind walls during a siege and might sally against our entrenchments. It's possible, but they would take casualties in any such attacks on our defensive positions. I don't believe they have enough men to do this. They would have to use most of their men and cannon, which would leave the city vulnerable. Thirty thousand clansmen could hold off their army, while another ten thousand sack Preddi City, so I believe they'll be stuck in the city.

"They also must know they would face a much different foe than before. They would have to factor in that we have cannon and more experience. In a few months, we might outgun them, even if they're better at maneuvering."

"It all sounds so logical, Yozef," said Maera, pausing in her recording. "But it assumes a lot."

"These three objectives are only the 'strategic' goals, as Yozef terms them," said Culich. "The 'tactics,' or how we actually go about achieving those three objectives, will be worked out later."

"Even those will change with circumstances," said Denes. "The 'fog of war' is another of Yozef's favorite expressions, along with 'No plan survives the first shot.' Still, we have to start somewhere, and these three objectives will guide us."

Orosz City

This time the trip to Orosz City took four days. Culich's leg was healing, but it would be several more months before the medicants allowed him to try using a peg extension on his leg stump. A modified carriage made the trip as easy as possible for the hetman, and the driver took care to minimize jostling. Most of the rest of the Keelan delegation rode in a second carriage, with each man taking turns keeping Culich company and continuing discussions.

The All-Clan Conclave itself was almost anti-climactic. Culich had warned Yozef not to get his expectations too high, and that it might take many days of arguing and posturing before they made any major decisions. Yozef girded himself for a grueling time and multiple frustrations. Therefore, they were both caught by surprise when Hetman Orosz called the conclave to order and asked Culich for a statement. Culich was helped by Vortig Luwis and Denes Vegga to a chair on an elevated two-foot-tall platform facing the rest of the conclave, so everyone could see him clearly.

Culich only got to the sentence "I propose we commit here and now to eradicate the Narthani presence on Caedellium," before exultations drowned out his next words. He stopped, stunned, until Orosz let the clamor die and called the hetmen to order.

The destruction of the Swavebroke capital, Shullick, the attacks on three hetmen, the two raids now viewed as successes, and the killing of a Narthani colonel swept away any remaining resistance to the idea of making a unified effort against the Narthani. Enthusiasm tempered only slightly when Yozef presented the three-objective proposal devised in Caernford.

Not that there weren't questions, comments, and arguments, but they occurred over details, not the fundamental plan. Granted, those details took them the next three days to settle each point to the satisfaction of enough hetmen to move on to the next point, but settle they did.

At the conclusion, Yozef held out one qualm on the issue he knew would cause major problems—command. A majority of clans favored a single overall command structure, to be worked out later, but there were enough holdouts for each clan maintaining total control of their own men to block that part of Yozef's proposal.

The vote was twelve clans to six, short of the number required by conclave rules for a compulsory decision. Culich put a hand on Yozef's forearm, when he was about to object to the vote.

"Not now, Yozef," he whispered. "We've come further than I dared hope. Wait for what comes next."

Hetman Orosz then asserted that events might dictate the need to make decisions faster than they could achieve via conclaves. The Stent and Farkesh hetmen made strong statements in support. By a sixteen to two vote, it was approved that future votes could be held via semaphore, with the Seaborn clan's vote to be cast by their hetman's heir, a son who would reside in Pewitt Province and who would attempt to stay in monthly contact with his father on the Seaborn Islands off the Caedellium northwest coast.

"Now we only need to convince four clans to change their vote," whispered Culich. "Several are already wavering or need more time to think. Once things are in motion, some of the holdouts will recognize the necessity and not want to be considered obstructionists. I think best we don't get into too rancorous of discussions about your ideas of command, since some hetmen consider you a Keelander and already resent too much Keelan influence. Orosz, Stent, Farkesh, and I will continue working on the other hetmen."

Yozef sat back in his chair, nursing admiration for the connivance of his father-in-law with the other hetmen and hoping Culich was right in his assessment and that the clans had enough time.

The immediate action for all clans remained clear. Fighting men were to be organized into Yozef's unit hierarchy. The clans that wished to would train on developing mixed-clan units. Firearms, gunpowder, and cannon production would be ramped up where already in production and expanded to other provinces wherever practical. In Yozef's view, perhaps the most important action was that the hetmen charged him with expanding his proposed campaign plan against the Narthani. Although he had no formal authority, the charge came with the expectation that all clans would provide him with whatever assistance he required. Each hetman would review the plan, which reminded Yozef of the inability of the European Union on Earth to take almost any action, because one member could veto any decision. However, Culich's assurance that the four hetmen conspirators would work on getting those four additional votes left Yozef no option but to trust that they would work out a central command in the next four to five months, the target date to launch the all-out attack on Preddi Province.

Preddi City

"It should be soon," said Okan Akuyun.

He sat with his wife on a second-floor balcony of their villa, enjoying the evening and the breeze coming off the ocean. They often sat together like this, if dinner was still being prepared. The difference now, and for the last six days, was the increased number of guards since Memas Erdelin had been killed. Reports estimated that the assassins numbered fewer than ten, but because the Narthani strike teams had twenty members, Akuyun had ordered that all senior staff, from major on up, and Administrator Tuzere and Assessor Hizer maintain twenty guards at all times. It often made for more orchestrated movements, an unavoidable awkwardness.

"That's what you've been saying for the last month," said Rabia.

Akuyun smiled. "And it's just as true this time as all the others you so rudely reminded me of."

"I'd ask if you had any more clues about how the High Command will respond to your report," said Rabia, "if I thought you had any more idea than all the other times I've asked. I know you say I shouldn't worry, since there's nothing either of us can do about it—but, well, you know."

"Yes, dear. I know. This time I *really* believe it will be soon. If it's not soon, we might find ourselves in serious trouble."

"Do the others share your concern?" Rabia knew Okan listened to his subordinates, and she probed to know whether he had just divulged his view alone or the consensus opinion.

"Hizer does and, I think, Tuzere and Zulfa. The colonels and Kalcan are having a hard time getting around the idea that the clans are a serious threat to even Preddi City. The two raids surprised us. Either the clans didn't expect to do as much damage as they did, or, what I suspect, they did exactly what they intended—showed us they could do it and let it serve as a warning against further attacks by us on clan territory.

"Those two raids were only about a thousand men each, but I can't ignore the possibility it could have been ten thousand, which is something well within the clans' capabilities. With ten thousand, the northern attack might not have been a raid, but a serious attempt to destroy the fifteen-hundred-man garrison at Hanslow and neutralize the Eywell clan.

"The results of the southern raid could have been worse. With ten thousand men, they could have ravaged much of Preddi Province before we could stop them. Then, with their greater mobility, they could have avoided a battle and withdrawn to threaten a repeat any time they wanted. I'm afraid I'm reduced to hoping the clan leaders aren't aware of the opportunities."

"You've told me how you've been working on the scenario where you slowly pull all troops and civilians into the fortifications here in Preddi City. Do you think the time is here for that?" asked Rabia.

"Not yet, and I hope it doesn't come to that. Only Tuzere and Ketin are involved in the planning. Tuzere wants to wait at least another few sixdays before we decide if it's a plausible option, and I've agreed. I've ordered intense patrols as far out as possible. If the clans start pushing our patrols back aggressively toward Preddi, I'll be forced to activate the consolidation here, if we're to get most of our people behind the fortifications."

CHAPTER 41

THE BEST LAID PLANS

Great Ocean

Although it wasn't Jaako Rintala's first sea voyage, it was the longest. By the time they reached Caedellium, the squadron would have circumnavigated almost three-quarters of Anyar, most of the trip spent sailing over the Great Ocean, the water that covered an entire hemisphere of the planet. They took this longer route to avoid the Narthani, whose increasing number of ships made traversing the Throat, the belt of sea separating the northern and southern continents, a riskier endeavor every year. The longer route also minimized the Narthani realizing that ships of one of their foes were snooping around an island of little interest to the rest of Anyar and of no relevance to wars with the Narthani, until now.

They had already been at sea for four months after leaving Kahmo, the largest port in eastern Fuomon. If Commodore Kyllo was correct, they had another month to go. Then they would see what they would see. Why were the Narthani so interested in Caedellium, and what was happening on that otherwise out-of-the-way island? Only in the last months had Fuomi intelligence uncovered that the Narthani had been up to something on the island for several years, exactly how long wasn't known. With new developments, Rintala was charged with finding out what was going on.

The Fuomi higher-ups didn't expect his command to engage the Narthani. The lack of information dictated that Rintala have flexibility in action, which was why the squadron had enough firepower to fight off any Narthani force of their size and the speed to escape otherwise. They also had a thousand Fuomi marines on five troop ships, because they would attempt to make contact with the inhabitants of Caedellium. Based on scanty information, the Caedelli reportedly consisted of clans having no central island authority.

"Wishing the wind were stronger or weaker, Jaako?" said a woman's voice. He turned and smiled at Eina Saisannin, one of only three women in the squadron. Saisannin was a linguist and an experienced ambassador. The other two women worked as surgeons with the marines.

"Both," said Rintala. "I wish for stronger winds to get us where we're going faster and weaker winds to make the voyage calmer. I know Fuomi are supposed to be Anyar's greatest seamen, but I'd prefer that others demonstrate that talent."

"I agree, Jaako. I've sailed before, though always shorter trips and on single ships." She motioned to the lines of ships arrayed right and left of the flagship they rode on. "It's impressive to see so many ships under sail and so orderly."

Rintala agreed, though he didn't say so. Their frigate was followed by a line of five troop ships, each one carrying two hundred marines. Fuomi troop ships were nothing like the lumbering troop ships of the Narthani. Fuomi naval doctrine mandated that every ship be capable of running with frigates, even if it sacrificed other features.

Following the troop ships were two supply ships, two more frigates flanked the central line right and left, and three sloops picketed forward and to the flanks. They didn't need any sloops astern, because no navy in the world could catch a Fuomi squadron or fleet.

Saisannin braced herself as the ship rolled over a large wave. "I've been going over all the reports and information we have on Caedellium and speculations on why the Narthani are so interested. Whatever is going on won't be good for the poor islanders. I'm afraid they're going to learn what it's like to become part of the Narthon Empire. If they were closer to us or one of the Narthani's other enemies, they might have gotten aid, but out where they are, they're on their own."

"It's a shame," agreed Rintala. "There's nothing we can do for them. We'll see if there's any part of the island not already subjugated, so we can try to understand the longer-term plans the Narthani have for the island. They don't make moves like this without having something in mind. Something we're sure not to like."

"Well," said Saisannin, "if the Narthani have completely put down the Caedellium inhabitants by now, it'll have been a long voyage to no purpose. Here's hoping there's some part of the island not yet subjugated."

Narthani Sloop *Saber*, 100 Miles Northeast of Caedellium

"Sail to the northeast!" shouted a lookout on the top mast.

All motion stopped, as crew and officers heard the call.

"Any identification yet?" the watch officer called up.

"Too far to tell, but it's headed this way."

Five minutes later the watch officer alerted the captain, who'd been awake all night because of a series of squalls.

"Captain, lookout reports a Narthani sloop under full sail headed straight to Caedellium. Do you think it's the one Admiral Kalcan has been waiting for?"

"How would I know?" groused the captain. "But orders are clear. I'll be on deck shortly. Begin turning us around and make all sail to Preddi City. If it's word from Narthon, Admiral Kalcan will want General Akuyun to be prepared."

END OF BOOK 3

MAJOR CHARACTERS

Akuyun, Okan. Commander of Narthani mission to conquer Caedellium.
Akuyun, Rabia. Wife of Okan.
Bakalacs, Feren. Hetman of Farkesh Clan.
Balcan, Mamduk. Narthani religious prelate.
Beynom, Cadwulf. Mathematics scholastic. Son of Diera and Sistian. Friend and employee of Yozef.
Beynom, Diera. A medicant. Abbess of St. Sidryn's abbey. Wife of Sistian.
Beynom, Sistian. A theophist. Abbot of St. Sidryn's abbey. Husband of Diera.
Bolwyn, Elton. A medicant at St. Sidryn's abbey.
Brison, Rhaedri. Most respected theophist on Caedellium.
Bultecki, Teresz. Hetman of Bultecki Clan.
Drifwich, Gethin (a.k.a. Eluk Sargol). Nyvaks clansman spying for the Narthani
Dyllis, Saoul. A medicant at St. Sidryn's abbey.
Erdelin, Memas. Narthani colonel.
Eywell, Brandor. Hetman of Eywell Clan.
Eywell, Biltin. Son of Brandor Eywell.
Faughns, Brak and Elian. Elderly home staff couple of Yozef.
Fitham, Petros. Elderly theophist at St. Sidryn's abbey.
Fuller, Filtin. Skilled worker and friend to Yozef.
Gwillamer, Cadoc. Hetman of Gwillamer Clan.
Harlie. Name given by Yozef to alien artificial intelligence created to interact with Yozef.
Havant, Esyl (a.k.a. Istem Sokulu). Narthani spy.
Hewell, Lordum. Hetman of Hewell Clan.
Hizer, Sadek. Narthani Assessor reporting direct to Narthani High Command.
Kalcan, Morfred. Narthani naval commander.
Kales, Wyfor. Abersford citizen. Tutor to Yozef for blade fighting and occasional bodyguard.
Keelan, Breda. Wife of Culich. Mother of Maera.
Keelan, Ceinwyn. 2nd daughter of Culich and Breda.
Keelan, Culich. Hetman of Clan Keelan. Father of Maera.
Keelan, Anid. 3rd daughter of Culich and Breda.
Keelan, Maera. Eldest daughter of Culich and Breda.
Keelan, Mared. Youngest daughter of Culich and Breda.
Kennrick, Pedr. Advisor to Hetman Culich Keelan.

Ketin, Erkan. Narthani colonel.

Kolsko, Yozef (a.k.a. Joseph Colsco). California chemistry graduate student who boards an ill-fated flight to a conference and meets an unimagined future.

Linton (Merton), Bronwyn. Owner of farm near Abersford. Mother of Aragorn, Yozef's son.

Metin, Nuthrat. Narthani colonel.

Mittack, Hulwyn. Hetman of Mittack Clan.

Moreland, Anarynd (a.k.a. Ana). Friend of Maera Keelan. Related to Moreland Clan hetman.

Moreland, Brym. Father of Anarynd. Cousin to Moreland hetman.

Moreland, Gynfor. Hetman of Moreland Clan.

Orosz, Tomis. Hetman of Orosz Clan.

Stent, Welman. Hetman of Stent Clan.

Puvey, Carnigan. Physically imposing member of abbey staff. Friend of Yozef.

Tuzere, Nizam. Narthani civilian administrator.

Vega, Denes. Magistrate and sheriff-equivalent in town of Abersford. Commander of Abersford fighting levy.

Vortig, Luwis. Advisor to Hetman Culich Keelan.

Luwis, Mulron. Son of Vortig Luwis. Commander Caernford garrison.

Vorwich, Longnor. Keelan Clan boyerman (district chief) of Abersford and St. Sidryn's area.

Walstyn, Gwyned. Ex-Narthani slave, friend of Anarynd.

Watchers. Name given by Yozef to alien creators of Harlie and whose spaceship destroyed Yozef's flight to Chicago.

Zulfa, Aivacs. Brigadier. Commander of Narthani group troops on Caedellium.

About the Author

Olan Thorensen is a pen name. He's a long-time science fiction fan (emphasis on 'long') who has jumped into independent publication with all its pitfalls and unknowns. He thinks all colors go together: clash, what clash? A fan of Dilbert, Non Sequitur, Peanuts (even if old strips), and still thinks the end of The Far Side was a tragedy. In his youth, served in the US Special Forces (Vietnam:SOG). Has a Phd in Genetics, around 200 science publications as author and co-author, and is a Fellow of the American Association for the Advancement of Science (AAAS). Lives in the Blue Ridge country of Virginia. Thinks it's totally cool someone can read his stories and enjoy them. Loves fireflies, thunderstorms, is eclectic in music, and thinks four seasons are better than one. His web page is olanthorensen.com and he hopes his books sell enough he can afford a better web site, better maps, and faster publication. All input from readers is appreciated.

Please email me with any comments at olanthorensen@gmail.com or through my web site at olanthorensen.com where color maps of Anyar are available. I promise to read all emails, though I won't be able to answer personally every one. Also, if you enjoyed the story, please leave a comment/review on appropriate venues, such as Amazon and Goodreads.

Made in the USA
Lexington, KY
15 February 2019